PENGUIN CLASSICS

ADAM BEDE

MARY ANN (MARIAN) EVANS was born in 1819 in Warwickshire. She attended schools in Nuneaton and Coventry, coming under the influence of evangelical teachers and clergymen. In 1836 her mother died and Marian became her father's housekeeper, educating herself in her spare time. In 1841 she moved to Coventry, and met Charles and Caroline Bray, local progressive intellectuals. Through them she was commissioned to translate Strauss's *Life of Jesus* and met the radical publisher John Chapman, who, when he purchased the *Westminster Review* in 1851, made her his managing editor. Having lost her Christian faith and thereby alienated her family, she moved to London where she met Herbert Spencer and the versatile man-of-letters George Henry Lewes. Lewes was separated from his wife, but with no possibility of divorce. In 1854 he and Marian decided to live together, and did so until Lewes's death in 1878. It was he who encouraged her to turn from philosophy and journalism to fiction, and she subsequently wrote, under the name of George Eliot, *Scenes of Clerical Life*, *Adam Bede*, *The Mill on the Floss*, *Silas Marner*, *Romola*, *Felix Holt*, *Middlemarch* and *Daniel Deronda*, as well as numerous essays, articles and reviews. George Eliot died in 1880, only a few months after marrying J. W. Cross, an old friend and admirer, who became her first biographer. She was buried beside Lewes at Highgate. George Eliot combined a formidable intelligence with imaginative sympathy and acute powers of observation, and became one of the greatest and most influential of English novelists. Her choice of material widened the horizons of the novel and her psychological insights radically changed the nature of fictional characterization.

MARGARET REYNOLDS is Reader in English and Contemporary Culture at Queen Mary, University of London, and a Life Member of Clare Hall, Cambridge. Previous posts were at the University of Birmingham and the University of Leeds. She is the author of *The Sappho History* (Palgrave, 2003) and *The Sappho Companion* (Chatto and Windus, 2000), and – with Angela Leighton – edited *Victorian Women Poets* (Blackwell, 1995). Her edition of Elizabeth Barrett Browning's *Aurora Leigh* (Ohio University Press, 1993) won the British Academy's Rose Mary Crawshay Prize. She is the presenter of BBC Radio 4's *Adventures in Poetry*, and has a weekly column on classic books in the Saturday *Times*.

GEORGE ELIOT

Adam Bede

Edited with an Introduction and Notes by
MARGARET REYNOLDS

PENGUIN BOOKS

PENGUIN CLASSICS

Published by the Penguin Group
Penguin Books Ltd, 80 Strand, London WC2R ORL, England
Penguin Group (USA) Inc., 375 Hudson Street, New York, New York 10014, USA
Penguin Group (Canada), 90 Eglinton Avenue East, Suite 700, Toronto, Ontario, Canada M4P 2Y3
(a division of Pearson Penguin Canada Inc.)
Penguin Ireland, 25 St Stephen's Green, Dublin 2, Ireland (a division of Penguin Books Ltd)
Penguin Group (Australia), 250 Camberwell Road, Camberwell, Victoria 3124, Australia
(a division of Pearson Australia Group Pty Ltd)
Penguin Books India Pvt Ltd, 11 Community Centre, Panchsheel Park, New Delhi – 110 017, India
Penguin Group (NZ), 67 Apollo Drive, Rosedale, North Shore 0632, New Zealand
(a division of Pearson New Zealand Ltd)
Penguin Books (South Africa) (Pty) Ltd, 24 Sturdee Avenue, Rosebank, Johannesburg 2196, South Africa

Penguin Books Ltd, Registered Offices: 80 Strand, London WC2R ORL, England

www.penguin.com

First published 1859
This edition first published in Penguin Classics 2008
2

Introduction and notes copyright © Margaret Reynolds, 2008
All rights reserved

The moral right of the editor has been asserted.

Set in 10.25/12.25pt PostScript Adobe Sabon
Typeset by Rowland Phototypesetting Ltd, Bury St Edmunds, Suffolk
Printed in England by Clays Ltd, St Ives plc

ISBN: 978-0-140-43664-8

www.greenpenguin.co.uk

Penguin Books is committed to a sustainable future
for our business, our readers and our planet.
The book in your hands is made from paper
certified by the Forest Stewardship Council.

Contents

Acknowledgements

Thanks are due first of all to the late and much missed Julia Briggs who invited me to undertake this edition of *Adam Bede*. The work of Stephen Gill, Valentine Cunningham, Doreen Roberts and Carol A. Martin has been an invaluable resource. I am grateful to Josephine McDonagh for kindly sending me material and for her readings of George Eliot. I owe much to friends and colleagues with whom I discussed various questions or who read parts of my work: Charlotte Dormandy, Edith Hall, Lisa Jardine, Leonee Ormond, Jacqueline Rose. I thank the staffs of the British Library, the Bodleian Library and the University of London Library for their courtesy and helpfulness. I am especially grateful to Lindeth Vasey, an exemplary copy-editor, and finally to Marcella Edwards at Penguin Classics who is an attentive and perceptive editor and, more than that, a good friend.

Chronology

1819 22 *November*, born at Arbury, Warwickshire.

1824–36 Attends boarding schools in Attleborough, Nuneaton and Coventry.

1836 3 *February*, mother dies.

1837 After sister Christiana marries, becomes father's house-keeper.

1841 Moves with her father to Coventry where she meets Charles and Caroline ('Cara') Bray. Reads Charles Hennell's *An Inquiry Concerning the Origin of Christianity* (1838) which leads her to question her religious faith.

1842 *January–May*, the 'Holy War' with her father when she refuses to attend church. Beginning of friendship with Charles Hennell and his sister Sara.

1844 Begins a translation of Strauss's *Das Leben Jesu* (4th edn, 1840).

1846 *The Life of Jesus* published.

1846–7 'Poetry and Prose, from the Notebook of an Eccentric', published in the Coventry *Herald and Observer*.

1847–8 Nurses father.

1849 Begins to translate Spinoza's *Tractatus theologico-politicus*. *31 May*, death of father. *June*, sets off for France, Italy and Switzerland with the Brays; they return to England in July. Remains in Geneva, lodging, from *October*, with the painter M. D'Albert-Durade and his wife. Begins journal.

1850 *March*, returns to England. Feels unwanted by her family and resides with the Brays. Decides to earn her living by writing. *October*, visits John Chapman in London.

1851 *January*, her first major article, 'The Progress of the

Intellect', published in the *Westminster Review*. *September*, moves to London and becomes assistant editor of the *Westminster*.

1852 *January*, her first number of the *Westminster* published. Close friendship with Herbert Spencer.

1853 Working hard on the *Westminster*. *October*, intimacy with George Henry Lewes begins.

1854 *July*, translation of Feuerbach's *Essence of Christianity* published. Leaves for Germany with Lewes. Begins translation of Spinoza's *Ethics*.

1855 *March*, returns to England with Lewes, and they set up house together.

1856 Trips to Ilfracombe and Tenby to collect materials for Lewes's *Sea-side Studies* (1858). Begins to write fiction, 'The Sad Fortunes of Amos Barton'. 'The Natural History of German Life' and 'Silly Novels by Lady Novelists', published in the *Westminster*.

1857 'Amos Barton', 'Mr Gilfil's Love-Story' and 'Janet's Repentance', published in *Blackwood's Edinburgh Magazine*. Assumes pseudonym, George Eliot. Writes to her brother of her relationship with Lewes and he breaks off communication. *October*, begins *Adam Bede*.

1858 *January, Scenes of Clerical Life*. Travels with Lewes to Munich, then to Dresden via Salzburg, Vienna and Prague.

1859 *February, Adam Bede*. *April*, interrupts composition of *The Mill on the Floss* to write 'The Lifted Veil', published in *Blackwood's* in *July*. *June*, pressured into unveiling the identity of 'George Eliot'.

1860 *April, The Mill on the Floss*. Trip to Italy where she conceives the idea of *Romola*. *August*, writes 'Brother Jacob'. Begins *Silas Marner*.

1861 *April, Silas Marner*. Further trip to Italy for research on *Romola* which she starts to write in *October*.

1862 *July, Romola* begins serialization in *Cornhill Magazine*.

1863 *July, Romola*. She and Lewes buy the Priory, Regent's Park.

1864 Begins verse play *The Spanish Gypsy*. *July*, 'Brother Jacob' published in the *Cornhill*.

1865 *February*, temporarily abandons her verse play, which is making her ill. *March*, starts writing *Felix Holt*.

1866 *June, Felix Holt*. Returns to work on *The Spanish Gypsy*.

1867 Trip to Spain to collect material. Subscribes £50 to the foundation of Girton College, Cambridge.

1868 *May, The Spanish Gypsy*.

1869 Writes 'Brother and Sister' sonnets, and begins *Middlemarch*.

1870 'The Legend of Jubal' published in *Macmillan's Magazine*.

1871 '*Armgart*' published in *Macmillan's*.

1871–2 *Middlemarch* published in eight parts.

1874 *The Legend of Jubal and Other Poems*.

1876 *Daniel Deronda* published in eight parts. Purchases the Heights in Witley, Surrey.

1878 *30 November*, Lewes dies.

1879 Preparing last volume of Lewes's *Problems of Life and Mind* for publication. *The Impressions of Theophrastus Such*.

1880 *6 May*, marries John Walter Cross. *22 December*, dies in London.

Introduction

(New readers should be aware that this introduction discusses details of the plot)

'With this drop of ink at the end of my pen, I will show you . . .'

With a single drop of ink for a mirror, the Egyptian sorcerer undertakes to reveal to any chance comer far-reaching visions of the past. This is what I undertake to do for you, reader. With this drop of ink at the end of my pen, I will show you . . .

The opening lines of George Eliot's *Adam Bede* are enticing and memorable. However, as the beginning of the first full-length novel by the nineteenth-century's foremost practitioner of 'realist fiction', they are bizarre. To be sure, we pretty quickly get to the historical setting of Jonathan Burge's workshop on 18 June 1799 in which we are required to believe. But Eliot's narrator has literally 'conjured' this vision out of the air by using magic borrowed from an exotic 'Egyptian sorcerer', even if she then brings it down to the practical magic of writing – 'with this drop of ink . . .' Commentators and annotators of *Adam Bede* have paid little attention to Eliot's strange image, but in fact her metaphoric 'mirror' reflects a story which she would have read in 1852 at a crucial stage in the development of her career as a novelist.

From 17 January to 27 March 1852 Wilkie Collins published a series of letters addressed to George Henry Lewes in the *Leader*, a radical weekly newspaper which Lewes had founded two years previously in 1850 with Thornton Leigh Hunt. Entitled 'Magnetic Evenings at Home', the letters related a 'scientific' enquiry into mesmerism and clairvoyance – as displayed by Count P— and his assistant Mademoiselle V—

– that took place while Collins was staying with friends at Weston-super-Mare. In the Fifth Letter he tells of the use of the mirror or 'wishing-stone' which was 'a piece of wood . . . shaped like a hand-mirror . . . [with] a highly-polished oval piece of coal attached to one side of the wood, instead of the ordinary looking-glass'. A 'wishing-stone', Collins explains, had once belonged to the Elizabethan gnostic John Dee, and Count P— had provided himself with a copy of this object:

> Convinced that the old Doctor's evil reputation among his con-
> temporaries as a sorcerer had been solely derived from his know-
> ledge and practice of animal magnetism, in days when new
> sciences of all kinds were fathered upon the devil, as a matter of
> course, our host [Count P—] conceived the idea of procuring as
> good an imitation of this 'wishing-stone' as could be obtained,
> and of rivalling the magic achievements of Dr Dee, by applying
> to it the magnetic process necessary to produce the phenomenon
> of *clairvoyance*.[1]

Here, then, are George Eliot's 'mirror' that allows for 'far-reaching visions', and her 'sorcerer'. For the 'ink', that is equivalent to the dark surface of the 'wishing-stone' and the exotic source of the clairvoyant practice, an 1867 article on 'Indo-Mohammedan Folk Lore' in *Notes and Queries* explains: '. . . the Lubbis in the South of India used the *unjun*, or shining globule, placed in the hand of a boy, to discover hidden treasure or stolen property.'[2] In Chapter 3 of his own novel *The Moonstone* (1868), Wilkie Collins describes the mysterious Indians using just such a method in order to find out the whereabouts of the diamond by pouring a splash of ink into a boy's hand.[3]

In 1852, Lewes was not impressed, and replied to Collins's account in 'The Fallacy of Clairvoyance', published on 27 March:

> In conclusion, let me say that the fallacy of clairvoyance is, I take
> it, the interpretation of a *dreaming* power as a *seeing* power. The
> clairvoyante (when not a charlatan) sees the objects of her
> dreams, and describes them; *what* those objects are depend

mainly upon the suggestion of external stimulus, in the shape of words, tones, hesitations, &c.[4]

Marian Evans also was likely to have been sceptical. Nonetheless, seven years later she used this image to describe her own 'dreaming power' as a novelist, adapting the clairvoyant's more usual visions of present and future to her own purpose in giving us 'far-reaching visions of the past'.[5] In *Adam Bede* Eliot looked not only into the long past of the nation, but into the past of her elders – her father and her aunt by marriage Elizabeth, Mrs Samuel Evans (whom Eliot always called 'Aunt Samuel'). More importantly still, she also looked into her own immediate past – the past that had made her into a writer.

Marian Evans into 'George Eliot'

After the death of her father in 1849 the twenty-nine-year-old Mary Ann Evans had gone to live in Switzerland. In 1850 she returned to England, and the next year moved to London where she went to live in the household of the publisher John Chapman, and started working for him as managing editor of his *Westminster Review*. In 1852 Marian met Herbert Spencer, a social philosopher and journalist, and they soon became so close that there were rumours of an engagement. Whatever her feelings, they were not reciprocated. Spencer, however, introduced her to a man who certainly was interested – George Henry Lewes. But again, there were obstacles.

Lewes had been married to Agnes Jervis since 1841 and they had four sons. In 1850, when Agnes began a relationship with his business partner Thornton Hunt, Lewes had accepted the resulting child as his own. When a second child was born of the liaison, Lewes ceased to regard Agnes as his wife but, having condoned the affair, he was not in a position to sue, retrospectively, for divorce citing adultery.

Marian Evans was also a radical thinker, though one rather more hampered by the conventional strictures which bound respectable women's behaviour. Even so, she did the only thing she could: she let her relationship with Lewes grow. With him, she shared her reading, her aspirations, her fears, her desires, her table and her bed. When and where this first began to happen we do not know, but it was probably sometime in the winter of 1853 when Marian moved out of Chapman's house and into lodgings in Cambridge Street, off the Edgware Road. Then, in 1854, at the age of thirty-four, Marian Evans let this secret life become known when she left England for Germany in company with Lewes and – as it is politely put in all the biographies – she lived with him as his wife.

Though she was already an accomplished journalist and a successful translator of David Strauss's *Das Leben Jesu*, from this time forward Lewes encouraged Marian Evans to fulfil her ambition and write fiction. She was soon at work on the first of the three long stories that were to make up *Scenes of Clerical Life*, and 'The Sad Fortunes of the Reverend Amos Barton' was published in *Blackwood's Edinburgh Magazine* in January and February 1857. Given Marian's peculiar situation, it was Lewes who offered this story to the publisher John Blackwood, saying that he was acting on behalf of 'a friend'.[6] Soon Blackwood was corresponding with Marian herself, addressing his letters to 'George Eliot Esq.' 'Mr Gilfil's Love Story' followed in March to June 1857, and 'Janet's Repentance' appeared from July to November.

Confident now in her own ability, and wanting a freer hand, on 5 September 1857 'George Eliot' wrote to Blackwood: 'I have a subject in my mind which will not come under the limitations of the title "Clerical Life," and I am inclined to take a large canvas for it, and write a novel.'[7]

In a journal entry entitled 'How I came to write Fiction', Marian Evans recollected that 'It had always been a vague dream of mine that some time or other I might write a novel . . . But I never went farther towards the actual writing of the novel than an introductory chapter describing a Staffordshire village and the life of the neighbouring farm houses.' Evans had kept the paper, however, and carried it with her when she went abroad with Lewes in 1854 'and one evening at Berlin, something led me to read it to George'.[8] Although this text does not survive, it may be that the sketch went on to become the opening to *Adam Bede* for Eliot was to retain that country setting in her first novel. Writing to Blackwood on 17 October 1857, she said, 'My new story haunts me a good deal . . . It will be a country story – full of the breath of cows and the scent of hay . . .'[9]

But it wasn't just the country setting that gave Eliot the impetus for her tale.

'My Aunt's Story'

In December 1856 Marian Evans had told Lewes the story about her aunt Elizabeth Evans and the young woman named Mary Voce who was found guilty of killing her child, and how her aunt had prayed with Mary the night before her execution and had gone with her in the cart to the gallows. In the next year, 1857 – so three years after she had begun living with Lewes – George Eliot told her family, including her beloved brother Isaac, the truth about her own relationship. Her family immediately broke off all communication. In October Eliot began to write *Adam Bede*.

We can trace this precise chronology for the composition of *Adam Bede* because Eliot wrote up what she called the 'History of Adam Bede' in her journal for 30 November 1858.[10] What we can only speculate on are the questions of why her aunt's story came back to her at just this time, and why it meant so much to her.

It is true that other women writers had tackled the subject of the 'fallen' woman and the unmarried mother. Elizabeth Gaskell had published *Ruth* in 1853; Elizabeth Barrett Browning had published *Aurora Leigh* – with its tale of Marian Erle's rape and consequent pregnancy – at the end of 1856. Eliot had read both books, and when she reviewed Barrett Browning's verse-novel, she remarked on 'its far-stretching thoughts, its abundant treasure of well digested learning, its acute observation of life, its yearning sympathy with multiform human sorrow . . .'.[11] It is tempting to wonder how far the story of Marian Erle spoke to Marian Evans.

Whatever the personal element in her need to retell her aunt's tale, Eliot's decision to publish the story of Hetty Sorel was brave. Elizabeth Gaskell and Elizabeth Barrett Browning were respectable married women.[12] As 'George Eliot', Marian Evans retained – for the moment – her privacy, but she could have no idea how long that might last and, as it turned out, she was soon forced to acknowledge the fact that she was the author of *Adam Bede*. In tackling this subject, she was also taking the risk of exposing herself, and her precious relationship with Lewes, to the most prurient comment. But still she had to do it, and in some hidden way the fact of her taking on this particular subject, at this particularly difficult moment in her life, was deeply connected both to Marian Evans's sense of self, and 'George Eliot's self-construction as a writer. 'I love it very much,' Eliot wrote about *Adam Bede* in her journal, 'and am deeply thankful to have written it, whatever the public may say of it' ('History').

In *Child Murder and British Culture 1720–1900*, Josephine McDonagh points to an extraordinary fairy-tale account of her own young self that Marian Evans gave her friend Sara Hennell in 1848:

Now over a quarter of a century ago there was a very young sprite who forsooth having turned out some respectable toads and a few indifferent lemurs and marmosets must fain try his hand on a human article and one 22[d] of November he presented to Dame Nature at her evening levee a rough though unmistakeable sketch of a human baby. The Old Mother had been rollicking all the autumn in the vintage and wanted no less than a winter's sleep to sober her. Being rather cross-grained in her cups she was in no humour to make the best of a bad business so she said, What have we here? in such a snappish tone, flourishing a bunch of nettles all the while, that the poor little Prometheus of a sprite began to look very snubbed. 'A pretty piece of work I should have to patch up this thing into a human soul and body that would hang together! Here,' she called to one of her Vishnu-sprites, 'smother it at once to save further harm.'[13]

In the end, the child is saved by the intervention of her friends: 'The poor sketch of a soul was found by the dark eyed maiden and those other bright and good mortals and they pitied and helped it, so that at last it grew to think and to love.'

McDonagh argues that the three key dates that are wrapped around George Eliot's account of her 'Aunt's Story' – 1802 when her Aunt Elizabeth prayed with Mary Voce, 1839 when her aunt told Marian about it, and 1856 when Marian told the story to Lewes – are all coincidentally significant dates in the legal and social history of infanticide.[14] But they are also key dates in Eliot's own memory of her self-making, taking her right back to her father's life – from which she would draw some elements in Adam's story – and her aunt's, and on to her own momentous life-decisions made in the mid 1850s.

The editors of George Eliot's *Journals* remark that during Lewes and Evans's second trip to Germany – when she was writing *Adam Bede* – Eliot's accounts of the art that they saw in various picture galleries suggest that 'Babies and children seem[ed] particularly fascinating to [her] at this time'.[15] The fascination – especially with children who are threatened or displaced – was to go into her fiction.

If, as McDonagh argues, *Adam Bede* functions around repressed memories and the return of things buried and forgotten, then no wonder 'My Aunt's Story' about a lost child was the one that 'haunted' Marian Evans as she turned herself into the writer 'George Eliot'. She had already imagined her adult self as a child escaping infanticide. Now, in the 1850s, Evans was remaking herself as an independent being and a writer – but the personal price was high. For in making that choice Evans had to sacrifice both the memory of the child that she had been – as she forfeited her childhood connection with her brother Isaac because of the irregular character of her union with Lewes – and – for the same reason – she felt that she had to relinquish the possibility of having children of her own. No wonder then that Hetty's predicament appealed to her imagination.

Mary Voce into Hetty Sorrel

When you look at George Eliot's own accounts of how she wrote *Adam Bede*, it is plain that it is the idea of Hetty that was the central point of her inspiration. The first piece of evidence is the 'History of Adam Bede' where she tells how she heard the story of Aunt Elizabeth Evans's night with Mary Voce for the first time in 1839 and how she told it to Lewes in December 1856. At that time, she noted, he 'remarked that the scene in the prison would make a fine element in a story'. Afterwards, came the idea of 'blending this and some other recollections of my aunt', and then, last of all, because she had to think of how 'to make the unhappy girl one of the chief *dramatis personae* and connect her with the hero', she invented the character of Adam based on 'one or two incidents' which were suggested by her father's early life.

So the imaginative progression in Eliot's mind goes Hetty, Dinah, Adam. Adam may have come to take on the title role, but Hetty was the wellspring. In detailing the process of composition Eliot happens to say that 'The opening of the third volume – Hetty's journeys – was, I think written more rapidly than the rest of the book, and was left without the slightest alteration of the first draught' ('History'). In fact, Carol A. Martin, the editor of the Clarendon Edition of *Adam Bede*, argues that the state of the manuscript does not bear this out for it includes many alterations and corrections.[16] All the same, it is revealing that what Eliot (mis)remembered was the ease with which she wrote those sections.

The second piece of evidence is George Eliot's note in the fair-copy manuscript, now in the British Library, written on 23 March 1859, after the manuscript had been returned from the printers. When she decided to dedicate the manuscript to Lewes, she added this account of the composition of the novel. Some parts of it, she says, were written 'only once', 'among these the description of Dinah & a good deal of her sermon, the love-scene between her & Seth, "Hetty's World", most of the scene in the Two Bedchambers, the talk between Arthur & Adam, various parts in the second volume which I can recal less easily, & in the third, Hetty's journeys, her confession and the cottage scenes'.[17] This account of the readily rising parts of the composition also suggests Eliot's absorption in certain elements of her tale: Hetty again, Dinah, Adam and Arthur.

In creating the character of Hetty, George Eliot relied only for the barest details on her Aunt Elizabeth's story. The facts in the case of Mary Voce were entirely different from Hetty's, for Mary was older, married, of rough character, had been deserted by her husband, had had other men, had borne several children, had committed a number of petty crimes, and seems to have purchased rat poison with the intention either of murdering her child – or of taking her own life. Even at the time of Mary Voce's trial and execution there were discrepancies in the way her story was told: the three contemporary broadsheets give quite different versions of the tale.[18] Add to that the fourth story told by Elizabeth Evans, and then the fifth, as it is retold by Eliot in *Adam Bede*, and Mary Voce is lost to our sight.

But Hetty is fully in our view. I am not at all on the side of the critics who object to Hetty: to her prettiness, to her self-indulgence, to her daydreams, to her passivity in her predicament, to her obduracy. On the contrary, I find that I sympathize with Hetty, not because I care about her in any old-fashioned way as I 'make friends' with this literary sign, but because she – or rather George Eliot through her – makes me imaginatively realize what it is, or what it might be, to be a woman in a society and a cultural context that values certain kinds of women, and condones certain kinds of behaviour and condemns others.

If readers now are sometimes surprised by the revelation of Hetty's pregnancy, some readers then professed to be shocked by the novel's forthrightness. Far from the facts of Hetty's sexual life being secret, it seems to me that Eliot's account of what happens and how and when is as explicit as it could possibly have been in 1859. Certainly, many of those revelations are signalled in a literary code of symbols, or displaced imagery or metaphoric language. You have to calculate the timing of months and seasons, for instance, or you have to think

about Hetty's red cloak, or note clues like Arthur's deciding not
to worry about 'any bad consequence that was not demonstrably inevitable', or the reference to Hetty's 'more luxuriant
womanliness' (Chapters XXIX, XXXIV). Or else you have
to understand that drowning was so commonly a method of
suicide for the unmarried and pregnant girl in the nineteenth
century that 'Found Drowned' – as Hetty imagines herself
(XXXIV) – meant much more than it said.

All these hints were obvious to contemporary readers of both
sexes. Eliot's publisher John Blackwood guessed early on in his
reading that 'The Captain's unfortunate attachment to Hetty
will I suppose form a main element in the Tragic part of the
story. I am not quite sure how far I like the scenes in the wood
and I hope things will not come to the usual sad catastrophe!'[19]
While the book was delayed in the press in December 1858,
Eliot was worried about the 'evil' consequences that might
attend on the possible disclosure of her identity because of the
sexual element in the plot.[20] When the book did appear on
1 February 1859, the *Saturday Review* deplored the novel as
part of the 'literature of pregnancy', while the *Examiner* felt
'bound to protest against the depiction in a novel of the stages
of childbirth, related with almost obstetric accuracy of detail'.[21]
For the modern reader, however, the untangling of these hints
is part of the perverse pleasure of the novel, in that the reader's
knowledge of what is happening and where it will lead, so soon
overtakes the ignorance of the other characters.[22]

'the great crime'

But the thing that makes Hetty so important for our time –
for any time of course, but still relevant now – is the fact of
her having murdered her child. The very crime has different
definitions in different social and historical circumstances
and might be called by many names: abandonment, neglect,
diminished responsibility, failure of care, abuse, murder.

Because most societies have a vested interest in sustaining the
ideal of the sanctity of motherhood, child murder is often a
taboo, and there are comparatively few infanticides in litera-

ture. There are many child-killers who are men – from the myth
of Cronus devouring his own children in Greek legend, to
Agamemnon surrendering Iphigenia to the altar, or Abraham
preparing to sacrifice Isaac. But mothers who murder are rarer
and more monstrous. In legend, Medea kills the offspring of
her marriage to Jason, but she is also a witch who has sex
outside marriage, betrays her country and her father, cuts her
brother into pieces, has the rival to her lover's throne boiled in
a pot, and sends a poisoned garment to her husband's new
bride.

Josephine McDonagh describes the two specific literary
infanticides that form a background to George Eliot's *Adam
Bede*.[23] The first is that by Martha Ray in William Wordsworth's poem 'The Thorn' published in the *Lyrical Ballads*
in 1798. This is of course the year preceding the opening date
of *Adam Bede*, and, in Chapter V, Arthur Donnithorne re-
ceives a copy of the *Lyrical Ballads*, which he describes as
'queer, wizard-like stories', commenting that they 'seem to be
twaddling stuff'. The remark is a clue for the reader, and suggests Arthur's shallow understanding, for Wordsworth was a
favourite poet of Eliot's and many of her epigraphs – including
that for *Adam Bede* – were drawn from his work.[24]

The second (supposed) infanticide is by Effie Deans in Walter
Scott's novel *The Heart of Midlothian* (1818). During the last
four years of her ailing father's life, Marian Evans had been
accustomed to read aloud to him for long hours every evening,
and their favourite author was Scott. Though of course, as it
turns out, Effie was innocent and her child survives.

Another literary infanticide that George Eliot would have
known is by the speaker in Elizabeth Barrett Browning's 1846
poem 'The Runaway Slave at Pilgrim's Point'. Here the child
definitely does die, strangled by his mother. But even while the
poem makes clear that the despairing mother's motives are
political – the child is the result of rape, he is too white, he is
one of those who will possess the 'master-right' – the horror of
the act itself is mitigated by the slave's residual instinct to love
her 'own, own' child.[25]

As far as the legal story of infanticide goes, the statute which

Hetty contravened and which condemned her, was the Stuart Bastardy Act of 1624 which decreed the death penalty for any woman who should 'either by drowning or secret burying thereof' kill her newborn child. If the child had been born dead, the onus was on the mother to 'make proof by one Witness at least, that the Child . . . was born dead'.[26] This act was passed at a time when there was much public anxiety about the rising rate of illegitimate births and about infant mortality and child abandonment. By the eighteenth century urbanization and more efficient modes of transport meant that the problem was much worse as women travelled to some place other than their home town to abandon their (live or dead) baby.[27] As it turned out, comparatively few women were tried, let alone executed, for this crime, in spite of the fact that the legal burden of proof required to show that the child was born dead was firmly placed with the mother.

In 1784 William Hunter, a surgeon and midwife, who was sympathetic to the plight of the unmarried woman, published an address to the Medical Society, where he pointed out that many women, giving birth under these extreme conditions, were likely to be deprived of 'all judgement and rational conduct'.[28] Lawyers argued that the assumptions of the law as it stood were unworkable and inappropriate. It was eventually repealed in 1803 – just a year after Mary Voce's death. At this stage, the reason given for the change was specifically that judges were so often disposed to be lenient, finding increasingly ingenious ways of accepting the slightest evidence that the child was stillborn, thus bringing the law into disrepute. All the same, cases still continued to be brought under the Act, and the last execution of a woman for newborn child murder took place in 1849 – ten years after Elizabeth Evans told Marian her story, and just ten years before the publication of *Adam Bede*.[29]

'you don't get extra points for killing a baby . . .'

One hundred and fifty years on, and women who are accused of killing their baby may not be executed, but they are often condemned to a living death. In recent years in Britain much publicity has surrounded the conviction and jailing of women such as Angela Cannings and the late Sally Clark – both found guilty of murdering their infant children, and later released when some of the prosecution's evidence (and, in particular, the reliability of one of their key medical witnesses) was discovered to be unsound.

In September 1994 Caroline Beale was arrested at John F. Kennedy airport in New York where she was found to be carrying a bag bound to her stomach containing the body of her baby, a little girl, to whom she had given birth the night before in an hotel room. Her boyfriend had been out drinking. She delivered the baby, by herself, in the bath. She tried to wash out some of the towels she had used to mop up the mess. In the end she wrapped the bloodiest inside the other towels, and left them on the floor. She picked the dead floating baby out of the bath and put it in a bag. No one had known that Caroline was pregnant.

She was arraigned for second-degree murder and spent eight months in prison in New York's Rikers Island. Eventually she was released on bail but was only allowed to return home to England after she was persuaded to plead guilty to manslaughter. 'In the United States,' said the District Attorney who prosecuted her, 'you don't get extra points for killing a baby.'[30]

When my students read George Eliot's *Adam Bede* they often complain that it is just not possible. It is too unbelievable, they say, that no one noticed that Hetty was pregnant. But the fact is that it happens all the time. And, just like Hetty, all the time, frightened women – young, old, married, not married, clever or foolish, well-off or poor – try to get rid of that secret baby.

In Britain today, at the beginning of the twenty-first century, babies are abandoned every week. In Germany and Japan, local authorities are trying out a scheme, based on an idea used by medieval churches, where a designated hole in the wall allows mothers to give up their babies anonymously.[31] Not all of these women are trying to kill their baby. Quite often they are trying to save that tiny life. In March 2001 an elderly couple living in Sawtry found a newborn baby boy on their doorstep. A few days later, after the police had asked the mother to come forward, the couple found a note on the same doorstep which said: 'Please forgive me. I had the baby on Saturday night while my parents were out. I am not bad.'

A Stage Adaptation, 1862

While it will always be an important issue, the topic of unwanted babies and child murder was a particularly fraught question when *Adam Bede* was published. The book was widely and respectfully reviewed, in spite of various papers exclaiming over the close attention to Hetty's pregnancy and delivery. All the same, the general reaction to the novel was so favourable that an adaptation was made for the stage and it was performed at the Royal Surrey Theatre in February 1862.[32]

As ever with such adaptations, it is not the faithfulness to the original text that is revealing, but the departures therefrom. In true melodramatic fashion the play hints at the catastrophe which will result from Arthur and Hetty's relationship early in the first scene. Parson Irwine reminds his mother that Arthur's uncle (not his grandfather) has made a will which disinherits him if he marries without his uncle's consent. The reason for this stricture is that 'the Colonel in his youth married below his position – misery was the consequence. His wife eloped with a scoundrel. The Colonel shot him and he has been a hard man ever since.' The scene ends, however, with Arthur and Irwine setting off for Hall Farm, and, as Arthur swears that he has no interest in the 'two pretty girls' there – 'Don't fear. I'm a stoic, a very St Anthony. They shan't tempt me' – Mrs Irwine brings the curtain down with the exclamation 'Oh these boys'.

Shortly afterward follows a scene where Hetty first meets Arthur in the wood, and then, on the evening of the dance, he takes her to the Hermitage where they are seen by Adam and the fight takes place. The curtain comes down on Act II as Adam cries 'Good heaven! He has struck his head against a stone', and ends with the stage direction 'Picture'.

Act III begins with Mrs Poyser remarking specifically that it is now *two years* since the unhappy events of the dance when

Adam fought with Arthur. Arthur, we are told, did not die, but left to join the army and has not been seen since. If you know the book – though, of course, many people in the audience in 1862 would *not* have read it – this seems very strange. Is this 'two years' just a mistake then? Or some peculiar foil set up for the sake of Victorian decency?

As Act III continues, Hetty is found to have disappeared, and then the plot more or less follows the book, except for Seth attempting to reassure Adam that there is 'a gleam of hope':

'There was found near the body of Hetty's child,' he says, 'a pack of old playing cards and a fortune telling Book. Of these Hetty disclaims all knowledge tho' it is suspected she must have got her living by fortune telling. I have ascertained that there was a gang of gipsies in the neighbourhood and to them doubtless these articles belonged.'

Scene 3 of Act III takes place in a prison ward-room and replays the scene between Dinah and Hetty which is so central to George Eliot's story. But here Hetty protests her innocence and tells Dinah that she simply put the baby down for a moment to go and beg some milk and that when she returned 'it was not crying – and there was a child – it was dead – not my child – no Dinah – not my child'. Dinah assumes that Hetty's reaction was one of extreme anguish – 'it was enough to deprive you of reason' – but when Hetty tells how she buried the dead baby and left it, Dinah says, 'If this is known it will go terribly against you', before she asks, 'Hetty, tell me were you married to him?' and Hetty faints without replying.

In the following scenes, which return the action to Hall Farm, Dinah and Adam come to an understanding rather earlier than they do in the novel. Then we go back to the scene of the trial where Hetty protests her innocence: 'I didn't desert it. I couldn't. I went to beg for it a cup of milk – and then when I came back it was gone – they had stolen it – give me my child.' In another curious departure from the original, Rachel Poyser is called to give evidence for Hetty's character, and she manages a little homily: 'The sin lies at the door o' them as tempted her and of your laws that are only to punish the weaker sex. The sooner they're altered the better.'

The play reaches a climax as Adam prepares to name the absent Arthur as the father of Hetty's child. At this point Arthur himself appears to announce . . . that he and Hetty are married. The judge insists that this is irrelevant, sends the jury out to consider whether or not Hetty is guilty of child murder, and they return with a verdict of 'Guilty'. Then, just as the judge prepares to pronounce the death sentence, Seth rushes in with a band of gipsies and . . . sure enough, Hetty's child . . . alive and well. 'She is acquitted,' says the judge: 'Tableaux. Curtain falls.'

And a Radio Adaptation, 2001

If Hetty's story needed some revision and a different ending (notably a marriage and a live baby) in 1862, the new set of historical and cultural forces at work in the early twenty-first century make George Eliot's novel similarly subject to revision and change.

In July 2001 the BBC broadcast a dramatization, adapted by Robert Forest and directed by Patrick Rayner, in a prime daily slot on BBC Radio 4. In one sense, this adaptation was true to George Eliot, for great attention was paid to the episode between Hetty and Dinah in the prison cell, and four whole episodes played out their conversation. In another sense, this was very much a production for a modern audience: Hetty came across as feisty, difficult, wanting more of life. She was allowed to be pretty explicit about what went on between her and Arthur in the Hermitage, and a heart-rending cry was put into her mouth as she complained that during those months of her hidden pregnancy, no one cared enough to notice: 'no one could *see me*'.[33] Her claim to a modern notion of the value of the individual life was also emphasized by the fact that, in the prison cell, it is Hetty who also forces Dinah to a 'confession', and that confession (using the scenes that actually come later in the book after Hetty's conviction) turns out to be that Dinah has fallen in love with Adam Bede.

However, as usual, it is the ending that tells. As in the original novel, Hetty's sentence is commuted and Dinah, we hear, goes to see Hetty on board the ship that will carry her to Australia. She reports that Hetty appeared eager to be away. Adam grudgingly meets with Arthur. Then he begs Dinah to marry him, pleading that it is her call to take him because he will 'be her cross' in life, given that he still cannot come to terms with his vengeful desire to kill Arthur.

But that wasn't quite the end of the story. In the last scene we heard waves and seagulls and the voice of Hetty singing one of Wesley's hymns. Someone – a sailor or another convict – asks her what she is, if she's 'No dissenter, and no churchgoer'. He goes on, 'What are you then? . . . Jew or Hindu?' And we hear her reply, 'Hetty Sorrel', to which he says, 'Hetty Sorrel, eh? And that's all?', and she says, 'Enough to be going on with – Hetty Sorrel.'

In 1862 it was Hetty's character that needed cleaning up for public presentation, so she had to be married and innocent of the crime. In 2001 it still has to be Hetty's character that is transformed as she becomes an independent woman, with a strong sense of self that will see her through, whatever her destiny. In both cases, interestingly, she survives.

George Eliot does not let Hetty live. It has often been remarked that Hetty's abrupt dismissal from the story, dying – as we are told in the Epilogue – just when her sentence of transportation has come to an end, is something of a letdown. Maybe it does seem so to a latterday audience. But Eliot's contemporary audience would have understood rather better. They would have known that the fate of a pretty young convict, subject both to the attentions and the cruelties of officers and other convicts, was hardly going to be a happy one. They would also have known that rehabilitation was impossible. A quiet life of penitence and reproach – away from her family – would have been the only one open to Hetty on return to England.

So Hetty disappears out of the story and Dinah's words end the novel, as they have dominated the story. For this is the other half of Eliot's inspiration for *Adam Bede*.

'George Eliot' into Dinah Morris

Before the novel was named, Eliot and Lewes referred to it between themselves as her 'Aunt's Story'. Her story, in that it was something that happened to Elizabeth Evans; her story, in that it was a tale she told to the young Mary Ann.[34] And it is words and storytelling, and the art of persuasion and rhetoric that become important here. 'Preaching' by another name. That is the essence of Aunt Elizabeth's story, and it is the essence of George Eliot's art.

Eliot is said to be a realist writer. It looks like an easy term. There are, in fact, only two ways in which fiction can be 'real'. The first is an emotional reality: for readers can indeed be made to feel by words, and that feeling – when it happens – is true. The second is a literary reality. For fiction is made with words, with structure and with form, and that certainly is real . . . 'With this drop of ink at the end my pen, I will show you . . .'

The way that Dinah speaks in the novel was closely connected in Eliot's own mind with the way that she herself wrote – and the way in which she genuinely felt as she wrote. In a revealing letter to Sara Hennell, Eliot said, 'How curious it seems to me that people should think Dinah's sermon, prayers, and speeches were *copied* – when they were written with hot tears, as they surged up in my own mind!'[35]

Dinah's two major speeches frame the action. The first takes place on the village green at Hayslope, the evening sun making a picturesque setting as the rays illuminate her face and light up her impassioned features. Here Dinah's audience is a whole community. But she makes only one convert, Bess Cranage. Her second 'sermon' takes place in the darkness of the night, enclosed, in the condemned cell, and alone with Hetty. And again, Dinah makes one convert – Hetty herself.

The method of each of these two speeches is the same; and that too is the same as the technique Dinah uses in the smaller virtuoso outbursts that punctuate the novel, whether her appeal to Hetty (Chapter XV), or her self-justification to Adam (Chapter LII).

The range of quotations in the two major framing speeches

is also the same. Dinah's text for her sermon in Chapter II, 'The Preaching', is Luke 4:18 where Jesus says, 'The Spirit of the Lord is upon me, because he hath anointed me to preach the gospel to the poor; he hath sent me . . . to preach deliverance to the captives, and recovering of sight to the blind, to set at liberty them that are bruised' (Authorized Version). It is a manifesto entirely in accord with George Eliot's own assessment of the moral role she adopted for her fiction. In addition, she draws on many other biblical references so that Dinah's sermon starts with a story from the Bible, then a quotation, then there is a story about herself which parallels the present situation, then she implicates her audience – 'you and me, dear friends, are poor' – and explains how God is already in their lives in everyday clichés, then she builds on that by describing how they might allow him a larger, more active place in their lives, and she goes on to refer – effectively for the fourth time – to a preaching situation (Jesus, John Wesley, her own present, Jesus again), and she introduces another biblical quotation.

The technique sets out a theme, reverses it, writes variations on it, then introduces a second and third, returning always to all the different themes even where they are worked through in a number of different keys, major and minor, until the whole climaxes in a virtuoso crescendo which blends quotation, reference to 'you and me' and the preaching scene:

'See!' she exclaimed, turning to the left, with her eyes fixed on a point above the heads of the people – 'see where our blessed Lord stands and weeps, and stretches out his arms towards you. Hear what he says . . . See the print of the nails on his dear hands . . .'

George Eliot read widely in preparing her research for *Adam Bede*, and the works of John Wesley and, especially, Henry Moore's *Life of Mrs Mary Fletcher* (Birmingham, 1817) were her sources. In March 1839 Eliot borrowed a copy of the latter from her aunt, and 'Miss Bosanquet' – as Mary Fletcher was before her marriage – is mentioned in Chapter VIII of *Adam Bede*. The early Methodist preachers, but the women in particular, employed a rhetoric of preaching which became a familiar pattern, mixing public and private reference, including biblical allusion, personal testimony, direct appeal, surrender and submission and a call to active entry into a spiritual life.[36]

Dinah's preaching also carries a musical analogy that is built into the narrative, offered to us through the medium of 'the stranger' who witnesses this first scene of Dinah's preaching in Chapter II. He provides a discriminating focus on Dinah's performance. He is the one who gives us eyes and ears. He is connected also with Dinah's second large framing 'sermon', and that is the one that takes place in Chapter XLV, which is also introduced by a curious encounter with an 'elderly gentleman'. In the case of the first encounter in Chapter II, we don't know who that stranger is. He is simply a rider who happens across the pretty scene on the village green and who stays to be impressed by Dinah's performance. The stranger takes on the role of informal witness. Or maybe he is even a formal witness, the representative of the reader, who does not move among the village people described, but who discerns their various relations, who can impartially criticize and assess, not only the village, but the impression Dinah makes on the village.

In the second case the stranger – who turns out to be the same man – is known and named. He is the governing Magistrate, Colonel Townley, the one and only person who has the authority to decree that Dinah may indeed be allowed to spend the night with Hetty in her cell. On this occasion, he does not witness Dinah's speech, but we do, because the imaginative intervention of the novelist has allowed us into that cell to hear Dinah's words. On the first occasion of his two brief appearances the stranger-Magistrate represents the reader. And Eliot herself does not know who that reader – those readers – might be, so it is appropriate that he has no name. But on the second occasion of his appearance the Magistrate represents the writer – and so it becomes relevant that he plays an authoritative role. Only through the imaginative licence of the writer can the reader be permitted access to the dark and seclusion of Hetty's cell, and to the secret scene of Dinah's persuasion and Hetty's repentance.

In one of her best-known essays George Eliot includes a statement of realist intent:

> The greatest benefit we owe to the artist, whether painter, poet, or novelist, is the extension of our sympathies ... Art is the nearest thing to life; it is a mode of amplifying experience and extending our contact with our fellow-men beyond the bounds of our personal lot. All the more sacred is the task of the artist when he undertakes to paint the life of the People. Falsification here is far more pernicious than in the more artificial aspects of life. It is not so very serious that we should have false ideas about evanescent fashions ... but it *is* serious that our sympathy with the perennial joys and struggles, the toil, the tragedy, and the humour in the life of our more heavily-laden fellow-men, should be perverted, and turned toward a false object instead of the true one ...[37]

For all that this presents itself as a plea for realism, it takes the form of a marked pattern of religious vocation in its vocabulary, and especially in the use of the word 'sacred'. If George Eliot's project is similar to Dinah's – the one by saving souls, the other by extending sympathies – then so is her form.

Dinah's spoken method – paralleling Eliot's literary method – is one characterized by collage and improvisation. Fragments and scraps of images, of pictures, of quotations, of allusions, asides and qualifications make up the weave of Dinah's sermons just as they make up the substance of Eliot's novel. Dinah's textual fragments are stories and allusions. In a similar way George Eliot herself kept notebooks of stray facts and ideas when she was preparing to write a novel.

And Eliot expects her reader to follow the complex web of her references. On the surface of Chapter XII we see Arthur beginning to succumb to the temptation presented by Hetty. But in Eliot's buried allusions we can foresee the whole sorry story: a tapestry depicts Moses the foundling; Arthur sings a song from the *Beggar's Opera*, 'Would you have a young virgin of fifteen years?'; the narrator comments on his xxxii   INTRODUCTION

'soft-heartedness' to 'the whole sex', a favourite phrase with
the rakish likes of Lovelace in Samuel Richardson's *Clarissa*
(1747–9), and refers to the Centaurs, famed in legend for their
lusts; Arthur is reading *Zeluco*, the history of a seducer; and
his Hermitage retreat is furnished with an 'ottoman' with all
its suggestion of decadent luxury and enticing harems. The
reader does not need to have it spelt out. The supporting themes
woven into the allusive background of the text tell us that Hetty
has not got a chance.

In the same essay Eliot points out that it is not reason that
makes up the power of language, but the accretions of history:

> It must be admitted that the language of cultivated nations is in
> anything but a rational state; ... one word stands for many
> things, and many words for one thing; the subtle shades of mean-
> ing, and still subtler echoes of association, make language an
> instrument which scarcely anything short of genius can wield
> with definiteness and certainty ...

She goes on to imagine a 'clean' scientific language, but then
rejects that possibility:

> With the anomalies and inconveniences of historical language,
> you will have parted with its music and its passion, with its vital
> qualities as an expression of individual character, with its subtle
> capabilities of wit, with everything that gives it power over the
> imagination ... Language must be left to grow in precision,
> completeness, and unity, as minds grow in clearness, comprehen-
> siveness, and sympathy.[38]

Her reader, then, must work to hear the 'music' that is in the
layering of her text. Music in language is something that
George Eliot believed in, partly because she knew that the
musical form was one closely related to her own method in
writing.

In an intriguing essay 'Notes on Form in Art' (1868) – not
published in her lifetime – Eliot analysed a mode of artistic
creation which is clearly related to her own. This method

must begin with the perception of separateness, derived principally from touch of which the other senses are modifications;
and ... things must be recognized as separate wholes before
they can be recognized as wholes composed of parts, or before
these wholes again can be regarded as relatively parts of a larger
whole.

She goes on to explain that it is this sustained discrimination
between likenesses and differences that makes 'form' in art:

as knowledge continues to grow by its alternating processes
of distinction and combination, seeing smaller and smaller un-
likenesses and grouping or associating these under a common
likeness, It arrives at the conception of wholes composed of
parts more and more multiplied and highly differenced, yet more
absolutely bound together by various conditions of common
likeness or mutual dependence.

Emotions – hers and ours – are what govern the shapes and
patterns of *Adam Bede*. Which is why the layering of reference, with its musical analogy of tune and accompaniment, aria
and chorus, is so important. It is, Eliot argues, an 'organic'
process:

Poetic Form was not begotten by thinking it out or framing it as
a shell which should hold emotional expression, any more than
the shell of an animal arises before the living creature; but emotion, by its tendency to repetition, i.e. rhythmic persistence in
proportion as diversifying thought is absent, creates a form by
the recurrence of its elements in adjustment with certain given
conditions of sound, language, action, or environment. Just as
the beautiful expanding curves of a bivalve shell are not first
made for the reception of the unstable inhabitant, but grow and
are limited by the simple rhythmic conditions of its growing
life.[39]

'The Two . . .'

George Eliot may be a moral realist and an exponent of literary
Realism, but she is also a stylist, even if she would describe her
method as one of 'emotional' style. One of the most interesting
things about *Adam Bede* is its elaborate structure in terms of
repetitions and doublenesses – a pattern which directly reflects
the philosophy of 'Poetic Form' that Eliot describes in her 1868
essay.

Many things in *Adam Bede* happen twice. Hetty makes two
journeys; Adam and Arthur meet in the wood on two occasions;
Arthur and Adam both make visits to Irwine with Hetty on
their mind. In Chapter XV there are the two bed-chambers
where a set of contrasts is explicitly worked out. Hetty peers
into an old tarnished mirror to see only the surface of herself,
while Dinah looks out of the window at the moonlit scene, then
closes her eyes 'that she might feel more intensely the presence
of a Love and Sympathy deeper and more tender than was
breathed from the earth and sky'. Hetty exerts her 'narrow bit
of an imagination' to luxuriate in a future where she wears
silks, where Arthur Donnithorne has his arm around her, while
Dinah's imagination creates 'a thorny thicket of sin and sorrow,
in which she saw the poor thing struggling torn and bleeding'.

Much later in the novel, in Chapter XLV, the essentials of
this scene will be repeated and revised when Dinah and Hetty
meet again, and weep together again in the darkness of the
prison. As the narrator says, 'What strange contrast the two
figures made!' (Chapter XV). But this method of comparing
and measuring is one that informs the shape of the whole novel
and one that the reader is, for the most part, expected to make,
without explicit pointers from the narrative.

Even the key fact of the melodramatic strand in the novel is
based on a doubleness – on a return. For, crucially, Hetty
'returns' to the site of the story of herself that she had tried to
'forget' when she buried her baby. And that return uncovers
what would otherwise have remained hidden. If Hetty had
never gone back to the wood and the hole under the nut-tree,
there would have been no story.

In one sense this technique employs both stylized and realistic techniques. It is a contrived artifice, but it draws the reader in, so that we acquire a memory of events and significances that make a pattern of reference points. In this way it is a method that insists on a series of engaged responses from the reader. This begins with an emotional response, grows to one which is contemplative, and finally on to one which includes the promotion of a moral perspective where the reader must evaluate and assess the actions of the characters in the light of his or her own opinions and conduct in life.

Even without her own two accounts of the process, it is easy to see how George Eliot's own fit range of 'emotions' grew into the story that was to become *Adam Bede* and her first full-length novel. Her 'Aunt's Story' was linked in her mind with her own personal situation from 1854 – and so Hetty Sorrel was born. And yet that very period, so personally fraught, anxious and painful in many ways, was also the time when Eliot was becoming a writer, finding a voice, speaking out to the world – and so Dinah Morris was born, becoming, at Lewes's suggestion, 'the principal figure at the last' ('History').

Adam and Arthur

That leaves Adam – and Arthur. We know, because Eliot says so in her account of the composition of *Adam Bede*, that 'The character of Adam and one or two incidents connected with him, were suggested by my Father's early life'. But it was George Henry Lewes who perceived that Adam's part was 'too passive', and that he needed to be 'brought into more direct collision with Arthur'. She went on, 'This doubt *haunted* me' (my italics), 'and out of it grew the scene in the Wood between Adam and Arthur' ('History'). It was, unsurprisingly, *music* that gave Eliot the clue.

In the summer of 1858 while she and Lewes were in Munich, she happened to see a production of Gioacchino Rossini's 1829 opera *William Tell*. As the opera opens Leuthold the shepherd rushes on stage. Switzerland is under the yoke of Gessler, the Austrian tyrant, and Leuthold is being pursued by soldiers because he has just killed one of their number as the soldier attempted to rape Leuthold's daughter. William Tell rescues him. This is the first of several confrontation scenes, most notably that in Act III, where a maypole is erected in the market-place of Altdorf to celebrate one hundred years of Austrian domination of Switzerland. Gessler has his hat placed on top of the pole and demands that the people bow down to it . . . which Tell, a Swiss patriot, refuses to do. As in *Adam Bede* the mix is one of sexual domination – effectively an invoking of *droit de seigneur* – and class conflict.

But I would suggest that it was the playing out of these oppositions in the *music* of Rossini's opera that spoke most potently to Eliot's creating mind. In the famous overture – the only part of the opera that figures regularly in the repertoire today – but also throughout the opera as a whole, there is a dramatic pattern of musical contrasts beginning with the evocation of the peaceful pastoral scene by the lake but then going on to the violence of armed conflict, then moving to the terror and pity of William Tell's defiance and the tender duets between the lovers, the patriot Arnold and the aristocratic Mathilde. Out of her encounter with this opera Eliot made the conflicted relation between Adam and Arthur. The doubt sown by Lewes about the need for a 'direct collision' between them led to 'the scene in the Wood between Arthur and Adam', said Eliot, and so 'the fight came to me as a *necessity* one night at the Munich opera when I was listening to *William Tell*' ('History').

So Eliot wrote the scene of the fight in Chapter XXVII and she offered a revised and reworked version of that episode in Chapter XLVIII. We are supposed to understand the parallels:

> The next day, at evening, two men were walking from opposite points towards the same scene, drawn thither by a common memory. The scene was the Grove by Donnithorne Chase: you know who the men are.

It is easy enough to read Adam and Arthur's relation as one 'between men' where the primary connection is to each other, and the woman over whom they compete is wiped out of the picture. But from the beginning it was 'their mutual relation to Hetty' ('History') that motivated Eliot's imagination, and Hetty is very much here in this second scene between the two men. And so the process comes full circle. Eliot's initial inspiration was the story of Hetty, and even when she makes the detour suggested by Lewes and brings Arthur and Adam into 'direct collision', Hetty is still her inspiration.

As ever, in a work of fiction that relies so heavily on the creative understanding and sympathetic response of the reader, Hetty's presence in signalled by a symbol that we recognize. In Chapter XXVIII, as Adam fetches water and brandy for Arthur, who is stricken by Adam's blow, Arthur rouses himself to find a light and search the Hermitage:

> At last he found a slight thing, which he put first in his pocket, and then, on a second thought, took it out again and thrust deep down into a waste-paper basket. It was a woman's little pink silk handkerchief . . .

It is the whole story of Arthur and Hetty's relation in miniature. But it is not the end of the story. In Chapter XLVIII Arthur is conscious of the whereabouts of the handkerchief as he re-enters the Hermitage with Adam: '. . . there was the waste-paper basket full of scraps, and deep down in it, Arthur felt in an instant, there was the little pink silk handkerchief'. And at the end of the scene – a scene in which Arthur says to Adam, 'Haven't I loved her too? Didn't I see her yesterday? Shan't I carry the thought of her about with me as much as you will?' – Arthur retrieves the handkerchief.

I think that we are meant to believe him. Just as Hetty had once buried her baby and yet returned to the site of forgetting and to the fate that she can never escape, so Arthur too buries the thing which symbolizes his love for Hetty and of his betrayal of her (the point being that she undressed in the hermitage and so came to leave her handkerchief behind), and yet he returns to retrieve it and acknowledge the consequences that he cannot escape.

And Arthur again

When I first read *Adam Bede* as a teenager I hated Arthur. I relished the terrible irony of Chapter XLIV.[40] I wanted him to suffer. Now, I'm not so sure.

In the end, it is Arthur who is true to Hetty. Adam is comforted. He has a new relation with his marriage to Dinah, he earns and retains the kind of life for which he had planned, he has his children.

But Arthur has none of this. He has to relinquish his dream of being the squire adored by his workers and tenant farmers. He loses his health. He does not marry. He is left only with regret and the eternal consciousness of the consequences of his wrongdoing, so that Hetty can never be out of his mind: 'I could never do anything for her . . . she lived long enough for all the suffering – and I'd thought so of the time when I might do something for her' (Epilogue).

And there's something else that Arthur loses – his child.

In the novel, we are never told whether this is a boy or a girl, but I believe that the child has to have been a boy. So, without an heir, Arthur loses his estate too and the line is broken as the land will go to his cousin. There's no legal logic to it, of course, because Hetty's baby, being illegitimate, would not be in line to inherit in any case. But there is a symbolic logic that makes the formal pattern so essential to George Eliot's method.

And there is also an emotional logic that connects this lost child to the artistic 'child' that Eliot created in writing *Adam Bede* . . . The story of Hetty – 'My Aunt's Story' – was the source of Eliot's inspiration in writing her first novel. It was a story of creation and destruction in a world where illegitimate offspring end up being sacrificed through fear and timidity in the face of social condemnation.

At one time in 1849 young Mary Ann Evans had imagined herself as a mortal scrap whose very existence was uncertain, fragile, and nearly brought to a premature end. Ten years later George Eliot's *Adam Bede* was a 'love-child', the product of her unsanctioned union with George Henry Lewes. But, unlike Hetty's child, Eliot was determined to allow hers to live, and her defiance of convention is there even in her story about her story: 'I love it very much and am deeply thankful to have written it, whatever the public may say to it' ('History').

NOTES

1. William Wilkie Collins (as W.W.C.), Fifth Letter, in 'Magnetic Evenings at Home', *Leader*, 3:101 (28 February 1852), pp. 207–8. During the 1840s and 1850s there was great interest throughout Europe in many different manifestations of spiritual powers. Franz Mesmer (1734–1815) developed a theory of 'animal magnetism' which later evolved into techniques of hypnosis. Other popular practices included mind-reading (or clairvoyance) and table-tapping (or spiritualism). For a full account of the Victorian obsession with clairvoyance and other psychological experiments, see Alison Winter, *Mesmerized: Powers of Mind in Victorian Britain* (Chicago: University of Chicago Press, 1998).

   Eliot's knowledge about the practices of the 'Egyptian sorcerer' also owes something to a book which she had read before writing *Adam Bede* and to which she returned many years later when she was preparing to write 'Stradivarius' (1873). In Edward William Lane's *An Account of the Manners and Customs of the Modern Egyptians*, 2 vols. (London: Charles Knight, 1837), vol. I, p. 373, he wrote, 'I asked the magician whether the objects appeared in the ink as if actually before the eyes, or as if in a glass, which makes the right appear left. He answered, that they appeared as in a mirror.' See Joseph Wiesenfarth, 'George Eliot's Notes for *Adam Bede*', *Nineteenth-Century Fiction*, 32:1 (September 1977), p. 128.

2. 'Indo-Mohammedan Folk Lore', 'Magic Mirrors' by H. C., *Notes and Queries*, 3rd series, 11 (January–June 1867), p. 180.

3. Wilkie Collins, *The Moonstone*, ed. Sandra Kemp (Harmondsworth: Penguin Books, 1998).

4. George Henry Lewes, 'The Fallacy of Clairvoyance', *Leader*, 3:105 (27 March 1852), p. 305.

5. The 'dreaming' character of the novelist at work was to become an image that Eliot often used, most notably in the opening sections of *The Mill on the Floss* (1860).

6. 6 November 1856, *Letters*, II, 269–70 (see Notes for complete citation).

7. *Letters*, II, 381. For a full account of Eliot's early life and the making of her career as a novelist, see the biographies by Kathryn Hughes, Rosemary Ashton and Gordon S. Haight; and Eliot's letters and journals.

8. 6 December 1857, *Journals*, ed. Harris and Johnston, p. 289. For the complete chronology of the history of the composition and publication of *Adam Bede*, see George Eliot, *Adam Bede*, ed. Carol A. Martin, Clarendon Edition (Oxford: Oxford University Press, 2001), pp. xi–liv.

9. *Letters*, II, 387.

10. See Appendix I: hereafter cited in the text as 'History'. The phrase 'My Aunt's Story' comes from the 'History'.

11. George Eliot, 'Aurora Leigh', *Westminster Review* (January 1857), pp. 306–10; reprinted in Elizabeth Barrett Browning, *Aurora Leigh*, ed. Margaret Reynolds (New York: W. W. Norton, 1996), pp. 407–8.

12. The famous story of Elizabeth Barrett's elopement with Robert Browning was a family secret at this time, and few people knew the details.

13. 23 November 1848, *Letters*, I, 272–3. Laura C. Berry also comments on this passage in *The Child, the State and the Victorian Novel* (Charlottesville: University of Virginia Press, 1999), pp. 149–50.

14. Josephine McDonagh, *Child Murder and British Culture 1720–1900* (Cambridge: Cambridge University Press, 2003), pp. 132–7. See also McDonagh, 'Child Murder Narratives in George Eliot's *Adam Bede*: Embedded Histories and Fictional Representation', *Nineteenth Century Literature*, 56:2 (2001), pp. 228–59.

15. *Journals*, ed. Harris and Johnston, p. 304. On this theme see also Rosemarie Bodenheimer, *The Real Life of Mary Ann Evans: George Eliot, Her Letters and Fiction* (Ithaca, NY: Cornell University Press, 1994).

16. Eliot, *Adam Bede*; ed. Martin, p. ciii.

17. George Eliot, Note on the composition of the novel, fair-copy manuscript of *Adam Bede*, British Library, Add MS. 34020.

18. See Appendix II.

19. 31 March 1858, *Letters*, II, 446.

20. 27 December 1858, *Letters*, II, 509.

21. *George Eliot: The Critical Heritage*, ed. David Carroll (London: Routledge and Kegan Paul, 1971), pp. 73–6; *Saturday Review* (26 February 1859), pp. 250–51; *Examiner* (5 March 1859), p. 149. Both quoted in Eliot, *Adam Bede*, ed. Martin, pp. vii, xlix.

22. John Sutherland works carefully through the chronology and the hints on Hetty's pregnancy in his literary puzzle essay, 'What is Hetty waiting for?', in *Is Heathcliff a Murderer?: Puzzles in Nineteenth-Century Fiction* (Oxford: Oxford University Press, 1996), pp. 110–16. His conclusion is that Hetty does not realize she is pregnant until Mrs Poyser gives her a lecture on the facts of life in view of her forthcoming marriage to Adam. I don't agree – Hetty lived on a farm, and doubtless knew what was what – and Eliot's novel is set in the late eighteenth century at a time when the legendary Victorian prudishness had not set in. That nobody *noticed* Hetty's pregnancy is another matter. But here Martin suggests that Eliot borrowed a detail from Walter Scott's *Heart of Midlothian* (1818) in that Mrs Poyser – who is the one person most likely to have noticed the latter stages of Hetty's pregnancy – is confined to her room throughout January in Chapter XXXV. In Scott's novel Mrs Saddletree, similarly sharp-eyed, is also got out of the way by this ruse (Eliot, *Adam Bede*, ed. Martin, p. xxii).

23. McDonagh, *Child Murder and British Culture*, pp. 123–53.

24. See Stephen Gill, *Wordsworth and the Victorians* (Oxford: Oxford University Press, 1998).

25. Elizabeth Barrett Browning, 'The Runaway Slave at Pilgrim's Point', lines 126 and 120, in *Victorian Women Poets*, ed. Angela Leighton and Margaret Reynolds (Oxford: Blackwell, 1995), pp. 80–88.

26. For a full account of the 1624 Act and the legal history of the crime of child murder, see Mark Jackson, *New Born Child Murder: Women, Illegitimacy and the Courts in Eighteenth-Century England* (Manchester: Manchester University Press, 1996).

27. See Daniel Defoe, *The Generous Protector; or, a Friendly Proposal to Prevent Murder and Other Enormous Abuses by Erecting an Hospital for Foundlings and Bastard Children* (London, 1731), and Gillian Wagner, *Thomas Coram, Gent* (Woodbridge Suffolk: Boydell Press, 2004). See also Lisa Zunshine, *Bastards and Foundlings*: Illegitimacy in Eighteenth-Century England (Columbus: Ohio State University Press, 2005).

28. William Hunter, 'On the Uncertainty of Signs of Murder, in the Case of Bastard Children' (1784), reprinted in *The Proofs of Infanticide Considered* (London, 1834), p. 8.

29. Jackson, *New Born Child Murder*. See also Lisa Zunshine, *Bastards and Foundlings*.

30. Duncan Campbell, *A Stranger and Afraid: The Story of Caroline Beale* (London: Macmillan, 1997), pp. 3–9, 35–7.

31. For this and other examples of current efforts to cope with relinquished children in various countries and cultures, see Kate Adie, *Nobody's Child: Who Are You When You Don't Know Your Past?* (London: Hodder and Stoughton, 2005).

32. The manuscript of the adaptation is in the Lord Chamberlain's collection, British Library. As Eliot refused an application to adapt *Adam Bede* for the stage in 1879, I take it that the 1862 version was unauthorized. See Eliot, *Adam Bede*, ed. Martin, p. lxxxvii, n. 7.

33. BBC Radio 4 Woman's Hour serial, 2–6, 9–13 and 16–20 July 2001, 10.45–11.00. Produced by Patrick Rayner, adapted by Robert Forrest with Thomas Arnold as Adam Bede, Katherine Igoe as Hetty Sorrel, Vicki Liddelle as Dinah Morris and Richard Greenwood as Arthur Donnithorne. I am indebted to Patrick Rayner and Robert Forrest for this information and their kind permission to refer to the script.

34. Eliot was baptized 'Mary Ann', and chose 'Marian' as an adult. She first used 'George Eliot' in a letter to John Blackwood written in February 1857.

35. 7 October 1859, *Letters*, III, 176. Quoted in Jennifer Uglow, *George Eliot* (London: Virago, 1987), p. 111.

36. See Mary Anne Schofield, ' "Women's Speaking Justified": The Feminine Quaker Voice, 1662–1797', *Tulsa Studies in Women's Literature*, 6:1 (Spring 1987), pp. 61–77.

37. George Eliot, 'The Natural History of German Life' (1856), in *George Eliot: Selected Critical Writings*, ed. Rosemary Ashton (Oxford: Oxford University Press, 1992), pp. 263–4.

38. Ibid., pp. 282–3.

39. George Eliot, 'Notes on Form in Art' (1868), in *Selected Critical Writings*, ed. Ashton, pp. 355–9.

40. According to Martin, foliation in Eliot's fair-copy manuscript suggests that Chapter XLIV, 'Arthur's Return', was originally to have followed Chapter XL, 'The Bitter Waters Spread', so that the full ghastliness of Hetty's predicament compared with Arthur's complacent anticipation was a second thought for Eliot (Eliot, *Adam Bede*, ed. Martin, p. xliii).

Further Reading

LETTERS, ESSAYS AND JOURNALS BY GEORGE ELIOT

George Eliot: Selected Critical Writings, ed. Rosemary Ashton (Oxford: Oxford University Press, 1992).
George Eliot: Selected Essays, Poems and Other Writings, ed. A. S. Byatt and Nicholas Warren (Harmondsworth: Penguin, 1990).
The George Eliot Letters, ed. Gordon S. Haight, 9 vols. (New Haven and London: Yale University Press, 1954–78).
The Journals of George Eliot, ed. Margaret Harris and Judith Johnston (Cambridge: Cambridge University Press, 1999).
Essays of George Eliot, ed. Thomas Pinney (London and New York: Routledge and Kegan Paul, 1963).
George Eliot: A Writer's Notebook 1854–1879 and Uncollected Writings, ed. Joseph Wiesenfarth (Charlottesville: University of Virginia Press, 1981).

BIOGRAPHIES

Rosemary Ashton, *George Eliot* (Oxford: Oxford University Press, 1993).
—, *G. H. Lewes: A Life* (Oxford: Oxford University Press, 1991).
Rosemarie Bodenheimer, *The Real Life of Mary Ann Evans:*

George Eliot, Her Letters and Fiction (Ithaca, New York: Cornell University Press, 1994).

Kristin Brady, *George Eliot* (Basingstoke and London: Macmillan, 1992).

J. W. Cross, *George Eliot's Life as Related in her Letters and Journals*, 3 vols. (Edinburgh and London: Blackwood's, 1885; reprinted with additions, 1886).

Valerie A. Dodd, *George Eliot: An Intellectual Life* (New York and London: St Martin's Press, 1990).

Tim Dolin, *George Eliot* (Oxford: Oxford World's Classics, 2005).

Gordon S. Haight, *George Eliot: A Biography* (Oxford: Oxford University Press, 1968; Harmondsworth: Penguin, 1992).

Kathryn Hughes, *George Eliot: The Last Victorian* (London: Fourth Estate, 1998).

Frederick Robert Karl, *George Eliot: A Biography* (New York: W. W. Norton, 1990).

Jennifer Uglow, *George Eliot* (London: Virago, 1987).

SELECTED EDITIONS OF *ADAM BEDE*

ed. Valentine Cunningham (Oxford: Oxford World's Classics, 1996).

ed. Stephen Gill (Harmondsworth: Penguin, 1980).

ed. Carol A. Martin (Oxford: Clarendon Press, 2001).

ed. Doreen Roberts (Ware, Hertfordshire: Wordsworth Classics, 2003).

SELECTED CRITICISM

Courtney Berger, 'When Bad Things Happen to Bad People: Liability and Individual Consciousness in *Adam Bede* and *Silas Marner*', *Novel: A Forum on Fiction*, 33:3 (Summer 2000), pp. 307–27.

Laura C. Berry, *The Child, the State and the Victorian Novel* (Charlottesville: University of Virginia Press, 1999).

David Carroll (ed.), *George Eliot: The Critical Heritage* (London: Routledge and Kegan Paul, 1971).

—, *George Eliot and the Conflict of Interpretations* (Cambridge: Cambridge University Press, 1992).

Michael Davis, *George Eliot and Nineteenth Century Psychology: Exploring the Unmapped Country* (Aldershot: Ashgate Publishing, 2006).

Stephen Gill, *Wordsworth and the Victorians* (Oxford: Clarendon Press, 1998).

Mark Jackson, *New Born Child Murder: Women, Illegitimacy and the Courts in Eighteenth-Century England* (Manchester: Manchester University Press, 1996).

Deanna K. Kreisel, 'Incognito, Intervention and Dismemberment in *Adam Bede*', *English Literary History*, 70:2 (Summer 2003), pp. 541–74.

Josephine McDonagh, *Child Murder and British Culture, 1720–1900* (Cambridge: Cambridge University Press, 2003).

—, 'Child Murder Narratives in George Eliot's *Adam Bede*: Embedded Histories and Fictional Representation', *Nineteenth Century Literature*, 56:2 (2001), pp. 228–59.

William Mottram, *The True Story of George Eliot in Relation to 'Adam Bede'* (Chicago: A. C. McClurg, 1906).

John Sutherland, 'What is Hetty waiting for?', in *Is Heathcliff a Murderer?: Puzzles in Nineteenth-Century Fiction* (Oxford: Oxford University Press, 1996), pp. 110–16.

Jerome Thale, '*Adam Bede*: Arthur Donnithorne and *Zeluco*', *Modern Language Notes*, 70:4 (April 1955), pp. 263–5.

Joseph Wiesenfarth, 'George Eliot's Notes for *Adam Bede*', *Nineteenth-Century Fiction*, 32:2 (September 1977), pp. 127–65.

Lisa Zunshine, *Bastards and Foundlings: Illegitimacy in Eighteenth-Century England* (Columbus: Ohio State University Press, 2005).

A Note on the Text

The copy-text for this edition is 'The New Edition' published by Blackwood's from 1873, both with and without illustrations, priced 31s. 6d. This edition was printed from plates of the first one-volume edition published on 31 January 1862 (called the 'Tenth Edition' on the title-page). George Eliot made substantial revisions to the text for the 1862 edition, writing her corrections in a copy of the so called 'Eighth Edition' (published in two volumes in 1860), which is now in the Harry Ransom Humanities Research Center at the University of Texas at Austin and which includes a note written by George Simpson of Blackwood's 'Corrected by Author Nov. 1861', recording the date of the publisher receiving the corrected copy. Eliot made hundreds of emendations to both words and punctuation, correcting inconsistencies in place and personal names, errors in dialect, and at least one anachronism.

While Eliot was making her list of changes for Blackwood's she wrote on 25 September 1861, 'I have read carefully all through "Adam Bede" and "The Mill [on the Floss]" and have marked all the *errata* I have discovered. I hope the new editions will be carefully printed after these corrected copies ... I am very glad ... that I have given the needful time to "Adam" ... for there were several mistakes which affected the sense in an important manner. It has moved me a good deal – reading the books again after a long interval, but it has done me good, for I can say a full Amen to everything I have written' (*Letters*, VIII, 291).

The copy-text has been amended to bring the text into line with Penguin Classics house-style, that is: 'ise' spellings have

been changed to 'ize'; 'judgment' changed to 'judgement';
double quotation marks to singles (with doubles inside);
unspaced M-dashes to spaced N, and 2M-dashes to M; the full
stop removed after part number, chapter number and title.
Hyphens at the end of a line in the copy-text have been emended
to the most usual form. Proper and personal names have been
corrected for the sake of consistency; so the town is Rosseter
throughout (not Drosseter), Irwine's butler is Carroll throughout (not Carrol), Dinah's Aunt is Judith (not Mary), Basan (not
Bashan) and Dacey (not Lacey). Some missing punctuation has
been silently corrected.

The first edition of *Adam Bede* was published by William
Blackwood and Sons of Edinburgh on 1 February 1859 in three
volumes, price 31s. 6d. Eliot maintained a close interest in both
the printing of the text and the sales of her work. Most notably,
she revised the passage about the willow wand and the nature of
Adam's superstition in the 'Fourth Edition' published *c.* 4 June
1859, and the substantial corrections that she made for the
1862 edition included her statement on the 'realist' project in
the opening paragraphs of Chapter XVII. *Adam Bede* sold more
than 15,000 copies in 10 editions over 3 years, and by 1879
some 80,000 copies had been printed. It was by far Eliot's most
consistently popular book, selling more than any other of her
titles which were often promoted as being 'by the author of
Adam Bede'.

ADAM BEDE

BY

GEORGE ELIOT

'So that ye may have
Clear images before your gladdened eyes
Of nature's unambitious underwood
And flowers that prosper in the shade. And when
I speak of such among the flock as swerved
Or fell, those only shall be singled out
Upon whose lapse, or error, something more
Than brotherly forgiveness may attend.'
— WORDSWORTH[1]

Contents

BOOK THIRD

BOOK FOURTH

BOOK FIFTH

BOOK SIXTH

BOOK FIRST

CHAPTER I

The Workshop

With a single drop of ink for a mirror, the Egyptian sorcerer undertakes to reveal to any chance comer far-reaching visions of the past.[1] This is what I undertake to do for you, reader. With this drop of ink at the end of my pen, I will show you the roomy workshop of Mr Jonathan Burge, carpenter and builder, in the village of Hayslope, as it appeared on the eighteenth of June, in the year of our Lord 1799.[2]

The afternoon sun was warm on the five workmen there, busy upon doors and window-frames and wainscoting.[3] A scent of pine-wood from a tent-like pile of planks outside the open door mingled itself with the scent of the elder-bushes which were spreading their summer snow close to the open window opposite; the slanting sunbeams shone through the transparent shavings that flew before the steady plane, and lit up the fine grain of the oak panelling which stood propped against the wall. On a heap of those soft shavings a rough grey shepherd-dog had made himself a pleasant bed, and was lying with his nose between his fore-paws, occasionally wrinkling his brows to cast a glance at the tallest of the five workmen, who was carving a shield in the centre of a wooden mantelpiece. It was to this workman that the strong barytone belonged which was heard above the sound of plane and hammer singing –

> 'Awake, my soul, and with the sun
> Thy daily stage of duty run;
> Shake off dull sloth. . . .'

Here some measurement was to be taken which required more concentrated attention, and the sonorous voice subsided into a low whistle; but it presently broke out again with renewed vigour –

> 'Let all thy converse be sincere,
> Thy conscience as the noonday clear.'[4]

Such a voice could only come from a broad chest, and the broad chest belonged to a large-boned muscular man nearly six feet high, with a back so flat and a head so well poised that when he drew himself up to take a more distant survey of his work, he had the air of a soldier standing at ease. The sleeve rolled up above the elbow showed an arm that was likely to win the prize for feats of strength; yet the long supple hand, with its broad finger-tips, looked ready for works of skill. In his tall stalwartness Adam Bede was a Saxon, and justified his name;[5] but the jet-black hair, made the more noticeable by its contrast with the light paper cap, and the keen glance of the dark eyes that shone from under strongly marked, prominent and mobile eyebrows, indicated a mixture of Celtic blood. The face was large and roughly hewn, and when in repose had no other beauty than such as belongs to an expression of good-humoured honest intelligence.

It is clear at a glance that the next workman is Adam's brother. He is nearly as tall; he has the same type of features, the same hue of hair and complexion; but the strength of the family likeness seems only to render more conspicuous the remarkable difference of expression both in form and face. Seth's[6] broad shoulders have a slight stoop; his eyes are grey; his eyebrows have less prominence and more repose than his brother's; and his glance, instead of being keen, is confiding and benignant. He has thrown off his paper cap, and you see that his hair is not thick and straight, like Adam's, but thin and wavy, allowing you to discern the exact contour of a coronal arch[7] that predominates very decidedly over the brow.

The idle tramps always felt sure they could get a copper from Seth; they scarcely ever spoke to Adam.

The concert of the tools and Adam's voice was at last broken by Seth, who, lifting the door at which he had been working intently, placed it against the wall, and said –

'There! I've finished my door to-day, anyhow.'

The workmen all looked up; Jim Salt, a burly red-haired man, known as Sandy Jim, paused from his planing, and Adam said to Seth, with a sharp glance of surprise –

'What! dost think thee'st[8] finished the door?'

'Ay, sure,' said Seth, with answering surprise; 'What's awanting to't?'

A loud roar of laughter from the other three workmen made Seth look round confusedly. Adam did not join in the laughter, but there was a slight smile on his face as he said, in a gentler tone than before –

'Why, thee'st forgot the panels.'

The laughter burst out afresh as Seth clapped his hands to his head, and coloured over brow and crown.

'Hoorray!' shouted a small lithe fellow, called Wiry Ben, running forward and seizing the door. 'We'll hang up th' door at fur end o' th' shop an' write on't "Seth Bede, the Methody,[9] his work". Here, Jim, lend's hould o' th' red-pot.'[10]

'Nonsense!' said Adam. 'Let it alone, Ben Cranage. You'll mayhap be making such a slip yourself some day; you'll laugh o' th' other side o' your mouth then.'

'Catch me at it, Adam. It'll be a good while afore my head's full o' th' Methodies,' said Ben.

'Nay, but it's often full o' drink, and that's worse.'

Ben, however, had now got the 'red-pot' in his hand, and was about to begin writing his inscription, making, by way of preliminary, an imaginary S in the air.

'Let it alone, will you?' Adam called out, laying down his tools, striding up to Ben, and seizing his right shoulder. 'Let it alone, or I'll shake the soul out o' your body.'

Ben shook in Adam's iron grasp, but, like a plucky small man as he was, he didn't mean to give in. With his left hand he snatched the brush from his powerless right, and made a movement as if he would perform the feat of writing with his left. In a moment Adam turned him round, seized his other

shoulder, and, pushing him along, pinned him against the wall.
But now Seth spoke.

'Let be, Addy, let be. Ben will be joking. Why, he's i' the
right to laugh at me – I canna help laughing at myself.'

'I shan't loose him, till he promises to let the door alone,'
said Adam.

'Come, Ben, lad,' said Seth, in a persuasive tone, 'don't let's
have a quarrel about it. You know Adam will have his way.
You may's well try to turn a waggon in a narrow lane. Say
you'll leave the door alone, and make an end on't.'

'I binna frighted at Adam,' said Ben, 'but I donna mind sayin'
as I'll let 't alone at your askin', Seth.'

'Come, that's wise of you, Ben,' said Adam, laughing and
relaxing his grasp.

They all returned to their work now; but Wiry Ben, having
had the worst in the bodily contest, was bent on retrieving that
humiliation by a success in sarcasm.

'Which was ye thinkin' on, Seth,' he began – 'the pretty
parson's face or her sarmunt,[11] when ye forgot the panels?'

'Come and hear her, Ben,' said Seth, good-humouredly; 'she's
going to preach on the Green to-night; happen ye'd get something to think on yourself then, instead o' those wicked songs
you're so fond on. Ye might get religion, and that 'ud be the
best day's earnings y' ever made.'

'All i' good time for that, Seth; I'll think about that when I'm
agoin' to settle i' life; bachelors doesn't want such heavy earnins.
Happen I shall do the coortin' an' the religion both together, as
ye do, Seth; but ye wouldna ha' me get converted an' chop in
atween ye an' the pretty preacher, an' carry her aff?'

'No fear o' that, Ben; she's neither for you nor for me to win,
I doubt. Only you come and hear her, and you won't speak
lightly on her again.'

'Well, I'n half a mind t' ha' a look at her to-night, if there
isn't good company at th' Holly Bush. What'll she take for her
text? Happen ye can tell me, Seth, if so be as I shouldna come
up i' time for't. Will't be, – What come ye out for to see? A
prophetess? Yea, I say unto you, and more than a prophetess[12]
– a uncommon pretty young woman.'

'Come, Ben,' said Adam, rather sternly, 'you let the words o' the Bible alone; you're going too far now.'

'What! are *ye* a-turnin' roun', Adam? I thought ye war dead again th' women preachin',[13] a while agoo?'

'Nay, I'm not turnin' noway. I said nought about the women preachin': I said, You let the Bible alone: you've got a jest-book,[14] han't you, as you're rare and proud on? Keep your dirty fingers to that.'

'Why, y' are gettin' as big a saint as Seth. Y' are goin' to th' preachin' to-night, I should think. Ye'll do finely t' lead the singin'. But I don' know what Parson Irwine 'ull say at his gran' favright Adam Bede a-turnin' Methody.'

'Never do you bother yourself about me, Ben. I'm not a-going to turn Methodist any more nor you are – though it's like enough you'll turn to something worse. Mester Irwine's got more sense nor to meddle wi' people's doing as they like in religion. That's between themselves and God, as he's said to me many a time.'

'Ay, ay; but he's none so fond o' your dissenters,[15] for all that.'

'Maybe; I'm none so fond o' Josh Tod's thick ale, but I don't hinder you from making a fool o' yourself wi't.'

There was a laugh at this thrust of Adam's, but Seth said, very seriously –

'Nay, nay, Addy, thee mustna say as anybody's religion's like thick ale. Thee dostna believe but what the dissenters and the Methodists have got the root o' the matter as well as the church folks.'

'Nay, Seth, lad; I'm not for laughing at no man's religion. Let 'em follow their consciences, that's all. Only I think it 'ud be better if their consciences 'ud let 'em stay quiet i' the church – there's a deal to be learnt there. And there's such a thing as being over-speritial; we must have something beside Gospel i' this world. Look at the canals, an' th' aqueducs, an' th' coal-pit engines, and Arkwright's mills there at Cromford;[16] a man must learn summat beside Gospel to make them things, I reckon. But t' hear some o' them preachers, you'd think as a man must be doing nothing all's life but shutting's eyes and looking what's a-going on inside him. I know a man must have the love o' God

in his soul, and the Bible's God's word. But what does the Bible
say? Why, it says as God put his sperrit into the workman as
built the tabernacle,[17] to make him do all the carved work and
things as wanted a nice hand. And this is my way o' looking at
it: there's the sperrit o' God in all things and all times – weekday
as well as Sunday – and i' the great works and inventions, and
i' the figuring and the mechanics. And God helps us with our
headpieces and our hands as well as with our souls; and if a
man does bits o' jobs out o' working hours – builds a oven for
's wife to save her from going to the bakehouse,[18] or scrats at
his bit o' garden and makes two potatoes grow istead o' one,
he's doing more good, and he's just as near to God, as if he was
running after some preacher and a-praying and a-groaning.'[19]

'Well done, Adam!' said Sandy Jim, who had paused from
his planing to shift his planks while Adam was speaking; 'that's
the best sarmunt I've heared this long while. By th' same token,
my wife's been a-plaguin' on me to build her a oven this
twelvemont.'

'There's reason in what thee say'st, Adam,' observed Seth,
gravely. 'But thee know'st thyself as it's hearing the preachers
thee find'st so much fault with has turned many an idle fellow
into an industrious un. It's the preacher as empties th' alehouse;
and if a man gets religion, he'll do his work none the worse for
that.'

'On'y he'll lave the panels out o' th' doors sometimes, eh,
Seth?' said Wiry Ben.

'Ah, Ben, you've got a joke again' me as 'll last you your life.
But it isna religion as was i' fault there; it was Seth Bede, as was
allays a wool-gathering chap,[20] and religion hasna cured him,
the more's the pity.'

'Ne'er heed me, Seth,' said Wiry Ben, 'y' are a downright
good-hearted chap, panels or no panels; an' ye donna set up
your bristles at every bit o' fun, like some o' your kin, as is
mayhap cliverer.'

'Seth, lad,' said Adam, taking no notice of the sarcasm against
himself, 'thee mustna take me unkind. I wasna driving at thee
in what I said just now. Some 's got one way o' looking at
things and some 's got another.'

'Nay, nay, Addy, thee mean'st me no unkindness,' said Seth, 'I know that well enough. Thee't like thy dog Gyp – thee bark'st at me sometimes, but thee allays lick'st my hand after.'

All hands worked on in silence for some minutes, until the church clock began to strike six. Before the first stroke had died away, Sandy Jim had loosed his plane and was reaching his jacket; Wiry Ben had left a screw half driven in, and thrown his screwdriver into his tool-basket; Mum Taft, who, true to his name, had kept silence[21] throughout the previous conversation, had flung down his hammer as he was in the act of lifting it; and Seth, too, had straightened his back, and was putting out his hand towards his paper cap. Adam alone had gone on with his work as if nothing had happened. But observing the cessation of the tools, he looked up, and said, in a tone of indignation –

'Look there, now! I can't abide to see men throw away their tools i' that way, the minute the clock begins to strike, as if they took no pleasure i' their work, and was afraid o' doing a stroke too much.'

Seth looked a little conscious, and began to be slower in his preparations for going, but Mum Taft broke silence, and said –

'Ay, ay, Adam lad, ye talk like a young un. When y' are six-an'-forty like me, istid o' six-an'-twenty, ye wonna be so flush o' workin' for nought.'

'Nonsense,' said Adam, still wrathful; 'what's age got to do with it, I wonder? Ye arena getting stiff yet, I reckon. I hate to see a man's arms drop down as if he was shot, before the clock's fairly struck, just as if he'd never a bit o' pride and delight in 's work. The very grindstone[22] 'ull go on turning a bit after you loose it.'

'Bodderation, Adam!' exclaimed Wiry Ben; 'lave a chap aloon, will 'ee? Ye war a-finding faut wi' preachers a while agoo – y' are fond enough o' preachin' yoursen. Ye may like work better nor play, but I like play better nor work; that'll 'commodate ye – it laves ye th' more to do.'

With this exit speech, which he considered effective, Wiry Ben shouldered his basket and left the workshop, quickly followed by Mum Taft and Sandy Jim. Seth lingered, and looked wistfully at Adam, as if he expected him to say something.

'Shalt go home before thee go'st to the preaching?' Adam asked, looking up.

'Nay; I've got my hat and things at Will Maskery's. I shan't be home before going for ten. I'll happen see Dinah Morris safe home, if she's willing. There's nobody comes with her from Poyser's, thee know'st.'

'Then I'll tell mother not to look for thee,' said Adam.

'Thee artna going to Poyser's thyself to-night?' said Seth, rather timidly, as he turned to leave the workshop.

'Nay, I'm going to th' school.'

Hitherto Gyp had kept his comfortable bed, only lifting up his head and watching Adam more closely as he noticed the other workmen departing. But no sooner did Adam put his ruler in his pocket, and begin to twist his apron round his waist, than Gyp ran forward and looked up in his master's face with patient expectation. If Gyp had had a tail he would doubtless have wagged it, but being destitute of that vehicle for his emotions, he was like many other worthy personages, destined to appear more phlegmatic than nature had made him.

'What! art ready for the basket, eh, Gyp?' said Adam, with the same gentle modulation of voice as when he spoke to Seth.

Gyp jumped and gave a short bark, as much as to say, 'Of course.' Poor fellow, he had not a great range of expression.

The basket was the one which on workdays held Adam's and Seth's dinner; and no official, walking in procession, could look more resolutely unconscious of all acquaintances than Gyp with his basket, trotting at his master's heels.

On leaving the workshop Adam locked the door, took the key out, and carried it to the house on the other side of the woodyard. It was a low house, with smooth grey thatch and buff walls, looking pleasant and mellow in the evening light. The leaded windows were bright and speckless, and the door-stone[23] was as clean as a white boulder at ebb tide. On the door-stone stood a clean old woman, in a dark-striped linen gown, a red kerchief, and a linen cap, talking to some speckled fowls which appeared to have been drawn towards her by an illusory expectation of cold potatoes or barley. The old woman's sight seemed to be dim, for she did not recognize Adam till he said –

'Here's the key, Dolly; lay it down for me in the house, will you?'

'Ay, sure; but wunna ye come in, Adam? Miss Mary's i' th' house, an' Mester Burge 'ull be back anon; he'd be glad t' ha' ye to supper wi'm, I'll be's warrand.'

'No, Dolly, thank you; I'm off home. Good-evening.'

Adam hastened with long strides, Gyp close to his heels, out of the workyard, and along the highroad leading away from the village and down to the valley. As he reached the foot of the slope, an elderly horseman, with his portmanteau[24] strapped behind him, stopped his horse when Adam had passed him, and turned round to have another long look at the stalwart workman in paper cap, leather breeches, and dark-blue worsted stockings.

Adam, unconscious of the admiration he was exciting, presently struck across the fields, and now broke out into the tune which had all day long been running in his head:–

> 'Let all thy converse he sincere,
> Thy conscience as the noonday clear;
> For God's all-seeing eye surveys
> Thy secret thoughts, thy works and ways.'

CHAPTER II

The Preaching

About a quarter to seven there was an unusual appearance of excitement in the village of Hayslope, and through the whole length of its little street, from the Donnithorne Arms to the churchyard gate, the inhabitants had evidently been drawn out of their houses by something more than the pleasure of lounging in the evening sunshine. The Donnithorne Arms stood at the entrance of the village, and a small farmyard and stackyard which flanked it, indicating that there was a pretty take of land[1] attached to the inn, gave the traveller a promise of good feed for himself and his horse, which might well console him for the ignorance in which the weatherbeaten sign left him as to the heraldic bearings of that ancient family, the Donnithornes. Mr Casson, the landlord, had been for some time standing at the door with his hands in his pockets, balancing himself on his heels and toes, and looking towards a piece of unenclosed ground,[2] with a maple in the middle of it, which he knew to be the destination of certain grave-looking men and women whom he had observed passing at intervals.

Mr Casson's person was by no means of that common type which can be allowed to pass without description. On a front view it appeared to consist principally of two spheres, bearing about the same relation to each other as the earth and the moon: that is to say, the lower sphere might be said, at a rough guess, to be thirteen times larger than the upper, which naturally performed the function of a mere satellite and tributary. But here the resemblance ceased, for Mr Casson's head was not at all a melancholy-looking satellite, nor was it a 'spotty globe', as Milton[3] has irreverently called the moon; on the contrary,

no head and face could look more sleek and healthy, and its
expression, which was chiefly confined to a pair of round and
ruddy cheeks, the slight knot and interruptions forming the
nose and eyes being scarcely worth mention, was one of jolly
contentment, only tempered by that sense of personal dignity
which usually made itself felt in his attitude and bearing. This
sense of dignity could hardly be considered excessive in a man
who had been butler to 'the family' for fifteen years, and who,
in his present high position, was necessarily very much in
contact with his inferiors. How to reconcile his dignity with the
satisfaction of his curiosity by walking towards the Green, was
the problem that Mr Casson had been revolving in his mind for
the last five minutes; but when he had partly solved it by
taking his hands out of his pockets, and thrusting them into the
armholes of his waistcoat, by throwing his head on one side,
and providing himself with an air of contemptuous indifference
to whatever might fall under his notice, his thoughts were
diverted by the approach of the horseman whom we lately saw
pausing to have another look at our friend Adam, and who
now pulled up at the door of the Donnithorne Arms.

'Take off the bridle and give him a drink, ostler,' said the
traveller to the lad in a smock-frock,[4] who had come out of the
yard at the sound of the horse's hoofs.

'Why, what's up in your pretty village, landlord?' he
continued, getting down. 'There seems to be quite a stir.'

'It's a Methodis, preaching, sir; it's been gev hout as a young
woman's a-going to preach on the Green,' answered Mr
Casson, in a treble and wheezy voice, with a slightly mincing
accent. 'Will you please to step in, sir, an' tek somethink?'

'No, I must be getting on to Rosseter. I only want a drink for
my horse. And what does your parson say, I wonder, to a young
woman preaching just under his nose?'

'Parson Irwine, sir, doesn't live here;[5] he lives at Brox'on,
over the hill there. The parsonage here's a tumble-down place,
sir, not fit for gentry to live in. He comes here to preach of a
Sunday afternoon, sir, an' puts up his hoss here. It's a grey cob,[6]
sir, an' he sets great store by't. He's allays put up his hoss here,
sir, iver since before I hed the Donnithorne Arms. I'm not this

countryman, you may tell by my tongue, sir. They're cur'ous talkers i' this country, sir; the gentry's hard work to hunderstand 'em. I was brought hup among the gentry, sir, an' got the turn o' their tongue when I was a bye. Why, what do you think the folks here says for "hevn't you"? – the gentry, you know, says, "hevn't you" – well, the people about here says "hanna yey". It's what they call the dileck as is spoke hereabout, sir. That's what I've heard Squire Donnithorne say many a time; it's the dileck, says he.'

'Ay, ay,' said the stranger, smiling. 'I know it very well. But you've not got many Methodists about here, surely – in this agricultural spot? I should have thought there would hardly be such a thing as a Methodist to be found about here. You're all farmers, aren't you? The Methodists can seldom lay much hold on *them*.'

'Why, sir, there's a pretty lot o' workmen round about, sir. There's Mester Burge as owns the timber-yard over there, he underteks a good bit o' building an' repairs. An' there's the stone-pits not far off. There's plenty of emply i' this countryside, sir. An' there's a fine batch o' Methodisses at Treddles'on – that's the market-town about three mile off – you'll maybe ha' come through it, sir. There's pretty nigh a score of 'em on the Green now, as come from there. That's where our people gets it from, though there's only two men of 'em in all Hayslope: that's Will Maskery, the wheelwright, and Seth Bede, a young man as works at the carpenterin'.'

'The preacher comes from Treddleston, then, does she?'

'Nay, sir, she comes out o' Stonyshire, pretty nigh thirty mile off. But she's a-visitin' hereabout at Mester Poyser's at the Hall Farm – it's them barns an' big walnut trees, right away to the left, sir. She's own niece to Poyser's wife, an' they'll be fine an' vexed at her for making a fool of herself i' that way. But I've heared as there's no holding these Methodisses when the maggit's once got i' their head: many of 'em goes stark starin' mad wi' their religion. Though this young woman's quiet enough to look at, by what I can make out; I've not seen her myself.'

'Well, I wish I had time to wait and see her, but I must get on. I've been out of my way for the last twenty minutes, to have

a look at that place in the valley. It's Squire Donnithorne's,
I suppose?'

'Yes, sir, that's Donnithorne Chase, that is. Fine hoaks there,
isn't there, sir? I should know what it is, sir, for I've lived butler
there a-going i' fifteen year. It's Captain Donnithorne as is th'
heir, sir – Squire Donnithorne's grandson. He'll be comin' of
hage this 'ay-'arvest, sir, an' we shall hev fine doins. He owns
all the land about here, sir, Squire Donnithorne does.'

'Well, it's a pretty spot, whoever may own it,' said the traveller, mounting his horse; 'and one meets some fine strapping
fellows about too. I met as fine a young fellow as ever I saw in
my life, about half an hour ago, before I came up the hill – a
carpenter, a tall broad-shouldered fellow with black hair and
black eyes, marching along like a soldier. We want such fellows
as he to lick the French.'

'Ay, sir, that's Adam Bede, that is, I'll be bound – Thias
Bede's son – everybody knows him hereabout. He's an
uncommon clever stiddy fellow, an' wonderful strong. Lord
bless you, sir – if you'll hexcuse me for saying so – he can
walk forty mile a-day, an' lift a matter o' sixty ston'. He's an
uncommon favourite wi' the gentry, sir: Captain Donnithorne
and Parson Irwine meks a fine fuss wi' him. But he's a little
lifted up an' peppery-like.'

'Well, good evening to you, landlord; I must get on.'

'Your servant, sir; good evenin'.'

The traveller put his horse into a quick walk up the village,
but when he approached the Green, the beauty of the view that
lay on his right hand, the singular contrast presented by the
groups of villagers with the knot of Methodists near the maple,
and perhaps yet more, curiosity to see the young female
preacher, proved too much for his anxiety to get to the end of
his journey, and he paused.

The Green lay at the extremity of the village, and from it the
road branched off in two directions, one leading farther up the
hill by the church, and the other winding gently down towards
the valley. On the side of the Green that led towards the church,
the broken line of thatched cottages was continued nearly
to the churchyard gate; but on the opposite, north-western side,

there was nothing to obstruct the view of gently-swelling
meadow, and wooded valley, and dark masses of distant hill.
That rich undulating district of Loamshire to which Hayslope
belonged, lies close to a grim outskirt of Stonyshire, overlooked
by its barren hills as a pretty blooming sister may sometimes
be seen linked in the arm of a rugged, tall, swarthy brother;
and in two or three hours' ride the traveller might exchange a
bleak treeless region, intersected by lines of cold grey stone, for
one where his road wound under the shelter of woods, or up
swelling hills, muffled with hedgerows and long meadow-grass
and thick corn; and where at every turn he came upon some
fine old country-seat nestled in the valley or crowning the slope,
some homestead with its long length of barn and its cluster
of golden ricks, some grey steeple looking out from a pretty
confusion of trees and thatch and dark-red tiles. It was just
such a picture as this last that Hayslope Church had made to
the traveller as he began to mount the gentle slope leading to
its pleasant uplands, and now from his station near the Green
he had before him in one view nearly all the other typical
features of this pleasant land. High up against the horizon were
the huge conical masses of hill, like giant mounds intended
to fortify this region of corn and grass against the keen and
hungry winds of the north; not distant enough to be clothed in
purple mystery, but with sombre greenish sides visibly specked
with sheep, whose motion was only revealed by memory, not
detected by sight; wooed from day to day by the changing
hours, but responding with no change in themselves – left for
ever grim and sullen after the flush of morning, the winged
gleams of the April noonday, the parting crimson glory of the
ripening summer sun. And directly below them the eye rested
on a more advanced line of hanging woods, divided by bright
patches of pasture or furrowed crops, and not yet deepened into
the uniform leafy curtains of high summer, but still showing the
warm tints of the young oak and the tender green of the ash
and lime. Then came the valley, where the woods grew thicker,
as if they had rolled down and hurried together from the patches
left smooth on the slope, that they might take the better care of
the tall mansion which lifted its parapets and sent its faint blue

summer smoke among them. Doubtless there was a large sweep
of park and a broad glassy pool in front of that mansion, but
the swelling slope of meadow would not let our traveller see
them from the village green. He saw instead a foreground which
was just as lovely – the level sunlight lying like transparent gold
among the gently-curving stems of the feathered grass and the
tall red sorrel, and the white umbels[7] of the hemlocks lining
the bushy hedgerows. It was that moment in summer when the
sound of the scythe being whetted makes us cast more lingering
looks at the flower-sprinkled tresses of the meadows.

He might have seen other beauties in the landscape if he
had turned a little in his saddle and looked eastward, beyond
Jonathan Burge's pasture and woodyard towards the green
corn-fields and walnut-trees of the Hall Farm; but apparently
there was more interest for him in the living groups close at
hand. Every generation in the village was there, from old
'Feyther Taft' in his brown worsted night-cap, who was bent
nearly double, but seemed tough enough to keep on his legs a
long while, leaning on his short stick, down to the babies with
their little round heads lolling forward in quilted linen caps.
Now and then there was a new arrival; perhaps a slouching
labourer, who, having eaten his supper, came out to look at the
unusual scene with a slow bovine gaze, willing to hear what
any one had to say in explanation of it, but by no means excited
enough to ask a question. But all took care not to join the
Methodists on the Green, and identify themselves in that way
with the expectant audience, for there was not one of them that
would not have disclaimed the imputation of having come out
to hear the 'preacher-woman', – they had only come out to see
'what war a-goin' on, like'. The men were chiefly gathered
in the neighbourhood of the blacksmith's shop. But do not
imagine them gathered in a knot. Villagers never swarm: a
whisper is unknown among them, and they seem almost as
incapable of an undertone as a cow or a stag. Your true rustic
turns his back on his interlocutor, throwing a question over
his shoulder as if he meant to run away from the answer,
and walking a step or two farther off when the interest of
the dialogue culminates. So the group in the vicinity of the

blacksmith's door was by no means a close one, and formed no
screen in front of Chad Cranage, the blacksmith himself, who
stood with his black brawny arms folded, leaning against the
door-post, and occasionally sending forth a bellowing laugh at
his own jokes, giving them a marked preference over the sarcasms of Wiry Ben, who had renounced the pleasures of the
Holly Bush for the sake of seeing life under a new form. But
both styles of wit were treated with equal contempt by Mr
Joshua Rann. Mr Rann's leathern apron and subdued griminess
can leave no one in any doubt that he is the village shoemaker;
the thrusting out of his chin and stomach, and the twirling of
his thumbs, are more subtle indications, intended to prepare
unwary strangers for the discovery that they are in the presence
of the parish clerk. 'Old Joshway', as he is irreverently called
by his neighbours, is in a state of simmering indignation; but
he has not yet opened his lips except to say, in a resounding
bass undertone, like the tuning of a violoncello, 'Sehon, King
of the Amorites: for His mercy endureth for ever; and Og the
King of Basan: for His mercy endureth for ever',[8] – a quotation
which may seem to have slight bearing on the present occasion,
but, as with every other anomaly, adequate knowledge will
show it to be a natural sequence. Mr Rann was inwardly maintaining the dignity of the Church in the face of this scandalous
irruption of Methodism, and as that dignity was bound up with
his own sonorous utterance of the responses, his argument
naturally suggested a quotation from the psalm he had read the
last Sunday afternoon.

The stronger curiosity of the women had drawn them quite
to the edge of the Green, where they could examine more closely
the Quaker-like costume[9] and odd deportment of the female
Methodists. Underneath the maple there was a small cart which
had been brought from the wheelwright's to serve as a pulpit,
and round this a couple of benches and a few chairs had been
placed. Some of the Methodists were resting on these, with
their eyes closed, as if wrapt in prayer or meditation. Others
chose to continue standing, and had turned their faces towards
the villagers with a look of melancholy compassion, which
was highly amusing to Bessy Cranage, the blacksmith's buxom

daughter, known to her neighbours as Chad's Bess, who wondered 'why the folks war a-makin' faces a that'ns'. Chad's Bess
was the object of peculiar compassion, because her hair, being
turned back under a cap which was set at the top of her head,
exposed to view an ornament of which she was much prouder
than of her red cheeks, namely, a pair of large round earrings
with false garnets in them, ornaments contemned not only by
the Methodists, but by her own cousin and namesake Timothy's
Bess, who, with much cousinly feeling, often wished 'them
earrings' might come to good.

Timothy's Bess, though retaining her maiden appellation
among her familiars, had long been the wife of Sandy Jim, and
possessed a handsome set of matronly jewels, of which it is
enough to mention the heavy baby she was rocking in her arms,
and the sturdy fellow of five in knee-breeches, and red legs,
who had a rusty milk-can round his neck by way of drum, and
was very carefully avoided by Chad's small terrier. This young
olive-branch,[10] notorious under the name of Timothy's Bess's
Ben, being of an inquiring disposition, unchecked by any false
modesty, had advanced beyond the group of women and children, and was walking round the Methodists, looking up in
their faces with his mouth wide open, and beating his stick
against the milk-can by way of musical accompaniment. But
one of the elderly women bending down to take him by the
shoulder, with an air of grave remonstrance, Timothy's Bess's
Ben first kicked out vigorously, then took to his heels and
sought refuge behind his father's legs.

'Ye gallows young dog,'[11] said Sandy Jim, with some paternal
pride, 'if ye donna keep that stick quiet, I'll tek it from ye. What
d'ye mane by kickin' foulks?'

'Here! gie him here to me, Jim,' said Chad Cranage; 'I'll tie
him up an' shoe him as I do th' hosses. Well, Mester Casson,'
he continued, as that personage sauntered up towards the group
of men, 'how are ye t' naight? Are ye coom t' help groon?[12]
They say folks allays groon when they're hearkenin' to th'
Methodys, as if they war bad i' th' inside. I mane to groon as
loud as your cow did th' other naight, an' then the praicher 'ull
think I'm i' th' raight way.'

'I'd advise you not to be up to no nonsense, Chad,' said Mr Casson, with some dignity; 'Poyser wouldn't like to hear as his wife's niece was treated any ways disrespectful, for all he mayn't be fond of her taking on herself to preach.'

'Ay, an' she's a pleasant-looked un too,' said Wiry Ben. 'I'll stick up for the pretty women preachin'; I know they'd persuade me over a deal sooner nor th' ugly men. I shouldna wonder if I turn Methody afore the night's out, an' begin to coort the preacher, like Seth Bede.'

'Why, Seth's looking rather too high, I should think,' said Mr Casson. 'This woman's kin wouldn't like her to demean herself to a common carpenter.'

'Tchu!' said Ben, with a long treble intonation, 'what's folks's kin got to do wi't? – Not a chip. Poyser's wife may turn her nose up an' forget bygones, but this Dinah[13] Morris, they tell me, 's as poor as iver she was – works at a mill,[14] an's much ado to keep hersen. A strappin' young carpenter as is a ready-made Methody, like Seth, wouldna be a bad match for her. Why, Poysers make as big a fuss wi' Adam Bede as if he war a nevvy o' their own.'

'Idle talk! idle talk!' said Mr Joshua Rann. 'Adam an' Seth's two men; you wunna fit them two wi' the same last.'

'Maybe,' said Wiry Ben, contemptuously, 'but Seth's the lad for me, though he war a Methody twice o'er. I'm fair beat wi' Seth, for I've been teazin' him iver sin' we've been workin' together, an' he bears me no more malice nor a lamb. An' he's a stout-hearted feller too, for when we saw the old tree all a-fire a-comin' across the fields one night, an' we thought as it war a boguy, Seth made no more ado, but he up to't as bold as a constable. Why, there he comes out o' Will Maskery's; an' there's Will hisself, lookin' as meek as if he couldna knock a nail o' the head for fear o' hurtin't. An' there's the pretty preacher-woman! My eye, she's got her bonnet off. I mun go a bit nearer.'

Several of the men followed Ben's lead, and the traveller pushed his horse on to the Green, as Dinah walked rather quickly, and in advance of her companions, towards the cart under the maple-tree. While she was near Seth's tall figure, she

looked short, but when she had mounted the cart, and was
away from all comparison, she seemed above the middle height
of woman, though in reality she did not exceed it – an effect
which was due to the slimness of her figure, and the simple line
of her black stuff dress. The stranger was struck with surprise
as he saw her approach and mount the cart – surprise, not so
much at the feminine delicacy of her appearance, as at the total
absence of self-consciousness in her demeanour. He had made
up his mind to see her advance with a measured step, and a
demure solemnity of countenance; he had felt sure that her face
would be mantled with the smile of conscious saintship, or else
charged with denunciatory bitterness. He knew but two types
of Methodist – the ecstatic and the bilious. But Dinah walked
as simply as if she were going to market, and seemed as unconscious of her outward appearance as a little boy: there was no
blush, no tremulousness, which said, 'I know you think me a
pretty woman, too young to preach'; no casting up or down of
the eyelids, no compression of the lips, no attitude of the arms,
that said, 'But you must think of me as a saint.' She held no
book in her ungloved hands, but let them hang down lightly
crossed before her, as she stood and turned her grey eyes on
the people. There was no keenness in the eyes; they seemed
rather to be shedding love than making observations; they had
the liquid look which tells that the mind is full of what it has
to give out, rather than impressed by external objects. She stood
with her left hand towards the descending sun, and leafy boughs
screened her from its rays; but in this sober light the delicate
colouring of her face seemed to gather a calm vividness, like
flowers at evening. It was a small oval face, of a uniform
transparent whiteness, with an egg-like line of cheek and chin,
a full but firm mouth, a delicate nostril, and a low perpendicular
brow, surmounted by a rising arch of parting between smooth
locks of pale reddish hair. The hair was drawn straight back
behind the ears, and covered, except for an inch or two, above
the brow, by a net Quaker cap. The eyebrows, of the same
colour as the hair, were perfectly horizontal and firmly pen-
cilled; the eyelashes, though no darker, were long and abundant; nothing was left blurred or unfinished. It was one of those

faces that make one think of white flowers with light touches of colour on their pure petals. The eyes had no peculiar beauty, beyond that of expression; they looked so simple, so candid, so gravely loving, that no accusing scowl, no light sneer could help melting away before their glance. Joshua Rann gave a long cough, as if he were clearing his throat in order to come to a new understanding with himself; Chad Cranage lifted up his leather skull-cap and scratched his head; and Wiry Ben wondered how Seth had the pluck to think of courting her.

'A sweet woman,' the stranger said to himself, 'but surely nature never meant her for a preacher.'

Perhaps he was one of those who think that nature has theatrical properties, and, with the considerate view of facilitating art and psychology, 'makes up' her characters, so that there may be no mistake about them. But Dinah began to speak.

'Dear friends,' she said, in a clear but not loud voice, 'let us pray for a blessing.'

She closed her eyes, and hanging her head down a little, continued in the same moderate tone, as if speaking to some one quite near her: –

'Saviour of sinners! when a poor woman, laden with sins, went out to the well to draw water, she found Thee sitting at the well.[15] She knew Thee not; she had not sought Thee; her mind was dark; her life was unholy. But Thou didst speak to her, Thou didst teach her, Thou didst show her that her life lay open before Thee, and yet Thou wast ready to give her that blessing which she had never sought. Jesus! Thou art in the midst of us, and Thou knowest all men: if there is any here like that poor woman – if their minds are dark, their lives unholy – if they have come out not seeking Thee, not desiring to be taught; deal with them according to the free mercy which Thou didst show to her. Speak to them, Lord; open their ears to my message; bring their sins to their minds, and make them thirst for that salvation which Thou art ready to give.

'Lord! Thou art with Thy people still: they see Thee in the night-watches, and their hearts burn within them as Thou talkest with them by the way. And Thou art near to those who have not known Thee: open their eyes that they may see Thee

– see Thee weeping over them, and saying "Ye will not come unto me that ye might have life" – see Thee hanging on the cross and saying, "Father, forgive them, for they know not what they do" – see Thee as Thou wilt come again in Thy glory to judge them at the last. Amen.'

Dinah opened her eyes again and paused, looking at the group of villagers, who were now gathered rather more closely on her right hand.

'Dear friends,' she began, raising her voice a little, 'you have all of you been to church, and I think you must have heard the clergyman read these words: "The Spirit of the Lord is upon me, because he hath anointed me to preach the gospel to the poor." Jesus Christ spoke those words – he said he came *to preach the Gospel to the poor*: I don't know whether you ever thought about those words much; but I will tell you when I remember first hearing them. It was on just such a sort of evening as this, when I was a little girl, and my aunt as brought me up, took me to hear a good man preach out of doors, just as we are here. I remember his face well: he was a very old man, and had very long white hair; his voice was very soft and beautiful, not like any voice I had ever heard before. I was a little girl, and scarcely knew anything, and this old man seemed to me such a different sort of a man from anybody I had ever seen before, that I thought he had perhaps come down from the sky to preach to us, and I said, "Aunt, will he go back to the sky to-night, like the picture in the Bible?"

'That man of God was Mr Wesley, who spent his life in doing what our blessed Lord did – preaching the Gospel to the poor – and he entered into his rest eight years ago. I came to know more about him years after, but I was a foolish thoughtless child then, and I remembered only one thing he told us in his sermon. He told us as "Gospel" meant "good news". The Gospel, you know, is what the Bible tells us about God.

'Think of that now! Jesus Christ did really come down from heaven, as I, like a silly child, thought Mr Wesley did; and what he came down for, was to tell good news about God to the poor. Why, you and me, dear friends, are poor. We have been brought up in poor cottages, and have been reared on oat-cake,[16] and lived coarse; and we haven't been to school much, nor read books, and we don't know much about anything but what happens just round us. We are just the sort of people that want to hear good news. For when anybody's well off, they don't much mind about hearing news from distant parts; but if a poor man or woman's in trouble and has hard work to make out a living, they like to have a letter to tell 'em they've got a friend as will help 'em. To be sure, we can't help knowing something about God, even if we've never heard the Gospel, the good news that our Saviour brought us. For we know everything comes from God: don't you say almost every day, "This and that will happen, please God"; and "We shall begin to cut the grass soon, please God to send us a little more sunshine"? We know very well we are altogether in the hands of God: we didn't bring ourselves into the world, we can't keep ourselves alive while we're sleeping; the daylight, and the wind, and the corn, and the cows to give us milk – everything we have comes from God. And he gave us our souls, and put love between parents and children, and husband and wife. But is that as much as we want to know about God? We see he is great and mighty, and can do what he will: we are lost, as if we was struggling in great waters, when we try to think of him.

'But perhaps doubts come into your mind like this: Can God take much notice of us poor people? Perhaps he only made the world for the great and the wise and the rich. It doesn't cost him much to give us our little handful of victual and bit of clothing; but how do we know he cares for us any more than we care for the worms and things in the garden, so as we rear our carrots and onions? Will God take care of us when we die? and has he any comfort for us when we are lame and sick and helpless? Perhaps, too, he is angry with us; else why does the blight come, and the bad harvests, and the fever, and all sorts of pain and trouble? For our life is full of trouble, and if God sends us good, he seems to send bad too. How is it? how is it?

'Ah! dear friends, we are in sad want of good news about God; and what does other good news signify if we haven't that? For everything else comes to an end, and when we die we leave it all. But God lasts when everything else is gone. What shall we do if he is not our friend?'

Then Dinah told how the good news had been brought, and how the mind of God towards the poor had been made manifest in the life of Jesus, dwelling on its lowliness and its acts of mercy.

'So you see, dear friends,' she went on, 'Jesus spent his time almost all in doing good to poor people; he preached out of doors to them, and he made friends of poor workmen, and taught them and took pains with them. Not but what he did good to the rich too, for he was full of love to all men, only he saw as the poor were more in want of his help. So he cured the lame and the sick and the blind, and he worked miracles, to feed the hungry, because, he said, he was sorry for them; and he was very kind to the little children, and comforted those who had lost their friends: and he spoke very tenderly to poor sinners that were sorry for their sins.

'Ah! wouldn't you love such a man if you saw him – if he was here in this village? What a kind heart he must have! What a friend he would be to go to in trouble! How pleasant it must be to be taught by him.

'Well, dear friends, who *was* this man? Was he only a good man – a very good man, and no more – like our dear Mr Wesley, who has been taken from us? . . . He was the son of God – "in the image of the Father", the Bible says; that means, just like God, who is the beginning and end of all things – the God we want to know about. So then, all the love that Jesus showed to the poor is the same love that God has for us. We can under- stand what Jesus felt, because he came in a body like ours, and spoke words such as we speak to each other. We were afraid to think what God was before – the God who made the world and the sky and the thunder and lightning. We could never see him; we could only see the things he had made; and some of these things was very terrible, so as we might well tremble when we thought of him. But our blessed Saviour has showed us what God is in a way us poor ignorant people can understand; he has showed us what God's heart is, what are his feelings towards us.

'But let us see a little more about what Jesus came on earth for. Another time he said, "I came to seek and to save that which was lost"; and another time, "I came not to call the righteous but sinners to repentance."

'The *lost!* . . . *Sinners!* . . . Ah! dear friends, does that mean you and me?'

Hitherto the traveller had been chained to the spot against his will by the charm of Dinah's mellow treble tones, which had a variety of modulation like that of a fine instrument touched with the unconscious skill of musical instinct. The simple things she said seemed like novelties, as a melody strikes us with a new feeling when we hear it sung by the pure voice of a boyish chorister; the quiet depth of conviction with which she spoke seemed in itself an evidence for the truth of her message. He saw that she had thoroughly arrested her hearers. The villagers had pressed nearer to her, and there was no longer anything but grave attention on all faces. She spoke slowly, though quite fluently, often pausing after a question, or before any transition of ideas. There was no change of attitude, no gesture; the effect of her speech was produced entirely by the inflections of her voice, and when she came to the question, 'Will God take care of us when we die?' she uttered it in such a tone of plaintive appeal that the tears came into some of the hardest eyes. The stranger had ceased to doubt, as he had done at the first glance, that she could fix the attention of her rougher hearers, but still he wondered whether she could have that power of rousing their more violent emotions, which must surely be a necessary seal of her vocation as a Methodist preacher, until she came to the words, 'Lost! – Sinners!' when there was a great change in her voice and manner. She had made a long pause before the exclamation, and the pause seemed to be filled by agitating thoughts that showed themselves in her features. Her pale face became paler; the circles under her eyes deepened, as they do when tears half gather without falling; and the mild loving eyes took an expression of appalled pity, as if she had suddenly discerned a destroying angel hovering over the heads of the people. Her voice became deep and muffled, but there was still no gesture. Nothing could be less like the ordinary type of the Ranter[17] than Dinah. She was not preaching as she heard others preach, but speaking directly from her own emotions, and under the inspiration of her own simple faith.

But now she had entered into a new current of feeling. Her manner became less calm, her utterance more rapid and agitated, as she tried to bring home to the people their guilt, their wilful darkness, their state of disobedience to God – as she dwelt on the hatefulness of sin, the Divine holiness, and the sufferings of the Saviour, by which a way had been opened for their salvation. At last it seemed as if, in her yearning desire to reclaim the lost sheep, she could not be satisfied by addressing her hearers as a body. She appealed first to one and then to another, beseeching them with tears to turn to God while there was yet time; painting to them the desolation of their souls, lost in sin, feeding on the husks of this miserable world, far away from God their Father; and then the love of the Saviour, who was waiting and watching for their return.

There was many a responsive sigh and groan from her fellow-Methodists, but the village mind does not easily take fire, and a little smouldering vague anxiety, that might easily die out again, was the utmost effect Dinah's preaching had wrought in them at present. Yet no one had retired, except the children and 'old Feyther Taft', who being too deaf to catch many words, had some time ago gone back to his ingle-nook. Wiry Ben was feeling very uncomfortable, and almost wishing he had not come to hear Dinah; he thought what she said would haunt him somehow. Yet he couldn't help liking to look at her and listen to her, though he dreaded every moment that she would fix her eyes on him, and address him in particular. She had already addressed Sandy Jim, who was now holding the baby to relieve his wife, and the big soft-hearted man had rubbed away some tears with his fist, with a confused intention of being a better fellow, going less to the Holly Bush down by the Stone-pits, and cleaning himself more regularly of a Sunday.

In front of Sandy Jim stood Chad's Bess, who had shown an unwonted quietude and fixity of attention ever since Dinah had begun to speak. Not that the matter of the discourse had arrested her at once, for she was lost in a puzzling speculation as to what pleasure and satisfaction there could be in life to a young woman who wore a cap like Dinah's. Giving up this inquiry in despair, she took to studying Dinah's nose, eyes, mouth, and hair, and wondering whether it was better to have such a sort of pale face as that, or fat red cheeks and round black eyes like her own. But gradually the influence of the general gravity told upon her, and she became conscious of what Dinah was saying. The gentle tones, the loving persuasion, did not touch her, but when the more severe appeals came she began to be frightened. Poor Bessy had always been considered a naughty girl; she was conscious of it; if it was necessary to be very good, it was clear she must be in a bad way. She couldn't find her places at church as Sally Rann could; she had often been tittering when she 'curcheyed'[18] to Mr Irwine; and these religious deficiencies were accompanied by a corresponding slackness in the minor morals, for Bessy belonged unquestionably to that unsoaped, lazy class of feminine characters with whom you may venture to 'eat an egg, an apple, or a nut'.[19] All this she was generally conscious of, and hitherto had not been greatly ashamed of it. But now she began to feel very much as if the constable had come to take her up and carry her before the justice for some undefined offence. She had a terrified sense that God, whom she had always thought of as very far off, was very near to her, and that Jesus was close by looking at her, though she could not see him. For Dinah had that belief in visible manifestations of Jesus,[20] which is common among the Methodists, and she communicated it irresistibly to her hearers: she made them feel that he was among them bodily, and might at any moment show himself to them in some way that would strike anguish and penitence into their hearts.

'See!' she exclaimed, turning to the left, with her eyes fixed on a point above the heads of the people – 'see where our blessed Lord stands and weeps, and stretches out his arms towards you. Hear what he says: "How often would I have gathered you as a hen gathereth her chickens under her wings, and ye would not!" . . . and ye would not,' she repeated, in a tone of pleading reproach, turning her eyes on the people again. 'See the print of the nails on his dear hands and feet. It is your sins that made them! Ah! how pale and worn he looks! He has gone through all that great agony in the garden, when his soul was exceeding sorrowful even unto death, and the great drops of sweat fell like blood to the ground. They spat upon him and buffeted him, they scourged him, they mocked him, they laid the heavy cross on his bruised shoulders. Then they nailed him up. Ah! what pain! His lips are parched with thirst, and they mock him still in this great agony; yet with those parched lips he prays for them, "Father, forgive them, for they know not what they do." Then a horror of great darkness fell upon him, and he felt what sinners feel when they are for ever shut out from God. That was the last drop in the cup of bitterness. "My God, my God!" he cries, "why hast Thou forsaken me?"

'All this he bore for you! For you – and you never think of him; for you – and you turn your backs on him; you don't care what he has gone through for you. Yet he is not weary of toiling for you: he has risen from the dead, he is praying for you at the right hand of God – "Father, forgive them, for they know not what they do." And he is upon this earth too; he is among us; he is there close to you now; I see his wounded body and his look of love.'

Here Dinah turned to Bessy Cranage, whose bonny youth and evident vanity had touched her with pity.

'Poor child! poor child! He is beseeching you, and you don't listen to him. You think of ear-rings and fine gowns and caps, and you never think of the Saviour who died to save your precious soul. Your cheeks will be shrivelled one day, your hair will be grey, your poor body will be thin and tottering! Then you will begin to feel that your soul is not saved; then you will have to stand before God dressed in your sins, in your evil tempers and vain thoughts. And Jesus, who stands ready to help you now, won't help you then: because you won't have him to be your Saviour, he will be your judge. Now he looks at you with love and mercy, and says, "Come to me that you may have life"; then he will turn away from you, and say, "Depart from me into everlasting fire!"'

Poor Bessy's wide-open black eyes began to fill with tears, her great red cheeks and lips became quite pale, and her face was distorted like a little child's before a burst of crying.

'Ah! poor blind child!' Dinah went on, 'think if it should happen to you as it once happened to a servant of God in the days of her vanity. *She* thought of her lace caps, and saved all her money to buy 'em; she thought nothing about how she might get a clean heart and a right spirit, she only wanted to have better lace than other girls. And one day when she put her new cap on and looked in the glass, she saw a bleeding Face crowned with thorns. That face is looking at you now,' – here Dinah pointed to a spot close in front of Bessy. – 'Ah! tear off those follies! cast them away from you, as if they were stinging adders. They *are* stinging you – they are poisoning your soul – they are dragging you down into a dark bottomless pit, where you will sink for ever, and for ever, and for ever, further away from light and God.'

Bessy could bear it no longer: a great terror was upon her, and wrenching her ear-rings from her ears, she threw them down before her, sobbing aloud. Her father, Chad, frightened lest he should be 'laid hold on' too, this impression on the rebellious Bess striking him as nothing less than a miracle, walked hastily away, and began to work at his anvil by way of reassuring himself. 'Folks mun ha' hoss-shoes, praichin' or no praichin': the divil canna lay hould o' me for that,' he muttered to himself.

But now Dinah began to tell of the joys that were in store for the penitent, and to describe in her simple way the divine peace and love with which the soul of the believer is filled – how the sense of God's love turns poverty into riches, and satisfies the soul, so that no uneasy desire vexes it, no fear alarms it: how, at last, the very temptation to sin is extinguished, and heaven is begun upon earth, because no cloud passes between the soul and God, who is its eternal sun.

'Dear friends,' she said at last, 'brothers and sisters, whom I love as those for whom my Lord has died, believe me, I know what this great blessedness is; and because I know it, I want you to have it too. I am poor, like you: I have to get my living with my hands; but no lord nor lady can be so happy as me, if they haven't got the love of God in their souls. Think what it is – not to hate anything but sin; to be full of love to every creature; to be frightened at nothing; to be sure that all things will turn to good; not to mind pain, because it is our Father's will; to know that nothing – no, not if the earth was to be burnt up, or the waters come and drown us – nothing could part us from God who loves us, and who fills our souls with peace and joy, because we are sure that whatever he wills is holy, just, and good.

'Dear friends, come and take this blessedness; it is offered to you; it is the good news that Jesus came to preach to the poor. It is not like the riches of this world, so that the more one gets the less the rest can have. God is without end; his love is without end –

> "Its streams the whole creation reach,
>   So plenteous is the store;
>   Enough for all, enough for each,
>   Enough for evermore." '21

Dinah had been speaking at least an hour, and the reddening light of the parting day seemed to give a solemn emphasis to her closing words. The stranger, who had been interested in the course of her sermon, as if it had been the development of a drama – for there is this sort of fascination in all sincere unpremeditated eloquence, which opens to one the inward drama of the speaker's emotions – now turned his horse aside, and pursued his way, while Dinah said, 'Let us sing a little, dear friends'; and as he was still winding down the slope, the voices of the Methodists reached him, rising and falling in that strange blending of exultation and sadness which belongs to the cadence of a hymn.

CHAPTER III

After the Preaching

In less than an hour from that time Seth Bede was walking by
Dinah's side along the hedgerow-path that skirted the pastures
and green corn-fields which lay between the village and the
Hall Farm. Dinah had taken off her little Quaker bonnet again,
and was holding it in her hands that she might have a freer
enjoyment of the cool evening twilight, and Seth could see the
expression of her face quite clearly as he walked by her side,
timidly revolving something he wanted to say to her. It was an
expression of unconscious placid gravity – of absorption in
thoughts that had no connection with the present moment or
with her own personality: an expression that is most of all
discouraging to a lover. Her very walk was discouraging: it had
that quiet elasticity that asks for no support. Seth felt this dimly;
he said to himself, 'She's too good and holy for any man, let
alone me', and the words he had been summoning rushed back
again before they had reached his lips. But another thought
gave him courage: 'There's no man could love her better, and
leave her freer to follow the Lord's work.' They had been silent
for many minutes now, since they had done talking about
Bessy Cranage; Dinah seemed almost to have forgotten Seth's
presence, and her pace was becoming so much quicker, that
the sense of their being only a few minutes' walk from the
yard-gates of the Hall Farm at last gave Seth courage to speak.

'You've quite made up your mind to go back to Snowfield o'
Saturday, Dinah?'

'Yes,' said Dinah, quietly. 'I'm called there. It was borne in
upon my mind[1] while I was meditating on Sunday night, as
sister Allen, who's in a decline, is in need of me. I saw her as

plain as we see that bit of thin white cloud, lifting up her poor
thin hand and beckoning to me. And this morning when I
opened the Bible for direction, the first words my eyes fell
on were, "And after we had seen the vision, immediately we
endeavoured to go into Macedonia."[2] If it wasn't for that clear
showing of the Lord's will I should be loth to go, for my
heart yearns over my aunt and her little ones, and that poor
wandering lamb Hetty Sorrel.[3] I've been much drawn out in
prayer for her of late, and I look on it as a token that there may
be mercy in store for her.'

'God grant it,' said Seth. 'For I doubt Adam's heart is so set
on her, he'll never turn to anybody else; and yet it 'ud go to my
heart if he was to marry her, for I canna think as she'd make
him happy. It's a deep mystery – the way the heart of man turns
to one woman out of all the rest he's seen i' the world, and
makes it easier for him to work seven year for *her*, like Jacob
did for Rachel; sooner than have any other woman for th'
asking. I often think of them words, "And Jacob served seven
years for Rachel; and they seemed to him but a few days for
the love he had to her."[4] I know those words 'ud come true
with me, Dinah, if so be you'd give me hope as I might win you
after seven years was over. I know you think a husband 'ud be
taking up too much o' your thoughts, because St Paul says,
"She that's married careth for the things of the world how she
may please her husband";[5] and may happen you'll think me
over-bold to speak to you about it again, after what you told
me o' your mind last Saturday. But I've been thinking it over
again by night and by day, and I've prayed not to be blinded
by my own desires, to think what's only good for me must be
good for you too. And it seems to me there's more texts for
your marrying than ever you can find against it. For St Paul
says as plain as can be in another place, "I will that the younger
women marry, bear children, guide the house, give none
occasion to the adversary to speak reproachfully"; and then
"two are better than one"; and that holds good with marriage
as well as with other things. For we should be o' one heart and
o' one mind, Dinah. We both serve the same Master, and are
striving after the same gifts; and I'd never be the husband to

make a claim on you as could interfere with your doing the work God has fitted you for. I'd make a shift, and fend indoor and out, to give you more liberty – more than you can have now, for you've got to get your own living now, and I'm strong enough to work for us both.'

When Seth had once begun to urge his suit, he went on earnestly, and almost hurriedly, lest Dinah should speak some decisive word before he had poured forth all the arguments he had prepared. His cheeks became flushed as he went on, his mild grey eyes filled with tears, and his voice trembled as he spoke the last sentence. They had reached one of those very narrow passes between two tall stones, which performed the office of a stile[6] in Loamshire, and Dinah paused as she turned towards Seth and said, in her tender but calm treble notes –

'Seth Bede, I thank you for your love towards me, and if I could think of any man as more than a Christian brother, I think it would be you. But my heart is not free to marry. That is good for other women, and it is a great and a blessed thing to be a wife and mother; but "as God has distributed to every man, as the Lord hath called every man, so let him walk".[7] God has called me to minister to others, not to have any joys or sorrows of my own, but to rejoice with them that do rejoice, and to weep with those that weep. He has called me to speak his word, and he has greatly owned my work. It could only be on a very clear showing that I could leave the brethren and sisters at Snowfield, who are favoured with very little of this world's good; where the trees are few, so that a child might count them, and there's very hard living for the poor in the winter. It has been given me to help, to comfort, and strengthen the little flock there, and to call in many wanderers; and my soul is filled with these things from my rising up till my lying down. My life is too short, and God's work is too great for me to think of making a home for myself in this world. I've not turned a deaf ear to your words, Seth, for when I saw as your love was given to me, I thought it might be a leading of Providence[8] for me to change my way of life, and that we should be fellow-helpers; and I spread the matter before the Lord. But whenever I tried to fix my mind on marriage, and our living together, other thoughts always came in – the times when I've prayed by the sick and dying, and the happy hours I've had preaching, when my heart was filled with love, and the Word was given to me abundantly. And when I've opened the Bible for direction, I've always lighted on some clear word to tell me where my work lay. I believe what you say, Seth, that you would try to be a help and not a hindrance to my work; but I see that our marriage is not God's will – He draws my heart another way. I desire to live and die without husband or children. I seem to have no room in my soul for wants and fears of my own, it has pleased God to fill my heart so full with the wants and sufferings of his poor people.'

Seth was unable to reply, and they walked on in silence. At last, as they were nearly at the yard-gate, he said –

'Well, Dinah, I must seek for strength to bear it, and to endure as seeing Him who is invisible. But I feel now how weak my faith is. It seems as if, when you are gone, I could never joy in anything any more. I think it's something passing the love of women[9] as I feel for you, for I could be content without your marrying me if I could go and live at Snowfield, and be near you. I trusted as the strong love God had given me towards you was a leading for us both; but it seems it was only meant for my trial. Perhaps I feel more for you than I ought to feel for any creature, for I often can't help saying of you what the hymn says –

> "In darkest shades if she appear,
>   My dawning is begun;
> She is my soul's bright morning-star,
>   And she my rising sun."[10]

That may be wrong, and I am to be taught better. But you wouldn't be displeased with me if things turned out so as I could leave this country and go to live at Snowfield?'

'No, Seth; but I counsel you to wait patiently, and not lightly to leave your own country and kindred. Do nothing without the Lord's clear bidding. It's a bleak and barren country there, not like this land of Goshen[11] you've been used to. We mustn't

be in a hurry to fix and choose our own lot; we must wait to be
guided.'

'But you'd let me write you a letter, Dinah, if there was
anything I wanted to tell you?'

'Yes, sure; let me know if you're in any trouble. You'll be
continually in my prayers.'

They had now reached the yard-gate, and Seth said, 'I won't
go in, Dinah; so farewell.' He paused and hesitated after she
had given him her hand, and then said, 'There's no knowing
but what you may see things different after a while. There may
be a new leading.'

'Let us leave that, Seth. It's good to live only a moment at a
time, as I've read in one of Mr Wesley's books. It isn't for you
and me to lay plans; we've nothing to do but to obey and to
trust. Farewell.'

Dinah pressed his hand with rather a sad look in her loving
eyes and then passed through the gate, while Seth turned away
to walk lingeringly home. But instead of taking the direct road,
he chose to turn back along the fields through which he and
Dinah had already passed; and I think his blue linen handkerchief was very wet with tears long before he had made up his
mind that it was time for him to set his face steadily homewards.
He was but three-and-twenty, and had only just learned what
it is to love – to love with that adoration which a young man
gives to a woman whom he feels to be greater and better than
himself. Love of this sort is hardly distinguishable from religious
feeling. What deep and worthy love is so? whether of woman
or child, or art or music. Our caresses, our tender words, our
still rapture under the influence of autumn sunsets, or pillared
vistas, or calm majestic statues, or Beethoven symphonies, all
bring with them the consciousness that they are mere waves
and ripples in an unfathomable ocean of love and beauty; our
emotion in its keenest moment passes from expression into
silence, our love at its highest flood rushes beyond its object,
and loses itself in the sense of divine mystery. And this blessed
gift of venerating love has been given to too many humble
craftsmen since the world began, for us to feel any surprise that
it should have existed in the soul of a Methodist carpenter half

a century ago, while there was yet a lingering after-glow from the time when Wesley and his fellow-labourer fed on the hips and haws of the Cornwall hedges, after exhausting limbs and lungs in carrying a divine message to the poor.

That after-glow has long faded away; and the picture we are apt to make of Methodism in our imagination is not an amphitheatre of green hills, or the deep shade of broad-leaved sycamores, where a crowd of rough men and weary-hearted women drank in a faith which was a rudimentary culture, which linked their thoughts with the past, lifted their imagination above the sordid details of their own narrow lives, and suffused their souls with the sense of a pitying, loving, infinite Presence, sweet as summer to the houseless needy. It is too possible that to some of my readers Methodism may mean nothing more than low-pitched gables up dingy streets, sleek grocers, sponging preachers, and hypocritical jargon – elements which are regarded as an exhaustive analysis of Methodism in many fashionable quarters.

That would be a pity; for I cannot pretend that Seth and Dinah were anything else than Methodists – not indeed of that modern type which reads quarterly reviews and attends in chapels with pillared porticoes; but of a very old-fashioned kind. They believed in present miracles, in instantaneous conversions, in revelations by dreams and visions; they drew lots, and sought for Divine guidance by opening the Bible at hazard; having a literal way of interpreting the Scriptures, which is not at all sanctioned by approved commentators; and it is impossible for me to represent their diction as correct, or their instruction as liberal. Still – if I have read religious history aright – faith, hope, and charity have not always been found in a direct ratio with a sensibility to the three concords;[12] and it is possible, thank Heaven! to have very erroneous theories and very sublime feelings. The raw bacon which clumsy Molly spares from her own scanty store, that she may carry it to her neighbour's child to 'stop the fits', may be a piteously inefficacious remedy; but the generous stirring of neighbourly kindness that prompted the deed has a beneficent radiation that is not lost.

Considering these things, we can hardly think Dinah and Seth beneath our sympathy, accustomed as we may be to weep over the loftier sorrows of heroines in satin boots and crinoline, and of heroes riding fiery horses, themselves ridden by still more fiery passions.[13]

Poor Seth! he was never on horseback in his life except once, when he was a little lad, and Mr Jonathan Burge took him up behind, telling him to 'hold on tight'; and instead of bursting out into wild accusing apostrophes to God and destiny, he is resolving, as he now walks homeward under the solemn starlight, to repress his sadness, to be less bent on having his own will, and to live more for others, as Dinah does.

CHAPTER IV

Home and its Sorrows

A green valley with a brook running through it, full almost to overflowing with the late rains; overhung by low stooping willows. Across this brook a plank is thrown, and over this plank Adam Bede is passing with his undoubting step, followed close by Gyp with the basket; evidently making his way to the thatched house, with a stack of timber by the side of it, about twenty yards up the opposite slope.

The door of the house is open, and an elderly woman is looking out; but she is not placidly contemplating the evening sunshine; she has been watching with dim eyes the gradually enlarging speck which for the last few minutes she has been quite sure is her darling son Adam. Lisbeth Bede loves her son with the love of a woman to whom her first-born has come late in life. She is an anxious, spare, yet vigorous old woman, clean as a snowdrop. Her grey hair is turned neatly back under a pure linen cap with a black band round it; her broad chest is covered with a buff neckerchief, and below this you see a sort of short bed-gown made of blue-checkered linen, tied round the waist and descending to the hips, from whence there is a considerable length of linsey-wolsey[1] petticoat. For Lisbeth is tall, and in other points too there is a strong likeness between her and her son Adam. Her dark eyes are somewhat dim now – perhaps from too much crying – but her broadly-marked eyebrows are still black, her teeth are sound, and as she stands knitting rapidly and unconsciously with her work-hardened hands, she has as firmly-upright an attitude as when she is carrying a pail of water on her head from the spring. There is the same type of frame and the same keen activity of

temperament in mother and son, but it was not from her that
Adam got his well-filled brow and his expression of large-
hearted intelligence.

Family likeness has often a deep sadness in it. Nature, that
great tragic dramatist, knits us together by bone and muscle,
and divides us by the subtler web of our brains; blends yearning
and repulsion; and ties us by our heart-strings to the beings
that jar us at every movement. We hear a voice with the very
cadence of our own uttering the thoughts we despise; we see
eyes – ah! so like our mother's – averted from us in cold
alienation; and our last darling child startles us with the air and
gestures of the sister we parted from in bitterness long years ago.
The father to whom we owe our best heritage – the mechanical
instinct, the keen sensibility to harmony, the unconscious skill
of the modelling hand – galls us, and puts us to shame by his
daily errors; the long-lost mother, whose face we begin to see
in the glass as our own wrinkles come, once fretted our young
souls with her anxious humours and irrational persistence.

It is such a fond anxious mother's voice that you hear, as
Lisbeth says –

'Well, my lad, it's gone seven by th' clock. Thee't allays stay
till the last child's born.[2] Thee wants thy supper, I'll warrand.
Where's Seth? gone arter some o's chapellin',[3] I reckon?'

'Ay, ay, Seth's at no harm, mother, thee mayst be sure. But
where's father?' said Adam quickly, as he entered the house
and glanced into the room on the left hand, which was used as
a workshop. 'Hasn't he done the coffin for Tholer? There's the
stuff standing just as I left it this morning.'

'Done the coffin?' said Lisbeth, following him, and knitting
uninterruptedly, though she looked at her son very anxiously.
'Eh, my lad, he went off to Treddles' on this forenoon, an's niver
come back. I doubt he's got to th' "Waggin Overthrow" again.'

A deep flush of anger passed rapidly over Adam's face. He
said nothing, but threw off his jacket, and began to roll up his
shirt-sleeves again.

'What art goin' to do, Adam?' said the mother, with a tone
and look of alarm. 'Thee wouldstna go to work again, wi'out
ha'in thy bit o' supper?'

Adam, too angry to speak, walked into the workshop. But his mother threw down her knitting, and, hurrying after him, took hold of his arm, and said in a tone of plaintive remonstrance –

'Nay, my lad, my lad, thee munna go wi'out thy supper; there's the taters wi' the gravy in 'em, just as thee lik'st 'em. I saved 'em o' purpose for thee. Come an' ha' thy supper, come.'

'Let be!' said Adam impetuously, shaking her off, and seizing one of the planks that stood against the wall. 'It's fine talking about having supper when here's a coffin promised to be ready at Brox'on by seven o'clock to-morrow morning, and ought to ha' been there now, and not a nail struck yet. My throat's too full to swallow victuals.'

'Why, thee canstna get the coffin ready,' said Lisbeth. 'Thee't work thyself to death. It 'ud take thee all night to do't.'

'What signifies how long it takes me? Isn't the coffin promised? Can they bury the man without a coffin? I'd work my right hand off sooner than deceive people with lies i' that way. It makes me mad to think on't. I shall overrun these doings before long. I've stood enough of 'em.'

Poor Lisbeth did not hear this threat for the first time, and if she had been wise she would have gone away quietly, and said nothing for the next hour. But one of the lessons a woman most rarely learns, is never to talk to an angry or a drunken man. Lisbeth sat down on the chopping bench and began to cry, and by the time she had cried enough to make her voice very piteous, she burst out into words.

'Nay, my lad, my lad, thee wouldstna go away an' break thy mother's heart, an' leave thy feyther to ruin. Thee wouldstna ha' 'em carry me to th' churchyard, an' thee not to follow me. I shanna rest i' my grave if I donna see thee at th' last; an' how's they to let thee know as I'm a-dyin', if thee't gone a-workin' i' distant parts, an' Seth belike gone arter thee, and thy feyther not able to hold a pen for's hand shakin', besides not knowin' where thee art? Thee mun forgie thy feyther – thee munna be so bitter again' him. He war a good feyther to thee afore he took to th' drink. He's a clever workman, an' taught thee thy trade, remember, an's niver gen me a blow nor so much as an

ill word – no, not even in's drink. Thee wouldstna ha'm go to
the workhus[4] – thy own feyther – an' him as was a fine-growed
man an' handy at everythin' amost as thee art thysen, five-
an'-twenty 'ear ago, when thee wast a baby at the breast.'

Lisbeth's voice became louder, and choked with sobs: a sort
of wail, the most irritating of all sounds where real sorrows
are to be borne, and real work to be done. Adam broke in
impatiently.

'Now, mother, don't cry and talk so. Haven't I got enough
to vex me without that? What's th' use o' telling me things as I
only think too much on every day? If I didna think on 'em why
should I do as I do, for the sake o' keeping things together here?
But I hate to be talking where it's no use: I like to keep my
breath for doing istead o' talking.'

'I know thee dost things as nobody else 'ud do, my lad. But
thee't allys so hard upo' thy feyther, Adam. Thee think'st
nothing too much to do for Seth: thee snapp'st me up if iver I
find faut wi' th' lad. But thee't so angered wi' thy feyther, more
nor wi' anybody else.'

'That's better than speaking soft, and letting things go the
wrong way, I reckon, isn't it? If I wasn't sharp with him, he'd
sell every bit o' stuff i' th' yard, and spend it on drink. I know
there's a duty to be done by my father, but it isn't my duty to
encourage him in running headlong to ruin. And what has Seth
got to do with it? The lad does no harm as I know of. But leave
me alone, mother, and let me get on with the work.'

Lisbeth dared not say any more; but she got up and called
Gyp, thinking to console herself somewhat for Adam's refusal
of the supper she had spread out in the loving expectation of
looking at him while he ate it, by feeding Adam's dog with
extra liberality. But Gyp was watching his master with wrinkled
brow and ears erect, puzzled at this unusual course of things;
and though he glanced at Lisbeth when she called him, and
moved his fore-paws uneasily, well knowing that she was inviting him to supper, he was in a divided state of mind, and
remained seated on his haunches, again fixing his eyes anxiously
on his master. Adam noticed Gyp's mental conflict, and though
his anger had made him less tender than usual to his mother, it

did not prevent him from caring as much as usual for his dog. We are apt to be kinder to the brutes that love us than to the women that love us. Is it because the brutes are dumb?

'Go, Gyp; go, lad!' Adam said, in a tone of encouraging command; and Gyp, apparently satisfied that duty and pleasure were one, followed Lisbeth into the house-place.[5]

But no sooner had he licked up his supper than he went back to his master, while Lisbeth sat down alone to cry over her knitting. Women who are never bitter and resentful are often the most querulous; and if Solomon was as wise as he is reputed to be, I feel sure that when he compared a contentious woman to a continual dropping on a very rainy day,[6] he had not a vixen in his eye – a fury with long nails, acrid and selfish. Depend upon it, he meant a good creature, who had no joy but in the happiness of the loved ones whom she contributed to make uncomfortable, putting by all the tid-bits for them, and spending nothing on herself. Such a woman as Lisbeth, for example – at once patient and complaining, self-renouncing and exacting, brooding the livelong day over what happened yesterday, and what is likely to happen to-morrow, and crying very readily both at the good and the evil. But a certain awe mingled itself with her idolatrous love of Adam, and when he said, 'Leave me alone', she was always silenced.

So the hours passed, to the loud ticking of the old day-clock[7] and the sound of Adam's tools. At last he called for a light and a draught of water (beer was a thing only to be drunk on holidays), and Lisbeth ventured to say as she took it in, 'Thy supper stans ready for thee, when thee lik'st.'

'Donna thee sit up, mother,' said Adam, in a gentle tone. He had worked off his anger now, and whenever he wished to be especially kind to his mother, he fell into his strongest native accent and dialect, with which at other times his speech was less deeply tinged. 'I'll see to father when he comes home; maybe he wonna come at all to-night. I shall be easier if thee't i' bed.'

'Nay, I'll bide till Seth comes. He wonna be long now, I reckon.'

It was then past nine by the clock, which was always in

advance of the day, and before it had struck ten the latch was lifted and Seth entered. He had heard the sound of the tools as he was approaching.

'Why, mother,' he said, 'how is it as father's working so late?'

'It's none o' thy feyther as is a-workin' – thee might know that well anoof if thy head warna full o' chapellin' – it's thy brother as does iverything, for there's niver nobody else i' th' way to do nothin'.'

Lisbeth was going on, for she was not at all afraid of Seth, and usually poured into his ears all the querulousness which was repressed by her awe of Adam. Seth had never in his life spoken a harsh word to his mother, and timid people always wreak their peevishness on the gentle. But Seth, with an anxious look, had passed into the workshop and said –

'Addy, how's this? What! father's forgot the coffin?'

'Ay, lad, th' old tale; but I shall get it done,' said Adam, looking up, and casting one of his bright keen glances at his brother. 'Why, what's the matter with thee? Thee't in trouble.'

Seth's eyes were red, and there was a look of deep depression on his mild face.

'Yes, Addy, but it's what must be borne, and can't be helped. Why, thee'st never been to the school,[8] then?'

'School? no; that screw can wait,' said Adam, hammering away again.

'Let me take my turn now, and do thee go to bed,' said Seth.

'No, lad, I'd rather go on, now I'm in harness. Thee't help me to carry it to Brox'on when it's done. I'll call thee up at sunrise. Go and eat thy supper, and shut the door, so as I mayn't hear mother's talk.'

Seth knew that Adam always meant what he said, and was not to be persuaded into meaning anything else. So he turned, with rather a heavy heart, into the house-place.

'Adam's niver touched a bit o' victual sin' home he's come,' said Lisbeth. 'I reckon thee'st hed thy supper at some o' thy Methody folks.'

'Nay, mother,' said Seth, 'I've had no supper yet.'

'Come, then,' said Lisbeth, 'but donna thee ate the taters, for Adam 'ull happen ate 'em if I leave 'em stannin'. He loves a bit o' taters an' gravy. But he's been so sore an' angered, he wouldn't ate 'em, for all I'd putten 'em by o' purpose for him. An' he's been a-threatenin' to go away again,' she went on, whimpering, 'an' I'm fast sure he'll go some dawnin' afore I'm up, an' niver let me know aforehand, an' he'll niver come back again when once he's gone. An' I'd better niver ha' had a son, as is like no other body's son for the deftness an' th' handiness, an' so looked on by th' grit folks, an' tall an' upright like a poplar-tree, an' me to be parted from him, an' niver see 'm no more.'

'Come, mother, donna grieve thyself in vain,' said Seth, in a soothing voice. 'Thee'st not half so good reason to think as Adam 'ull go away as to think he'll stay with thee. He may say such a thing when he's in wrath – and he's got excuse for being wrathful sometimes – but his heart 'ud never let him go. Think how he's stood by us all when it's been none so easy – paying his savings to free me from going for a soldier,[9] an' turnin' his earnins into wood for father, when he's got plenty o' uses for his money, and many a young man like him 'ud ha' been married and settled before now. He'll never turn round and knock down his own work, and forsake them as it's been the labour of his life to stand by.'

'Donna talk to me about's marr'in',' said Lisbeth, crying afresh. 'He's set's heart on that Hetty Sorrel, as 'ull niver save a penny, an' 'ull toss up her head at's old mother. An' to think as he might ha' Mary Burge, an' be took partners, an' be a big man wi' workmen under him, like Mester Burge – Dolly's told me so o'er an' o'er again – if it warna as he's set's heart on that bit of a wench, as is o' no more use nor the gillyflower on the wall. An' he so wise at bookin' an' figurin', an' not to know no better nor that!'

'But, mother, thee know'st we canna love just where other folks 'ud have us. There's nobody but God can control the heart of man. I could ha' wished myself as Adam could ha' made another choice, but I wouldn't reproach him for what he can't help. And I'm not sure but what he tries to o'ercome it. But it's a matter as he doesn't like to be spoke to about, and I can only pray to the Lord to bless and direct him.'

'Ay, thee't allays ready enough at prayin', but I donna see as thee gets much wi' thy prayin'. Thee wotna get double earnins o' this side Yule. Th' Methodies 'll niver make thee half the man thy brother is, for all they're a-makin' a preacher on thee.'

'It's partly truth thee speak'st there, mother,' said Seth, mildly; 'Adam's far before me, an's done more for me than I can ever do for him. God distributes talents to every man according as He sees good. But thee mustna undervally prayer. Prayer mayna bring money, but it brings us what no money can buy – a power to keep from sin, and be content with God's will, whatever He may please to send. If thee wouldst pray to God to help thee, and trust in His goodness, thee wouldstna be so uneasy about things.'

'Unaisy? I'm i' th' right on't to be unaisy. It's well seen on *thee* what it is niver to be unaisy. Thee't gi' away all thy earnins, an' niver be unaisy as thee'st nothin' laid up again' a rainy day. If Adam had been as aisy as thee, he'd niver ha' had no money to pay for thee. Take no thought for the morrow[10] – take no thought – that's what thee't allays sayin'; an' what comes on't? Why, as Adam has to take thought for thee.'

'Those are the words o' the Bible, mother,' said Seth. 'They don't mean as we should be idle. They mean we shouldn't be over anxious and worreting ourselves about what'll happen tomorrow, but do our duty, and leave the rest to God's will.'

'Ay, ay, that's the way wi' thee: thee allays makes a peck o' thy own words out o' a pint o' the Bible's.[11] I donna see how thee't to know as "take no thought for the morrow" means all that. An' when the Bible's such a big book, an' thee canst read all thro't, an' ha' the pick o' the texes, I canna think why thee dostna pick better words as donna mean so much more nor they say. Adam doesna pick a that'n; I can understan' the tex as he's allays a-sayin', "God helps them as helps theirsens."'[12]

'Nay, mother,' said Seth, 'that's no text o' the Bible. It comes out of a book as Adam picked up at the stall at Treddles'on. It was wrote by a knowing man, but over-worldly, I doubt.

However, that saying's partly true; for the Bible tells us we must be workers together with God.'

'Well, how'm I to know? It sounds like a tex. But what's th' matter wi' th' lad? Thee't hardly atin' a bit o' supper. Dostna mean to ha' no more nor that bit o' oat-cake? An' thee lookst as white as a flick[13] o' new bacon. What's th' matter wi' thee?'

'Nothing to mind about, mother; I'm not hungry. I'll just look in at Adam again, and see if he'll let me go on with the coffin.'

'Ha' a drop o' warm broth?' said Lisbeth, whose motherly feeling now got the better of her 'nattering' habit. 'I'll set two-three sticks a-light in a minute.'

'Nay, mother, thank thee; thee't very good,' said Seth, gratefully; and encouraged by this touch of tenderness, he went on: 'Let me pray a bit with thee for father, and Adam, and all of us – it'll comfort thee, happen, more than thee thinkst.'

'Well, I've nothin' to say again' it.'

Lisbeth, though disposed always to take the negative side in her conversations with Seth, had a vague sense that there was some comfort and safety in the fact of his piety, and that it somehow relieved her from the trouble of any spiritual transactions on her own behalf.

So the mother and son knelt down together, and Seth prayed for the poor wandering father, and for those who were sorrowing for him at home. And when he came to the petition that Adam might never be called to set up his tent in a far country, but that his mother might be cheered and comforted by his presence all the days of her pilgrimage,[14] Lisbeth's ready tears flowed again, and she wept aloud.

When they rose from their knees, Seth went to Adam again, and said, 'Wilt only lie down for an hour or two, and let me go on the while?'

'No, Seth, no. Make mother go to bed, and go thyself.'

Meantime Lisbeth had dried her eyes, and now followed Seth, holding something in her hands. It was the brown-and-yellow platter containing the baked potatoes with the gravy in them and bits of meat which she had cut and mixed among them. Those were dear times,[15] when wheaten bread and fresh meat

were delicacies to working people. She set the dish down rather
timidly on the bench by Adam's side, and said, 'Thee canst pick
a bit while thee't workin'. I'll bring thee another drop o' water.'

'Ay, mother, do,' said Adam, kindly; 'I'm getting very thirsty.'

In half an hour all was quiet; no sound was to be heard in
the house but the loud ticking of the old day-clock, and the
ringing of Adam's tools. The night was very still: when Adam
opened the door to look out at twelve o'clock, the only motion
seemed to be in the glowing, twinkling stars: every blade of
grass was asleep.

Bodily haste and exertion usually leave our thoughts very
much at the mercy of our feelings and imagination; and it was
so to-night with Adam. While his muscles were working lustily,
his mind seemed as passive as a spectator at a diorama:[16] scenes
of the sad past, and probably sad future, floating before him,
and giving place one to the other in swift succession.

He saw how it would be to-morrow morning, when he had
carried the coffin to Broxton and was at home again, having
his breakfast: his father perhaps would come in ashamed to
meet his son's glance – would sit down, looking older and more
tottering than he had done the morning before, and hang down
his head, examining the floor-quarries; while Lisbeth would ask
him how he supposed the coffin had been got ready, that he
had slinked off and left undone – for Lisbeth was always the
first to utter the word of reproach, although she cried at Adam's
severity towards his father.

'So it will go on, worsening and worsening,' thought Adam;
'there's no slipping up-hill again, and no standing still when
once you've begun to slip down.' And then the day came back
to him when he was a little fellow and used to run by his father's
side, proud to be taken out to work, and prouder still to hear
his father boasting to his fellow-workmen how 'the little chap
had an uncommon notion o' carpentering'. What a fine active
fellow his father was then! When people asked Adam whose
little lad he was, he had a sense of distinction as he answered,
'I'm Thias Bede's lad' – he was quite sure everybody knew Thias
Bede: didn't he make the wonderful pigeon-house at Broxton
parsonage?[17] Those were happy days, especially when Seth,

who was three years the younger, began to go out working too, and Adam began to be a teacher as well as a learner. But then came the days of sadness, when Adam was someway on in his teens, and Thias began to loiter at the public-houses, and Lisbeth began to cry at home, and to pour forth her plaints in the hearing of her sons. Adam remembered well the night of shame and anguish when he first saw his father quite wild and foolish, shouting a song out fitfully among his drunken companions at the 'Waggon Overthrown'. He had run away once when he was only eighteen, making his escape in the morning twilight with a little blue bundle over his shoulder, and his 'mensuration book'[18] in his pocket, and saying to himself very decidedly that he could bear the vexations of home no longer – he would go and seek his fortune, setting up his stick at the crossways and bending his steps the way it fell. But by the time he got to Stoniton, the thought of his mother and Seth, left behind to endure everything without him, became too importunate, and his resolution failed him. He came back the next day, but the misery and terror his mother had gone through in those two days had haunted her ever since.

'No!' Adam said to himself to-night, 'that must never happen again. It'ud make a poor balance when my doings are cast up at the last, if my poor old mother stood o' the wrong side. My back's broad enough and strong enough; I should be no better than a coward to go away and leave the troubles to be borne by them as aren't half so able. "They that are strong ought to bear the infirmities of those that are weak, and not to please themselves."[19] There's a text wants no candle to show't; it shines by its own light. It's plain enough you get into the wrong road i' this life if you run after this and that only for the sake o' making things easy and pleasant to yourself. A pig may poke his nose into the trough and think o' nothing outside it; but if you've got a man's heart and soul in you, you can't be easy a-making your own bed an' leaving the rest to lie on the stones. Nay, nay, I'll never slip my neck out o' the yoke, and leave the load to be drawn by the weak uns. Father's a sore cross to me, an's likely to be for many a long year to come. What then? I've got th' health, and the limbs, and the sperrit to bear it.'

At this moment a smart rap, as if with a willow wand, was given at the house door, and Gyp, instead of barking, as might have been expected, gave a loud howl. Adam, very much startled, went at once to the door and opened it. Nothing was there; all was still, as when he opened it an hour before; the leaves were motionless, and the light of the stars showed the placid fields on both sides of the brook quite empty of visible life. Adam walked round the house, and still saw nothing except a rat which darted into the woodshed as he passed. He went in again, wondering; the sound was so peculiar, that the moment he heard it, it called up the image of the willow wand striking the door. He could not help a little shudder, as he remembered how often his mother had told him of just such a sound coming as a sign when some one was dying. Adam was not a man to be gratuitously superstitious; but he had the blood of the peasant in him as well as of the artisan, and a peasant can no more help believing in a traditional superstition than a horse can help trembling when he sees a camel. Besides, he had that mental combination which is at once humble in the region of mystery, and keen in the region of knowledge: it was the depth of his reverence quite as much as his hard common-sense, which gave him his disinclination to doctrinal religion, and he often checked Seth's argumentative spiritualism by saying, 'Eh, it's a big mystery; thee know'st but little about it.' And so it happened that Adam was at once penetrating and credulous. If a new building had fallen down and he had been told that this was a divine judgment, he would have said, 'May be; but the bearing o' the roof and walls wasn't right, else it wouldn't ha' come down'; yet he believed in dreams and prognostics, and to his dying day he bated his breath a little when he told the story of the stroke with the willow wand.[20] I tell it as he told it, not attempting to reduce it to its natural elements: in our eagerness to explain impressions, we often lose our hold of the sympathy that comprehends them.

But he had the best antidote against imaginative dread in the necessity for getting on with the coffin, and for the next ten minutes his hammer was ringing so uninterruptedly, that other sounds, if there were any, might well be overpowered. A pause came, however, when he had to take up his ruler, and now again came the strange rap, and again Gyp howled. Adam was at the door without the loss of a moment; but again all was still, and the starlight showed there was nothing but the dew-laden grass in front of the cottage.

Adam for a moment thought uncomfortably about his father; but of late years he had never come home at dark hours from Treddleston, and there was every reason for believing that he was then sleeping off his drunkenness at the 'Waggon Over-thrown'. Besides, to Adam, the conception of the future was so inseparable from the painful image of his father, that the fear of any fatal accident to him was excluded by the deeply-infixed fear of his continual degradation. The next thought that occurred to him was one that made him slip off his shoes and tread lightly up-stairs, to listen at the bedroom doors. But both Seth and his mother were breathing regularly.

Adam came down and set to work again, saying to himself, 'I won't open the door again. It's no use staring about to catch sight of a sound. Maybe there's a world about us as we can't see, but th' ear's quicker than the eye, and catches a sound from't now and then. Some people think they get a sight on't too, but they're mostly folks whose eyes are not much use to 'em at anything else. For my part, I think it's better to see when your perpendicular's true, than to see a ghost.'

Such thoughts as these are apt to grow stronger and stronger as daylight quenches the candles and the birds begin to sing. By the time the red sunlight shone on the brass nails that formed the initials on the lid of the coffin, any lingering foreboding from the sound of the willow wand was merged in satisfaction that the work was done and the promise redeemed. There was no need to call Seth, for he was already moving overhead, and presently came down-stairs.

'Now, lad,' said Adam, as Seth made his appearance, 'the coffin's done, and we can take it over to Brox'on, and be back again before half after six. I'll take a mouthful o' oat-cake, and then we'll be off.'

The coffin was soon propped on the tall shoulders of the two brothers, and they were making their way, followed close by

Gyp, out of the little woodyard into the lane at the back of the
house. It was but about a mile and a half to Broxton over the
opposite slope, and their road wound very pleasantly along
lanes and across fields, where the pale woodbines and the dog-
roses were scenting the hedgerows, and the birds were twittering and trilling in the tall leafy boughs of oak and elm. It
was a strangely-mingled picture – the fresh youth of the summer
morning, with its Eden-like peace and loveliness, the stalwart
strength of the two brothers in their rusty working clothes, and
the long coffin on their shoulders. They paused for the last time
before a small farmhouse outside the village of Broxton. By six
o'clock the task was done, the coffin nailed down, and Adam
and Seth were on their way home. They chose a shorter way
homeward, which would take them across the fields and the
brook in front of the house. Adam had not mentioned to Seth
what had happened in the night, but he still retained sufficient
impression from it himself to say –

'Seth, lad, if father isn't come home by the time we've had
our breakfast, I think it'll be as well for thee to go over to
Treddles'on and look after him, and thee canst get me the brass
wire I want. Never mind about losing an hour at thy work; we
can make that up. What dost say?'

'I'm willing,' said Seth. 'But see what clouds have gathered
since we set out. I'm thinking we shall have more rain. It'll be
a sore time for th' haymaking if the meadows are flooded again.
The brook's fine and full now: another day's rain 'ud cover the
plank, and we should have to go round by the road.'

They were coming across the valley now, and had entered
the pasture through which the brook ran.

'Why, what's that sticking against the willow?' continued
Seth, beginning to walk faster. Adam's heart rose to his mouth:
the vague anxiety about his father was changed into a great
dread. He made no answer to Seth, but ran forward, preceded
by Gyp, who began to bark uneasily; and in two moments he
was at the bridge.

This was what the omen meant, then! And the grey-haired
father, of whom he had thought with a sort of hardness a few
hours ago, as certain to live to be a thorn in his side, was

perhaps even then struggling with that watery death! This was
the first thought that flashed through Adam's conscience, before
he had time to seize the coat and drag out the tall heavy body.
Seth was already by his side, helping him, and when they had
it on the bank, the two sons in the first moments knelt and
looked with mute awe at the glazed eyes, forgetting that there
was need for action – forgetting everything but that their father
lay dead before them. Adam was the first to speak.

'I'll run to mother,' he said, in a loud whisper. 'I'll be back
to thee in a minute.'

Poor Lisbeth was busy preparing her sons' breakfast, and
their porridge was already steaming on the fire. Her kitchen
always looked the pink of cleanliness, but this morning she was
more than usually bent on making her hearth and breakfast-
table look comfortable and inviting.

'The lads 'ull be fine an' hungry,' she said, half aloud, as she
stirred the porridge. 'It's a good step to Brox'on, an' it's hungry
air o'er the hill – wi' that heavy coffin too. Eh! it's heavier now,
wi' poor Bob Tholer in't. Howiver, I've made a drap more
porridge nor common this mornin'. The feyther 'ull happen
come in arter a bit. Not as he'll ate much porridge. He swallers
sixpenn'orth o' ale, an' saves a hap'orth o'porridge – that's his
way o' layin' by money, as I've told him many a time, an' am
likely to tell him again afore the day's out. Eh! poor mon, he
takes it quiet enough; there's no denyin' that.'

But now Lisbeth heard the heavy 'thud' of a running footstep
on the turf, and, turning quickly towards the door, she saw
Adam enter, looking so pale and overwhelmed that she
screamed aloud and rushed towards him before he had time to
speak.

'Hush, mother,' Adam said, rather hoarsely, 'don't be frightened. Father's tumbled into the water. Belike we may bring him
round again. Seth and me are going to carry him in. Get a
blanket and make it hot at the fire.'

In reality Adam was convinced that his father was dead, but
he knew there was no other way of repressing his mother's
impetuous wailing grief than by occupying her with some active
task which had hope in it.

He ran back to Seth, and the two sons lifted the sad burden in heartstricken silence. The wide-open glazed eyes were grey, like Seth's, and had once looked with mild pride on the boys before whom Thias had lived to hang his head in shame. Seth's chief feeling was awe and distress at this sudden snatching away of his father's soul; but Adam's mind rushed back over the past in a flood of relenting and pity. When death, the great Reconciler, has come, it is never our tenderness that we repent of, but our severity.

CHAPTER V

The Rector

Before twelve o'clock there had been some heavy storms of rain, and the water lay in deep gutters on the sides of the gravel-walks in the garden of Broxton Parsonage; the great Provence roses[1] had been cruelly tossed by the wind and beaten by the rain, and all the delicate-stemmed border flowers had been dashed down and stained with the wet soil. A melancholy morning – because it was nearly time hay-harvest should begin, and instead of that the meadows were likely to be flooded.

But people who have pleasant homes get indoor enjoyments that they would never think of but for the rain. If it had not been a wet morning, Mr Irwine would not have been in the dining-room playing at chess with his mother, and he loves both his mother and chess quite well enough to pass some cloudy hours very easily by their help. Let me take you into that dining-room, and show you the Rev. Adolphus Irwine, Rector of Broxton, Vicar of Hayslope, and Vicar of Blythe, a pluralist at whom the severest Church-reformer[2] would have found it difficult to look sour. We will enter very softly, and stand still in the open doorway, without awaking the glossy brown setter who is stretched across the hearth, with her two puppies beside her; or the pug, who is dosing, with his black muzzle aloft, like a sleepy president.[3]

The room is a large and lofty one, with an ample mullioned oriel window at one end; the walls, you see, are new, and not yet painted;[4] but the furniture, though originally of an expensive sort, is old and scanty, and there is no drapery about the window. The crimson cloth over the large dining-table is very threadbare, though it contrasts pleasantly enough with the dead hue of the plaster on the walls; but on this cloth there is a massive silver waiter[5] with a decanter of water on it, of the same pattern as two larger ones that are propped up on the sideboard with a coat of arms conspicuous[6] in their centre. You suspect at once that the inhabitants of this room have inherited more blood than wealth, and would not be surprised to find that Mr Irwine had a finely-cut nostril and upper lip; but at present we can only see that he has a broad flat back and an abundance of powdered hair,[7] all thrown backward and tied behind with a black ribbon – a bit of conservatism in costume which tells you that he is not a young man. He will perhaps turn round by-and-by, and in the meantime we can look at that stately old lady, his mother, a beautiful aged brunette, whose rich-toned complexion is well set off by the complex wrappings of pure white cambric and lace about her head and neck. She is as erect in her comely embonpoint as a statue of Ceres;[8] and her dark face, with its delicate aquiline nose, firm proud mouth, and small intense black eye, is so keen and sarcastic in its expression that you instinctively substitute a pack of cards for the chess-men, and imagine her telling your fortune. The small brown hand with which she is lifting her queen is laden with pearls, diamonds, and turquoises; and a large black veil is very carefully adjusted over the crown of her cap, and falls in sharp contrast on the white folds about her neck. It must take a long time to dress that old lady in the morning! But it seems a law of nature that she should be dressed so: she is clearly one of those children of royalty who have never doubted their right divine,[9] and never met with any one so absurd as to question it.

'There, Dauphin,[10] tell me what that is!' says this magnificent old lady, as she deposits her queen very quietly and folds her arms. 'I should be sorry to utter a word disagreeable to your feelings.'

'Ah! you witch-mother, you sorceress![11] How is a Christian man to win a game off you? I should have sprinkled the board with holy water before we began. You've not won that game by fair means, now, so don't pretend it.'

'Yes, yes, that's what the beaten have always said of great conquerors. But see, there's the sunshine falling on the board,

to show you more clearly what a foolish move you made with
that pawn. Come, shall I give you another chance?'

'No, mother, I shall leave you to your own conscience, now
it's clearing up. We must go and plash up the mud a little,
mustn't we, Juno?'[12] This was addressed to the brown setter,
who had jumped up at the sound of the voices and laid her
nose in an insinuating way on her master's leg. 'But I must go
up-stairs first and see Anne. I was called away to Tholer's
funeral just when I was going before.'

'It's of no use, child; she can't speak to you. Kate says she
has one of her worst headaches this morning.'

'Oh, she likes me to go and see her just the same; she's never
too ill to care about that.'

If you know how much of human speech is mere purposeless
impulse or habit, you will not wonder when I tell you that this
identical objection had been made, and had received the same
kind of answer, many hundred times in the course of the fifteen
years that Mr Irwine's sister Anne had been an invalid. Splendid
old ladies, who take a long time to dress in the morning, have
often slight sympathy with sickly daughters.

But while Mr Irwine was still seated, leaning back in his chair
and stroking Juno's head, the servant came to the door and
said, 'If you please, sir, Joshua Rann wishes to speak with you,
if you're at liberty.'

'Let him be shown in here,' said Mrs Irwine, taking up her
knitting. 'I always like to hear what Mr Rann has got to say.
His shoes will be dirty, but see that he wipes them, Carroll.'

In two minutes Mr Rann appeared at the door with very
deferential bows, which, however, were far from conciliating
Pug, who gave a sharp bark, and ran across the room to recon-
noitre the stranger's legs; while the two puppies, regarding Mr
Rann's prominent calf and ribbed worsted stockings from a
more sensuous point of view, plunged and growled over them
in great enjoyment. Meantime, Mr Irwine turned round his
chair and said –

'Well, Joshua, anything the matter at Hayslope, that you've
come over this damp morning? Sit down, sit down. Never mind
the dogs; give them a friendly kick. Here, Pug, you rascal!'

It is very pleasant to see some men turn round; pleasant as a sudden rush of warm air in winter, or the flash of firelight in the chill dusk. Mr Irwine was one of those men. He bore the same sort of resemblance to his mother that our loving memory of a friend's face often bears to the face itself: the lines were all more generous, the smile brighter, the expression heartier. If the outline had been less finely cut, his face might have been called jolly; but that was not the right word for its mixture of bonhommie and distinction.

'Thank your reverence,' answered Mr Rann, endeavouring to look unconcerned about his legs, but shaking them alternately to keep off the puppies; 'I'll stand, if you please, as more becoming. I hope I see you and Mrs Irwine well, an' Miss Irwine – an' Miss Anne, I hope's as well as usual.'

'Yes, Joshua, thank you. You see how blooming my mother looks. She beats us younger people hollow. But what's the matter?'

'Why, sir, I had to come to Brox'on to deliver some work, and I thought it but right to call and let you know the goins-on as there's been i' the village, such as I hanna seen i' my time, and I've lived in it man and boy sixty year come St Thomas, and collected th' Easter dues[13] for Mr Blick before your reverence come into the parish, and been at the ringin' o' every bell, and the diggin' o' every grave, and sung i' the quire long afore Bartle Massey come from nobody knows where, wi' his counter-singin',[14] and fine anthems, as puts everybody out but himself – one takin' it up after another like sheep a-bleatin' i' th' fold. I know what belongs to bein' a parish clerk, and I know as I should be wantin' i' respect to your reverence, an' church, an' king, if I was t' allow such goins-on wi'out speakin'. I was took by surprise, an' knowed nothin' on it beforehand, an' I was so flustered, I was clean as if I'd lost my tools. I hanna slep more nor four hour this night as is past an' gone; an' then it was nothin' but nightmare, as tired me worse nor wakin'.'

'Why, what in the world is the matter, Joshua? Have the thieves been at the church lead[15] again?'

'Thieves! no, sir, – an' yet, as I may say, it *is* thieves, an' a-thievin' the church, too. It's the Methodisses as is like to get th' upper hand i' th' parish, if your reverence an' his honour, Squire Donnithorne, doesna think well to say the word an' forbid it. Not as I'm a-dictatin' to you, sir; I'm not forgettin' myself so far as to be wise above my betters. Howiver, whether I'm wise or no, that's neither here nor there, but what I've got to say I say – as the young Methodis woman, as is at Mester Poyser's, was a-preachin' an' a-praying on the Green last night, as sure as I'm a-stannin' afore your reverence now.'

'Preaching on the Green!' said Mr Irwine, looking surprised but quite serene. 'What, that pale pretty young woman I've seen at Poyser's? I saw she was a Methodist, or Quaker, or something of that sort, by her dress, but I didn't know she was a preacher.'

'It's a true word as I say, sir,' rejoined Mr Rann, compressing his mouth into a semicircular form, and pausing long enough to indicate three notes of exclamation. 'She preached on the Green last night; an' she's laid hold of Chad's Bess, as the girl's been i' fits welly iver sin'.'

'Well, Bessy Cranage is a hearty-looking lass; I daresay she'll come round again, Joshua. Did anybody else go into fits?'

'No, sir, I canna say as they did. But there's no knowin' what'll come, if we're t' have such preachins as that agoin' on ivery week – there'll be no livin' i' th' village. For them Methodisses make folks believe as if they take a mug o' drink extry, an' make theirselves a bit comfortable, they'll have to go to hell for't as sure as they're born. I'm not a tipplin' man nor a drunkard – nobody can say it on me – but I like a extry quart at Easter or Christmas time, as is nat'ral when we're goin' the rounds a-singin', an' folks offer't you for nothin'; or when I'm a-collectin' the dues; an' I like a pint wi' my pipe, an' a neighbourly chat at Mester Casson's now an' then, for I was brought up i' the Church, thank God, an' ha' been a parish clerk this two-an'-thirty year: I should know what the church religion is.'

'Well, what's your advice, Joshua? What do you think should be done?'

'Well, your reverence, I'm not for takin' any measures again

the young woman. She's well enough if she'd let alone preachin';
an' I hear as she's a-goin' away back to her own country soon.
She's Mr Poyser's own niece, an' I donna wish to say what's
anyways disrespectful o' th' family at th' Hall Farm, as I've
measured for shoes, little an' big, welly iver sin' I've been a
shoemaker. But there's that Will Maskery, sir, as is the ram-
pageousest Methodis as can be, an' I make no doubt it was
him as stirred up th' young woman to preach last night, an'
he'll be a bringin' other folks to preach from Treddles'on, if his
comb isn't cut a bit;[16] an' I think as he should be let know as
he isna t' have the makin' an' mendin' o' church carts an'
implemens, let alone stayin' i' that house an' yard as is Squire
Donnithorne's.'

'Well, but you say yourself, Joshua, that you never knew any
one come to preach on the Green before; why should you think
they'll come again? The Methodists don't come to preach in
little villages like Hayslope, where there's only a handful of
labourers, too tired to listen to them. They might almost as well
go and preach on the Binton Hills. Will Maskery is no preacher
himself, I think.'

'Nay, sir, he's no gift at stringin' the words together wi'out
book; he'd be stuck fast like a cow i' wet clay. But he's got
tongue enough to speak disrespectful about's neebors, for he
said as I was a blind Pharisee;[17] – a-usin' the Bible i' that way
to find nicknames for folks as are his elders an' betters! – and
what's worse, he's been heard to say very unbecomin' words
about your reverence; for I could bring them as 'ud swear as he
called you a "dumb dog", an' a "idle shepherd".[18] You'll forgi'e
me for sayin' such things over again.'

'Better not, better not, Joshua. Let evil words die as soon as
they're spoken. Will Maskery might be a great deal worse fellow
than he is. He used to be a wild drunken rascal, neglecting his
work and beating his wife, they told me; now he's thrifty and
decent, and he and his wife look comfortable together. If you
can bring me any proof that he interferes with his neighbours,
and creates any disturbance, I shall think it my duty as a clergyman and a magistrate to interfere. But it wouldn't become wise
people, like you and me, to be making a fuss about trifles, as if

we thought the Church was in danger because Will Maskery
lets his tongue wag rather foolishly, or a young woman talks in
a serious way to a handful of people on the Green. We must
"live and let live", Joshua, in religion as well as in other things.
You go on doing your duty, as parish clerk and sexton, as well
as you've always done it, and making those capital thick boots
for your neighbours, and things won't go far wrong in Hayslope, depend upon it.'

'Your reverence is very good to say so; an' I'm sensable as,
you not livin' i' the parish, there's more upo' my shoulders.'

'To be sure; and you must mind and not lower the Church
in people's eyes by seeming to be frightened about it for a little
thing, Joshua. I shall trust to your good sense, now, to take no
notice at all of what Will Maskery says, either about you or
me. You and your neighbours can go on taking your pot of
beer soberly, when you've done your day's work, like good
churchmen; and if Will Maskery doesn't like to join you, but
to go to a prayer-meeting at Treddleston instead, let him; that's
no business of yours, so long as he doesn't hinder you from
doing what you like. And as to people saying a few idle words
about us, we must not mind that, any more than the old church-
steeple minds the rooks cawing about it. Will Maskery comes
to church every Sunday afternoon, and does his wheelwright's
business steadily in the week-days, and as long as he does that
he must be let alone.'

'Ah, sir, but when he comes to church, he sits an' shakes his
head, an' looks as sour an' as coxy[19] when we're a-singin', as I
should like to fetch him a rap across the jowl – God forgi'e me
– an' Mrs Irwine, an' your reverence, too, for speakin' so afore
you. An' he said as our Christmas singin' was no better nor the
cracklin' o' thorns under a pot.'[20]

'Well, he's got a bad ear for music, Joshua. When people
have wooden heads, you know, it can't be helped. He won't
bring the other people in Hayslope round to his opinion, while
you go on singing as well as you do.'

'Yes, sir, but it turns a man's stomach t' hear the Scripture
misused i' that way. I know as much o' the words o' the Bible
as he does, an' could say the Psalms right through i' my sleep

if you was to pinch me; but I know better nor to take 'em to say my own say wi'. I might as well take the Sacriment-cup[21] home and use it at meals.'

'That's a very sensible remark of yours, Joshua; but, as I said before—'

While Mr Irwine was speaking, the sound of a booted step, and the clink of a spur, were heard on the stone floor of the entrance-hall, and Joshua Rann moved hastily aside from the doorway to make room for some one who paused there, and said, in a ringing tenor voice,

'Godson Arthur; – may he come in?'

'Come in, come in, godson!' Mrs Irwine answered, in the deep half-masculine tone which belongs to the vigorous old woman, and there entered a young gentleman in a riding-dress, with his right arm in a sling; whereupon followed that pleasant confusion of laughing interjections, and hand-shakings, and 'How are you's?' mingled with joyous short barks and wagging of tails on the part of the canine members of the family, which tells that the visitor is on the best terms with the visited. The young gentleman was Arthur Donnithorne, known in Hayslope, variously, as 'the young squire', 'the heir', and 'the captain'. He was only a captain in the Loamshire Militia; but to the Hayslope tenants he was more intensely a captain than all the young gentlemen of the same rank in his Majesty's regulars[22] – he outshone them as the planet Jupiter outshines the Milky Way. If you want to know more particularly how he looked, call to your remembrance some tawny-whiskered, brown-locked, clear-complexioned young Englishman whom you have met with in a foreign town, and been proud of as a fellow-countryman – well-washed, high-bred, white-handed, yet looking as if he could deliver well from the left shoulder, and floor his man: I will not be so much of a tailor as to trouble your imagination with the difference of costume, and insist on the striped waistcoat, long-tailed coat, and low top-boots.

Turning round to take a chair, Captain Donnithorne said, 'But don't let me interrupt Joshua's business – he has something to say.'

'Humbly begging your honour's pardon,' said Joshua, bowing

low, 'there was one thing I had to say to his reverence as other things had drove out o' my head.'

'Out with it, Joshua, quickly!' said Mr Irwine.

'Belike, sir, you havena heared as Thias Bede's dead – drownded this morning, or more like overnight, i' the Willow Brook, again' the bridge right i' front o' the house.'

'Ah!' exclaimed both the gentlemen at once, as if they were a good deal interested in the information.

'An' Seth Bede's been to me this morning to say he wished me to tell your reverence as his brother Adam begged of you particular t' allow his father's grave to be dug by the White Thorn, because his mother's set her heart on it, on account of a dream as she had; an' they'd ha' come theirselves to ask you, but they've so much to see after with the crowner,[23] an' that; an' their mother's took on so, an' wants 'em to make sure o' the spot for fear somebody else should take it. An' if your reverence sees well and good, I'll send my boy to tell 'em as soon as I get home; an' that's why I make bold to trouble you wi' it, his honour being present.'

'To be sure, Joshua, to be sure, they shall have it. I'll ride round to Adam myself, and see him. Send your boy, however, to say they shall have the grave, lest anything should happen to detain me. And now, good morning, Joshua; go into the kitchen and have some ale.'

'Poor old Thias!' said Mr Irwine, when Joshua was gone, 'I'm afraid the drink helped the brook to drown him. I should have been glad for the load to have been taken off my friend Adam's shoulders in a less painful way. That fine fellow has been propping up his father from ruin for the last five or six years.'

'He's a regular trump, is Adam,' said Captain Donnithorne. 'When I was a little fellow, and Adam was a strapping lad of fifteen, and taught me carpentering, I used to think if ever I was a rich sultan, I would make Adam my grand-vizier.[24] And I believe now, he would bear the exaltation as well as any poor wise man in an Eastern story. If ever I live to be a large-acred man instead of a poor devil with a mortgaged allowance of pocket-money, I'll have Adam for my right-hand. He shall manage my woods for me, for he seems to have a better notion of those things than any man I ever met with; and I know he would make twice the money of them that my grandfather does, with that miserable old Satchell to manage, who understands no more about timber than an old carp. I've mentioned the subject to my grandfather once or twice, but for some reason or other he has a dislike to Adam, and *I* can do nothing. But come, your reverence, are you for a ride with me? It's splendid out of doors now. We can go to Adam's together, if you like; but I want to call at the Hall Farm on my way, to look at the whelps Poyser is keeping for me.'

'You must stay and have lunch first, Arthur,' said Mrs Irwine. 'It's nearly two. Carroll will bring it in directly.'

'I want to go to the Hall Farm too,' said Mr Irwine, 'to have another look at the little Methodist who is staying there. Joshua tells me she was preaching on the Green last night.'

'Oh, by Jove!' said Captain Donnithorne, laughing. 'Why, she looks as quiet as a mouse. There's something rather striking about her, though. I positively felt quite bashful the first time I saw her: she was sitting stooping over her sewing in the sunshine outside the house, when I rode up and called out, without noticing that she was a stranger, "Is Martin Poyser at home?" I declare, when she got up and looked at me, and just said, "He's in the house, I believe: I'll go and call him", I felt quite ashamed of having spoken so abruptly to her. She looked like St Catherine[25] in a Quaker dress. It's a type of face one rarely sees among our common people.'

'I should like to see the young woman, Dauphin,' said Mrs Irwine. 'Make her come here on some pretext or other.'

'I don't know how I can manage that, mother; it will hardly do for me to patronize a Methodist preacher, even if she would consent to be patronized by an idle shepherd, as Will Maskery calls me. You should have come in a little sooner, Arthur, to hear Joshua's denunciation of his neighbour Will Maskery. The old fellow wants me to excommunicate the wheelwright, and then deliver him over to the civil arm – that is to say, to your grandfather – to be turned out of house and yard. If I chose to interfere in this business, now, I might get up as pretty a story of hatred and persecution as the Methodists need desire to publish in the next number of their magazine.[26] It wouldn't take me much trouble to persuade Chad Cranage and half-a-dozen other bull-headed fellows, that they would be doing an acceptable service to the Church by hunting Will Maskery out of the village with rope-ends and pitchforks; and then, when I had furnished them with half a sovereign to get gloriously drunk after their exertions, I should have put the climax to as pretty a farce as any of my brother clergy have set going in their parishes for the last thirty years.'

'It is really insolent of the man, though, to call you an "idle shepherd", and a "dumb dog",' said Mrs Irwine: 'I should be inclined to check him a little there. You are too easy-tempered, Dauphin.'

'Why, mother, you don't think it would be a good way of sustaining my dignity to set about vindicating myself from the aspersions of Will Maskery? Besides, I'm not so sure that they *are* aspersions. I *am* a lazy fellow, and get terribly heavy in my saddle; not to mention that I'm always spending more than I can afford in bricks and mortar, so that I get savage at a lame beggar when he asks me for sixpence. Those poor lean cobblers,[27] who think they can help to regenerate mankind by setting out to preach in the morning twilight before they begin their day's work, may well have a poor opinion of me. But come, let us have our luncheon. Isn't Kate coming to lunch?'

'Miss Irwine told Bridget to take her lunch up-stairs,' said Carroll; 'she can't leave Miss Anne.'

'Oh, very well. Tell Bridget to say I'll go up and see Miss Anne presently. You can use your right arm quite well, now, Arthur,' Mr Irwine continued, observing that Captain Donnithorne had taken his arm out of the sling.

'Yes, pretty well; but Godwin insists on my keeping it up constantly for some time to come. I hope I shall be able to get away to the regiment, though, in the beginning of August. It's a desperately dull business being shut up at the Chase in the summer months, when one can neither hunt nor shoot, so as to make one's self pleasantly sleepy in the evening. However, we are to astonish the echoes on the 30th of July. My grandfather has given me *carte blanche* for once, and I promise you the entertainment shall be worthy of the occasion. The world will not see the grand epoch of my majority[28] twice. I think I shall have a lofty throne for you, godmamma, or rather two, one on the lawn and another in the ball-room, that you may sit and look down upon us like an Olympian goddess.'[29]

'I mean to bring out my best brocade, that I wore at your christening twenty years ago,' said Mrs Irwine. 'Ah, I think I shall see your poor mother flitting about in her white dress, which looked to me almost like a shroud that very day; and it *was* her shroud only three months after; and your little cap and christening dress were buried with her too. She had set her heart on that, sweet soul! Thank God you take after your mother's family, Arthur. If you had been a puny, wiry, yellow baby, I wouldn't have stood godmother to you. I should have been sure you would turn out a Donnithorne. But you were such a broad-faced, broad-chested, loud-screaming rascal, I knew you were every inch of you a Tradgett.'

'But you might have been a little too hasty there, mother,' said Mr Irwine, smiling. 'Don't you remember how it was with Juno's last pups? One of them was the very image of its mother, but it had two or three of its father's tricks notwithstanding. Nature is clever enough to cheat even you, mother.'

'Nonsense, child! Nature never makes a ferret in the shape of a mastiff. You'll never persuade me that I can't tell what men are by their outsides. If I don't like a man's looks, depend upon it I shall never like *him*. I don't want to know people that look ugly and disagreeable, any more than I want to taste dishes that look disagreeable. If they make me shudder at the first glance, I say, take them away. An ugly, piggish, or fishy eye, now, makes me feel quite ill; it's like a bad smell.'

'Talking of eyes,' said Captain Donnithorne, 'that reminds me that I've got a book I meant to bring you, godmamma. It came down in a parcel from London the other day. I know you are fond of queer, wizard-like stories. It's a volume of poems, "Lyrical Ballads": most of them seem to be twaddling stuff; but the first is in a different style – "The Ancient Mariner"[30] is the title. I can hardly make head or tail of it as a story, but it's a

strange, striking thing. I'll send it over to you; and there are some
other books that *you* may like to see, Irwine – pamphlets about
Antinomianism and Evangelicalism,³¹ whatever they may be. I
can't think what the fellow means by sending such things to me.
I've written to him, to desire that from henceforth he will send
me no book or pamphlet on anything that ends in *ism*.'

'Well, I don't know that I'm very fond of *isms* myself; but I
may as well look at the pamphlets; they let one see what is
going on. I've a little matter to attend to, Arthur,' continued
Mr Irwine, rising to leave the room, 'and then I shall be ready
to set out with you.'

The little matter that Mr Irwine had to attend to took him
up the old stone staircase (part of the house was very old), and
made him pause before a door at which he knocked gently.
'Come in,' said a woman's voice, and he entered a room so
darkened by blinds and curtains that Miss Kate, the thin middle-
aged lady standing by the bedside, would not have had light
enough for any other sort of work than the knitting which lay
on the little table near her. But at present she was doing what
required only the dimmest light – sponging the aching head
that lay on the pillow with fresh vinegar. It was a small face,
that of the poor sufferer; perhaps it had once been pretty, but
now it was worn and sallow. Miss Kate came towards her
brother and whispered, 'Don't speak to her; she can't bear to
be spoken to to-day.' Anne's eyes were closed, and her brow
contracted as if from intense pain. Mr Irwine went to the
bedside, and took up one of the delicate hands and kissed it; a
slight pressure from the small fingers told him that it was worth
while to have come up-stairs for the sake of doing that. He
lingered a moment, looking at her, and then turned away and
left the room, treading very gently – he had taken off his boots
and put on slippers before he came up-stairs. Whoever remembers how many things he has declined to do even for himself,
rather than have the trouble of putting on or taking off his
boots, will not think this last detail insignificant.

And Mr Irwine's sisters, as any person of family within ten
miles of Broxton could have testified, were such stupid, uninteresting women! It was quite a pity handsome, clever Mrs Irwine

should have had such commonplace daughters. That fine old lady herself was worth driving ten miles to see, any day; her beauty, her well-preserved faculties, and her old-fashioned dignity, made her a graceful subject for conversation in turn with the King's health, the sweet new patterns in cotton dresses, the news from Egypt, and Lord Dacey's lawsuit,[32] which was fretting poor Lady Dacey to death. But no one ever thought of mentioning the Miss Irwines, except the poor people in Broxton village, who regarded them as deep in the science of medicine, and spoke of them vaguely as 'the gentlefolks'. If any one had asked old Job Dummilow who gave him his flannel jacket, he would have answered, 'the gentlefolks, last winter'; and widow Steene dwelt much on the virtues of the 'stuff' the gentlefolks gave her for her cough. Under this name, too, they were used with great effect as a means of taming refractory children, so that at the sight of poor Miss Anne's sallow face, several small urchins had a terrified sense that she was cognisant of all their worst misdemeanours, and knew the precise number of stones with which they had intended to hit farmer Britton's ducks. But for all who saw them through a less mythical medium, the Miss Irwines were quite superfluous existences; inartistic figures crowding the canvas of life without adequate effect. Miss Anne, indeed, if her chronic headaches could have been accounted for by a pathetic story of disappointed love, might have had some romantic interest attached to her; but no such story had either been known or invented concerning her, and the general impression was quite in accordance with the fact, that both the sisters were old maids for the prosaic reason that they had never received an eligible offer.

Nevertheless, to speak paradoxically, the existence of insignificant people has very important consequences in the world. It can be shown to affect the price of bread and the rate of wages, to call forth many evil tempers from the selfish, and many heroisms from the sympathetic, and, in other ways, to play no small part in the tragedy of life. And if that handsome, generous-blooded clergyman, the Rev. Adolphus Irwine, had not had these two hopelessly-maiden sisters, his lot would have been shaped quite differently: he would very likely have taken a comely wife in his youth, and now, when his hair was getting grey under the powder, would have had tall sons and blooming daughters – such possessions, in short, as men commonly think will repay them for all the labour they take under the sun. As it was – having with all his three livings no more than seven hundred a-year, and seeing no way of keeping his splendid mother and his sickly sister, not to reckon a second sister, who was usually spoken of without any adjective, in such lady-like ease as became their birth and habits, and at the same time providing for a family of his own – he remained, you see, at the age of eight-and-forty, a bachelor, not making any merit of that renunciation, but saying laughingly, if any one alluded to it, that he made it an excuse for many indulgences which a wife would never have allowed him. And perhaps he was the only person in the world who did not think his sisters uninteresting and superfluous; for his was one of those large-hearted, sweet-blooded natures that never know a narrow or a grudging thought; epicurean,[33] if you will, with no enthusiasm, no self-scourging sense of duty; but yet, as you have seen, of a sufficiently subtle moral fibre to have an unwearying tenderness for obscure and monotonous suffering. It was his large-hearted indulgence that made him ignore his mother's hardness towards her daughters, which was the more striking from its contrast with her doting fondness towards himself: he held it no virtue to frown at irremediable faults.

See the difference between the impression a man makes on you when you walk by his side in familiar talk, or look at him in his home, and the figure he makes when seen from a lofty historical level, or even in the eyes of a critical neighbour who thinks of him as an embodied system or opinion rather than as a man. Mr Roe, the 'travelling preacher'[34] stationed at Treddleston, had included Mr Irwine in a general statement concerning the Church clergy in the surrounding district, whom he described as men given up to the lusts of the flesh and the pride of life; hunting and shooting, and adorning their own houses; asking what shall we eat, and what shall we drink, and wherewithal shall we be clothed? – careless of dispensing the bread of life to their flocks, preaching at best but a carnal and

soul-benumbing morality, and trafficking in the souls of men by
receiving money[35] for discharging the pastoral office in parishes
where they did not so much as look on the faces of the people
more than once a-year. The ecclesiastical historian, too, looking
into parliamentary reports of that period, finds honourable
members[36] zealous for the Church, and untainted with any
sympathy for the 'tribe of canting Methodists', making state-
ments scarcely less melancholy than that of Mr Roe. And it is
impossible for me to say that Mr Irwine was altogether belied
by the generic classification assigned him. He really had no
very lofty aims, no theological enthusiasm: if I were closely
questioned, I should be obliged to confess that he felt no serious
alarms about the souls of his parishioners, and would have
thought it a mere loss of time to talk in a doctrinal and awakening manner to old 'Feyther Taft', or even to Chad Cranage the
blacksmith. If he had been in the habit of speaking theoretically,
he would perhaps have said that the only healthy form religion
could take in such minds was that of certain dim but strong
emotions, suffusing themselves as a hallowing influence over
the family affections and neighbourly duties. He thought the
custom of baptism more important than its doctrine, and that
the religious benefits the peasant drew from the church where
his fathers worshipped and the sacred piece of turf where they
lay buried, were but slightly dependent on a clear understanding
of the Liturgy or the sermon. Clearly the Rector was not what
is called in these days an 'earnest' man: he was fonder of church
history than of divinity, and had much more insight into men's
characters than interest in their opinions; he was neither labori-
ous, nor obviously self-denying, nor very copious in almsgiving,
and his theology, you perceive, was lax. His mental palate,
indeed, was rather pagan, and found a savouriness in a quotation from Sophocles or Theocritus[37] that was quite absent from
any text in Isaiah or Amos. But if you feed your young setter
on raw flesh, how can you wonder at its retaining a relish for
uncooked partridge in after-life? and Mr Irwine's recollections
of young enthusiasm and ambition were all associated with
poetry and ethics that lay aloof from the Bible.

On the other hand, I must plead, for I have an affectionate

partiality towards the Rector's memory, that he was not vindic-
tive – and some philanthropists have been so; that he was not
intolerant – and there is a rumour that some zealous theologians
have not been altogether free from that blemish; that although
he would probably have declined to give his body to be burned
in any public cause, and was far from bestowing all his goods
to feed the poor, he had that charity[38] which has sometimes
been lacking to very illustrious virtue – he was tender to other
men's failings, and unwilling to impute evil. He was one of
those men, and they are not the commonest, of whom we
can know the best only by following them away from the
market-place, the platform, and the pulpit, entering with them
into their own homes, hearing the voice with which they speak
to the young and aged about their own hearthstone, and witnessing their thoughtful care for the everyday wants of everyday
companions, who take all their kindness as a matter of course,
and not as a subject for panegyric.[39]

Such men, happily, have lived in times when great abuses
flourished, and have sometimes even been the living representa-
tives of the abuses. That is a thought which might comfort us
a little under the opposite fact – that it is better sometimes *not*
to follow great reformers of abuses beyond the threshold of
their homes.

But whatever you may think of Mr Irwine now, if you had
met him that June afternoon riding on his grey cob, with his
dogs running beside him – portly, upright, manly, with a good-
natured smile on his finely-turned lips as he talked to his dashing
young companion on the bay mare, you must have felt that,
however ill he harmonized with sound theories of the clerical
office, he somehow harmonized extremely well with that peaceful landscape.

See them in the bright sunlight, interrupted every now and
then by rolling masses of cloud, ascending the slope from the
Broxton side, where the tall gables and elms of the rectory
predominate over the tiny white-washed church. They will soon
be in the parish of Hayslope; the grey church-tower and village
roofs lie before them to the left, and farther on, to the right,
they can just see the chimneys of the Hall Farm.

CHAPTER VI

The Hall Farm

Evidently that gate is never opened: for the long grass and the great hemlocks grow close against it; and if it were opened, it is so rusty, that the force necessary to turn it on its hinges would be likely to pull down the square stone-built pillars, to the detriment of the two stone lionesses which grin with a doubtful carnivorous affability above a coat of arms, surmounting each of the pillars. It would be easy enough, by the aid of the nicks in the stone pillars, to climb over the brick wall with its smooth stone coping; but by putting our eyes close to the rusty bars of the gate, we can see the house well enough, and all but the very corners of the grassy enclosure.

It is a very fine old place, of red brick, softened by a pale powdery lichen, which has dispersed itself with happy irregularity, so as to bring the red brick into terms of friendly companionship with the limestone ornaments surrounding the three gables, the windows, and the door-place. But the windows are patched with wooden panes, and the door, I think, is like the gate – it is never opened: how it would groan and grate against the stone floor if it were! For it is a solid, heavy, handsome door, and must once have been in the habit of shutting with a sonorous bang behind a liveried lackey, who had just seen his master and mistress off the grounds in a carriage and pair.

But at present one might fancy the house in the early stage of a chancery suit,[1] and that the fruit from that grand double row of walnut-trees on the right hand of the enclosure would fall and rot among the grass, if it were not that we heard the booming bark of dogs echoing from great buildings at the back. And now the half-weaned calves that have been sheltering themselves in a gorse-built hovel against the left-hand wall, come out and set up a silly answer to that terrible bark, doubtless supposing that it has reference to buckets of milk.

Yes, the house must be inhabited, and we will see by whom; for imagination is a licensed trespasser: it has no fear of dogs, but may climb over walls and peep in at windows with impunity. Put your face to one of the glass panes in the right-hand window: what do you see? A large open fireplace, with rusty dogs[2] in it, and a bare-boarded floor; at the far end, fleeces of wool stacked up; in the middle of the floor, some empty corn bags. That is the furniture of the dining-room. And what through the left-hand window? Several clothes-horses, a pillion,[3] spinning-wheel, and an old box wide open, and stuffed full of coloured rags. At the edge of this box there lies a great wooden doll, which, so far as mutilation is concerned, bears a strong resemblance to the finest Greek sculpture,[4] and especially in the total loss of its nose. Near it there is a little chair, and the butt-end of a boy's leather long-lashed whip.

The history of the house is plain now. It was once the residence of a country squire, whose family, probably dwindling down to mere spinsterhood, got merged in the more territorial name of Donnithorne. It was once the Hall; it is now the Hall Farm. Like the life in some coast-town that was once a watering-place,[5] and is now a port, where the genteel streets are silent and grass-grown, and the docks and warehouses busy and resonant, the life at the Hall has changed its focus, and no longer radiates from the parlour, but from the kitchen and the farmyard.

Plenty of life there! though this is the drowsiest time of the year, just before hay-harvest; and it is the drowsiest time of the day too, for it is close upon three by the sun, and it is half-past three by Mrs Poyser's handsome eight-day clock.[6] But there is always a stronger sense of life when the sun is brilliant after rain; and now he is pouring down his beams, and making sparkles among the wet straw, and lighting up every patch of vivid green moss on the red tiles of the cow-shed, and turning even the muddy water that is hurrying along the channel to the drain into a mirror for the yellow-billed ducks, who are seizing the opportunity of getting a drink with as much body in it as possible. There is quite a concert of noises: the great bull-dog, chained against the stables, is thrown into furious exasperation by the unwary approach of a cock too near the mouth of his kennel, and sends forth a thundering bark, which is answered by two fox-hounds shut up in the opposite cow-house; the old top-knotted hens, scratching with their chicks among the straw, set up a sympathetic croaking as the discomfited cock joins them; a sow with her brood, all very muddy as to the legs, and curled as to the tail, throws in some deep staccato notes; our friends the calves are bleating from the home croft; and, under all, a fine ear discerns the continuous hum of human voices.

For the great barn-doors are thrown wide open, and men are busy there mending the harness, under the superintendence of Mr Goby the 'whittaw',[7] otherwise saddler, who entertains them with the latest Treddleston gossip. It is certainly rather an unfortunate day that Alick, the shepherd, has chosen for having the whittaws, since the morning turned out so wet; and Mrs Poyser has spoken her mind pretty strongly as to the dirt which the extra number of men's shoes brought into the house at dinner-time. Indeed, she has not yet recovered her equanimity on the subject, though it is now nearly three hours since dinner, and the house-floor is perfectly clean again; as clean as everything else in that wonderful house-place, where the only chance of collecting a few grains of dust would be to climb on the salt-coffer, and put your finger on the high mantel-shelf on which the glittering brass candle-sticks are enjoying their summer sinecure; for at this time of year, of course, every one goes to bed while it is yet light, or at least light enough to discern the outline of objects after you have bruised your shins against them. Surely nowhere else could an oak clock-case and an oak table have got to such a polish by the hand: genuine 'elbow polish', as Mrs Poyser called it, for she thanked God she never had any of your varnished rubbish in her house. Hetty Sorrel often took the opportunity, when her aunt's back was turned, of looking at the pleasing reflection of herself in those polished surfaces, for the oak table was usually turned up like a screen, and was more for ornament than for use; and she could see herself sometimes in the great round pewter dishes that were ranged on the shelves above the long deal dinner-table, or in the hobs of the grate, which always shone like jasper.[8]

Everything was looking at its brightest at this moment, for the sun shone right on the pewter dishes, and from their reflecting surfaces pleasant jets of light were thrown on mellow oak and bright brass; – and on a still pleasanter object than these; for some of the rays fell on Dinah's finely moulded cheek, and lit up her pale red hair to auburn, as she bent over the heavy household linen which she was mending for her aunt. No scene could have been more peaceful, if Mrs Poyser, who was ironing a few things that still remained from the Monday's wash, had not been making a frequent clinking with her iron, and moving to and fro whenever she wanted it to cool; carrying the keen glance of her blue-grey eye from the kitchen to the dairy, where Hetty was making up the butter, and from the dairy to the back-kitchen, where Nancy was taking the pies out of the oven. Do not suppose, however, that Mrs Poyser was elderly or shrewish in her appearance; she was a good-looking woman, not more than eight-and-thirty, of fair complexion and sandy hair, well-shapen, light-footed: the most conspicuous article in her attire was an ample checkered linen apron, which almost covered her skirt; and nothing could be plainer or less noticeable than her cap and gown, for there was no weakness of which she was less tolerant than feminine vanity, and the preference of ornament to utility. The family likeness between her and her niece Dinah Morris, with the contrast between her keenness and Dinah's seraphic gentleness of expression, might have served a painter as an excellent suggestion for a Martha and Mary.[9] Their eyes were just of the same colour, but a striking test of the difference in their operation was seen in the demeanour of Trip, the black-and-tan terrier, whenever that much-suspected dog unwarily exposed himself to the freezing arctic ray of Mrs Poyser's glance. Her tongue was not less keen than her eye, and, whenever a damsel came within earshot, seemed to take up an unfinished lecture, as a barrel-organ takes up a tune, precisely at the point where it had left off.

The fact that it was churning-day[10] was another reason why

it was inconvenient to have the 'whittaws', and why, con-
sequently, Mrs Poyser should scold Molly the housemaid
with unusual severity. To all appearance Molly had got through
her after-dinner work in an exemplary manner, had 'cleaned
herself' with great despatch, and now came to ask, sub-
missively, if she should sit down to her spinning till milking-
time. But this blameless conduct, according to Mrs Poyser,
shrouded a secret indulgence of unbecoming wishes, which she
now dragged forth and held up to Molly's view with cutting
eloquence.

'Spinning, indeed! It isn't spinning as you'd be at, I'll be
bound, and let you have your own way. I never knew your
equals for gallowsness.[11] To think of a gell o' your age wanting
to go and sit with half-a-dozen men! I'd ha' been ashamed to
let the words pass over my lips if I'd been you. And you, as
have been here ever since last Michaelmas, and I hired you at
Treddles'on stattits, without a bit o' character[12] – as I say, you
might be grateful to be hired in that way to a respectable place;
and you knew no more o' what belongs to work when you
come here than the mawkin[13] i' the field. As poor a two-fisted
thing as ever I saw, you know you was. Who taught you to
scrub a floor, I should like to know? Why, you'd leave the dirt
in heaps i' the corners – anybody 'ud think you'd never been
brought up among Christians. And as for spinning, why, you've
wasted as much as your wage i' the flax you've spoiled learning
to spin.[14] And you've a right to feel that, and not to go about
as gaping and as thoughtless as if you was beholding to nobody.
Comb the wool for the whittaws,[15] indeed! That's what you'd
like to be doing is it? That's the way with you – that's the road
you'd all like to go, headlongs to ruin. You're never easy till
you've got some sweetheart as is as big a fool as yourself: you
think you'll be finely off when you're married, I daresay, and
have got a three-legged stool to sit on, and never a blanket to
cover you, and a bit o' oat-cake for your dinner, as three
children are a-snatching at.'

'I'm sure I donna want t' go wi' the whittaws,' said Molly,
whimpering, and quite overcome by this Dantean picture[16] of
her future, 'on'y we allays used to comb the wool for'n at

Mester Ottley's; an' so I just axed ye. I donna want to set eyes
on the whittaws again; I wish I may never stir if I do.'

'Mr Ottley's, indeed! It's fine talking o' what you did at Mr
Ottley's. Your missis there might like her floors dirted wi'
whittaws for what I know. There's no knowing what people
wonna like – such ways as I've heard of! I never had a gell come
into my house as seemed to know what cleaning was; I think
people live like pigs, for my part. And as to that Betty as was
dairymaid at Trent's before she come to me, she'd ha' left the
cheeses without turning from week's end to week's end, and
the dairy thralls,[17] I might ha' wrote my name on 'em when I
come down-stairs after my illness, as the doctor said it was
inflammation – it was a mercy I got well of it. And to think o'
your knowing no better, Molly, and been here a-going i' nine
months, and not for want o' talking to, neither – and what are
you stanning there for, like a jack as is run down, istead o'
getting your wheel out?[18] You're a rare un for sitting down to
your work a little while after it's time to put by.'

'Munny, my iron's twite told; pease put it down to warm.'

The small chirruping voice that uttered this request came
from a little sunny-haired girl between three and four, who,
seated on a high chair at the end of the ironing-table, was
arduously clutching the handle of a miniature iron with her
tiny fat fist, and ironing rags with an assiduity that required
her to put her little red tongue out as far as anatomy would
allow.

'Cold, is it, my darling? Bless your sweet face!' said Mrs
Poyser, who was remarkable for the facility with which she
could relapse from her official objurgatory tone to one of
fondness or of friendly converse. 'Never mind! Mother's done
her ironing now. She's going to put the ironing things away.'

'Munny, I tould 'ike to do into de barn to Tommy, to see de
whittawd.'

'No, no, no; Totty 'ud get her feet wet,' said Mrs Poyser,
carrying away her iron. 'Run into the dairy, and see cousin
Hetty make the butter.'

'I tould 'ike a bit o' pum-take,' rejoined Totty, who seemed
to be provided with several relays of requests; at the same time,

taking the opportunity of her momentary leisure, to put her fingers into a bowl of starch, and drag it down, so as to empty the contents with tolerable completeness on to the ironing-sheet.

'Did ever anybody see the like?' screamed Mrs Poyser, running towards the table when her eye had fallen on the blue stream. 'The child's allays i' mischief if your back's turned a minute. What shall I do to you, you naughty, naughty gell?'

Totty, however, had descended from her chair with great swiftness, and was already in retreat towards the dairy with a sort of waddling run, and an amount of fat on the nape of her neck, which made her look like the metamorphosis of a white sucking-pig.

The starch having been wiped up by Molly's help, and the ironing apparatus put by, Mrs Poyser took up her knitting, which always lay ready at hand, and was the work she liked best, because she could carry it on automatically as she walked to and fro. But now she came and sat down opposite Dinah, whom she looked at in a meditative way, as she knitted her grey worsted stocking.

'You look th' image o' your aunt Judith, Dinah, when you sit a-sewing. I could almost fancy it was thirty years back, and I was a little gell at home, looking at Judith as she sat at her work, after she'd done th' house up; only it was a little cottage, father's was, and not a big rambling house as gets dirty i' one corner as fast as you clean it in another; but for all that, I could fancy you was your aunt Judith, only her hair was a deal darker than yours, and she was stouter and broader i' the shoulders. Judith and me allays hung together, though she had such queer ways, but your mother and her never could agree. Ah! your mother little thought as she'd have a daughter just cut out after the very pattern o' Judith, and leave her an orphan, too, for Judith to take care on, and bring up with a spoon[19] when *she* was in the graveyard at Stoniton. I allays said that o' Judith, as she'd bear a pound weight any day, to save anybody else carrying a ounce. And she was just the same from the first o' my remembering her; it made no difference in her, as I could see, when she took to the Methodists, only she talked a bit different,

VI THE HALL FARM 85

and wore a different sort o'cap; but she'd never in her life spent
a penny on herself more than keeping herself decent.'

'She was a blessed woman,' said Dinah; 'God had given her
a loving, self-forgetting nature, and He perfected it by grace.
And she was very fond of you too, aunt Rachel. I've often heard
her talk of you in the same sort of way. When she had that bad
illness, and I was only eleven years old, she used to say, "You'll
have a friend on earth in your aunt Rachel, if I'm taken from
you; for she has a kind heart"; and I'm sure I've found it so.'

'I don't know how, child; anybody 'ud be cunning[20] to do
anything for you, I think; you're like the birds o' th' air, and
live nobody knows how. I'd ha' been glad to behave to you like
a mother's sister, if you'd come and live i' this country, where
there's some shelter and victual for man and beast, and folks
don't live on the naked hills, like poultry a-scratching on a
gravel bank. And then you might get married to some decent
man, and there'd be plenty ready to have you, if you'd only
leave off that preaching as is ten times worse than anything
your aunt Judith ever did. And even if you'd marry Seth Bede,
as is a poor wool-gathering Methodist, and's never like to have
a penny beforehand, I know your uncle 'ud help you with a
pig, and very like a cow, for he's allays been good-natur'd to
my kin, for all they're poor, and made 'em welcome to the
house; and 'ud do for you, I'll be bound, as much as ever he'd
do for Hetty, though she's his own niece. And there's linen in
the house as I could well spare you, for I've got lots o' sheeting
and table-clothing, and towelling, as isn't made up. There's a
piece o' sheeting I could give you as that squinting Kitty spun
– she was a rare girl to spin, for all she squinted, and the
children couldn't abide her; and, you know, the spinning's
going on constant, and there's new linen wove twice as fast as
the old wears out. But where's the use o' talking, if ye wonna
be persuaded, and settle down like any other woman in her
senses, istead o' wearing yourself out with walking and preaching, and giving away every penny you get, so as you've nothing
saved against sickness; and all the things you've got i' the world,
I verily believe, 'ud go into a bundle no bigger nor a double
cheese. And all because you've got notions i' your head about

religion more nor what's i' the Catechism and the Prayer-book.'

'But not more than what's in the Bible,[21] aunt,' said Dinah.

'Yes, and the Bible too, for that matter,' Mrs Poyser rejoined, rather sharply; 'else why shouldn't them as know best what's in the Bible – the parsons and people as have got nothing to do but learn it – do the same as you do? But, for the matter o' that, if everybody was to do like you, the world must come to a standstill; for if everybody tried to do without house and home, and with poor eating and drinking, and was allays talking as we must despise the things o' the world, as you say, I should like to know where the pick o' the stock, and the corn, and the best new-milk cheeses 'ud have to go. Everybody 'ud be wanting bread made o' tail-ends, and everybody 'ud be running after everybody else to preach to 'em, istead o' bringing up their families, and laying by against a bad harvest. It stands to sense as that can't be the right religion.'

'Nay, dear aunt, you never heard me say that all people are called to forsake their work and their families. It's quite right the land should be ploughed and sowed, and the precious corn stored, and the things of this life cared for, and right that people should rejoice in their families, and provide for them, so that this is done in the fear of the Lord, and that they are not unmindful of the soul's wants while they are caring for the body. We can all be servants of God wherever our lot is cast, but He gives us different sorts of work, according as He fits us for it and calls us to it. I can no more help spending my life in trying to do what I can for the souls of others, than you could help running if you heard little Totty crying at the other end of the house; the voice would go to your heart, you would think the dear child was in trouble or in danger, and you couldn't rest without running to help her and comfort her.'

'Ah,' said Mrs Poyser, rising and walking towards the door, 'I know it 'ud be just the same if I was to talk to you for hours. You'd make me the same answer at th' end. I might as well talk to the running brook, and tell it to stan' still.'

The causeway outside the kitchen door was dry enough now for Mrs Poyser to stand there quite pleasantly and see what was going on in the yard, the grey worsted stocking making a steady progress in her hands all the while. But she had not been standing there more than five minutes before she came in again, and said to Dinah, in rather a flurried, awe-stricken tone –

'If there isn't Captain Donnithorne and Mr Irwine a-coming into the yard! I'll lay my life they're come to speak about your preaching on the Green, Dinah; it's you must answer 'em, for I'm dumb. I've said enough a'ready about your bringing such disgrace upo' your uncle's family. I wouldn't ha' minded if you'd been Mr Poyser's own niece – folks must put up wi' their own kin, as they put up wi' their own noses – it's their own flesh and blood. But to think of a niece o' mine being cause o' my husband's being turned out of his farm, and me brought him no fortin but my savins—'

'Nay, dear aunt Rachel,' said Dinah gently, 'you've no cause for such fears. I've strong assurance that no evil will happen to you and my uncle and the children from anything I've done. I didn't preach without direction.'[22]

'Direction! I know very well what you mean by direction,' said Mrs Poyser, knitting in a rapid and agitated manner. 'When there's a bigger maggot than usial in your head you call it "direction"; and then nothing can stir you – you look like the statty[23] o' the outside o' Treddles'on church, a-starin' and a-smilin' whether it's fair weather or foul. I hanna common patience with you.'

By this time the two gentlemen had reached the palings, and had got down from their horses; it was plain they meant to come in. Mrs Poyser advanced to the door to meet them, curtsying low, and trembling between anger with Dinah and anxiety to conduct herself with perfect propriety on the occasion. For in those days the keenest of bucolic minds felt a whispering awe at the sight of the gentry, such as of old men felt when they stood on tip-toe to watch the gods passing by in tall human shape.

'Well, Mrs Poyser, how are you after this stormy morning?' said Mr Irwine, with his stately cordiality. 'Our feet are quite dry; we shall not soil your beautiful floor.'

'Oh, sir, don't mention it,' said Mrs Poyser. 'Will you and the Captain please to walk into the parlour?'

'No, indeed, thank you, Mrs Poyser,' said the Captain, looking eagerly round the kitchen, as if his eye were seeking something it could not find. 'I delight in your kitchen. I think it is
the most charming room I know. I should like every farmer's
wife to come and look at it for a pattern.'

'Oh, you're pleased to say so, sir. Pray take a seat,' said Mrs
Poyser, relieved a little by this compliment and the Captain's
evident good-humour, but still glancing anxiously at Mr Irwine,
who, she saw, was looking at Dinah and advancing towards her.

'Poyser is not at home, is he?' said Captain Donnithorne,
seating himself where he could see along the short passage to
the open dairy-door.

'No, sir, he isn't; he's gone to Rosseter to see Mr West, the
factor,[24] about the wool. But there's father i' the barn, sir, if
he'd be of any use.'

'No, thank you; I'll just look at the whelps and leave a
message about them with your shepherd. I must come another
day and see your husband; I want to have a consultation with
him about horses. Do you know when he's likely to be at
liberty?'

'Why, sir, you can hardly miss him, except it's o' Treddles'on
market-day – that's of a Friday, you know. For if he's anywhere
on the farm we can send for him in a minute. If we'd got rid o'
the Scantlands we should have no outlying fields; and I should
be glad of it, for if ever anything happens he's sure to be gone
to the Scantlands. Things allays happen so contrairy, if they've
a chance; and it's an unnat'ral thing to have one bit o' your
farm in one county and all the rest in another.'

'Ah, the Scantlands would go much better with Choyce's
farm, especially as he wants dairy-land and you've got plenty.
I think yours is the prettiest farm on the estate, though; and do
you know, Mrs Poyser, if I were going to marry and settle, I
should be tempted to turn you out, and do up this fine old
house, and turn farmer myself.'

'Oh, sir,' said Mrs Poyser, rather alarmed, 'you wouldn't like
it at all. As for farming, it's putting money into your pocket wi'
your right hand and fetching it out wi' your left. As fur as I can
see, it's raising victual for other folks, and just getting a mouth-

ful for yourself and your children as you go along. Not as you'd
be like a poor man as wants to get his bread: you could afford
to lose as much money as you liked i' farming; but it's poor fun
losing money, I should think, though I understan' it's what the
great folks i' London play at more than anything. For my
husband heard at market as Lord Dacey's eldest son had lost
thousands upo' thousands to the Prince o' Wales, and they said
my lady was going to pawn her jewels to pay for him. But you
know more about that than I do, sir. But, as for farming, sir, I
canna think as you'd like it; and this house – the draughts in it
are enough to cut you through, and it's my opinion the floors
up-stairs are very rotten, and the rats i' the cellar are beyond
anything.'

'Why, that's a terrible picture, Mrs Poyser. I think I should
be doing you a service to turn you out of such a place. But
there's no chance of that. I'm not likely to settle for the next
twenty years, till I'm a stout gentleman of forty; and my grandfather would never consent to part with such good tenants
as you.'

'Well, sir, if he thinks so well o' Mr Poyser for a tenant, I
wish you could put in a word for him to allow us some new
gates for the Five closes, for my husband's been asking and
asking till he's tired, and to think o' what he's done for the
farm, and's never had a penny allowed him, be the times bad
or good. And as I've said to my husband often and often, I'm
sure if the Captain had anything to do with it, it wouldn't be
so. Not as I wish to speak disrespectful o' them as have got the
power i' their hands, but it's more than flesh and blood 'ull
bear sometimes, to be toiling and striving, and up early and
down late, and hardly sleeping a wink when you lie down for
thinking as the cheese may swell, or the cows may slip their
calf, or the wheat may grow green again i' the sheaf – and after
all, at th' end o' the year, it's like as if you'd been cooking a
feast and had got the smell of it for your pains.'

Mrs Poyser, once launched into conversation, always sailed
along without any check from her preliminary awe of the
gentry. The confidence she felt in her own powers of exposition
was a motive force that overcame all resistance.

ADAM BEDE

'I'm afraid I should only do harm instead of good, if I were to speak about the gates, Mrs Poyser,' said the Captain, 'though I assure you there's no man on the estate I would sooner say a word for than your husband. I know his farm is in better order than any other within ten miles of us; and as for the kitchen,' he added, smiling, 'I don't believe there's one in the kingdom to beat it. By the by, I've never seen your dairy: I must see your dairy, Mrs Poyser.'

'Indeed, sir, it's not fit for you to go in, for Hetty's in the middle o' making the butter, for the churning was thrown late, and I'm quite ashamed.' This Mrs Poyser said blushing, and believing that the Captain was really interested in her milk-pans, and would adjust his opinion of her to the appearance of her dairy.

'Oh, I've no doubt it's in capital order. Take me in,' said the Captain, himself leading the way, while Mrs Poyser followed.

CHAPTER VII

The Dairy

The dairy was certainly worth looking at; it was a scene to sicken for with a sort of calenture[1] in hot and dusty streets – such coolness, such purity, such fresh fragrance of new-pressed cheese, of firm butter, of wooden vessels perpetually bathed in pure water; such soft colouring of red earthenware and creamy surfaces, brown wood and polished tin, grey limestone and rich orange-red rust on the iron weights and hooks and hinges. But one gets only a confused notion of these details when they surround a distractingly pretty girl of seventeen, standing on little pattens[2] and rounding her dimpled arm to lift a pound of butter out of the scale.

Hetty blushed a deep rose-colour when Captain Donnithorne entered the dairy and spoke to her; but it was not at all a distressed blush, for it was inwreathed with smiles and dimples, and with sparkles from under long curled dark eyelashes; and while her aunt was discoursing to him about the limited amount of milk that was to be spared for butter and cheese so long as the calves were not all weaned, and a large quantity but inferior quality of milk yielded by the short-horn, which had been bought on experiment, together with other matters which must be interesting to a young gentleman who would one day be a landlord, Hetty tossed and patted her pound of butter with quite a self-possessed, coquettish air, slily conscious that no turn of her head was lost.

There are various orders of beauty, causing men to make fools of themselves in various styles, from the desperate to the sheepish; but there is one order of beauty which seems made to turn the heads not only of men, but of all intelligent mammals,

even of women. It is a beauty like that of kittens, or very small
downy ducks making gentle rippling noises with their soft bills,
or babies just beginning to toddle and to engage in conscious
mischief – a beauty with which you can never be angry, but
that you feel ready to crush for inability to comprehend the
state of mind into which it throws you. Hetty Sorrel's was that
sort of beauty. Her aunt, Mrs Poyser, who professed to despise
all personal attractions, and intended to be the severest of
mentors, continually gazed at Hetty's charms by the sly, fascinated in spite of herself; and after administering such a scolding
as naturally flowed from her anxiety to do well by her husband's
niece – who had no mother of her own to scold her, poor thing!
– she would often confess to her husband, when they were safe
out of hearing, that she firmly believed 'the naughtier the little
huzzy behaved, the prettier she looked'.

It is of little use for me to tell you that Hetty's cheek was like
a rose-petal, that dimples played about her pouting lips, that
her large dark eyes hid a soft roguishness under their long
lashes, and that her curly hair, though all pushed back under
her round cap while she was at work, stole back in dark delicate
rings on her forehead, and about her white shell-like ears; it is
of little use for me to say how lovely was the contour of her
pink-and-white neckerchief, tucked into her low plum-coloured
stuff boddice, or how the linen butter-making apron, with its
bib, seemed a thing to be imitated in silk by duchesses, since it
fell in such charming lines, or how her brown stockings and
thick-soled buckled shoes lost all that clumsiness which they
must certainly have had when empty of her foot and ankle; –
of little use, unless you have seen a woman who affected you
as Hetty affected her beholders, for otherwise, though you
might conjure up the image of a lovely woman, she would not
in the least resemble that distracting kitten-like maiden. I might
mention all the divine charms of a bright spring day, but if you
had never in your life utterly forgotten yourself in straining
your eyes after the mounting lark, or in wandering through the
still lanes when the fresh-opened blossoms fill them with a
sacred silent beauty like that of fretted aisles, where would be
the use of my descriptive catalogue? I could never make you

know what I meant by a bright spring day. Hetty's was a
spring-tide beauty; it was the beauty of young frisking things,
round-limbed, gambolling, circumventing you by a false air of
innocence – the innocence of a young star-browed calf, for
example, that, being inclined for a promenade out of bounds,
leads you a severe steeple-chase over hedge and ditch, and only
comes to a stand in the middle of a bog.

And they are the prettiest attitudes and movements into
which a pretty girl is thrown in making up butter – tossing
movements that give a charming curve to the arm, and a side-
ward inclination of the round white neck; little patting and
rolling movements with the palm of the hand, and nice adaptations and finishings which cannot at all be effected without a
great play of the pouting mouth and the dark eyes. And then
the butter itself seems to communicate a fresh charm – it is so
pure, so sweet-scented; it is turned off the mould with such a
beautiful firm surface, like marble in a pale yellow light! Moreover, Hetty was particularly clever at making up the butter; it
was the one performance of hers that her aunt allowed to pass
without severe criticism; so she handled it with all the grace
that belongs to mastery.

'I hope you will be ready for a great holiday on the thirtieth
of July, Mrs Poyser,' said Captain Donnithorne, when he had
sufficiently admired the dairy, and given several improvised
opinions on Swede turnips and short-horns. 'You know what
is to happen then, and I shall expect you to be one of the guests
who come earliest and leave latest. Will you promise me your
hand for two dances, Miss Hetty? If I don't get your promise
now, I know I shall hardly have a chance, for all the smart
young farmers will take care to secure you.'

Hetty smiled and blushed, but before she could answer, Mrs
Poyser interposed, scandalized at the mere suggestion that the
young squire could be excluded by any meaner partners.

'Indeed, sir, you are very kind to take that notice of her. And
I'm sure, whenever you're pleased to dance with her, she'll be
proud and thankful, if she stood still all the rest o' th' evening.'

'Oh no, no, that would be too cruel to all the other young
fellows who can dance. But you will promise me two dances,

won't you?' the Captain continued, determined to make Hetty
look at him and speak to him.

Hetty dropped the prettiest little curtsy, and stole a half-shy,
half-coquettish glance at him as she said –

'Yes, thank you, sir.'

'And you must bring all your children, you know, Mrs
Poyser; your little Totty, as well as the boys. I want all the
youngest children on the estate to be there – all those who will
be fine young men and women when I'm a bald old fellow.'

'Oh dear, sir, that 'ull be a long time first,' said Mrs Poyser,
quite overcome at the young squire's speaking so lightly of
himself, and thinking how her husband would be interested in
hearing her recount this remarkable specimen of high-born
humour. The Captain was thought to be 'very full of his jokes',
and was a great favourite throughout the estate on account of
his free manners. Every tenant was quite sure things would be
different when the reins got into his hands – there was to be a
millennial abundance[3] of new gates, allowances of lime, and
returns of ten per cent.

'But where is Totty to-day?' he said. 'I want to see her.'

'Where *is* the little un, Hetty?' said Mrs Poyser. 'She came in
here not long ago.'

'I don't know. She went into the brewhouse to Nancy,
I think.'

The proud mother, unable to resist the temptation to show
her Totty, passed at once into the back-kitchen, in search of
her, not, however, without misgivings lest something should
have happened to render her person and attire unfit for presentation.

'And do you carry the butter to market when you've made
it?' said the Captain to Hetty, meanwhile.

'Oh no, sir; not when it's so heavy: I'm not strong enough to
carry it. Alick takes it on horseback.'

'No, I'm sure your pretty arms were never meant for such
heavy weights. But you go out a walk sometimes these pleasant
evenings, don't you? Why don't you have a walk in the Chase
sometimes, now it's so green and pleasant? I hardly ever see
you anywhere except at home and at church.'

'Aunt doesn't like me to go a-walking only when I'm going somewhere,' said Hetty. 'But I go through the Chase sometimes.'

'And don't you ever go to see Mrs Best, the housekeeper? I think I saw you once in the housekeeper's room.'

'It isn't Mrs Best, it's Mrs Pomfret, the lady's maid, as I go to see. She's teaching me tent-stitch and the lace-mending. I'm going to tea with her to-morrow afternoon.'

The reason why there had been space for this *tête-à-tête* can only be known by looking into the back-kitchen, where Totty had been discovered rubbing a stray blue-bag[4] against her nose, and in the same moment allowing some liberal indigo drops to fall on her afternoon pinafore. But now she appeared holding her mother's hand – the end of her round nose rather shiny from a recent and hurried application of soap and water.

'Here she is!' said the Captain, lifting her up and setting her on the low stone shelf. 'Here's Totty! By the by, what's her other name? She wasn't christened Totty.'

'Oh, sir, we call her sadly out of her name. Charlotte's her christened name. It's a name i' Mr Poyser's family: his grandmother was named Charlotte. But we began with calling her Lotty, and now it's got to Totty. To be sure it's more like a name for a dog than a Christian child.'

'Totty's a capital name. Why, she looks like a Totty. Has she got a pocket on?' said the Captain, feeling in his own waistcoat pockets.

Totty immediately with great gravity lifted up her frock, and showed a tiny pink pocket at present in a state of collapse.

'It dot notin in it,' she said, as she looked down at it very earnestly.

'No! what a pity! such a pretty pocket. Well, I think I've got some things in mine that will make a pretty jingle in it. Yes! I declare I've got five little round silver things, and hear what a pretty noise they make in Totty's pink pocket.' Here he shook the pocket with the five sixpences in it, and Totty showed her teeth and wrinkled her nose in great glee; but, divining that there was nothing more to be got by staying, she jumped off the shelf and ran away to jingle her pocket in the hearing of

Nancy, while her mother called after her, 'Oh for shame, you naughty gell! not to thank the Captain for what he's given you. I'm sure, sir, it's very kind of you; but she's spoiled shameful; her father won't have her said nay in anything, and there's no managing her. It's being the youngest, and th' only gell.'

'Oh, she's a funny little fatty; I wouldn't have her different. But I must be going now, for I suppose the Rector is waiting for me.'

With a 'good-bye', a bright glance, and a bow to Hetty, Arthur left the dairy. But he was mistaken in imagining himself waited for. The Rector had been so much interested in his conversation with Dinah, that he would not have chosen to close it earlier; and you shall hear now what they had been saying to each other.

CHAPTER VIII

A Vocation

Dinah, who had risen when the gentlemen came in, but still kept hold of the sheet she was mending, curtsied respectfully when she saw Mr Irwine looking at her and advancing towards her. He had never yet spoken to her, or stood face to face with her, and her first thought, as her eyes met his, was, 'What a well-favoured countenance! Oh that the good seed might fall on that soil,[1] for it would surely flourish.' The agreeable impression must have been mutual, for Mr Irwine bowed to her with a benignant deference, which would have been equally in place if she had been the most dignified lady of his acquaintance.

'You are only a visitor in this neighbourhood, I think?' were his first words, as he seated himself opposite to her.

'No, sir, I come from Snowfield, in Stonyshire. But my aunt was very kind, wanting me to have rest from my work there, because I'd been ill, and she invited me to come and stay with her for a while.'

'Ah, I remember Snowfield very well; I once had occasion to go there. It's a dreary bleak place. They were building a cotton-mill there; but that's many years ago now: I suppose the place is a good deal changed by the employment that mill must have brought.'

'It *is* changed so far as the mill has brought people there, who get a livelihood for themselves by working in it, and make it better for the tradesfolks. I work in it myself, and have reason to be grateful, for thereby I have enough and to spare. But it's still a bleak place, as you say, sir – very different from this country.'

'You have relations living there probably, so that you are attached to the place as your home?'

'I had an aunt there once; she brought me up, for I was an orphan. But she was taken away seven years ago, and I have no other kindred that I know of, besides my aunt Poyser, who is very good to me, and would have me come and live in this country, which to be sure is a good land, wherein they eat bread without scarceness.[2] But I'm not free to leave Snowfield, where I was first planted, and have grown deep into it, like the small grass on the hill-top.'

'Ah, I daresay you have many religious friends and companions there; you are a Methodist – a Wesleyan,[3] I think?'

'Yes, my aunt at Snowfield belonged to the Society, and I have cause to be thankful for the privileges I have had thereby from my earliest childhood.'

'And have you been long in the habit of preaching? – for I understand you preached at Hayslope last night.'

'I first took to the work four years since, when I was twenty-one.'

'Your Society sanctions women's preaching, then?'

'It doesn't forbid them, sir, when they've a clear call to the work, and when their ministry is owned by the conversion of sinners, and the strengthening of God's people. Mrs Fletcher, as you may have heard about, was the first woman to preach in the Society, I believe, before she was married, when she was Miss Bosanquet;[4] and Mr Wesley approved of her undertaking the work. She had a great gift, and there are many others now living who are precious fellow-helpers in the work of the ministry. I understand there's been voices raised against it in the Society of late, but I cannot but think their counsel will come to nought. It isn't for men to make channels for God's Spirit, as they make channels for the water-courses, and say, "Flow here, but flow not there."'

'But don't you find some danger among your people – I don't mean to say that it is so with you, far from it – but don't you find sometimes that both men and women fancy themselves channels for God's Spirit, and are quite mistaken, so that they set about a work for which they are unfit, and bring holy things into contempt?'

'Doubtless it is so sometimes; for there have been evil-doers among us who have sought to deceive the brethren, and some there are who deceive their own selves. But we are not without discipline and correction to put a check upon these things. There's a very strict order kept among us, and the brethren and sisters watch for each other's souls as they that must give account. They don't go every one his own way⁵ and say, "Am I my brother's keeper?"'⁶

'But tell me – if I may ask, and I am really interested in knowing it – how you first came to think of preaching?'

'Indeed, sir, I didn't think of it at all – I'd been used from the time I was sixteen to talk to the little children and teach them, and sometimes I had had my heart enlarged to speak in class, and was much drawn out in prayer with the sick. But I had felt no call to preach; for when I'm not greatly wrought upon, I'm too much given to sit still and keep by myself; it seems as if I could sit silent all day long with the thought of God overflowing my soul – as the pebbles lie bathed in the Willow Brook. For thoughts are so great – aren't they, sir? They seem to lie upon us like a deep flood; and it's my besetment⁷ to forget where I am and everything about me, and lose myself in thoughts that I could give no account of, for I could neither make a beginning nor ending of them in words. That was my way as long as I can remember; but sometimes it seemed as if speech came to me without any will of my own, and words were given to me that came out as the tears come, because our hearts are full and we can't help it. And those were always times of great blessing, though I had never thought it could be so with me before a congregation of people. But, sir, we are led on, like the little children, by a way that we know not. I was called to preach quite suddenly, and since then I have never been left in doubt about the work that was laid upon me.'

'But tell me the circumstances – just how it was, the very day you began to preach.'

'It was one Sunday I walked with brother Marlowe, who

was an aged man, one of the local preachers, all the way to
Hetton-Deeps – that's a village where the people get their living
by working in the lead-mines, and where there's no church nor
preacher, but they live like sheep without a shepherd. It's better
than twelve miles from Snowfield, so we set out early in the
morning, for it was summer-time; and I had a wonderful sense
of the Divine love as we walked over the hills, where there's no
trees, you know, sir, as there is here, to make the sky look
smaller, but you see the heavens stretched out like a tent, and
you feel the everlasting arms around you. But before we got to
Hetton, brother Marlowe was seized with a dizziness that made
him afraid of falling, for he overworked himself sadly, at his
years, in watching and praying, and walking so many miles to
speak the Word, as well as carrying on his trade of linen-
weaving. And when we got to the village, the people were
expecting him, for he'd appointed the time and the place when
he was there before, and such of them as cared to hear the
Word of Life were assembled on a spot where the cottages was
thickest, so as others might be drawn to come. But he felt as he
couldn't stand up to preach, and he was forced to lie down in
the first of the cottages we came to. So I went to tell the people,
thinking we'd go into one of the houses, and I would read and
pray with them. But as I passed along by the cottages and saw
the aged and trembling women at the doors, and the hard looks
of the men, who seemed to have their eyes no more filled with
the sight of the Sabbath morning than if they had been dumb
oxen that never looked up to the sky, I felt a great movement
in my soul, and I trembled as if I was shaken by a strong spirit
entering into my weak body. And I went to where the little
flock of people was gathered together, and stepped on the low
wall that was built against the green hillside, and I spoke the
words that were given to me abundantly.[8] And they all came
round me out of all the cottages, and many wept over their
sins, and have since been joined to the Lord. That was the
beginning of my preaching, sir, and I've preached ever since.'

Dinah had let her work fall during this narrative, which she
uttered in her usual simple way, but with that sincere, articulate,
thrilling treble, by which she always mastered her audience. She

stooped now to gather up her sewing, and then went on with it as before. Mr Irwine was deeply interested. He said to himself, 'He must be a miserable prig who would act the pedagogue here: one might as well go and lecture the trees for growing in their own shape.'

'And you never feel any embarrassment from the sense of your youth – that you are a lovely young woman on whom men's eyes are fixed?'[9] he said aloud.

'No, I've no room for such feelings, and I don't believe the people ever take notice about that. I think, sir, when God makes His presence felt through us, we are like the burning bush: Moses never took any heed what sort of bush it was – he only saw the brightness of the Lord.[10] I've preached to as rough ignorant people as can be in the villages about Snowfield – men that looked very hard and wild; but they never said an uncivil word to me, and often thanked me kindly as they made way for me to pass through the midst of them.'

'*That* I can believe – that I can well believe,' said Mr Irwine, emphatically. 'And what did you think of your hearers last night, now? Did you find them quiet and attentive?'

'Very quiet, sir; but I saw no signs of any great work upon them, except in a young girl named Bessy Cranage, towards whom my heart yearned greatly, when my eyes first fell on her blooming youth, given up to folly and vanity. I had some private talk and prayer with her afterwards, and I trust her heart is touched. But I've noticed, that in these villages where the people lead a quiet life among the green pastures and the still waters,[11] tilling the ground and tending the cattle, there's a strange deadness to the Word, as different as can be from the great towns, like Leeds, where I once went to visit a holy woman who preaches there. It's wonderful how rich is the harvest of souls up those high-walled streets, where you seemed to walk as in a prison-yard, and the ear is deafened with the sounds of worldly toil. I think maybe it is because the promise is sweeter when this life is so dark and weary, and the soul gets more hungry when the body is ill at ease.'

'Why, yes, our farm-labourers are not easily roused. They take life almost as slowly as the sheep and cows. But we have some intelligent workmen about here. I daresay you know the Bedes; Seth Bede, by the by, is a Methodist.'

'Yes, I know Seth well, and his brother Adam a little. Seth is a gracious young man – sincere and without offence; and Adam is like the patriarch Joseph,[12] for his great skill and knowledge, and the kindness he shows to his brother and his parents.'

'Perhaps you don't know the trouble that has just happened to them? Their father, Matthias Bede, was drowned in the Willow Brook last night, not far from his own door. I'm going now to see Adam.'

'Ah, their poor aged mother!' said Dinah, dropping her hands, and looking before her with pitying eyes, as if she saw the object of her sympathy. 'She will mourn heavily; for Seth has told me she's of an anxious troubled heart. I must go and see if I can give her any help.'

As she rose and was beginning to fold up her work, Captain Donnithorne, having exhausted all plausible pretexts for remaining among the milk-pans, came out of the dairy, followed by Mrs Poyser. Mr Irwine now rose also, and, advancing towards Dinah, held out his hand, and said –

'Good-by. I hear you are going away soon; but this will not be the last visit you will pay your aunt – so we shall meet again, I hope.'

His cordiality towards Dinah set all Mrs Poyser's anxieties at rest, and her face was brighter than usual, as she said –

'I've never asked after Mrs Irwine and the Miss Irwines, sir; I hope they're as well as usual.'

'Yes, thank you, Mrs Poyser, except that Miss Anne has one of her bad headaches to-day. By the by, we all liked that nice cream-cheese you sent us – my mother especially.'

'I'm very glad, indeed, sir. It is but seldom I make one, but I remembered Mrs Irwine was fond of 'em. Please to give my duty to her, and to Miss Kate and Miss Anne. They've never been to look at my poultry this long while, and I've got some beautiful speckled chickens, black and white, as Miss Kate might like to have some of amongst hers.'

'Well, I'll tell her; she must come and see them. Good-by,' said the Rector, mounting his horse.

'Just ride slowly on, Irwine,' said Captain Donnithorne, mounting also. 'I'll overtake you in three minutes. I'm only going to speak to the shepherd about the whelps. Good-by, Mrs Poyser; tell your husband I shall come and have a long talk with him soon.'

Mrs Poyser curtsied duly, and watched the two horses until they had disappeared from the yard, amidst great excitement on the part of the pigs and the poultry, and under the furious indignation of the bull-dog, who performed a Pyrrhic dance,[13] that every moment seemed to threaten the breaking of his chain. Mrs Poyser delighted in this noisy exit; it was a fresh assurance to her that the farmyard was well guarded, and that no loiterers could enter unobserved; and it was not until the gate had closed behind the Captain that she turned into the kitchen again, where Dinah stood with her bonnet in her hand, waiting to speak to her aunt, before she set out for Lisbeth Bede's cottage.

Mrs Poyser, however, though she noticed the bonnet, deferred remarking on it until she had disburdened herself of her surprise at Mr Irwine's behaviour.

'Why, Mr Irwine wasn't angry, then? What did he say to you, Dinah? Didn't he scold you for preaching?'

'No, he was not at all angry; he was very friendly to me. I was quite drawn out to speak to him; I hardly know how, for I had always thought of him as a worldly Sadducee.[14] But his countenance is as pleasant as the morning sunshine.'

'Pleasant! and what else did y' expect to find him but pleasant?' said Mrs Poyser, impatiently, resuming her knitting. 'I should think his countenance is pleasant indeed! and him a gentleman born, and's got a mother like a picter. You may go the country round, and not find such another woman turned sixty-six. It's summat-like to see such a man as that i' the desk of a Sunday! As I say to Poyser, it's like looking at a full crop o' wheat, or a pasture with a fine dairy o' cows in it; it makes you think the world's comfortable-like. But as for such creaturs as you Methodisses run after, I'd as soon go to look at a lot o' bare-ribbed runts on a common.[15] Fine folks they are to tell you what's right, as look as if they'd never tasted nothing better than bacon-sword and sour-cake[16] i' their lives. But what did

Mr Irwine say to you about that fool's trick o' preaching on
the Green?'

'He only said he'd heard of it; he didn't seem to feel any
displeasure about it. But, dear aunt, don't think any more about
that. He told me something that I'm sure will cause you sorrow,
as it does me. Thias Bede was drowned last night in the Willow
Brook, and I'm thinking that the aged mother will be greatly in
need of comfort. Perhaps I can be of use to her, so I have fetched
my bonnet and am going to set out.'

'Dear heart, dear heart! But you must have a cup o' tea first,
child,' said Mrs Poyser, falling at once from the key of B with
five sharps to the frank and genial C.[17] 'The kettle's boiling –
we'll have it ready in a minute; and the young uns 'ull be in and
wanting theirs directly. I'm quite willing you should go and see
th' old woman, for you're one as is allays welcome in trouble,
Methodist or no Methodist; but, for the matter o' that, it's the
flesh and blood folks are made on as makes the difference.
Some cheeses are made o' skimmed milk and some o' new milk,
and it's no matter what you call 'em, you may tell which is
which by the look and the smell. But as to Thias Bede, he's
better out o' the way nor in – God forgi' me for saying so – for
he's done little this ten year but make trouble for them as
belonged to him; and I think it 'ud be well for you to take a
little bottle o' rum for th' old woman, for I daresay she's got
never a drop o' nothing to comfort her inside. Sit down, child,
and be easy, for you shan't stir out till you've had a cup o' tea,
and so I tell you.'

During the latter part of this speech, Mrs Poyser had been
reaching down the tea-things from the shelves, and was on her
way towards the pantry for the loaf (followed close by Totty,
who had made her appearance on the rattling of the tea-cups),
when Hetty came out of the dairy relieving her tired arms by
lifting them up, and clasping her hands at the back of her head.

'Molly,' she said, rather languidly, 'just run out and get me
a bunch of dock-leaves:[18] the butter's ready to pack up now.'

'D' you hear what's happened, Hetty?' said her aunt.

'No; how should I hear anything?' was the answer, in a
pettish tone.

'Not as you'd care much, I daresay, if you did hear; for you're too feather-headed to mind if everybody was dead, so as you could stay up-stairs a-dressing yourself for two hours by the clock. But anybody besides yourself 'ud mind about such things happening to them as think a deal more of you than you deserve. But Adam Bede and all his kin might be drownded for what you'd care – you'd be perking at the glass the next minute.'

'Adam Bede – drowned?' said Hetty, letting her arms fall, and looking rather bewildered, but suspecting that her aunt was as usual exaggerating with a didactic purpose.

'No, my dear, no,' said Dinah, kindly, for Mrs Poyser had passed on to the pantry without deigning more precise information. 'Not Adam. Adam's father, the old man, is drowned. He was drowned last night in the Willow Brook. Mr Irwine has just told me about it.'

'Oh, how dreadful!' said Hetty, looking serious, but not deeply affected; and as Molly now entered with the dock-leaves, she took them silently and returned to the dairy without asking further questions.

CHAPTER IX

Hetty's World

While she adjusted the broad leaves that set off the pale fragrant butter as the primrose is set off by its nest of green, I am afraid Hetty was thinking a great deal more of the looks Captain Donnithorne had cast at her than of Adam and his troubles. Bright, admiring glances from a handsome young gentleman, with white hands, a gold chain, occasional regimentals,[1] and wealth and grandeur immeasurable – those were the warm rays that set poor Hetty's heart vibrating, and playing its little foolish tunes over and over again. We do not hear that Memnon's statue[2] gave forth its melody at all under the rushing of the mightiest wind, or in response to any other influence divine or human than certain shortlived sunbeams of morning; and we must learn to accommodate ourselves to the discovery that some of those cunningly-fashioned instruments called human souls have only a very limited range of music, and will not vibrate in the least under a touch that fills others with tremulous rapture or quivering agony.

Hetty was quite used to the thought that people liked to look at her. She was not blind to the fact that young Luke Britton of Broxton came to Hayslope Church on a Sunday afternoon on purpose that he might see her; and that he would have made much more decided advances if her uncle Poyser, thinking but lightly of a young man whose father's land was so foul as old Luke Britton's, had not forbidden her aunt to encourage him by any civilities. She was aware, too, that Mr Craig, the gardener at the Chase, was over head and ears in love with her, and had lately made unmistakable avowals in luscious strawberries and hyperbolical peas. She knew still better, that Adam Bede – tall,

upright, clever, brave Adam Bede – who carried such authority
with all the people round about, and whom her uncle was
always delighted to see of an evening, saying that 'Adam knew
a fine sight more o' the natur o' things than those as thought
themselves his betters' – she knew that this Adam, who was
often rather stern to other people, and not much given to run
after the lasses, could be made to turn pale or red any day by a
word or a look from her. Hetty's sphere of comparison was
not large, but she couldn't help perceiving that Adam was
'something like' a man; always knew what to say about things,
could tell her uncle how to prop the hovel, and had mended
the churn in no time; knew, with only looking at it, the value
of the chestnut tree that was blown down, and why the damp
came in the walls, and what they must do to stop the rats; and
wrote a beautiful hand that you could read off, and could do
figures in his head – a degree of accomplishment totally
unknown among the richest farmers of that country-side. Not
at all like that slouching Luke Britton, who, when she once
walked with him all the way from Broxton to Hayslope, had
only broken silence to remark that the grey goose had begun to
lay. And as for Mr Craig, the gardener, he was a sensible man
enough, to be sure, but he was knock-kneed, and had a queer
sort of sing-song in his talk; moreover, on the most charitable
supposition, he must be far on the way to forty.

Hetty was quite certain her uncle wanted her to encourage
Adam, and would be pleased for her to marry him. For those
were times when there was no rigid demarcation of rank
between the farmer and the respectable artisan, and on the
home hearth, as well as in the public-house, they might be seen
taking their jug of ale together; the farmer having a latent sense
of capital, and of weight in parish affairs, which sustained
him under his conspicuous inferiority in conversation. Martin
Poyser was not a frequenter of public-houses, but he liked a
friendly chat over his own home-brewed; and though it was
pleasant to lay down the law to a stupid neighbour who had
no notion how to make the best of his farm, it was also an
agreeable variety to learn something from a clever fellow like
Adam Bede. Accordingly, for the last three years – ever since

he had superintended the building of the new barn – Adam had always been made welcome at the Hall Farm, especially of a winter evening, when the whole family, in patriarchal fashion, master and mistress, children and servants, were assembled in that glorious kitchen, at well-graduated distances from the blazing fire. And for the last two years, at least, Hetty had been in the habit of hearing her uncle say, 'Adam Bede may be working for wage now, but he'll be a master-man[3] some day, as sure as I sit in this chair. Mester Burge is in the right on't to want him to go partners and marry his daughter, if it's true what they say; the woman as marries him 'ull have a good take, be't Lady-day[4] or Michaelmas', – a remark which Mrs Poyser always followed up with her cordial assent. 'Ah!' she would say, 'it's all very fine having a ready-made rich man, but may-happen he'll be a ready-made fool; and it's no use filling your pocket full of money if you've got a hole in the corner. It'll do you no good to sit in a spring-cart o' your own, if you've got a soft to drive you: he'll soon turn you over into the ditch. I allays said I'd never marry a man as had got no brains; for where's the use of a woman having brains of her own if she's tackled to a geck[5] as everybody's a-laughing at? She might as well dress herself fine to sit back'ards on a donkey.'

These expressions, though figurative, sufficiently indicated the bent of Mrs Poyser's mind with regard to Adam; and though she and her husband might have viewed the subject differently if Hetty had been a daughter of their own, it was clear that they would have welcomed the match with Adam for a penniless niece. For what could Hetty have been but a servant elsewhere, if her uncle had not taken her in and brought her up as a domestic help to her aunt, whose health since the birth of Totty had not been equal to more positive labour than the superintendence of servants and children? But Hetty had never given Adam any steady encouragement. Even in the moments when she was most thoroughly conscious of his superiority to her other admirers, she had never brought herself to think of accepting him. She liked to feel that this strong, skilful, keen-eyed man was in her power, and would have been indignant if he had shown the least sign of slipping from under the yoke of

her coquettish tyranny, and attaching himself to the gentle
Mary Burge, who would have been grateful enough for the
most trifling notice from him. 'Mary Burge, indeed! such a
sallow-faced girl: if she put on a bit of pink ribbon, she looked
as yellow as a crow-flower, and her hair was as straight as a
hank of cotton.' And always when Adam stayed away for several weeks from the Hall Farm, and otherwise made some show
of resistance to his passion as a foolish one, Hetty took care to
entice him back into the net by little airs of meekness and
timidity, as if she were in trouble at his neglect. But as to
marrying Adam, that was a very different affair! There was
nothing in the world to tempt her to do that. Her cheeks never
grew a shade deeper when his name was mentioned; she felt no
thrill when she saw him passing along the causeway by the
window, or advancing towards her unexpectedly in the foot-
path across the meadow; she felt nothing when his eyes rested
on her, but the cold triumph of knowing that he loved her, and
would not care to look at Mary Burge: he could no more stir
in her the emotions that make the sweet intoxication of young
love, than the mere picture of a sun can stir the spring sap in
the subtle fibres of the plant. She saw him as he was – a poor
man, with old parents to keep, who would not be able, for a
long while to come, to give her even such luxuries as she shared
in her uncle's house. And Hetty's dreams were all of luxuries:
to sit in a carpeted parlour, and always wear white stockings;
to have some large beautiful earrings such as were all the
fashion; to have Nottingham lace[6] round the top of her gown,
and something to make her handkerchief smell nice, like Miss
Lydia Donnithorne's when she drew it out at church; and not
to be obliged to get up early or be scolded by anybody. She
thought, if Adam had been rich and could have given her these
things, she loved him well enough to marry him.

But for the last few weeks a new influence had come over
Hetty – vague, atmospheric, shaping itself into no self-confessed
hopes or prospects, but producing a pleasant narcotic effect,
making her tread the ground and go about her work in a sort
of dream, unconscious of weight or effort, and showing her all
things through a soft, liquid veil, as if she were living not in

this solid world of brick and stone, but in a beatified world, such as the sun lights up for us in the waters. Hetty had become aware that Mr Arthur Donnithorne would take a good deal of trouble for the chance of seeing her; that he always placed himself at church so as to have the fullest view of her both sitting and standing; that he was constantly finding reasons for calling at the Hall Farm, and always would contrive to say something for the sake of making her speak to him and look at him. The poor child no more conceived at present the idea that the young squire could ever be her lover, than a baker's pretty daughter in the crowd, whom a young emperor distinguishes by an imperial but admiring smile, conceives that she shall be made empress. But the baker's daughter goes home and dreams of the handsome young emperor, and perhaps weighs the flour amiss while she is thinking what a heavenly lot it must be to have him for a husband: and so poor Hetty had got a face and a presence haunting her waking and sleeping dreams; bright, soft glances had penetrated her, and suffused her life with a strange, happy languor. The eyes that shed those glances were really not half so fine as Adam's, which sometimes looked at her with a sad, beseeching tenderness; but they had found a ready medium in Hetty's little silly imagination, whereas Adam's could get no entrance through that atmosphere. For three weeks, at least, her inward life had consisted of little else than living through in memory the looks and words Arthur had directed towards her – of little else than recalling the sensations with which she heard his voice outside the house, and saw him enter, and became conscious that his eyes were fixed on her, and then became conscious that a tall figure, looking down on her with eyes that seemed to touch her, was coming nearer in clothes of beautiful texture, with an odour like that of a flower-garden borne on the evening breeze. Foolish thoughts! but all this happened, you must remember, nearly sixty years ago, and Hetty was quite uneducated – a simple farmer's girl, to whom a gentleman with a white hand was dazzling as an Olympian god. Until to-day, she had never looked farther into the future than to the next time Captain Donnithorne would come to the Farm, or the next Sunday when she should see him at church; but now she thought, perhaps he would try to meet her when she went to the Chase to-morrow – and if he should speak to her, and walk a little way, when nobody was by! That had never happened yet; and now her imagination, instead of retracing the past, was busy fashioning what would happen to-morrow – whereabout in the Chase she should see him coming towards her, how she should put her new rose-coloured ribbon on, which he had never seen, and what he would say to her to make her return his glance – a glance which she would be living through in her memory, over and over again, all the rest of the day.

In this state of mind, how could Hetty give any feeling to Adam's troubles, or think much about poor old Thias being drowned? Young souls, in such pleasant delirium as hers, are as unsympathetic as butterflies sipping nectar; they are isolated from all appeals by a barrier of dreams – by invisible looks and impalpable arms.

While Hetty's hands were busy packing up the butter, and her head filled with these pictures of the morrow, Arthur Donni-thorne, riding by Mr Irwine's side towards the valley of the Willow Brook, had also certain indistinct anticipations, running as an under-current in his mind while he was listening to Mr Irwine's account of Dinah; – indistinct, yet strong enough to make him feel rather conscious when Mr Irwine suddenly said –

'What fascinated you so in Mrs Poyser's dairy, Arthur? Have you become an amateur of damp quarries and skimming-dishes?'[7]

Arthur knew the Rector too well to suppose that a clever invention would be of any use, so he said, with his accustomed frankness –

'No, I went to look at the pretty butter-maker, Hetty Sorrel. She's a perfect Hebe;[8] and if I were an artist, I would paint her. It's amazing what pretty girls one sees among the farmers' daughters, when the men are such clowns. That common round red face one sees sometimes in the men – all cheek and no features, like Martin Poyser's – comes out in the women of the family as the most charming phiz[9] imaginable.'

'Well, I have no objection to your contemplating Hetty in an

artistic light, but I must not have you feeding her vanity, and
filling her little noddle with the notion that she's a great beauty,
attractive to fine gentlemen, or you will spoil her for a poor
man's wife – honest Craig's, for example, whom I have seen
bestowing soft glances on her. The little puss seems already to
have airs enough to make a husband as miserable as it's a law
of nature for a quiet man to be when he marries a beauty.
Apropos of marrying, I hope our friend Adam will get settled,
now the poor old man's gone. He will only have his mother to
keep in future, and I've a notion that there's a kindness between
him and that nice modest girl, Mary Burge, from something
that fell from old Jonathan one day when I was talking to him.
But when I mentioned the subject to Adam he looked uneasy,
and turned the conversation. I suppose the love-making doesn't
run smooth, or perhaps Adam hangs back till he's in a better
position. He has independence of spirit enough for two men –
rather an excess of pride if anything.'

'That would be a capital match for Adam. He would slip
into old Burge's shoes, and make a fine thing of that building
business, I'll answer for him. I should like to see him well settled
in this parish; he would be ready then to act as my grand-vizier
when I wanted one. We could plan no end of repairs and
improvements together. I've never seen the girl, though, I think
– at least I've never looked at her.'

'Look at her next Sunday at church – she sits with her father
on the left of the reading-desk. You needn't look quite so much
at Hetty Sorrel then. When I've made up my mind that I can't
afford to buy a tempting dog, I take no notice of him, because
if he took a strong fancy to me, and looked lovingly at me,
the struggle between arithmetic and inclination might become
unpleasantly severe. I pique myself on my wisdom there,
Arthur, and as an old fellow to whom wisdom has become
cheap, I bestow it upon you.'

'Thank you. It may stand me in good stead some day, though
I don't know that I have any present use for it. Bless me! how
the brook has overflowed. Suppose we have a canter, now we're
at the bottom of the hill.'

That is the great advantage of dialogue on horseback; it can be merged any minute into a trot or canter, and one might have escaped from Socrates himself[10] in the saddle. The two friends were free from the necessity of further conversation till they pulled up in the lane behind Adam's cottage.

CHAPTER X

Dinah Visits Lisbeth

At five o'clock Lisbeth came down-stairs with a large key in her hand: it was the key of the chamber where her husband lay dead. Throughout the day, except in her occasional outbursts of wailing grief, she had been in incessant movement, performing the initial duties to her dead with the awe and exactitude that belong to religious rites. She had brought out her little store of bleached linen, which she had for long years kept in reserve for this supreme use. It seemed but yesterday – that time so many midsummers ago, when she had told Thias where this linen lay, that he might be sure and reach it out for her when *she* died, for she was the elder of the two. Then there had been the work of cleansing to the strictest purity every object in the sacred chamber, and of removing from it every trace of common daily occupation. The small window which had hitherto freely let in the frosty moonlight or the warm summer sunrise on the working-man's slumber, must now be darkened with a fair white sheet, for this was the sleep which is as sacred under the bare rafters as in ceiled houses.[1] Lisbeth had even mended a long-neglected and unnoticeable rent in the checkered bit of bed-curtain; for the moments were few and precious now in which she would be able to do the smallest office of respect or love for the still corpse, to which in all her thoughts she attributed some consciousness. Our dead are never dead to us until we have forgotten them: they can be injured by us, they can be wounded; they know all our penitence, all our aching sense that their place is empty, all the kisses we bestow on the smallest relic of their presence. And the aged peasant-woman most of all believes that her dead are conscious. Decent burial

was what Lisbeth had been thinking of for herself through years
of thrift, with an indistinct expectation that she should know
when she was being carried to the churchyard, followed by her
husband and her sons; and now she felt as if the greatest work
of her life were to be done in seeing that Thias was buried
decently before her – under the white thorn, where once, in a
dream, she had thought she lay in the coffin, yet all the while
saw the sunshine above, and smelt the white blossoms that
were so thick upon the thorn the Sunday she went to be
churched[2] after Adam was born.

But now she had done everything that could be done to-day
in the chamber of death – had done it all herself, with some aid
from her sons in lifting, for she would let no one be fetched to
help her from the village, not being fond of female neighbours
generally; and her favourite Dolly, the old housekeeper at Mr
Burge's, who had come to condole with her in the morning as
soon as she heard of Thias's death, was too dim-sighted to be
of much use. She had locked the door, and now held the key in
her hand, as she threw herself wearily into a chair that stood
out of its place in the middle of the house floor, where in
ordinary times she would never have consented to sit. The
kitchen had had none of her attention that day; it was soiled
with the tread of muddy shoes, and untidy with clothes and
other objects out of place. But what at another time would have
been intolerable to Lisbeth's habits of order and cleanliness,
seemed to her now just what should be: it was right that things
should look strange and disordered and wretched, now the old
man had come to his end in that sad way: the kitchen ought
not to look as if nothing had happened. Adam, overcome with
the agitations and exertions of the day after his night of hard
work, had fallen asleep on a bench in the workshop; and Seth
was in the back kitchen making a fire of sticks that he might
get the kettle to boil, and persuade his mother to have a cup of
tea, an indulgence which she rarely allowed herself.

There was no one in the kitchen when Lisbeth entered and
threw herself into the chair. She looked round with blank eyes
at the dirt and confusion on which the bright afternoon's sun
shone dismally; it was all of a piece with the sad confusion of

her mind – that confusion which belongs to the first hours of a sudden sorrow, when the poor human soul is like one who has been deposited sleeping among the ruins of a vast city, and wakes up in dreary amazement, not knowing whether it is the growing or the dying day – not knowing why and whence came this illimitable scene of desolation, or why he too finds himself desolate in the midst of it.

At another time Lisbeth's first thought would have been, 'Where is Adam?' but the sudden death of her husband had restored him in these hours to that first place in her affections which he had held six-and-twenty years ago: she had forgotten his faults as we forget the sorrows of our departed childhood, and thought of nothing but the young husband's kindness and the old man's patience. Her eyes continued to wander blankly until Seth came in and began to remove some of the scattered things, and clear the small round deal table that he might set out his mother's tea upon it.

'What art goin' to do?' she said, rather peevishly.

'I want thee to have a cup of tea, mother,' answered Seth, tenderly. 'It'll do thee good; and I'll put two or three of these things away, and make the house look more comfortable.'

'Comfortable! How canst talk o' ma'in' things comfortable? Let a-be, let a-be. There's no comfort for me no more,' she went on, the tears coming when she began to speak, 'now thy poor feyther's gone, as I'n washed for and mended, an' got's victual for him for thirty 'ear, an' him allays so pleased wi' iverything I done for him, an' used to be so handy an' do the jobs for me when I war ill an' cumbered wi' th' babby, an' made me the posset³ an' brought it up-stairs as proud as could be, an' carried the lad as war as heavy as two children for five mile an' ne'er grumbled, all the way to Warson Wake, 'cause I wanted to go an' see my sister, as war dead an' gone the very next Christmas as e'er come. An' him to be drownded in the brook as we passed o'er the day we war married an' come home together, an' he'd made them lots o' shelves for me to put my plates an' things on, an' showed 'em me as proud as could be, 'cause he know'd I should be pleased. An' he war to die an' me not to know, but to be a-sleepin' i' my bed, as if I caredna nought about it. Eh!

an' me to live to see that! An' us as war young folks once, an' thought we should do rarely when we war married. Let a-be, lad, let a-be! I wonna ha' no tay: I carena if I ne'er ate nor drink no more. When one end o' th' bridge tumbles down, where's th' use o' th' other stannin'? I may's well die, an' foller my old man. There's no knowin' but he'll want me.'

Here Lisbeth broke from words into moans, swaying herself backwards and forwards on her chair. Seth, always timid in his behaviour towards his mother, from the sense that he had no influence over her, felt it was useless to attempt to persuade or soothe her, till this passion was past; so he contented himself with tending the back-kitchen fire, and folding up his father's clothes, which had been hanging out to dry since morning; afraid to move about in the room where his mother was, lest he should irritate her further.

But after Lisbeth had been rocking herself and moaning for some minutes, she suddenly paused, and said aloud to herself –

'I'll go an' see arter Adam, for I canna think where he's gotten; an' I want him to go up-stairs wi' me afore it's dark, for the minutes to look at the corpse is like the meltin' snow.'

Seth overheard this, and coming into the kitchen again, as his mother rose from her chair, he said –

'Adam's asleep in the workshop, mother. Thee'dst better not wake him. He was o'erwrought with work and trouble.'

'Wake him? Who's a-goin' to wake him? I shanna wake him wi' lookin' at him. I hanna seen the lad this two hour – I'd welly forgot as he'd e'er growed up from a babby when's feyther carried him.'

Adam was seated on a rough bench, his head supported by his arm, which rested from the shoulder to the elbow on the long planing-table in the middle of the workshop. It seemed as if he had sat down for a few minutes' rest, and had fallen asleep without slipping from his first attitude of sad, fatigued thought. His face, unwashed since yesterday, looked pallid and clammy; his hair was tossed shaggily about his forehead, and his closed eyes had the sunken look which follows upon watching and sorrow. His brow was knit, and his whole face had an expression of weariness and pain. Gyp was evidently uneasy, for he sat on his haunches resting his nose on his master's stretched-out leg, and dividing the time between licking the hand that hung listlessly down, and glancing with a listening air towards the door. The poor dog was hungry and restless, but would not leave his master, and was waiting impatiently for some change in the scene. It was owing to this feeling on Gyp's part, that when Lisbeth came into the workshop, and advanced towards Adam as noiselessly as she could, her intention not to awake him was immediately defeated; for Gyp's excitement was too great to find vent in anything short of a sharp bark, and in a moment Adam opened his eyes and saw his mother standing before him. It was not very unlike his dream, for his sleep had been little more than living through again, in a fevered delirious way, all that had happened since daybreak, and his mother with her fretful grief was present to him through it all. The chief difference between the reality and the vision was, that in his dream Hetty was continually coming before him in bodily presence – strangely mingling herself as an actor in scenes with which she had nothing to do. She was even by the Willow Brook; she made his mother angry by coming into the house; and he met her with her smart clothes quite wet through, as he walked in the rain to Treddleston, to tell the coroner. But wherever Hetty came, his mother was sure to follow soon; and when he opened his eyes, it was not at all startling to see her standing near him.

'Eh, my lad, my lad!' Lisbeth burst out immediately, her wailing impulse returning, for grief in its freshness feels the need of associating its loss and its lament with every change of scene and incident, 'thee'st got nobody now but thy old mother to torment thee and be a burden to thee: thy poor feyther 'ull ne'er anger thee no more; an' thy mother may's well go arter him – the sooner the better – for I'm no good to nobody now. One old coat 'ull do to patch another, but it's good for nought else. Thee'dst like to ha' a wife to mend thy clothes an' get thy victual, better nor thy old mother. An' I shall be nought but cumber,[4] a-sittin' i' th' chimney-corner. (Adam winced and moved uneasily; he dreaded, of all things, to hear his mother

speak of Hetty.) But if thy feyther had lived, he'd ne'er ha'
wanted me to go to make room for another, for he could no
more ha' done wi'out me nor one side o' the scissars can do
wi'out th' other. Eh, we should ha' been both flung away
together, an' then I shouldna ha' seen this day, an' one buryin'
'ud ha' done for us both.'

Here Lisbeth paused, but Adam sat in pained silence: he
could not speak otherwise than tenderly to his mother to-day;
but he could not help being irritated by this plaint. It was not
possible for poor Lisbeth to know how it affected Adam, any
more than it is possible for a wounded dog to know how his
moans affect the nerves of his master. Like all complaining
women, she complained in the expectation of being soothed,
and when Adam said nothing, she was only prompted to
complain more bitterly.

'I know thee couldst do better wi'out me, for thee couldst go
where thee likedst, an' marry them as thee likedst. But I donna
want to say thee nay, let thee bring home who thee wut; I'd
ne'er open my lips to find faut, for when folks is old an' o' no
use, they may think theirsens well off to get the bit an' the sup,
though they'n to swallow ill words wi't. An' if thee'st set thy
heart on a lass as'll bring thee nought and waste all, when thee
mightst ha' them as 'ud make a man on thee, I'll say nought,
now thy feyther's dead an' drownded, for I'm no better nor an
old haft[5] when the blade's gone.'

Adam, unable to bear this any longer, rose silently from the
bench, and walked out of the workshop into the kitchen. But
Lisbeth followed him.

'Thee wutna go up-stairs an' see thy feyther, then? I'n done
everythin' now, an' he'd like thee to go an' look at him, for he
war allays so pleased when thee wast mild to him.'

Adam turned round at once, and said, 'Yes, mother; let us
go up-stairs. Come, Seth, let us go together.'

They went up-stairs, and for five minutes all was silence.
Then the key was turned again, and there was a sound of
footsteps on the stairs. But Adam did not come down again; he
was too weary and worn-out to encounter more of his mother's
querulous grief, and he went to rest on his bed. Lisbeth no

sooner entered the kitchen and sat down than she threw her
apron over her head, and began to cry and moan, and rock
herself as before. Seth thought, 'She will be quieter by-and-by,
now we have been up-stairs'; and he went into the back-kitchen
again, to tend his little fire, hoping that he should presently
induce her to have some tea.

Lisbeth had been rocking herself in this way for more than
five minutes, giving a low moan with every forward movement
of her body, when she suddenly felt a hand placed gently on
hers, and a sweet treble voice said to her, 'Dear sister, the Lord
has sent me to see if I can be a comfort to you.'

Lisbeth paused, in a listening attitude, without removing her
apron from her face. The voice was strange to her. Could it be
her sister's spirit come back to her from the dead after all those
years? She trembled, and dared not look.

Dinah, believing that this pause of wonder was in itself a
relief for the sorrowing woman, said no more just yet, but
quietly took off her bonnet, and then, motioning silence to Seth,
who, on hearing her voice, had come in with a beating heart,
laid one hand on the back of Lisbeth's chair, and leaned over
her, that she might be aware of a friendly presence.

Slowly Lisbeth drew down her apron, and timidly she opened
her dim dark eyes. She saw nothing at first but a face – a pure,
pale face, with loving grey eyes, and it was quite unknown to
her. Her wonder increased; perhaps it *was* an angel. But in the
same instant Dinah had laid her hand on Lisbeth's again, and
the old woman looked down at it. It was a much smaller hand
than her own, but it was not white and delicate, for Dinah had
never worn a glove in her life, and her hand bore the traces of
labour from her childhood upwards. Lisbeth looked earnestly
at the hand for a moment, and then, fixing her eyes again on
Dinah's face, said, with something of restored courage, but in
a tone of surprise –

'Why, ye're a workin' woman!'

'Yes, I am Dinah Morris, and I work in the cotton-mill when
I am at home.'

'Ah!' said Lisbeth slowly, still wondering; 'ye comed in so
light, like the shadow on the wall, an' spoke i' my ear, as I

thought ye might be a sperrit. Ye've got a' most the face o' one as is a-sittin' on the grave i' Adam's new Bible.'

'I come from the Hall Farm now. You know Mrs Poyser – she's my aunt, and she has heard of your great affliction, and is very sorry; and I'm come to see if I can be any help to you in your trouble; for I know your sons Adam and Seth, and I know you have no daughter; and when the clergyman told me how the hand of God was heavy upon you, my heart went out towards you, and I felt a command to come and be to you in the place of a daughter in this grief, if you will let me.'

'Ah! I know who y' are now; y' are a Methody, like Seth; he's tould me on you,' said Lisbeth, fretfully, her overpowering sense of pain returning, now her wonder was gone. 'Ye'll make it out as trouble's a good thing, like *he* allays does. But where's the use o' talkin' to me a-that'n? Ye canna make the smart less wi' talkin'. Ye'll ne'er make me believe as it's better for me not to ha' my old man die in's bed, if he must die, an' ha' the parson to pray by him, an' me to sit by him, an' tell him ne'er to mind th' ill words I've gi'en him sometimes when I war angered, an' to gi' him a bit an' a sup, as long as a bit an' a sup he'd swallow. But eh! to die i' the cold water, an' us close to him, an' ne'er to know; an' me a-sleepin', as if I ne'er belonged to him no more nor if he'd been a journeyman tramp⁶ from nobody knows where!'

Here Lisbeth began to cry and rock herself again; and Dinah said –

'Yes, dear friend, your affliction is great. It would be hardness of heart to say that your trouble was not heavy to bear. God didn't send me to you to make light of your sorrow, but to mourn with you, if you will let me. If you had a table spread for a feast, and was making merry with your friends, you would think it was kind to let me come and sit down and rejoice with you, because you'd think I should like to share those good things; but I should like better to share in your trouble and your labour, and it would seem harder to me if you denied me that. You won't send me away? You're not angry with me for coming?'

'Nay, nay; angered! who said I war angered? It war good on

you to come. An' Seth, why donna ye get her some tay? Ye war
in a hurry to get some for me, as had no need, but ye donna
think o' gettin' 't for them as wants it. Sit ye down; sit ye down.
I thank you kindly for comin', for it's little wage ye get by
walkin' through the wet fields to see an old woman like me. . . .
Nay, I'n got no daughter o' my own – ne'er had one – an I
warna sorry, for they're poor queechy[7] things, gells is; I allays
wanted to ha' lads, as could fend for theirsens. An' the lads 'ull
be marryin' – I shall ha' daughters eno', an' too many. But now,
do ye make the tay as ye like it, for I'n got no taste i' my mouth
this day – it's all one what I swaller – it's all got the taste o'
sorrow wi't.'

Dinah took care not to betray that she had had her tea,
and accepted Lisbeth's invitation very readily, for the sake of
persuading the old woman herself to take the food and drink
she so much needed after a day of hard work and fasting.

Seth was so happy now Dinah was in the house that he could
not help thinking her presence was worth purchasing with a
life in which grief incessantly followed upon grief; but the next
moment he reproached himself – it was almost as if he were
rejoicing in his father's sad death. Nevertheless the joy of being
with Dinah *would* triumph: it was like the influence of climate,
which no resistance can overcome. And the feeling even suffused itself over his face so as to attract his mother's notice,
while she was drinking her tea.

'Thee may'st well talk o' trouble bein' a good thing, Seth, for
thee thriv'st on't. Thee look'st as if thee know'dst no more o'
care an' cumber nor when thee wast a babby a-lyin' awake i'
th' cradle. For thee'dst allays lie still wi' thy eyes open, an'
Adam ne'er 'ud lie still a minute when he wakened. Thee wast
allays like a bag o' meal as can ne'er be bruised – though, for
the matter o' that, thy poor feyther war just such another. But
ye've got the same look too' (here Lisbeth turned to Dinah). 'I
reckon it's wi' bein' a Methody. Not as I'm a-findin' faut wi'
ye for't, for ye've no call to be frettin', an' somehow ye looken
sorry too. Eh! well, if the Methodies are fond o' trouble, they're
like to thrive: it's a pity they canna ha't all, an' take it away
from them as donna like it. I could ha' gi'en 'em plenty; for

when I'd gotten my old man I war worreted from morn till night; and now's he's gone, I'd be glad for the worst o'er again.'

'Yes,' said Dinah, careful not to oppose any feeling of Lisbeth's, for her reliance, in her smallest words and deeds, on a divine guidance, always issued in that finest woman's tact which proceeds from acute and ready sympathy – 'yes; I remember, too, when my dear aunt died, I longed for the sound of her bad cough in the nights, instead of the silence that came when she was gone. But now, dear friend, drink this other cup of tea and eat a little more.'

'What!' said Lisbeth, taking the cup, and speaking in a less querulous tone, 'had ye got no feyther and mother, then, as ye war so sorry about your aunt?'

'No, I never knew a father or mother; my aunt brought me up from a baby. She had no children, for she was never married, and she brought me up as tenderly as if I'd been her own child.'

'Eh, she'd fine work wi' ye, I'll warrant, bringin' ye up from a babby, an' her a lone woman – it's ill bringin' up a cade lamb. But I daresay ye warna franzy,[8] for ye look as if ye'd ne'er been angered i' your life. But what did ye do when your aunt died, an' why didna ye come to live in this country, bein' as Mrs Poyser's your aunt too?'

Dinah, seeing that Lisbeth's attention was attracted, told her the story of her early life – how she had been brought up to work hard, and what sort of place Snowfield was, and how many people had a hard life there – all the details that she thought likely to interest Lisbeth. The old woman listened, and forgot to be fretful, unconsciously subject to the soothing influence of Dinah's face and voice. After a while she was persuaded to let the kitchen be made tidy; for Dinah was bent on this, believing that the sense of order and quietude around her would help in disposing Lisbeth to join in the prayer she longed to pour forth at her side. Seth, meanwhile, went out to chop wood; for he surmised that Dinah would like to be left alone with his mother.

Lisbeth sat watching her as she moved about in her still quick way, and said at last, 'Ye've got a notion o' cleanin' up. I wouldna mind ha'in ye for a daughter, for ye wouldna spend the lad's wage i' fine clothes an' waste. Ye're not like the lasses o' this country-side. I reckon folks is different at Snowfield from what they are here.'

'They have a different sort of life, many of 'em,' said Dinah; 'they work at different things – some in the mill, and many in the mines, in the villages round about. But the heart of man is the same everywhere, and there are the children of this world and the children of light there as well as elsewhere. But we've many more Methodists there than in this country.'

'Well, I didna know as the Methody women war like ye, for there's Will Maskery's wife, as they say's a big Methody, isna pleasant to look at, at all. I'd as lief look at a tooad. An' I'm thinkin' I wouldna mind if ye'd stay an' sleep here, for I should like to see ye i' th' house i' th' mornin'. But may-happen they'll be lookin' for ye at Mester Poyser's.'

'No,' said Dinah, 'they don't expect me, and I should like to stay, if you'll let me.'

'Well, there's room; I'n got my bed laid i' th' little room o'er the back-kitchen, an' ye can lie beside me. I'd be glad to ha' ye wi' me to speak to i' th' night, for ye've got a nice way o' talkin'. It puts me i' mind o' the swallows as was under the thack[9] last 'ear, when they fust begun to sing low an' soft-like i' th' mornin'. Eh, but my old man war fond o' them birds! an' so war Adam, but they'n ne'er comed again this 'ear. Happen *they*'re dead too.'

'There,' said Dinah, 'now the kitchen looks tidy, and now, dear mother – for I'm your daughter to-night, you know – I should like you to wash your face and have a clean cap on. Do you remember what David did, when God took away his child from him?[10] While the child was yet alive he fasted and prayed to God to spare it, and he would neither eat nor drink, but lay on the ground all night, beseeching God for the child. But when he knew it was dead, he rose up from the ground and washed and anointed himself, and changed his clothes, and ate and drank; and when they asked him how it was that he seemed to have left off grieving now the child was dead, he said, "While the child was yet alive, I fasted and wept; for I said, Who can tell whether God will be gracious to me, that the child may live? But now he is dead, wherefore should I fast? can I bring him back again? I shall go to him, but he shall not return to me."'

'Eh, that's a true word,' said Lisbeth. 'Yea, my old man wonna come back to me, but I shall go to him – the sooner the better. Well, ye may do as ye like wi' me: there's a clean cap i' that drawer, an' I'll go i' the back-kitchen an' wash my face. An' Seth, thee may'st reach down Adam's new Bible wi' th' picters in, an' she shall read us a chapter. Eh, I like them words – "I shall go to him, but he wonna come back to me."'

Dinah and Seth were both inwardly offering thanks for the greater quietness of spirit that had come over Lisbeth. This was what Dinah had been trying to bring about, through all her still sympathy and absence from exhortation. From her girlhood upwards she had had experience among the sick and the mourning, among minds hardened and shrivelled through poverty and ignorance, and had gained the subtlest perception of the mode in which they could best be touched, and softened into willingness to receive words of spiritual consolation or warning. As Dinah expressed it, 'she was never left to herself; but it was always given her when to keep silence and when to speak'. And do we not all agree to call rapid thought and noble impulse by the name of inspiration? After our subtlest analysis of the mental process, we must still say, as Dinah did, that our highest thoughts and our best deeds are all given to us.

And so there was earnest prayer – there was faith, love, and hope pouring itself forth that evening in the little kitchen. And poor aged fretful Lisbeth, without grasping any distinct idea, without going through any course of religious emotions, felt a vague sense of goodness and love, and of something right lying underneath and beyond all this sorrowing life. She couldn't understand the sorrow; but, for these moments, under the subduing influence of Dinah's spirit, she felt that she must be patient and still.

CHAPTER XI

In the Cottage

It was but half-past four the next morning, when Dinah, tired of lying awake listening to the birds, and watching the growing light through the little window in the garret roof, rose and began to dress herself very quietly, lest she should disturb Lisbeth. But already some one else was astir in the house, and had gone down-stairs, preceded by Gyp. The dog's pattering step was a sure sign that it was Adam who went down; but Dinah was not aware of this, and she thought it was more likely to be Seth, for he had told her how Adam had stayed up working the night before. Seth, however, had only just awakened at the sound of the opening door. The exciting influence of the previous day, heightened at last by Dinah's unexpected presence, had not been counteracted by any bodily weariness, for he had not done his ordinary amount of hard work; and so when he went to bed, it was not till he had tired himself with hours of tossing wakefulness that drowsiness came, and led on a heavier morning sleep than was usual with him.

But Adam had been refreshed by his long rest, and, with his habitual impatience of mere passivity, he was eager to begin the new day, and subdue sadness by his strong will and strong arm. The white mist lay in the valley; it was going to be a bright, warm day, and he would start to work again when he had had his breakfast.

'There's nothing but what's bearable as long as a man can work,' he said to himself: 'the natur o' things doesn't change, though it seems as if one's own life was nothing but change. The square o' four is sixteen, and you must lengthen your lever in proportion to your weight, is as true when a man's miserable as when he's happy; and the best o' working is, it gives you a grip hold o' things outside your own lot.'

As he dashed the cold water over his head and face, he felt completely himself again, and with his black eyes as keen as ever, and his thick black hair all glistening with the fresh moisture, he went into the workshop to look out the wood for his father's coffin, intending that he and Seth should carry it with them to Jonathan Burge's, and have the coffin made by one of the workmen there, so that his mother might not see and hear the sad task going forward at home.

He had just gone into the workshop, when his quick ear detected a light rapid foot on the stairs – certainly not his mother's. He had been in bed and asleep when Dinah had come in, in the evening, and now he wondered whose step this could be. A foolish thought came, and moved him strangely. As if it could be Hetty! She was the last person likely to be in the house. And yet he felt reluctant to go and look, and have the clear proof that it was some one else. He stood leaning on a plank he had taken hold of, listening to sounds which his imagination interpreted for him so pleasantly, that the keen strong face became suffused with a timid tenderness. The light footstep moved about the kitchen, followed by the sound of the sweeping brush, hardly making so much noise as the lightest breeze that chases the autumn leaves along the dusty path; and Adam's imagination saw a dimpled face, with dark bright eyes and roguish smiles, looking backward at this brush, and a rounded figure just leaning a little to clasp the handle. A very foolish thought – it could not be Hetty; but the only way of dismissing such nonsense from his head was to go and see *who* it was, for his fancy only got nearer and nearer to belief while he stood there listening. He loosed the plank, and went to the kitchen door.

'How do you do, Adam Bede?' said Dinah, in her calm treble, pausing from her sweeping, and fixing her mild grave eyes upon him. 'I trust you feel rested and strengthened again to bear the burthen and heat of the day.'[1]

It was like dreaming of the sunshine, and awaking in the moonlight. Adam had seen Dinah several times, but always at the Hall Farm, where he was not very vividly conscious of any woman's presence except Hetty's, and he had only in the last day or two begun to suspect that Seth was in love with her, so that his attention had not hitherto been drawn towards her for his brother's sake. But now her slim figure, her plain black gown, and her pale serene face, impressed him with all the force that belongs to a reality contrasted with a preoccupying fancy. For the first moment or two he made no answer, but looked at her with the concentrated, examining glance which a man gives to an object in which he has suddenly begun to be interested. Dinah, for the first time in her life, felt a painful self-consciousness; there was something in the dark penetrating glance of this strong man so different from the mildness and timidity of his brother Seth. A faint blush came, which deepened as she wondered at it. This blush recalled Adam from his forgetfulness.

'I was quite taken by surprise; it was very good of you to come and see my mother in her trouble,' he said, in a gentle grateful tone, for his quick mind told him at once how she came to be there. 'I hope my mother was thankful to have you,' he added, wondering rather anxiously what had been Dinah's reception.

'Yes,' said Dinah, resuming her work, 'she seemed greatly comforted after a while, and she's had a good deal of rest in the night, by times. She was fast asleep when I left her.'

'Who was it took the news to the Hall Farm?' said Adam, his thoughts reverting to some one there; he wondered whether *she* had felt anything about it.

'It was Mr Irwine, the clergyman, told me, and my aunt was grieved for your mother when she heard it, and wanted me to come; and so is my uncle, I'm sure, now he's heard it, but he was gone out to Rosseter all yesterday. They'll look for you there as soon as you've got time to go, for there's nobody round that hearth but what's glad to see you.'

Dinah, with her sympathetic divination, knew quite well that Adam was longing to hear if Hetty had said anything about their trouble; she was too rigorously truthful for benevolent invention, but she had contrived to say something in which

Hetty was tacitly included. Love has a way of cheating itself consciously, like a child who plays at solitary hide-and-seek; it is pleased with assurances that it all the while disbelieves. Adam liked what Dinah had said so much that his mind was directly full of the next visit he should pay to the Hall Farm, when Hetty would perhaps behave more kindly to him than she had ever done before.

'But you won't be there yourself any longer?' he said to Dinah.

'No, I go back to Snowfield on Saturday, and I shall have to set out to Treddleston early, to be in time for the Oakbourne carrier.[2] So I must go back to the farm to-night, that I may have the last day with my aunt and her children. But I can stay here all to-day, if your mother would like me; and her heart seemed inclined towards me last night.'

'Ah, then, she's sure to want you to-day. If mother takes to people at the beginning, she's sure to get fond of 'em; but she's a strange way of not liking young women. Though, to be sure,' Adam went on, smiling, 'her not liking other young women is no reason why she shouldn't like you.'

Hitherto Gyp had been assisting at this conversation in motionless silence, seated on his haunches, and alternately looking up in his master's face to watch its expression, and observing Dinah's movements about the kitchen. The kind smile with which Adam uttered the last words was apparently decisive with Gyp of the light in which the stranger was to be regarded, and as she turned round after putting aside her sweeping-brush, he trotted towards her, and put up his muzzle against her hand in a friendly way.

'You see Gyp bids you welcome,' said Adam, 'and he's very slow to welcome strangers.'

'Poor dog!' said Dinah, patting the rough grey coat, 'I've a strange feeling about the dumb things as if they wanted to speak, and it was a trouble to 'em because they couldn't. I can't help being sorry for the dogs always, though perhaps there's no need. But they may well have more in them than they know how to make us understand, for we can't say half what we feel, with all our words.'

Seth came down now, and was pleased to find Adam talking with Dinah; he wanted Adam to know how much better she was than all other women. But after a few words of greeting, Adam drew him into the workshop to consult about the coffin, and Dinah went on with her cleaning.

By six o'clock they were all at breakfast with Lisbeth in a kitchen as clean as she could have made it herself. The window and door were open, and the morning air brought with it a mingled scent of southernwood, thyme, and sweetbriar from the patch of garden by the side of the cottage. Dinah did not sit down at first, but moved about, serving the others with the warm porridge and the toasted oat-cake, which she had got ready in the usual way, for she had asked Seth to tell her just what his mother gave them for breakfast. Lisbeth had been unusually silent since she came down-stairs, apparently requiring some time to adjust her ideas to a state of things in which she came down like a lady to find all the work done, and sat still to be waited on. Her new sensations seemed to exclude the remembrance of her grief. At last, after tasting the porridge, she broke silence –

'Ye might ha' made the parridge worse,' she said to Dinah; 'I can ate it wi'out it's turnin' my stomach. It might ha' been a trifle thicker an' no harm, an' I allays putten a sprig o' mint in mysen; but how's ye t' know that? The lads arena like to get folks as 'll make their parridge as I'n made it for 'em; it's well if they get onybody as 'll make parridge at all. But ye might do, wi' a bit o' showin'; for ye're a stirrin' body in a mornin', an' ye've a light heel, an' ye've cleaned th' house well enough for a ma'-shift.'

'Makeshift, mother?' said Adam. 'Why, I think the house looks beautiful. I don't know how it could look better.'

'Thee dostna know? – nay; how's thee to know? Th' men ne'er know whether the floor's clean or cat-licked. But thee'lt know when thee gets thy parridge burnt, as it's like enough to be when I'n gi'en o'er makin' it. Thee'lt think thy mother war good for summat then.'

'Dinah,' said Seth, 'do come and sit down now and have your breakfast. We're all served now.'

'Ay, come an' sit ye down – do,' said Lisbeth, 'an' ate a
morsel; ye'd need, arter bein' upo' your legs this hour an' half
a'ready. Come, then,' she added, in a tone of complaining
affection, as Dinah sat down by her side, 'I'll be loath for ye t'
go, but ye canna stay much longer, I doubt. I could put up wi'
ye i' th' house better nor wi' most folks.'

'I'll stay till to-night if you're willing,' said Dinah. 'I'd stay
longer, only I'm going back to Snowfield on Saturday, and I
must be with my aunt to-morrow.'

'Eh, I'd ne'er go back to that country. My old man come
from that Stonyshire side, but he left it when he war a young
un, an' i' the right on't too; for he said as there war no wood
there, an' it 'ud ha' been a bad country for a carpenter.'

'Ah,' said Adam, 'I remember father telling me when I was a
little lad, that he made up his mind if ever he moved it should
be south'ard. But I'm not so sure about it. Bartle Massey says
– and he knows the South – as the northern men are a finer
breed than the southern, harder-headed and stronger-bodied,
and a deal taller. And then he says, in some o' those counties
it's as flat as the back o' your hand, and you can see nothing of
a distance, without climbing up the highest trees. I couldn't
abide that: I like to go to work by a road that'll take me up a
bit of a hill, and see the fields for miles round me, and a bridge,
or a town, or a bit of a steeple here and there. It makes you feel
the world's a big place, and there's other men working in it
with their heads and hands besides yourself.'

'I like th' hills best,' said Seth, 'when the clouds are over your
head, and you see the sun shining ever so far off, over the
Loamford way, as I've often done o' late, on the stormy days:
it seems to me as if that was heaven where there's always joy
and sunshine, though this life's dark and cloudy.'

'Oh, I love the Stonyshire side,' said Dinah; 'I shouldn't like
to set my face towards the countries where they're rich in corn
and cattle, and the ground so level and easy to tread; and to
turn my back on the hills where the poor people have to live
such a hard life, and the men spend their days in the mines
away from the sunlight. It's very blessed on a bleak cold day,
when the sky is hanging dark over the hill, to feel the love of

God in one's soul, and carry it to the lonely, bare, stone houses, where there's nothing else to give comfort.'

'Eh!' said Lisbeth, 'that's very well for ye to talk, as looks welly like the snowdrop-flowers as ha' lived for days an' days when I'n gethered 'em, wi' nothin' but a drop o' water an' a peep o' daylight; but the hungry foulks had better leave th' hungry country. It makes less mouths for the scant cake. But,' she went on, looking at Adam, 'donna thee talk o' goin' south'ard or north'ard, an' leavin' thy feyther and mother i' the churchyard, an' goin' to a country as they know nothin' on. I'll ne'er rest i' my grave if I donna see thee i' the churchyard of a Sunday.'

'Donna fear, mother,' said Adam. 'If I hadna made up my mind not to go, I should ha' been gone before now.'

He had finished his breakfast now, and rose as he was speaking.

'What art goin' to do?' asked Lisbeth. 'Set about thy feyther's coffin?'

'No, mother,' said Adam; 'we're going to take the wood to the village, and have it made there.'

'Nay, my lad, nay,' Lisbeth burst out in an eager, wailing tone; 'thee wotna let nobody make thy feyther's coffin but thysen? Who'd make it so well? An' him as know'd what good work war, an's got a son as is the head o' the village, an' all Treddles'on too, for cleverness.'

'Very well, mother, if that's thy wish, I'll make the coffin at home; but I thought thee wouldstna like to hear the work going on.'

'An' why shouldna I like't? It's the right thing to be done. An' what's liking got to do wi't? It's choice o' mislikings is all I'n got i' this world. One morsel's as good as another when your mouth's out o' taste. Thee mun set about it now this mornin' fust thing. I wonna ha' nobody to touch the coffin but thee.'

Adam's eyes met Seth's, which looked from Dinah to him rather wistfully.

'No, mother,' he said, 'I'll not consent but Seth shall have a hand in it too, if it's to be done at home. I'll go to the village this forenoon, because Mr Burge 'ull want to see me, and Seth shall stay at home and begin the coffin. I can come back at noon, and then he can go.'

'Nay, nay,' persisted Lisbeth, beginning to cry, 'I'n set my heart on't as thee shalt ma' thy feyther's coffin. Thee't so stiff an' masterful, thee't ne'er do as thy mother wants thee. Thee wast often angered wi' thy feyther when he war alive; thee must be the better to him now he's gone. He'd ha' thought nothin' on't for Seth to ma's coffin.'

'Say no more, Adam, say no more,' said Seth, gently, though his voice told that he spoke with some effort; 'mother's in the right. I'll go to work, and do thee stay at home.'

He passed into the workshop immediately, followed by Adam; while Lisbeth, automatically obeying her old habits, began to put away the breakfast things, as if she did not mean Dinah to take her place any longer. Dinah said nothing, but presently used the opportunity of quietly joining the brothers in the workshop.

They had already got on their aprons and paper-caps, and Adam was standing with his left hand on Seth's shoulder, while he pointed with the hammer in his right to some boards which they were looking at. Their backs were turned towards the door by which Dinah entered, and she came in so gently that they were not aware of her presence till they heard her voice saying, 'Seth Bede!' Seth started, and they both turned round. Dinah looked as if she did not see Adam, and fixed her eyes on Seth's face, saying with calm kindness –

'I won't say farewell. I shall see you again when you come from work. So as I'm at the farm before dark, it will be quite soon enough.'

'Thank you, Dinah; I should like to walk home with you once more. It'll perhaps be the last time.'

There was a little tremor in Seth's voice. Dinah put out her hand and said, 'You'll have sweet peace in your mind to-day, Seth, for your tenderness and long-suffering towards your aged mother.'

She turned round and left the workshop as quickly and quietly as she had entered it. Adam had been observing her closely all the while, but she had not looked at him. As soon as she was gone, he said –

'I don't wonder at thee for loving her, Seth. She's got a face like a lily.'

Seth's soul rushed to his eyes and lips: he had never yet confessed his secret to Adam, but now he felt a delicious sense of disburthenment, as he answered –

'Ay, Addy, I do love her – too much, I doubt. But she doesna love me, lad, only as one child o' God loves another. She'll never love any man as a husband – that's my belief.'

'Nay, lad, there's no telling; thee mustna lose heart. She's made out o' stuff with a finer grain than most o' the women; I can see that clear enough. But if she's better than they are in other things, I canna think she'll fall short of 'em in loving.'

No more was said. Seth set out to the village, and Adam began his work on the coffin.

'God help the lad, and me too,' he thought, as he lifted the board. 'We're like enough to find life a tough job – hard work inside and out. It's a strange thing to think of a man as can lift a chair with his teeth, and walk fifty mile on end, trembling and turning hot and cold at only a look from one woman out of all the rest i' the world. It's a mystery we can give no account of; but no more we can of the sprouting o' the seed, for that matter.'

CHAPTER XII

In the Wood

That same Thursday morning, as Arthur Donnithorne was moving about in his dressing-room, seeing his well-looking British person reflected in the old-fashioned mirrors, and stared at, from a dingy olive-green piece of tapestry, by Pharaoh's daughter and her maidens, who ought to have been minding the infant Moses,[1] he was holding a discussion with himself, which, by the time his valet was tying the black silk sling over his shoulder, had issued in a distinct practical resolution.

'I mean to go to Eagledale and fish for a week or so,' he said aloud. 'I shall take you with me, Pym, and set off this morning; so be ready by half-past eleven.'

The low whistle, which had assisted him in arriving at this resolution, here broke out into his loudest ringing tenor, and the corridor, as he hurried along it, echoed to his favourite song from the 'Beggar's Opera', 'When the heart of a man is oppressed with care.'[2] Not an heroic strain; nevertheless Arthur felt himself very heroic as he strode towards the stables to give his orders about the horses. His own approbation was necessary to him, and it was not an approbation to be enjoyed quite gratuitously; it must be won by a fair amount of merit. He had never yet forfeited that approbation, and he had considerable reliance on his own virtues. No young man could confess his faults more candidly; candour was one of his favourite virtues; and how can a man's candour be seen in all its lustre unless he has a few failings to talk of? But he had an agreeable confidence that his faults were all of a generous kind – impetuous, warm-blooded, leonine; never crawling, crafty, reptilian. It was not possible for Arthur Donnithorne to do anything mean,

dastardly, or cruel. 'No! I'm a devil of a fellow for getting
myself into a hobble,[3] but I always take care the load shall fall
on my own shoulders.' Unhappily there is no inherent poetical
justice in hobbles, and they will sometimes obstinately refuse
to inflict their worst consequences on the prime offender, in
spite of his loudly expressed wish. It was entirely owing to this
deficiency in the scheme of things that Arthur had ever brought
any one into trouble besides himself. He was nothing, if not
good-natured; and all his pictures of the future, when he should
come into the estate, were made up of a prosperous, contented
tenantry, adoring their landlord, who would be the model of
an English gentleman – mansion in first-rate order, all elegance
and high taste – jolly housekeeping, finest stud in Loamshire –
purse open to all public objects – in short, everything as different as possible from what was now associated with the name
of Donnithorne. And one of the first good actions he would
perform in that future should be to increase Irwine's income
for the vicarage of Hayslope,[4] so that he might keep a carriage
for his mother and sisters. His hearty affection for the Rector
dated from the age of frocks and trousers.[5] It was an affection
partly filial, partly fraternal; – fraternal enough to make him
like Irwine's company better than that of most younger men,
and filial enough to make him shrink strongly from incurring
Irwine's disapprobation.

You perceive that Arthur Donnithorne was 'a good fellow' –
all his college[6] friends thought him such: he couldn't bear to
see any one uncomfortable; he would have been sorry even in
his angriest moods for any harm to happen to his grandfather;
and his aunt Lydia herself had the benefit of that soft-
heartedness which he bore towards the whole sex.[7] Whether he
would have self-mastery enough to be always as harmless and
purely beneficent as his good nature led him to desire, was a
question that no one had yet decided against him: he was but
twenty-one, you remember; and we don't inquire too closely
into character in the case of a handsome generous young fellow,
who will have property enough to support numerous pecca-
dilloes – who, if he should unfortunately break a man's legs in
his rash driving, will be able to pension him handsomely; or if

he should happen to spoil a woman's existence for her, will make it up to her with expensive *bon-bons*, packed up and directed by his own hand. It would be ridiculous to be prying and analytic in such cases, as if one were inquiring into the character of a confidential clerk. We use round, general, gentle-manly epithets about a young man of birth and fortune; and ladies, with that fine intuition which is the distinguishing attribute of their sex, see at once that he is 'nice'. The chances are that he will go through life without scandalizing any one; a seaworthy vessel that no one would refuse to insure. Ships, certainly, are liable to casualties, which sometimes make ter-ribly evident some flaw in their construction, that would never have been discoverable in smooth water; and many a 'good fellow', through a disastrous combination of circumstances, has undergone a like betrayal.

But we have no fair ground for entertaining unfavourable auguries concerning Arthur Donnithorne, who this morning proves himself capable of a prudent resolution founded on conscience. One thing is clear: Nature has taken care that he shall never go far astray with perfect comfort and satisfaction to himself; he will never get beyond that border-land of sin, where he will be perpetually harassed by assaults from the other side of the boundary. He will never be a courtier of Vice, and wear her orders in his button-hole.

It was about ten o'clock, and the sun was shining brilliantly; everything was looking lovelier for the yesterday's rain. It is a pleasant thing on such a morning to walk along the well-rolled gravel on one's way to the stables, meditating an excursion. But the scent of the stables, which, in a natural state of things, ought to be among the soothing influences of a man's life, always brought with it some irritation to Arthur. There was no having his own way in the stables; everything was managed in the stingiest fashion. His grandfather persisted in retaining as head groom an old dolt whom no sort of lever could move out of his old habits, and who was allowed to hire a succession of raw Loamshire lads as his subordinates, one of whom had lately tested a new pair of shears by clipping an oblong patch on Arthur's bay mare. This state of things is naturally embittering;

one can put up with annoyances in the house, but to have the stable made a scene of vexation and disgust, is a point beyond what human flesh and blood can be expected to endure long together without danger of misanthropy.

Old John's wooden, deep-wrinkled face was the first object that met Arthur's eyes as he entered the stable-yard, and it quite poisoned for him the bark of the two bloodhounds that kept watch there. He could never speak quite patiently to the old blockhead.

'You must have Meg saddled for me and brought to the door at half-past eleven, and I shall want Rattler saddled for Pym at the same time. Do you hear?'

'Yes, I hear, I hear, Cap'n,' said old John, very deliberately, following the young master into the stable. John considered a young master as the natural enemy of an old servant, and young people in general as a poor contrivance for carrying on the world.

Arthur went in for the sake of patting Meg, declining as far as possible to see anything in the stables, lest he should lose his temper before breakfast. The pretty creature was in one of the inner stables, and turned her mild head as her master came beside her. Little Trot, a tiny spaniel, her inseparable companion in the stable, was comfortably curled up on her back.

'Well, Meg, my pretty girl,' said Arthur, patting her neck, 'we'll have a glorious canter this morning.'

'Nay, your honour, I donna see as that can be,' said John.

'Not be? Why not?'

'Why, she's got lamed.'

'Lamed, confound you! what do you mean?'

'Why, th' lad took her too close to Dalton's hosses, an' one on 'em flung out at her, an' she's got her shank bruised o' the near fore-leg.'

The judicious historian abstains from narrating precisely what ensued. You understand that there was a great deal of strong language, mingled with soothing 'who-ho's' while the leg was examined; that John stood by with quite as much emotion as if he had been a cunningly carved crab-tree walking-

stick, and that Arthur Donnithorne presently repassed the iron
gates of the pleasure-ground without singing as he went.

He considered himself thoroughly disappointed and annoyed.
There was not another mount in the stable for himself and his
servant besides Meg and Rattler. It was vexatious; just when
he wanted to get out of the way for a week or two. It seemed
culpable in Providence to allow such a combination of circumstances. To be shut up at the Chase with a broken arm, when
every other fellow in his regiment was enjoying himself at Windsor – shut up with his grandfather, who had the same sort of
affection for him as for his parchment deeds! And to be dis-
gusted at every turn with the management of the house and the
estate! In such circumstances a man necessarily gets in an ill
humour, and works off the irritation by some excess or other.
'Salkeld would have drunk a bottle of port every day,' he
muttered to himself; 'but I'm not well seasoned enough for that.
Well, since I can't go to Eagledale, I'll have a gallop on Rattler
to Norburne this morning, and lunch with Gawaine.'

Behind this explicit resolution there lay an implicit one. If he
lunched with Gawaine and lingered chatting, he should not
reach the Chase again till nearly five, when Hetty would be safe
out of his sight in the housekeeper's room; and when she set
out to go home, it would be his lazy time after dinner, so he
should keep out of her way altogether. There really would have
been no harm in being kind to the little thing, and it was worth
dancing with a dozen ball-room belles only to look at Hetty for
half an hour. But perhaps he had better not take any more
notice of her; it might put notions into her head, as Irwine had
hinted; though Arthur, for his part, thought girls were not by
any means so soft and easily bruised; indeed, he had generally
found them twice as cool and cunning as he was himself. As for
any real harm in Hetty's case, it was out of the question: Arthur
Donnithorne accepted his own bond for himself with perfect
confidence.

So the twelve o'clock sun saw him galloping towards
Norburne; and by good fortune Halsell Common lay in his
road, and gave him some fine leaps for Rattler. Nothing like
'taking' a few bushes and ditches for exorcising a demon; and

it is really astonishing that the Centaurs,[8] with their immense advantages in this way, have left so bad a reputation in history.

After this, you will perhaps be surprised to hear, that although Gawaine was at home, the hand of the dial in the courtyard had scarcely cleared the last stroke of three, when Arthur returned through the entrance-gates, got down from the panting Rattler, and went into the house to take a hasty luncheon. But I believe there have been men since his day who have ridden a long way to avoid a rencontre, and then galloped hastily back lest they should miss it. It is the favourite stratagem of our passions to sham a retreat, and to turn sharp round upon us at the moment we have made up our minds that the day is our own.

'The Cap'n's been ridin' the devil's own pace,' said Dalton the coachman, whose person stood out in high relief as he smoked his pipe against the stable wall, when John brought up Rattler.

'An' I wish he'd get the devil to do's grooming for'n,' growled John.

'Ay; he'd hev a deal haimabler[9] groom nor what he has now,' observed Dalton; and the joke appeared to him so good, that, being left alone upon the scene, he continued at intervals to take his pipe from his mouth in order to wink at an imaginary audience, and shake luxuriously with a silent, ventral laughter; mentally rehearsing the dialogue from the beginning, that he might recite it with effect in the servants' hall.

When Arthur went up to his dressing-room again after luncheon, it was inevitable that the debate he had had with himself there earlier in the day should flash across his mind; but it was impossible for him now to dwell on the remembrance – impossible to recall the feelings and reflections which had been decisive with him then, any more than to recall the peculiar scent of the air that had freshened him when he first opened his window. The desire to see Hetty had rushed back like an ill-stemmed current; he was amazed himself at the force with which this trivial fancy seemed to grasp him: he was even rather tremulous as he brushed his hair – pooh! it was riding in that breakneck way. It was because he had made a serious affair of an idle matter, by thinking of it as if it were of any consequence. He would amuse himself by seeing Hetty to-day, and get rid of the whole thing from his mind. It was all Irwine's fault. 'If Irwine had said nothing, I shouldn't have thought half so much of Hetty as of Meg's lameness.' However, it was just the sort of day for lolling in the Hermitage, and he would go and finish Dr Moore's *Zeluco*[10] there before dinner. The Hermitage stood in Fir-tree Grove – the way Hetty was sure to come in walking from the Hall Farm. So nothing could be simpler and more natural: meeting Hetty was a mere circumstance of his walk, not its object.

Arthur's shadow flitted rather faster among the sturdy oaks of the Chase than might have been expected from the shadow of a tired man on a warm afternoon, and it was still scarcely four o'clock when he stood before the tall narrow gate leading into the delicious labyrinthine wood which skirted one side of the Chase, and which was called Fir-tree Grove, not because the firs were many, but because they were few. It was a wood of beeches and limes, with here and there a light, silver-stemmed birch – just the sort of wood most haunted by the nymphs: you see their white sunlit limbs gleaming athwart the boughs, or peeping from behind the smooth-sweeping outline of a tall lime; you hear their soft liquid laughter – but if you look with a too curious sacrilegious eye, they vanish behind the silvery beeches, they make you believe that their voice was only a running brooklet, perhaps they metamorphose themselves into a tawny squirrel that scampers away and mocks you from the topmost bough. It was not a grove with measured grass or rolled gravel for you to tread upon, but with narrow, hollow-shaped, earthy paths, edged with faint dashes of delicate moss – paths which look as if they were made by the free-will of the trees and underwood, moving reverently aside to look at the tall queen of the white-footed nymphs.

It was along the broadest of these paths that Arthur Donnithorne passed, under an avenue of limes and beeches. It was a still afternoon – the golden light was lingering languidly among the upper boughs, only glancing down here and there on the purple pathway and its edge of faintly sprinkled moss:

an afternoon in which destiny disguises her cold awful face
behind a hazy radiant veil, encloses us in warm downy wings,
and poisons us with violet-scented breath. Arthur strolled along
carelessly, with a book under his arm, but not looking on the
ground as meditative men are apt to do; his eyes *would* fix
themselves on the distant bend in the road, round which a little
figure must surely appear before long. Ah! there she comes: first
a bright patch of colour, like a tropic bird among the boughs,
then a tripping figure, with a round hat on, and a small basket
under her arm; then a deep-blushing, almost frightened, but
bright-smiling girl, making her curtsy with a fluttered yet happy
glance, as Arthur came up to her. If Arthur had had time to
think at all, he would have thought it strange that he should
feel fluttered too, be conscious of blushing too – in fact, look
and feel as foolish as if he had been taken by surprise instead
of meeting just what he expected. Poor things! It was a pity
they were not in that golden age of childhood when they would
have stood face to face, eyeing each other with timid liking,
then given each other a little butterfly kiss, and toddled off to
play together. Arthur would have gone home to his silk-
curtained cot, and Hetty to her home-spun pillow, and both
would have slept without dreams, and to-morrow would have
been a life hardly conscious of a yesterday.

Arthur turned round and walked by Hetty's side without
giving a reason. They were alone together for the first time.
What an overpowering presence that first privacy is! He actually
dared not look at this little buttermaker for the first minute or
two. As for Hetty, her feet rested on a cloud, and she was borne
along by warm zephyrs; she had forgotten her rose-coloured
ribbons; she was no more conscious of her limbs than if her
childish soul had passed into a water-lily, resting on a liquid
bed, and warmed by the midsummer sunbeams. It may seem a
contradiction, but Arthur gathered a certain carelessness and
confidence from his timidity: it was an entirely different state
of mind from what he had expected in such a meeting with
Hetty; and full as he was of vague feeling, there was room, in
those moments of silence, for the thought that his previous
debates and scruples were needless.

'You are quite right to choose this way of coming to the Chase,' he said at last, looking down at Hetty, 'it is so much prettier as well as shorter than coming by either of the lodges.'

'Yes, sir,' Hetty answered, with a tremulous, almost whispering voice. She didn't know one bit how to speak to a gentleman like Mr Arthur, and her very vanity made her more coy of speech.

'Do you come every week to see Mrs Pomfret?'

'Yes, sir, every Thursday, only when she's got to go out with Miss Donnithorne.'

'And she's teaching you something, is she?'

'Yes, sir, the lace-mending as she learnt abroad, and the stocking-mending – it looks just like the stocking, you can't tell it's been mended; and she teaches me cutting-out too.'

'What, are *you* going to be a lady's-maid?'

'I should like to be one very much indeed.' Hetty spoke more audibly now, but still rather tremulously; she thought, perhaps she seemed as stupid to Captain Donnithorne as Luke Britton did to her.

'I suppose Mrs Pomfret always expects you at this time?'

'She expects me at four o'clock. I'm rather late to-day, because my aunt couldn't spare me; but the regular time is four, because that gives us time before Miss Donnithorne's bell rings.'

'Ah, then, I must not keep you now, else I should like to show you the Hermitage. Did you ever see it?'

'No, sir.'

'This is the walk where we turn up to it. But we must not go now. I'll show it you some other time, if you'd like to see it?'

'Yes, please, sir.'

'Do you always come back this way in the evening, or are you afraid to come so lonely a road?'

'Oh no, sir, it's never late; I always set out by eight o'clock, and it's so light now in the evening. My aunt would be angry with me if I didn't get home before nine.'

'Perhaps Craig, the gardener, comes to take care of you?'

A deep blush overspread Hetty's face and neck. 'I'm sure he doesn't; I'm sure he never did; I wouldn't let him; I don't like him,' she said hastily, and the tears of vexation had come so

fast, that before she had done speaking a bright drop rolled
down her hot cheek. Then she felt ashamed to death that she
was crying, and for one long instant her happiness was all gone.
But in the next she felt an arm steal round her, and a gentle
voice said –

'Why, Hetty, what makes you cry? I didn't mean to vex you.
I wouldn't vex you for the world, you little blossom. Come,
don't cry; look at me, else I shall think you won't forgive me.'

Arthur had laid his hand on the soft arm that was nearest to
him, and was stooping towards Hetty with a look of coaxing
entreaty. Hetty lifted her long dewy lashes, and met the eyes
that were bent towards her with a sweet, timid, beseeching
look. What a space of time those three moments were, while
their eyes met and his arms touched her! Love is such a simple
thing when we have only one-and-twenty summers and a sweet
girl of seventeen trembles under our glance, as if she were a
bud first opening her heart with wondering rapture to the
morning. Such young unfurrowed souls roll to meet each other
like two velvet peaches that touch softly and are at rest; they
mingle as easily as two brooklets that ask for nothing but to
entwine themselves and ripple with ever-interlacing curves in
the leafiest hiding-places. While Arthur gazed into Hetty's dark
beseeching eyes, it made no difference to him what sort of
English she spoke; and even if hoops and powder had been in
fashion, he would very likely not have been sensible just then
that Hetty wanted those signs of high breeding.

But they started asunder with beating hearts: something had
fallen on the ground with a rattling noise; it was Hetty's basket;
all her little workwoman's matters were scattered on the path,
some of them showing a capability of rolling to great lengths.
There was much to be done in picking up, and not a word was
spoken; but when Arthur hung the basket over her arm again,
the poor child felt a strange difference in his look and manner.
He just pressed her hand, and said, with a look and tone that
were almost chilling to her –

'I have been hindering you; I must not keep you any longer
now. You will be expected at the house. Good-bye.'

Without waiting for her to speak, he turned away from her

and hurried back towards the road that led to the Hermitage, leaving Hetty to pursue her way in a strange dream, that seemed to have begun in bewildering delight, and was now passing into contrarieties and sadness. Would he meet her again as she came home? Why had he spoken almost as if he were displeased with her? and then run away so suddenly? She cried, hardly knowing why.

Arthur too was very uneasy, but his feelings were lit up for him by a more distinct consciousness. He hurried to the Hermitage, which stood in the heart of the wood, unlocked the door with a hasty wrench, slammed it after him, pitched *Zeluco* into the most distant corner, and, thrusting his right hand into his pocket, first walked four or five times up and down the scanty length of the little room, and then seated himself on the ottoman[11] in an uncomfortable stiff way, as we often do when we wish not to abandon ourselves to feeling.

He was getting in love with Hetty – that was quite plain. He was ready to pitch everything else – no matter where – for the sake of surrendering himself to this delicious feeling which had just disclosed itself. It was no use blinking the fact now – they would get too fond of each other, if he went on taking notice of her – and what would come of it? He should have to go away in a few weeks, and the poor little thing would be miserable. He *must not* see her alone again; he must keep out of her way. What a fool he was for coming back from Gawaine's!

He got up and threw open the windows to let in the soft breath of the afternoon, and the healthy scent of the firs that made a belt round the Hermitage. The soft air did not help his resolutions, as he leaned out and looked into the leafy distance. But he considered his resolution sufficiently fixed: there was no need to debate with himself any longer. He had made up his mind not to meet Hetty again; and now he might give himself up to thinking how immensely agreeable it would be if circumstances were different – how pleasant it would have been to meet her this evening as she came back, and put his arm round her again and look into her sweet face. He wondered if the dear little thing were thinking of him too – twenty to one she was. How beautiful her eyes were with the tear on their lashes! He would like to satisfy his soul for a day with looking at them, and he *must* see her again: – he must see her, simply to remove any false impression from her mind about his manner to her just now. He would behave in a quiet, kind way to her – just to prevent her from going home with her head full of wrong fancies. Yes, that would be the best thing to do after all.

It was a long while – more than an hour – before Arthur had brought his meditations to this point; but once arrived there, he could stay no longer at the Hermitage. The time must be filled up with movement until he should see Hetty again. And it was already late enough to go and dress for dinner, for his grandfather's dinner-hour was six.

CHAPTER XIII

Evening in the Wood

It happened that Mrs Pomfret had had a slight quarrel with Mrs Best, the housekeeper, on this Thursday morning – a fact which had two consequences highly convenient to Hetty. It caused Mrs Pomfret to have tea sent up to her own room, and it inspired that exemplary lady's-maid with so lively a recollection of former passages in Mrs Best's conduct, and of dialogues in which Mrs Best had decidedly the inferiority as an interlocutor with Mrs Pomfret, that Hetty required no more presence of mind than was demanded for using her needle, and throwing in an occasional 'yes' or 'no'. She would have wanted to put on her hat earlier than usual; only she had told Captain Donnithorne that she usually set out about eight o'clock, and if he *should* go to the Grove again expecting to see her, and she should be gone! Would he come? Her little butterfly-soul fluttered incessantly between memory and dubious expectation. At last the minute-hand of the old-fashioned brazen-faced time-piece was on the last quarter to eight, and there was every reason for its being time to get ready for departure. Even Mrs Pomfret's preoccupied mind did not prevent her from noticing what looked like a new flush of beauty in the little thing as she tied on her hat before the looking-glass.

'That child gets prettier and prettier every day, I do believe,' was her inward comment. 'The more's the pity. She'll get neither a place nor a husband any the sooner for it. Sober well-to-do men don't like such pretty wives. When I was a girl, I was more admired than if I had been so very pretty. However, she's reason to be grateful to me for teaching her something to get her bread with, better than farmhouse work. They always told me I was

good-natured – and that's the truth, and to my hurt, too, else
there's them in this house that wouldn't be here now to lord it
over me in the housekeeper's room.'

Hetty walked hastily across the short space of pleasure-
ground which she had to traverse, dreading to meet Mr Craig,
to whom she could hardly have spoken civilly. How relieved
she was when she had got safely under the oaks and among the
fern of the Chase! Even then she was as ready to be startled as
the deer that leaped away at her approach. She thought nothing
of the evening light that lay gently in the grassy alleys between
the fern, and made the beauty of their living green more visible
than it had been in the overpowering flood of noon: she thought
of nothing that was present. She only saw something that was
possible: Mr Arthur Donnithorne coming to meet her again
along the Fir-tree Grove. That was the foreground of Hetty's
picture; behind it lay a bright hazy something – days that were
not to be as the other days of her life had been. It was as if she
had been wooed by a river-god, who might any time take her
to his wondrous halls below a watery heaven. There was no
knowing what would come, since this strange entrancing
delight had come. If a chest full of lace and satin and jewels
had been sent her from some unknown source,[1] how could she
but have thought that her whole lot was going to change, and
that tomorrow some still more bewildering joy would befall
her? Hetty had never read a novel; if she had ever seen one, I
think the words would have been too hard for her; how then
could she find a shape for her expectations? They were as
formless as the sweet languid odours of the garden at the Chase,
which had floated past her as she walked by the gate.

She is at another gate now – that leading into Fir-tree Grove.
She enters the wood, where it is already twilight, and at every
step she takes, the fear at her heart becomes colder. If he should
not come! Oh how dreary it was – the thought of going out at
the other end of the wood, into the unsheltered road, without
having seen him. She reaches the first turning towards the
Hermitage, walking slowly – he is not there. She hates the
leveret[2] that runs across the path: she hates everything that is
not what she longs for. She walks on, happy whenever she

is coming to a bend in the road, for perhaps he is behind it. No. She is beginning to cry: her heart has swelled so, the tears stand in her eyes; she gives one great sob, while the corners of her mouth quiver, and the tears roll down.

She doesn't know that there is another turning to the Hermitage, that she is close against it, and that Arthur Donnithorne is only a few yards from her, full of one thought, and a thought of which she only is the object. He is going to see Hetty again; that is the longing which has been growing through the last three hours to a feverish thirst. Not, of course, to speak in the caressing way into which he had unguardedly fallen before dinner, but to set things right with her by a kindness which would have the air of friendly civility, and prevent her from running away with wrong notions about their mutual relation.

If Hetty had known he was there, she would not have cried; and it would have been better, for then Arthur would perhaps have behaved as wisely as he had intended. As it was, she started when he appeared at the end of the side-alley, and looked up at him with two great drops rolling down her cheeks. What else could he do but speak to her in a soft, soothing tone, as if she were a bright-eyed spaniel with a thorn in her foot?

'Has something frightened you, Hetty? Have you seen anything in the wood? Don't be frightened – I'll take care of you now.'

Hetty was blushing so, she didn't know whether she was happy or miserable. To be crying again – what did gentlemen think of girls who cried in that way? She felt unable even to say 'no', but could only look away from him, and wipe the tears from her cheek. Not before a great drop had fallen on her rose-coloured strings; she knew that quite well.

'Come, be cheerful again. Smile at me, and tell me what's the matter. Come, tell me.'

Hetty turned her head towards him, whispered, 'I thought you wouldn't come,' and slowly got courage to lift her eyes to him. That look was too much: he must have had eyes of Egyptian granite not to look too lovingly in return.

'You little frightened bird! little tearful rose! silly pet! You won't cry again, now I'm with you, will you?'

Ah, he doesn't know in the least what he is saying. This is not what he meant to say. His arm is stealing round the waist again, it is tightening its clasp; he is bending his face nearer and nearer to the round cheek, his lips are meeting those pouting child-lips, and for a long moment time has vanished. He may be a shepherd in Arcadia for aught he knows, he may be the first youth kissing the first maiden, he may be Eros himself, sipping the lips of Psyche[3] – it is all one.

There was no speaking for minutes after. They walked along with beating hearts till they came within sight of the gate at the end of the wood. Then they looked at each other, not quite as they had looked before, for in their eyes there was the memory of a kiss.

But already something bitter had begun to mingle itself with the fountain of sweets: already Arthur was uncomfortable. He took his arm from Hetty's waist, and said –

'Here we are, almost at the end of the Grove. I wonder how late it is,' he added, pulling out his watch. 'Twenty minutes past eight – but my watch is too fast. However, I'd better not go any further now. Trot along quickly with your little feet, and get home safely. Good-bye.'

He took her hand, and looked at her half sadly, half with a constrained smile. Hetty's eyes seemed to beseech him not to go away yet; but he patted her cheek and said 'Good-bye' again. She was obliged to turn away from him, and go on.

As for Arthur, he rushed back through the wood, as if he wanted to put a wide space between himself and Hetty. He would not go to the Hermitage again; he remembered how he had debated with himself there before dinner, and it had all come to nothing – worse than nothing. He walked right on into the Chase, glad to get out of the Grove, which surely was haunted by his evil genius. Those beeches and smooth limes – there was something enervating in the very sight of them; but the strong knotted old oaks had no bending languor in them – the sight of them would give a man some energy. Arthur lost himself among the narrow openings in the fern, winding about without seeking any issue, till the twilight deepened almost to night under the great boughs, and the hare looked black as it darted across his path.

He was feeling much more strongly than he had done in the morning: it was as if his horse had wheeled round from a leap, and dared to dispute his mastery. He was dissatisfied with himself, irritated, mortified. He no sooner fixed his mind on the probable consequences of giving way to the emotions which had stolen over him to-day – of continuing to notice Hetty, of allowing himself any opportunity for such slight caresses as he had been betrayed into already – than he refused to believe such a future possible for himself. To flirt with Hetty was a very different affair from flirting with a pretty girl of his own station: that was understood to be an amusement on both sides; or, if it became serious, there was no obstacle to marriage. But this little thing would be spoken ill of directly, if she happened to be seen walking with him; and then those excellent people, the Poysers, to whom a good name was as precious as if they had the best blood in the land in their veins – he should hate himself if he made a scandal of that sort, on the estate that was to be his own some day, and among tenants by whom he liked, above all, to be respected. He could no more believe that he should so fall in his own esteem than that he should break both his legs and go on crutches all the rest of his life. He couldn't imagine himself in that position; it was too odious, too unlike him.

And even if no one knew anything about it, they might get too fond of each other, and then there could be nothing but the misery of parting, after all. No gentleman, out of a ballad, could marry a farmer's niece. There must be an end to the whole thing at once. It was too foolish.

And yet he had been so determined this morning, before he went to Gawaine's; and while he was there something had taken hold of him and made him gallop back. It seemed, he couldn't quite depend on his own resolution, as he had thought he could: he almost wished his arm would get painful again, and then he should think of nothing but the comfort it would be to get rid of the pain. There was no knowing what impulse might seize

him to-morrow, in this confounded place, where there was
nothing to occupy him imperiously through the live-long day.
What could he do to secure himself from any more of this folly?

There was but one resource. He would go and tell Irwine –
tell him everything. The mere act of telling it would make it
seem trivial; the temptation would vanish, as the charm of fond
words vanishes when one repeats them to the indifferent. In
every way it would help him, to tell Irwine. He would ride to
Broxton Rectory the first thing after breakfast to-morrow.

Arthur had no sooner come to this determination than he
began to think which of the paths would lead him home, and
made as short a walk thither as he could. He felt sure he should
sleep now: he had had enough to tire him, and there was no
more need for him to think.

CHAPTER XIV

The Return Home

While that parting in the wood was happening, there was a parting in the cottage too, and Lisbeth had stood with Adam at the door, straining her aged eyes to get the last glimpse of Seth and Dinah, as they mounted the opposite slope.

'Eh, I'm loath to see the last on her,' she said to Adam, as they turned into the house again. 'I'd ha' been willin' t' ha' her about me till I died and went to lie by my old man. She'd make it easier dyin' – she spakes so gentle an' moves about so still. I could be fast sure that pictur was drawed for her i' thy new Bible – th' angel a-sittin' on the big stone by the grave. Eh, I wouldna mind ha'in' a daughter like that; but nobody ne'er marries them as is good for aught.'

'Well, mother, I hope thee *wilt* have her for a daughter; for Seth's got a liking for her, and I hope she'll get a liking for Seth in time.'

'Where's th' use o' talkin' a-that'n? She caresna for Seth. She's goin' away twenty mile aff. How's she to get a likin' for him, I'd like to know? No more nor the cake 'ull come wi'out the leaven.[1] Thy figurin' books might ha' tould thee better nor that, I should think, else thee mightst as well read the commin print, as Seth allays does.'

'Nay, mother,' said Adam, laughing, 'the figures tell us a fine deal, and we couldn't go far without 'em, but they don't tell us about folk's feelings. It's a nicer job to calculate *them*. But Seth's as good-hearted a lad as ever handled a tool, and plenty o' sense, and good-looking too; and he's got the same way o' thinking as Dinah. He deserves to win her, though there's no denying she's a rare bit o' workmanship. You don't see such women turned off the wheel every day.'

'Eh, thee't allays stick up for thy brother. Thee'st been just the same, e'er sin' ye war little uns together. Thee wart allays for halving iverything wi' him. But what's Seth got to do with marryin', as is on'y three-an'-twenty? He'd more need to learn an' lay by sixpence. An' as for his desarving her – she's two 'ear older nor Seth: she's pretty near as old as thee. But that's the way; folks mun allays choose by contrairies, as if they must be sorted like the pork – a bit o' good meat wi' a bit o' offal.'

To the feminine mind in some of its moods, all things that might be, receive a temporary charm from comparison with what is; and since Adam did not want to marry Dinah himself, Lisbeth felt rather peevish on that score – as peevish as she would have been if he *had* wanted to marry her, and so shut himself out from Mary Burge and the partnership as effectually as by marrying Hetty.

It was more than half-past eight when Adam and his mother were talking in this way, so that when, about ten minutes later, Hetty reached the turning of the lane that led to the farmyard gate, she saw Dinah and Seth approaching it from the opposite direction, and waited for them to come up to her. They, too, like Hetty, had lingered a little in their walk, for Dinah was trying to speak words of comfort and strength to Seth in these parting moments. But when they saw Hetty, they paused and shook hands: Seth turned homewards, and Dinah came on alone.

'Seth Bede would have come and spoken to you, my dear,' she said, as she reached Hetty, 'but he's very full of trouble to-night.'

Hetty answered with a dimpled smile, as if she did not quite know what had been said; and it made a strange contrast to see that sparkling self-engrossed loveliness looked at by Dinah's calm pitying face, with its open glance which told that her heart lived in no cherished secrets of its own, but in feelings which it longed to share with all the world. Hetty liked Dinah as well as she had ever liked any woman; how was it possible to feel otherwise towards one who always put in a kind word for her when her aunt was finding fault, and who was always ready to take Totty off her hands – little tiresome Totty, that was made such a pet of by every one, and that Hetty could see no interest in at all? Dinah had never said anything disapproving or reproachful to Hetty during her whole visit to the Hall Farm; she had talked to her a great deal in a serious way, but Hetty didn't mind that much, for she never listened: whatever Dinah might say, she almost always stroked Hetty's cheek after it, and wanted to do some mending for her. Dinah was a riddle to her; Hetty looked at her much in the same way as one might imagine a little perching bird that could only flutter from bough to bough, to look at the swoop of the swallow or the mounting of the lark; but she did not care to solve such riddles, any more than she cared to know what was meant by the pictures in the 'Pilgrim's Progress',[2] or in the old folio Bible that Marty and Tommy always plagued her about on a Sunday.

Dinah took her hand now and drew it under her own arm.

'You look very happy to-night, dear child,' she said. 'I shall think of you often when I'm at Snowfield, and see your face before me as it is now. It's a strange thing – sometimes when I'm quite alone, sitting in my room with my eyes closed, or walking over the hills, the people I've seen and known, if it's only been for a few days, are brought before me, and I hear their voices and see them look and move almost plainer than I ever did when they were really with me so as I could touch them. And then my heart is drawn out towards them, and I feel their lot as if it was my own, and I take comfort in spreading it before the Lord and resting in His love, on their behalf as well as my own. And so I feel sure you will come before me.'

She paused a moment, but Hetty said nothing.

'It has been a very precious time to me,' Dinah went on, 'last night and to-day – seeing two such good sons as Adam and Seth Bede. They are so tender and thoughtful for their aged mother. And she has been telling me what Adam has done, for these many years, to help his father and his brother; it's wonderful what a spirit of wisdom and knowledge[3] he has, and how he's ready to use it all in behalf of them that are feeble. And I'm sure he has a loving spirit too. I've noticed it often among my own people around Snowfield, that the strong, skilful men are often the gentlest to the women and children; and it's pretty to see 'em carrying the little babies as if they were no heavier than little birds. And the babies always seem to like the strong arm best. I feel sure it would be so with Adam Bede. Don't you think so, Hetty?'

'Yes,' said Hetty, abstractedly, for her mind had been all the while in the wood, and she would have found it difficult to say what she was assenting to. Dinah saw she was not inclined to talk, but there would not have been time to say much more, for they were now at the yard-gate.

The still twilight, with its dying western red, and its few faint struggling stars, rested on the farmyard, where there was not a sound to be heard but the stamping of the cart-horses in the stable. It was about twenty minutes after sunset: the fowls were all gone to roost, and the bull-dog lay stretched on the straw outside his kennel, with the black-and-tan terrier by his side, when the falling-to of the gate disturbed them, and set them barking, like good officials, before they had any distinct knowledge of the reason.

The barking had its effect in the house, for, as Dinah and Hetty approached, the doorway was filled by a portly figure, with a ruddy black-eyed face, which bore in it the possibility of looking extremely acute, and occasionally contemptuous, on market-days, but had now a predominant after-supper expression of hearty good nature. It is well known that great scholars who have shown the most pitiless acerbity in their criticism of other men's scholarship, have yet been of a relenting and indulgent temper in private life; and I have heard of a learned man meekly rocking the twins in the cradle with his left hand, while with his right he inflicted the most lacerating sarcasms on an opponent who had betrayed a brutal ignorance of Hebrew. Weaknesses and errors must be forgiven – alas! they are not alien to us – but the man who takes the wrong side on the momentous subject of the Hebrew points[4] must be treated as the enemy of his race. There was the same sort of antithetic mixture in Martin Poyser: he was of so excellent a disposition that he had been kinder and more respectful than ever to his old father since he had made a deed of gift of all his property, and no man judged his neighbours more charitably on all personal matters; but for a farmer, like Luke Britton, for example, whose fallows were not well cleaned, who didn't know the rudiments of hedging and ditching, and showed but a small share of judgment in the purchase of winter stock, Martin Poyser was as hard and implacable as the north-east wind. Luke Britton could not make a remark, even on the weather, but Martin Poyser detected in it a taint of that unsoundness and general ignorance which was palpable in all his farming operations. He hated to see the fellow lift the pewter pint to his mouth in the bar of the Royal George on market-day, and the mere sight of him on the other side of the road brought a severe and critical expression into his black eyes, as different as possible from the fatherly glance he bent on his two nieces as they approached the door. Mr Poyser had smoked his evening pipe, and now held his hands in his pockets, as the only resource of a man who continues to sit up after the day's business is done.

'Why, lasses, ye're rather late to-night,' he said, when they reached the little gate leading into the causeway. 'The mother's begun to fidget about you, an' she's got the little un ill. An' how did you leave the old woman Bede, Dinah? Is she much down about the old man? He'd been but a poor bargain to her this five year.'

'She's been greatly distressed for the loss of him,' said Dinah; 'but she's seemed more comforted to-day. Her son Adam's been at home all day, working at his father's coffin, and she loves to have him at home. She's been talking about him to me almost all the day. She has a loving heart, though she's sorely given to fret and be fearful. I wish she had a surer trust to comfort her in her old age.'

'Adam's sure enough,' said Mr Poyser, misunderstanding Dinah's wish. 'There's no fear but he'll yield well i' the threshing. He's not one o' them as is all straw and no grain. I'll be bond for him any day, as he'll be a good son to the last. Did he say he'd be coming to see us soon? But come in, come in,' he added, making way for them; 'I hadn't need keep y' out any longer.'

The tall buildings round the yard shut out a good deal of the sky, but the large window let in abundant light to show every corner of the house-place.

Mrs Poyser, seated in the rocking-chair, which had been brought out of the 'right-hand parlour', was trying to soothe Totty to sleep. But Totty was not disposed to sleep; and when her cousins entered, she raised herself up, and showed a pair of flushed cheeks, which looked fatter than ever now they were defined by the edge of her linen night-cap.

In the large wicker-bottomed arm-chair in the left-hand chimney-nook sat old Martin Poyser, a hale but shrunken and bleached image of his portly black-haired son – his head hanging forward a little, and his elbows pushed backwards so as to allow the whole of his fore-arm to rest on the arm of the chair. His blue handkerchief was spread over his knees, as was usual indoors, when it was not hanging over his head; and he sat watching what went forward with the quiet *outward* glance of healthy old age, which, disengaged from any interest in an inward drama, spies out pins upon the floor, follows one's minutest motions with an unexpectant purposeless tenacity, watches the flickering of the flame or the sun-gleams on the wall, counts the quarries on the floor, watches even the hand of the clock, and pleases itself with detecting a rhythm in the tick.

'What a time o' night this is to come home, Hetty,' said Mrs Poyser. 'Look at the clock, do; why, it's going on for half-past nine, and I've sent the gells to bed this half-hour, and late enough too; when they've got to get up at half after four, and the mowers' bottles to fill, and the baking; and here's this blessed child wi' the fever for what I know, and as wakeful as if it was dinner-time, and nobody to help me to give her the physic but your uncle, and fine work there's been, and half of it spilt on her night-gown – it's well if she's swallowed more nor 'ull make her worse istead o' better. But folks as have no mind to be o' use have allays the luck to be out o' the road when there's anything to be done.'

'I did set out before eight, aunt,' said Hetty, in a pettish tone, with a slight toss of her head. 'But this clock's so much before the clock at the Chase, there's no telling what time it'll be when I get here.'

'What! you'd be wanting the clock set by gentle-folks's time, would you? an' sit up burnin' candle, an' lie a-bed wi' the sun a-bakin' you like a cowcumber[5] i' the frame? The clock hasn't been put forrard for the first time to-day, I reckon.'

The fact was, Hetty had really forgotten the difference of the clocks when she told Captain Donnithorne that she set out at eight, and this, with her lingering pace, had made her nearly half an hour later than usual. But here her aunt's attention was diverted from this tender subject by Totty, who, perceiving at length that the arrival of her cousins was not likely to bring anything satisfactory to her in particular, began to cry, 'Munny, munny', in an explosive manner.

'Well, then, my pet, mother's got her, mother won't leave her; Totty be a good dilling,[6] and go to sleep now,' said Mrs Poyser, leaning back and rocking the chair, while she tried to make Totty nestle against her. But Totty only cried louder, and said 'Don't yock!' So the mother, with that wondrous patience which love gives to the quickest temperament, sat up again, and pressed her cheek against the linen night-cap and kissed it, and forgot to scold Hetty any longer.

'Come, Hetty,' said Martin Poyser, in a conciliatory tone, 'go and get your supper i' the pantry, as the things are all put away; an' then you can come an' take the little un while your aunt undresses herself, for she won't lie down in bed without her mother. An' I reckon *you* could eat a bit, Dinah, for they don't keep much of a house down there.'

'No, thank you, uncle,' said Dinah; 'I ate a good meal before I came away, for Mrs Bede would make a kettle-cake[7] for me.'

'I don't want any supper,' said Hetty, taking off her hat. 'I can hold Totty now, if aunt wants me.'

'Why, what nonsense that is to talk!' said Mrs Poyser. 'Do you think you can live wi'out eatin', an' nourish your inside wi' stickin' red ribbons on your head? Go an' get your supper this minute, child; there's a nice bit o' cold pudding i' the safe[8] – just what you're fond of.'

Hetty complied silently by going towards the pantry, and Mrs Poyser went on speaking to Dinah.

'Sit down, my dear, an' look as if you knowed what it was to make yourself a bit comfortable i' the world. I warrant the old woman was glad to see you, since you stayed so long.'

'She seemed to like having me there at last; but her sons say she doesn't like young women about her commonly; and I thought just at first she was almost angry with me for going.'

'Eh, it's a poor look-out when th' ould foulks doesna like the young uns,' said old Martin, bending his head down lower, and seeming to trace the pattern of the quarries with his eye.

'Ay, it's ill livin' in a hen-roost for them as doesn't like fleas,' said Mrs Poyser. 'We've all had our turn at bein' young, I reckon, be't good luck or ill.'

'But she must learn to 'commodate herself to young women,' said Mr Poyser, 'for it isn't to be counted on as Adam and Seth 'ull keep bachelors for the next ten year to please their mother. That 'ud be unreasonable. It isn't right for old nor young nayther to make a bargain all o' their own side. What's good for one's good all round i' the long-run. I'm no friend to young fellows a-marrying afore they know the difference atween a crab⁹ an' a apple; but they may wait o'er long.'

'To be sure,' said Mrs Poyser; 'if you go past your dinner-time, there'll be little relish o' your meat. You turn it o'er an' o'er wi' your fork, an' don't eat it after all. You find faut wi' your meat, an' the faut's all i' your own stomach.'

Hetty now came back from the pantry, and said, 'I can take Totty now, aunt, if you like.'

'Come, Rachel,' said Mr Poyser, as his wife seemed to hesitate, seeing that Totty was at last nestling quietly, 'thee'dst better let Hetty carry her up-stairs, while thee tak'st thy things off. Thee't tired. It's time thee wast in bed. Thee't bring on the pain in thy side again.'

'Well, she may hold her if the child 'ull go to her,' said Mrs Poyser.

Hetty went close to the rocking-chair, and stood without her usual smile, and without any attempt to entice Totty, simply waiting for her aunt to give the child into her hands.

'Wilt go to cousin Hetty, my dilling, while mother gets ready
to go to bed? Then Totty shall go into mother's bed, and sleep
there all night.'

Before her mother had done speaking, Totty had given her
answer in an unmistakable manner, by knitting her brow, setting her tiny teeth against her under-lip, and leaning forward
to slap Hetty on the arm with her utmost force. Then, without
speaking, she nestled to her mother again.

'Hey, hey,' said Mr Poyser, while Hetty stood without
moving, 'not go to cousin Hetty? That's like a babby: Totty's
a little woman, an' not a babby.'

'It's no use trying to persuade her,' said Mrs Poyser. 'She
allays takes against Hetty when she isn't well. Happen she'll go
to Dinah.'

Dinah, having taken off her bonnet and shawl, had hitherto
kept quietly seated in the background, not liking to thrust
herself between Hetty and what was considered Hetty's proper
work. But now she came forward, and, putting out her arms,
said, 'Come, Totty, come and let Dinah carry her up-stairs
along with mother: poor, poor mother! she's so tired – she
wants to go to bed.'

Totty turned her face towards Dinah, and looked at her an
instant, then lifted herself up, put out her little arms, and let
Dinah lift her from her mother's lap. Hetty turned away without
any sign of ill-humour, and taking her hat from the table, stood
waiting with an air of indifference, to see if she should be told
to do anything else.

'You may make the door fast now, Poyser; Alick's been come
in this long while,' said Mrs Poyser, rising with an appearance
of relief from her low chair. 'Get me the matches down, Hetty,
for I must have the rushlight[10] burning i' my room. Come,
father.'

The heavy wooden bolts began to roll in the house doors,
and old Martin prepared to move, by gathering up his blue
handkerchief, and reaching his bright knobbed walnut-tree
stick from the corner. Mrs Poyser then led the way out of the
kitchen, followed by the grandfather, and Dinah with Totty in
her arms – all going to bed by twilight, like the birds. Mrs

Poyser, on her way, peeped into the room where her two boys lay, just to see their ruddy round cheeks on the pillow, and to hear for a moment their light regular breathing.

'Come, Hetty, get to bed,' said Mr Poyser, in a soothing tone, as he himself turned to go up-stairs. 'You didna mean to be late, I'll be bound, but your aunt's been worried to-day. Good-night, my wench, good-night.'

CHAPTER XV

The Two Bed-Chambers

Hetty and Dinah both slept in the second story, in rooms adjoining each other, meagrely-furnished rooms, with no blinds to shut out the light, which was now beginning to gather new strength from the rising of the moon – more than enough strength to enable Hetty to move about and undress with perfect comfort. She could see quite well the pegs in the old painted linen-press on which she hung her hat and gown; she could see the head of every pin on her red cloth pin-cushion; she could see a reflection of herself in the old-fashioned looking-glass, quite as distinct as was needful, considering that she had only to brush her hair and put on her night-cap. A queer old looking-glass! Hetty got into an ill-temper with it almost every time she dressed. It had been considered a handsome glass in its day, and had probably been bought into the Poyser family a quarter of a century before, at a sale of genteel household furniture. Even now an auctioneer could say something for it: it had a great deal of tarnished gilding about it; it had a firm mahogany base, well supplied with drawers, which opened with a decided jerk, and sent the contents leaping out from the farthest corners, without giving you the trouble of reaching them; above all, it had a brass candle-socket on each side, which would give it an aristocratic air to the very last. But Hetty objected to it because it had numerous dim blotches sprinkled over the mirror, which no rubbing would remove, and because, instead of swinging backwards and forwards, it was fixed in an upright position, so that she could only get one good view of her head and neck, and that was to be had only by sitting down on a low chair before her dressing-table. And the dressing-table was no dressing-table at all, but a small old chest of drawers, the most awkward thing in the world to sit down before, for the big brass handles quite hurt her knees, and she couldn't get near the glass at all comfortably. But devout worshippers never allow inconveniences to prevent them from performing their religious rites, and Hetty this evening was more bent on her peculiar form of worship than usual.

Having taken off her gown and white kerchief, she drew a key from the large pocket that hung outside her petticoat, and, unlocking one of the lower drawers in the chest, reached from it two short bits of wax candle – secretly bought at Treddleston – and stuck them in the two brass sockets. Then she drew forth a bundle of matches, and lighted the candles; and last of all, a small red-framed shilling looking-glass, without blotches. It was into this small glass that she chose to look first after seating herself. She looked into it, smiling, and turning her head on one side, for a minute, then laid it down and took out her brush and comb from an upper drawer. She was going to let down her hair, and make herself look like that picture of a lady in Miss Lydia Donnithorne's dressing-room. It was soon done, and the dark hyacinthine[1] curves fell on her neck. It was not heavy, massive, merely rippling hair, but soft and silken, running at every opportunity into delicate rings. But she pushed it all backward to look like the picture, and form a dark curtain, throwing into relief her round white neck. Then she put down her brush and comb, and looked at herself, folding her arms before her, still like the picture. Even the old mottled glass couldn't help sending back a lovely image, none the less lovely because Hetty's stays were not of white satin – such as I feel sure heroines must generally wear – but of a dark greenish cotton texture.

O yes! she was very pretty: Captain Donnithorne thought so. Prettier than anybody about Hayslope – prettier than any of the ladies she had ever seen visiting at the Chase – indeed it seemed fine ladies were rather old and ugly – and prettier than Miss Bacon, the miller's daughter, who was called the beauty of Treddleston. And Hetty looked at herself tonight with quite a different sensation from what she had ever felt before; there

was an invisible spectator whose eye rested on her like morning
on the flowers. His soft voice was saying over and over again
those pretty things she had heard in the wood; his arm was
round her, and the delicate rose-scent of his hair was with her
still. The vainest woman is never thoroughly conscious of her
own beauty till she is loved by the man who sets her own
passion vibrating in return.

But Hetty seemed to have made up her mind that something
was wanting, for she got up and reached an old black lace scarf
out of the linen-press, and a pair of large earrings out of the
sacred drawer from which she had taken her candles. It was an
old old scarf, full of rents, but it would make a becoming border
round her shoulders, and set off the whiteness of her upper
arm. And she would take out the little earrings she had in her
ears – oh, how her aunt had scolded her for having her ears
bored! – and put in those large ones: they were but coloured
glass and gilding; but if you didn't know what they were made
of, they looked just as well as what the ladies wore. And so she
sat down again, with the large earrings in her ears, and the
black lace scarf adjusted round her shoulders. She looked down
at her arms: no arms could be prettier down to a little way
below the elbow – they were white and plump, and dimpled to
match her cheeks; but towards the wrist, she thought with
vexation that they were coarsened by butter-making, and other
work that ladies never did.

Captain Donnithorne couldn't like her to go on doing work:
he would like to see her in nice clothes, and thin shoes and
white stockings, perhaps with silk clocks[2] to them; for he must
love her very much – no one else had ever put his arm round
her and kissed her in that way. He would want to marry her,
and make a lady of her; she could hardly dare to shape the
thought – yet how else could it be? Marry her quite secretly, as
Mr James, the Doctor's assistant, married the Doctor's niece,
and nobody ever found it out for a long while after, and then
it was of no use to be angry. The Doctor had told her aunt all
about it in Hetty's hearing. She didn't know how it would be,
but it was quite plain the old Squire could never be told anything
about it, for Hetty was ready to faint with awe and fright if she

came across him at the Chase. He might have been earth-born, for what she knew: it had never entered her mind that he had been young like other men; he had always been the old Squire at whom everybody was frightened. Oh, it was impossible to think how it would be! But Captain Donnithorne would know; he was a great gentleman, and could have his way in everything, and could buy everything he liked. And nothing could be as it had been again: perhaps some day she should be a grand lady, and ride in her coach, and dress for dinner in a brocaded silk, with feathers in her hair, and her dress sweeping the ground, like Miss Lydia and Lady Dacey, when she saw them going into the dining-room one evening, as she peeped through the little round window in the lobby; only she should not be old and ugly like Miss Lydia, or all the same thickness like Lady Dacey, but very pretty, with her hair done in a great many different ways, and sometimes in a pink dress, and sometimes in a white one – she didn't know which she liked best; and Mary Burge and everybody would perhaps see her going out in her carriage – or rather, they would *hear* of it: it was impossible to imagine these things happening at Hayslope in sight of her aunt. At the thought of all this splendour, Hetty got up from her chair, and in doing so caught the little red-framed glass with the edge of her scarf, so that it fell with a bang on the floor; but she was too eagerly occupied with her vision to care about picking it up; and after a momentary start, began to pace with a pigeon-like stateliness backwards and forwards along her room, in her coloured stays and coloured skirt, and the old black lace scarf round her shoulders, and the great glass earrings in her ears.

How pretty the little puss looks in that odd dress! It would be the easiest folly in the world to fall in love with her: there is such a sweet baby-like roundness about her face and figure; the delicate dark rings of hair lie so charmingly about her ears and neck; her great dark eyes with their long eyelashes touch one so strangely, as if an imprisoned frisky sprite looked out of them.

Ah, what a prize the man gets who wins a sweet bride like Hetty! How the men envy him who come to the wedding breakfast, and see her hanging on his arm in her white lace and orange blossoms. The dear, young, round, soft, flexible thing! Her heart must be just as soft, her temper just as free from angles, her character just as pliant. If anything ever goes wrong, it must be the husband's fault there: he can make her what he likes – that is plain. And the lover himself thinks so too: the little darling is so fond of him, her little vanities are so bewitching, he wouldn't consent to her being a bit wiser; those kitten-like glances and movements are just what one wants to make one's hearth a paradise. Every man under such circumstances is conscious of being a great physiognomist. Nature, he knows, has a language of her own, which she uses with strict veracity, and he considers himself an adept in the language. Nature has written out his bride's character for him in those exquisite lines of cheek and lip and chin, in those eyelids delicate as petals, in those long lashes curled like the stamen of a flower, in the dark liquid depths of those wonderful eyes. How she will dote on her children! She is almost a child herself, and the little pink round things will hang about her like florets round the central flower; and the husband will look on, smiling benignly, able, whenever he chooses, to withdraw into the sanctuary of his wisdom, towards which his sweet wife will look reverently, and never lift the curtain. It is a marriage such as they made in the golden age, when the men were all wise and majestic, and the women all lovely and loving.

It was very much in this way that our friend Adam Bede thought about Hetty; only he put his thoughts into different words. If ever she behaved with cold vanity towards him, he said to himself, it is only because she doesn't love me well enough; and he was sure that her love, whenever she gave it, would be the most precious thing a man could possess on earth. Before you despise Adam as deficient in penetration, pray ask yourself if you were ever predisposed to believe evil of any pretty woman – if you ever *could*, without hard head-breaking demonstration, believe evil of the *one* supremely pretty woman who has bewitched you. No: people who love downy peaches are apt not to think of the stone, and sometimes jar their teeth terribly against it.

Arthur Donnithorne, too, had the same sort of notion about

Hetty, so far as he had thought of her nature at all. He felt sure she was a dear, affectionate, good little thing. The man who awakes the wondering tremulous passion of a young girl always thinks her affectionate; and if he chances to look forward to future years, probably imagines himself being virtuously tender to her, because the poor thing is so clingingly fond of him. God made these dear women so – and it is a convenient arrangement in case of sickness.

After all, I believe the wisest of us must be beguiled in this way sometimes, and must think both better and worse of people than they deserve. Nature has her language, and she is not unveracious; but we don't know all the intricacies of her syntax just yet, and in a hasty reading we may happen to extract the very opposite of her real meaning. Long dark eyelashes, now: what can be more exquisite? I find it impossible not to expect some depth of soul behind a deep grey eye with a long dark eyelash, in spite of an experience which has shown me that they may go along with deceit, peculation,[3] and stupidity. But if, in the reaction of disgust, I have betaken myself to a fishy eye,[4] there has been a surprising similarity of result. One begins to suspect at length that there is no direct correlation between eyelashes and morals; or else, that the eyelashes express the disposition of the fair one's grandmother, which is on the whole less important to us.

No eyelashes could be more beautiful than Hetty's; and now, while she walks with her pigeon-like stateliness along the room and looks down on her shoulders bordered by the old black lace, the dark fringe shows to perfection on her pink cheek. They are but dim ill-defined pictures that her narrow bit of an imagination can make of the future; but of every picture she is the central figure in fine clothes; Captain Donnithorne is very close to her, putting his arm round her, perhaps kissing her, and everybody else is admiring and envying her – especially Mary Burge, whose new print dress looks very contemptible by the side of Hetty's resplendent toilette. Does any sweet or sad memory mingle with this dream of the future – any loving thought of her second parents – of the children she had helped to tend – of any youthful companion, any pet animal, any relic of her own childhood even? Not one. There are some plants that have hardly any roots: you may tear them from their native nook of rock or wall, and just lay them over your ornamental flower-pot, and they blossom none the worse. Hetty could have cast all her past life behind her, and never cared to be reminded of it again. I think she had no feeling at all towards the old house, and did not like the Jacob's Ladder[5] and the long row of hollyhocks in the garden better than other flowers – perhaps not so well. It was wonderful how little she seemed to care about waiting on her uncle, who had been a good father to her: she hardly ever remembered to reach him his pipe at the right time without being told, unless a visitor happened to be there, who would have a better opportunity of seeing her as she walked across the hearth. Hetty did not understand how any-body could be very fond of middle-aged people. And as for those tiresome children, Marty and Tommy and Totty, they had been the very nuisance of her life – as bad as buzzing insects that will come teasing you on a hot day when you want to be quiet. Marty, the eldest, was a baby when she first came to the farm, for the children born before him had died, and so Hetty had had them all three, one after the other, toddling by her side in the meadow, or playing about her on wet days in the half-empty rooms of the large old house. The boys were out of hand now, but Totty was still a day-long plague, worse than either of the others had been, because there was more fuss made about her. And there was no end to the making and mending of clothes. Hetty would have been glad to hear that she should never see a child again; they were worse than the nasty little lambs that the shepherd was always bringing in to be taken special care of in lambing time; for the lambs *were* got rid of sooner or later. As for the young chickens and turkeys, Hetty would have hated the very word 'hatching', if her aunt had not bribed her to attend to the young poultry by promising her the proceeds of one out of every brood. The round downy chicks peeping out from under their mother's wing never touched Hetty with any pleasure; that was not the sort of prettiness she cared about, but she did care about the prettiness of the new things she would buy for herself at Treddleston fair with the

money they fetched. And yet she looked so dimpled, so charming, as she stooped down to put the soaked bread under the
hencoop, that you must have been a very acute personage
indeed to suspect her of that hardness. Molly, the housemaid,
with a turn-up nose and a protuberant jaw, was really a tender-
hearted girl, and, as Mrs Poyser said, a jewel to look after the
poultry; but her stolid face showed nothing of this maternal
delight, any more than a brown earthenware pitcher will show
the light of the lamp within it.

It is generally a feminine eye that first detects the moral
deficiencies hidden under the 'dear deceit' of beauty: so it is not
surprising that Mrs Poyser, with her keenness and abundant
opportunity for observation, should have formed a tolerably
fair estimate of what might be expected from Hetty in the way
of feeling, and in moments of indignation she had sometimes
spoken with great openness on the subject to her husband.

'She's no better than a peacock, as 'ud strut about on the
wall, and spread its tail when the sun shone if all the folks i'
the parish was dying: there's nothing seems to give her a turn
i' th' inside, not even when we thought Totty had tumbled into
the pit. To think o' that dear cherub! And we found her wi' her
little shoes stuck i' the mud and crying fit to break her heart by
the far horse-pit. But Hetty niver minded it, I could see, though
she's been at the nussin' o' the child ever since it was a babby.
It's my belief her heart's as hard as a pebble.'

'Nay, nay,' said Mr Poyser, 'thee mustn't judge Hetty too
hard. Them young gells are like th' unripe grain; they'll make
good meal by-and-by, but they're squashy as yet. Thee't see
Hetty 'll be all right when she's got a good husband and children
of her own.'

'*I* don't want to be hard upo' the gell. She's got cliver fingers
of her own, and can be useful enough when she likes, and I
should miss her wi' the butter, for she's got a cool hand. An'
let be what may, I'd strive to do my part by a niece o' yours,
an' *that* I've done: for I've taught her everything as belongs to
a house, an' I've told her her duty often enough, though, God
knows, I've no breath to spare, an' that catchin' pain comes on
dreadful by times. Wi' them three gells in the house I'd need

have twice the strength, to keep 'em up to their work. It's like having roast-meat at three fires; as soon as you've basted one, another's burnin'.'

Hetty stood sufficiently in awe of her aunt to be anxious to conceal from her so much of her vanity as could be hidden without too great a sacrifice. She could not resist spending her money in bits of finery which Mrs Poyser disapproved; but she would have been ready to die with shame, vexation, and fright, if her aunt had this moment opened the door, and seen her with her bits of candle lighted, and strutting about decked in her scarf and earrings. To prevent such a surprise, she always bolted her door, and she had not forgotten to do so to-night. It was well: for there now came a light tap, and Hetty, with a leaping heart, rushed to blow out the candles and throw them into the drawer. She dared not stay to take out her earrings, but she threw off her scarf, and let it fall on the floor, before the light tap came again. We shall know how it was that the light tap came, if we leave Hetty for a short time, and return to Dinah, at the moment when she had delivered Totty to her mother's arms, and was come up-stairs to her bedroom, adjoining Hetty's.

Dinah delighted in her bedroom window. Being on the second story of that tall house, it gave her a wide view over the fields. The thickness of the wall formed a broad step about a yard below the window, where she could place her chair. And now the first thing she did, on entering her room, was to seat herself in this chair, and look out on the peaceful fields beyond which the large moon was rising, just above the hedgerow elms. She liked the pasture best where the milch cows[6] were lying, and next to that the meadow where the grass was half mown, and lay in silvered sweeping lines. Her heart was very full, for there was to be only one more night on which she would look out on those fields for a long time to come; but she thought little of leaving the mere scene, for, to her, bleak Snowfield had just as many charms: she thought of all the dear people whom she had learned to care for among these peaceful fields, and who would now have a place in her loving remembrance for ever. She thought of the struggles and the weariness that might lie before them in the rest of their life's journey, when she would be away

from them, and know nothing of what was befalling them; and
the pressure of this thought soon became too strong for her to
enjoy the unresponding stillness of the moonlit fields. She closed
her eyes, that she might feel more intensely the presence of a
Love and Sympathy deeper and more tender than was breathed
from the earth and sky. That was often Dinah's mode of praying
in solitude. Simply to close her eyes, and to feel herself enclosed
by the Divine Presence; then gradually her fears, her yearning
anxieties for others, melted away like ice-crystals in a warm
ocean. She had sat in this way perfectly still, with her hands
crossed on her lap, and the pale light resting on her calm face,
for at least ten minutes, when she was startled by a loud sound,
apparently of something falling in Hetty's room. But like all
sounds that fall on our ears in a state of abstraction, it had no
distinct character, but was simply loud and startling, so that
she felt uncertain whether she had interpreted it rightly. She
rose and listened, but all was quiet afterwards, and she reflected
that Hetty might merely have knocked something down in
getting into bed. She began slowly to undress; but now, owing
to the suggestions of this sound, her thought became concentrated on Hetty: that sweet young thing, with life and all its
trials before her – the solemn daily duties of the wife and mother
– and her mind so unprepared for them all; bent merely on little
foolish, selfish pleasures, like a child hugging its toys in the
beginning of a long toilsome journey, in which it will have to
bear hunger and cold and unsheltered darkness. Dinah felt a
double care for Hetty, because she shared Seth's anxious interest in his brother's lot, and she had not come to the conclusion
that Hetty did not love Adam well enough to marry him. She
saw too clearly the absence of any warm, self-devoting love in
Hetty's nature, to regard the coldness of her behaviour towards
Adam as any indication that he was not the man she would like
to have for a husband. And this blank in Hetty's nature, instead
of exciting Dinah's dislike, only touched her with a deeper pity:
the lovely face and form affected her as beauty always affects a
pure and tender mind, free from selfish jealousies: it was an
excellent divine gift, that gave a deeper pathos to the need, the
sin, the sorrow with which it was mingled, as the canker in a

lily-white bud is more grievous to behold than in a common pot-herb.

By the time Dinah had undressed and put on her night-gown, this feeling about Hetty had gathered a painful intensity; her imagination had created a thorny thicket of sin and sorrow, in which she saw the poor thing struggling torn and bleeding, looking with tears for rescue and finding none. It was in this way that Dinah's imagination and sympathy acted and reacted habitually, each heightening the other. She felt a deep longing to go now and pour into Hetty's ear all the words of tender warning and appeal that rushed into her mind. But perhaps Hetty was already asleep. Dinah put her ear to the partition, and heard still some slight noises, which convinced her that Hetty was not yet in bed. Still she hesitated; she was not quite certain of a divine direction; the voice that told her to go to Hetty seemed no stronger than the other voice which said that Hetty was weary, and that going to her now in an unseasonable moment would only tend to close her heart more obstinately. Dinah was not satisfied without a more unmistakable guidance than those inward voices. There was light enough for her, if she opened her Bible, to discern the text sufficiently to know what it would say to her. She knew the physiognomy of every page, and could tell on what book she opened, sometimes on what chapter, without seeing title or number. It was a small thick Bible, worn quite round at the edges. Dinah laid it sideways on the window ledge, where the light was strongest, and then opened it with her forefinger. The first words she looked at were those at the top of the left-hand page: 'And they all wept sore, and fell on Paul's neck and kissed him.' That was enough for Dinah; she had opened on that memorable parting at Ephesus, when Paul had felt bound to open his heart in a last exhortation and warning.[7] She hesitated no longer, but, opening her own door gently, went and tapped at Hetty's. We know she had to tap twice, because Hetty had to put out her candles and throw off her black lace scarf; but after the second tap the door was opened immediately. Dinah said, 'Will you let me come in, Hetty?' and Hetty, without speaking, for she was confused and vexed, opened the door wider and let her in.

What a strange contrast the two figures made! Visible enough in that mingled twilight and moonlight. Hetty, her cheeks flushed and her eyes glistening from her imaginary drama, her beautiful neck and arms bare, her hair hanging in a curly tangle down her back, and the baubles in her ears. Dinah, covered with her long white dress, her pale face full of subdued emotion, almost like a lovely corpse into which the soul has returned charged with sublimer secrets and a sublimer love. They were nearly of the same height; Dinah evidently a little the taller as she put her arm round Hetty's waist, and kissed her forehead.

'I knew you were not in bed, my dear,' she said, in her sweet clear voice, which was irritating to Hetty, mingling with her own peevish vexation like music with jangling chains, 'for I heard you moving; and I longed to speak to you again to-night, for it is the last but one that I shall be here, and we don't know what may happen to-morrow to keep us apart. Shall I sit down with you while you do up your hair?'

'Oh yes,' said Hetty, hastily turning round and reaching the second chair in the room, glad that Dinah looked as if she did not notice her earrings.

Dinah sat down, and Hetty began to brush together her hair before twisting it up, doing it with that air of excessive indifference which belongs to confused self-consciousness. But the expression of Dinah's eyes gradually relieved her; they seemed unobservant of all details.

'Dear Hetty,' she said, 'it has been borne in upon my mind to-night that you may some day be in trouble – trouble is appointed for us all here below,[8] and there comes a time when we need more comfort and help than the things of this life[9] can give. I want to tell you that if ever you are in trouble, and need a friend that will always feel for you and love you, you have got that friend in Dinah Morris at Snowfield; and if you come to her, or send for her, she'll never forget this night and the words she is speaking to you now. Will you remember it, Hetty?'

'Yes,' said Hetty, rather frightened. 'But why should you think I shall be in trouble? Do you know of anything?'

Hetty had seated herself as she tied on her cap, and now

Dinah leaned forwards and took her hands as she answered –

'Because, dear, trouble comes to us all in this life: we set our hearts on things which it isn't God's will for us to have,[10] and then we go sorrowing; the people we love are taken from us, and we can joy in nothing because they are not with us; sickness comes, and we faint under the burden of our feeble bodies; we go astray and do wrong, and bring ourselves into trouble with our fellow-men. There is no man or woman born into this world to whom some of these trials do not fall, and so I feel that some of them must happen to you; and I desire for you, that while you are young you should seek for strength from your Heavenly Father, that you may have a support which will not fail you in the evil day.'[11]

Dinah paused and released Hetty's hands, that she might not hinder her. Hetty sat quite still; she felt no response within herself to Dinah's anxious affection; but Dinah's words, uttered with solemn pathetic distinctness, affected her with a chill fear. Her flush had died away almost to paleness; she had the timidity of a luxurious pleasure-seeking nature, which shrinks from the hint of pain. Dinah saw the effect, and her tender anxious pleading became the more earnest, till Hetty, full of a vague fear that something evil was some time to befall her, began to cry.

It is our habit to say that while the lower nature can never understand the higher, the higher nature commands a complete view of the lower. But I think the higher nature has to learn this comprehension, as we learn the art of vision, by a good deal of hard experience, often with bruises and gashes incurred in taking things up by the wrong end, and fancying our space wider than it is. Dinah had never seen Hetty affected in this way before, and, with her usual benignant hopefulness, she trusted it was the stirring of a divine impulse. She kissed the sobbing thing, and began to cry with her for grateful joy. But Hetty was simply in that excitable state of mind in which there is no calculating what turn the feelings may take from one moment to another, and for the first time she became irritated under Dinah's caress. She pushed her away impatiently, and said, with a childish sobbing voice –

'Don't talk to me so, Dinah. Why do you come to frighten me? I've never done anything to you. Why can't you let me be?'

Poor Dinah felt a pang. She was too wise to persist, and only said mildly, 'Yes, my dear, you're tired; I won't hinder you any longer. Make haste and get into bed. Good-night.'

She went out of the room almost as quietly and quickly as if she had been a ghost; but once by the side of her own bed, she threw herself on her knees, and poured out in deep silence all the passionate pity that filled her heart.

As for Hetty, she was soon in the wood again – her waking dreams being merged in a sleeping life scarcely more fragmentary and confused.

CHAPTER XVI

Links

Arthur Donnithorne, you remember, is under an engagement with himself to go and see Mr Irwine this Friday morning, and he is awake and dressing so early, that he determines to go before breakfast, instead of after. The Rector, he knows, breakfasts alone at half-past nine, the ladies of the family having a different breakfast-hour; Arthur will have an early ride over the hill and breakfast with him. One can say everything best over a meal.

The progress of civilization has made a breakfast or a dinner an easy and cheerful substitute for more troublesome and disagreeable ceremonies. We take a less gloomy view of our errors now our father confessor listens to us over his egg and coffee. We are more distinctly conscious that rude penances are out of the question for gentlemen in an enlightened age, and that mortal sin is not incompatible with an appetite for muffins. An assault on our pockets, which in more barbarous times would have been made in the brusque form of a pistol-shot, is quite a well-bred and smiling procedure now it has become a request for a loan thrown in as an easy parenthesis between the second and third glasses of claret.

Still, there was this advantage in the old rigid forms, that they committed you to the fulfilment of a resolution by some outward deed: when you have put your mouth to one end of a hole in a stone wall, and are aware that there is an expectant ear at the other end,[1] you are more likely to say what you came out with the intention of saying, than if you were seated with your legs in an easy attitude under the mahogany, with a companion who will have no reason to be surprised if you have nothing particular to say.

However, Arthur Donnithorne, as he winds among the pleasant lanes on horseback in the morning sunshine, has a sincere determination to open his heart to the Rector, and the swirling sound of the scythe as he passes by the meadow is all the pleasanter to him because of this honest purpose. He is glad to see the promise of settled weather now, for getting in the hay, about which the farmers have been fearful; and there is something so healthful in the sharing of a joy that is general and not merely personal, that this thought about the hay-harvest reacts on his state of mind, and makes his resolution seem an easier matter. A man about town might perhaps consider that these influences were not to be felt out of a child's storybook; but when you are among the fields and hedgerows, it is impossible to maintain a consistent superiority to simple natural pleasures.

Arthur had passed the village of Hayslope, and was approaching the Broxton side of the hill, when, at a turning in the road, he saw a figure about a hundred yards before him which it was impossible to mistake for any one else than Adam Bede, even if there had been no grey, tailless shepherd-dog at his heels. He was striding along at his usual rapid pace; and Arthur pushed on his horse to overtake him, for he retained too much of his boyish feeling for Adam to miss an opportunity of chatting with him. I will not say that his love for that good fellow did not owe some of its force to the love of patronage: our friend Arthur liked to do everything that was handsome, and to have his handsome deeds recognized.

Adam looked round as he heard the quickening clatter of the horse's heels, and waited for the horseman, lifting his paper cap from his head with a bright smile of recognition. Next to his own brother Seth, Adam would have done more for Arthur Donnithorne than for any other young man in the world. There was hardly anything he would not rather have lost than the two-feet ruler which he always carried in his pocket; it was Arthur's present, bought with his pocket-money when he was a fair-haired lad of eleven, and when he had profited so well by Adam's lessons in carpentering and turning, as to embarrass

every female in the house with gifts of superfluous thread-reels
and round boxes. Adam had quite a pride in the little squire in
those early days, and the feeling had only become slightly modified as the fair-haired lad had grown into the whiskered young
man. Adam, I confess, was very susceptible to the influence of
rank, and quite ready to give an extra amount of respect to
every one who had more advantages than himself, not being a
philosopher, or a proletaire with democratic ideas,[2] but simply
a stout-limbed clever carpenter with a large fund of reverence
in his nature, which inclined him to admit all established claims
unless he saw very clear grounds for questioning them. He had
no theories about setting the world to rights, but he saw there
was a great deal of damage done by building with ill-seasoned
timber – by ignorant men in fine clothes making plans for
outhouses and workshops and the like, without knowing the
bearings of things – by slovenly joiners' work, and by hasty
contracts that could never be fulfilled without ruining somebody; and he resolved, for his part, to set his face against such
doings. On these points he would have maintained his opinion
against the largest landed proprietor in Loamshire or Stonyshire
either; but he felt that beyond these it would be better for him
to defer to people who were more knowing than himself. He
saw as plainly as possible how ill the woods on the estate were
managed, and the shameful state of the farm-buildings; and
if old Squire Donnithorne had asked him the effect of this
mismanagement, he would have spoken his opinion without
flinching, but the impulse to a respectful demeanour towards a
'gentleman' would have been strong within him all the while.
The word 'gentleman' had a spell for Adam, and, as he often
said, he 'couldn't abide a fellow who thought he made himself
fine by being coxy to's betters'. I must remind you again that
Adam had the blood of the peasant in his veins, and that since
he was in his prime half a century ago, you must expect some
of his characteristics to be obsolete.

Towards the young squire this instinctive reverence of
Adam's was assisted by boyish memories and personal regard;
so you may imagine that he thought far more of Arthur's good
qualities, and attached far more value to very slight actions of

his, than if they had been the qualities and actions of a common workman like himself. He felt sure it would be a fine day for everybody about Hayslope when the young squire came into the estate – such a generous open-hearted disposition as he had, and an 'uncommon' notion about improvements and repairs, considering he was only just coming of age. Thus there was both respect and affection in the smile with which he raised his paper cap as Arthur Donnithorne rode up.

'Well, Adam, how are you?' said Arthur, holding out his hand. He never shook hands with any of the farmers, and Adam felt the honour keenly. 'I could swear to your back a long way off. It's just the same back, only broader, as when you used to carry me on it. Do you remember?'

'Ay, sir, I remember. It 'ud be a poor look-out if folks didn't remember what they did and said when they were lads. We should think no more about old friends than we do about new uns, then.'

'You're going to Broxton, I suppose?' said Arthur, putting his horse on at a slow pace while Adam walked by his side. 'Are you going to the Rectory?'

'No, sir, I'm going to see about Bradwell's barn. They're afraid of the roof pushing the walls out; and I'm going to see what can be done with it before we send the stuff and the workmen.'

'Why, Burge trusts almost everything to you now, Adam, doesn't he? I should think he will make you his partner soon. He will, if he's wise.'

'Nay, sir, I don't see as he'd be much the better off for that. A foreman, if he's got a conscience, and delights in his work, will do his business as well as if he was a partner. I wouldn't give a penny for a man as 'ud drive a nail in slack because he didn't get extra pay for it.'

'I know that, Adam; I know you work for him as well as if you were working for yourself. But you would have more power than you have now, and could turn the business to better account perhaps. The old man must give up his business some time, and he has no son; I suppose he'll want a son-in-law who can take to it. But he has rather grasping fingers of his own, I fancy: I daresay he wants a man who can put some money into the business. If I were not as poor as a rat, I would gladly invest some money in that way, for the sake of having you settled on the estate. I'm sure I should profit by it in the end. And perhaps I shall be better off in a year or two. I shall have a larger allowance now I'm of age; and when I've paid off a debt or two, I shall be able to look about me.'

'You're very good to say so, sir, and I'm not unthankful. But' – Adam continued, in a decided tone – 'I shouldn't like to make any offers to Mr Burge, or t' have any made for me. I see no clear road to a partnership. If he should ever want to dispose of the business, that 'ud be a different matter. I should be glad of some money at a fair interest then, for I feel sure I could pay it off in time.'

'Very well, Adam,' said Arthur, remembering what Mr Irwine had said about a probable hitch in the love-making between Adam and Mary Burge, 'we'll say no more about it at present. When is your father to be buried?'

'On Sunday, sir; Mr Irwine's coming earlier on purpose. I shall be glad when it's over, for I think my mother 'ull perhaps get easier then. It cuts one sadly to see the grief of old people; they've no way o' working it off; and the new spring brings no new shoots out on the withered tree.'

'Ah, you've had a good deal of trouble and vexation in your life, Adam. I don't think you've ever been harebrained and light-hearted, like other youngsters. You've always had some care on your mind.'

'Why, yes, sir; but that's nothing to make a fuss about. If we're men, and have men's feelings, I reckon we must have men's troubles. We can't be like the birds, as fly from their nest as soon as they've got their wings, and never know their kin when they see 'em, and get a fresh lot every year. I've had enough to be thankful for: I've allays had health and strength and brains to give me a delight in my work; and I count it a great thing as I've had Bartle Massey's night-school to go to. He's helped me to knowledge I could never ha' got by myself.'

'What a rare fellow you are, Adam!' said Arthur, after a pause, in which he had looked musingly at the big fellow walking by his side. 'I could hit out better than most men at

Oxford, and yet I believe you would knock me into next week if I were to have a battle with you.'

'God forbid I should ever do that, sir,' said Adam, looking round at Arthur, and smiling. 'I used to fight for fun; but I've never done that since I was the cause o' poor Gil Tranter being laid up for a fortnight. I'll never fight any man again, only when he behaves like a scoundrel. If you get hold of a chap that's got no shame nor conscience to stop him, you must try what you can do by bunging his eyes up.'

Arthur did not laugh, for he was preoccupied with some thought that made him say presently –

'I should think now, Adam, you never have any struggles within yourself. I fancy you would master a wish that you had made up your mind it was not quite right to indulge, as easily as you would knock down a drunken fellow who was quarrelsome with you. I mean, you are never shilly-shally, first making up your mind that you won't do a thing, and then doing it after all?'

'Well,' said Adam, slowly, after a moment's hesitation – 'no. I don't remember ever being see-saw in that way, when I'd made my mind up, as you say, that a thing was wrong. It takes the taste out o' my mouth for things, when I know I should have a heavy conscience after 'em. I've seen pretty clear, ever since I could cast up a sum, as you can never do what's wrong without breeding sin and trouble more than you can ever see. It's like a bit o' bad workmanship – you never see th' end o' the mischief it'll do. And it's a poor look-out to come into the world to make your fellow-creatures worse off instead o' better. But there's a difference between the things folks call wrong. I'm not for making a sin of every little fool's trick, or bit o' nonsense anybody may be let into, like some o' them dissenters. And a man may have two minds whether it isn't worth while to get a bruise or two for the sake of a bit o' fun. But it isn't my way to be see-saw about anything: I think my fault lies th' other way. When I've said a thing, if it's only to myself, it's hard for me to go back.'

'Yes, that's just what I expected of you,' said Arthur. 'You've got an iron will, as well as an iron arm. But however strong a man's resolution may be, it costs him something to carry it out, now and then. We may determine not to gather any cherries, and keep our hands sturdily in our pockets, but we can't prevent our mouths from watering.'

'That's true, sir; but there's nothing like settling with ourselves as there's a deal we must do without i' this life. It's no use looking on life as if it was Treddles'on fair, where folks only go to see shows and get fairings.³ If we do, we shall find it different. But where's the use o' me talking to you, sir? You know better than I do.'

'I'm not so sure of that, Adam. You've had four or five years of experience more than I've had, and I think your life has been a better school to you than college has been to me.'

'Why, sir, you seem to think o' college something like what Bartle Massey does. He says college mostly makes people like bladders – just good for nothing but t' hold the stuff as is poured into 'em. But he's got a tongue like a sharp blade, Bartle has: it never touches anything but it cuts. Here's the turning, sir. I must bid you good-morning, as you're going to the Rectory.'

'Good-bye, Adam, good-bye.'

Arthur gave his horse to the groom at the Rectory gate, and walked along the gravel towards the door which opened on the garden. He knew that the Rector always breakfasted in his study, and the study lay on the left hand of this door, opposite the dining-room. It was a small low room, belonging to the old part of the house – dark with the sombre covers of the books that lined the walls; yet it looked very cheery this morning as Arthur reached the open window. For the morning sun fell aslant on the great glass globe with gold fish in it, which stood on a scagliola pillar⁴ in front of the ready-spread bachelor breakfast-table, and by the side of this breakfast-table was a group which would have made any room enticing. In the crimson damask easy-chair sat Mr Irwine, with that radiant freshness which he always had when he came from his morning toilet; his finely-formed plump white hand was playing along Juno's brown curly back; and close to Juno's tail, which was wagging with calm matronly pleasure, the two brown pups were rolling over each other in an ecstatic duet of worrying noises. On a cushion a little removed sat Pug, with the air of a maiden lady, who looked on these familiarities as animal weaknesses, which she made as little show as possible of observ-ing. On the table, at Mr Irwine's elbow, lay the first volume of the Foulis Æschylus,[5] which Arthur knew well by sight; and the silver coffee-pot, which Carroll was bringing in, sent forth a fragrant steam which completed the delights of a bachelor breakfast.

'Hallo, Arthur, that's a good fellow! You're just in time,' said Mr Irwine, as Arthur paused and stepped in over the low window-sill. 'Carroll, we shall want more coffee and eggs, and haven't you got some cold fowl for us to eat with that ham? Why, this is like old days, Arthur; you haven't been to breakfast with me these five years.'

'It was a tempting morning for a ride before breakfast,' said Arthur; 'and I used to like breakfasting with you so when I was reading with you. My grandfather is always a few degrees colder at breakfast than at any other hour in the day. I think his morning bath doesn't agree with him.'

Arthur was anxious not to imply that he came with any special purpose. He had no sooner found himself in Mr Irwine's presence than the confidence which he had thought quite easy before, suddenly appeared the most difficult thing in the world to him, and at the very moment of shaking hands he saw his purpose in quite a new light. How could he make Irwine understand his position unless he told him those little scenes in the wood; and how could he tell them without looking like a fool? And then his weakness in coming back from Gawaine's, and doing the very opposite of what he intended! Irwine would think him a shilly-shally fellow ever after. However, it must come out in an unpremeditated way; the conversation might lead up to it.

'I like breakfast-time better than any other moment in the day,' said Mr Irwine. 'No dust has settled on one's mind then, and it presents a clear mirror to the rays of things. I always have a favourite book by me at breakfast, and I enjoy the bits I pick up then so much, that regularly every morning it seems to me as if I should certainly become studious again. But pres-

ently Dent brings up a poor fellow who has killed a hare, and
when I've got through my "justicing", as Carroll calls it, I'm
inclined for a ride round the glebe,[6] and on my way back I meet
with the master of the workhouse, who has got a long story of
a mutinous pauper to tell me; and so the day goes on, and I'm
always the same lazy fellow before evening sets in. Besides, one
wants the stimulus of sympathy, and I have never had that since
poor D'Oyley left Treddleston. If you had stuck to your books
well, you rascal, I should have had a pleasanter prospect before
me. But scholarship doesn't run in your family blood.'

'No indeed. It's well if I can remember a little inapplicable
Latin to adorn my maiden speech in Parliament six or seven
years hence. "Cras ingens iterabimus aequor",[7] and a few shreds
of that sort, will perhaps stick to me, and I shall arrange my
opinions so as to introduce them. But I don't think a knowledge
of the classics is a pressing want to a country gentleman; as far
as I can see, he'd much better have a knowledge of manures.
I've been reading your friend Arthur Young's books[8] lately, and
there's nothing I should like better than to carry out some of
his ideas in putting the farmers on a better management of their
land; and, as he says, making what was a wild country, all of
the same dark hue, bright and variegated with corn and cattle.
My grandfather will never let me have any power while he lives;
but there's nothing I should like better than to undertake the
Stonyshire side of the estate – it's in a dismal condition – and
set improvements on foot, and gallop about from one place
to another and overlook them. I should like to know all the
labourers, and see them touching their hats to me with a look
of goodwill.'

'Bravo, Arthur! a man who has no feeling for the classics
couldn't make a better apology for coming into the world than
by increasing the quantity of food to maintain scholars – and
rectors who appreciate scholars. And whenever you enter on
your career of model landlord may I be there to see. You'll
want a portly rector to complete the picture, and take his tithe[9]
of all the respect and honour you get by your hard work. Only
don't set your heart too strongly on the goodwill you are to get
in consequence. I'm not sure that men are the fondest of those

who try to be useful to them. You know Gawaine has got
the curses of the whole neighbourhood upon him about that
enclosure. You must make it quite clear to your mind which
you are most bent upon, old boy – popularity or usefulness –
else you may happen to miss both.'

'Oh! Gawaine is harsh in his manners; he doesn't make himself personally agreeable to his tenants. I don't believe there's
anything you can't prevail on people to do with kindness. For
my part, I couldn't live in a neighbourhood where I was not
respected and beloved; and it's very pleasant to go among the
tenants here, they seem all so well inclined to me. I suppose it
seems only the other day to them since I was a little lad, riding
on a pony about as big as a sheep. And if fair allowances
were made to them, and their buildings attended to, one could
persuade them to farm on a better plan, stupid as they are.'

'Then mind you fall in love in the right place, and don't get
a wife who will drain your purse and make you niggardly in
spite of yourself. My mother and I have a little discussion about
you sometimes: she says, "I'll never risk a single prophecy on
Arthur until I see the woman he falls in love with." She thinks
your lady-love will rule you as the moon rules the tides. But I
feel bound to stand up for you, as my pupil, you know; and
I maintain that you're not of that watery quality. So mind you
don't disgrace my judgment.'

Arthur winced under this speech, for keen old Mrs Irwine's
opinion about him had the disagreeable effect of a sinister
omen. This, to be sure, was only another reason for persevering
in his intention, and getting an additional security against himself. Nevertheless, at this point in the conversation, he was
conscious of increased disinclination to tell his story about
Hetty. He was of an impressible nature, and lived a great deal
in other people's opinions and feelings concerning himself; and
the mere fact that he was in the presence of an intimate friend,
who had not the slightest notion that he had had any such
serious internal struggle as he came to confide, rather shook his
own belief in the seriousness of the struggle. It was not, after
all, a thing to make a fuss about; and what could Irwine do for
him that he could not do for himself? He would go to Eagledale

in spite of Meg's lameness – go on Rattler, and let Pym follow as well as he could on the old hack. That was his thought as he sugared his coffee; but the next minute, as he was lifting the cup to his lips, he remembered how thoroughly he had made up his mind last night to tell Irwine. No! he would not be vacillating again – he *would* do what he had meant to do, this time. So it would be well not to let the personal tone of the conversation altogether drop. If they went to quite indifferent topics, his difficulty would be heightened. It had required no noticeable pause for this rush and rebound of feeling, before he answered –

'But I think it is hardly an argument against a man's general strength of character, that he should be apt to be mastered by love. A fine constitution doesn't insure one against small-pox or any other of those inevitable diseases. A man may be very firm in other matters, and yet be under a sort of witchery from a woman.'

'Yes; but there's this difference between love and small-pox, or bewitchment either – that if you detect the disease at an early stage and try change of air, there is every chance of complete escape without any further development of symptoms. And there are certain alterative doses which a man may administer to himself by keeping unpleasant consequences before his mind: this gives you a sort of smoked glass through which you may look at the resplendent fair one and discern her true outline; though I'm afraid, by the by, the smoked glass is apt to be missing just at the moment it is most wanted. I daresay, now, even a man fortified with a knowledge of the classics might be lured into an imprudent marriage, in spite of the warning given him by the chorus in the Prometheus.'[10]

The smile that flitted across Arthur's face was a faint one, and instead of following Mr Irwine's playful lead, he said, quite seriously – 'Yes, that's the worst of it. It's a desperately vexatious thing, that after all one's reflections and quiet determinations, we should be ruled by moods that one can't calculate on beforehand. I don't think a man ought to be blamed so much if he is betrayed into doing things in that way, in spite of his resolutions.'

'Ah, but the moods lie in his nature, my boy, just as much as his reflections did, and more. A man can never do anything at variance with his own nature. He carries within him the germ of his most exceptional action; and if we wise people make eminent fools of ourselves on any particular occasion, we must endure the legitimate conclusion that we carry a few grains of folly to our ounce of wisdom.'

'Well, but one may be betrayed into doing things by a combination of circumstances, which one might never have done otherwise.'

'Why, yes, a man can't very well steal a bank-note unless the bank-note lies within convenient reach; but he won't make us think him an honest man because he begins to howl at the bank-note for falling in his way.'

'But surely you don't think a man who struggles against a temptation into which he falls at last, as bad as the man who never struggles at all?'

'No, certainly; I pity him in proportion to his struggles, for they foreshadow the inward suffering which is the worst form of Nemesis.[11] Consequences are unpitying. Our deeds carry their terrible consequences, quite apart from any fluctuations that went before – consequences that are hardly ever confined to ourselves. And it is best to fix our minds on that certainty, instead of considering what may be the elements of excuse for us. But I never knew you so inclined for moral discussion, Arthur? Is it some danger of your own that you are considering in this philosophical, general way?'

In asking this question, Mr Irwine pushed his plate away, threw himself back in his chair, and looked straight at Arthur. He really suspected that Arthur wanted to tell him something, and thought of smoothing the way for him by this direct question. But he was mistaken. Brought suddenly and involuntarily to the brink of confession, Arthur shrank back, and felt less disposed towards it than ever. The conversation had taken a more serious tone than he had intended – it would quite mislead Irwine – he would imagine there was a deep passion for Hetty, while there was no such thing. He was conscious of colouring, and was annoyed at his boyishness.

'Oh no, no danger,' he said as indifferently as he could. 'I don't know that I am more liable to irresolution than other people; only there are little incidents now and then that set one speculating on what might happen in the future.'

Was there a motive at work under this strange reluctance of Arthur's which had a sort of backstairs influence, not admitted to himself? Our mental business is carried on much in the same way as the business of the State: a great deal of hard work is done by agents who are not acknowledged. In a piece of machinery, too, I believe there is often a small unnoticeable wheel which has a great deal to do with the motion of the large obvious ones. Possibly there was some such unrecognized agent secretly busy in Arthur's mind at this moment – possibly it was the fear lest he might hereafter find the fact of having made a confession to the Rector a serious annoyance, in case he should *not* be able quite to carry out his good resolutions? I dare not assert that it was not so. The human soul is a very complex thing.

The idea of Hetty had just crossed Mr Irwine's mind as he looked inquiringly at Arthur, but his disclaiming, indifferent answer confirmed the thought which had quickly followed – that there could be nothing serious in that direction. There was no probability that Arthur ever saw her except at church, and at her own home under the eye of Mrs Poyser; and the hint he had given Arthur about her the other day had no more serious meaning than to prevent him from noticing her so as to rouse the little chit's vanity, and in this way perturb the rustic drama of her life. Arthur would soon join his regiment, and be far away: no, there could be no danger in that quarter, even if Arthur's character had not been a strong security against it. His honest, patronizing pride in the goodwill and respect of everybody about him was a safeguard even against foolish romance, still more against a lower kind of folly. If there had been anything special on Arthur's mind in the previous conversation, it was clear he was not inclined to enter into details, and Mr Irwine was too delicate to imply even a friendly curiosity. He perceived a change of subject would be welcome, and said –

'By the way, Arthur, at your colonel's birthday *fête* there

were some transparencies that made a great effect in honour of
Britannia, and Pitt, and the Loamshire Militia, and, above all,
the "generous youth",[12] the hero of the day. Don't you think
you should get up something of the same sort to astonish our
weak minds?'

The opportunity was gone. While Arthur was hesitating, the
rope to which he might have clung had drifted away – he must
trust now to his own swimming.

In ten minutes from that time, Mr Irwine was called for on
business, and Arthur, bidding him good-bye, mounted his horse
again with a sense of dissatisfaction, which he tried to quell by
determining to set off for Eagledale without an hour's delay.

BOOK SECOND

CHAPTER XVII

In Which the Story Pauses a Little[1]

'This Rector of Broxton is little better than a pagan!' I hear one of my readers exclaim. 'How much more edifying it would have been if you had made him give Arthur some truly spiritual advice. You might have put into his mouth the most beautiful things – quite as good as reading a sermon.'

Certainly I could, if I held it the highest vocation of the novelist to represent things as they never have been and never will be. Then, of course, I might refashion life and character entirely after my own liking; I might select the most unexceptionable type of clergyman, and put my own admirable opinions into his mouth on all occasions. But it happens, on the contrary, that my strongest effort is to avoid any such arbitrary picture, and to give a faithful account of men and things as they have mirrored themselves in my mind. The mirror is doubtless defective; the outlines will sometimes be disturbed, the reflection faint or confused; but I feel as much bound to tell you as precisely as I can what that reflection is, as if I were in the witness-box narrating my experience on oath.

Sixty years ago – it is a long time, so no wonder things have changed – all clergymen were not zealous; indeed there is reason to believe that the number of zealous clergymen was small, and it is probable that if one among the small minority had owned the livings of Broxton and Hayslope in the year 1799, you would have liked him no better than you like Mr Irwine. Ten to one, you would have thought him a tasteless, indiscreet, methodistical man. It is so very rarely that facts hit that nice medium required by our own enlightened opinions and refined taste! Perhaps you will say, 'Do improve the facts a little, then;

make them more accordant with those correct views which it is our privilege to possess. The world is not just what we like; do touch it up with a tasteful pencil, and make believe it is not quite such a mixed entangled affair. Let all people who hold unexceptionable opinions act unexceptionably. Let your most faulty characters always be on the wrong side, and your virtuous ones on the right. Then we shall see at a glance whom we are to condemn, and whom we are to approve. Then we shall be able to admire, without the slightest disturbance of our prepossessions: we shall hate and despise with that true ruminant relish which belongs to undoubting confidence.'

But, my good friend, what will you do then with your fellow-parishioner who opposes your husband in the vestry? – with your newly-appointed vicar, whose style of preaching you find painfully below that of his regretted predecessor? – with the honest servant who worries your soul with her one failing? – with your neighbour, Mrs Green, who was really kind to you in your last illness, but has said several ill-natured things about you since your convalescence? – nay, with your excellent husband himself, who has other irritating habits besides that of not wiping his shoes? These fellow-mortals, every one, must be accepted as they are: you can neither straighten their noses, nor brighten their wit, nor rectify their dispositions; and it is these people – amongst whom your life is passed – that it is needful you should tolerate, pity, and love: it is these more or less ugly, stupid, inconsistent people, whose movements of goodness you should be able to admire – for whom you should cherish all possible hopes, all possible patience. And I would not, even if I had the choice, be the clever novelist who could create a world so much better than this, in which we get up in the morning to do our daily work, that you would be likely to turn a harder, colder eye on the dusty streets and the common green fields – on the real breathing men and women, who can be chilled by your indifference or injured by your prejudice; who can be cheered and helped onward by your fellow-feeling, your forbearance, your outspoken, brave justice.

So I am content to tell my simple story, without trying to make things seem better than they were; dreading nothing, indeed, but falsity, which, in spite of one's best efforts, there is reason to dread. Falsehood is so easy, truth so difficult. The pencil is conscious of a delightful facility in drawing a griffin – the longer the claws, and the larger the wings, the better; but that marvellous facility which we mistook for genius is apt to forsake us when we want to draw a real unexaggerated lion. Examine your words well, and you will find that even when you have no motive to be false, it is a very hard thing to say the exact truth, even about your own immediate feelings – much harder than to say something fine about them which is *not* the exact truth.

It is for this rare, precious quality of truthfulness that I delight in many Dutch paintings,[2] which lofty-minded people despise. I find a source of delicious sympathy in these faithful pictures of a monotonous homely existence, which has been the fate of so many more among my fellow-mortals than a life of pomp or of absolute indigence, of tragic suffering or of world-stirring actions. I turn, without shrinking, from cloud-borne angels, from prophets, sibyls, and heroic warriors, to an old woman bending over her flower-pot, or eating her solitary dinner, while the noonday light, softened perhaps by a screen of leaves, falls on her mob-cap, and just touches the rim of her spinning-wheel, and her stone jug, and all those cheap common things which are the precious necessaries of life to her; – or I turn to that village wedding, kept between four brown walls, where an awkward bridegroom opens the dance with a high-shouldered, broad-faced bride, while elderly and middle-aged friends look on, with very irregular noses and lips, and probably with quart-pots in their hands, but with an expression of unmistakable contentment and goodwill. 'Foh!' says my idealistic friend, 'what vulgar details! What good is there in taking all these pains to give an exact likeness of old women and clowns? What a low phase of life! – what clumsy, ugly people!'

But bless us, things may be lovable that are not altogether handsome, I hope? I am not at all sure that the majority of the human race have not been ugly, and even among those 'lords of their kind', the British, squat figures, ill-shapen nostrils, and dingy complexions are not startling exceptions. Yet there is a great deal of family love amongst us. I have a friend or two whose class of features is such that the Apollo curl on the summit of their brows would be decidedly trying; yet to my certain knowledge tender hearts have beaten for them, and their miniatures – flattering, but still not lovely – are kissed in secret by motherly lips. I have seen many an excellent matron, who could never in her best days have been handsome, and yet she had a packet of yellow love-letters in a private drawer, and sweet children showered kisses on her sallow cheeks. And I believe there have been plenty of young heroes, of middle stature and feeble beards, who have felt quite sure they could never love anything more insignificant than a Diana,[3] and yet have found themselves in middle life happily settled with a wife who waddles. Yes! thank God; human feeling is like the mighty rivers that bless the earth: it does not wait for beauty – it flows with resistless force and brings beauty with it.

All honour and reverence to the divine beauty of form! Let us cultivate it to the utmost in men, women, and children – in our gardens and in our houses. But let us love that other beauty too, which lies in no secret of proportion, but in the secret of deep human sympathy. Paint us an angel, if you can, with a floating violet robe, and a face paled by the celestial light; paint us yet oftener a Madonna, turning her mild face upward and opening her arms to welcome the divine glory; but do not impose on us any aesthetic rules which shall banish from the region of Art those old women scraping carrots with their work-worn hands, those heavy clowns taking holiday in a dingy pot-house,[4] those rounded backs and stupid weather-beaten faces that have bent over the spade and done the rough work of the world – those homes with their tin pans, their brown pitchers, their rough curs, and their clusters of onions. In this world there are so many of these common coarse people, who have no picturesque sentimental wretchedness! It is so needful we should remember their existence, else we may happen to leave them quite out of our religion and philosophy, and frame lofty theories which only fit a world of extremes. Therefore let Art always remind us of them; therefore let us always have men ready to give the loving pains of a life to the faithful representing

of commonplace things – men who see beauty in these commonplace things, and delight in showing how kindly the light of
heaven falls on them. There are few prophets in the world; few
sublimely beautiful women; few heroes. I can't afford to give
all my love and reverence to such rarities: I want a great deal
of those feelings for my everyday fellow-men, especially for the
few in the foreground of the great multitude, whose faces I
know, whose hands I touch, for whom I have to make way with
kindly courtesy. Neither are picturesque lazzaroni[5] or romantic
criminals half so frequent as your common labourer, who gets
his own bread, and eats it vulgarly but creditably with his own
pocket-knife. It is more needful that I should have a fibre of
sympathy connecting me with that vulgar citizen who weighs
out my sugar in a vilely-assorted cravat and waistcoat, than
with the handsomest rascal in red scarf and green feathers; –
more needful that my heart should swell with loving admiration
at some trait of gentle goodness in the faulty people who sit at
the same hearth with me, or in the clergyman of my own parish,
who is perhaps rather too corpulent, and in other respects is
not an Oberlin or a Tillotson,[6] than at the deeds of heroes
whom I shall never know except by hearsay, or at the sublimest
abstract of all clerical graces that was ever conceived by an able
novelist.

And so I come back to Mr Irwine, with whom I desire you
to be in perfect charity, far as he may be from satisfying your
demands on the clerical character. Perhaps you think he was
not – as he ought to have been – a living demonstration of the
benefits attached to a national church? But I am not sure of
that; at least I know that the people in Broxton and Hayslope
would have been very sorry to part with their clergyman, and
that most faces brightened at his approach; and until it can be
proved that hatred is a better thing for the soul than love, I
must believe that Mr Irwine's influence in his parish was a more
wholesome one than that of the zealous Mr Ryde, who came
there twenty years afterwards, when Mr Irwine had been gathered to his fathers. It is true, Mr Ryde insisted strongly on the
doctrines of the Reformation,[7] visited his flock a great deal in
their own homes, and was severe in rebuking the aberrations

of the flesh – put a stop, indeed, to the Christmas rounds of
the church singers, as promoting drunkenness, and too light a
handling of sacred things. But I gathered from Adam Bede, to
whom I talked of these matters in his old age, that few clergymen could be less successful in winning the hearts of their
parishioners than Mr Ryde. They learned a great many notions
about doctrine from him, so that almost every churchgoer under
fifty began to distinguish as well between the genuine gospel
and what did not come precisely up to that standard, as if he
had been born and bred a Dissenter; and for some time after
his arrival there seemed to be quite a religious movement in
that quiet rural district. 'But,' said Adam, 'I've seen pretty clear,
ever since I was a young un, as religion's something else besides
notions. It isn't notions sets people doing the right thing – it's
feelings. It's the same with the notions in religion as it is with
math'matics, – a man may be able to work problems straight
off in's head as he sits by the fire and smokes his pipe; but if he
has to make a machine or a building, he must have a will and
a resolution, and love something else better than his own ease.
Somehow, the congregation began to fall off, and people began
to speak light o' Mr Ryde. I believe he meant right at bottom;
but, you see, he was sourish-tempered, and was for beating
down prices with the people as worked for him; and his preaching wouldn't go down well with that sauce. And he wanted to
be like my lord judge i' the parish, punishing folks for doing
wrong; and he scolded 'em from the pulpit as if he'd been a
Ranter, and yet he couldn't abide the Dissenters, and was a
deal more set against 'em than Mr Irwine was. And then he
didn't keep within his income, for he seemed to think at first
go-off that six hundred a-year was to make him as big a man
as Mr Donnithorne: that's a sore mischief I've often seen with
the poor curates jumping into a bit of a living all of a sudden.
Mr Ryde was a deal thought on at a distance, I believe, and he
wrote books; but as for math'matics and the natur o' things he
was as ignorant as a woman. He was very knowing about
doctrines, and used to call 'em the bulwarks of the Reformation;
but I've always mistrusted that sort o' learning as leaves folks
foolish and unreasonable about business. Now Mester Irwine

was as different as could be: as quick! – he understood what
you meant in a minute; and he knew all about building, and
could see when you'd made a good job. And he behaved as
much like a gentleman to the farmers, and th' old women and
the labourers, as he did to the gentry. You never saw *him*
interfering and scolding, and trying to play th' emperor. Ah! he
was a fine man as ever you set eyes on; and so kind to's mother
and sisters. That poor sickly Miss Anne – he seemed to think
more of her than of anybody else in the world. There wasn't a
soul in the parish had a word to say against him; and his
servants stayed with him till they were so old and pottering, he
had to hire other folks to do their work.'

'Well,' I said, 'that was an excellent way of preaching in the
week-days; but I daresay, if your old friend Mr Irwine were to
come to life again, and get into the pulpit next Sunday, you
would be rather ashamed that he didn't preach better after all
your praise of him.'

'Nay, nay,' said Adam, broadening his chest and throwing
himself back in his chair, as if he were ready to meet all infer-
ences, 'nobody has ever heard me say Mr Irwine was much of
a preacher. He didn't go into deep speritial experience; and I
know there's a deal in a man's inward life as you can't measure
by the square, and say, "Do this and that 'll follow", and, "Do
that and this 'll follow." There's things go on in the soul, and
times when feelings come into you like a rushing mighty wind,
as the Scripture says, and part your life in two a'most, so as
you look back on yourself as if you was somebody else. Those
are things as you can't bottle up in a "do this" and "do that";
and I'll go so far with the strongest Methodist ever you'll find.
That shows me there's deep speritial things in religion. You
can't make much out wi' talking about it, but you feel it. Mr
Irwine didn't go into those things: he preached short moral
sermons, and that was all. But then he acted pretty much up to
what he said; he didn't set up for being so different from other
folks one day, and then be as like 'em as two peas the next.
And he made folks love him and respect him, and that was
better nor stirring up their gall wi' being overbusy. Mrs Poyser
used to say – you know she would have her word about

everything – she said, Mr Irwine was like a good meal o' victual, you were the better for him without thinking on it, and Mr Ryde was like a dose o' physic, he gripped you and worreted you, and after all he left you much the same.'

'But didn't Mr Ryde preach a great deal more about that spiritual part of religion than you talk of, Adam? Couldn't you get more out of his sermons than out of Mr Irwine's?'

'Eh, I knowna. He preached a deal about doctrines. But I've seen pretty clear ever since I was a young un, as religion's something else besides doctrines and notions. I look at it as if the doctrines was like finding names for your feelings, so as you can talk of 'em when you've never known 'em, just as a man may talk o' tools when he knows their names, though he's never so much as seen 'em, still less handled 'em. I've heard a deal o' doctrine i' my time, for I used to go after the Dissenting preachers along wi' Seth, when I was a lad o' seventeen, and got puzzling myself a deal about th' Arminians and the Calvinists.[8] The Wesleyans, you know, are strong Arminians; and Seth, who could never abide anything harsh, and was always for hoping the best, held fast by the Wesleyans from the very first; but I thought I could pick a hole or two in their notions, and I got disputing wi' one o' the class leaders down at Treddles'on, and harassed him so, first o' this side and then o' that, till at last he said, "Young man, it's the devil making use o' your pride and conceit as a weapon to war against the simplicity o' the truth." I couldn't help laughing then, but as I was going home, I thought the man wasn't far wrong. I began to see as all this weighing and sifting what this text means and that text means, and whether folks are saved all by God's grace, or whether there goes an ounce o' their own will to 't, was no part o' real religion at all. You may talk o' these things for hours on end, and you'll only be all the more coxy and conceited for't. So I took to going nowhere but to church, and hearing nobody but Mr Irwine, for he said nothing but what was good, and what you'd be the wiser for remembering. And I found it better for my soul to be humble before the mysteries o' God's dealings, and not be making a clatter about what I could never understand. And they're poor foolish questions after all; for what have we got either inside or outside of us but what comes from God? If we've got a resolution to do right, He gave it us, I reckon, first or last; but I see plain enough we shall never do it without a resolution, and that's enough for me.'

Adam, you perceive, was a warm admirer, perhaps a partial judge, of Mr Irwine, as, happily, some of us still are of the people we have known familiarly. Doubtless it will be despised as a weakness by that lofty order of minds who pant after the ideal, and are oppressed by a general sense that their emotions are of too exquisite a character to find fit objects among their everyday fellow-men. I have often been favoured with the confidence of these select natures, and find them concur in the experience that great men are over-estimated and small men are insupportable; that if you would love a woman without ever looking back on your love as a folly, she must die while you are courting her; and if you would maintain the slightest belief in human heroism, you must never make a pilgrimage to see the hero. I confess I have often meanly shrunk from confessing to these accomplished and acute gentlemen what my own experience has been. I am afraid I have often smiled with hypocritical assent, and gratified them with an epigram on the fleeting nature of our illusions, which any one moderately acquainted with French literature⁹ can command at a moment's notice. Human converse, I think some wise man has remarked, is not rigidly sincere. But I herewith discharge my conscience, and declare, that I have had quite enthusiastic movements of admiration towards old gentlemen who spoke the worst English, who were occasionally fretful in their temper, and who had never moved in a higher sphere of influence than that of parish overseer; and that the way in which I have come to the conclusion that human nature is lovable – the way I have learnt something of its deep pathos, its sublime mysteries – has been by living a great deal among people more or less commonplace and vulgar, of whom you would perhaps hear nothing very surprising if you were to inquire about them in the neighbourhoods where they dwelt. Ten to one most of the small shopkeepers in their vicinity saw nothing at all in them. For I have observed this remarkable coincidence, that the select natures

who pant after the ideal, and find nothing in pantaloons or
petticoats great enough to command their reverence and love,
are curiously in unison with the narrowest and pettiest. For
example, I have often heard Mr Gedge, the landlord of the
Royal Oak, who used to turn a bloodshot eye on his neighbours
in the village of Shepperton, sum up his opinion of the people
in his own parish – and they were all the people he knew – in
these emphatic words: 'Ay, sir, I've said it often, and I'll say it
again, they're a poor lot i' this parish – a poor lot, sir, big and
little.' I think he had a dim idea that if he could migrate to a
distant parish, he might find neighbours worthy of him; and
indeed he did subsequently transfer himself to the Saracen's
Head, which was doing a thriving business in the back street of
a neighbouring market-town. But, oddly enough, he has found
the people up that back street of precisely the same stamp as
the inhabitants of Shepperton – 'a poor lot, sir, big and little,
and them as comes for a go o' gin are no better than them as
comes for a pint o' twopenny – a poor lot'.

CHAPTER XVIII

Church

'Hetty, Hetty, don't you know church begins at two, and it's gone half after one a'ready? Have you got nothing better to think on this good Sunday, as poor old Thias Bede's to be put into the ground, and him drownded i' th' dead o' the night, as it's enough to make one's back run cold, but you must be 'dizening[1] yourself as if there was a wedding istid of a funeral?'

'Well, aunt,' said Hetty, 'I can't be ready so soon as everybody else, when I've got Totty's things to put on. And I'd ever such work to make her stand still.'

Hetty was coming down-stairs, and Mrs Poyser, in her plain bonnet and shawl, was standing below. If ever a girl looked as if she had been made of roses, that girl was Hetty in her Sunday hat and frock. For her hat was trimmed with pink, and her frock had pink spots, sprinkled on a white ground. There was nothing but pink and white about her, except in her dark hair and eyes and her little buckled shoes. Mrs Poyser was provoked at herself, for she could hardly keep from smiling, as any mortal is inclined to do at the sight of pretty round things. So she turned without speaking, and joined the group outside the house door, followed by Hetty, whose heart was fluttering so at the thought of some one she expected to see at church, that she hardly felt the ground she trod on.

And now the little procession set off. Mr Poyser was in his Sunday suit of drab,[2] with a red-and-green waistcoat, and a green watch-ribbon having a large cornelian seal[3] attached, pendant like a plumb-line from that promontory where his watch-pocket was situated; a silk handkerchief of a yellow tone round his neck; and excellent grey ribbed stockings, knitted by

Mrs Poyser's own hand, setting off the proportions of his leg. Mr Poyser had no reason to be ashamed of his leg, and suspected that the growing abuse of top-boots and other fashions tending to disguise the nether limbs, had their origin in a pitiable degeneracy of the human calf. Still less had he reason to be ashamed of his round jolly face, which was good-humour itself as he said, 'Come, Hetty – come, little uns!' and, giving his arm to his wife, led the way through the causeway gate into the yard.

The 'little uns' addressed were Marty and Tommy, boys of nine and seven, in little fustian tailed coats and knee-breeches, relieved by rosy cheeks and black eyes; looking as much like their father as a very small elephant is like a very large one. Hetty walked between them, and behind came patient Molly, whose task it was to carry Totty through the yard, and over all the wet places on the road; for Totty, having speedily recovered from her threatened fever, had insisted on going to church today, and especially on wearing her red-and-black necklace outside her tippet.[4] And there were many wet places for her to be carried over this afternoon, for there had been heavy showers in the morning, though now the clouds had rolled off and lay in towering silvery masses on the horizon.

You might have known it was Sunday if you had only waked up in the farmyard. The cocks and hens seemed to know it, and made only crooning subdued noises; the very bull-dog looked less savage, as if he would have been satisfied with a smaller bite than usual. The sunshine seemed to call all things to rest and not to labour; it was asleep itself on the moss-grown cowshed; on the group of white ducks nestling together with their bills tucked under their wings; on the old black sow stretched languidly on the straw, while her largest young one found an excellent spring-bed on his mother's fat ribs; on Alick, the shepherd, in his new smock-frock, taking an uneasy siesta, half-sitting half-standing on the granary steps. Alick was of opinion that church, like other luxuries, was not to be indulged in often by a foreman who had the weather and the ewes on his mind. 'Church! nay – I'n gotten summat else to think on,' was an answer which he often uttered in a tone of bitter significance that silenced further question. I feel sure Alick meant no irreverence; indeed, I know that his mind was not of a speculative negative cast, and he would on no account have missed going to church on Christmas Day, Easter Sunday, and 'Whissuntide'.[5] But he had a general impression that public worship and religious ceremonies, like other non-productive employments, were intended for people who had leisure.

'There's father a-standing at the yard-gate,' said Martin Poyser. 'I reckon he wants to watch us down the field. It's wonderful what sight he has, and him turned seventy-five.'

'Ah, I often think it's wi' th' old folks as it is wi' the babbies,' said Mrs Poyser; 'they're satisfied wi' looking, no matter what they're looking at. It's God A'mighty's way o' quietening 'em, I reckon, afore they go to sleep.'

Old Martin opened the gate as he saw the family procession approaching, and held it wide open, leaning on his stick – pleased to do this bit of work; for, like all old men whose life has been spent in labour, he liked to feel that he was still useful – that there was a better crop of onions in the garden because he was by at the sowing – and that the cows would be milked the better if he stayed at home on a Sunday afternoon to look on. He always went to church on Sacrament Sundays, but not very regularly at other times; on wet Sundays, or whenever he had a touch of rheumatism, he used to read the three first chapters of Genesis instead.

'They'll ha' putten Thias Bede i' the ground afore ye get to the churchyard,' he said, as his son came up. 'It 'ud ha' been better luck if they'd ha' buried him i' the forenoon when the rain was fallin'; there's no likelihoods of a drop now; an' the moon lies like a boat there, dost see? That's a sure sign o' fair weather – there's a many as is false, but that's sure.'

'Ay, ay,' said the son, 'I'm in hopes it'll hold up now.'

'Mind what the parson says, mind what the parson says, my lads,' said Grandfather to the black-eyed youngsters in knee-breeches, conscious of a marble or two in their pockets, which they looked forward to handling a little, secretly, during the sermon.

'Dood-bye, dandad,' said Totty. 'Me doin to church. Me dot my netlace on. Dive me a peppermint.'

Grandad, shaking with laughter at this 'deep little wench', slowly transferred his stick to his left hand, which held the gate open, and slowly thrust his finger into the waistcoat-pocket on which Totty had fixed her eyes with a confident look of expectation.

And when they were all gone, the old man leaned on the gate again, watching them across the lane along the Home Close, and through the far gate, till they disappeared behind a bend in the hedge. For the hedgerows in those days shut out one's view, even on the better-managed farms; and this afternoon, the dog-roses were tossing out their pink wreaths, the night-shade was in its yellow and purple glory, the pale honeysuckle grew out of reach, peeping high up out of a holly bush, and over all an ash or a sycamore every now and then threw its shadow across the path.

There were acquaintances at other gates who had to move aside and let them pass: at the gate of the Home Close there was half the dairy of cows standing one behind the other, extremely slow to understand that their large bodies might be in the way; at the far gate there was the mare holding her head over the bars, and beside her the liver-coloured foal with its head towards its mother's flank, apparently still much embarrassed by its own straddling existence. The way lay entirely through Mr Poyser's own fields till they reached the main road leading to the village, and he turned a keen eye on the stock and the crops as they went along, while Mrs Poyser was ready to supply a running commentary on them all. The woman who manages a dairy has a large share in making the rent, so she may well be allowed to have her opinion on stock and their 'keep' – an exercise which strengthens her understanding so much that she finds herself able to give her husband advice on most other subjects.

'There's that short-horned Sally,' she said, as they entered the Home Close, and she caught sight of the meek beast that lay chewing the cud, and looking at her with a sleepy eye. 'I begin to hate the sight o' the cow; and I say now what I said three weeks ago, the sooner we get rid of her the better, for there's that little yallow cow as doesn't give half the milk, and yet I've twice as much butter from her.'

'Why, thee't not like the women in general,' said Mr Poyser; 'they like the short-horns, as give such a lot o' milk. There's Chowne's wife wants him to buy no other sort.'

'What's it sinnify what Chowne's wife likes? – a poor soft thing, wi' no more head-piece nor a sparrow. She'd take a big cullender to strain her lard wi', and then wonder as the scratchins run through. I've seen enough of her to know as I'll niver take a servant from her house again – all hugger-mugger – and you'd niver know, when you went in, whether it was Monday or Friday, the wash draggin' on to th' end o' the week; and as for her cheese, I know well enough it rose like a loaf in a tin last year. And then she talks o' the weather bein' i' fault, as there's folks 'ud stand on their heads and then say the fault was i' their boots.'

'Well, Chowne's been wanting to buy Sally, so we can get rid of her if thee lik'st,' said Mr Poyser, secretly proud of his wife's superior power of putting two and two together; indeed, on recent market-days he had more than once boasted of her discernment in this very matter of short-horns.

'Ay, them as choose a soft for a wife may's well buy up the short-horns, for if you get your head stuck in a bog your legs may's well go after it. Eh! talk o' legs, there's legs for you,' Mrs Poyser continued, as Totty, who had been set down now the road was dry, toddled on in front of her father and mother. 'There's shapes! An' she's got such a long foot, she'll be her father's own child.'

'Ay, she'll be welly such a one as Hetty i' ten years' time, on'y she's got *thy* coloured eyes. I niver remember a blue eye i' my family; my mother had eyes as black as sloes, just like Hetty's.'

'The child 'ull be none the worse for having summat as isn't like Hetty. An' I'm none for having her so over pretty. Though, for the matter o' that, there's people wi' light hair an' blue eyes as pretty as them wi' black. If Dinah had got a bit o' colour in her cheeks, an' didn't stick that Methodist cap on her head, enough to frighten the cows, folks 'ud think her as pretty as Hetty.'

'Nay, nay,' said Mr Poyser, with rather a contemptuous

emphasis, 'thee dostna know the pints of a woman. The men 'ud niver run after Dinah as they would after Hetty.'

'What care I what the men 'ud run after? It's well seen what choice the most of 'em know how to make, by the poor draggle-tails o' wives you see, like bits o' gauze ribbin, good for nothing when the colour's gone.'

'Well, well, thee canstna say but what I knowed how to make a choice when I married thee,' said Mr Poyser, who usually settled little conjugal disputes by a compliment of this sort; 'and thee wast twice as buxom as Dinah ten year ago.'

'I niver said as a woman had need to be ugly to make a good missis of a house. There's Chowne's wife ugly enough to turn the milk an' save the rennet,[6] but she'll niver save nothing any other way. But as for Dinah, poor child, she's niver likely to be buxom as long as she'll make her dinner o' cake and water, for the sake o' giving to them as want. She provoked me past bearing sometimes; and, as I told her, she went clean again' the Scriptur', for that says, "Love your neighbour as yourself";[7] "but," I said, "if you loved your neighbour no better nor you do yourself, Dinah, it's little enough you'd do for him. You'd be thinking he might do well enough on a half-empty stomach." Eh, I wonder where she is this blessed Sunday! – sitting by that sick woman, I daresay, as she'd set her heart on going to all of a sudden.'

'Ah, it was a pity she should take such megrims[8] into her head, when she might ha' stayed wi' us all summer, and eaten twice as much as she wanted, and it 'ud niver ha' been missed. She made no odds in th' house at all, for she sat as still at her sewing as a bird on the nest, and was uncommon nimble at running to fetch anything. If Hetty gets married, theed'st like to ha' Dinah wi' thee constant.'

'It's no use thinking o' that,' said Mrs Poyser. 'You might as well beckon to the flying swallow, as ask Dinah to come an' live here comfortable, like other folks. If anything could turn her, I should ha' turned her, for I've talked to her for a hour on end, and scolded her too; for she's my own sister's child, and it behoves me to do what I can for her. But eh, poor thing, as soon as she'd said us "good-bye", an' got into the cart, an' looked back at me with her pale face, as is welly like her aunt Judith come back from heaven, I begun to be frightened to think o' the set-downs I had given her; for it comes over you sometimes as if she'd a way o' knowing the rights o' things more nor other folks have. But I'll niver give in as that's 'cause she's a Methodist, no more nor a white calf's white 'cause it eats out o' the same bucket wi' a black un.'

'Nay,' said Mr Poyser, with as near an approach to a snarl as his good-nature would allow; 'I'n no opinion o' the Methodists. It's on'y tradesfolks as turn Methodists; you niver knew a farmer bitten wi' them maggots. There's maybe a work-man now an' then, as isn't over clever at's work, takes to preachin' an' that, like Seth Bede. But you see Adam, as has got one o' the best head-pieces hereabout, knows better; he's a good Churchman, else I'd never encourage him for a sweetheart for Hetty.'

'Why, goodness me,' said Mrs Poyser, who had looked back while her husband was speaking, 'look where Molly is with them lads. They're the field's length behind us. How *could* you let 'em do so, Hetty? Anybody might as well set a pictur to watch the children as you. Run back, and tell 'em to come on.'

Mr and Mrs Poyser were now at the end of the second field, so they set Totty on the top of one of the large stones forming the true Loamshire stile, and awaited the loiterers; Totty observing with complacency, 'Dey naughty, naughty boys – me dood.'

The fact was that this Sunday walk through the fields was fraught with great excitement to Marty and Tommy, who saw a perpetual drama going on in the hedgerows, and could no more refrain from stopping and peeping than if they had been a couple of spaniels or terriers. Marty was quite sure he saw a yellowhammer on the boughs of the great ash, and while he was peeping, he missed the sight of a white-throated stoat, which had run across the path and was described with much fervour by the junior Tommy. Then there was a little greenfinch, just fledged, fluttering along the ground, and it seemed quite possible to catch it, till it managed to flutter under the black-berry bush. Hetty could not be got to give any heed to these things, so Molly was called on for her ready sympathy, and peeped with open mouth wherever she was told, and said 'Lawks!' whenever she was expected to wonder.

Molly hastened on with some alarm when Hetty had come back and called to them that her aunt was angry; but Marty ran on first, shouting, 'We've found the speckled turkey's nest, mother!' with the instinctive confidence that people who bring good news are never in fault.

'Ah,' said Mrs Poyser, really forgetting all discipline in this pleasant surprise, 'that's a good lad; why, where is it?'

'Down in ever such a hole, under the hedge. I saw it first, looking after the greenfinch, and she sat on the nest.'

'You didn't frighten her, I hope,' said the mother, 'else she'll forsake it.'

'No, I went away as still as still, and whispered to Molly – didn't I, Molly?'

'Well, well, now come on,' said Mrs Poyser, 'and walk before father and mother, and take your little sister by the hand. We must go straight on now. Good boys don't look after the birds of a Sunday.'

'But, mother,' said Marty, 'you said you'd give half-a-crown to find the speckled turkey's nest. Mayn't I have the half-crown put into my money-box?'

'We'll see about that, my lad, if you walk along now like a good boy.'

The father and mother exchanged a significant glance of amusement at their eldest-born's acuteness; but on Tommy's round face there was a cloud.

'Mother,' he said, half crying, 'Marty's got ever so much more money in his box nor I've got in mine.'

'Munny, *me* want half-a-toun in *my* bots,' said Totty.

'Hush, hush, hush,' said Mrs Poyser, 'did ever anybody hear such naughty children? Nobody shall ever see their money-boxes any more, if they don't make haste and go on to church.'

This dreadful threat had the desired effect, and through the two remaining fields the three pair of small legs trotted on without any serious interruption, notwithstanding a small pond full of tadpoles, alias 'bullhead', which the lads looked at wistfully.

The damp hay that must be scattered and turned afresh tomorrow was not a cheering sight to Mr Poyser, who during hay and corn harvest had often some mental struggles as to the benefits of a day of rest; but no temptation would have induced him to carry on any field-work, however early in the morning, on a Sunday; for had not Michael Holdsworth had a pair of oxen 'sweltered'⁹ while he was ploughing on Good Friday? That was a demonstration that work on sacred days was a wicked thing; and with wickedness of any sort Martin Poyser was quite clear that he would have nothing to do, since money got by such means would never prosper.

'It a'most makes your fingers itch to be at the hay now the sun shines so,' he observed, as they passed through the 'Big Meadow'. 'But it's poor foolishness to think o' saving by going against your conscience. There's that Jim Wakefield, as they used to call "Gentleman Wakefield", used to do the same of a Sunday as o' week-days, and took no heed to right or wrong, as if there was nayther God nor devil. An' what's he come to? Why, I saw him myself last market-day a-carrying a basket wi' oranges in't.'

'Ah, to be sure,' said Mrs Poyser, emphatically, 'you make but a poor trap to catch luck if you go and bait it wi' wickedness. The money as is got so's like to burn holes i' your pocket. I'd niver wish us to leave our lads a sixpence but what was got i' the rightful way. And as for the weather, there's One above makes it, and we must put up wi't: it's nothing of a plague to what the wenches are.'

Notwithstanding the interruption in their walk, the excellent habit which Mrs Poyser's clock had of taking time by the forelock, had secured their arrival at the village while it was still a quarter to two, though almost every one who meant to go to church was already within the churchyard gates. Those who stayed at home were chiefly mothers, like Timothy's Bess, who stood at her own door nursing her baby, and feeling as women feel in that position – that nothing else can be expected of them.

It was not entirely to see Thias Bede's funeral that the people were standing about the churchyard so long before service began; that was their common practice. The women, indeed, usually entered the church at once, and the farmers' wives talked in an under-tone to each other, over the tall pews, about their illnesses and the total failure of doctor's stuff, recommending dandelion-tea, and other home-made specifics, as far preferable – about the servants, and their growing exorbitance as to wages, whereas the quality of their services declined from year to year, and there was no girl nowadays to be trusted any further than you could see her – about the bad price Mr Dingall, the Treddleston grocer, was giving for butter, and the reasonable doubts that might be held as to his solvency, notwithstanding that Mrs Dingall was a sensible woman, and they were all sorry for *her*, for she had very good kin. Meantime the men lingered outside, and hardly any of them except the singers, who had a humming and fragmentary rehearsal to go through, entered the church until Mr Irwine was in the desk. They saw no reason for that premature entrance, – what could they do in church, if they were there before service began? – and they did not conceive that any power in the universe could take it ill of them if they stayed out and talked a little about 'bus'ness'.

Chad Cranage looks like quite a new acquaintance to-day, for he has got his clean Sunday face, which always makes his little granddaughter cry at him as a stranger. But an experienced eye would have fixed on him at once as the village blacksmith, after seeing the humble deference with which the big saucy fellow took off his hat and stroked his hair to the farmers; for Chad was accustomed to say that a working man must hold a candle to – a personage understood to be as black as he was himself on week-days; by which evil-sounding rule of conduct he meant what was, after all, rather virtuous than otherwise, namely, that men who had horses to be shod must be treated with respect. Chad and the rougher sort of workmen kept aloof from the grave under the white thorn, where the burial was going forward; but Sandy Jim, and several of the farm-labourers, made a group round it, and stood with their hats off, as fellow-mourners with the mother and sons. Others held a midway position, sometimes watching the group at the grave, sometimes listening to the conversation of the farmers, who

stood in a knot near the church door, and were now joined by
Martin Poyser, while his family passed into the church. On the
outside of this knot stood Mr Casson, the landlord of the
Donnithorne Arms, in his most striking attitude – that is to say,
with the forefinger of his right hand thrust between the buttons
of his waistcoat, his left hand in his breeches-pocket, and his
head very much on one side; looking, on the whole, like an
actor who has only a monosyllabic part intrusted to him, but
feels sure that the audience discern his fitness for the leading
business; curiously in contrast with old Jonathan Burge, who
held his hands behind him, and leaned forward coughing asth-
matically, with an inward scorn of all knowingness that could
not be turned into cash. The talk was in rather a lower tone
than usual to-day, hushed a little by the sound of Mr Irwine's
voice reading the final prayers of the burial-service. They had
all had their word of pity for poor Thias, but now they had got
upon the nearer subject of their own grievances against Satchell,
the Squire's bailiff, who played the part of steward so far as it
was not performed by old Mr Donnithorne himself, for that
gentleman had the meanness to receive his own rents and make
bargains about his own timber. This subject of conversation
was an additional reason for not being loud, since Satchell
himself might presently be walking up the paved road to the
church door. And soon they became suddenly silent; for Mr
Irwine's voice had ceased, and the group round the white thorn
was dispersing itself towards the church.

They all moved aside, and stood with their hats off, while
Mr Irwine passed. Adam and Seth were coming next with
their mother between them; for Joshua Rann officiated as head
sexton as well as clerk, and was not yet ready to follow the
rector into the vestry. But there was a pause before the three
mourners came on: Lisbeth had turned round to look again
towards the grave! Ah! there was nothing now but the brown
earth under the white thorn. Yet she cried less to-day than she
had done any day since her husband's death: along with all her
grief there was mixed an unusual sense of her own importance
in having a 'burial', and in Mr Irwine's reading a special service
for her husband; and besides, she knew the funeral psalm was

going to be sung for him. She felt this counter-excitement to her sorrow still more strongly as she walked with her sons towards the church door, and saw the friendly sympathetic nods of their fellow-parishioners.

The mother and sons passed into the church, and one by one the loiterers followed, though some still lingered without; the sight of Mr Donnithorne's carriage, which was winding slowly up the hill, perhaps helping to make them feel that there was no need for haste.

But presently the sound of the bassoon and the key-bugles[10] burst forth; the evening hymn, which always opened the service, had begun, and every one must now enter and take his place.

I cannot say that the interior of Hayslope Church was remarkable for anything except for the grey age of its oaken pews – great square pews mostly, ranged on each side of a narrow aisle. It was free, indeed, from the modern blemish of galleries. The choir had two narrow pews to themselves in the middle of the right-hand row, so that it was a short process for Joshua Rann to take his place among them as principal bass, and return to his desk after the singing was over. The pulpit and desk, grey and old as the pews, stood on one side of the arch leading into the chancel, which also had its grey square pews for Mr Donnithorne's family and servants. Yet I assure you these grey pews, with the buff-washed walls, gave a very pleasing tone to this shabby interior, and agreed extremely well with the ruddy faces and bright waistcoats. And there were liberal touches of crimson toward the chancel, for the pulpit and Mr Donnithorne's own pew had handsome crimson cloth cushions; and, to close the vista, there was a crimson altar-cloth, embroidered with golden rays by Miss Lydia's own hand.

But even without the crimson cloth, the effect must have been warm and cheering when Mr Irwine was in the desk, looking benignly round on that simple congregation – on the hardy old men, with bent knees and shoulders, perhaps, but with vigour left for much hedge-clipping and thatching; on the tall stalwart frames and roughly-cut bronzed faces of the stone-cutters and carpenters; on the half-dozen well-to-do farmers, with their apple-cheeked families; and on the clean old women, mostly farm-labourers' wives, with their bit of snow-white cap-border under their black bonnets, and with their withered arms, bare from the elbow, folded passively over their chests. For none of the old people held books – why should they? not one of them could read. But they knew a few 'good words' by heart, and their withered lips now and then moved silently, following the service without any very clear comprehension indeed, but with a simple faith in its efficacy to ward off harm and bring blessing. And now all faces were visible, for all were standing up – the little children on the seats, peeping over the edge of the grey pews, while good Bishop Ken's evening hymn[11] was being sung to one of those lively psalm-tunes which died out with the last generation of rectors and choral parish-clerks. Melodies die out, like the pipe of Pan,[12] with the ears that love them and listen for them. Adam was not in his usual place among the singers to-day, for he sat with his mother and Seth, and he noticed with surprise that Bartle Massey was absent too: all the more agreeable for Mr Joshua Rann, who gave out his bass notes with unusual complacency, and threw an extra ray of severity into the glances he sent over his spectacles at the recusant Will Maskery.

I beseech you to imagine Mr Irwine looking round on this scene, in his ample white surplice, that became him so well, with his powdered hair thrown back, his rich brown complexion, and his finely-cut nostril and upper lip; for there was a certain virtue in that benignant yet keen countenance, as there is in all human faces from which a generous soul beams out. And over all streamed the delicious June sunshine through the old windows, with their desultory patches of yellow, red, and blue, that threw pleasant touches of colour on the opposite wall.

I think, as Mr Irwine looked round to-day, his eyes rested an instant longer than usual on the square pew occupied by Martin Poyser and his family. And there was another pair of dark eyes that found it impossible not to wander thither, and rest on that round pink-and-white figure. But Hetty was at that moment quite careless of any glances – she was absorbed in the thought that Arthur Donnithorne would soon be coming into church, for the carriage must surely be at the church gate by this time. She had never seen him since she parted with him in the wood on Thursday evening, and oh! how long the time had seemed! Things had gone on just the same as ever since that evening; the wonders that had happened then had brought no changes after them; they were already like a dream. When she heard the church door swinging, her heart beat so, she dared not look up. She felt that her aunt was curtsying; she curtsied herself. That must be old Mr Donnithorne – he always came first, the wrinkled small old man, peering round with short-sighted glances at the bowing and curtsying congregation; then she knew Miss Lydia was passing, and though Hetty liked so much to look at her fashionable little coal-scuttle bonnet, with the wreath of small roses round it, she didn't mind it to-day. But there were no more curtsies – no, he was not come; she felt sure there was nothing else passing the pew door but the house-keeper's black bonnet, and the lady's-maid's beautiful straw that had once been Miss Lydia's, and then the powdered heads of the butler and footman. No, he was not there; yet she would look now – she might be mistaken – for, after all, she had not looked. So she lifted up her eyelids and glanced timidly at the cushioned pew in the chancel: – there was no one but old Mr Donnithorne rubbing his spectacles with his white handker-chief, and Miss Lydia opening the large gilt-edged prayer-book. The chill disappointment was too hard to bear: she felt herself turning pale, her lips trembling; she was ready to cry. Oh, what *should* she do? Everybody would know the reason; they would know she was crying because Arthur was not there. And Mr Craig, with the wonderful hot-house plant in his button-hole, was staring at her, she knew. It was dreadfully long before the General Confession[13] began, so that she could kneel down. Two great drops *would* fall then, but no one saw them except good-natured Molly, for her aunt and uncle knelt with their backs towards her. Molly, unable to imagine any cause for tears in church except faintness, of which she had a vague traditional knowledge, drew out of her pocket a queer little flat blue smelling-bottle,[14] and after much labour in pulling the cork out, thrust the narrow neck against Hetty's nostrils. 'It donna smell,'

she whispered, thinking this was a great advantage which old
salts had over fresh ones: they did you good without biting
your nose. Hetty pushed it away peevishly; but this little flash
of temper did what the salts could not have done – it roused
her to wipe away the traces of her tears, and try with all her
might not to shed any more. Hetty had a certain strength in her
vain little nature: she would have borne anything rather than
be laughed at, or pointed at with any other feeling than admiration; she would have pressed her own nails into her tender
flesh rather than people should know a secret she did not want
them to know.

What fluctuations there were in her busy thoughts and feelings, while Mr Irwine was pronouncing the solemn 'Absolution'
in her deaf ears, and through all the tones of petition that
followed! Anger lay very close to disappointment, and soon
won the victory over the conjectures her small ingenuity could
devise to account for Arthur's absence on the supposition that
he really wanted to come, really wanted to see her again. And
by the time she rose from her knees mechanically, because all
the rest were rising, the colour had returned to her cheeks even
with a heightened glow, for she was framing little indignant
speeches to herself, saying she hated Arthur for giving her this
pain – she would like him to suffer too. Yet while this selfish
tumult was going on in her soul, her eyes were bent down on
her prayer-book, and the eyelids with their dark fringe looked
as lovely as ever. Adam Bede thought so, as he glanced at her
for a moment on rising from his knees.

But Adam's thoughts of Hetty did not deafen him to the
service; they rather blended with all the other deep feelings for
which the church service was a channel to him this afternoon,
as a certain consciousness of our entire past and our imagined
future blends itself with all our moments of keen sensibility.
And to Adam the church service was the best channel he could
have found for his mingled regret, yearning, and resignation;
its interchange of beseeching cries for help, with outbursts of
faith and praise – its recurrent responses and the familiar
rhythm of its collects, seemed to speak for him as no other form
of worship could have done; as, to those early Christians who

had worshipped from their childhood upward in catacombs,[15] the torch-light and shadows must have seemed nearer the Divine presence than the heathenish daylight of the street. The secret of our emotions never lies in the bare object, but in its subtle relations to our own past: no wonder the secret escapes the unsympathizing observer, who might as well put on his spectacles to discern odours.

But there was one reason why even a chance comer would have found the service in Hayslope Church more impressive than in most other village nooks in the kingdom – a reason, of which I am sure you have not the slightest suspicion. It was the reading of our friend Joshua Rann. Where that good shoemaker got his notion of reading from, remained a mystery even to his most intimate acquaintances. I believe, after all, he got it chiefly from Nature, who had poured some of her music into this honest conceited soul, as she had been known to do into other narrow souls before his. She had given him, at least, a fine bass voice and a musical ear; but I cannot positively say whether these alone had sufficed to inspire him with the rich chant in which he delivered the responses. The way he rolled from a rich deep forte into a melancholy cadence, subsiding, at the end of the last word, into a sort of faint resonance, like the lingering vibrations of a fine violoncello, I can compare to nothing for its strong calm melancholy but the rush and cadence of the wind among the autumn boughs. This may seem a strange mode of speaking about the reading of a parish-clerk – a man in rusty spectacles, with stubbly hair, a large occiput, and a prominent crown.[16] But that is Nature's way: she will allow a gentleman of splendid physiognomy and poetic aspirations to sing woefully out of tune, and not give him the slightest hint of it; and takes care that some narrow-browed fellow, trolling a ballad in the corner of a pot-house, shall be as true to his intervals as a bird.

Joshua himself was less proud of his reading than of his singing, and it was always with a sense of heightened importance that he passed from the desk to the choir. Still more to-day: it was a special occasion; for an old man, familiar to all the parish, had died a sad death – not in his bed, a circumstance

the most painful to the mind of the peasant – and now the
funeral psalm was to be sung in memory of his sudden departure. Moreover, Bartle Massey was not at church, and Joshua's
importance in the choir suffered no eclipse. It was a solemn
minor strain they sang. The old psalm-tunes have many a wail
among them, and the words –

> 'Thou sweep'st us off as with a flood;
>   We vanish hence like dreams'[17]

– seemed to have a closer application than usual, in the death
of poor Thias. The mother and sons listened, each with peculiar
feelings. Lisbeth had a vague belief that the psalm was doing
her husband good; it was part of that decent burial which she
would have thought it a greater wrong to withhold from him
than to have caused him many unhappy days while he was
living. The more there was said about her husband, the more
there was done for him, surely the safer he would be. It was
poor Lisbeth's blind way of feeling that human love and pity
are a ground of faith in some other love. Seth, who was easily
touched, shed tears, and tried to recall, as he had done continually since his father's death, all that he had heard of the possibility that a single moment of consciousness at the last might be a
moment of pardon and reconcilement; for was it not written in
the very psalm they were singing, that the divine dealings were
not measured and circumscribed by time? Adam had never been
unable to join in a psalm before. He had known plenty of
trouble and vexation since he had been a lad; but this was the
first sorrow that had hemmed in his voice, and strangely enough
it was sorrow because the chief source of his past trouble and
vexation was for ever gone out of his reach. He had not been
able to press his father's hand before their parting, and say,
'Father, you know it was all right between us; I never forgot
what I owed you when I was a lad; you forgive me if I have
been too hot and hasty now and then!' Adam thought but little
to-day of the hard work and the earnings he had spent on his
father: his thoughts ran constantly on what the old man's feelings had been in moments of humiliation, when he had held

down his head before the rebukes of his son. When our indignation is borne in submissive silence, we are apt to feel twinges of doubt afterwards as to our own generosity, if not justice; how much more when the object of our anger has gone into everlasting silence, and we have seen his face for the last time in the meekness of death!

'Ah! I was always too hard,' Adam said to himself. 'It's a sore fault in me as I'm so hot and out o' patience with people when they do wrong, and my heart gets shut up against 'em, so as I can't bring myself to forgive 'em. I see clear enough there's more pride nor love in my soul, for I could sooner make a thousand strokes with th' hammer for my father than bring myself to say a kind word to him. And there went plenty o' pride and temper to the strokes, as the devil *will* be having his finger in what we call our duties as well as our sins. Mayhap the best thing I ever did in my life was only doing what was easiest for myself. It's allays been easier for me to work nor to sit still, but the real tough job for me 'ud be to master my own will and temper, and go right against my own pride. It seems to me now, if I was to find father at home to-night, I should behave different; but there's no knowing – perhaps nothing 'ud be a lesson to us if it didn't come too late. It's well we should feel as life's a reckoning we can't make twice over; there's no real making amends in this world, any more nor you can mend a wrong subtraction by doing your addition right.'

This was the key-note to which Adam's thoughts had perpetually returned since his father's death, and the solemn wail of the funeral psalm was only an influence that brought back the old thoughts with stronger emphasis. So was the sermon, which Mr Irwine had chosen with reference to Thias's funeral. It spoke briefly and simply of the words, 'In the midst of life we are in death'[18] – how the present moment is all we can call our own for works of mercy, of righteous dealing, and of family tenderness. All very old truths – but what we thought the oldest truth becomes the most startling to us in the week when we have looked on the dead face of one who has made a part of our own lives. For when men want to impress us with the effect of a new and wonderfully vivid light, do they not let it fall on the most familiar objects, that we may measure its intensity by remembering the former dimness?

Then came the moment of the final blessing, when the forever sublime words, 'The peace of God, which passeth all understanding', seemed to blend with the calm afternoon sunshine that fell on the bowed heads of the congregation; and then the quiet rising, the mothers tying on the bonnets of the little maidens who had slept through the sermon, the fathers collecting the prayer-books, until all streamed out through the old archway into the green churchyard, and began their neighbourly talk, their simple civilities, and their invitations to tea; for on a Sunday every one was ready to receive a guest – it was the day when all must be in their best clothes and their best humour.

Mr and Mrs Poyser paused a minute at the church gate: they were waiting for Adam to come up, not being contented to go away without saying a kind word to the widow and her sons.

'Well, Mrs Bede,' said Mrs Poyser, as they walked on together, 'you must keep up your heart; husbands and wives must be content when they've lived to rear their children and see one another's hair grey.'

'Ay, ay,' said Mr Poyser; 'they wonna have long to wait for one another then, anyhow. And ye've got two o' the strapping'st sons i' th' country; and well you may, for I remember poor Thias as fine a broad-shouldered fellow as need to be; and as for you, Mrs Bede, why you're straighter i' the back nor half the young women now.'

'Eh,' said Lisbeth, 'it's poor luck for the platter to wear well when it's broke i' two. The sooner I'm laid under the thorn the better. I'm no good to nobody now.'

Adam never took notice of his mother's little unjust plaints; but Seth said, 'Nay, mother, thee mustna say so. Thy sons 'ull never get another mother.'

'That's true, lad, that's true,' said Mr Poyser; 'and it's wrong on us to give way to grief, Mrs Bede; for it's like the children cryin' when the fathers and mothers take things from 'em. There's One above knows better nor us.'

'Ah,' said Mrs Poyser, 'an' it's poor work allays settin' the dead above the livin'. We shall all on us be dead some time, I reckon – it 'ud be better if folks 'ud make much on us before-hand, istid o' beginnin' when we're gone. It's but little good you'll do a-watering the last year's crop.'

'Well, Adam,' said Mr Poyser, feeling that his wife's words were, as usual, rather incisive than soothing, and that it would be well to change the subject, 'you'll come and see us again now, I hope. I hanna had a talk with you this long while, and the missis here wants you to see what can be done with her best spinning-wheel, for it's got broke, and it'll be a nice job to mend it – there'll want a bit o' turning. You'll come as soon as you can now, will you?'

Mr Poyser paused and looked round while he was speaking, as if to see where Hetty was; for the children were running on before. Hetty was not without a companion, and she had, besides, more pink and white about her than ever; for she held in her hand the wonderful pink-and-white hot-house plant, with a very long name – a Scotch name, she supposed,[19] since people said Mr Craig the gardener was Scotch. Adam took the opportunity of looking round too; and I am sure you will not require of him that he should feel any vexation in observing a pouting expression on Hetty's face as she listened to the gar-dener's small-talk. Yet in her secret heart she was glad to have him by her side, for she would perhaps learn from him how it was Arthur had not come to church. Not that she cared to ask him the question, but she hoped the information would be given spontaneously; for Mr Craig, like a superior man, was very fond of giving information.

Mr Craig was never aware that his conversation and advances were received coldly, for to shift one's point of view beyond certain limits is impossible to the most liberal and expansive mind; we are none of us aware of the impression we produce on Brazilian monkeys of feeble understanding – it is possible they see hardly anything in us. Moreover, Mr Craig was a man of sober passions, and was already in his tenth year of hesitation as to the relative advantages of matrimony and bachelorhood. It is true that, now and then, when he had been a little heated by an extra glass of grog, he had been heard to say of Hetty

that the 'lass was well enough', and that 'a man might do worse';
but on convivial occasions men are apt to express themselves
strongly.

Martin Poyser held Mr Craig in honour, as a man who 'knew
his business', and who had great lights concerning soils and
compost; but he was less of a favourite with Mrs Poyser, who
had more than once said in confidence to her husband, 'You're
mighty fond o' Craig; but for my part, I think he's welly like a
cock as thinks the sun's rose o' purpose to hear him crow.' For
the rest, Mr Craig was an estimable gardener, and was not
without reasons for having a high opinion of himself. He had
also high shoulders and high cheek-bones, and hung his head
forward a little, as he walked along with his hands in his
breeches-pockets. I think it was his pedigree only that had the
advantage of being Scotch, and not his 'bringing up'; for except
that he had a stronger burr in his accent, his speech differed
little from that of the Loamshire people about him. But a
gardener is Scotch, as a French teacher is Parisian.

'Well, Mr Poyser,' he said, before the good slow farmer had
time to speak, 'ye'll not be carrying your hay to-morrow, I'm
thinking: the glass sticks at "change", and ye may rely upo' my
word as we'll ha' more downfall afore twenty-four hours is
past. Ye see that darkish blue cloud there upo' the 'rizon – ye
know what I mean by the 'rizon, where the land and sky seems
to meet?'

'Ay, ay, I see the cloud,' said Mr Poyser, ' 'rizon or no 'rizon.
It's right o'er Mike Holdsworth's fallow, and a foul fallow
it is.'

'Well, you mark my words, as that cloud 'ull spread o'er the
sky pretty nigh as quick as you'd spread a tarpaulin over one
o' your hay-ricks. It's a great thing to ha' studied the look o'
the clouds. Lord bless you! th' met'orological almanecks can
learn me nothing, but there's a pretty sight o' things I could let
them up to, if they'd just come to me. And how are *you*, Mrs
Poyser? – thinking o' getherin' the red currants soon, I reckon.
You'd a deal better gether 'em afore they're o'er-ripe, wi' such
weather as we've got to look forward to. How do ye do,
Mistress Bede?' Mr Craig continued, without a pause, nodding

by the way to Adam and Seth. 'I hope y' enjoyed them spinach
and gooseberries as I sent Chester with th' other day. If ye want
vegetables while ye're in trouble, ye know where to come to.
It's well known I'm not giving other folks' things away; for
when I've supplied the house, the garden's my own spekilation,
and it isna every man th' old Squire could get as 'ud be equil to
the undertaking, let alone asking whether he'd be willing. I've
got to run my calkilation fine, I can tell you, to make sure o'
getting back the money as I pay the Squire. I should like to see
some o' them fellows as make the almanecks looking as far
before their noses as I've got to do every year as comes.'

'They look pretty fur, though,' said Mr Poyser, turning his
head on one side, and speaking in rather a subdued reverential
tone. 'Why, what could come truer nor that pictur o' the cock
wi' the big spurs, as has got its head knocked down wi' th'
anchor, an' th' firin', an' the ships behind? Why, that pictur
was made afore Christmas, and yit it's come as true as th' Bible.
Why, th' cock's France, an' th' anchor's Nelson[20] – an' they
told us that beforehand.'

'Pee – ee-eh!' said Mr Craig. 'A man doesna want to see fur
to know as th' English 'ull beat the French. Why, I know upo'
good authority as it's a big Frenchman as reaches five foot high,
an' they live upo' spoon-meat[21] mostly. I knew a man as his
father had a particular knowledge o' the French. I should like
to know what them grasshoppers are to do against such fine
fellows as our young Captain Arthur. Why, it 'ud astonish
a Frenchman only to look at him; his arm's thicker nor a
Frenchman's body, I'll be bound, for they pinch theirsells in wi'
stays; and it's easy enough, for they've got nothing i' their
insides.'

'Where *is* the Captain, as he wasna at church to-day?' said
Adam. 'I was talking to him o' Friday, and he said nothing
about his going away.'

'Oh, he's only gone to Eagledale for a bit o' fishing; I reckon
he'll be back again afore many days are o'er, for he's to be at
all th' arranging and preparing o' things for the comin' o' age
o' the 30th o' July. But he's fond o' getting away for a bit, now

XVIII CHURCH   225

and then. Him and th' old Squire fit one another like frost and flowers.'

Mr Craig smiled and winked slowly as he made this last observation, but the subject was not developed farther, for now they had reached the turning in the road where Adam and his companions must say 'good-bye'. The gardener, too, would have had to turn off in the same direction if he had not accepted Mr Poyser's invitation to tea. Mrs Poyser duly seconded the invitation, for she would have held it a deep disgrace not to make her neighbours welcome to her house: personal likes and dislikes must not interfere with that sacred custom. Moreover, Mr Craig had always been full of civilities to the family at the Hall Farm, and Mrs Poyser was scrupulous in declaring that she had 'nothing to say again' him, on'y it was a pity he couldna be hatched o'er again, an' hatched different'.

So Adam and Seth, with their mother between them, wound their way down to the valley and up again to the old house, where a saddened memory had taken the place of a long, long anxiety – where Adam would never have to ask again as he entered, 'Where's father?'

And the other family party, with Mr Craig for company, went back to the pleasant bright house-place at the Hall Farm – all with quiet minds, except Hetty, who knew now where Arthur was gone, but was only the more puzzled and uneasy. For it appeared that his absence was quite voluntary; he need not have gone – he would not have gone if he had wanted to see her. She had a sickening sense that no lot could ever be pleasant to her again if her Thursday night's vision was not to be fulfilled; and in this moment of chill, bare, wintry disappointment and doubt, she looked towards the possibility of being with Arthur again, of meeting his loving glance, and hearing his soft words, with that eager yearning which one may call the 'growing pain' of passion.

CHAPTER XIX

Adam on a Working Day

Notwithstanding Mr Craig's prophecy, the dark-blue cloud dispersed itself without having produced the threatened consequences. 'The weather,' as he observed the next morning – 'the weather, you see, 's a ticklish thing, an' a fool 'ull hit on't sometimes when a wise man misses; that's why the almanecks get so much credit. It's one o' them chancy things as fools thrive on.'

This unreasonable behaviour of the weather, however, could displease no one else in Hayslope beside Mr Craig. All hands were to be out in the meadows this morning as soon as the dew had risen; the wives and daughters did double work in every farmhouse, that the maids might give their help in tossing the hay; and when Adam was marching along the lanes, with his basket of tools over his shoulder, he caught the sound of jocose talk and ringing laughter from behind the hedges. The jocose talk of haymakers is best at a distance; like those clumsy bells round the cows' necks, it has rather a coarse sound when it comes close, and may even grate on your ears painfully; but heard from far off, it mingles very prettily with the other joyous sounds of nature. Men's muscles move better when their souls are making merry music, though their merriment is of a poor blundering sort, not at all like the merriment of birds.

And perhaps there is no time in a summer's day more cheering, than when the warmth of the sun is just beginning to triumph over the freshness of the morning – when there is just a lingering hint of early coolness to keep off languor under the delicious influence of warmth. The reason Adam was walking along the lanes at this time was because his work for the rest

of the day lay at a country house about three miles off, which
was being put in repair for the son of a neighbouring squire;
and he had been busy since early morning with the packing of
panels, doors, and chimney-pieces, in a waggon which was now
gone on before him, while Jonathan Burge himself had ridden
to the spot on horseback, to await its arrival and direct the
workmen.

   This little walk was a rest to Adam, and he was unconsciously
under the charm of the moment. It was summer morning in his
heart, and he saw Hetty in the sunshine: a sunshine without
glare – with slanting rays that tremble between the delicate
shadows of the leaves. He thought, yesterday, when he put out
his hand to her as they came out of church, that there was a
touch of melancholy kindness in her face, such as he had not
seen before, and he took it as a sign that she had some sympathy
with his family trouble. Poor fellow! that touch of melancholy
came from quite another source; but how was he to know? We
look at the one little woman's face we love, as we look at the
face of our mother earth, and see all sorts of answers to our
own yearnings. It was impossible for Adam not to feel that
what had happened in the last week had brought the prospect
of marriage nearer to him. Hitherto he had felt keenly the
danger that some other man might step in and get possession
of Hetty's heart and hand, while he himself was still in a position
that made him shrink from asking her to accept him. Even if
he had had a strong hope that she was fond of him – and his
hope was far from being strong – he had been too heavily
burthened with other claims to provide a home for himself and
Hetty – a home such as he could expect her to be content with
after the comfort and plenty of the Farm. Like all strong
natures, Adam had confidence in his ability to achieve something in the future; he felt sure he should some day, if he lived,
be able to maintain a family, and make a good broad path for
himself; but he had too cool a head not to estimate to the full
the obstacles that were to be overcome. And the time would be
so long! And there was Hetty, like a bright-cheeked apple hanging over the orchard wall, within sight of everybody, and everybody must long for her![1] To be sure, if she loved him very

much, she would be content to wait for him: but *did* she love him? His hopes had never risen so high that he had dared to ask her. He was clear-sighted enough to be aware that her uncle and aunt would have looked kindly on his suit, and indeed without this encouragement he would never have persevered in going to the Farm; but it was impossible to come to any but fluctuating conclusions about Hetty's feelings. She was like a kitten, and had the same distractingly pretty looks, that meant nothing, for everybody that came near her.

But now he could not help saying to himself that the heaviest part of his burden was removed, and that even before the end of another year his circumstances might be brought into a shape that would allow him to think of marrying. It would always be a hard struggle with his mother, he knew: she would be jealous of any wife he might choose, and she had set her mind especially against Hetty – perhaps for no other reason than that she suspected Hetty to be the woman he *had* chosen. It would never do, he feared, for his mother to live in the same house with him when he was married; and yet how hard she would think it if he asked her to leave him! Yes, there was a great deal of pain to be gone through with his mother, but it was a case in which he must make her feel that his will was strong – it would be better for her in the end. For himself, he would have liked that they should all live together till Seth was married, and they might have built a bit themselves to the old house, and made more room. He did not like 'to part wi' th' lad': they had hardly ever been separated for more than a day since they were born.

But Adam had no sooner caught his imagination leaping forward in this way – making arrangements for an uncertain future – than he checked himself. 'A pretty building I'm making, without either bricks or timber. I'm up i' the garret a'ready, and haven't so much as dug the foundation.' Whenever Adam was strongly convinced of any proposition, it took the form of a principle in his mind: it was knowledge to be acted on, as much as the knowledge that damp will cause rust. Perhaps here lay the secret of the hardness he had accused himself of: he had too little fellow-feeling with the weakness that errs in spite of foreseen consequences. Without this fellow-feeling, how are we to get enough patience and charity towards our stumbling, falling companions in the long and changeful journey? And there is but one way in which a strong determined soul can learn it – by getting his heart-strings bound round the weak and erring, so that he must share not only the outward consequence of their error, but their inward suffering. That is a long and hard lesson, and Adam had at present only learned the alphabet of it in his father's sudden death, which, by annihilating in an instant all that had stimulated his indignation, had sent a sudden rush of thought and memory over what had claimed his pity and tenderness.

But it was Adam's strength, not its correlative hardness, that influenced his meditations this morning. He had long made up his mind that it would be wrong as well as foolish for him to marry a blooming young girl, so long as he had no other prospect than that of growing poverty with a growing family. And his savings had been so constantly drawn upon (besides the terrible sweep of paying for Seth's substitute in the militia), that he had not enough money beforehand to furnish even a small cottage, and keep something in reserve against a rainy day. He had good hope that he should be 'firmer on his legs' by-and-by; but he could not be satisfied with a vague confidence in his arm and brain; he must have definite plans, and set about them at once. The partnership with Jonathan Burge was not to be thought of at present – there were things implicitly tacked to it that he could not accept; but Adam thought that he and Seth might carry on a little business for themselves in addition to their journeyman's work, by buying a small stock of superior wood and making articles of household furniture, for which Adam had no end of contrivances. Seth might gain more by working at separate jobs under Adam's direction than by his journeyman's work, and Adam, in his over-hours, could do all the 'nice' work, that required peculiar skill. The money gained in this way, with the good wages he received as foreman, would soon enable them to get beforehand with the world, so sparingly as they would all live now. No sooner had this little plan shaped itself in his mind than he began to be busy with exact calculations about the wood to be bought, and the particular article of furniture that should be undertaken first – a kitchen cupboard of his own contrivance, with such an ingenious arrangement of sliding-doors and bolts, such convenient nooks for stowing household provender, and such a symmetrical result to the eye, that every good housewife would be in raptures with it, and fall through all the gradations of melancholy longing till her husband promised to buy it for her. Adam pictured to himself Mrs Poyser examining it with her keen eye, and trying in vain to find out a deficiency; and, of course, close to Mrs Poyser stood Hetty, and Adam was again beguiled from calculations and contrivances into dreams and hopes. Yes, he would go and see her this evening – it was so long since he had been at the Hall Farm. He would have liked to go to the night-school, to see why Bartle Massey had not been at church yesterday, for he feared his old friend was ill; but, unless he could manage both visits, this last must be put off till to-morrow – the desire to be near Hetty, and to speak to her again, was too strong.

As he made up his mind to this, he was coming very near to the end of his walk, within the sound of the hammers at work on the refitting of the old house. The sound of tools to a clever workman who loves his work is like the tentative sounds of the orchestra to the violinist who has to bear his part in the overture: the strong fibres begin their accustomed thrill, and what was a moment before joy, vexation, or ambition, begins its change into energy. All passion become strength when it has an outlet from the narrow limits of our personal lot in the labour of our right arm, the cunning of our right hand, or the still, creative activity of our thought. Look at Adam through the rest of the day, as he stands on the scaffolding with the two-feet ruler in his hand, whistling low while he considers how a difficulty about a floor-joist or a window-frame is to be overcome; or as he pushes one of the younger workmen aside, and takes his place in upheaving a weight of timber, saying, 'Let alone, lad! thee'st got too much gristle i' thy bones yet'; or as he fixes his keen black eyes on the motions of a workman on the other side of the room, and warns him that his distances are not right. Look at this broad-shouldered man with the bare muscular arms, and the thick firm black hair tossed about like trodden meadow-grass whenever he takes off his paper cap, and with the strong barytone voice bursting every now and then into loud and solemn psalm-tunes, as if seeking an outlet for superfluous strength, yet presently checking himself, apparently crossed by some thought which jars with the singing. Perhaps, if you had not been already in the secret, you might not have guessed what sad memories, what warm affection, what tender fluttering hopes, had their home in this athletic body with the broken finger-nails – in this rough man, who knew no better lyrics than he could find in the Old and New Version[2] and an occasional hymn; who knew the smallest possible amount of profane history; and for whom the motion and shape of the earth, the course of the sun, and the changes of the seasons, lay in the region of mystery just made visible by fragmentary knowledge. It had cost Adam a great deal of trouble, and work in over-hours, to know what he knew over and above the secrets of his handicraft, and that acquaintance with mechanics and figures, and the nature of the materials he worked with, which was made easy to him by inborn inherited faculty – to get the mastery of his pen, and write a plain hand, to spell without any other mistakes than must in fairness be attributed to the unreasonable character of orthography rather than to any deficiency in the speller, and, moreover, to learn his musical notes and part-singing. Besides all this, he had read his Bible, including the apocryphal books; 'Poor Richard's Almanac', Taylor's 'Holy Living and Dying', 'The Pilgrim's Progress', with Bunyan's Life and 'Holy War', a great deal of Bailey's Dictionary, 'Valentine and Orson', and part of a 'History of Babylon',[3] which Bartle Massey had lent him. He might have had many more books from Bartle Massey, but he had no time for reading 'the commin print', as Lisbeth called it, so busy as he was with figures in all the leisure moments which he did not fill up with extra carpentry.

Adam, you perceive, was by no means a marvellous man, nor, properly speaking, a genius, yet I will not pretend that his was an ordinary character among workmen; and it would not be at all a safe conclusion that the next best man you may happen to see with a basket of tools over his shoulder and a paper cap on his head has the strong conscience and the strong sense, the blended susceptibility and self-command, of our friend Adam. He was not an average man. Yet such men as he are reared here and there in every generation of our peasant artisans – with an inheritance of affections nurtured by a simple family life of common need and common industry, and an inheritance of faculties trained in skilful courageous labour: they make their way upward, rarely as geniuses, most commonly as painstaking honest men, with the skill and conscience to do well the tasks that lie before them. Their lives have no discernible echo beyond the neighbourhood where they dwelt, but you are almost sure to find there some good piece of road, some building, some application of mineral produce, some improvement in farming practice, some reform of parish abuses, with which their names are associated by one or two generations after them. Their employers were the richer for them, the work of their hands has worn well, and the work of their brains has guided well the hands of other men. They went about in their youth in flannel or paper caps, in coats black with coal-dust or streaked with lime and red paint; in old age their white hairs are seen in a place of honour at church and at market, and they tell their well-dressed sons and daughters, seated round the bright hearth on winter evenings, how pleased they were when they first earned their twopence a-day. Others there are who die poor, and never put off the workman's coat on week-days: they have not had the art of getting rich; but they are men of trust, and when they die before the work is all out of them, it is as if some main screw had got loose in a machine; the master who employed them says, 'Where shall I find their like?'[4]

CHAPTER XX

Adam Visits the Hall Farm

Adam came back from his work in the empty waggon; that was why he had changed his clothes, and was ready to set out to the Hall Farm when it still wanted a quarter to seven.

'What's thee got thy Sunday cloose on for?' said Lisbeth, complainingly, as he came down-stairs. 'Thee artna goin' to th' school i' thy best coat?'

'No, mother,' said Adam, quietly. 'I'm going to the Hall Farm, but mayhap I may go to the school after, so thee mustna wonder if I'm a bit late. Seth 'ull be at home in half an hour – he's only gone to the village; so thee wutna mind.'

'Eh, an' what's thee got thy best cloose on for to go to th' Hall Farm? The Poyser folks see'd thee in 'em yesterday, I warrand. What dost mean by turnin' worki'day into Sunday a-that'n? It's poor keepin' company wi' folks as donna like to see thee i' thy workin' jacket.'

'Good-bye, mother, I can't stay,' said Adam, putting on his hat and going out.

But he had no sooner gone a few paces beyond the door than Lisbeth became uneasy at the thought that she had vexed him. Of course, the secret of her objection to the best clothes was her suspicion that they were put on for Hetty's sake; but deeper than all her peevishness lay the need that her son should love her. She hurried after him, and laid hold of his arm before he had got half-way down to the brook, and said, 'Nay, my lad, thee wutna go away angered wi' thy mother, an' her got nought to do but to sit by hersen an' think on thee?'

'Nay, nay, mother,' said Adam, gravely, and standing still while he put his arm on her shoulder, 'I'm not angered. But

I wish, for thy own sake, thee'dst be more contented to let me do what I've made up my mind to do. I'll never be no other than a good son to thee as long as we live. But a man has other feelings besides what he owes to's father and mother; and thee oughtna to want to rule over me body and soul. And thee must make up thy mind, as I'll not give way to thee where I've a right to do what I like. So let us have no more words about it.'

'Eh,' said Lisbeth, not willing to show that she felt the real bearing of Adam's words, 'an' who likes to see thee i' thy best cloose better nor thy mother? An' when thee'st got thy face washed as clean as the smooth white pibble, an' thy hair combed so nice, and thy eyes a-sparklin' – what else is there as thy old mother should like to look at half so well? An' thee sha't put on thy Sunday cloose when thee lik'st for me – I'll ne'er plague thee no moor about'n.'

'Well, well; good-bye, mother,' said Adam, kissing her, and hurrying away. He saw there was no other means of putting an end to the dialogue. Lisbeth stood still on the spot, shading her eyes and looking after him till he was quite out of sight. She felt to the full all the meaning that had lain in Adam's words, and, as she lost sight of him and turned back slowly into the house, she said aloud to herself – for it was her way to speak her thoughts aloud in the long days when her husband and sons were at their work – 'Eh, he'll be tellin' me as he's goin' to bring her home one o' these days; an' she'll be missis o'er me, and I mun look on, belike, while she uses the blue-edged platters, and breaks 'em, mayhap, though there's ne'er been one broke sin' my old man an' me bought 'em at the fair twenty 'ear come next Whissuntide. Eh!' she went on, still louder, as she caught up her knitting from the table, 'but she'll ne'er knit the lads' stockins, nor foot 'em nayther, while I live; an' when I'm gone, he'll bethink him as nobody 'ull ne'er fit's leg an' foot as his old mother did. She'll know nothin' o' narrowin' an' heelin,' I warrand, an' she'll make a long toe as he canna get's boot on. That's what comes o' marr'in' young wenches. I war gone thirty, an' th' feyther too, afore we war married; an' young enough too. She'll be a poor dratchell[1] by then *she's* thirty, a-marr'in' a-that'n, afore her teeth's all come.'

Adam walked so fast that he was at the yard gate before seven. Martin Poyser and the grandfather were not yet come in from the meadow: every one was in the meadow, even to the black-and-tan terrier – no one kept watch in the yard but the bull-dog; and when Adam reached the house-door, which stood wide open, he saw there was no one in the bright clean house-place. But he guessed where Mrs Poyser and some one else would be, quite within hearing; so he knocked on the door and said in his strong voice, 'Mrs Poyser within?'

'Come in, Mr Bede, come in,' Mrs Poyser called out from the dairy. She always gave Adam this title when she received him in her own house. 'You may come into the dairy if you will, for I canna justly leave the cheese.'

Adam walked into the dairy, where Mrs Poyser and Nancy were crushing the first evening cheese.

'Why, you might think you war come to a dead-house,' said Mrs Poyser, as he stood in the open doorway; 'they're all i' the meadow; but Martin's sure to be in afore long, for they're leaving the hay cocked to-night, ready for carrying first thing to-morrow. I've been forced t' have Nancy in, upo' 'count as Hetty must gether the red currans to-night; the fruit allays ripens so contrairy, just when every hand's wanted. An' there's no trustin' the children to gether it, for they put more into their own mouths nor into the basket; you might as well set the wasps to gether the fruit.'

Adam longed to say he would go into the garden till Mr Poyser came in, but he was not quite courageous enough, so he said, 'I could be looking at your spinning-wheel, then, and see what wants doing to it. Perhaps it stands in the house, where I can find it?'

'No, I've put it away in the right-hand parlour; but let it be till I can fetch it and show it you. I'd be glad now, if you'd go into the garden, and tell Hetty to send Totty in. The child 'ull run in if she's told, an' I know Hetty's lettin' her eat too many currans. I'll be much obliged to you, Mr Bede, if you'll go and send her in; an' there's the York and Lankester roses beautiful in the garden now – you'll like to see 'em. But you'd like a drink o' whey first, p'r'aps; I know you're fond o' whey, as most folks is when they hanna got to crush it out.'

'Thank you, Mrs Poyser,' said Adam; 'a drink o' whey's allays a treat to me. I'd rather have it than beer any day.'

'Ay, ay,' said Mrs Poyser, reaching a small white basin that stood on the shelf, and dipping it into the whey-tub, 'the smell o' bread's sweet t' everybody but the baker. The Miss Irwines allays say, "Oh, Mrs Poyser, I envy you your dairy; and I envy you your chickens; and what a beautiful thing a farmhouse is, to be sure!" An' I say, "Yes; a farmhouse is a fine thing for them as look on, an' don't know the liftin', an' the stannin', an' the worritin' o' th' inside, as belongs to't."'

'Why, Mrs Poyser, you wouldn't like to live anywhere else but in a farmhouse, so well as you manage it,' said Adam, taking the basin; 'and there can be nothing to look at pleasanter nor a fine milch cow, standing up to'ts knees in pasture, and the new milk frothing in the pail, and the fresh butter ready for market, and the calves, and the poultry. Here's to your health, and may you allays have strength to look after your own dairy, and set a pattern t' all the farmers' wives in the country.'

Mrs Poyser was not to be caught in the weakness of smiling at a compliment, but a quiet complacency overspread her face like a stealing sunbeam, and gave a milder glance than usual to her blue-grey eyes, as she looked at Adam drinking the whey. Ah! I think I taste that whey now – with a flavour so delicate that one can hardly distinguish it from an odour, and with that soft gliding warmth that fills one's imagination with a still, happy dreaminess. And the light music of the dropping whey is in my ears, mingling with the twittering of a bird outside the wire network window – the window overlooking the garden, and shaded by tall Gueldres roses.[2]

'Have a little more, Mr Bede?' said Mrs Poyser, as Adam set down the basin.

'No, thank you; I'll go into the garden now, and send in the little lass.'

'Ay, do; and tell her to come to her mother in the dairy.'

Adam walked round by the rick-yard, at present empty of ricks, to the little wooden gate leading into the garden – once

the well-tended kitchen-garden of a manor-house; now, but
for the handsome brick wall with stone coping that ran along
one side of it, a true farmhouse garden, with hardy perennial
flowers, unpruned fruit-trees, and kitchen vegetables growing
together in careless, half-neglected abundance. In that leafy,
flowery, bushy time, to look for any one in this garden was
like playing at 'hide-and-seek'. There were the tall hollyhocks
beginning to flower, and dazzle the eye with their pink, white,
and yellow; there were the syringas and Gueldres roses, all large
and disorderly for want of trimming; there were leafy walls of
scarlet beans and late peas; there was a row of bushy filberts
in one direction, and in another a huge apple-tree making a
barren circle under its low-spreading boughs. But what signified
a barren patch or two? The garden was so large. There was
always a superfluity of broad beans – it took nine or ten of
Adam's strides to get to the end of the uncut grass walk that
ran by the side of them; and as for other vegetables, there was
so much more room than was necessary for them, that in the
rotation of crops a large flourishing bed of groundsel was of
yearly occurrence on one spot or other. The very rose-trees, at
which Adam stopped to pluck one, looked as if they grew wild;
they were all huddled together in bushy masses, now flaunting
with wide open petals, almost all of them of the streaked pink-
and-white kind, which doubtless dated from the union of the
houses of York and Lancaster.[3] Adam was wise enough to
choose a compact Provence rose that peeped out half-smothered
by its flaunting scentless neighbours, and held it in his hand –
he thought he should be more at ease holding something in his
hand – as he walked on to the far end of the garden, where he
remembered there was the largest row of currant-trees, not far
off from the great yew-tree arbour.

But he had not gone many steps beyond the roses, when he
heard the shaking of a bough, and a boy's voice saying –

'Now, then, Totty, hold out your pinny – there's a duck.'

The voice came from the boughs of a tall cherry-tree, where
Adam had no difficulty in discerning a small blue-pinafored
figure perched in a commodious position where the fruit was
thickest. Doubtless Totty was below, behind the screen of peas.

Yes – with her bonnet hanging down her back, and her fat face, dreadfully smeared with red juice, turned up towards the cherry-tree, while she held her little round hole of a mouth and her red-stained pinafore to receive the promised downfall. I am sorry to say, more than half the cherries that fell were hard and yellow instead of juicy and red; but Totty spent no time in useless regrets, and she was already sucking the third juiciest when Adam said, 'There now, Totty, you've got your cherries. Run into the house with 'em to mother – she wants you – she's in the dairy. Run in this minute – there's a good little girl.'

He lifted her up in his strong arms and kissed her as he spoke, a ceremony which Totty regarded as a tiresome interruption to cherry-eating; and when he set her down she trotted off quite silently towards the house, sucking her cherries as she went along.

'Tommy, my lad, take care you're not shot for a little thieving bird,' said Adam, as he walked on towards the currant-trees.

He could see there was a large basket at the end of the row: Hetty would not be far off, and Adam already felt as if she were looking at him. Yet when he turned the corner she was standing with her back towards him, and stooping to gather the low-hanging fruit. Strange that she had not heard him coming! perhaps it was because she was making the leaves rustle. She started when she became conscious that some one was near – started so violently that she dropped the basin with the currants in it, and then, when she saw it was Adam, she turned from pale to deep red. That blush made his heart beat with a new happiness. Hetty had never blushed at seeing him before.

'I frightened you,' he said, with a delicious sense that it didn't signify what he said, since Hetty seemed to feel as much as he did; 'let *me* pick the currants up.'

That was soon done, for they had only fallen in a tangled mass on the grass-plot, and Adam, as he rose and gave her the basin again, looked straight into her eyes with the subdued tenderness that belongs to the first moments of hopeful love.

Hetty did not turn away her eyes; her blush had subsided and she met his glance with a quiet sadness, which contented

Adam, because it was so unlike anything he had seen in her before.

'There's not many more currants to get,' she said; 'I shall soon ha' done now.'

'I'll help you,' said Adam; and he fetched the large basket which was nearly full of currants, and set it close to them.

Not a word more was spoken as they gathered the currants. Adam's heart was too full to speak, and he thought Hetty knew all that was in it. She was not indifferent to his presence after all; she had blushed when she saw him, and then there was that touch of sadness about her which must surely mean love, since it was the opposite of her usual manner, which had often impressed him as indifference. And he could glance at her continually as she bent over the fruit, while the level evening sunbeams stole through the thick apple-tree boughs, and rested on her round cheek and neck as if they too were in love with her. It was to Adam the time that a man can least forget in after-life, – the time when he believes that the first woman he has ever loved betrays by a slight something – a word, a tone, a glance, the quivering of a lip or an eyelid – that she is at least beginning to love him in return. The sign is so slight, it is scarcely perceptible to the ear or eye – he could describe it to no one – it is a mere feather-touch, yet it seems to have changed his whole being, to have merged an uneasy yearning into a delicious unconsciousness of everything but the present moment. So much of our early gladness vanishes utterly from our memory: we can never recall the joy with which we laid our heads on our mother's bosom or rode on our father's back in childhood; doubtless that joy is wrought up into our nature, as the sunlight of long-past mornings is wrought up in the soft mellowness of the apricot; but it is gone for ever from our imagination, and we can only *believe* in the joy of childhood. But the first glad moment in our first love is a vision which returns to us to the last, and brings with it a thrill of feeling intense and special as the recurrent sensation of a sweet odour breathed in a far-off hour of happiness. It is a memory that gives a more exquisite touch to tenderness, that feeds the madness of jealousy, and adds the last keenness to the agony of despair.

Hetty bending over the red bunches, the level rays piercing the screen of apple-tree boughs, the length of bushy garden beyond, his own emotion as he looked at her and believed that she was thinking of him, and that there was no need for them to talk – Adam remembered it all to the last moment of his life.

And Hetty? You know quite well that Adam was mistaken about her. Like many other men, he thought the signs of love for another were signs of love towards himself. When Adam was approaching unseen by her, she was absorbed as usual in thinking and wondering about Arthur's possible return: the sound of any man's footstep would have affected her just in the same way – she would have *felt* it might be Arthur before she had time to see, and the blood that forsook her cheek in the agitation of that momentary feeling would have rushed back again at the sight of any one else just as much as at the sight of Adam. He was not wrong in thinking that a change had come over Hetty: the anxieties and fears of a first passion, with which she was trembling, had become stronger than vanity, had given her for the first time that sense of helpless dependence on another's feeling which awakens the clinging deprecating womanhood even in the shallowest girl that can ever experience it, and creates in her a sensibility to kindness which found her quite hard before. For the first time Hetty felt that there was something soothing to her in Adam's timid yet manly tenderness: she wanted to be treated lovingly – oh, it was very hard to bear this blank of absence, silence, apparent indifference, after those moments of glowing love! She was not afraid that Adam would tease her with love-making and flattering speeches like her other admirers: he had always been so reserved to her: she could enjoy without any fear the sense that this strong brave man loved her, and was near her. It never entered into her mind that Adam was pitiable too – that Adam, too, must suffer one day.

Hetty, we know, was not the first woman that had behaved more gently to the man who loved her in vain, because she had herself begun to love another. It was a very old story; but Adam knew nothing about it, so he drank in the sweet delusion.

'That'll do,' said Hetty, after a little while. 'Aunt wants me to leave some on the trees. I'll take 'em in now.'

'It's very well I came to carry the basket,' said Adam, 'for it 'ud ha' been too heavy for your little arms.'

'No; I could ha' carried it with both hands.'

'Oh, I daresay,' said Adam, smiling, 'and been as long getting into the house as a little ant carrying a caterpillar. Have you ever seen those tiny fellows carrying things four times as big as themselves?'

'No,' said Hetty, indifferently, not caring to know the difficulties of ant-life.

'Oh, I used to watch 'em often when I was a lad. But now, you see, I can carry the basket with one arm, as if it was an empty nutshell, and give you th' other arm to lean on. Won't you? Such big arms as mine were made for little arms like yours to lean on.'

Hetty smiled faintly, and put her arm within his. Adam looked down at her, but her eyes were turned dreamily towards another corner of the garden.

'Have you ever been to Eagledale?' she said, as they walked slowly along.

'Yes,' said Adam, pleased to have her ask a question about himself; 'ten years ago, when I was a lad, I went with father to see about some work there. It's a wonderful sight – rocks and caves such as you never saw in your life. I never had a right notion o' rocks till I went there.'

'How long did it take to get there?'

'Why, it took us the best part o' two days' walking. But it's nothing of a day's journey for anybody as has got a first-rate nag. The Captain 'ud get there in nine or ten hours, I'll be bound, he's such a rider. And I shouldn't wonder if he's back again to-morrow; he's too active to rest long in that lonely place, all by himself, for there's nothing but a bit of a inn i' that part where he's gone to fish. I wish he'd got th' estate in his hands; that 'ud be the right thing for him, for it 'ud give him plenty to do, and he'd do't well too, for all he's so young; he's got better notions o' things than many a man twice his age. He spoke very handsome to me th' other day about lending me money to set up i' business; and if things came round that way, I'd rather be beholding to him nor to any man i' the world.'

Poor Adam was led on to speak about Arthur because he thought Hetty would be pleased to know that the young squire was so ready to befriend him; the fact entered into his future prospects, which he would like to seem promising in her eyes. And it was true that Hetty listened with an interest which brought a new light into her eyes and a half smile upon her lips.

'How pretty the roses are now!' Adam continued, pausing to look at them. 'See! I stole the prettiest, but I didna mean to keep it myself. I think these as are all pink, and have got a finer sort o' green leaves, are prettier than the striped uns, don't you?'

He set down the basket, and took the rose from his button-hole.

'It smells very sweet,' he said; 'those striped uns have no smell. Stick it in your frock, and then you can put it in water after. It 'ud be a pity to let it fade.'

Hetty took the rose, smiling as she did so at the pleasant thought that Arthur could so soon get back if he liked. There was a flash of hope and happiness in her mind, and with a sudden impulse of gaiety she did what she had very often done before – stuck the rose in her hair a little above the left ear. The tender admiration in Adam's face was slightly shadowed by reluctant disapproval. Hetty's love of finery was just the thing that would most provoke his mother, and he himself disliked it as much as it was possible for him to dislike anything that belonged to her.

'Ah,' he said, 'that's like the ladies in the pictures at the Chase; they've mostly got flowers or feathers or gold things i' their hair, but somehow I don't like to see 'em: they allays put me i' mind o' the painted women outside the shows at Treddles'on fair. What can a woman have to set her off better than her own hair, when it curls so, like yours? If a woman's young and pretty, I think you can see her good looks all the better for her being plain dressed. Why, Dinah Morris looks very nice, for all she wears such a plain cap and gown. It seems to me as a woman's face doesna want flowers; it's almost like a flower itself. I'm sure yours is.'

'Oh, very well,' said Hetty, with a little playful pout, taking the rose out of her hair. 'I'll put one o' Dinah's caps on when we go in, and you'll see if I look better in it. She left one behind, so I can take the pattern.'

'Nay, nay, I don't want you to wear a Methodist cap like Dinah's. I daresay it's a very ugly cap, and I used to think when I saw her here, as it was nonsense for her to dress different t' other people; but I never rightly noticed her till she came to see mother last week, and then I thought the cap seemed to fit her face somehow as th' acorn cup fits th' acorn, and I shouldn't like to see her so well without it. But you've got another sort o' face; I'd have you just as you are now, without anything t' interfere with your own looks. It's like when a man's singing a good tune, you don't want t' hear bells tinkling and interfering wi' the sound.'

He took her arm and put it within his again, looking down on her fondly. He was afraid she should think he had lectured her; imagining, as we are apt to do, that she had perceived all the thoughts he had only half expressed. And the thing he dreaded most was lest any cloud should come over this evening's happiness. For the world he would not have spoken of his love to Hetty yet, till this commencing kindness towards him should have grown into unmistakable love. In his imagination he saw long years of his future life stretching before him, blest with the right to call Hetty his own: he could be content with very little at present. So he took up the basket of currants once more, and they went on towards the house.

The scene had quite changed in the half-hour that Adam had been in the garden. The yard was full of life now: Marty was letting the screaming geese through the gate, and wickedly provoking the gander by hissing at him; the granary-door was groaning on its hinges as Alick shut it, after dealing out the corn; the horses were being led out to watering, amidst much barking of all the three dogs, and many 'whups' from Tim the ploughman, as if the heavy animals who held down their meek, intelligent heads, and lifted their shaggy feet so deliberately, were likely to rush wildly in every direction but the right. Everybody was come back from the meadow; and when Hetty and Adam entered the house-place, Mr Poyser was seated in the three-cornered chair, and the grandfather in the large arm-chair opposite, looking on with pleasant expectation while the supper was being laid on the oak table. Mrs Poyser had laid the cloth herself – a cloth made of homespun linen, with a shining checkered pattern on it, and of an agreeable whitey-brown hue, such as all sensible housewives like to see – none of your bleached 'shop-rag' that would wear into holes in no time, but good homespun that would last for two generations. The cold veal, the fresh lettuces, and the stuffed chine, might well look tempting to hungry men who had dined at half-past twelve o'clock. On the large deal table against the wall there were bright pewter plates and spoons and cans, ready for Alick and his companions; for the master and servants ate their supper not far off each other; which was all the pleasanter, because if a remark about to-morrow morning's work occurred to Mr Poyser, Alick was at hand to hear it.

'Well, Adam, I'm glad to see ye,' said Mr Poyser. 'What! ye've been helping Hetty to gether the currans, eh? Come, sit ye down, sit ye down. Why, it's pretty near a three-week since y' had your supper with us; and the missis has got one of her rare stuffed chines. I'm glad ye're come.'

'Hetty,' said Mrs Poyser, as she looked into the basket of currants to see if the fruit was fine, 'run up-stairs, and send Molly down. She's putting Totty to bed, and I want her to draw th' ale, for Nancy's busy yet i' the dairy. You can see to the child. But whativer did you let her run away from you along wi' Tommy for, and stuff herself wi' fruit as she can't eat a bit o' good victual?'

This was said in a lower tone than usual, while her husband was talking to Adam; for Mrs Poyser was strict in adherence to her own rules of propriety, and she considered that a young girl was not to be treated sharply in the presence of a respectable man who was courting her. That would not be fair-play: every woman was young in her turn, and had her chances of matri-mony, which it was a point of honour for other women not to spoil – just as one market-woman who has sold her own eggs must not try to balk another of a customer.

Hetty made haste to run away up-stairs, not easily finding an answer to her aunt's question, and Mrs Poyser went out to see after Marty and Tommy, and bring them in to supper.

Soon they were all seated – the two rosy lads, one on each side, by the pale mother, a place being left for Hetty between Adam and her uncle. Alick too was come in, and was seated in his far corner, eating cold broad beans out of a large dish with his pocket-knife, and finding a flavour in them which he would not have exchanged for the finest pine-apple.

'What a time that gell is drawing th' ale, to be sure!' said Mrs Poyser, when she was dispensing her slices of stuffed chine. 'I think she sets the jug under and forgets to turn the tap, as there's nothing you can't believe o' them wenches: they'll set the empty kettle o' the fire, and then come an hour after to see if the water boils.'

'She's drawin' for the men too,' said Mr Poyser. 'Thee shouldst ha' told her to bring our jug up first.'

'Told her?' said Mrs Poyser: 'Yes, I might spend all the wind i' my body, an' take the bellows too, if I was to tell them gells everything as their own sharpness wonna tell 'em. Mr Bede, will you take some vinegar with your lettuce? Ay, you're i' the right not. It spoils the flavour o' the chine, to my thinking. It's poor eating where the flavour o' the meat lies i' the cruets. There's folks as make bad butter, and trusten to the salt t' hide it.'

Mrs Poyser's attention was here diverted by the appearance of Molly, carrying a large jug, two small mugs, and four drinking-cans, all full of ale or small beer – an interesting example of the prehensile power possessed by the human hand. Poor Molly's mouth was rather wider open than usual, as she walked along with her eyes fixed on the double cluster of vessels in her hands, quite innocent of the expression in her mistress's eye.

'Molly, I niver knew your equils – to think o' your poor mother as is a widow, an' I took you wi' as good as no character, an' the times an' times I've told you'. . . .

Molly had not seen the lightning, and the thunder shook her

nerves the more for the want of that preparation. With a vague alarmed sense that she must somehow comport herself differently, she hastened her step a little towards the far deal table, where she might set down her cans – caught her foot in her apron, which had become untied, and fell with a crash and a splash into a pool of beer; whereupon a tittering explosion from Marty and Tommy, and a serious 'Ello!' from Mr Poyser, who saw his draught of ale unpleasantly deferred.

'There you go!' resumed Mrs Poyser, in a cutting tone, as she rose and went towards the cupboard while Molly began dolefully to pick up the fragments of pottery. 'It's what I told you 'ud come, over and over again; and there's your month's wage gone, and more, to pay for that jug as I've had i' the house this ten year, and nothing ever happened to't before; but the crockery you've broke sin' here in th' house you've been 'ud make a parson swear – God forgi' me for saying so; an' if it had been boiling wort⁴ out o' the copper, it 'ud ha' been the same, and you'd ha' been scalded, and very like lamed for life, as there's no knowing but what you will be some day if you go on; for anybody 'ud think you'd got the St Vitus's Dance,⁵ to see the things you've throwed down. It's a pity but what the bits was stacked up for you to see, though it's neither seeing nor hearing as 'ull make much odds to you – anybody 'ud think you war case-hardened.'

Poor Molly's tears were dropping fast by this time, and in her desperation at the lively movement of the beer-stream towards Alick's legs, she was converting her apron into a mop, while Mrs Poyser, opening the cupboard, turned a blighting eye upon her.

'Ah,' she went on, 'you'll do no good wi' crying an' making more wet to wipe up. It's all your own wilfulness, as I tell you, for there's nobody no call to break anything if they'll only go the right way to work. But wooden folks had need ha' wooden things t' handle. And here must I take the brown-and-white jug, as it's niver been used three times this year, and go down i' the cellar myself, and belike catch my death, and be laid up wi' inflammation'. . . .

Mrs Poyser had turned round from the cupboard with the

brown-and-white jug in her hand, when she caught sight of something at the other end of the kitchen; perhaps it was because she was already trembling and nervous that the appar- ition had so strong an effect on her; perhaps jug-breaking, like other crimes, has a contagious influence. However it was, she stared and started like a ghost-seer, and the precious brown- and-white jug fell to the ground, parting for ever with its spout and handle.

'Did ever anybody see the like?' she said, with a suddenly lowered tone, after a moment's bewildered glance round the room. 'The jugs are bewitched, I think. It's them nasty glazed handles – they slip o'er the finger like a snail.'

'Why, thee'st let thy own whip fly i' thy face,' said her hus- band, who had now joined in the laugh of the young ones.

'It's all very fine to look on and grin,' rejoined Mrs Poyser; 'but there's times when the crockery seems alive, an' flies out o' your hand like a bird. It's like the glass, sometimes, 'ull crack as it stands. What is to be broke *will* be broke, for I never dropped a thing i' my life for want o' holding it, else I should never ha' kept the crockery all these 'ears as I bought at my own wedding. And Hetty, are you mad? Whativer do you mean by coming down i' that way, and making one think as there's a ghost a-walking i' th' house?'

A new outbreak of laughter, while Mrs Poyser was speaking, was caused, less by her sudden conversion to a fatalistic view of jug-breaking, than by that strange appearance of Hetty, which had startled her aunt. The little minx had found a black gown of her aunt's, and pinned it close round her neck to look like Dinah's, had made her hair as flat as she could, and had tied on one of Dinah's high-crowned borderless net-caps. The thought of Dinah's pale grave face and mild grey eyes, which the sight of the gown and cap brought with it, made it a laughable surprise enough to see them replaced by Hetty's round rosy cheeks and coquettish dark eyes. The boys got off their chairs and jumped round her, clapping their hands, and even Alick gave a low ventral laugh as he looked up from his beans. Under cover of the noise, Mrs Poyser went into the back kitchen to send Nancy into the cellar with the great pewter measure, which had some chance of being free from bewitchment.

'Why, Hetty, lass, are ye turned Methodist?' said Mr Poyser, with that comfortable slow enjoyment of a laugh which one only sees in stout people. 'You must pull your face a deal longer before you'll do for one; mustna she, Adam? How come you to put them things on, eh?'

'Adam said he liked Dinah's cap and gown better nor my clothes,' said Hetty, sitting down demurely. 'He says folks look better in ugly clothes.'

'Nay, nay,' said Adam, looking at her admiringly; 'I only said they seemed to suit Dinah. But if I'd said you'd look pretty in 'em, I should ha' said nothing but what was true.'

'Why, thee thought'st Hetty war a ghost, didstna?' said Mr Poyser to his wife, who now came back and took her seat again. 'Thee look'dst as scared as scared.'

'It little sinnifies how I looked,' said Mrs Poyser; 'looks 'ull mend no jugs, nor laughing neither, as I see. Mr Bede, I'm sorry you've to wait so long for your ale, but it's coming in a minute. Make yourself at home wi' th' cold potatoes: I know you like 'em. Tommy, I'll send you to bed this minute, if you don't give over laughing. What is there to laugh at, I should like to know? I'd sooner cry nor laugh at the sight o' that poor thing's cap; and there's them as 'ud be better if they could make theirselves like her i' more ways nor putting on her cap. It little becomes anybody i' this house to make fun o' my sister's child, an' her just gone away from us, as it went to my heart to part wi' her: an' I know one thing, as if trouble was to come, an' I was to be laid up i' my bed, an' the children was to die – as there's no knowing but what they will – an' the murrain was to come among the cattle again, an' everything went to rack an' ruin – I say we might be glad to get sight o' Dinah's cap again, wi' her own face under it, border or no border. For she's one o' them things as looks the brightest on a rainy day, and loves you the best when you're most i' need on't.'

Mrs Poyser, you perceive, was aware that nothing would be so likely to expel the comic as the terrible. Tommy, who was of a susceptible disposition, and very fond of his mother, and

who had, besides, eaten so many cherries as to have his feelings
less under command than usual, was so affected by the dreadful
picture she had made of the possible future, that he began to
cry; and the good-natured father, indulgent to all weaknesses
but those of negligent farmers, said to Hetty –

'You'd better take the things off again, my lass; it hurts your
aunt to' see 'em.'

Hetty went up-stairs again, and the arrival of the ale made
an agreeable diversion; for Adam had to give his opinion of the
new tap, which could not be otherwise than complimentary to
Mrs Poyser; and then followed a discussion on the secrets of
good brewing, the folly of stinginess in 'hopping', and the
doubtful economy of a farmer's making his own malt. Mrs
Poyser had so many opportunities of expressing herself with
weight on these subjects, that by the time supper was ended,
the ale jug refilled, and Mr Poyser's pipe alight, she was once
more in high good-humour, and ready, at Adam's request, to
fetch the broken spinning-wheel for his inspection.

'Ah,' said Adam, looking at it carefully, 'here's a nice bit o'
turning wanted. It's a pretty wheel. I must have it up at the
turning-shop in the village, and do it there, for I've no convenence for turning at home. If you'll send it to Mr Burge's
shop i' the morning, I'll get it done for you by Wednesday. I've
been turning it over in my mind,' he continued, looking at Mr
Poyser, 'to make a bit more convenence at home for nice jobs
o' cabinet-making. I've always done a deal at such little things
in odd hours, and they're profitable, for there's more workmanship nor material in 'em. I look for me and Seth to get a little
business for ourselves i' that way, for I know a man at Rosseter
as 'ull take as many things as we should make, besides what we
could get orders for round about.'

Mr Poyser entered with interest into a project which seemed
a step towards Adam's becoming a 'master-man'; and Mrs
Poyser gave her approbation to the scheme of the movable
kitchen cupboard, which was to be capable of containing
grocery, pickles, crockery, and house-linen, in the utmost com-
pactness, without confusion. Hetty, once more in her own dress,
with her neckerchief pushed a little backwards on this warm

evening, was seated picking currants near the window, where Adam could see her quite well. And so the time passed pleasantly till Adam got up to go. He was pressed to come again soon, but not to stay longer, for at this busy time sensible people would not run the risk of being sleepy at five o'clock in the morning.

'I shall take a step farther,' said Adam, 'and go on to see Mester Massey, for he wasn't at church yesterday, and I've not seen him for a week past. I've never hardly known him to miss church before.'

'Ay,' said Mr Poyser, 'we've heared nothing about him, for it's the boys' hollodays⁶ now, so we can give you no account.'

'But you'll niver think o' going there at this hour o' the night?' said Mrs Poyser, folding up her knitting.

'Oh, Mester Massey sits up late,' said Adam. 'An' the night-school's not over yet. Some o' the men don't come till late – they've got so far to walk. And Bartle himself's never in bed till it's gone eleven.'

'I wouldna have him to live wi' me, then,' said Mrs Poyser, 'a-dropping candle-grease about, as you're like to tumble down o' the floor the first thing i' the morning.'

'Ay, eleven o'clock's late – it's late,' said old Martin. 'I ne'er sot up so i' *my* life, not to say as it warna a marr'in', or a christenin', or a wake, or th' harvest-supper. Eleven o'clock's late.'

'Why, I sit up till after twelve often,' said Adam, laughing, 'but it isn't t' eat and drink extry, it's to work extry. Good-night, Mrs Poyser; good-night, Hetty.'

Hetty could only smile and not shake hands, for hers were dyed and damp with currant juice; but all the rest gave a hearty shake to the large palm that was held out to them, and said, 'Come again, come again!'

'Ay, think o' that now,' said Mr Poyser, when Adam was out on the causeway. 'Sitting up till past twelve to do extry work! Ye'll not find many men o' six-an'-twenty as 'ull do to put i' the shafts wi' him. If you can catch Adam for a husband, Hetty, you'll ride i' your own spring-cart some day, I'll be your warrant.'

Hetty was moving across the kitchen with the currants, so her uncle did not see the little toss of the head with which she answered him. To ride in a spring-cart seemed a very miserable lot indeed to her now.

CHAPTER XXI

The Night-School and the Schoolmaster

Bartle Massey's was one of a few scattered houses on the edge of a common, which was divided by the road to Treddleston. Adam reached it in a quarter of an hour after leaving the Hall Farm; and when he had his hand on the door-latch, he could see, through the curtainless window, that there were eight or nine heads bending over the desks, lighted by thin dips.[1]

When he entered, a reading lesson was going forward, and Bartle Massey merely nodded, leaving him to take his place where he pleased. He had not come for the sake of a lesson to-night, and his mind was too full of personal matters, too full of the last two hours he had passed in Hetty's presence, for him to amuse himself with a book till school was over; so he sat down in a corner, and looked on with an absent mind. It was a sort of scene which Adam had beheld almost weekly for years; he knew by heart every arabesque flourish in the framed specimen of Bartle Massey's handwriting which hung over the schoolmaster's head, by way of keeping a lofty ideal before the minds of his pupils; he knew the backs of all the books on the shelf running along the whitewashed wall above the pegs for the slates; he knew exactly how many grains were gone out of the ear of Indian-corn that hung from one of the rafters; he had long ago exhausted the resources of his imagination in trying to think how the bunch of leathery sea-weed had looked and grown in its native element; and from the place where he sat, he could make nothing of the old map of England that hung against the opposite wall, for age had turned it of a fine yellow brown, something like that of a well-seasoned meer-schaum.[2] The drama that was going on was almost as familiar as the scene, nevertheless habit had not made him indifferent to it, and even in his present self-absorbed mood, Adam felt a momentary stirring of the old fellow-feeling, as he looked at the rough men painfully holding pen or pencil with their cramped hands, or humbly labouring through their reading lesson.

The reading class now seated on the form in front of the schoolmaster's desk, consisted of the three most backward pupils. Adam would have known it, only by seeing Bartle Massey's face as he looked over his spectacles, which he had shifted to the ridge of his nose, not requiring them for present purposes. The face wore its mildest expression: the grizzled bushy eyebrows had taken their more acute angle of compassionate kindness, and the mouth, habitually compressed with a pout of the lower lip, was relaxed so as to be ready to speak a helpful word or syllable in a moment. This gentle expression was the more interesting because the schoolmaster's nose, an irregular aquiline twisted a little on one side, had rather a formidable character; and his brow, moreover, had that peculiar tension which always impresses one as a sign of a keen impatient temperament: the blue veins stood out like cords under the transparent yellow skin, and this intimidating brow was softened by no tendency to baldness, for the grey bristly hair, cut down to about an inch in length, stood round it in as close ranks as ever.

'Nay, Bill, nay,' Bartle was saying in a kind tone, as he nodded to Adam, 'begin that again, and then perhaps, it'll come to you what d, r, y, spells. It's the same lesson you read last week, you know.'

'Bill' was a sturdy fellow, aged four-and-twenty, an excellent stone-sawyer, who could get as good wages as any man in the trade of his years; but he found a reading lesson in words of one syllable a harder matter to deal with than the hardest stone he had ever had to saw. The letters, he complained, were so 'uncommon alike, there was no tellin' 'em one from another', the sawyer's business not being concerned with minute differences such as exist between a letter with its tail turned up and a letter with its tail turned down. But Bill had a firm determination that he would learn to read, founded chiefly on two reasons: first, that Tom Hazelow, his cousin, could read

anything 'right off', whether it was print or writing, and Tom
had sent him a letter from twenty miles off, saying how he was
prospering in the world, and had got an overlooker's place;
secondly, that Sam Phillips, who sawed with him, had learned
to read when he was turned twenty; and what could be done
by a little fellow like Sam Phillips, Bill considered, could be
done by himself, seeing that he could pound Sam into wet clay
if circumstances required it. So here he was, pointing his big
finger towards three words at once, and turning his head on
one side that he might keep better hold with his eye of the one
word which was to be discriminated out of the group. The
amount of knowledge Bartle Massey must possess was something so dim and vast that Bill's imagination recoiled before it:
he would hardly have ventured to deny that the schoolmaster
might have something to do in bringing about the regular return
of daylight and the changes in the weather.

The man seated next to Bill was of a very different type: he
was a Methodist brickmaker, who, after spending thirty years
of his life in perfect satisfaction with his ignorance, had lately
'got religion', and along with it the desire to read the Bible. But
with him, too, learning was a heavy business, and on his way
out to-night he had offered as usual a special prayer for help,
seeing that he had undertaken this hard task with a single eye
to the nourishment of his soul – that he might have a greater
abundance of texts and hymns wherewith to banish evil memories and the temptations of old habit; or, in brief language,
the devil. For the brickmaker had been a notorious poacher,
and was suspected, though there was no good evidence against
him, of being the man who had shot a neighbouring gamekeeper
in the leg. However that might be, it is certain that shortly after
the accident referred to, which was coincident with the arrival
of an awakening Methodist preacher at Treddleston, a great
change had been observed in the brickmaker; and though he
was still known in the neighbourhood by his old sobriquet of
'Brimstone',[3] there was nothing he held in so much horror
as any farther transactions with that evil-smelling element.
He was a broad-chested fellow, with a fervid temperament,
which helped him better in imbibing religious ideas than in

the dry process of acquiring the mere human knowledge of the alphabet. Indeed, he had been already a little shaken in his resolution by a brother Methodist, who assured him that the letter was a mere obstruction to the Spirit, and expressed a fear that Brimstone was too eager for the knowledge that puffeth up.

The third beginner was a much more promising pupil. He was a tall but thin and wiry man, nearly as old as Brimstone, with a very pale face, and hands stained a deep blue. He was a dyer, who, in the course of dipping homespun wool and old women's petticoats, had got fired with the ambition to learn a great deal more about the strange secrets of colour. He had already a high reputation in the district for his dyes, and he was bent on discovering some method by which he could reduce the expense of crimsons and scarlets. The druggist at Treddleston had given him a notion that he might save himself a great deal of labour and expense if he could learn to read, and so he had begun to give his spare hours to the night-school, resolving that his 'little chap' should lose no time in coming to Mr Massey's day-school as soon as he was old enough.

It was touching to see these three big men, with the marks of their hard labour about them, anxiously bending over the worn books, and painfully making out, 'The grass is green', 'The sticks are dry', 'The corn is ripe' – a very hard lesson to pass to after columns of single words all alike except in the first letter. It was almost as if three rough animals were making humble efforts to learn how they might become human. And it touched the tenderest fibre in Bartle Massey's nature, for such full-grown children as these were the only pupils for whom he had no severe epithets, and no impatient tones. He was not gifted with an imperturbable temper, and on music-nights it was apparent that patience could never be an easy virtue to him; but this evening, as he glances over his spectacles at Bill Downes, the sawyer, who is turning his head on one side with a desperate sense of blankness before the letters d, r, y, his eyes shed their mildest and most encouraging light.

After the reading class, two youths, between sixteen and nineteen, came up with imaginary bills of parcels, which they had been writing out on their slates, and were now required to

calculate 'off-hand' – a test which they stood with such imperfect success that Bartle Massey, whose eyes had been glaring at
them ominously through his spectacles for some minutes, at
length burst out in a bitter, high-pitched tone, pausing between
every sentence to rap the floor with a knobbed stick which
rested between his legs.

'Now, you see, you don't do this thing a bit better than you
did a fortnight ago; and I'll tell you what's the reason. You
want to learn accounts; that's well and good. But you think all
you need do to learn accounts is to come to me and do sums
for an hour or so, two or three times a-week; and no sooner do
you get your caps on and turn out of doors again, than you
sweep the whole thing clean out of your mind. You go whistling
about, and take no more care what you're thinking of than if
your heads were gutters for any rubbish to swill through that
happened to be in the way; and if you get a good notion in 'em,
it's pretty soon washed out again. You think knowledge is to
be got cheap – you'll come and pay Bartle Massey sixpence
a-week, and he'll make you clever at figures without your taking
any trouble. But knowledge isn't to be got with paying sixpence,
let me tell you: if you're to know figures, you must turn 'em
over in your own heads, and keep your thoughts fixed on 'em.
There's nothing you can't turn into a sum, for there's nothing
but what's got number in it – even a fool. You may say to
yourselves, "I'm one fool, and Jack's another; if my fool's head
weighed four pound, and Jack's three pound three ounces and
three quarters, how many pennyweights heavier would my head
be than Jack's?" A man that had got his heart in learning figures
would make sums for himself, and work 'em in his head: when
he sat at his shoemaking, he'd count his stitches by fives, and
then put a price on his stitches, say half a farthing, and then see
how much money he could get in an hour; and then ask himself
how much money he'd get in a day at that rate; and then how
much ten workmen would get working three, or twenty, or a
hundred years at that rate – and all the while his needle would
be going just as fast as if he left his head empty for the devil to
dance in. But the long and the short of it is – I'll have nobody
in my night-school that doesn't strive to learn what he comes

to learn, as hard as if he was striving to get out of a dark hole into broad daylight. I'll send no man away because he's stupid: if Billy Taft, the idiot, wanted to learn anything, I'd not refuse to teach him. But I'll not throw away good knowledge on people who think they can get it by the sixpenn'orth, and carry it away with 'em as they would an ounce of snuff. So never come to me again, if you can't show that you've been working with your own heads, instead of thinking you can pay for mine to work for you. That's the last word I've got to say to you.'

With this final sentence, Bartle Massey gave a sharper rap than ever with his knobbed stick, and the discomfited lads got up to go with a sulky look. The other pupils had happily only their writing-books to show, in various stages of progress from pot-hooks to round text; and mere pen-strokes, however perverse, were less exasperating to Bartle than false arithmetic. He was a little more severe than usual on Jacob Storey's Z's, of which poor Jacob had written a pageful, all with their tops turned the wrong way, with a puzzled sense that they were not right 'somehow'. But he observed in apology, that it was a letter you never wanted hardly, and he thought it had only been put there 'to finish off th' alphabet, like, though ampus-and (&) would ha' done as well, for what he could see'.

At last the pupils had all taken their hats and said their 'Good-nights', and Adam, knowing his old master's habits, rose and said, 'Shall I put the candles out, Mr Massey?'

'Yes, my boy, yes, all but this, which I'll carry into the house; and just lock the outer door, now you're near it,' said Bartle, getting his stick in the fitting angle to help him in descending from his stool. He was no sooner on the ground than it became obvious why the stick was necessary – the left leg was much shorter than the right. But the schoolmaster was so active with his lameness, that it was hardly thought of as a misfortune; and if you had seen him make his way along the schoolroom floor, and up the step into his kitchen, you would perhaps have understood why the naughty boys sometimes felt that his pace might be indefinitely quickened, and that he and his stick might overtake them even in their swiftest run.

The moment he appeared at the kitchen door with the candle in his hand, a faint whimpering began in the chimney-corner, and a brown-and-tan-coloured bitch, of that wise-looking breed with short legs and long body, known to an unmechanical generation as turnspits, came creeping along the floor, wagging her tail, and hesitating at every other step, as if her affections were painfully divided between the hamper in the chimney-corner and the master, whom she could not leave without a greeting.

'Well, Vixen, well then, how are the babbies?' said the school-master, making haste towards the chimney-corner, and holding the candle over the low hamper, where two extremely blind puppies lifted up their heads towards the light, from a nest of flannel and wool. Vixen could not even see her master look at them without painful excitement: she got into the hamper and got out again the next moment, and behaved with true feminine folly, though looking all the while as wise as a dwarf with a large old-fashioned head and body on the most abbreviated legs.

'Why, you've got a family, I see, Mr Massey?' said Adam, smiling, as he came into the kitchen. 'How's that? I thought it was against the law here.'

'Law? What's the use o' law when a man's once such a fool as to let a woman into his house?' said Bartle, turning away from the hamper with some bitterness. He always called Vixen a woman, and seemed to have lost all consciousness that he was using a figure of speech. 'If I'd known Vixen was a woman, I'd never have held the boys from drowning her; but when I'd got her into my hand, I was forced to take to her. And now you see what she's brought me to – the sly, hypocritical wench' – Bartle spoke these last words in a rasping tone of reproach, and looked at Vixen, who poked down her head and turned up her eyes towards him with a keen sense of opprobrium – 'and contrived to be brought to bed on a Sunday at church-time. I've wished again and again I'd been a bloody-minded man, that I could have strangled the mother and the brats with one cord.'

'I'm glad it was no worse a cause kept you from church,' said Adam. 'I was afraid you must be ill for the first time i' your life.

And I was particular sorry not to have you at church yesterday.'

'Ah, my boy, I know why, I know why,' said Bartle, kindly, going up to Adam, and raising his hand up to the shoulder that was almost on a level with his own head. 'You've had a rough bit o' road to get over since I saw you – a rough bit o' road. But I'm in hopes there are better times coming for you. I've got some news to tell you. But I must get my supper first, for I'm hungry, I'm hungry. Sit down, sit down.'

Bartle went into his little pantry, and brought out an excellent home-baked loaf; for it was his one extravagance in these dear times to eat bread once a-day instead of oat-cake; and he justi-fied it by observing, that what a schoolmaster wanted was brains, and oat-cake ran too much to bone instead of brains. Then came a piece of cheese and a quart jug with a crown of foam upon it. He placed them all on the round deal table which stood against his large arm-chair in the chimney-corner, with Vixen's hamper on one side of it, and a window-shelf with a few books piled up in it on the other. The table was as clean as if Vixen had been an excellent housewife in a checkered apron; so was the quarry floor; and the old carved oaken press, table, and chairs, which in these days would be bought at a high price in aristocratic houses,[4] though, in that period of spider-legs and inlaid cupids, Bartle had got them for an old song, were as free from dust as things could be at the end of a summer's day.

'Now, then, my boy, draw up, draw up. We'll not talk about business till we've had our supper. No man can be wise on an empty stomach. But,' said Bartle, rising from his chair again, 'I must give Vixen her supper too, confound her! though she'll do nothing with it but nourish those unnecessary babbies. That's the way with these women, they've got no head-pieces to nourish, and so their food all runs either to fat or to brats.'

He brought out of the pantry a dish of scraps, which Vixen at once fixed her eyes on, and jumped out of her hamper to lick up with the utmost despatch.

'I've had my supper, Mr Massey,' said Adam, 'so I'll look on while you eat yours. I've been at the Hall Farm, and they always have their supper betimes, you know: they don't keep your late hours.'

'I know little about their hours,' said Bartle, dryly, cutting his bread and not shrinking from the crust. 'It's a house I seldom go into, though I'm fond of the boys, and Martin Poyser's a good fellow. There's too many women in the house for me: I hate the sound of women's voices; they're always either a-buzz or a-squeak – always either a-buzz or a-squeak. Mrs Poyser keeps at the top o' the talk like a fife; and as for the young lasses, I'd as soon look at water-grubs – I know what they'll turn to – stinging gnats, stinging gnats. Here, take some ale, my boy: it's been drawn for you – it's been drawn for you.'

'Nay, Mr Massey,' said Adam, who took his old friend's whim more seriously than usual to-night, 'don't be so hard on the creaturs God has made to be companions for us. A working man 'ud be badly off without a wife to see to th' house and the victual, and make things clean and comfortable.'

'Nonsense! It's the silliest lie a sensible man like you ever believed, to say a woman makes a house comfortable. It's a story got up, because the women are there, and something must be found for 'em to do. I tell you there isn't a thing under the sun that needs to be done at all, but what a man can do better than a woman, unless it's bearing children, and they do that in a poor make-shift way; it had better ha' been left to the men – it had better ha' been left to the men. I tell you, a woman 'ull bake you a pie every week of her life, and never come to see that the hotter th' oven the shorter the time. I tell you, a woman 'ull make your porridge every day for twenty years, and never think of measuring the proportion between the meal and the milk – a little more or less, she'll think, doesn't signify: the porridge *will* be awk'ard now and then: if it's wrong, it's summat in the meal, or it's summat in the milk, or it's summat in the water. Look at me! I make my own bread, and there's no difference between one batch and another from year's end to year's end; but if I'd got any other woman besides Vixen in the house, I must pray to the Lord every baking to give me patience if the bread turned out heavy. And as for cleanliness, my house is cleaner than any other house on the Common, though the half of 'em swarm with women. Will Baker's lad comes to help me in a morning, and we get as much cleaning done in one hour without any fuss, as a woman 'ud get done in three, and all the while be sending buckets o' water after your ankles, and let the fender and the fire-irons stand in the middle o' the floor half the day, for you to break your shins against 'em. Don't tell me about God having made such creatures to be companions for us! I don't say but He might make Eve to be a companion to Adam in Paradise – there was no cooking to be spoilt there, and no other woman to cackle with and make mischief; though you see what mischief she did as soon as she'd an opportunity. But it's an impious, unscriptural opinion to say a woman's a blessing to a man now; you might as well say adders and wasps, and foxes and wild beasts, are a blessing, when they're only the evils that belong to this state o' probation, which it's lawful for a man to keep as clear of as he can in this life, hoping to get quit of 'em for ever in another – hoping to get quit of 'em for ever in another.'

Bartle had become so excited and angry in the course of his invective that he had forgotten his supper, and only used the knife for the purpose of rapping the table with the haft. But towards the close, the raps became so sharp and frequent, and his voice so quarrelsome, that Vixen felt it incumbent on her to jump out of the hamper and bark vaguely.

'Quiet, Vixen!' snarled Bartle, turning round upon her. 'You're like the rest o' the women – always putting in *your* word before you know why.'

Vixen returned to her hamper again in humiliation, and her master continued his supper in a silence which Adam did not choose to interrupt; he knew the old man would be in a better humour when he had had his supper and lighted his pipe. Adam was used to hear him talk in this way, but had never learned so much of Bartle's past life as to know whether his view of married comfort was founded on experience. On that point Bartle was mute; and it was even a secret where he had lived previous to the twenty years in which, happily for the peasants and artisans of this neighbourhood, he had been settled among them as their only schoolmaster. If anything like a question was ventured on this subject, Bartle always replied, 'Oh, I've seen many places – I've been a deal in the south' – and the Loamshire men would as soon have thought of asking for a particular town or village in Africa as in 'the south'.

'Now then, my boy,' said Bartle, at last, when he had poured out his second mug of ale and lighted his pipe – 'now then, we'll have a little talk. But tell me first, have you heard any particular news to-day?'

'No,' said Adam, 'not as I remember.'

'Ah, they'll keep it close, they'll keep it close, I daresay. But I found it out by chance; and it's news that may concern you, Adam, else I'm a man that don't know a superficial square foot from a solid.'

Here Bartle gave a series of fierce and rapid puffs, looking earnestly the while at Adam. Your impatient loquacious man has never any notion of keeping his pipe alight by gentle measured puffs; he is always letting it go nearly out, and then punishing it for that negligence. At last he said –

'Satchell's got a paralytic stroke. I found it out from the lad they sent to Treddleston for the doctor, before seven o'clock this morning. He's a good way beyond sixty, you know; it's much if he gets over it.'

'Well,' said Adam, 'I daresay there'd be more rejoicing than sorrow in the parish at his being laid up. He's been a selfish, tale-bearing, mischievous fellow; but, after all, there's nobody he's done so much harm to as to th' old Squire. Though it's the Squire himself as is to blame – making a stupid fellow like that a sort o' man-of-all-work, just to save th' expense of having a proper steward to look after th' estate. And he's lost more by ill-management o' the woods, I'll be bound, than 'ud pay for two stewards. If he's laid on the shelf, it's to be hoped he'll make way for a better man, but I don't see how it's like to make any difference to me.'

'But I see it, but I see it,' said Bartle; 'and others besides me. The Captain's coming of age now – you know that as well as I do – and it's to be expected he'll have a little more voice in things. And I know, and you know too, what 'ud be the Captain's wish about the woods, if there was a fair opportunity for making a change. He's said in plenty of people's hearing that he'd make you manager of the woods to-morrow, if he'd the

power. Why, Carroll, Mr Irwine's butler, heard him say so to
the parson not many days ago. Carroll looked in when we were
smoking our pipes o' Saturday night at Casson's, and he told
us about it; and whenever anybody says a good word for you,
the parson's ready to back it, that I'll answer for. It was pretty
well talked over, I can tell you, at Casson's, and one and another
had their fling at you: for if donkeys set to work to sing, you're
pretty sure what the tune 'ull be.'

'Why, did they talk it over before Mr Burge?' said Adam; 'or
wasn't he there o' Saturday?'

'Oh, he went away before Carroll came; and Casson – he's
always for setting other folks right, you know – would have it
Burge was the man to have the management of the woods.
"A substantial man," says he, "with pretty near sixty years'
experience o' timber: it 'ud be all very well for Adam Bede to
act under him, but it isn't to be supposed the Squire 'ud appoint
a young fellow like Adam, when there's his elders and betters
at hand!" But I said, "That's a pretty notion o' yours, Casson.
Why, Burge is the man to *buy* timber; would you put the woods
into his hands, and let him make his own bargains? I think you
don't leave your customers to score their own drink, do you?
And as for age, what that's worth depends on the quality o' the
liquor. It's pretty well known who's the backbone of Jonathan
Burge's business."'

'I thank you for your good word, Mr Massey,' said Adam.
'But, for all that, Casson was partly i' the right for once. There's
not much likelihood that th' old Squire 'ud ever consent t'
employ me: I offended him about two years ago, and he's never
forgiven me.'

'Why, how was that? You never told me about it,' said Bartle.

'Oh, it was a bit o' nonsense. I'd made a frame for a screen
for Miss Lyddy – she's allays making something with her
worsted-work, you know – and she'd given me particular orders
about this screen, and there was as much talking and measuring
as if we'd been planning a house. However, it was a nice bit o'
work, and I liked doing it for her. But, you know, those little
friggling[5] things take a deal o' time. I only worked at it in
over-hours – often late at night – and I had to go to Treddleston

over an' over again, about little bits o' brass nails and such
gear; and I turned the little knobs and the legs, and carved th'
open work, after a pattern, as nice as could be. And I was
uncommon pleased with it when it was done. And when I
took it home, Miss Lyddy sent for me to bring it into her
drawing-room, so as she might give me directions about fastening on the work – very fine needlework, Jacob and Rachel
a-kissing one another among the sheep,[6] like a picture – and th'
old Squire was sitting there, for he mostly sits with her. Well,
she was mighty pleased with the screen, and then she wanted
to know what pay she was to give me. I didn't speak at random
– you know it's not my way; I'd calculated pretty close, though
I hadn't made out a bill, and I said, One pound thirteen. That
was paying for the mater'als and paying me, but none too
much, for my work. Th' old Squire looked up at this, and
peered in his way at the screen, and said, "One pound thirteen
for a gimcrack like that! Lydia, my dear, if you must spend
money on these things, why don't you get them at Rosseter,
instead of paying double price for clumsy work here? Such
things are not work for a carpenter like Adam. Give him a
guinea,[7] and no more." Well, Miss Lyddy, I reckon, believed
what he told her, and she's not over-fond o' parting with the
money herself – she's not a bad woman at bottom, but she's
been brought up under his thumb; so she began fidgeting with
her purse, and turned as red as her ribbon. But I made a bow,
and said, "No, thank you, madam; I'll make you a present o'
the screen, if you please. I've charged the regular price for my
work, and I know it's done well; and I know, begging his
honour's pardon, that you couldn't get such a screen at Rosseter
under two guineas. I'm willing to give you my work – it's been
done in my own time, and nobody's got anything to do with it
but me; but if I'm paid, I can't take a smaller price than I asked,
because that 'ud be like saying, I'd asked more than was just.
With your leave, madam, I'll bid you good-morning." I made
my bow and went out before she'd time to say any more, for
she stood with the purse in her hand, looking almost foolish. I
didn't mean to be disrespectful, and I spoke as polite as I could;
but I can give in to no man, if he wants to make it out as I'm

trying t' overreach him. And in the evening the footman brought me the one pound thirteen wrapped in paper. But since then I've seen pretty clear as th' old Squire can't abide me.'

'That's likely enough, that's likely enough,' said Bartle, meditatively. 'The only way to bring him round would be to show him what was for his own interest, and that the Captain may do – that the Captain may do.'

'Nay, I don't know,' said Adam; 'the Squire's 'cute[8] enough, but it takes something else besides 'cuteness to make folks see what'll be their interest in the long-run. It takes some conscience and belief in right and wrong, I see that pretty clear. You'd hardly ever bring round th' old Squire to believe he'd gain as much in a straightfor'ard way as by tricks and turns. And, besides, I've not much mind to work under him: I don't want to quarrel with any gentleman, more particular an old gentleman turned eighty, and I know we couldn't agree long. If the Captain was master o' th' estate, it 'ud be different: he's got a conscience and a will to do right, and I'd sooner work for him nor for any man living.'

'Well, well, my boy, if good luck knocks at your door, don't you put your head out at window and tell it to be gone about its business, that's all. You must learn to deal with odd and even in life, as well as in figures. I tell you now, as I told you ten years ago, when you pommelled young Mike Holdsworth for wanting to pass a bad shilling, before you knew whether he was in jest or earnest – you're over-hasty and proud, and apt to set your teeth against folks that don't square to your notions. It's no harm for *me* to be a bit fiery and stiff-backed: I'm an old schoolmaster, and shall never want to get on to a higher perch. But where's the use of all the time I've spent in teaching you writing and mapping and mensuration, if you're not to get for'ard in the world, and show folks there's some advantage in having a head on your shoulders, instead of a turnip? Do you mean to go on turning up your nose at every opportunity, because it's got a bit of a smell about it that nobody finds out but yourself? It's as foolish as that notion o' yours that a wife is to make a working man comfortable. Stuff and nonsense! – stuff and nonsense! Leave that to fools that never got beyond a

sum in simple addition. Simple addition enough! Add one fool
to another fool, and in six years' time six fools more – they're
all of the same denomination, big and little's nothing to do with
the sum!'

During this rather heated exhortation to coolness and discretion the pipe had gone out, and Bartle gave the climax to his
speech by striking a light furiously, after which he puffed with
fierce resolution, fixing his eye still on Adam, who was trying
not to laugh.

'There's a good deal o' sense in what you say, Mr Massey,'
Adam began, as soon as he felt quite serious, 'as there always
is. But you'll give in that it's no business o' mine to be building
on chances that may never happen. What I've got to do is to
work as well as I can with the tools and mater'als I've got in
my hands. If a good chance comes to me, I'll think o' what
you've been saying; but till then, I've got nothing to do but to
trust to my own hands and my own head-piece. I'm turning
over a little plan for Seth and me to go into the cabinet-making
a bit by ourselves, and win a extra pound or two in that way.
But it's getting late now – it'll be pretty near eleven before I'm
at home, and mother may happen to lie awake; she's more
fidgety nor usual now. So I'll bid you good-night.'

'Well, well, we'll go to the gate with you – it's a fine night,'
said Bartle, taking up his stick. Vixen was at once on her
legs, and without further words the three walked out into the
starlight, by the side of Bartle's potato-beds, to the little gate.

'Come to the music o' Friday night, if you can, my boy,' said
the old man, as he closed the gate after Adam, and leaned
against it.

'Ay, ay,' said Adam, striding along towards the streak of pale
road. He was the only object moving on the wide common. The
two grey donkeys, just visible in front of the gorse bushes, stood
as still as limestone images – as still as the grey-thatched roof
of the mud cottage a little farther on. Bartle kept his eye on the
moving figure till it passed into the darkness, while Vixen, in a
state of divided affection, had twice run back to the house to
bestow a parenthetic lick on her puppies.

'Ay, ay,' muttered the schoolmaster, as Adam disappeared;

'there you go, stalking along – stalking along; but you wouldn't have been what you are if you hadn't had a bit of old lame Bartle inside you. The strongest calf must have something to suck at. There's plenty of these big, lumbering fellows 'ud never have known their A B C, if it hadn't been for Bartle Massey. Well, well, Vixen, you foolish wench, what is it, what is it? I must go in, must I? Ay, ay, I'm never to have a will o' my own any more. And those pups, what do you think I'm to do with 'em, when they're twice as big as you? – for I'm pretty sure the father was that hulking bull-terrier of Will Baker's – wasn't he now, eh, you sly hussey?' (Here Vixen tucked her tail between her legs, and ran forward into the house. Subjects are sometimes broached which a well-bred female will ignore.)

'But where's the use of talking to a woman with babbies?' continued Bartle: 'she's got no conscience – no conscience; it's all run to milk.'

BOOK THIRD

CHAPTER XXII

Going to the Birthday Feast

The thirtieth of July was come, and it was one of those half-dozen warm days which sometimes occur in the middle of a rainy English summer. No rain had fallen for the last three or four days, and the weather was perfect for that time of the year: there was less dust than usual on the dark-green hedgerows, and on the wild camomile that starred the roadside, yet the grass was dry enough for the little children to roll on it, and there was no cloud but a long dash of light, downy ripple, high, high up in the far-off blue sky. Perfect weather for an outdoor July merrymaking, yet surely not the best time of year to be born in. Nature seems to make a hot pause just then – all the loveliest flowers are gone; the sweet time of early growth and vague hopes is past; and yet the time of harvest and ingathering is not come, and we tremble at the possible storms that may ruin the precious fruit in the moment of its ripeness. The woods are all one dark monotonous green; the waggon-loads of hay no longer creep along the lanes, scattering their sweet-smelling fragments on the blackberry branches; the pastures are often a little tanned, yet the corn has not got its last splendour of red and gold; the lambs and calves have lost all traces of their innocent frisky prettiness, and have become stupid young sheep and cows. But it is a time of leisure on the farm – that pause between hay and corn harvest, and so the farmers and labourers in Hayslope and Broxton thought the Captain did well to come of age just then, when they could give their undivided minds to the flavour of the great cask of ale which had been brewed the autumn after 'the heir' was born, and was to be tapped on his twenty-first birthday. The air had been merry with the ringing of church-bells very early this morning, and every one had made haste to get through the needful work before twelve, when it would be time to think of getting ready to go to the Chase.

The mid-day sun was streaming into Hetty's bed-chamber, and there was no blind to temper the heat with which it fell on her head as she looked at herself in the old specked glass. Still, that was the only glass she had in which she could see her neck and arms, for the small hanging glass she had fetched out of the next room – the room that had been Dinah's – would show her nothing below her little chin, and that beautiful bit of neck where the roundness of her cheek melted into another roundness shadowed by dark delicate curls. And to-day she thought more than usual about her neck and arms; for at the dance this evening she was not to wear any neckerchief, and she had been busy yesterday with her spotted pink-and-white frock, that she might make the sleeves either long or short at will. She was dressed now just as she was to be in the evening, with a tucker made of 'real' lace, which her aunt had lent her for this unparalleled occasion, but with no ornaments besides; she had even taken out her small round earrings which she wore every day. But there was something more to be done, apparently, before she put on her neckerchief and long sleeves, which she was to wear in the day-time, for now she unlocked the drawer that held her private treasures. It is more than a month since we saw her unlock that drawer before, and now it holds new treasures, so much more precious than the old ones that these are thrust into the corner. Hetty would not care to put the large coloured glass earrings into her ears now; for see! she has got a beautiful pair of gold and pearls and garnet, lying snugly in a pretty little box lined with white satin. Oh the delight of taking out that little box and looking at the earrings! Do not reason about it, my philosophical reader, and say that Hetty, being very pretty, must have known that it did not signify whether she had on any ornaments or not; and that, moreover, to look at earrings which she could not possibly wear out of her bedroom could hardly be a satisfaction, the essence of vanity being a reference to the impressions produced on others; you will never understand women's natures if you are so excessively rational. Try rather to divest yourself of all your rational prejudices, as much as if you were studying the psychology of a canary bird,[1] and only watch the movements of this pretty round creature as she turns her head on one side with an unconscious smile at the earrings nestled in the little box. Ah, you think, it is for the sake of the person who has given them to her, and her thoughts are gone back now to the moment when they were put into her hands. No; else why should she have cared to have earrings rather than anything else? and I know that she had longed for earrings from among all the ornaments she could imagine.

'Little, little ears!' Arthur had said, pretending to pinch them one evening, as Hetty sat beside him on the grass without her hat. 'I wish I had some pretty earrings!' she said in a moment, almost before she knew what she was saying – the wish lay so close to her lips, it *would* flutter past them at the slightest breath. And the next day – it was only last week – Arthur had ridden over to Rosseter on purpose to buy them. That little wish so *naïvely* uttered, seemed to him the prettiest bit of childishness; he had never heard anything like it before; and he had wrapped the box up in a great many covers, that he might see Hetty unwrapping it with growing curiosity, till at last her eyes flashed back their new delight into his.

No, she was not thinking most of the giver when she smiled at the earrings, for now she is taking them out of the box, not to press them to her lips, but to fasten them in her ears, – only for one moment, to see how pretty they look, as she peeps at them in the glass against the wall, with first one position of the head and then another, like a listening bird. It is impossible to be wise on the subject of earrings as one looks at her; what should those delicate pearls and crystals be made for, if not for such ears? One cannot even find fault with the tiny round hole which they leave when they are taken out; perhaps water-nixies, and such lovely things without souls,[2] have these little round holes in their ears by nature, ready to hang jewels in. And Hetty must be one of them: it is too painful to think that she is a woman, with a woman's destiny before her – a woman spinning in young ignorance a light web of folly and vain hopes which may one day close round her and press upon her, a rancorous poisoned garment,[3] changing all at once her fluttering, trivial butterfly sensations into a life of deep human anguish.

But she cannot keep in the earrings long, else she may make her uncle and aunt wait. She puts them quickly into the box again, and shuts them up. Some day she will be able to wear any earrings she likes, and already she lives in an invisible world of brilliant costumes, shimmering gauze, soft satin, and velvet, such as the lady's-maid at the Chase has shown her in Miss Lydia's wardrobe: she feels the bracelets on her arms, and treads on a soft carpet in front of a tall mirror. But she has one thing in the drawer which she can venture to wear to-day, because she can hang it on the chain of dark-brown berries which she has been used to wear on grand days, with a tiny flat scent-bottle at the end of it tucked inside her frock; and she *must* put on her brown berries – her neck would look so unfinished without it. Hetty was not quite as fond of the locket as of the earrings, though it was a handsome large locket, with enamelled flowers at the back and a beautiful gold border round the glass, which showed a light-brown slightly waving lock, forming a background for two little dark rings. She must keep it under her clothes, and no one would see it. But Hetty had another passion, only a little less strong than her love of finery; and that other passion made her like to wear the locket even hidden in her bosom. She would always have worn it, if she had dared to encounter her aunt's questions about a ribbon round her neck. So now she slipped it on along her chain of dark-brown berries, and snapped the chain round her neck. It was not a very long chain, only allowing the locket to hang a little way below the edge of her frock. And now she had nothing to do but to put on her long sleeves, her new white gauze neckerchief, and her straw hat trimmed with white to-day instead of the pink, which had become rather faded under the July sun. That hat made the drop of bitterness in Hetty's cup to-day, for it was not quite new – everybody would see that it was a little tanned against the white ribbon – and Mary Burge, she felt sure, would have a new hat or bonnet on. She looked for consolation at her fine white cotton stockings: they really were very nice indeed, and she had given almost all her spare money for them. Hetty's dream of the future could not make her insensible to triumph in the present: to be sure, Captain Donnithorne loved her so, that he would never care about looking at other people, but then those other people didn't know how he loved her, and she was not satisfied to appear shabby and insignificant in their eyes even for a short space.

The whole party was assembled in the house-place when Hetty went down, all of course in their Sunday clothes; and the bells had been ringing so this morning in honour of the Captain's twenty-first birthday, and the work had all been got done so early, that Marty and Tommy were not quite easy in their minds until their mother had assured them that going to church was not part of the day's festivities. Mr Poyser had once suggested that the house should be shut up, and left to take care of itself; 'for,' said he, 'there's no danger of anybody's breaking in – everybody'll be at the Chase, thieves an' all. If we lock th' house up, all the men can go: it's a day they wonna see twice i' their lives.' But Mrs Poyser answered with great decision: 'I never left th' house to take care of itself since I was a missis, and I never will. There's been ill-looking tramps enoo' about the place this last week, to carry off every ham an' every spoon we'n got; and they all collogue[4] together, them tramps, as it's a mercy they hanna come and pisoned the dogs and murdered us all in our beds afore we knowed, some Friday night when we'n got the money in th' house to pay the men. And it's like enough the tramps know where we're going as well as we do oursens; for if Old Harry[5] wants any work done, you may be sure he'll find the means.'

'Nonsense about murdering us in our beds,' said Mr Poyser; 'I've got a gun i' our room, hanna I? and thee'st got ears as 'ud find it out if a mouse was gnawing the bacon. Howiver, if thee wouldstna be easy, Alick can stay at home i' the forepart o' the day, and Tim can come back tow'rds five o'clock, and let Alick have his turn. They may let Growler loose if anybody offers to do mischief, and there's Alick's dog, too, ready enough to set his tooth in a tramp if Alick gives him a wink.'

Mrs Poyser accepted this compromise, but thought it advisable to bar and bolt to the utmost; and now, at the last moment before starting, Nancy, the dairymaid, was closing the shutters of the house-place, although the window, lying under the immediate observation of Alick and the dogs, might have been supposed the least likely to be selected for a burglarious attempt.

The covered cart, without springs, was standing ready to carry the whole family except the men-servants: Mr Poyser and the grandfather sat on the seat in front, and within there was room for all the women and children; the fuller the cart the better, because then the jolting would not hurt so much, and Nancy's broad person and thick arms were an excellent cushion to be pitched on. But Mr Poyser drove at no more than a walking pace, that there might be as little risk of jolting as possible on this warm day; and there was time to exchange greetings and remarks with the foot-passengers who were going the same way, specking the paths between the green meadows and the golden cornfields with bits of movable bright colour – a scarlet waistcoat to match the poppies that nodded a little too thickly among the corn, or a dark-blue neckerchief with ends flaunting across a bran-new white smock-frock. All Broxton and all Hayslope were to be at the Chase, and make merry there in honour of 'th' heir';[6] and the old men and women, who had never been so far down this side of the hill for the last twenty years, were being brought from Broxton and Hayslope in one of the farmer's waggons, at Mr Irwine's suggestion. The church-bells had struck up again now – a last tune, before the ringers came down the hill to have their share in the festival; and before the bells had finished, other music was heard approaching, so that even Old Brown, the sober horse that was drawing Mr Poyser's cart, began to prick up his ears. It was the band of the Benefit Club,[7] which had mustered in all its glory; that is to say, in bright-blue scarfs and blue favours, and carrying its banner with the motto, 'Let brotherly love continue', encircling a picture of a stone-pit.

The carts, of course, were not to enter the Chase. Every one must get down at the lodges, and the vehicles must be sent back.

'Why, the Chase is like a fair a'ready,' said Mrs Poyser, as she got down from the cart, and saw the groups scattered under the great oaks, and the boys running about in the hot sunshine to survey the tall poles surmounted by the fluttering garments that were to be the prize of the successful climbers. 'I should ha' thought there wasna so many people i' the two parishes. Mercy on us! how hot it is out o' the shade! Come here, Totty, else your little face 'ull be burnt to a scratchin'! They might ha' cooked the dinners i' that open space, an' saved the fires. I shall go to Mrs Best's room an' sit down.'

'Stop a bit, stop a bit,' said Mr Poyser. 'There's th' waggin coming wi' th' old folks in't; it'll be such a sight as wonna come o'er again, to see 'em get down an' walk along all together. You remember some on 'em i' their prime, eh, father?'

'Ay, ay,' said old Martin, walking slowly under the shade of the lodge porch, from which he could see the aged party descend. 'I remember Jacob Taft walking fifty mile after the Scotch raybels,[8] when they turned back from Stoniton.'

He felt himself quite a youngster, with a long life before him, as he saw the Hayslope patriarch, old Feyther Taft, descend from the waggon and walk towards him, in his brown nightcap, and leaning on his two sticks.

'Well, Mester Taft,' shouted old Martin, at the utmost stretch of his voice, – for though he knew the old man was stone deaf, he could not omit the propriety of a greeting, – 'you're hearty yet. You can enjoy yoursen to-day, for-all you're ninety an' better.'

'Your sarvant, mesters, your sarvant,' said Feyther Taft in a treble tone, perceiving that he was in company.

The aged group, under care of sons or daughters, themselves worn and grey, passed on along the least-winding carriage-road towards the house, where a special table was prepared for them; while the Poyser party wisely struck across the grass under the shade of the great trees, but not out of view of the house-front, with its sloping lawn and flower-beds, or of the pretty striped marquee at the edge of the lawn, standing at right angles with two larger marquees on each side of the open green space where the games were to be played. The house would have been nothing but a plain square mansion of Queen Anne's time, but for the remnant of an old abbey to which it was united at one end, in much the same way as one may sometimes see a new farmhouse rising high and prim at the end of older and lower farm-offices. The fine old remnant stood a little backward and under the shadow of tall beeches, but the sun was now on the taller and more advanced front, the blinds were all down, and the house seemed asleep in the hot mid-day: it made Hetty quite sad to look at it: Arthur must be somewhere in the back rooms, with the grand company, where he could not possibly know that she was come, and she should not see him for a long, long while – not till after dinner, when they said he was to come up and make a speech.

But Hetty was wrong in part of her conjecture. No grand company was come except the Irwines, for whom the carriage had been sent early, and Arthur was at that moment not in a back room, but walking with the Rector into the broad stone cloisters of the old abbey, where the long tables were laid for all the cottage tenants and the farm-servants. A very handsome young Briton he looked to-day, in high spirits and a bright-blue frock-coat, the highest mode – his arm no longer in a sling. So open-looking and candid, too; but candid people have their secrets, and secrets leave no lines in young faces.

'Upon my word,' he said, as they entered the cool cloisters, 'I think the cottagers have the best of it: these cloisters make a delightful dining-room on a hot day. That was capital advice of yours, Irwine, about the dinners – to let them be as orderly and comfortable as possible, and only for the tenants: especially as I had only a limited sum after all; for though my grandfather talked of a *carte blanche*, he couldn't make up his mind to trust me, when it came to the point.'

'Never mind, you'll give more pleasure in this quiet way,' said Mr Irwine. 'In this sort of thing people are constantly confounding liberality with riot and disorder. It sounds very grand to say that so many sheep and oxen were roasted whole, and everybody ate who liked to come; but in the end it generally happens that no one has had an enjoyable meal. If the people get a good dinner and a moderate quantity of ale in the middle

of the day, they'll be able to enjoy the games as the day cools.
You can't hinder some of them from getting too much towards
evening, but drunkenness and darkness go better together than
drunkenness and daylight.'

'Well, I hope there won't be much of it. I've kept the Treddleston people away, by having a feast for them in the town; and
I've got Casson and Adam Bede, and some other good fellows,
to look to the giving out of ale in the booths, and to take care
things don't go too far. Come, let us go up above now, and see
the dinner-tables for the large tenants.'

They went up the stone staircase leading simply to the long
gallery above the cloisters, a gallery where all the dusty worth-
less old pictures had been banished for the last three generations
– mouldy portraits of Queen Elizabeth and her ladies, General
Monk with his eye knocked out, Daniel very much in the dark
among the lions, and Julius Caesar on horseback, with a high
nose and laurel crown, holding his Commentaries in his hand.[9]

'What a capital thing it is that they saved this piece of the
old abbey!' said Arthur. 'If I'm ever master here, I shall do up
the gallery in first-rate style: we've got no room in the house a
third as large as this. That second table is for the farmers' wives
and children: Mrs Best said it would be more comfortable for
the mothers and children to be by themselves. I was determined
to have the children, and make a regular family thing of it. I
shall be the "old squire" to those little lads and lasses some
day, and they'll tell their children what a much finer young
fellow I was than my own son. There's a table for the women
and children below as well. But you will see them all – you will
come up with me after dinner, I hope?'

'Yes, to be sure,' said Mr Irwine. 'I wouldn't miss your
maiden speech to the tenantry.'

'And there will be something else you'll like to hear,' said
Arthur. 'Let us go into the library and I'll tell you all about it
while my grandfather is in the drawing-room with the ladies.
Something that will surprise you,' he continued, as they sat
down. 'My grandfather has come round after all.'

'What, about Adam?'

'Yes; I should have ridden over to tell you about it, only

I was so busy. You know I told you I had quite given up arguing the matter with him – I thought it was hopeless; but yesterday morning he asked me to come in here to him before I went out, and astonished me by saying that he had decided on all the new arrangements he should make in consequence of old Satchell being obliged to lay by work, and that he intended to employ Adam in superintending the woods at a salary of a guinea a-week, and the use of a pony to be kept here. I believe the secret of it is, he saw from the first it would be a profitable plan, but he had some particular dislike of Adam to get over – and besides, the fact that I propose a thing is generally a reason with him for rejecting it. There's the most curious contradiction in my grandfather: I know he means to leave me all the money he has saved, and he is likely enough to have cut off poor aunt Lydia, who has been a slave to him all her life, with only five hundred a-year, for the sake of giving me all the more; and yet I sometimes think he positively hates me because I'm his heir. I believe if I were to break my neck, he would feel it the greatest misfortune that could befall him, and yet it seems a pleasure to him to make my life a series of petty annoyances.'

'Ah, my boy, it is not only woman's love that is ἀπέρωτος ἔρως, as old Æschylus calls it.[10] There's plenty of "unloving love" in the world of a masculine kind. But tell me about Adam. Has he accepted the post? I don't see that it can be much more profitable than his present work, though, to be sure, it will leave him a good deal of time on his own hands.'

'Well, I felt some doubt about it when I spoke to him, and he seemed to hesitate at first. His objection was, that he thought he should not be able to satisfy my grandfather. But I begged him as a personal favour to me not to let any reason prevent him from accepting the place, if he really liked the employment, and would not be giving up anything that was more profitable to him. And he assured me he should like it of all things; – it would be a great step forward for him in business, and it would enable him to do what he had long wished to do – to give up working for Burge. He says he shall have plenty of time to superintend a little business of his own, which he and Seth will carry on, and will perhaps be able to enlarge by degrees. So he has agreed at last, and I have arranged that he shall dine with the large tenants to-day; and I mean to announce the appointment to them, and ask them to drink Adam's health. It's a little drama I've got up in honour of my friend Adam. He's a fine fellow, and I like the opportunity of letting people know that I think so.'

'A drama in which friend Arthur piques himself on having a pretty part to play,' said Mr Irwine, smiling. But when he saw Arthur colour, he went on relentingly, 'My part, you know, is always that of the old Fogy[11] who sees nothing to admire in the young folks. I don't like to admit that I'm proud of my pupil when he does graceful things. But I must play the amiable old gentleman for once, and second your toast in honour of Adam. Has your grandfather yielded on the other point too, and agreed to have a respectable man as steward?'

'Oh, no,' said Arthur, rising from his chair with an air of impatience, and walking along the room with his hands in his pockets. 'He's got some project or other about letting the Chase Farm, and bargaining for a supply of milk and butter for the house. But I ask no questions about it – it makes me too angry. I believe he means to do all the business himself, and have nothing in the shape of a steward. It's amazing what energy he has, though.'

'Well, we'll go to the ladies now,' said Mr Irwine, rising too. 'I want to tell my mother what a splendid throne you've prepared for her under the marquee.'

'Yes, and we must be going to luncheon too,' said Arthur. 'It must be two o'clock, for there is the gong beginning to sound for the tenants' dinners.'

CHAPTER XXIII

Dinner-Time

When Adam heard that he was to dine up-stairs with the large tenants, he felt rather uncomfortable at the idea of being exalted in this way above his mother and Seth, who were to dine in the cloisters below. But Mr Mills, the butler, assured him that Captain Donnithorne had given particular orders about it, and would be very angry if Adam was not there.

Adam nodded, and went up to Seth, who was standing a few yards off. 'Seth, lad,' he said, 'the Captain has sent to say I'm to dine up-stairs – he wishes it particular, Mr Mills says, so I suppose it 'ud be behaving ill for me not to go. But I don't like sitting up above thee and mother, as if I was better than my own flesh and blood. Thee't not take it unkind, I hope?'

'Nay, nay, lad,' said Seth, 'thy honour's our honour; and if thee get'st respect, thee'st won it by thy own deserts. The further I see thee above me, the better, so long as thee feel'st like a brother to me. It's because o' thy being appointed over the woods, and it's nothing but what's right. That's a place o' trust, and thee't above a common workman now.'

'Ay,' said Adam, 'but nobody knows a word about it yet. I haven't given notice to Mr Burge about leaving him, and I don't like to tell anybody else about it before he knows, for he'll be a good bit hurt, I doubt. People 'ull be wondering to see me there, and they'll like enough be guessing the reason, and asking questions, for there's been so much talk up and down about my having the place, this last three weeks.'

'Well, thee canst say thee wast ordered to come without being told the reason. That's the truth. And mother 'ull be fine and joyful about it. Let's go and tell her.'

Adam was not the only guest invited to come up-stairs on other grounds than the amount he contributed to the rent-roll. There were other people in the two parishes who derived dignity from their functions rather than from their pocket, and of these Bartle Massey was one. His lame walk was rather slower than usual on this warm day, so Adam lingered behind when the bell rang for dinner, that he might walk up with his old friend; for he was a little too shy to join the Poyser party on this public occasion. Opportunities of getting to Hetty's side would be sure to turn up in the course of the day, and Adam contented himself with that, for he disliked any risk of being 'joked' about Hetty; – the big, outspoken, fearless man was very shy and diffident as to his love-making.

'Well, Mester Massey,' said Adam, as Bartle came up, 'I'm going to dine up-stairs with you to-day: the Captain's sent me orders.'

'Ah!' said Bartle, pausing, with one hand on his back. 'Then there's something in the wind – there's something in the wind. Have you heard anything about what the old Squire means to do?'

'Why, yes,' said Adam; 'I'll tell you what I know, because I believe you can keep a still tongue in your head if you like; and I hope you'll not let drop a word till it's common talk, for I've particular reasons against its being known.'

'Trust to me, my boy, trust to me. I've got no wife to worm it out of me and then run out and cackle it in everybody's hearing. If you trust a man, let him be a bachelor – let him be a bachelor.'

'Well, then, it was so far settled yesterday, that I'm to take the management o' the woods. The Captain sent for me, t' offer it me, when I was seeing to the poles and things here, and I've agreed to't. But if anybody asks any questions up-stairs, just you take no notice, and turn the talk to something else, and I'll be obliged to you. Now, let us go on, for we're pretty nigh the last, I think.'

'I know what to do, never fear,' said Bartle, moving on. 'The news will be good sauce to my dinner. Ay, ay, my boy, you'll get on. I'll back you for an eye at measuring, and a head-piece

for figures, against any man in this county; and you've had
good teaching – you've had good teaching.'

When they got up-stairs, the question which Arthur had left
unsettled, as to who was to be president, and who vice, was
still under discussion, so that Adam's entrance passed without
remark.

'It stands to sense,' Mr Casson was saying, 'as old Mr Poyser,
as is th' oldest man i' the room, should sit at top o' the table. I
wasn't butler fifteen year without learning the rights and the
wrongs about dinner.'

'Nay, nay,' said old Martin, 'I'n gi'en up to my son; I'm no
tenant now; let my son take my place. Th' ould folks ha' had
their turn: they mun make way for the young uns.'

'I should ha' thought the biggest tenant had the best right,
more nor th' oldest,' said Luke Britton, who was not fond of
the critical Mr Poyser; 'there's Mester Holdsworth has more
land nor anybody else on th' estate.'

'Well,' said Mr Poyser, 'suppose we say th' man wi' the
foulest land shall sit at top; then whoever gets th' honour,
there'll be no envying on him.'

'Eh, here's Mester Massey,' said Mr Craig, who, being a
neutral in the dispute, had no interest but in conciliation; 'the
schoolmaster ought to be able to tell you what's right. Who's
to sit at top o' the table, Mr Massey?'

'Why, the broadest man,' said Bartle; 'and then he won't take
up other folks' room; and the next broadest must sit at bottom.'

This happy mode of settling the dispute produced much
laughter – a smaller joke would have sufficed for that. Mr
Casson, however, did not feel it compatible with his dignity
and superior knowledge to join in the laugh, until it turned out
that he was fixed on as the second broadest man. Martin Poyser,
the younger, as the broadest, was to be president, and Mr
Casson, as next broadest, was to be vice.

Owing to this arrangement, Adam, being, of course, at the
bottom of the table, fell under the immediate observation of
Mr Casson, who, too much occupied with the question of
precedence, had not hitherto noticed his entrance. Mr Casson,
we have seen, considered Adam 'rather lifted up and peppery-

like': he thought the gentry made more fuss about this young carpenter than was necessary; they made no fuss about Mr Casson, although he had been an excellent butler for fifteen years.

'Well, Mr Bede, you're one o' them as mounts hup'ards apace,' he said, when Adam sat down. 'You've niver dined here before, as I remember.'

'No, Mr Casson,' said Adam, in his strong voice, that could be heard along the table; 'I've never dined here before, but I come by Captain Donnithorne's wish, and I hope it's not disagreeable to anybody here.'

'Nay, nay,' said several voices at once, 'we're glad ye're come. Who's got anything to say again' it?'

'And ye'll sing us, "Over the hills and far away",[1] after dinner, wonna ye?' said Mr Chowne. 'That's a song I'm uncommon fond on.'

'Peeh!' said Mr Craig; 'it's not to be named by side o' the Scotch tunes. I've never cared about singing myself; I've had something better to do. A man that's got the names and the nature o' plants in's head isna likely to keep a hollow place t' hold tunes in. But a second cousin o' mine, a drovier, was a rare hand at remembering the Scotch tunes. He'd got nothing else to think on.'

'The Scotch tunes!' said Bartle Massey, contemptuously; 'I've heard enough o' the Scotch tunes to last me while I live. They're fit for nothing but to frighten the birds with – that's to say, the English birds, for the Scotch birds may sing Scotch for what I know. Give the lads a bagpipes instead of a rattle, and I'll answer for it the corn 'll be safe.'[2]

'Yes, there's folks as find a pleasure in undervallying what they know but little about,' said Mr Craig.

'Why, the Scotch tunes are just like a scolding, nagging woman,' Bartle went on, without deigning to notice Mr Craig's remark. 'They go on with the same thing over and over again, and never come to a reasonable end. Anybody 'ud think the Scotch tunes had always been asking a question of somebody as deaf as old Taft, and had never got an answer yet.'

Adam minded the less about sitting by Mr Casson, because

this position enabled him to see Hetty, who was not far off him at the next table. Hetty, however, had not even noticed his presence yet, for she was giving angry attention to Totty, who insisted on drawing up her feet on to the bench in antique fashion, and thereby threatened to make dusty marks on Hetty's pink-and-white frock. No sooner were the little fat legs pushed down than up they came again, for Totty's eyes were too busy in staring at the large dishes to see where the plum-pudding was, for her to retain any consciousness of her legs. Hetty got quite out of patience, and at last, with a frown and pout, and gathering tears, she said –

'Oh dear, aunt, I wish you'd speak to Totty; she keeps putting her legs up so, and messing my frock.'

'What's the matter wi' the child? She can niver please you,' said the mother. 'Let her come by the side o' me, then: *I* can put up wi' her.'

Adam was looking at Hetty, and saw the frown and pout, and the dark eyes seeming to grow larger with pettish half-gathered tears. Quiet Mary Burge, who sat near enough to see that Hetty was cross, and that Adam's eyes were fixed on her, thought that so sensible a man as Adam must be reflecting on the small value of beauty in a woman whose temper was bad. Mary was a good girl, not given to indulge in evil feelings, but she said to herself, that, since Hetty had a bad temper, it was better Adam should know it. And it was quite true, that if Hetty had been plain she would have looked very ugly and unamiable at that moment, and no one's moral judgment upon her would have been in the least beguiled. But really there was something quite charming in her pettishness: it looked so much more like innocent distress than ill-humour; and the severe Adam felt no movement of disapprobation; he only felt a sort of amused pity, as if he had seen a kitten setting up its back, or a little bird with its feathers ruffled. He could not gather what was vexing her, but it was impossible to him to feel otherwise than that she was the prettiest thing in the world, and that if he could have his way, nothing should ever vex her any more. And presently, when Totty was gone, she caught his eye, and her face broke into one of its brightest smiles, as she nodded to him. It was a bit of flirtation: she knew Mary Burge was looking at them. But the smile was like wine to Adam.

CHAPTER XXIV

The Health-Drinking

When the dinner was over, and the first draughts from the great cask of birthday ale were brought up, room was made for the broad Mr Poyser at the side of the table, and two chairs were placed at the head. It had been settled very definitely what Mr Poyser was to do when the young Squire should appear, and for the last five minutes he had been in a state of abstraction, with his eyes fixed on the dark picture opposite, and his hands busy with the loose cash and other articles in his breeches-pockets.

When the young Squire entered, with Mr Irwine by his side, every one stood up, and this moment of homage was very agreeable to Arthur. He liked to feel his own importance, and besides that, he cared a great deal for the goodwill of these people: he was fond of thinking that they had a hearty, special regard for him. The pleasure he felt was in his face as he said –

'My grandfather and I hope all our friends here have enjoyed their dinner, and find my birthday ale good. Mr Irwine and I are come to taste it with you, and I am sure we shall all like anything the better that the Rector shares with us.'

All eyes were now turned on Mr Poyser, who, with his hands still busy in his pockets, began with the deliberateness of a slow-striking clock. 'Captain, my neighbours have put it upo' me to speak for 'em to-day, for where folks think pretty much alike, one spokesman's as good as a score. And though we've mayhappen got contrairy ways o' thinking about a many things – one man lays down his land one way, an' another another – an' I'll not take it upon me to speak to no man's farming, but my own – this I'll say, as we're all o' one mind about our young

Squire. We've pretty nigh all on us known you when you war a little un, an' we've niver known anything on you but what was good an' honourable. You speak fair an' y' act fair, an' we're joyful when we look forrard to your being our landlord, for we b'lieve you mean to do right by everybody, an' 'ull make no man's bread bitter to him if you can help it. That's what I mean, an' that's what we all mean; and when a man's said what he means, he'd better stop, for th' ale 'ull be none the better for stannin'. An' I'll not say how we like th' ale yet, for we couldna well taste it till we'd drunk your health in it; but the dinner was good, an' if there's anybody hasna enjoyed it, it must be the fault of his own inside. An' as for the Rector's company, it's well known as that's welcome t' all the parish wherever he may be; an' I hope, an' we all hope, as he'll live to see us old folks, an' our children grown to men an' women, an' your honour a family man. I've no more to say as concerns the present time, an' so we'll drink our young Squire's health – three times three.'

Hereupon a glorious shouting, a rapping, a jingling, a clattering, and a shouting, with plentiful *da capo*,[1] pleasanter than a strain of sublimest music in the ears that receive such a tribute for the first time. Arthur had felt a twinge of conscience during Mr Poyser's speech, but it was too feeble to nullify the pleasure he felt in being praised. Did he not deserve what was said of him on the whole? If there was something in his conduct that Poyser wouldn't have liked if he had known it, why, no man's conduct will bear too close an inspection; and Poyser was not likely to know it; and, after all, what had he done? Gone a little too far, perhaps, in flirtation, but another man in his place would have acted much worse; and no harm could come – no harm *should* come, for the next time he was alone with Hetty, he would explain to her that she must not think seriously of him or of what had passed. It was necessary to Arthur, you perceive, to be satisfied with himself: uncomfortable thoughts must be got rid of by good intentions for the future, which can be formed so rapidly, that he had time to be uncomfortable and to become easy again before Mr Poyser's slow speech was finished, and when it was time for him to speak he was quite light-hearted.

'I thank you all, my good friends and neighbours,' Arthur said, 'for the good opinion of me, and the kind feelings towards me which Mr Poyser has been expressing on your behalf and on his own, and it will always be my heartiest wish to deserve them. In the course of things we may expect that, if I live, I shall one day or other be your landlord; indeed it is on the ground of that expectation that my grandfather has wished me to celebrate this day and to come among you now; and I look forward to this position, not merely as one of power and pleasure for myself, but as a means of benefiting my neighbours. It hardly becomes so young a man as I am, to talk much about farming to you, who are most of you so much older, and are men of experience; still, I have interested myself a good deal in such matters, and learned as much about them as my opportunities have allowed; and when the course of events shall place the estate in my hands, it will be my first desire to afford my tenants all the encouragement a landlord can give them, in improving their land, and trying to bring about a better practice of husbandry. It will be my wish to be looked on by all my deserving tenants as their best friend, and nothing would make me so happy as to be able to respect every man on the estate, and to be respected by him in return. It is not my place at present to enter into particulars; I only meet your good hopes concerning me by telling you that my own hopes correspond to them – that what you expect from me I desire to fulfil; and I am quite of Mr Poyser's opinion, that when a man has said what he means, he had better stop. But the pleasure I feel in having my own health drunk by you would not be perfect if we did not drink the health of my grandfather, who has filled the place of both parents to me. I will say no more, until you have joined me in drinking his health on a day when he has wished me to appear among you as the future representative of his name and family.'

Perhaps there was no one present except Mr Irwine who thoroughly understood and approved Arthur's graceful mode of proposing his grandfather's health. The farmers thought the young Squire knew well enough that they hated the old Squire, and Mrs Poyser said, 'he'd better not ha' stirred a kettle o' sour broth'. The bucolic mind does not readily apprehend the refinements of good taste. But the toast could not be rejected, and when it had been drunk, Arthur said –

'I thank you, both for my grandfather and myself; and now there is one more thing I wish to tell you, that you may share my pleasure about it, as I hope and believe you will. I think there can be no man here who has not a respect, and some of you, I am sure, have a very high regard, for my friend Adam Bede. It is well known to every one in this neighbourhood that there is no man whose word can be more depended on than his; that whatever he undertakes to do, he does well, and is as careful for the interests of those who employ him as for his own. I'm proud to say that I was very fond of Adam when I was a little boy, and I have never lost my old feeling for him – I think that shows that I know a good fellow when I find him. It has long been my wish that he should have the management of the woods on the estate, which happen to be very valuable; not only because I think so highly of his character, but because he has the knowledge and the skill which fit him for the place. And I am happy to tell you that it is my grandfather's wish too, and it is now settled that Adam shall manage the woods – a change which I am sure will be very much for the advantage of the estate; and I hope you will by-and-by join me in drinking his health, and in wishing him all the prosperity in life that he deserves. But there is a still older friend of mine than Adam Bede present, and I need not tell you that it is Mr Irwine. I'm sure you will agree with me that we must drink no other person's health until we have drunk his. I know you have all reason to love him, but no one of his parishioners has so much reason as I. Come, charge your glasses, and let us drink to our excellent Rector – three times three!'

This toast was drunk with all the enthusiasm that was wanting to the last, and it certainly was the most picturesque moment in the scene when Mr Irwine got up to speak, and all the faces in the room were turned towards him. The superior refinement of his face was much more striking than that of Arthur's when seen in comparison with the people round them. Arthur's was a much commoner British face, and the splendour of his new-fashioned clothes was more akin to the young farmer's taste in

costume than Mr Irwine's powder, and the well-brushed but
well-worn black, which seemed to be his chosen suit for great
occasions; for he had the mysterious secret of never wearing a
new-looking coat.

'This is not the first time, by a great many,' he said, 'that I
have had to thank my parishioners for giving me tokens of their
goodwill, but neighbourly kindness is among those things that
are the more precious the older they get. Indeed, our pleasant
meeting to-day is a proof that when what is good comes of age
and is likely to live, there is reason for rejoicing, and the relation
between us as clergyman and parishioners came of age two
years ago, for it is three-and-twenty years since I first came
among you, and I see some tall fine-looking young men here,
as well as some blooming young women, that were far from
looking as pleasantly at me when I christened them, as I am
happy to see them looking now. But I'm sure you will not
wonder when I say, that among all those young men, the one
in whom I have the strongest interest is my friend Mr Arthur
Donnithorne, for whom you have just expressed your regard. I
had the pleasure of being his tutor for several years, and have
naturally had opportunities of knowing him intimately which
cannot have occurred to any one else who is present; and I have
some pride as well as pleasure in assuring you that I share
your high hopes concerning him, and your confidence in his
possession of those qualities which will make him an excellent
landlord when the time shall come for him to take that important position among you. We feel alike on most matters on
which a man who is getting towards fifty can feel in common
with a young man of one-and-twenty, and he has just been
expressing a feeling which I share very heartily, and I would
not willingly omit the opportunity of saying so. That feeling is
his value and respect for Adam Bede. People in a high station
are of course more thought of and talked about, and have their
virtues more praised, than those whose lives are passed in
humble everyday work; but every sensible man knows how
necessary that humble everyday work is, and how important it
is to us that it should be done well. And I agree with my friend
Mr Arthur Donnithorne in feeling that when a man whose duty

lies in that sort of work shows a character which would make him an example in any station, his merit should be acknowledged. He is one of those to whom honour is due, and his friends should delight to honour him. I know Adam Bede well – I know what he is as a workman, and what he has been as a son and brother – and I am saying the simplest truth when I say that I respect him as much as I respect any man living. But I am not speaking to you about a stranger; some of you are his intimate friends, and I believe there is not one here who does not know enough of him to join heartily in drinking his health.'

As Mr Irwine paused, Arthur jumped up, and, filling his glass, said, 'A bumper to Adam Bede, and may he live to have sons as faithful and clever as himself!'

No hearer, not even Bartle Massey, was so delighted with this toast as Mr Poyser: 'tough work' as his first speech had been, he would have started up to make another if he had not known the extreme irregularity of such a course. As it was, he found as outlet for his feeling in drinking his ale unusually fast, and setting down his glass with a swing of his arm, and a determined rap. If Jonathan Burge and a few others felt less comfortable on the occasion, they tried their best to look contented, and so the toast was drunk with a goodwill apparently unanimous.

Adam was rather paler than usual when he got up to thank his friends. He was a good deal moved by this public tribute – very naturally, for he was in the presence of all his little world, and it was uniting to do him honour. But he felt no shyness about speaking, not being troubled with small vanity or lack of words; he looked neither awkward nor embarrassed, but stood in his usual firm upright attitude, with his head thrown a little backward and his hands perfectly still, in that rough dignity which is peculiar to intelligent, honest, well-built workmen, who are never wondering what is their business in the world.

'I'm quite taken by surprise,' he said. 'I didn't expect anything o' this sort, for it's a good deal more than my wages. But I've the more reason to be grateful to you, Captain, and to you, Mr Irwine, and to all my friends here, who've drunk my health and wished me well. It 'ud be nonsense for me to be saying, I don't at all deserve th' opinion you have of me; that 'ud be poor thanks to you, to say that you've known me all these years, and yet haven't sense enough to find out a great deal o' the truth about me. You think, if I undertake to do a bit o' work, I'll do it well, be my pay big or little – and that's true. I'd be ashamed to stand before you here if it wasna true. But it seems to me, that's a man's plain duty, and nothing to be conceited about, and it's pretty clear to me as I've never done more than my duty; for let us do what we will, it's only making use o' the sperrit and the powers that ha' been given to us. And so this kindness o' yours, I'm sure, is no debt you owe me, but a free gift, and as such I accept it and am thankful. And as to this new employment I've taken in hand, I'll only say that I took it at Captain Donnithorne's desire, and that I'll try to fulfil his expectations. I'd wish for no better lot than to work under him, and to know that while I was getting my own bread I was taking care of his int'rests. For I believe he's one o' those gentlemen as wishes to do the right thing, and to leave the world a bit better than he found it, which it's my belief every man may do, whether he's gentle or simple, whether he sets a good bit o' work going and finds the money, or whether he does the work with his own hands. There's no occasion for me to say any more about what I feel towards him: I hope to show it through the rest o' my life in my actions.'

There were various opinions about Adam's speech: some of the women whispered that he didn't show himself thankful enough, and seemed to speak as proud as could be; but most of the men were of opinion that nobody could speak more straightfor'ard, and that Adam was as fine a chap as need to be. While such observations were being buzzed about, mingled with wonderings as to what the old Squire meant to do for a bailiff, and whether he was going to have a steward,[2] the two gentlemen had risen, and were walking round to the table where the wives and children sat. There was none of the strong ale here, of course, but wine and dessert – sparkling gooseberry for the young ones, and some good sherry for the mothers. Mrs Poyser was at the head of this table, and Totty was now seated in her lap, bending her small nose deep down into a wine-glass in search of the nuts floating there.

'How do you do, Mrs Poyser?' said Arthur. 'Weren't you pleased to hear your husband make such a good speech to-day?'

'Oh, sir, the men are mostly so tongue-tied – you're forced partly to guess what they mean, as you do wi' the dumb creaturs.'

'What! you think you could have made it better for him?' said Mr Irwine, laughing.

'Well, sir, when I want to say anything, I can mostly find words to say it in, thank God. Not as I'm a-finding faut wi' my husband, for if he's a man o' few words, what he says he'll stand to.'

'I'm sure I never saw a prettier party than this,' Arthur said, looking round at the apple-cheeked children. 'My aunt and the Miss Irwines will come up and see you presently. They were afraid of the noise of the toasts, but it would be a shame for them not to see you at table.'

He walked on, speaking to the mothers and patting the children, while Mr Irwine satisfied himself with standing still, and nodding at a distance, that no one's attention might be disturbed from the young Squire, the hero of the day. Arthur did not venture to stop near Hetty, but merely bowed to her as he passed along the opposite side. The foolish child felt her heart swelling with discontent; for what woman was ever satisfied with apparent neglect, even when she knows it to be the mask of love? Hetty thought this was going to be the most miserable day she had had for a long while; a moment of chill daylight and reality came across her dream: Arthur, who had seemed so near to her only a few hours before, was separated from her, as the hero of a great procession is separated from a small outsider in the crowd.

CHAPTER XXV

The Games

The great dance was not to begin until eight o'clock; but for any lads and lasses who liked to dance on the shady grass before then, there was music always at hand; for was not the band of the Benefit Club capable of playing excellent jigs, reels, and hornpipes?[1] And, besides this, there was a grand band hired from Rosseter, who, with their wonderful wind-instruments and puffed-out cheeks, were themselves a delightful show to the small boys and girls. To say nothing of Joshua Rann's fiddle, which, by an act of generous forethought, he had provided himself with, in case any one should be of sufficiently pure taste to prefer dancing to a solo on that instrument.

Meantime, when the sun had moved off the great open space in front of the house, the games began. There were of course well-soaped poles to be climbed by the boys and youths, races to be run by the old women, races to be run in sacks, heavy weights to be lifted by the strong men, and a long list of challenges to such ambitious attempts as that of walking as many yards as possible on one leg – feats in which it was generally remarked that Wiry Ben, being 'the lissom'st, springest fellow i' the country', was sure to be pre-eminent. To crown all, there was to be a donkey-race – that sublimest of all races, conducted on the grand socialistic idea[2] of everybody encouraging everybody else's donkey, and the sorriest donkey winning.

And soon after four o'clock, splendid old Mrs Irwine, in her damask satin and jewels and black lace, was led out by Arthur, followed by the whole family party, to her raised seat under the striped marquee, where she was to give out the prizes to the victors. Staid, formal Miss Lydia had requested to resign that queenly office to the royal old lady, and Arthur was pleased with this opportunity of gratifying his godmother's taste for stateliness. Old Mr Donnithorne, the delicately-clean, finely-scented, withered old man, led out Miss Irwine, with his air of punctilious, acid politeness; Mr Gawaine brought Miss Lydia, looking neutral and stiff in an elegant peach-blossom silk; and Mr Irwine came last with his pale sister Anne. No other friend of the family, besides Mr Gawaine, was invited to-day; there was to be a grand dinner for the neighbouring gentry on the morrow, but to-day all the forces were required for the entertainment of the tenants.

There was a sunk fence in front of the marquee, dividing the lawn from the park, but a temporary bridge had been made for the passage of the victors, and the groups of people standing, or seated here and there on benches, stretched on each side of the open space from the white marquees up to the sunk fence.

'Upon my word it's a pretty sight,' said the old lady, in her deep voice, when she was seated, and looked round on the bright scene with its dark-green background; 'and it's the last fête-day I'm likely to see, unless you make haste and get married, Arthur. But take care you get a charming bride, else I would rather die without seeing her.'

'You're so terribly fastidious, godmother,' said Arthur, 'I'm afraid I should never satisfy you with my choice.'

'Well, I won't forgive you if she's not handsome. I can't be put off with amiability, which is always the excuse people are making for the existence of plain people. And she must not be silly; that will never do, because you'll want managing, and a silly woman can't manage you. Who is that tall young man, Dauphin, with the mild face? There, standing without his hat, and taking such care of that tall old woman by the side of him – his mother, of course. I like to see that.'

'What, don't you know him, mother?' said Mr Irwine. 'That is Seth Bede, Adam's brother – a Methodist, but a very good fellow. Poor Seth has looked rather down-hearted of late; I thought it was because of his father's dying in that sad way; but Joshua Rann tells me he wanted to marry that sweet little

Methodist preacher who was here about a month ago, and I suppose she refused him.'

'Ah, I remember hearing about her: but there are no end of people here that I don't know, for they're grown up and altered so since I used to go about.'

'What excellent sight you have!' said old Mr Donnithorne, who was holding a double glass up to his eyes, 'to see the expression of that young man's face so far off. His face is nothing but a pale blurred spot to me. But I fancy I have the advantage of you when we come to look close. I can read small print without spectacles.'

'Ah, my dear sir, you began with being very near-sighted, and those near-sighted eyes always wear the best. I want very strong spectacles to read with, but then I think my eyes get better and better for things at a distance. I suppose if I could live another fifty years, I should be blind to everything that wasn't out of other people's sight, like a man who stands in a well, and sees nothing but the stars.'

'See,' said Arthur, 'the old women are ready to set out on their race now. Which do you bet on, Gawaine?'

'The long-legged one, unless they're going to have several heats, and then the little wiry one may win.'

'There are the Poysers, mother, not far off on the right hand,' said Miss Irwine. 'Mrs Poyser is looking at you. Do take notice of her.'

'To be sure I will,' said the old lady, giving a gracious bow to Mrs Poyser. 'A woman who sends me such excellent cream-cheese is not to be neglected. Bless me! what a fat child that is she is holding on her knee! But who is that pretty girl with dark eyes?'

'That is Hetty Sorrel,' said Miss Lydia Donnithorne, 'Martin Poyser's niece – a very likely young person, and well-looking too. My maid has taught her fine needle-work, and she has mended some lace of mine very respectably indeed – very respectably.'

'Why, she has lived with the Poysers six or seven years, mother; you must have seen her,' said Miss Irwine.

'No, I've never seen her, child; at least not as she is now,' said Mrs Irwine, continuing to look at Hetty. 'Well-looking, indeed! She's a perfect beauty! I've never seen anything so pretty since my young days. What a pity such beauty as that should be thrown away among the farmers, when it's wanted so terribly among the good families without fortune! I daresay, now, she'll marry a man who would have thought her just as pretty if she had had round eyes and red hair.'

Arthur dared not turn his eyes towards Hetty while Mrs Irwine was speaking of her. He feigned not to hear, and to be occupied with something on the opposite side. But he saw her plainly enough without looking; saw her in heightened beauty, because he heard her beauty praised – for other men's opinion, you know, was like a native climate to Arthur's feelings: it was the air on which they thrived the best, and grew strong. Yes! she *was* enough to turn any man's head: any man in his place would have done and felt the same. And to give her up after all, as he was determined to do, would be an act that he should always look back upon with pride.

'No, mother,' said Mr Irwine, replying to her last words; 'I can't agree with you there. The common people are not quite so stupid as you imagine. The commonest man, who has his ounce of sense and feeling, is conscious of the difference between a lovely, delicate woman, and a coarse one. Even a dog feels a difference in their presence. The man may be no better able than the dog to explain the influence the more refined beauty has on him, but he feels it.'

'Bless me, Dauphin, what does an old bachelor like you know about it?'

'Oh, that is one of the matters in which old bachelors are wiser than married men, because they have time for more general contemplation. Your fine critic of women must never shackle his judgment by calling one woman his own. But, as an example of what I was saying, that pretty Methodist preacher I mentioned just now, told me that she had preached to the roughest miners, and had never been treated with anything but the utmost respect and kindness by them. The reason is – though she doesn't know it – that there's so much tenderness, refinement, and purity about her. Such a woman as that brings with her "airs from heaven"³ that the coarsest fellow is not insensible to.'

'Here's a delicate bit of womanhood, or girlhood, coming to receive a prize, I suppose,' said Mr Gawaine. 'She must be one of the racers in the sacks, who had set off before we came.'

The 'bit of womanhood' was our old acquaintance Bessy Cranage, otherwise Chad's Bess, whose large red cheeks and blowsy person had undergone an exaggeration of colour, which, if she had happened to be a heavenly body, would have made her sublime. Bessy, I am sorry to say, had taken to her earrings again since Dinah's departure, and was otherwise decked out in such small finery as she could muster. Any one who could have looked into poor Bessy's heart would have seen a striking resemblance between her little hopes and anxieties and Hetty's. The advantage, perhaps, would have been on Bessy's side in the matter of feeling. But then, you see, they were so very different outside! You would have been inclined to box Bessy's ears, and you would have longed to kiss Hetty.

Bessy had been tempted to run the arduous race, partly from mere hoidenish gaiety, partly because of the prize. Some one had said there were to be cloaks and other nice clothes for prizes, and she approached the marquee, fanning herself with her handkerchief, but with exultation sparkling in her round eyes.

'Here is the prize for the first sack-race,' said Miss Lydia, taking a large parcel from the table where the prizes were laid, and giving it to Mrs Irwine before Bessy came up; 'an excellent grogram gown and a piece of flannel.'⁴

'You didn't think the winner was to be so young, I suppose, aunt?' said Arthur. 'Couldn't you find something else for this girl, and save that grim-looking gown for one of the older women?'

'I have bought nothing but what is useful and substantial,' said Miss Lydia, adjusting her own lace; 'I should not think of encouraging a love of finery in young women of that class. I have a scarlet cloak, but that is for the old woman who wins.'

This speech of Miss Lydia's produced rather a mocking

expression in Mrs Irwine's face as she looked at Arthur, while Bessy came up and dropped a series of curtsies.

'This is Bessy Cranage, mother,' said Mr Irwine, kindly, 'Chad Cranage's daughter. You remember Chad Cranage, the blacksmith?'

'Yes, to be sure,' said Mrs Irwine. 'Well, Bessy, here is your prize – excellent warm things for winter. I'm sure you have had hard work to win them this warm day.'

Bessy's lip fell as she saw the ugly, heavy gown, – which felt so hot and disagreeable, too, on this July day, and was such a great ugly thing to carry. She dropped her curtsies again, without looking up, and with a growing tremulousness about the corners of her mouth, and then turned away.

'Poor girl,' said Arthur; 'I think she's disappointed. I wish it had been something more to her taste.'

'She's a bold-looking young person,' observed Miss Lydia. 'Not at all one I should like to encourage.'

Arthur silently resolved that he would make Bessy a present of money before the day was over, that she might buy something more to her mind; but she, not aware of the consolation in store for her, turned out of the open space, where she was visible from the marquee, and throwing down the odious bundle under a tree, began to cry – very much tittered at the while by the small boys. In this situation she was descried by her discreet matronly cousin, who lost no time in coming up, having just given the baby into her husband's charge.

'What's the matter wi' ye?' said Bess the matron, taking up the bundle and examining it. 'Ye'n sweltered yoursen, I reckon, running that fool's race. An' here, they'n gi'en you lots o' good grogram and flannel, as should ha' been gi'en by good rights to them as had the sense to keep away from such foolery. Ye might spare me a bit o' this grogram to make clothes for the lad – ye war ne'er ill-natured, Bess; I ne'er said that on ye.'

'Ye may take it all, for what I care,' said Bess the maiden with a pettish movement, beginning to wipe away her tears and recover herself.

'Well, I could do wi't, if so be ye want to get rid on't,' said the disinterested cousin, walking quickly away with the bundle, lest Chad's Bess should change her mind.

But that bonny-cheeked lass was blest with an elasticity of spirits that secured her from any rankling grief; and by the time the grand climax of the donkey-race came on, her disappointment was entirely lost in the delightful excitement of attempting to stimulate the last donkey by hisses, while the boys applied the argument of sticks. But the strength of the donkey mind lies in adopting a course inversely as the arguments urged, which, well considered, requires as great a mental force as the direct sequence; and the present donkey proved the first-rate order of his intelligence by coming to a dead stand-still just when the blows were thickest. Great was the shouting of the crowd, radiant the grinning of Bill Downes the stone-sawyer and the fortunate rider of this superior beast, which stood calm and stiff-legged in the midst of its triumph.

Arthur himself had provided the prizes for the men, and Bill was made happy with a splendid pocket-knife, supplied with blades and gimlets enough to make a man at home on a desert island. He had hardly returned from the marquee with the prize in his hand, when it began to be understood that Wiry Ben proposed to amuse the company, before the gentry went to dinner, with an impromptu and gratuitous performance – namely, a hornpipe, the main idea of which was doubtless borrowed; but this was to be developed by the dancer in so peculiar and complex a manner that no one could deny him the praise of originality. Wiry Ben's pride in his dancing – an accomplishment productive of great effect at the yearly Wake⁵ – had needed only slightly elevating by an extra quantity of good ale, to convince him that the gentry would be very much struck with his performance of the hornpipe; and he had been decidedly encouraged in this idea by Joshua Rann, who observed that it was nothing but right to do something to please the young Squire, in return for what he had done for them. You will be the less surprised at this opinion in so grave a personage when you learn that Ben had requested Mr Rann to accompany him on the fiddle, and Joshua felt quite sure that though there might not be much in the dancing, the music would make up

for it. Adam Bede, who was present in one of the large marquees, where the plan was being discussed, told Ben he had
better not make a fool of himself – a remark which at once
fixed Ben's determination: he was not going to let anything
alone because Adam Bede turned up his nose at it.

'What's this, what's this?' said old Mr Donnithorne. 'Is it
something you've arranged, Arthur? Here's the clerk coming
with his fiddle, and a smart fellow with a nosegay in his
button-hole.'

'No,' said Arthur; 'I know nothing about it. By Jove, he's
going to dance! It's one of the carpenters – I forget his name at
this moment.'

'It's Ben Cranage – wiry Ben, they call him,' said Mr Irwine;
'rather a loose fish, I think. Anne, my dear, I see that fiddle-
scraping is too much for you: you're getting tired. Let me take
you in now, that you may rest till dinner.'

Miss Anne rose assentingly, and the good brother took her
away, while Joshua's preliminary scrapings burst into the
'White Cockade',[6] from which he intended to pass to a variety
of tunes, by a series of transitions which his good ear really
taught him to execute with some skill. It would have been an
exasperating fact to him, if he had known it, that the general
attention was too thoroughly absorbed by Ben's dancing for
any one to give much heed to the music.

Have you ever seen a real English rustic perform a solo
dance? Perhaps you have only seen a ballet rustic, smiling like
a merry countryman in crockery, with graceful turns of the
haunch and insinuating movements of the head. That is as
much like the real thing as the 'Bird Waltz'[7] is like the song of
birds. Wiry Ben never smiled: he looked as serious as a dancing
monkey – as serious as if he had been an experimental philosopher ascertaining in his own person the amount of shaking
and the varieties of angularity that could be given to the human
limbs.

To make amends for the abundant laughter in the striped
marquee, Arthur clapped his hands continually and cried
'Bravo!' But Ben had one admirer whose eyes followed his
movements with a fervid gravity that equalled his own. It was

Martin Poyser, who was seated on a bench, with Tommy between his legs.

'What dost think o' that?' he said to his wife. 'He goes as pat to the music as if he was made o' clockwork. I used to be a pretty good un at dancing myself when I was lighter, but I could niver ha' hit it just to th' hair like that.'

'It's little matter what his limbs are, to my thinking,' returned Mrs Poyser. 'He's empty enough i' the upper story, or he'd niver come jigging an' stamping i' that way, like a mad grass-hopper, for the gentry to look at him. They're fit to die wi' laughing, I can see.'

'Well, well, so much the better, it amuses 'em,' said Mr Poyser, who did not easily take an irritable view of things. 'But they're going away now, t' have their dinner, I reckon. We'll move about a bit, shall we? and see what Adam Bede's doing. He's got to look after the drinking and things: I doubt he hasna had much fun.'

CHAPTER XXVI

The Dance

Arthur had chosen the entrance-hall for the ball-room: very wisely, for no other room could have been so airy, or would have had the advantage of the wide doors opening into the garden, as well as a ready entrance into the other rooms. To be sure, a stone floor was not the pleasantest to dance on, but then, most of the dancers had known what it was to enjoy a Christmas dance on kitchen quarries. It was one of those entrance-halls which make the surrounding rooms look like closets – with stucco angels, trumpets, and flower wreaths on the lofty ceiling, and great medallions of miscellaneous heroes on the walls, alternating with statues in niches. Just the sort of place to be ornamented well with green boughs, and Mr Craig had been proud to show his taste and his hot-house plants on the occasion. The broad steps of the stone staircase were covered with cushions to serve as seats for the children, who were to stay till half-past nine with the servant-maids, to see the dancing; and as this dance was confined to the chief tenants, there was abundant room for every one. The lights were charmingly disposed in coloured-paper lamps, high up among green boughs, and the farmers' wives and daughters, as they peeped in, believed no scene could be more splendid; they knew now quite well in what sort of rooms the king and queen lived, and their thoughts glanced with some pity towards cousins and acquaintances who had not this fine opportunity of knowing how things went on in the great world. The lamps were already lit, though the sun had not long set, and there was that calm light out of doors in which we seem to see all objects more distinctly than in the broad day.

It was a pretty scene outside the house: the farmers and their families were moving about the lawn, among the flowers and shrubs, or along the broad straight road leading from the east front, where a carpet of mossy grass spread on each side, studded here and there with a dark flat-boughed cedar, or a grand pyramidal fir sweeping the ground with its branches, all tipped with a fringe of paler green. The groups of cottagers in the park were gradually diminishing, the young ones being attracted towards the lights that were beginning to gleam from the windows of the gallery in the abbey, which was to be their dancing-room, and some of the sober elder ones thinking it time to go home quietly. One of these was Lisbeth Bede, and Seth went with her – not from filial attention only, for his conscience would not let him join in dancing. It had been rather a melancholy day to Seth: Dinah had never been more constantly present with him than in this scene, where everything was so unlike her. He saw her all the more vividly after looking at the thoughtless faces and gay-coloured dresses of the young women – just as one feels the beauty and the greatness of a pictured Madonna the more, when it has been for a moment screened from us by a vulgar head in a bonnet. But this presence of Dinah in his mind only helped him to bear the better with his mother's mood, which had been becoming more and more querulous for the last hour. Poor Lisbeth was suffering from a strange conflict of feelings. Her joy and pride in the honour paid to her darling son Adam was beginning to be worsted in the conflict with the jealousy and fretfulness which had revived when Adam came to tell her that Captain Donnithorne desired him to join the dancers in the hall. Adam was getting more and more out of her reach; she wished all the old troubles back again, for then it mattered more to Adam what his mother said and did.

'Eh, it's fine talkin' o' dancin',' she said, 'an' thy father not a five week in's grave. An' I wish I war there too, istid o' bein' left to take up merrier folks's room above ground.'

'Nay, don't look at it i' that way, mother,' said Adam, who was determined to be gentle to her to-day. 'I don't mean to dance – I shall only look on. And since the Captain wishes

me to be there, it 'ud look as if I thought I knew better than
him to say as I'd rather not stay. And thee know'st how he's
behaved to me to-day.'

'Eh, thee't do as thee lik'st, for thy old mother's got no right
t' hinder thee. She's nought but th' old husk, and thee'st slipped
away from her, like the ripe nut.'

'Well, mother,' said Adam, 'I'll go and tell the Captain as it
hurts thy feelings for me to stay, and I'd rather go home upo'
that account: he won't take it ill then, I daresay, and I'm willing.' He said this with some effort, for he really longed to be
near Hetty this evening.

'Nay, nay, I wonna ha' thee do that – the young Squire 'ull
be angered. Go an' do what thee't ordered to do, an' me and
Seth 'ull go whome. I know it's a grit honour for thee to be so
looked on – an' who's to be prouder on it nor thy mother?
Hadna she the cumber o' rearin' thee an' doin' for thee all these
'ears?'

'Well, good-bye, then, mother – good-bye, lad – remember
Gyp when you get home,' said Adam, turning away towards
the gate of the pleasure-grounds, where he hoped he might be
able to join the Poysers, for he had been so occupied throughout
the afternoon that he had had no time to speak to Hetty. His
eye soon detected a distant group, which he knew to be the
right one, returning to the house along the broad gravel road,
and he hastened on to meet them.

'Why, Adam, I'm glad to get sight on y' again,' said Mr
Poyser, who was carrying Totty on his arm. 'You're going t'
have a bit o' fun, I hope, now your work's all done. And here's
Hetty has promised no end o' partners, an' I've just been askin'
her if she'd agreed to dance wi' you, an' she says no.'

'Well, I didn't think o' dancing to-night,' said Adam, already
tempted to change his mind, as he looked at Hetty.

'Nonsense!' said Mr Poyser. 'Why, everybody's goin' to
dance to-night, all but the old Squire and Mrs Irwine. Mrs
Best's been tellin' us as Miss Lyddy and Miss Irwine 'ull dance,
an' the young Squire 'ull pick my wife for his first partner, t'
open the ball: so she'll be forced to dance, though she's laid by
ever sin' the Christmas afore the little un was born. You canna

for shame stand still, Adam, an' you a fine young fellow, and can dance as well as anybody.'

'Nay, nay,' said Mrs Poyser, 'it 'ud be unbecomin'. I know the dancin's nonsense; but if you stick at everything because it's nonsense, you wonna go far i' this life. When your broth's ready-made for you, you mun swallow the thickenin', or else let the broth alone.'

'Then if Hetty 'ull dance with me,' said Adam, yielding either to Mrs Poyser's argument or to something else, 'I'll dance whichever dance she's free.'

'I've got no partner for the fourth dance,' said Hetty; 'I'll dance that with you, if you like.'

'Ah,' said Mr Poyser, 'but you mun dance the first dance, Adam, else it'll look partic'ler. There's plenty o' nice partners to pick an' choose from, an' it's hard for the gells when the men stan' by and don't ask 'em.'

Adam felt the justice of Mr Poyser's observation: it would not do for him to dance with no one besides Hetty; and remembering that Jonathan Burge had some reason to feel hurt to-day, he resolved to ask Miss Mary to dance with him the first dance, if she had no other partner.

'There's the big clock strikin' eight,' said Mr Poyser; 'we must make haste in now, else the Squire and the ladies 'ull be in afore us, an' that wouldna look well.'

When they had entered the hall, and the three children under Molly's charge had been seated on the stairs, the folding-doors of the drawing-room were thrown open, and Arthur entered in his regimentals, leading Mrs Irwine to a carpet-covered dais ornamented with hothouse plants, where she and Miss Anne were to be seated with old Mr Donnithorne, that they might look on at the dancing, like the kings and queens in the plays. Arthur had put on his uniform to please the tenants, he said, who thought as much of his militia dignity as if it had been an elevation to the premiership. He had not the least objection to gratify them in that way: his uniform was very advantageous to his figure.

The old Squire, before sitting down, walked round the hall to greet the tenants and make polite speeches to the wives: he was always polite; but the farmers had found out, after long puzzling, that this polish was one of the signs of hardness. It was observed that he gave his most elaborate civility to Mrs Poyser to-night, inquiring particularly about her health, recommending her to strengthen herself with cold water as he did, and avoid all drugs. Mrs Poyser curtsied and thanked him with great self-command, but when he had passed on, she whispered to her husband, 'I'll lay my life he's brewin' some nasty turn against us. Old Harry doesna wag his tail so for nothin'.' Mr Poyser had no time to answer, for now Arthur came up and said, 'Mrs Poyser, I'm come to request the favour of your hand for the first dance; and, Mr Poyser, you must let me take you to my aunt, for she claims you as her partner.'

The wife's pale cheek flushed with a nervous sense of unwonted honour as Arthur led her to the top of the room; but Mr Poyser, to whom an extra glass had restored his youthful confidence in his good looks and good dancing, walked along with them quite proudly, secretly flattering himself that Miss Lydia had never had a partner in *her* life who could lift her off the ground as he would. In order to balance the honours given to the two parishes, Miss Irwine danced with Luke Britton, the largest Broxton farmer, and Mr Gawaine led out Mrs Britton. Mr Irwine, after seating his sister Anne, had gone to the abbey gallery, as he had agreed with Arthur beforehand, to see how the merriment of the cottagers was prospering. Meanwhile, all the less distinguished couples had taken their places: Hetty was led out by the inevitable Mr Craig, and Mary Burge by Adam; and now the music struck up, and the glorious country-dance, best of all dances, began.

Pity it was not a boarded floor! Then the rhythmic stamping of the thick shoes would have been better than any drums. That merry stamping, that gracious nodding of the head, that waving bestowal of the hand – where can we see them now? That simple dancing of well-covered matrons, laying aside for an hour the cares of house and dairy, remembering but not affecting youth, not jealous but proud of the young maidens by their side – that holiday sprightliness of portly husbands paying little compliments to their wives, as if their courting days were come again – those lads and lasses a little confused and awkward with their partners, having nothing to say – it would be a pleasant variety to see all that sometimes, instead of low dresses and large skirts, and scanning glances exploring costumes, and languid men in lackered boots smiling with double meaning.

There was but one thing to mar Martin Poyser's pleasure in this dance: it was, that he was always in close contact with Luke Britton, that slovenly farmer. He thought of throwing a little glazed coldness into his eye in the crossing of hands; but then, as Miss Irwine was opposite to him instead of the offensive Luke, he might freeze the wrong person. So he gave his face up to hilarity, unchilled by moral judgements.

How Hetty's heart beat as Arthur approached her! He had hardly looked at her to-day; now he *must* take her hand. Would he press it? would he look at her? She thought she would cry if he gave her no sign of feeling. Now he was there – he had taken her hand – yes, he was pressing it. Hetty turned pale as she looked up at him for an instant and met his eyes, before the dance carried him away. That pale look came upon Arthur like the beginning of a dull pain, which clung to him, though he must dance and smile and joke all the same. Hetty would look so, when he told her what he had to tell her; and he should never be able to bear it – he should be a fool and give way again. Hetty's look did not really mean so much as he thought: it was only the sign of a struggle between the desire for him to notice her, and the dread lest she should betray the desire to others. But Hetty's face had a language that transcended her feelings. There are faces which nature charges with a meaning and pathos not belonging to the single human soul that flutters beneath them, but speaking the joys and sorrows of foregone generations – eyes that tell of deep love which doubtless has been and is somewhere, but not paired with these eyes – perhaps paired with pale eyes that can say nothing; just as a national language may be instinct with poetry unfelt by the lips that use it. That look of Hetty's oppressed Arthur with a dread which yet had something of a terrible unconfessed delight in it, that she loved him too well. There was a hard task before him, for at that moment he felt he would have given up three years of his youth for the happiness of abandoning himself without remorse to his passion for Hetty.

These were the incongruous thoughts in his mind, as he led Mrs Poyser, who was panting with fatigue, and secretly resolving that neither judge nor jury should force her to dance another dance, to take a quiet rest in the dining-room, where supper was laid out for the guests to come and take it as they chose.

'I've desired Hetty to remember as she's got to dance wi' you, sir,' said the good innocent woman; 'for she's so thoughtless, she'd be like enough to go an' engage herself for ivery dance. So I told her not to promise too many.'

'Thank you, Mrs Poyser,' said Arthur, not without a twinge. 'Now, sit down in this comfortable chair, and here is Mills ready to give you what you would like best.'

He hurried away to seek another matronly partner, for due honour must be paid to the married women before he asked any of the young ones; and the country-dances, and the stamping, and the gracious nodding, and the waving of the hands, went on joyously.

At last the time had come for the fourth dance – longed for by the strong, grave Adam, as if he had been a delicate-handed youth of eighteen; for we are all very much alike when we are in our first love; and Adam had hardly ever touched Hetty's hand for more than a transient greeting – had never danced with her but once before. His eyes had followed her eagerly to-night in spite of himself, and had taken in deeper draughts of love. He thought she behaved so prettily, so quietly; she did not seem to be flirting at all, she smiled less than usual; there was almost a sweet sadness about her. 'God bless her!' he said inwardly; 'I'd make her life a happy un, if a strong arm to work for her, and a heart to love her, could do it.'

And then there stole over him delicious thoughts of coming home from work, and drawing Hetty to his side, and feeling her cheek softly pressed against his, till he forgot where he was, and the music and the tread of feet might have been the falling of rain and the roaring of the wind, for what he knew.

But now the third dance was ended, and he might go up to her and claim her hand. She was at the far end of the hall near the staircase, whispering with Molly, who had just given the sleeping Totty into her arms, before running to fetch shawls and bonnets from the landing. Mrs Poyser had taken the two boys away into the dining-room to give them some cake before they went home in the cart with grandfather, and Molly was to follow as fast as possible.

'Let me hold her,' said Adam, as Molly turned up-stairs: 'the children are so heavy when they're asleep.'

Hetty was glad of the relief, for to hold Totty in her arms, standing, was not at all a pleasant variety to her. But this second transfer had the unfortunate effect of rousing Totty, who was not behind any child of her age in peevishness at an unseasonable awaking. While Hetty was in the act of placing her in Adam's arms, and had not yet withdrawn her own, Totty opened her eyes, and forthwith fought out with her left fist at Adam's arm, and with her right caught at the string of brown beads round Hetty's neck. The locket leaped out from her frock, and the next moment the string was broken, and Hetty, helpless, saw beads and locket scattered wide on the floor.

'My locket, my locket!' she said, in a loud frightened whisper to Adam; 'never mind the beads.'

Adam had already seen where the locket fell, for it had attracted his glance as it leaped out of her frock. It had fallen on the raised wooden dais where the band sat, not on the stone floor; and as Adam picked it up, he saw the glass with the dark and light locks of hair under it. It had fallen that side upwards, so the glass was not broken. He turned it over on his hand, and saw the enamelled gold back.

'It isn't hurt,' he said, as he held it towards Hetty, who was unable to take it because both her hands were occupied with Totty.

'Oh, it doesn't matter, I don't mind about it,' said Hetty, who had been pale and was now red.

'Not matter?' said Adam, gravely. 'You seemed very frightened about it. I'll hold it till you're ready to take it,' he added, quietly closing his hand over it, that she might not think he wanted to look at it again.

By this time Molly had come with bonnet and shawl, and as

soon as she had taken Totty, Adam placed the locket in Hetty's hand. She took it with an air of indifference, and put it in her pocket; in her heart vexed and angry with Adam, because he had seen it, but determined now that she would show no more signs of agitation.

'See,' she said, 'they're taking their places to dance; let us go.'

Adam assented silently. A puzzled alarm had taken possession of him. Had Hetty a lover he didn't know of? – for none of her relations, he was sure, would give her a locket like that; and none of her admirers, with whom he was acquainted, was in the position of an accepted lover, as the giver of that locket must be. Adam was lost in the utter impossibility of finding any person for his fears to alight on: he could only feel with a terrible pang that there was something in Hetty's life unknown to him; that while he had been rocking himself in the hope that she would come to love him, she was already loving another. The pleasure of the dance with Hetty was gone; his eyes, when they rested on her, had an uneasy questioning expression in them; he could think of nothing to say to her; and she, too, was out of temper and disinclined to speak. They were both glad when the dance was ended.

Adam was determined to stay no longer; no one wanted him, and no one would notice if he slipped away. As soon as he got out of doors, he began to walk at his habitual rapid pace, hurrying along without knowing why, busy with the painful thought that the memory of this day, so full of honour and promise to him, was poisoned for ever. Suddenly, when he was far on through the Chase, he stopped, startled by a flash of reviving hope. After all, he might be a fool, making a great misery out of a trifle. Hetty, fond of finery as she was, might have bought the thing herself. It looked too expensive for that – it looked like the things on white satin in the great jeweller's shop at Rosseter. But Adam had very imperfect notions of the value of such things, and he thought it could certainly not cost more than a guinea. Perhaps Hetty had had as much as that in Christmas boxes,[1] and there was no knowing but she might have been childish enough to spend it in that way; she was such a young thing, and she couldn't help loving finery! But then, why had she been so frightened about it at first, and changed colour so, and afterwards pretended not to care? Oh, that was because she was ashamed of his seeing that she had such a smart thing – she was conscious that it was wrong for her to spend her money on it, and she knew that Adam disapproved of finery. It was a proof she cared about what he liked and disliked. She must have thought from his silence and gravity afterwards that he was very much displeased with her, that he was inclined to be harsh and severe towards her foibles. And as he walked on more quietly, chewing the cud of this new hope, his only uneasiness was that he had behaved in a way which might chill Hetty's feeling towards him. For this last view of the matter *must* be the true one. How could Hetty have an accepted lover, quite unknown to him? She was never away from her uncle's house for more than a day; she could have no acquaintances that did not come there, and no intimacies unknown to her uncle and aunt. It would be folly to believe that the locket was given to her by a lover. The little ring of dark hair he felt sure was her own; he could form no guess about the light hair under it, for he had not seen it very distinctly. It might be a bit of her father's or mother's, who had died when she was a child, and she would naturally put a bit of her own along with it.

And so Adam went to bed comforted, having woven for himself an ingenious web of probabilities – the surest screen a wise man can place between himself and the truth. His last waking thoughts melted into a dream that he was with Hetty again at the Hall Farm, and that he was asking her to forgive him for being so cold and silent.

And while he was dreaming this, Arthur was leading Hetty to the dance, and saying to her in low hurried tones, 'I shall be in the wood the day after to-morrow at seven; come as early as you can.' And Hetty's foolish joys and hopes, which had flown away for a little space, scared by a mere nothing, now all came fluttering back, unconscious of the real peril. She was happy for the first time this long day, and wished that dance would last for hours. Arthur wished it too; it was the last weakness he meant to indulge in; and a man never lies with more delicious languor under the influence of a passion, than when he has persuaded himself that he shall subdue it tomorrow.

But Mrs Poyser's wishes were quite the reverse of this, for her mind was filled with dreary forebodings as to the retardation of to-morrow morning's cheese in consequence of these late hours. Now that Hetty had done her duty and danced one dance with the young Squire, Mr Poyser must go out and see if the cart was come back to fetch them, for it was half-past ten o'clock, and notwithstanding a mild suggestion on his part that it would be bad manners for them to be the first to go, Mrs Poyser was resolute on the point, 'manners or no manners'.

'What! going already, Mrs Poyser?' said old Mr Donnithorne, as she came to curtsy and take leave; 'I thought we should not part with any of our guests till eleven: Mrs Irwine and I, who are elderly people, think of sitting out the dance till then.'

'Oh, your honour, it's all right and proper for gentlefolks to stay up by candle-light – they've got no cheese on their minds. We're late enough as it is, an' there's no lettin' the cows know as they mustn't want to be milked so early to-morrow mornin'. So, if you'll please t' excuse us, we'll take our leave.'

'Eh!' she said to her husband, as they set off in the cart, 'I'd sooner ha' brewin' day and washin' day together than one o' these pleasurin' days. There's no work so tirin' as danglin' about an' starin' an' not rightly knowin' what you're goin' to do next; and keepin' your face i' smilin' order like a grocer o' market-day for fear people shouldna think you civil enough. An' you've nothing to show for't when it's done, if it isn't a yallow face wi' eatin' things as disagree.'

'Nay, nay,' said Mr Poyser, who was in his merriest mood, and felt that he had had a great day, 'a bit o' pleasuring's good for thee sometimes. An' thee danc'st as well as any of 'em, for I'll back thee against all the wives i' the parish for a light foot an' ankle. An' it was a great honour for the young Squire to ask thee first – I reckon it was because I sat at th' head o' the table an' made the speech. An' Hetty too – *she* never had such a partner before – a fine young gentleman in reg'mentals. It'll serve you to talk on, Hetty, when you're an old woman – how you danced wi' th' young Squire the day he come o' age.'

BOOK FOURTH

CHAPTER XXVII

A Crisis

It was beyond the middle of August – nearly three weeks after the birthday feast. The reaping of the wheat had begun in our north midland county of Loamshire, but the harvest was likely still to be retarded by the heavy rains, which were causing inundations and much damage throughout the country. From this last trouble the Broxton and Hayslope farmers, on their pleasant uplands, and in their brook-watered valleys, had not suffered, and as I cannot pretend that they were such exceptional farmers as to love the general good better than their own, you will infer that they were not in very low spirits about the rapid rise in the price of bread, so long as there was hope of gathering in their own corn undamaged; and occasional days of sunshine and drying winds flattered this hope.

The eighteenth of August was one of these days, when the sunshine looked brighter in all eyes for the gloom that went before. Grand masses of cloud were hurried across the blue, and the great round hills behind the Chase seemed alive with their flying shadows; the sun was hidden for a moment, and then shone out warm again like a recovered joy; the leaves, still green, were tossed off the hedgerow trees by the wind; around the farmhouses there was a sound of clapping doors; the apples fell in the orchards; and the stray horses on the green sides of the lanes and on the common had their manes blown about their faces. And yet the wind seemed only part of the general gladness because the sun was shining. A merry day for the children, who ran and shouted to see if they could top the wind with their voices; and the grown-up people, too, were in good spirits, inclined to believe in yet finer days, when the wind had fallen. If only the corn were not ripe enough to be blown out of the husk and scattered as untimely seed!

And yet a day on which a blighting sorrow may fall upon a man. For if it be true that Nature at certain moments seems charged with a presentiment of one individual lot, must it not also be true that she seems unmindful, unconscious of another? For there is no hour that has not its births of gladness and despair, no morning brightness that does not bring new sickness to desolation as well as new forces to genius and love. There are so many of us, and our lots are so different: what wonder that Nature's mood is often in harsh contrast with the great crisis of our lives? We are children of a large family, and must learn, as such children do, not to expect that our hurts will be made much of – to be content with little nurture and caressing, and help each other the more.

It was a busy day with Adam, who of late had done almost double work; for he was continuing to act as foreman for Jonathan Burge, until some satisfactory person could be found to supply his place, and Jonathan was slow to find that person. But he had done the extra work cheerfully, for his hopes were buoyant again about Hetty. Every time she had seen him since the birthday, she had seemed to make an effort to behave all the more kindly to him, that she might make him understand she had forgiven his silence and coldness during the dance. He had never mentioned the locket to her again; too happy that she smiled at him – still happier because he observed in her a more subdued air, something that he interpreted as the growth of womanly tenderness and seriousness. 'Ah!' he thought, again and again, 'she's only seventeen; she'll be thoughtful enough after a while. And her aunt allays says how clever she is at the work. She'll make a wife as mother'll have no occasion to grumble at, after all.' To be sure, he had only seen her at home twice since the birthday; for one Sunday, when he was intending to go from church to the Hall Farm, Hetty had joined the party of upper servants from the Chase, and had gone home with them – almost as if she were inclined to encourage Mr Craig. 'She's takin' too much likin' to them folks i' the housekeeper's room,' Mrs Poyser remarked. 'For my part, I was never over-fond o' gentlefolks's servants – they're mostly like the fine ladies' fat dogs, nayther good for barking nor butcher's meat, but on'y for show.' And another evening she was gone to Treddleston to buy some things; though, to his great surprise, as he was returning home, he saw her at a distance getting over a stile quite out of the Treddleston road. But when he hastened to her, she was very kind, and asked him to go in again when he had taken her to the yard gate. She had gone a little farther into the fields after coming from Treddleston, because she didn't want to go in, she said: it was so nice to be out of doors, and her aunt always made such a fuss about it if she wanted to go out. 'Oh, do come in with me!' she said, as he was going to shake hands with her at the gate, and he could not resist that. So he went in, and Mrs Poyser was contented with only a slight remark on Hetty's being later than was expected; while Hetty, who had looked out of spirits when he met her, smiled and talked, and waited on them all with unusual promptitude.

That was the last time he had seen her; but he meant to make leisure for going to the Farm to-morrow. To-day, he knew, was her day for going to the Chase to sew with the lady's-maid, so he would get as much work done as possible this evening, that the next might be clear.

One piece of work that Adam was superintending was some slight repairs at the Chase Farm, which had been hitherto occupied by Satchell, as bailiff, but which it was now rumoured that the old Squire was going to let to a smart man in top-boots, who had been seen to ride over it one day. Nothing but the desire to get a tenant could account for the Squire's undertaking repairs, though the Saturday-evening party at Mr Casson's agreed over their pipes that no man in his senses would take the Chase Farm unless there was a bit more plough-land laid to it. However that might be, the repairs were ordered to be executed with all despatch; and Adam, acting for Mr Burge, was carrying out the order with his usual energy. But to-day, having been occupied elsewhere, he had not been able to arrive at the Chase Farm till late in the afternoon; and he then discovered that some old roofing, which he had calculated on preserving, had given way. There was clearly no good to be done with this part of the building without pulling it all down; and Adam immediately saw in his mind a plan for building it up again, so as to make the most convenient of cow-sheds and calf-pens, with a hovel for implements; and all without any great expense for materials. So, when the workmen were gone, he sat down, took out his pocket-book, and busied himself with sketching a plan, and making a specification of the expenses, that he might show it to Burge the next morning, and set him on persuading the Squire to consent. To 'make a good job' of anything, however small, was always a pleasure to Adam; and he sat on a block, with his book resting on a planing-table, whistling low every now and then, and turning his head on one side with a just perceptible smile of gratification – of pride, too, for if Adam loved a bit of good work, he loved also to think, 'I did it!' And I believe the only people who are free from that weakness are those who have no work to call their own. It was nearly seven before he had finished and put on his jacket again; and on giving a last look round, he observed that Seth, who had been working here to-day, had left his basket of tools behind him. 'Why, th' lad's forgot his tools,' thought Adam, 'and he's got to work up at the shop to-morrow. There never was such a chap for wool-gathering; he'd leave his head behind him, if it was loose. However, it's lucky I've seen 'em; I'll carry 'em home.'

The buildings of the Chase Farm lay at one extremity of the Chase, at about ten minutes' walking distance from the Abbey. Adam had come thither on his pony, intending to ride to the stables, and put up his nag on his way home. At the stables he encountered Mr Craig, who had come to look at the Captain's new horse, on which he was to ride away the day after tomorrow; and Mr Craig detained him to tell how all the servants were to collect at the gate of the courtyard to wish the young Squire luck as he rode out; so that, by the time Adam had got into the Chase, and was striding along with the basket of tools over his shoulder, the sun was on the point of setting, and was sending level crimson rays among the great trunks of the old oaks, and touching every bare patch of ground with a transient glory, that made it look like a jewel dropt upon the grass. The wind had fallen now, and there was only enough breeze to stir the delicate-stemmed leaves. Any one who had been sitting in the house all day would have been glad to walk now; but Adam had been quite enough in the open air to wish to shorten his way home; and he bethought himself that he might do so by striking across the Chase and going through the Grove, where he had never been for years. He hurried on across the Chase, stalking along the narrow paths between the fern, with Gyp at his heels, not lingering to watch the magnificent changes of the light – hardly once thinking of it – yet feeling its presence in a certain calm happy awe which mingled itself with his busy working-day thoughts. How could he help feeling it? The very deer felt it, and were more timid.

Presently Adam's thoughts recurred to what Mr Craig had said about Arthur Donnithorne, and pictured his going away, and the changes that might take place before he came back: then they travelled back affectionately over the old scenes of boyish companionship, and dwelt on Arthur's good qualities, which Adam had a pride in, as we all have in the virtues of the superior who honours us. A nature like Adam's, with a great need of love and reverence in it, depends for so much of its happiness on what it can believe and feel about others! And he had no ideal world of dead heroes; he knew little of the life of men in the past; he must find the beings to whom he could cling with loving admiration among those who came within speech of him. These pleasant thoughts about Arthur brought a milder expression than usual into his keen rough face: perhaps they were the reason why, when he opened the old green gate leading into the Grove, he paused to pat Gyp, and say a kind word to him.

After that pause, he strode on again along the broad winding path through the Grove. What grand beeches! Adam delighted in a fine tree of all things; as the fisherman's sight is keenest on the sea, so Adam's perceptions were more at home with trees than with other objects. He kept them in his memory, as a painter does, with all the flecks and knots in their bark, all the curves and angles of their boughs; and had often calculated the height and contents of a trunk to a nicety, as he stood looking at it. No wonder that, notwithstanding his desire to get on, he could not help pausing to look at a curious large beech which he had seen standing before him at a turning in the road, and convince himself that it was not two trees wedded together, but only one. For the rest of his life he remembered that moment when he was calmly examining the beech, as a man remembers his last glimpse of the home where his youth was passed, before the road turned, and he saw it no more. The beech stood at the last turning before the Grove ended in an archway of boughs that let in the eastern light; and as Adam stepped away from the tree to continue his walk, his eyes fell on two figures about twenty yards before him.

He remained as motionless as a statue, and turned almost as pale. The two figures were standing opposite to each other, with clasped hands, about to part; and while they were bending to kiss, Gyp, who had been running among the brushwood, came out, caught sight of them, and gave a sharp bark. They separated with a start – one hurried through the gate out of the Grove, and the other, turning round, walked slowly, with a sort of saunter, towards Adam, who still stood transfixed and pale, clutching tighter the stick with which he held the basket of tools over his shoulder, and looking at the approaching figure with eyes in which amazement was fast turning to fierceness.

Arthur Donnithorne looked flushed and excited; he had tried to make unpleasant feelings more bearable by drinking a little more wine than usual at dinner to-day, and was still enough under its flattering influence to think more lightly of this unwished-for rencontre with Adam than he would otherwise have done. After all, Adam was the best person who could have happened to see him and Hetty together: he was a sensible fellow, and would not babble about it to other people. Arthur felt confident that he could laugh the thing off, and explain it away. And so he sauntered forward with elaborate carelessness – his flushed face, his evening dress of fine cloth and fine linen, his hands half thrust into his waistcoat-pockets, all shone upon by the strange evening light which the light clouds had caught up even to the zenith, and were now shedding down between the topmost branches above him.

Adam was still motionless, looking at him as he came up. He understood it all now – the locket, and everything else that had been doubtful to him: a terrible scorching light showed him the hidden letters that changed the meaning of the past. If he had moved a muscle, he must inevitably have sprung upon Arthur like a tiger; and in the conflicting emotions that filled those long moments, he had told himself that he would not give loose to passion, he would only speak the right thing. He stood as if petrified by an unseen force, but the force was his own strong will.

'Well, Adam,' said Arthur, 'you've been looking at the fine old beeches, eh? They're not to be come near by the hatchet, though; this is a sacred grove. I overtook pretty little Hetty Sorrel as I was coming to my den – the Hermitage, there. She ought not to come home this way so late. So I took care of her to the gate, and asked for a kiss for my pains. But I must get back now, for this road is confoundedly damp. Good-night, Adam: I shall see you to-morrow – to say good-bye, you know.'

Arthur was too much preoccupied with the part he was playing himself to be thoroughly aware of the expression in Adam's face. He did not look directly at Adam, but glanced carelessly round at the trees, and then lifted up one foot to look at the sole of his boot. He cared to say no more; he had thrown quite dust enough into honest Adam's eyes; and as he spoke the last words, he walked on.

'Stop a bit, sir,' said Adam, in a hard peremptory voice, without turning round. 'I've got a word to say to you.'

Arthur paused in surprise. Susceptible persons are more affected by a change of tone than by unexpected words, and Arthur had the susceptibility of a nature at once affectionate and vain. He was still more surprised when he saw that Adam had not moved, but stood with his back to him, as if summoning him to return. What did he mean? He was going to make a serious business of this affair. Arthur felt his temper rising. A patronizing disposition always has its meaner side, and in the confusion of his irritation and alarm there entered the feeling that a man to whom he had shown so much favour as to Adam, was not in a position to criticize his conduct. And yet he was dominated, as one who feels himself in the wrong always is, by the man whose good opinion he cares for. In spite of pride and temper, there was as much deprecation as anger in his voice when he said –

'What do you mean, Adam?'

'I mean, sir,' answered Adam, in the same harsh voice, still without turning round, – 'I mean, sir, that you don't deceive me by your light words. This is not the first time you've met Hetty Sorrel in this grove, and this is not the first time you've kissed her.'

Arthur felt a startled uncertainty how far Adam was speaking from knowledge, and how far from mere inference. And this uncertainty, which prevented him from contriving a prudent answer, heightened his irritation. He said in a high sharp tone –

'Well, sir, what then?'

'Why, then, instead of acting like th' upright, honourable man we've all believed you to be, you've been acting the part of a selfish light-minded scoundrel. You know, as well as I do, what it's to lead to, when a gentleman like you kisses and makes love to a young woman like Hetty, and gives her presents as she's frightened for other folks to see. And I say it again, you're acting the part of a selfish, light-minded scoundrel, though it cuts me to th' heart to say so, and I'd rather ha' lost my right hand.'

'Let me tell you, Adam,' said Arthur, bridling his growing anger, and trying to recur to his careless tone, 'you're not only devilishly impertinent, but you're talking nonsense. Every pretty girl is not such a fool as you, to suppose that when a gentleman admires her beauty, and pays her a little attention, he must mean something particular. Every man likes to flirt with a pretty girl, and every pretty girl likes to be flirted with. The wider the distance between them the less harm there is, for then she's not likely to deceive herself.'

'I don't know what you mean by flirting,' said Adam, 'but if you mean behaving to a woman as if you loved her, and yet not loving her all the while, I say that's not the action of an honest man, and what isn't honest does come t' harm. I'm not a fool, and you're not a fool, and you know better than what you're saying. You know it couldn't be made public as you've

behaved to Hetty as y' have done without her losing her character, and bringing shame and trouble on her and her relations.
What if you meant nothing by your kissing and your presents?
Other folks won't believe as you've meant nothing; and don't
tell me about her not deceiving herself. I tell you as you've filled
her mind so with the thought of you as it'll mayhap poison her
life; and she'll never love another man as 'ud make her a good
husband.'

Arthur had felt a sudden relief while Adam was speaking; he
perceived that Adam had no positive knowledge of the past,
and that there was no irrevocable damage done by this evening's
unfortunate rencontre. Adam could still be deceived. The candid Arthur had brought himself into a position in which successful lying was his only hope. The hope allayed his anger a little.

'Well, Adam,' he said, in a tone of friendly concession, 'you're
perhaps right. Perhaps I've gone a little too far in taking notice
of the pretty little thing, and stealing a kiss now and then.
You're such a grave, steady fellow, you don't understand the
temptation to such trifling. I'm sure I wouldn't bring any trouble
or annoyance on her and the good Poysers on any account if I
could help it. But I think you look a little too seriously at it.
You know I'm going away immediately, so I shan't make any
more mistakes of the kind. But let us say good-night,' – Arthur
here turned round to walk on, – 'and talk no more about the
matter. The whole thing will soon be forgotten.'

'No, by God!' Adam burst out with rage that could be con-
trolled no longer, throwing down the basket of tools, and
striding forward till he was right in front of Arthur. All his
jealousy and sense of personal injury, which he had been
hitherto trying to keep under, had leaped up and mastered him.
What man of us, in the first moments of a sharp agony, could
ever feel that the fellow-man who has been the medium of
inflicting it, did not mean to hurt us? In our instinctive rebellion
against pain, we are children again, and demand an active will
to wreak our vengeance on. Adam at this moment could only
feel that he had been robbed of Hetty – robbed treacherously
by the man in whom he had trusted; and he stood close in front
of Arthur, with fierce eyes glaring at him, with pale lips and

clenched hands, the hard tones in which he had hitherto been constraining himself to express no more than a just indignation, giving way to a deep agitated voice that seemed to shake him as he spoke.

'No, it'll not be soon forgot, as you've come in between her and me, when she might ha' loved me – it'll not soon be forgot as you've robbed me o' my happiness, while I thought you was my best friend, and a noble-minded man, as I was proud to work for. And you've been kissing her, and meaning nothing, have you? And I never kissed her i' my life – but I'd ha' worked hard for years for the right to kiss her. And you make light of it. You think little o' doing what may damage other folks, so as you get your bit o' trifling, as means nothing. I throw back your favours, for you're not the man I took you for. I'll never count you my friend any more. I'd rather you'd act as my enemy, and fight me where I stand – it's all th' amends you can make me.'

Poor Adam, possessed by rage that could find no other vent, began to throw off his coat and his cap, too blind with passion to notice the change that had taken place in Arthur while he was speaking. Arthur's lips were now as pale as Adam's; his heart was beating violently. The discovery that Adam loved Hetty was a shock which made him for the moment see himself in the light of Adam's indignation, and regard Adam's suffering as not merely a consequence, but an element of his error. The words of hatred and contempt – the first he had ever heard in his life – seemed like scorching missiles that were making ineffaceable scars on him. All screening self-excuse, which rarely falls quite away while others respect us, forsook him for an instant, and he stood face to face with the first great irrevocable evil he had ever committed. He was only twenty-one – and three months ago – nay, much later – he had thought proudly that no man should ever be able to reproach him justly. His first impulse, if there had been time for it, would perhaps have been to utter words of propitiation; but Adam had no sooner thrown off his coat and cap, than he became aware that Arthur was standing pale and motionless, with his hands still thrust in his waistcoat-pockets.

'What!' he said, 'won't you fight me like a man? You know I won't strike you while you stand so.'

'Go away, Adam,' said Arthur, 'I don't want to fight you.'

'No,' said Adam, bitterly; 'you don't want to fight me, – you think I'm a common man, as you can injure without answering for it.'

'I never meant to injure you,' said Arthur, with returning anger. 'I didn't know you loved her.'

'But you've made her love *you*,' said Adam. 'You're a double-faced man – I'll never believe a word you say again.'

'Go away, I tell you,' said Arthur, angrily, 'or we shall both repent.'

'No,' said Adam, with a convulsed voice, 'I swear I won't go away without fighting you. Do you want provoking any more? I tell you you're a coward and a scoundrel, and I despise you.'

The colour had all rushed back to Arthur's face: in a moment his right hand was clenched, and dealt a blow like lightning, which sent Adam staggering backward. His blood was as thoroughly up as Adam's now, and the two men, forgetting the emotions that had gone before, fought with the instinctive fierceness of panthers in the deepening twilight darkened by the trees. The delicate-handed gentleman was a match for the workman in everything but strength, and Arthur's skill enabled him to protract the struggle for some long moments. But between unarmed men the battle is to the strong, where the strong is no blunderer, and Arthur must sink under a well-planted blow of Adam's, as a steel rod is broken by an iron bar. The blow soon came, and Arthur fell, his head lying concealed in a tuft of fern, so that Adam could only discern his darkly-clad body.

He stood still in the dim light waiting for Arthur to rise.

The blow had been given now, towards which he had been straining all the force of nerve and muscle – and what was the good of it? What had he done by fighting? Only satisfied his own passion, only wreaked his own vengeance. He had not rescued Hetty, nor changed the past – there it was just as it had been, and he sickened at the vanity of his own rage.

But why did not Arthur rise? He was perfectly motionless,

and the time seemed long to Adam. . . . Good God! had the blow been too much for him? Adam shuddered at the thought of his own strength, as with the oncoming of this dread he knelt down by Arthur's side and lifted his head from among the fern. There was no sign of life: the eyes and teeth were set. The horror that rushed over Adam completely mastered him, and forced upon him its own belief. He could feel nothing but that death was in Arthur's face, and that he was helpless before it. He made not a single movement, but knelt like an image of despair gazing at an image of death.

CHAPTER XXVIII

A Dilemma

It was only a few minutes measured by the clock – though Adam always thought it had been a long while – before he perceived a gleam of consciousness in Arthur's face and a slight shiver through his frame. The intense joy that flooded his soul brought back some of the old affection with it.

'Do you feel any pain, sir?' he said, tenderly, loosening Arthur's cravat.

Arthur turned his eyes on Adam with a vague stare which gave way to a slightly startled motion as if from the shock of returning memory. But he only shivered again and said nothing.

'Do you feel any hurt, sir?' Adam said again, with a trembling in his voice.

Arthur put his hand up to his waistcoat buttons, and when Adam had unbuttoned it, he took a longer breath. 'Lay my head down,' he said, faintly, 'and get me some water if you can.'

Adam laid the head down gently on the fern again, and emptying the tools out of the flag-basket, hurried through the trees to the edge of the Grove bordering on the Chase, where a brook ran below the bank.

When he returned with his basket leaking, but still half full, Arthur looked at him with a more thoroughly reawakened consciousness.

'Can you drink a drop out o' your hand, sir?' said Adam, kneeling down again to lift up Arthur's head.

'No,' said Arthur, 'dip my cravat in and souse it on my head.'

The water seemed to do him some good, for he presently raised himself a little higher, resting on Adam's arm.

'Do you feel any hurt inside, sir?' Adam asked again.

'No – no hurt,' said Arthur, still faintly, 'but rather done up.'
After a while he said, 'I suppose I fainted away when you
knocked me down.'

'Yes, sir, thank God,' said Adam. 'I thought it was worse.'

'What! you thought you'd done for me, eh? come, help me
on my legs.'

'I feel terribly shaky and dizzy,' Arthur said, as he stood
leaning on Adam's arm; 'that blow of yours must have come
against me like a battering-ram. I don't believe I can walk
alone.'

'Lean on me, sir; I'll get you along,' said Adam. 'Or, will you
sit down a bit longer, on my coat here? and I'll prop y' up.
You'll perhaps be better in a minute or two.'

'No,' said Arthur. 'I'll go to the Hermitage – I think I've got
some brandy there. There's a short road to it a little further on,
near the gate. If you'll just help me on.'

They walked slowly, with frequent pauses, but without
speaking again. In both of them, the concentration in the present which had attended the first moments of Arthur's revival,
had now given way to a vivid recollection of the previous scene.
It was nearly dark in the narrow path among the trees, but
within the circle of fir-trees round the Hermitage there was
room for the growing moonlight to enter in at the windows.
Their steps were noiseless on the thick carpet of fir-needles, and
the outward stillness seemed to heighten their inward consciousness, as Arthur took the key out of his pocket and placed it in
Adam's hand, for him to open the door. Adam had not known
before that Arthur had furnished the old Hermitage and made
it a retreat for himself, and it was a surprise to him when he
opened the door to see a snug room with all the signs of frequent
habitation.

Arthur loosed Adam's arm and threw himself on the ottoman. 'You'll see my hunting-bottle somewhere,' he said. 'A
leather case with a bottle and glass in.'

Adam was not long in finding the case. 'There's very little
brandy in it, sir,' he said, turning it downwards over the glass,
as he held it before the window, 'hardly this little glassful.'

'Well, give me that,' said Arthur, with the peevishness of physical depression. When he had taken some sips, Adam said, 'Hadn't I better run to th' house, sir, and get some more brandy? I can be there and back pretty soon. It'll be a stiff walk home for you, if you don't have something to revive you.'

'Yes – go. But don't say I'm ill. Ask for my man Pym, and tell him to get it from Mills, and not to say I'm at the Hermitage. Get some water too.'

Adam was relieved to have an active task – both of them were relieved to be apart from each other for a short time. But Adam's swift pace could not still the eager pain of thinking – of living again with concentrated suffering through the last wretched hour, and looking out from it over all the new, sad future.

Arthur lay still for some minutes after Adam was gone, but presently he rose feebly from the ottoman and peered about slowly in the broken moonlight, seeking something. It was a short bit of wax candle that stood amongst a confusion of writing and drawing materials. There was more searching for the means of lighting the candle, and when that was done, he went cautiously round the room as if wishing to assure himself of the presence or absence of something. At last he had found a slight thing, which he put first in his pocket, and then, on a second thought, took out again, and thrust deep down into a waste-paper basket. It was a woman's little pink silk neckerchief. He set the candle on the table, and threw himself down on the ottoman again, exhausted with the effort.

When Adam came back with his supplies, his entrance awoke Arthur from a doze.

'That's right,' Arthur said; 'I'm tremendously in want of some brandy-vigour.'

'I'm glad to see you've got a light, sir,' said Adam. 'I've been thinking I'd better have asked for a lanthorn.'

'No, no; the candle will last long enough – I shall soon be up to walking home now.'

'I can't go before I've seen you safe home, sir,' said Adam, hesitatingly.

'No: it will be better for you to stay – sit down.'

Adam sat down, and they remained opposite to each other in uneasy silence, while Arthur slowly drank brandy-and-water, with visibly renovating effect. He began to lie in a more voluntary position, and looked as if he were less overpowered by bodily sensations. Adam was keenly alive to these indications, and as his anxiety about Arthur's condition began to be allayed, he felt more of that impatience which every one knows who has had his just indignation suspended by the physical state of the culprit. Yet there was one thing on his mind to be done before he could recur to remonstrance: it was to confess what had been unjust in his own words. Perhaps he longed all the more to make this confession, that his indignation might be free again; and as he saw the signs of returning ease in Arthur, the words again and again came to his lips and went back, checked by the thought that it would be better to leave everything till to-morrow. As long as they were silent they did not look at each other, and a foreboding came across Adam that if they began to speak as though they remembered the past – if they looked at each with full recognition – they must take fire again. So they sat in silence till the bit of wax candle flickered low in the socket; the silence all the while becoming more irksome to Adam. Arthur had just poured out some more brandy-and-water, and he threw one arm behind his head and drew up one leg in an attitude of recovered ease, which was an irresistible temptation to Adam to speak what was on his mind.

'You begin to feel more yourself again, sir,' he said, as the candle went out, and they were half-hidden from each other in the faint moonlight.

'Yes: I don't feel good for much – very lazy, and not inclined to move; but I'll go home when I've taken this dose.'

There was a slight pause before Adam said –

'My temper got the better of me, and I said things as wasn't true. I'd no right to speak as if you'd known you was doing me an injury: you'd no grounds for knowing it; I've always kept what I felt for her as secret as I could.'

He paused again before he went on.

'And perhaps I judged you too harsh – I'm apt to be harsh; and you may have acted out o' thoughtlessness more than I should ha' believed was possible for a man with a heart and a conscience. We're not all put together alike, and we may misjudge one another. God knows, it's all the joy I could have now, to think the best of you.'

Arthur wanted to go home without saying any more – he was too painfully embarrassed in mind, as well as too weak in body, to wish for any further explanation to-night. And yet it was a relief to him that Adam reopened the subject in a way the least difficult for him to answer. Arthur was in the wretched position of an open, generous man, who has committed an error which makes deception seem a necessity. The native impulse to give truth in return for truth, to meet trust with frank confession, must be suppressed, and duty was become a question of tactics. His deed was reacting upon him – was already governing him tyrannously, and forcing him into a course that jarred with his habitual feelings. The only aim that seemed admissible to him now was to deceive Adam to the utmost: to make Adam think better of him than he deserved. And when he heard the words of honest retraction – when he heard the sad appeal with which Adam ended – he was obliged to rejoice in the remains of ignorant confidence it implied. He did not answer immediately, for he had to be judicious, and not truthful.

'Say no more about our anger, Adam,' he said, at last, very languidly, for the labour of speech was unwelcome to him; 'I forgive your momentary injustice – it was quite natural, with the exaggerated notions you had in your mind. We shall be none the worse friends in future, I hope, because we've fought: you had the best of it, and that was as it should be, for I believe I've been most in the wrong of the two. Come, let us shake hands.'

Arthur held out his hand, but Adam sat still.

'I don't like to say "No" to that, sir,' he said, 'but I can't shake hands till it's clear what we mean by't. I was wrong when I spoke as if you'd done me an injury knowingly, but I wasn't wrong in what I said before, about your behaviour t' Hetty, and I can't shake hands with you as if I held you my friend the same as ever, till you've cleared that up better.'

Arthur swallowed his pride and resentment as he drew back

his hand. He was silent for some moments, and then said, as indifferently as he could –

'I don't know what you mean by clearing up, Adam. I've told you already that you think too seriously of a little flirtation. But if you are right in supposing there is any danger in it – I'm going away on Saturday, and there will be an end of it. As for the pain it has given you, I'm heartily sorry for it. I can say no more.'

Adam said nothing, but rose from his chair, and stood with his face towards one of the windows, as if looking at the blackness of the moonlit fir-trees; but he was in reality conscious of nothing but the conflict within him. It was of no use now – his resolution not to speak till to-morrow: he must speak there and then. But it was several minutes before he turned round and stepped nearer to Arthur, standing and looking down on him as he lay.

'It'll be better for me to speak plain,' he said, with evident effort, 'though it's hard work. You see, sir, this isn't a trifle to me, whatever it may be to you. I'm none o' them men as can go making love first to one woman and then t' another, and don't think it much odds which of 'em I take. What I feel for Hetty's a different sort o' love, such as I believe nobody can know much about but them as feel it, and God as has given it to 'em. She's more nor everything else to me, all but my conscience and my good name. And if it's true what you've been saying all along – and if it's only been trifling and flirting as you call it, as'll be put an end to by your going away – why, then, I'd wait, and hope her heart 'ud turn to me after all. I'm loath to think you'd speak false to me, and I'll believe your word, however things may look.'

'You would be wronging Hetty more than me not to believe it,' said Arthur, almost violently, starting up from the ottoman, and moving away. But he threw himself into a chair again directly, saying, more feebly, 'You seem to forget that, in suspecting me, you are casting imputations upon her.'

'Nay, sir,' Adam said, in a calmer voice, as if he were half relieved – for he was too straightforward to make a distinction between a direct falsehood and an indirect one – 'Nay, sir, things don't lie level between Hetty and you. You're acting with your eyes open, whatever you may do; but how do you know what's been in her mind? She's all but a child – as any man with a conscience in him ought to feel bound to take care on. And whatever you may think, I know you've disturbed her mind. I know she's been fixing her heart on you; for there's a many things clear to me now as I didn't understand before. But you seem to make light o' what *she* may feel – you don't think o' that.'

'Good God, Adam, let me alone!' Arthur burst out impetuously; 'I feel it enough without your worrying me.'

He was aware of his indiscretion as soon as the words had escaped him.

'Well, then, if you feel it,' Adam rejoined eagerly; 'if you feel as you may ha' put false notions into her mind, and made her believe as you loved her, when all the while you meant nothing, I've this demand to make of you; – I'm not speaking for myself, but for her. I ask you t' undeceive her before you go away. Y'aren't going away for ever; and if you leave her behind with a notion in her head o' your feeling about her the same as she feels about you, she'll be hankering after you, and the mischief may get worse. It may be a smart to her now, but it'll save her pain i' th' end. I ask you to write a letter – you may trust to my seeing as she gets it: tell her the truth, and take blame to yourself for behaving as you'd no right to do to a young woman as isn't your equal. I speak plain, sir. But I can't speak any other way. There's nobody can take care o' Hetty in this thing but me.'

'I can do what I think needful in the matter,' said Arthur, more and more irritated by mingled distress and perplexity, 'without giving promises to you. I shall take what measures I think proper.'

'No,' said Adam, in an abrupt decided tone, 'that won't do. I must know what ground I'm treading on. I must be safe as you've put an end to what ought never to ha' been begun. I don't forget what's owing to you as a gentleman; but in this thing we're man and man, and I can't give up.'

There was no answer for some moments. Then Arthur said, 'I'll see you to-morrow. I can bear no more now; I'm ill.'

He rose as he spoke, and reached his cap, as if intending to go.

'You won't see her again!' Adam exclaimed, with a flash of recurring anger and suspicion, moving towards the door and placing his back against it. 'Either tell me she can never be my wife – tell me you've been lying – or else promise me what I've said.'

Adam, uttering this alternative, stood like a terrible fate before Arthur, who had moved forward a step or two, and now stopped, faint, shaken, sick in mind and body. It seemed long to both of them – that inward struggle of Arthur's – before he said, feebly, 'I promise; let me go.'

Adam moved away from the door and opened it, but when Arthur reached the step, he stopped again and leaned against the door-post.

'You're not well enough to walk alone, sir,' said Adam. 'Take my arm again.'

Arthur made no answer, and presently walked on, Adam following. But, after a few steps, he stood still again, and said coldly, 'I believe I must trouble you. It's getting late now, and there may be an alarm set up about me at home.'

Adam gave his arm, and they walked on without uttering a word, till they came where the basket and the tools lay.

'I must pick up the tools, sir,' Adam said. 'They're my brother's. I doubt they'll be rusted. If you'll please to wait a minute.'

Arthur stood still without speaking, and no other word passed between them till they were at the side entrance, where he hoped to get in without being seen by any one. He said then, 'Thank you; I needn't trouble you any further.'

'What time will it be conven'ent for me to see you to-morrow, sir?' said Adam.

'You may send me word that you're here at five o'clock,' said Arthur; 'not before.'

'Good-night, sir,' said Adam. But he heard no reply; Arthur had turned into the house.

CHAPTER XXIX

The Next Morning

Arthur did not pass a sleepless night; he slept long and well. For sleep comes to the perplexed – if the perplexed are only weary enough. But at seven he rang his bell and astonished Pym by declaring he was going to get up, and must have breakfast brought to him at eight.

'And see that my mare is saddled at half-past eight, and tell my grandfather when he's down that I'm better this morning, and am gone for a ride.'

He had been awake an hour, and could rest in bed no longer. In bed our yesterdays are too oppressive: if a man can only get up, though it be but to whistle or to smoke, he has a present which offers some resistance to the past – sensations which assert themselves against tyrannous memories. And if there were such a thing as taking averages of feeling, it would certainly be found that in the hunting and shooting seasons regret, self-reproach, and mortified pride, weigh lighter on country gentlemen than in late spring and summer. Arthur felt that he should be more of a man on horseback. Even the presence of Pym, waiting on him with the usual deference, was a reassurance to him after the scenes of yesterday. For, with Arthur's sensitiveness to opinion, the loss of Adam's respect was a shock to his self-contentment which suffused his imagination with the sense that he had sunk in all eyes; as a sudden shock of fear from some real peril makes a nervous woman afraid even to step, because all her perceptions are suffused with a sense of danger.

Arthur's, as you know, was a loving nature. Deeds of kindness were as easy to him as a bad habit; they were the common issue of his weaknesses and good qualities, of his egoism and his sympathy. He didn't like to witness pain, and he liked to have grateful eyes beaming on him as the giver of pleasure. When he was a lad of seven, he one day kicked down an old gardener's pitcher of broth, from no motive but a kicking impulse, not reflecting that it was the old man's dinner; but on learning that sad fact, he took his favourite pencil-case and a silver-hafted knife out of his pocket and offered them as compensation. He had been the same Arthur ever since, trying to make all offences forgotten in benefits. If there were any bitterness in his nature, it could only show itself against the man who refused to be conciliated by him. And perhaps the time was come for some of that bitterness to rise. At the first moment, Arthur had felt pure distress and self-reproach at discovering that Adam's happiness was involved in his relation to Hetty: if there had been a possibility of making Adam tenfold amends – if deeds of gift, or any other deeds, could have restored Adam's contentment and regard for him as a benefactor, Arthur would not only have executed them without hesitation, but would have felt bound all the more closely to Adam, and would never have been weary of making retribution. But Adam could receive no amends; his suffering could not be cancelled; his respect and affection could not be recovered by any prompt deeds of atonement. He stood like an immovable obstacle against which no pressure could avail; an embodiment of what Arthur most shrank from believing in – the irrevocableness of his own wrong-doing. The words of scorn, the refusal to shake hands, the mastery asserted over him in their last conversation in the Hermitage – above all, the sense of having been knocked down, to which a man does not very well reconcile himself, even under the most heroic circumstances – pressed on him with a galling pain which was stronger than compunction. Arthur would so gladly have persuaded himself that he had done no harm! And if no one had told him the contrary, he could have persuaded himself so much better. Nemesis can seldom forge a sword for herself out of our consciences – out of the suffering we feel in the suffering we may have caused: there is rarely metal enough there to make an effective weapon.

Our moral sense learns the manners of good society, and smiles when others smile; but when some rude person gives rough names to our actions, she is apt to take part against us. And so it was with Arthur: Adam's judgement of him, Adam's grating words, disturbed his self-soothing arguments.

Not that Arthur had been at ease before Adam's discovery. Struggles and resolves had transformed themselves into compunction and anxiety. He was distressed for Hetty's sake, and distressed for his own, that he must leave her behind. He had always, both in making and breaking resolutions, looked beyond his passion, and seen that it must speedily end in separation; but his nature was too ardent and tender for him not to suffer at this parting; and on Hetty's account he was filled with uneasiness. He had found out the dream in which she was living – that she was to be a lady in silks and satins; and when he had first talked to her about his going away, she had asked him tremblingly to let her go with him and be married. It was his painful knowledge of this which had given the most exasperating sting to Adam's reproaches. He had said no word with the purpose of deceiving her, her vision was all spun by her own childish fancy; but he was obliged to confess to himself that it was spun half out of his own actions. And to increase the mischief, on this last evening he had not dared to hint the truth to Hetty: he had been obliged to soothe her with tender, hopeful words, lest he should throw her into violent distress. He felt the situation acutely; felt the sorrow of the dear thing in the present, and thought with a darker anxiety of the tenacity which her feelings might have in the future. That was the one sharp point which pressed against him; every other he could evade by hopeful self-persuasion. The whole thing had been secret; the Poysers had not the shadow of a suspicion. No one, except Adam, knew anything of what had passed – no one else was likely to know; for Arthur had impressed on Hetty that it would be fatal to betray, by word or look, that there had been the least intimacy between them; and Adam, who knew half their secret, would rather help them to keep it than betray it. It was an unfortunate business altogether, but there was no use in making it worse than it was, by imaginary exaggerations and forebodings of evil that might never come. The temporary sadness for Hetty was the worst consequence; he resolutely turned away his eyes from any bad consequence that was not demonstrably inevitable. But – but Hetty might have had the trouble in some other way if not in this. And perhaps hereafter he might be able to do a great deal for her, and make up to her for all the tears she would shed about him. She would owe the advantage of his care for her in future years to the sorrow she had incurred now. *So* good comes out of evil. Such is the beautiful arrangement of things!

Are you inclined to ask whether this can be the same Arthur who, two months ago, had that freshness of feeling, that delicate honour which shrinks from wounding even a sentiment, and does not contemplate any more positive offence as possible for it? – who thought that his own self-respect was a higher tribunal than any external opinion? The same, I assure you, only under different conditions. Our deeds determine us, as much as we determine our deeds;[1] and until we know what has been or will be the peculiar combination of outward with inward facts, which constitutes a man's critical actions, it will be better not to think ourselves wise about his character. There is a terrible coercion in our deeds which may first turn the honest man into a deceiver, and then reconcile him to the change; for this reason – that the second wrong presents itself to him in the guise of the only practicable right. The action which before commission has been seen with that blended common-sense and fresh untarnished feeling which is the healthy eye of the soul, is looked at afterwards with the lens of apologetic ingenuity, through which all things that men call beautiful and ugly are seen to be made up of textures very much alike. Europe adjusts itself to a *fait accompli*,[2] and so does an individual character, – until the placid adjustment is disturbed by a convulsive retribution.

No man can escape this vitiating effect of an offence against his own sentiment of right, and the effect was the stronger in Arthur because of that very need of self-respect which, while his conscience was still at ease, was one of his best safeguards. Self-accusation was too painful to him – he could not face it. He must persuade himself that he had not been very much to blame; he began even to pity himself for the necessity he was under of deceiving Adam: it was a course so opposed to the honesty of his own nature. But then, it was the only right thing to do.

Well, whatever had been amiss in him, he was miserable enough in consequence: miserable about Hetty: miserable about this letter that he had promised to write, and that seemed at one moment to be a gross barbarity, at another perhaps the greatest kindness he could do to her. And across all this reflection would dart every now and then a sudden impulse of passionate defiance towards all consequences; he would carry Hetty away, and all other considerations might go to . . .

In this state of mind the four walls of his room made an intolerable prison to him; they seemed to hem in and press down upon him all the crowd of contradictory thoughts and conflicting feelings, some of which would fly away in the open air. He had only an hour or two to make up his mind in, and he must get clear and calm. Once on Meg's back, in the fresh air of that fine morning, he should be more master of the situation.

The pretty creature arched her bay neck in the sunshine, and pawed the gravel, and trembled with pleasure when her master stroked her nose, and patted her, and talked to her even in a more caressing tone than usual. He loved her the better because she knew nothing of his secrets. But Meg was quite as well acquainted with her master's mental state as many others of her sex with the mental condition of the nice young gentlemen towards whom their hearts are in a state of fluttering expectation.

Arthur cantered for five miles beyond the Chase, till he was at the foot of a hill where there were no hedges or trees to hem in the road. Then he threw the bridle on Meg's neck, and prepared to make up his mind.

Hetty knew that their meeting yesterday must be the last before Arthur went away; there was no possibility of their contriving another without exciting suspicion; and she was like a frightened child, unable to think of anything, only able to cry at the mention of parting, and then put her face up to have the tears kissed away. He *could* do nothing but comfort her, and lull her into dreaming on. A letter would be a dreadfully abrupt way of awakening her! Yet there was truth in what Adam said – that it would save her from a lengthened delusion, which might be worse than a sharp immediate pain. And it was the only way of satisfying Adam, who *must* be satisfied, for more reasons than one. If he could have seen her again! But that was impossible; there was such a thorny hedge of hindrances between them, and an imprudence would be fatal. And yet, if he *could* see her again, what good would it do? Only cause him to suffer more from the sight of her distress and the remembrance of it. Away from him, she was surrounded by all the motives to self-control.

A sudden dread here fell like a shadow across his imagination – the dread lest she should do something violent in her grief; and close upon that dread came another, which deepened the shadow. But he shook them off with the force of youth and hope. What was the ground for painting the future in that dark way? It was just as likely to be the reverse. Arthur told himself, he did not deserve that things should turn out badly – he had never meant beforehand to do anything his conscience disapproved – he had been led on by circumstances. There was a sort of implicit confidence in him that he was really such a good fellow at bottom, Providence would not treat him harshly.

At all events, he couldn't help what would come now: all he could do was to take what seemed the best course at the present moment. And he persuaded himself that that course was to make the way open between Adam and Hetty. Her heart might really turn to Adam, as he said, after a while; and in that case there would have been no great harm done, since it was still Adam's ardent wish to make her his wife. To be sure, Adam was deceived – deceived in a way that Arthur would have resented as a deep wrong if it had been practised on himself. That was a reflection that marred the consoling prospect. Arthur's cheeks even burned in mingled shame and irritation at the thought. But what could a man do in such a dilemma? He was bound in honour to say no word that could injure Hetty: his first duty was to guard *her*. He would never have told or acted a lie on his own account. Good God! what a miserable fool he was to have brought himself into such a dilemma; and yet, if ever a man had excuses, he had. (Pity that consequences are determined not by excuses but by actions!)

Well, the letter must be written; it was the only means that promised a solution of the difficulty. The tears came into Arthur's eyes as he thought of Hetty reading it; but it would be almost as hard for him to write it: he was not doing anything easy to himself; and this last thought helped him to arrive at a conclusion. He could never deliberately have taken a step which inflicted pain on another and left himself at ease. Even a movement of jealousy at the thought of giving up Hetty to Adam, went to convince him that he was making a sacrifice.

When once he had come to this conclusion, he turned Meg round, and set off home again in a canter. The letter should be written the first thing, and the rest of the day would be filled up with other business: he should have no time to look behind him. Happily Irwine and Gawaine were coming to dinner, and by twelve o'clock the next day he should have left the Chase miles behind him. There was some security in this constant occupation against an uncontrollable impulse seizing him to rush to Hetty, and thrust into her hand some mad proposition that would undo everything. Faster and faster went the sensitive Meg, at every slight sign from her rider, till the canter had passed into a swift gallop.

'I thought they said th' young mester war took ill last night,' said sour old John, the groom, at dinner-time in the servants' hall. 'He's been ridin' fit to split the mare i' two this forenoon.'

'That's happen one o' the symptims, John,' said the facetious coachman.

'Then I wish he war let blood[3] for't, that's all,' said John, grimly.

Adam had been early at the Chase to know how Arthur was, and had been relieved from all anxiety about the effects of his blow by learning that he was gone out for a ride. At five o'clock he was punctually there again, and sent up word of his arrival. In a few minutes Pym came down with a letter in his hand, and gave it to Adam, saying that the Captain was too busy to see

him, and had written everything he had to say. The letter
was directed to Adam, but he went out of doors again before
opening it. It contained a sealed enclosure directed to Hetty.
On the inside of the cover Adam read: –

'In the enclosed letter I have written everything you wish. I leave
it to you to decide whether you will be doing best to deliver it to
Hetty or to return it to me. Ask yourself once more whether you
are not taking a measure which may pain her more than mere
silence.

'There is no need for our seeing each other again now. We
shall meet with better feelings some months hence.

A. D.'

'Perhaps he's i' th' right on't not to see me,' thought Adam.
'It's no use meeting to say more hard words, and it's no use
meeting to shake hands and say we're friends again. We're not
friends, an' it's better not to pretend it. I know forgiveness is a
man's duty, but, to my thinking, that can only mean as you're
to give up all thoughts o' taking revenge: it can never mean as
you're t' have your old feelings back again, for that's not possible. He's not the same man to me, and I can't *feel* the same
towards him. God help me! I don't know whether I feel the
same towards anybody: I seem as if I'd been measuring my
work from a false line, and had got it all to measure over again.'
But the question about delivering the letter to Hetty soon
absorbed Adam's thoughts. Arthur had procured some relief to
himself by throwing the decision on Adam with a warning; and
Adam, who was not given to hesitation, hesitated here. He
determined to feel his way – to ascertain as well as he could
what was Hetty's state of mind before he decided on delivering
the letter.

CHAPTER XXX

The Delivery of the Letter

The next Sunday Adam joined the Poysers on their way out of church, hoping for an invitation to go home with them. He had the letter in his pocket, and was anxious to have an opportunity of talking to Hetty alone. He could not see her face at church, for she had changed her seat, and when he came up to her to shake hands, her manner was doubtful and constrained. He expected this, for it was the first time she had met him since she had been aware that he had seen her with Arthur in the Grove.

'Come, you'll go on with us, Adam,' Mr Poyser said when they reached the turning; and as soon as they were in the fields Adam ventured to offer his arm to Hetty. The children soon gave them an opportunity of lingering behind a little, and then Adam said –

'Will you contrive for me to walk out in the garden a bit with you this evening, if it keeps fine, Hetty? I've something partic'lar to talk to you about.'

Hetty said, 'Very well.' She was really as anxious as Adam was that she should have some private talk with him: she wondered what he thought of her and Arthur: he must have seen them kissing, she knew, but she had no conception of the scene that had taken place between Arthur and Adam. Her first feeling had been that Adam would be very angry with her, and perhaps would tell her aunt and uncle; but it never entered her mind that he would dare to say anything to Captain Donnithorne. It was a relief to her that he behaved so kindly to her to-day, and wanted to speak to *her* alone; for she had trembled when she found he was going home with them lest he should mean 'to tell'. But, now he wanted to talk to her by herself, she should

learn what he thought, and what he meant to do. She felt a
certain confidence that she could persuade him not to do anything she did not want him to do; she could perhaps even make
him believe that she didn't care for Arthur; and as long as Adam
thought there was any hope of her having him, he would do
just what she liked, she knew. Besides, she *must* go on seeming
to encourage Adam, lest her uncle and aunt should be angry,
and suspect her of having some secret lover.

Hetty's little brain was busy with this combination, as she
hung on Adam's arm, and said 'yes' or 'no' to some slight
observations of his about the many hawthorn-berries there
would be for the birds this next winter, and the low-hanging
clouds that would hardly hold up till morning. And when they
rejoined her aunt and uncle, she could pursue her thoughts
without interruption, for Mr Poyser held that though a young
man might like to have the woman he was courting on his arm,
he would nevertheless be glad of a little reasonable talk about
business the while; and, for his own part, he was curious to
hear the most recent news about the Chase Farm. So, through
the rest of the walk, he claimed Adam's conversation for himself; and Hetty laid her small plots, and imagined her little
scenes of cunning blandishment, as she walked along by the
hedgerows on honest Adam's arm, quite as well as if she had been
an elegantly clad coquette alone in her boudoir. For if a country
beauty in clumsy shoes be only shallow-hearted enough, it is
astonishing how closely her mental processes may resemble those
of a lady in society and crinoline, who applies her refined
intellect to the problem of committing indiscretions without
compromising herself. Perhaps the resemblance was not much
the less because Hetty felt very unhappy all the while. The
parting with Arthur was a double pain to her; mingling with
the tumult of passion and vanity, there was a dim undefined
fear that the future might shape itself in some way quite unlike
her dream. She clung to the comforting hopeful words Arthur
had uttered in their last meeting – 'I shall come again at Christmas, and then we will see what can be done.' She clung to the
belief that he was so fond of her, he would never be happy
without her; and she still hugged her secret – that a great

gentleman loved her – with gratified pride, as a superiority over all the girls she knew. But the uncertainty of the future, the possibilities to which she could give no shape, began to press upon her like the invisible weight of air; she was alone on her little island of dreams, and all around her was the dark unknown water where Arthur was gone. She could gather no elation of spirits now by looking forward, but only by looking backward to build confidence on past words and caresses. But occasionally, since Thursday evening, her dim anxieties had been almost lost behind the more definite fear that Adam might betray what he knew to her uncle and aunt, and his sudden proposition to talk with her alone had set her thoughts to work in a new way. She was eager not to lose this evening's opportunity; and after tea, when the boys were going into the garden, and Totty begged to go with them, Hetty said, with an alacrity that surprised Mrs Poyser –

'I'll go with her, aunt.'

It did not seem at all surprising that Adam said he would go too; and soon he and Hetty were left alone together on the walk by the filbert-trees, while the boys were busy elsewhere gathering the large unripe nuts to play at 'cob-nut'[1] with, and Totty was watching them with a puppy-like air of contemplation. It was but a short time – hardly two months – since Adam had had his mind filled with delicious hopes, as he stood by Hetty's side in this garden. The remembrance of that scene had often been with him since Thursday evening: the sunlight through the apple-tree boughs, the red bunches, Hetty's sweet blush. It came importunately now, on this sad evening, with the low-hanging clouds; but he tried to suppress it, lest some emotion should impel him to say more than was needful for Hetty's sake.

'After what I saw on Thursday night, Hetty,' he began, 'you won't think me making too free in what I'm going to say. If you was being courted by any man as 'ud make you his wife, and I'd known you was fond of him, and meant to have him, I should have no right to speak a word to you about it; but when I see you're being made love to by a gentleman as can never marry you, and doesna think o' marrying you, I feel bound t' interfere for you. I can't speak about it to them as are i' the place o' your parents, for that might bring worse trouble than's needful.'

Adam's words relieved one of Hetty's fears, but they also carried a meaning which sickened her with a strengthened foreboding. She was pale and trembling, and yet she would have angrily contradicted Adam, if she had dared to betray her feelings. But she was silent.

'You're so young, you know, Hetty,' he went on, almost tenderly, 'and y' haven't seen much o' what goes on in the world. It's right for me to do what I can to save you from getting into trouble for want o' your knowing where you're being led to. If anybody besides me knew what I know about your meeting a gentleman, and having fine presents from him, they'd speak light on you, and you'd lose your character. And besides that, you'll have to suffer in your feelings, wi' giving your love to a man as can never marry you, so as he might take care of you all your life.'

Adam paused, and looked at Hetty, who was plucking the leaves from the filbert-trees, and tearing them up in her hand. Her little plans and preconcerted speeches had all forsaken her, like an ill-learnt lesson, under the terrible agitation produced by Adam's words. There was a cruel force in their calm certainty which threatened to grapple and crush her flimsy hopes and fancies. She wanted to resist them – she wanted to throw them off with angry contradiction; but the determination to conceal what she felt still governed her. It was nothing more than a blind prompting now, for she was unable to calculate the effect of her words.

'You've no right to say as I love him,' she said, faintly, but impetuously, plucking another rough leaf and tearing it up. She was very beautiful in her paleness and agitation, with her dark childish eyes dilated, and her breath shorter than usual. Adam's heart yearned over her as he looked at her. Ah, if he could but comfort her, and soothe her, and save her from this pain; if he had but some sort of strength that would enable him to rescue her poor troubled mind, as he would have rescued her body in the face of all danger!

'I doubt it must be so, Hetty,' he said, tenderly; 'for I canna believe you'd let any man kiss you by yourselves, and give you a gold box with his hair, and go a-walking i' the Grove to meet him, if you didna love him. I'm not blaming you, for I know it 'ud begin by little and little, till at last you'd not be able to throw it off. It's him I blame for stealing your love i' that way, when he knew he could never make you the right amends. He's been trifling with you, and making a plaything of you, and caring nothing about you as a man ought to care.'

'Yes, he does care for me; I know better nor you,' Hetty burst out. Everything was forgotten but the pain and anger she felt at Adam's words.

'Nay, Hetty,' said Adam, 'if he'd cared for you rightly he'd never ha' behaved so. He told me himself he meant nothing by his kissing and presents, and he wanted to make me believe as you thought light of 'em too. But I know better nor that. I can't help thinking as you've been trusting to his loving you well enough to marry you, for all he's a gentleman. And that's why I must speak to you about it, Hetty, – for fear you should be deceiving yourself. It's never entered his head the thought o' marrying you.'

'How do you know? How durst you say so?' said Hetty, pausing in her walk and trembling. The terrible decision of Adam's tone shook her with fear. She had no presence of mind left for the reflection that Arthur would have his reasons for not telling the truth to Adam. Her words and look were enough to determine Adam: he must give her the letter.

'Perhaps you can't believe me, Hetty; because you think too well of him – because you think he loves you better than he does. But I've got a letter i' my pocket, as he wrote himself for me to give you. I've not read the letter, but he says he's told you the truth in it. But before I give you the letter, consider, Hetty, and don't let it take too much hold on you. It wouldna ha' been good for you if he'd wanted to do such a mad thing as marry you: it 'ud ha' led to no happiness i' th' end.'

Hetty said nothing: she felt a revival of hope at the mention of a letter which Adam had not read. There would be something quite different in it from what he thought.

Adam took out the letter, but he held it in his hand still, while he said, in a tone of tender entreaty –

'Don't you bear me ill-will, Hetty, because I'm the means o' bringing you this pain. God knows I'd ha' borne a good deal worse for the sake o' sparing it you. And think – there's nobody but me knows about this; and I'll take care of you as if I was your brother. You're the same as ever to me, for I don't believe you've done any wrong knowingly.'

Hetty had laid her hand on the letter, but Adam did not loose it till he had done speaking. She took no notice of what he said – she had not listened; but when he loosed the letter, she put it into her pocket, without opening it, and then began to walk more quickly, as if she wanted to go in.

'You're in the right not to read it just yet,' said Adam. 'Read it when you're by yourself. But stay out a little bit longer, and let us call the children: you look so white and ill; your aunt may take notice of it.'

Hetty heard the warning. It recalled to her the necessity of rallying her native powers of concealment, which had half given way under the shock of Adam's words. And she had the letter in her pocket: she was sure there was comfort in that letter, in spite of Adam. She ran to find Totty, and soon reappeared with recovered colour, leading Totty, who was making a sour face, because she had been obliged to throw away an unripe apple that she had set her small teeth in.

'Hegh, Totty,' said Adam, 'come and ride on my shoulder – ever so high – you'll touch the tops o' the trees.'

What little child ever refused to be comforted by that glorious sense of being seized strongly and swung upward? I don't believe Ganymede[2] cried when the eagle carried him away, and perhaps deposited him on Jove's shoulder at the end. Totty smiled down complacently from her secure height, and pleasant was the sight to the mother's eyes, as she stood at the house door and saw Adam coming with his small burthen.

'Bless your sweet face, my pet,' she said, the mother's strong love filling her keen eyes with mildness, as Totty leaned forward and put out her arms. She had no eyes for Hetty at that moment, and only said, without looking at her, 'You go and draw some ale, Hetty: the gells are both at the cheese.'

After the ale had been drawn and her uncle's pipe lighted, there was Totty to be taken to bed, and brought down again in her night-gown, because she would cry instead of going to sleep. Then there was supper to be got ready, and Hetty must be continually in the way to give help. Adam stayed till he knew Mrs Poyser expected him to go, engaging her and her husband in talk as constantly as he could, for the sake of leaving Hetty more at ease. He lingered, because he wanted to see her safely through that evening, and he was delighted to find how much self-command she showed. He knew she had not had time to read the letter, but he did not know she was buoyed up by a secret hope that the letter would contradict everything he had said. It was hard work for him to leave her – hard to think that he should not know for days how she was bearing her trouble. But he must go at last, and all he could do was to press her hand gently as he said 'Good-bye', and hope she would take that as a sign that if his love could ever be a refuge for her, it was there the same as ever. How busy his thoughts were, as he walked home, in devising pitying excuses for her folly; in referring all her weakness to the sweet lovingness of her nature; in blaming Arthur, with less and less inclination to admit that *his* conduct night be extenuated too! His exasperation at Hetty's suffering – and also at the sense that she was possibly thrust for ever out of his own reach – deafened him to any plea for the miscalled friend who had wrought this misery. Adam was a clear-sighted, fair-minded man – a fine fellow, indeed, morally as well as physically. But if Aristides the Just[3] was ever in love and jealous, he was at that moment not perfectly magnanimous. And I cannot pretend that Adam, in these painful days, felt nothing but righteous indignation and loving pity. He was bitterly jealous; and in proportion as his love made him indulgent in his judgment of Hetty, the bitterness found a vent in his feeling towards Arthur.

'Her head was allays likely to be turned,' he thought, 'when a gentleman, with his fine manners, and fine clothes, and his white hands, and that way o' talking gentlefolks have, came about her, making up to her in a bold way, as a man couldn't do that was only her equal; and it's much if she'll ever like a common man now.' He could not help drawing his own hands out of his pocket, and looking at them – at the hard palms and the broken finger-nails. 'I'm a roughish fellow, altogether: I don't know, now I come to think on't, what there is much for a woman to like about me; and yet I might ha' got another wife easy enough, if I hadn't set my heart on her. But it's little matter what other women think about me, if she can't love me. She might ha' loved me, perhaps, as likely as any other man – there's nobody hereabouts as I'm afraid of, if *he* hadn't come between us; but now I shall belike be hateful to her because I'm so different to him. And yet there's no telling – she may turn round the other way, when she finds he's made light of her all the while. She may come to feel the vally[4] of a man as 'ud be thankful to be bound to her all his life. But I must put up with it whichever way it is – I've only to be thankful it's been no worse: I am not th' only man that's got to do without much happiness i' this life. There's many a good bit o' work done with a sad heart. It's God's will, and that's enough for us: we shouldn't know better how things ought to be than He does, I reckon, if we was to spend our lives i' puzzling. But it 'ud ha' gone near to spoil my work for me, if I'd seen her brought to sorrow and shame, and through the man as I've always been proud to think on. Since I've been spared that, I've no right to grumble. When a man's got his limbs whole, he can bear a smart cut or two.'

As Adam was getting over a stile at this point in his reflections, he perceived a man walking along the field before him. He knew it was Seth, returning from an evening preaching, and made haste to overtake him.

'I thought thee'dst be at home before me,' he said, as Seth turned round to wait for him, 'for I'm later than usual tonight.'

'Well, I'm later too, for I got into talk, after meeting, with John Barnes, who has lately professed himself in a state of perfection,[5] and I'd a question to ask him about his experience.

It's one o' them subjects that lead you further than y' expect –
they don't lie along the straight road.'

They walked along together in silence two or three minutes.
Adam was not inclined to enter into the subtleties of religious
experience, but he *was* inclined to interchange a word or two
of brotherly affection and confidence with Seth. That was a
rare impulse in him, much as the brothers loved each other.
They hardly ever spoke of personal matters, or uttered more
than an allusion to their family troubles. Adam was by nature
reserved in all matters of feeling, and Seth felt a certain timidity
towards his more practical brother.

'Seth, lad,' Adam said, putting his arm on his brother's
shoulder, 'hast heard anything from Dinah Morris since she
went away?'

'Yes,' said Seth. 'She told me I might write her word after a
while, how we went on, and how mother bore up under her
trouble. So I wrote to her a fortnight ago, and told her about
thee having a new employment, and how mother was more
contented; and last Wednesday, when I called at the post at
Treddles'on I found a letter from her. I think thee'dst perhaps
like to read it; but I didna say anything about it, because thee'st
seemed so full of other things. It's quite easy t' read – she writes
wonderful for a woman.'

Seth had drawn the letter from his pocket and held it out to
Adam, who said, as he took it –

'Ay, lad, I've got a tough load to carry just now – thee mustna
take it ill if I'm a bit silenter and crustier nor usual. Trouble
doesna make me care the less for thee. I know we shall stick
together to the last.'

'I take nought ill o' thee, Adam: I know well enough what it
means if thee't a bit short wi' me now and then.'

'There's mother opening the door to look out for us,' said
Adam, as they mounted the slope. 'She's been sitting i' the dark
as usual. Well, Gyp, well! art glad to see me?'

Lisbeth went in again quickly and lighted a candle, for she
had heard the welcome rustling of footsteps on the grass, before
Gyp's joyful bark.

'Eh, my lads! th' hours war ne'er so long sin' I war born as

they'n been this blessed Sunday night. What can ye both ha'
been doin' till this time?'

'Thee shouldstna sit i' the dark, mother,' said Adam; 'that
makes the time seem longer.'

'Eh, what am I to do wi' burnin' candle of a Sunday, when
there's on'y me, an' it's sin to do a bit o' knittin'? The daylight's
long enough for me to stare i' th' booke as I canna read. It 'ud
be a fine way o' shortenin' the time, to make it waste the good
candle. But which on you's for ha'in' supper? Ye mun ayther be
clemmed[6] or full, I should think, seein' what time o' night it is.'

'I'm hungry, mother,' said Seth, seating himself at the little
table, which had been spread ever since it was light.

'I've had my supper,' said Adam. 'Here, Gyp,' he added,
taking some cold potato from the table, and rubbing the rough
grey head that looked up towards him.

'Thee needstna be gi'in' th' dog,' said Lisbeth: 'I'n fed him
well a'ready. I'm not like to forget him, I reckon, when he's all
o' thee I can get sight on.'

'Come, then, Gyp,' said Adam, 'we'll go to bed. Good-night,
mother; I'm very tired.'

'What ails him, dost know?' Lisbeth said to Seth, when Adam
was gone up-stairs. 'He's like as if he was struck for death this
day or two – he's so cast down. I found him i' the shop this
forenoon, arter thee wast gone, a-sittin' an' doin' nothin' – not
so much as a booke afore him.'

'He's a deal o' work upon him just now, mother,' said Seth,
'and I think he's a bit troubled in his mind. Don't you take
notice of it, because it hurts him when you do. Be as kind to
him as you can, mother, and don't say anything to vex him.'

'Eh, what dost talk o' my vexin' him? an' what am I like to
be but kind? I'll ma' him a kettle-cake for breakfast i' the
mornin'.'

Adam, meanwhile, was reading Dinah's letter by the light of
his dip candle.

'DEAR BROTHER SETH – Your letter lay three days beyond my
knowing of it at the Post, for I had not money enough by me to
pay the carriage,[7] this being a time of great need and sickness

here, with the rains that have fallen, as if the windows of heaven were opened again; and to lay by money, from day to day, in such a time, when there are so many in present need of all things, would be a want of trust like the laying up of the manna.[8] I speak of this, because I would not have you think me slow to answer, or that I had small joy in your rejoicing at the worldly good that has befallen your brother Adam. The honour and love you bear him is nothing but meet, for God has given him great gifts, and he uses them as the patriarch Joseph did, who, when he was exalted to a place of power and trust, yet yearned with tenderness towards his parent and his younger brother.

'My heart is knit to your aged mother since it was granted me to be near her in the day of trouble. Speak to her of me, and tell her I often bear her in my thoughts at evening time, when I am sitting in the dim light as I did with her, and we held one another's hands, and I spoke the words of comfort that were given to me. Ah, that is a blessed time, isn't it, Seth, when the outward light is fading, and the body is a little wearied with its work and its labour. Then the inward light shines the brighter, and we have a deeper sense of resting on the Divine strength. I sit on my chair in the dark room and close my eyes, and it is as if I was out of the body and could feel no want for evermore. For then, the very hardship, and the sorrow, and the blindness, and the sin, I have beheld and been ready to weep over, – yea, all the anguish of the children of men, which sometimes wraps me round like sudden darkness – I can bear with a willing pain, as if I was sharing the Redeemer's cross. For I feel it, I feel it – infinite love is suffering too – yea, in the fulness of knowledge it suffers, it yearns, it mourns; and that is a blind self-seeking which wants to be freed from the sorrow wherewith the whole creation groaneth and travaileth. Surely it is not true blessedness to be free from sorrow, while there is sorrow and sin in the world: sorrow is then a part of love, and love does not seek to throw it off. It is not the spirit only that tells me this – I see it in the whole work and word of the gospel. Is there not pleading in heaven? Is not the Man of Sorrows[9] there in that crucified body wherewith he ascended? And is He not one with the Infinite Love itself – as our love is one with our sorrow?

'These thoughts have been much borne in on me of late, and I have seen with new clearness the meaning of those words, "If any man love me, let him take up my cross." I have heard this enlarged on as if it meant the troubles and persecutions we bring on ourselves by confessing Jesus. But surely that is a narrow thought. The true cross of the Redeemer was the sin and sorrow of this world – *that* was what lay heavy on his heart – and that is the cross we shall share with him, that is the cup we must drink of with him, if we would have any part in that Divine Love which is one with his sorrow.

'In my outward lot, which you ask about, I have all things and abound. I have had constant work in the mill, though some of the other hands have been turned off for a time; and my body is greatly strengthened, so that I feel little weariness after long walking and speaking. What you say about staying in your own country with your mother and brother shows me that you have a true guidance: your lot is appointed there by a clear showing, and to seek a greater blessing elsewhere would be like laying a false offering on the altar and expecting the fire from heaven to kindle it. My work and my joy are here among the hills, and I sometimes think I cling too much to my life among the people here, and should be rebellious if I was called away.

'I was thankful for your tidings about the dear friends at the Hall Farm; for though I sent them a letter, by my aunt's desire, after I came back from my sojourn among them, I have had no word from them. My aunt has not the pen of a ready writer, and the work of the house is sufficient for the day,[10] for she is weak in body. My heart cleaves to her and her children as the nearest of all to me in the flesh; yea, and to all in that house. I am carried away to them continually in my sleep, and often in the midst of work, and even of speech, the thought of them is borne in on me as if they were in need and trouble, which yet is dark to me. There may be some leading here;[11] but I wait to be taught. You say they are all well.

'We shall see each other again in the body, I trust, – though, it may be, not for a long while; for the brethren and sisters at Leeds are desirous to have me for a short space among them, when I have a door opened me again to leave Snowfield.

'Farewell, dear brother – and yet not farewell. For those children of God whom it has been granted to see each other face to face and to hold communion together, and to feel the same spirit working in both, can never more be sundered, though the hills may lie between. For their souls are enlarged for evermore by that union, and they bear one another about in their thoughts continually as it were a new strength. – Your faithful Sister and fellow-worker in Christ,

"Dinah Morris."

'I have not skill to write the words so small as you do, and my pen moves slow. And so I am straitened, and say but little of what is in my mind. Greet your mother for me with a kiss. She asked me to kiss her twice when we parted.'

Adam had refolded the letter, and was sitting meditatively with his head resting on his arm at the head of the bed, when Seth came up-stairs.

'Hast read the letter?' said Seth.

'Yes,' said Adam. 'I don't know what I should ha' thought of her and her letter if I'd never seen her: I daresay I should ha' thought a preaching woman hateful. But she's one as makes everything seem right she says and does, and I seemed to see her and hear her speaking when I read the letter. It's wonderful how I remember her looks and her voice. She'd make thee rare and happy, Seth; she's just the woman for thee.'

'It's no use thinking o' that,' said Seth, despondingly. 'She spoke so firm, and she's not the woman to say one thing and mean another.'

'Nay, but her feelings may grow different. A woman may get to love by degrees – the best fire doesna flare up the soonest. I'd have thee go and see her by-and-by: I'd make it convenient for thee to be away three or four days, and it 'ud be no walk for thee – only between twenty and thirty mile.'

'I should like to see her again, whether or no, if she wouldna be displeased with me for going,' said Seth.

'She'll be none displeased,' said Adam, emphatically, getting up and throwing off his coat. 'It might be a great happiness to us all, if she'd have thee, for mother took to her so wonderful, and seemed so contented to be with her.'

'Ay,' said Seth, rather timidly, 'and Dinah's fond o' Hetty too; she thinks a deal about her.'

Adam made no reply to that, and no other word but 'good-night' passed between them.

CHAPTER XXXI

In Hetty's Bed-Chamber

It was no longer light enough to go to bed without a candle, even in Mrs Poyser's early household, and Hetty carried one with her as she went up at last to her bedroom soon after Adam was gone and bolted the door behind her.

Now she would read her letter. It must – it must have comfort in it. How was Adam to know the truth? It was always likely he should say what he did say.

She set down the candle, and took out the letter. It had a faint scent of roses, which made her feel as if Arthur were close to her. She put it to her lips, and a rush of remembered sensations for a moment or two swept away all fear. But her heart began to flutter strangely, and her hands to tremble as she broke the seal. She read slowly; it was not easy for her to read a gentleman's handwriting,[1] though Arthur had taken pains to write plainly.

'DEAREST HETTY, – I have spoken truly when I have said that I loved you, and I shall never forget our love. I shall be your true friend as long as life lasts, and I hope to prove this to you in many ways. If I say anything to pain you in this letter, do not believe it is for want of love and tenderness towards you, for there is nothing I would not do for you, if I knew it to be really for your happiness. I cannot bear to think of my little Hetty shedding tears when I am not there to kiss them away; and if I followed only my own inclinations, I should be with her at this moment instead of writing. It is very hard for me to part from her – harder still for me to write words which may seem unkind, though they spring from the truest kindness.

'Dear, dear Hetty, sweet as our love has been to me, sweet as it would be to me for you to love me always, I feel that it would have been better for us both if we had never had that happiness, and that it is my duty to ask you to love me and care for me as little as you can. The fault has all been mine, for though I have been unable to resist the longing to be near you, I have felt all the while that your affection for me might cause you grief. I ought to have resisted my feelings. I should have done so, if I had been a better fellow than I am; but now, since the past cannot be altered, I am bound to save you from any evil that I have power to prevent. And I feel it would be a great evil for you if your affections continued so fixed on me that you could think of no other man who might be able to make you happier by his love than I ever can, and if you continued to look towards something in the future which cannot possibly happen. For, dear Hetty, if I were to do what you one day spoke of, and make you my wife, I should do what you yourself would come to feel was for your misery instead of your welfare. I know you can never be happy except by marrying a man in your own station; and if I were to marry you now, I should only be adding to any wrong I have done, besides offending against my duty in the other relations of life. You know nothing, dear Hetty, of the world in which I must always live, and you would soon begin to dislike me, because there would be so little in which we should be alike.

'And since I cannot marry you, we must part – we must try not to feel like lovers any more. I am miserable while I say this, but nothing else can be. Be angry with me, my sweet one, I deserve it; but do not believe that I shall not always care for you – always be grateful to you – always remember my Hetty; and if any trouble should come that we do not now foresee, trust in me to do everything that lies in my power.

'I have told you where you are to direct a letter to, if you want to write, but I put it down below lest you should have forgotten. Do not write unless there is something I can really do for you; for, dear Hetty, we must try to think of each other as little as we can. Forgive me, and try to forget everything about me, except that I shall be, as long as I live, your affectionate friend,

ARTHUR DONNITHORNE.'

Slowly Hetty had read this letter; and when she looked up from it there was the reflection of a blanched face in the old dim glass – a white marble face with rounded childish forms, but with something sadder than a child's pain in it. Hetty did not see the face – she saw nothing – she only felt that she was cold and sick and trembling. The letter shook and rustled in her hand. She laid it down. It was a horrible sensation – this cold and trembling: it swept away the very ideas that produced it, and Hetty got up to reach a warm cloak from her clothes-press, wrapped it round her, and sat as if she were thinking of nothing but getting warm. Presently she took up the letter with a firmer hand, and began to read it through again. The tears came this time – great rushing tears, that blinded her and blotched the paper. She felt nothing but that Arthur was cruel– cruel to write so, cruel not to marry her. Reasons why he could not marry her had no existence for her mind; how could she believe in any misery that could come to her from the fulfilment of all she had been longing for and dreaming of? She had not the ideas that could make up the notion of that misery.

As she threw down the letter again, she caught sight of her face in the glass; it was reddened now, and wet with tears; it was almost like a companion that she might complain to – that would pity her. She leaned forward on her elbows, and looked into those dark overflooding eyes, and at that quivering mouth, and saw how the tears came thicker and thicker, and how the mouth became convulsed with sobs.

The shattering of all her little dream-world, the crushing blow on her new-born passion, afflicted her pleasure-craving nature with an overpowering pain that annihilated all impulse to resistance, and suspended her anger. She sat sobbing till the candle went out, and then, wearied, aching, stupefied with crying, threw herself on the bed without undressing, and went to sleep.

There was a feeble dawn in the room when Hetty awoke, a little after four o'clock, with a sense of dull misery, the cause of which broke upon her gradually, as she began to discern the objects round her in the dim light. And then came the frightening thought that she had to conceal her misery, as well as to

bear it, in this dreary daylight that was coming. She could lie
no longer: she got up and went towards the table: there lay the
letter; she opened her treasure-drawer: there lay the earrings
and the locket – the signs of all her short happiness – the signs
of the life-long dreariness that was to follow it. Looking at the
little trinkets which she had once eyed and fingered so fondly
as the earnest of her future paradise of finery, she lived back in
the moments when they had been given to her with such tender
caresses, such strangely pretty words, such glowing looks,
which filled her with a bewildering delicious surprise – they
were so much sweeter than she had thought anything could be.
And the Arthur who had spoken to her and looked at her in
this way, who was present with her now – whose arm she felt
round her, his cheek against hers, his very breath upon her –
was the cruel, cruel Arthur who had written that letter: – that
letter which she snatched and crushed and then opened again,
that she might read it once more. The half-benumbed mental
condition which was the effect of the last night's violent crying,
made it necessary to her to look again and see if her wretched
thoughts were actually true – if the letter was really so cruel.
She had to hold it close to the window, else she could not have
read it by the faint light. Yes! it was worse – it was more cruel.
She crushed it up again in anger. She hated the writer of that
letter – hated him for the very reason that she hung upon him
with all her love – all the girlish passion and vanity that made
up her love.

She had no tears this morning. She had wept them all away
last night, and now she felt that dry-eyed morning misery,
which is worse than the first shock, because it has the future in
it as well as the present. Every morning to come, as far as her
imagination could stretch, she would have to get up and feel
that the day would have no joy for her. For there is no despair
so absolute as that which comes with the first moments of our
first great sorrow, when we have not yet known what it is to
have suffered and be healed, to have despaired and to have
recovered hope. As Hetty began languidly to take off the clothes
she had worn all the night, that she might wash herself and
brush her hair, she had a sickening sense that her life would go

on in this way: she should always be doing things she had no
pleasure in, getting up to the old tasks of work, seeing people
she cared nothing about, going to church, and to Treddleston,
and to tea with Mrs Best, and carrying no happy thought with
her. For her short poisonous delights had spoiled for ever all
the little joys that had once made the sweetness of her life – the
new frock ready for Treddleston fair, the party at Mr Britton's
at Broxton wake, the beaux that she would say 'No' to for a
long while, and the prospect of the wedding that was to come
at last when she would have a silk gown and a great many
clothes all at once. These things were all flat and dreary to her
now: everything would be a weariness: and she would carry
about for ever a hopeless thirst and longing.

She paused in the midst of her languid undressing, and leaned
against the dark old clothes-press. Her neck and arms were
bare, her hair hung down in delicate rings; and they were just
as beautiful as they were that night two months ago, when she
walked up and down this bed-chamber glowing with vanity
and hope. She was not thinking of her neck and arms now;
even her own beauty was indifferent to her. Her eyes wandered
sadly over the dull old chamber, and then looked out vacantly
towards the growing dawn. Did a remembrance of Dinah come
across her mind? – of her foreboding words, which had made
her angry? – of Dinah's affectionate entreaty to think of her as
a friend in trouble? No, the impression had been too slight to
recur. Any affection or comfort Dinah could have given her
would have been as indifferent to Hetty this morning as everything else was except her bruised passion. She was only thinking
she could never stay here and go on with the old life – she could
better bear something quite new than sinking back into the old
everyday round. She would like to run away that very morning,
and never see any of the old faces again. But Hetty's was not a
nature to face difficulties – to dare to loose her hold on the
familiar, and rush blindly on some unknown condition. Hers
was a luxurious and vain nature, not a passionate one; and if she
were ever to take any violent measure, she must be urged to it
by the desperation of terror. There was not much room for her
thoughts to travel in the narrow circle of her imagination, and

she soon fixed on the one thing she would do to get away from
her old life: she would ask her uncle to let her go to be a
lady's-maid. Miss Lydia's maid would help her to get a situation, if she knew Hetty had her uncle's leave.

When she had thought of this, she fastened up her hair and
began to wash: it seemed more possible to her to go down-stairs
and try to behave as usual. She would ask her uncle this very
day. On Hetty's blooming health it would take a great deal of
such mental suffering as hers to leave any deep impress; and
when she was dressed as neatly as usual in her working-dress,
with her hair tucked up under her little cap, an indifferent
observer would have been more struck with the young roundness of her cheek and neck, and the darkness of her eyes and
eyelashes, than with any signs of sadness about her. But when
she took up the crushed letter and put it in her drawer, that she
might lock it out of sight, hard smarting tears, having no relief
in them as the great drops had that fell last night, forced their
way into her eyes. She wiped them away quickly: she must not
cry in the day-time: nobody should find out how miserable
she was, nobody should know she was disappointed about
anything; and the thought that the eyes of her aunt and uncle
would be upon her, gave her the self-command which often
accompanies a great dread. For Hetty looked out from her
secret misery towards the possibility of their ever knowing what
had happened, as the sick and weary prisoner might think of
the possible pillory. They would think her conduct shameful;
and shame was torture. That was poor little Hetty's conscience.

So she locked up her drawer and went away to her early
work.

In the evening, when Mr Poyser was smoking his pipe, and
his good-nature was therefore at its superlative moment, Hetty
seized the opportunity of her aunt's absence to say –

'Uncle, I wish you'd let me go for a lady's-maid.'

Mr Poyser took the pipe from his mouth, and looked at Hetty
in mild surprise for some moments. She was sewing, and went
on with her work industriously.

'Why, what's put that into your head, my wench?' he said at
last, after he had given one conservative puff.

'I should like it – I should like it better than farm-work.'

'Nay, nay; you fancy so because you donna know it, my wench. It wouldn't be half so good for your health, nor for your luck i' life. I'd like you to stay wi' us till you've got a good husband: you're my own niece, and I wouldn't have you go to service, though it was a gentleman's house, as long as I've got a home for you.'

Mr Poyser paused, and puffed away at his pipe.

'I like the needlework,' said Hetty, 'and I should get good wages.'

'Has your aunt been a bit sharp wi' you?' said Mr Poyser, not noticing Hetty's further argument. 'You mustna mind that, my wench – she does it for your good. She wishes you well; an' there isn't many aunts as are no kin to you 'ud ha' done by you as she has.'

'No, it isn't my aunt,' said Hetty, 'but I should like the work better.'

'It was all very well for you to learn the work a bit – an' I gev my consent to that fast enough, sin' Mrs Pomfret was willing to teach you. For if anything was t' happen, it's well to know how to turn your hand to different sorts o' things. But I niver meant you to go to service, my wench; my family's ate their own bread and cheese as fur back as anybody knows, hanna they, father? You wouldna like your grandchild to take wage?'

'Na-a-y,' said old Martin, with an elongation of the word, meant to make it bitter as well as negative, while he leaned forward and looked down on the floor. 'But the wench takes arter her mother. I'd hard work t' hould *her* in, an' she married i' spite o' me – a feller wi' on'y two head o' stock when there should ha' been ten on's farm – she might well die o' th' inflammation afore she war thirty.'

It was seldom the old man made so long a speech; but his son's question had fallen like a bit of dry fuel on the embers of a long unextinguished resentment, which had always made the grandfather more indifferent to Hetty than to his son's children. Her mother's fortune had been spent by that good-for-nought Sorrel, and Hetty had Sorrel's blood in her veins.

'Poor thing, poor thing!' said Martin the younger, who was sorry to have provoked this retrospective harshness. 'She'd but bad luck. But Hetty's got as good a chanche o' getting a solid, sober husband as any gell i' this country.'

After throwing out this pregnant hint, Mr Poyser recurred to his pipe and his silence, looking at Hetty to see if she did not give some sign of having renounced her ill-advised wish. But instead of that, Hetty, in spite of herself, began to cry, half out of ill-temper at the denial, half out of the day's repressed sadness.

'Hegh, hegh!' said Mr Poyser, meaning to check her playfully, 'don't let's have any crying. Crying's for them as ha' got no home, not for them as want to get rid o' one. What dost think?' he continued to his wife, who now came back into the house-place, knitting with fierce rapidity, as if that movement were a necessary function, like the twittering of a crab's antennae.

'Think? – why, I think we shall have the fowl stole before we are much older, wi' that gell forgetting to lock the pens up o' nights. What's the matter now, Hetty? What are you crying at?'

'Why, she's been wanting to go for a lady's-maid,' said Mr Poyser. 'I tell her we can do better for her nor that.'

'I thought she'd got some maggot in her head, she's gone about wi' her mouth buttoned up so all day. It's all wi' going so among them servants at the Chase, as we war fools for letting her. She thinks it 'ud be a finer life than being wi' them as are akin to her, and ha' brought her up sin' she war no bigger nor Marty. She thinks there's nothing belongs to being a lady's-maid, but wearing finer clothes nor she was born to, I'll be bound. It's what rag she can get to stick on her as she's thinking on from morning till night; as I often ask her if she wouldn't like to be the mawkin i' the field, for then she'd be made o' rags inside and out. I'll never gi' my consent to her going for a lady's-maid, while she's got good friends to take care on her till she's married to somebody better nor one o' them valets, as is neither a common man nor a gentleman, an' must live on the fat o' the land, an's like enough to stick his hands under his coat tails and expect his wife to work for him.'

XXXI IN HETTY'S BED-CHAMBER

'Ay, ay,' said Mr Poyser, 'we must have a better husband for her nor that, and there's better at hand. Come, my wench, give over crying, and get to bed. I'll do better for you nor letting you go for a lady's-maid. Let's hear no more on't.'

When Hetty was gone up-stairs he said –

'I canna make it out as she should want to go away, for I thought she'd got a mind t' Adam Bede. She's looked like it o' late.'

'Eh, there's no knowing what she's got a liking to, for things take no more hold on her than if she was a dried pea. I believe that gell Molly – as is aggravatin' enough, for the matter o' that – but I believe she'd care more about leaving us and the children, for all she's been here but a year come Michaelmas, nor Hetty would. But she's got this notion o' being a lady's-maid wi' going among them servants – we might ha' known what it 'ud lead to when we let her go to learn the fine work. But I'll put a stop to it pretty quick.'

'Thee'dst be sorry to part wi' her, if it wasn't for her good,' said Mr Poyser. 'She's useful to thee i' the work.'

'Sorry? yes; I'm fonder on her nor she deserves – a little hard-hearted hussy, wanting to leave us i' that way. I can't ha' had her about me these seven year, I reckon, and done for her, and taught her everything, wi'out caring about her. An' here I'm having linen spun, an' thinking all the while it'll make sheeting and table-clothing for her when she's married, an' she'll live i' the parish wi' us, and never go out of our sights – like a fool as I am for thinking aught about her, as is no better nor a cherry wi' a hard stone inside it.'

'Nay, nay, thee mustna make much of a trifle,' said Mr Poyser, soothingly. 'She's fond on us, I'll be bound; but she's young, an' gets things in her head as she can't rightly give account on. Them young fillies 'ull run away often wi'out knowing why.'

Her uncle's answers, however, had had another effect on Hetty besides that of disappointing her and making her cry. She knew quite well whom he had in his mind in his allusions to marriage, and to a sober, solid husband; and when she was in her bedroom again, the possibility of her marrying Adam presented itself to her in a new light. In a mind where no strong sympathies are at work, where there is no supreme sense of right to which the agitated nature can cling and steady itself to quiet endurance, one of the first results of sorrow is a desperate vague clutching after any deed that will change the actual condition. Poor Hetty's vision of consequences, at no time more than a narrow fantastic calculation of her own probable pleasures and pains, was now quite shut out by reckless irritation under present suffering, and she was ready for one of those convulsive, motiveless actions by which wretched men and women leap from a temporary sorrow into a life-long misery.

Why should she not marry Adam? She did not care what she did, so that it made some change in her life. She felt confident that he would still want to marry her, and any further thought about Adam's happiness in the matter had never yet visited her.

'Strange!' perhaps you will say, 'this rush of impulse towards a course that might have seemed the most repugnant to her present state of mind, and in only the second night of her sadness!'

Yes, the actions of a little trivial soul like Hetty's, struggling amidst the serious, sad destinies of a human being *are* strange. So are the motions of a little vessel without ballast tossed about on a stormy sea. How pretty it looked with its particoloured sail in the sunlight, moored in the quiet bay!

'Let that man bear the loss who loosed it from its moorings.'[2]

But that will not save the vessel – the pretty thing that might have been a lasting joy.

CHAPTER XXXII

Mrs Poyser 'Has Her Say Out'

The next Saturday evening there was much excited discussion at the Donnithorne Arms concerning an incident which had occurred that very day – no less than a second appearance of the smart man in top-boots, said by some to be a mere farmer in treaty for the Chase Farm, by others to be the future steward; but by Mr Casson himself, the personal witness to the stranger's visit, pronounced contemptuously to be nothing better than a bailiff, such as Satchell had been before him. No one had thought of denying Mr Casson's testimony to the fact that he had seen the stranger, nevertheless he proffered various corroborating circumstances.

'I see him myself,' he said; 'I see him coming along by the Crab-tree meadow on a bald-faced hoss. I'd just been t' hev a pint – it was half after ten i' the forenoon, when I hev my pint as reg'lar as the clock – and I says to Knowles, as druv up with his waggon, "You'll get a bit o' barley to-day, Knowles," I says, "if you look about you"; and then I went round by the rick-yard, and towart the Treddles'on road; and just as I come up by the big ash-tree, I see the man i' top-boots coming along on a bald-faced hoss – I wish I may never stir if I didn't. And I stood still till he come up, and I says, "Good morning, sir," I says, for I wanted to hear the turn of his tongue, as I might know whether he was a this-country-man; so I says, "Good morning, sir: it'll 'old hup for the barley this morning, I think. There'll be a bit got hin, if we've good luck." And he says, "Eh, ye may be raight, there's no tallin'," he says; and I knowed by that' – here Mr Casson gave a wink – 'as he didn't come from a hundred mile off. I daresay he'd think me a hodd talker, as

you Loamshire folks allays does hany one as talks the right
language.'

'The right language!' said Bartle Massey, contemptuously.
'You're about as near the right language as a pig's squeaking is
like a tune played on a key-bugle.'

'Well, I don't know,' answered Mr Casson, with an angry
smile. 'I should think a man as has lived among the gentry from
a boy, is likely to know what's the right language pretty nigh
as well as a schoolmaster.'

'Ay, ay, man,' said Bartle, with a tone of sarcastic consolation, 'you talk the right language for *you*. When Mike
Holdsworth's goat says ba-a-a, it's all right – it 'ud be unnatural
for it to make any other noise.'

The rest of the party being Loamshire men, Mr Casson had
the laugh strongly against him, and wisely fell back on the
previous question, which, far from being exhausted in a single
evening, was renewed in the churchyard, before service, the
next day, with the fresh interest conferred on all news when
there is a fresh person to hear it; and that fresh hearer was
Martin Poyser, who, as his wife said, 'never went boozin' with
that set at Casson's, a-sittin' soakin'-in drink, and looking as
wise as a lot o' cod-fish wi' red faces'.

It was probably owing to the conversation she had had
with her husband on their way from church, concerning this
problematic stranger, that Mrs Poyser's thoughts immediately
reverted to him when, a day or two afterwards, as she was
standing at the house-door with her knitting, in that eager
leisure which came to her when the afternoon cleaning was
done, she saw the old Squire enter the yard on his black pony,
followed by John the groom. She always cited it afterwards as
a case of prevision, which really had something more in it than
her own remarkable penetration, that the moment she set eyes
on the Squire, she said to herself, 'I shouldna wonder if he's
come about that man as is a-going to take the Chase Farm,
wanting Poyser to do something for him without pay. But
Poyser's a fool if he does.'

Something unwonted must clearly be in the wind, for the old
Squire's visits to his tenantry were rare; and though Mrs Poyser

had during the last twelvemonth recited many imaginary speeches, meaning even more than met the ear, which she was quite determined to make to him the next time he appeared within the gates of the Hall Farm, the speeches had always remained imaginary.

'Good-day, Mrs Poyser,' said the old Squire, peering at her with his short-sighted eyes – a mode of looking at her which, as Mrs Poyser observed, 'allays aggravated her: it was as if you was a insect, and he was going to dab his finger-nail on you.'

However, she said, 'Your servant, sir', and curtsied with an air of perfect deference as she advanced towards him: she was not the woman to misbehave towards her betters, and fly in the face of the catechism,[1] without severe provocation.

'Is your husband at home, Mrs Poyser?'

'Yes, sir; he's only i' the rick-yard. I'll send for him in a minute, if you'll please to get down and step in.'

'Thank you; I will do so. I want to consult him about a little matter; but you are quite as much concerned in it, if not more. I must have your opinion too.'

'Hetty, run and tell your uncle to come in,' said Mrs Poyser, as they entered the house, and the old gentleman bowed low in answer to Hetty's curtsy; while Totty, conscious of a pinafore stained with gooseberry jam, stood hiding her face against the clock, and peeping round furtively.

'What a fine old kitchen this is!' said Mr Donnithorne, looking round admiringly. He always spoke in the same deliberate, well-chiselled, polite way, whether his words were sugary or venomous. 'And you keep it so exquisitely clean, Mrs Poyser. I like these premises, do you know, beyond any on the estate.'

'Well, sir, since you're fond of 'em, I should be glad if you'd let a bit o' repairs be done to 'em, for the boarding's i' that state, as we're like to be eaten up wi' rats and mice; and the cellar, you may stan' up to your knees i' water in't, if you like to go down; but perhaps you'd rather believe my words. Won't you please to sit down, sir?'

'Not yet; I must see your dairy. I have not seen it for years, and I hear on all hands about your fine cheese and butter,' said the Squire, looking politely unconscious that there could be any question on which he and Mrs Poyser might happen to disagree. 'I think I see the door open, there: you must not be surprised if I cast a covetous eye on your cream and butter. I don't expect that Mrs Satchell's cream and butter will bear comparison with yours.'

'I can't say, sir, I'm sure. It's seldom I see other folks's butter, though there's some on it as one's no need to see – the smell's enough.'

'Ah, now this I like,' said Mr Donnithorne, looking round at the damp temple of cleanliness, but keeping near the door. 'I'm sure I should like my breakfast better if I knew the butter and cream came from this dairy. Thank you, that really is a pleasant sight. Unfortunately, my slight tendency to rheumatism makes me afraid of damp: I'll sit down in your comfortable kitchen. Ah, Poyser, how do you do? In the midst of business, I see, as usual. I've been looking at your wife's beautiful dairy – the best manager in the parish, is she not?'

Mr Poyser had just entered in shirt-sleeves and open waist-coat, with a face a shade redder than usual, from the exertion of 'pitching'.[2] As he stood, red, rotund, and radiant, before the small, wiry, cool, old gentleman, he looked like a prize apple by the side of a withered crab.[3]

'Will you please to take this chair, sir?' he said, lifting his father's arm-chair forward a little: 'you'll find it easy.'

'No, thank you, I never sit in easy-chairs,' said the old gentle-man, seating himself on a small chair near the door. 'Do you know, Mrs Poyser – sit down, pray, both of you – I've been far from contented, for some time, with Mrs Satchell's dairy management. I think she has not a good method, as you have.'

'Indeed, sir, I can't speak to that,' said Mrs Poyser, in a hard voice, rolling and unrolling her knitting, and looking icily out of the window, as she continued to stand opposite the Squire. Poyser might sit down if he liked, she thought: *she* wasn't going to sit down, as if she'd give in to any such smooth-tongued palaver.[4] Mr Poyser, who looked and felt the reverse of icy, did sit down in his three-cornered chair.

'And now, Poyser, as Satchell is laid up, I am intending to let the Chase Farm to a respectable tenant. I'm tired of having a

XXXII MRS POYSER 'HAS HER SAY OUT'

farm on my own hands – nothing is made the best of in such cases, as you know. A satisfactory bailiff is hard to find; and I think you and I, Poyser, and your excellent wife here, can enter into a little arrangement in consequence, which will be to our mutual advantage.'

'Oh,' said Mr Poyser, with a good-natured blankness of imagination as to the nature of the arrangement.

'If I'm called upon to speak, sir,' said Mrs Poyser, after glancing at her husband with pity at his softness, 'you know better than me; but I don't see what the Chase Farm is t' us – we've cumber enough wi' our own farm. Not but what I'm glad to hear o' anybody respectable coming into the parish: there's some as ha' been brought in as hasn't been looked on i' that character.'

'You're likely to find Mr Thurle an excellent neighbour, I assure you: such a one as you will feel glad to have accommodated by the little plan I'm going to mention; especially as I hope you will find it as much to your own advantage as his.'

'Indeed, sir, if it's anything to our advantage, it'll be the first offer o' the sort I've heared on. It's them as take advantage that get advantage i' this world, I think: folks have to wait long enough afore it's brought to 'em.'

'The fact is, Poyser,' said the Squire, ignoring Mrs Poyser's theory of worldly prosperity, 'there is too much dairy land, and too little plough land, on the Chase Farm, to suit Thurle's purpose – indeed, he will only take the farm on condition of some change in it: his wife, it appears, is not a clever dairy-woman, like yours. Now, the plan I'm thinking of is to effect a little exchange. If you were to have the Hollow Pastures, you might increase your dairy, which must be so profitable under your wife's management; and I should request you, Mrs Poyser, to supply my house with milk, cream, and butter at the market prices. On the other hand, Poyser, you might let Thurle have the Lower and Upper Ridges, which really, with our wet seasons, would be a good riddance for you. There is much less risk in dairy land than corn land.'

Mr Poyser was leaning forward, with his elbows on his knees, his head on one side, and his mouth screwed up – apparently absorbed in making the tips of his fingers meet so as to represent with perfect accuracy the ribs of a ship. He was much too acute a man not to see through the whole business, and to foresee perfectly what would be his wife's view of the subject; but he disliked giving unpleasant answers: unless it was on a point of farming practice, he would rather give up than have a quarrel, any day; and, after all, it mattered more to his wife than to him. So, after a few moments' silence, he looked up at her and said mildly. 'What dost say?'

Mrs Poyser had had her eyes fixed on her husband with cold severity during his silence, but now she turned away her head with a toss, looked icily at the opposite roof of the cow-shed, and spearing her knitting together with the loose pin, held it firmly between her clasped hands.

'Say? Why, I say you may do as you like about giving up any o' your corn land afore your lease is up, which it won't be for a year come next Michaelmas, but I'll not consent to take more dairy work into my hands, either for love or money; and there's nayther love nor money here, as I can see, on'y other folks's love o' theirselves, and the money as is to go into other folks's pockets. I know there's them as is born t' own the land, and them as is born to sweat on't' – here Mrs Poyser paused to gasp a little – 'and I know it's christened folks's duty to submit to their betters as fur as flesh and blood 'ull bear it; but I'll not make a martyr o' myself, and wear myself to skin and bone, and worret myself as if I was a churn wi' butter a-coming in't, for no landlord in England, not if he was King George himself.'

'No, no, my dear Mrs Poyser, certainly not,' said the Squire, still confident in his own powers of persuasion, 'you must not overwork yourself; but don't you think your work will rather be lessened than increased in this way? There is so much milk required at the Abbey, that you will have little increase of cheese and butter making from the addition to your dairy; and I believe selling the milk is the most profitable way of disposing of dairy produce, is it not?'

'Ay, that's true,' said Mr Poyser, unable to repress an opinion on a question of farming profits, and forgetting that it was not in this case a purely abstract question.

'I daresay,' said Mrs Poyser bitterly, turning her head half-way towards her husband, and looking at the vacant arm-chair – 'I daresay it's true for men as sit i' th' chimney-corner and make believe as everything's cut wi' ins an' outs to fit int' everything else. If you could make a pudding wi' thinking o' the batter, it 'ud be easy getting dinner. How do I know whether the milk 'ull be wanted constant? What's to make me sure as the house won't be put o' board wage⁵ afore we're many months older, and then I may have to lie awake o' nights wi' twenty gallons o' milk on my mind – and Dingall 'ull take no more butter, let alone paying for it; and we must fat pigs till we're obliged to beg the butcher on our knees to buy 'em, and lose half of 'em wi' the measles. And there's the fetching and carrying, as 'ud be welly half a day's work for a man an' hoss – *that's* to be took out o' the profits, I reckon? But there's folks 'ud hold a sieve under the pump and expect to carry away the water.'

'That difficulty – about the fetching and carrying – you will not have, Mrs Poyser,' said the Squire, who thought that this entrance into particulars indicated a distant inclination to compromise on Mrs Poyser's part – 'Bethell will do that regularly with the cart and pony.'

'Oh, sir, begging your pardon, I've never been used t' having gentlefolks's servants coming about my back places, a-making love to both the gells at once, and keeping 'em with their hands on their hips listening to all manner o' gossip when they should be down on their knees a-scouring. If we're to go to ruin, it shanna be wi' having our back kitchen turned into a public.'

'Well, Poyser,' said the Squire, shifting his tactics, and looking as if he thought Mrs Poyser had suddenly withdrawn from the proceedings and left the room, 'you can turn the Hollows into feeding-land. I can easily make another arrangement about supplying my house. And I shall not forget your readiness to accommodate your landlord as well as a neighbour. I know you will be glad to have your lease renewed for three years when the present one expires; otherwise, I daresay Thurle, who is a man of some capital, would be glad to take both the farms, as they could be worked so well together. But I don't want to part with an old tenant like you.'

To be thrust out of the discussion in this way would have been enough to complete Mrs Poyser's exasperation, even without the final threat. Her husband, really alarmed at the possibility of their leaving the old place where he had been bred and born – for he believed the old Squire had small spite enough for anything – was beginning a mild remonstrance explanatory of the inconvenience he should find in having to buy and sell more stock, with –

'Well, sir, I think as it's rether hard' ... when Mrs Poyser burst in with the desperate determination to have her say out this once, though it were to rain notices to quit, and the only shelter were the workhouse.

'Then, sir, if I may speak – as, for all I'm a woman, and there's folks as thinks a woman's fool enough to stan' by an' look on while the men sign her soul away, I've a right to speak, for I make one quarter o' the rent, and save another quarter – I say, if Mr Thurle's so ready to take farms under you, it's a pity but what he should take this, and see if he likes to live in a house wi' all the plagues o' Egypt⁶ in't – wi' the cellar full o' water, and frogs and toads hoppin' up the steps by dozens – and the floors rotten, and the rats and mice gnawing every bit o' cheese, and runnin' over our heads as we lie i' bed till we expect 'em to eat us up alive – as it's a mercy they hanna eat the children long ago. I should like to see if there's another tenant besides Poyser as 'ud put up wi' never having a bit o' repairs done till a place tumbles down – and not then, on'y wi' begging and praying, and having to pay half – and being strung up wi' the rent as it's much if he gets enough out o' the land to pay, for all he's put his own money into the ground beforehand. See if you'll get a stranger to lead such a life here as that: a maggot must be born i' the rotten cheese to like it, I reckon. You may run away from my words, sir,' continued Mrs Poyser, following the old Squire beyond the door – for after the first moments of stunned surprise he had got up, and, waving his hand towards her with a smile, had walked out towards his pony. But it was impossible for him to get away immediately, for John was walking the pony up and down the yard, and was some distance from the causeway when his master beckoned.

'You may run away from my words, sir, and you may go spinnin' underhand ways o' doing us a mischief, for you've got Old Harry to your friend, though nobody else is, but I tell you for once as we're not dumb creatures to be abused and made money on by them as ha' got the lash i' their hands, for want o' knowing how t' undo the tackle.⁷ An' if I'm the only one as speaks my mind, there's plenty o' the same way o' thinking i' this parish and the next to 't, for your name's no better than a brimstone match in everybody's nose – if it isna two-three old folks as you think o' saving your soul by giving 'em a bit o' flannel and a drop o' porridge.⁸ An' you may be right i' thinking it'll take but little to save your soul, for it'll be the smallest savin' y' iver made, wi' all your scrapin'.'

There are occasions on which two servant-girls and a waggoner may be a formidable audience, and as the Squire rode away on his black pony, even the gift of short-sightedness did not prevent him from being aware that Molly and Nancy and Tim were grinning not far from him. Perhaps he suspected that sour old John was grinning behind him – which was also the fact. Meanwhile the bull-dog, the black-and-tan terrier, Alick's sheep-dog, and the gander hissing at a safe distance from the pony's heels, carried out the idea of Mrs Poyser's solo in an impressive quartett.

Mrs Poyser, however, had no sooner seen the pony move off than she turned round, gave the two hilarious damsels a look which drove them into the back kitchen, and, unspearing her knitting, began to knit again with her usual rapidity, as she re-entered the house.

'Thee'st done it now,' said Mr Poyser, a little alarmed and uneasy, but not without some triumphant amusement at his wife's outbreak.

'Yes, I know I've done it,' said Mrs Poyser; 'but I've had my say out, and I shall be th' easier for't all my life. There's no pleasure i' living, if you're to be corked up for ever, and only dribble your mind out by the sly, like a leaky barrel. I shan't repent saying what I think, if I live to be as old as th' old Squire; and there's little likelihoods – for it seems as if them as aren't wanted here are th' only folks as aren't wanted i' th' other world.'

'But thee wutna like moving from th' old place this Michaelmas twelvemonth,' said Mr Poyser, 'and going into a strange parish, where thee know'st nobody. It'll be hard upon us both, and upo' father too.'

'Eh, it's no use worreting; there's plenty o' things may happen between this and Michaelmas twelvemonth. The Captain may be master afore then, for what we know,' said Mrs Poyser, inclined to take an unusually hopeful view of an embarrassment which had been brought about by her own merit, and not by other people's fault.

'*I'm* none for worreting,' said Mr Poyser, rising from his three-cornered chair, and walking slowly towards the door; 'but I should be loath to leave the old place, and the parish where I was bred and born, and father afore me. We should leave our roots behind us, I doubt, and niver thrive again.'

CHAPTER XXXIII

More Links

The barley was all carried at last, and the harvest suppers[1] went by without waiting for the dismal black crop of beans. The apples and nuts were gathered and stored; the scent of whey departed from the farmhouses, and the scent of brewing came in its stead. The woods behind the Chase, and all the hedgerow trees, took on a solemn splendour under the dark low-hanging skies. Michaelmas was come, with its fragrant basketfuls of purple damsons, and its paler purple daisies, and its lads and lasses leaving or seeking service, and winding along between the yellow hedges, with their bundles under their arms. But though Michaelmas was come, Mr Thurle, that desirable tenant, did not come to the Chase Farm, and the old Squire, after all, had been obliged to put in a new bailiff. It was known throughout the two parishes that the Squire's plan had been frustrated because the Poysers had refused to be 'put upon', and Mrs Poyser's outbreak was discussed in all the farmhouses with a zest which was only heightened by frequent repetition. The news that 'Bony' was come back from Egypt was comparatively insipid, and the repulse of the French in Italy[2] was nothing to Mrs Poyser's repulse of the old Squire. Mr Irwine had heard a version of it in every parishioner's house, with the one exception of the Chase. But since he had always, with marvellous skill, avoided any quarrel with Mr Donnithorne, he could not allow himself the pleasure of laughing at the old gentleman's discomfiture with any one besides his mother, who declared that if she were rich she should like to allow Mrs Poyser a pension for life, and wanted to invite her to the parsonage, that she might hear an account of the scene from Mrs Poyser's own lips.

'No, no, mother,' said Mr Irwine; 'it was a little bit of irregular justice on Mrs Poyser's part, but a magistrate like me must not countenance irregular justice. There must be no report spread that I have taken notice of the quarrel, else I shall lose the little good influence I have over the old man.'

'Well, I like that woman even better than her cream-cheeses,' said Mrs Irwine. 'She has the spirit of three men, with that pale face of hers; and she says such sharp things too.'

'Sharp! yes, her tongue is like a new-set razor. She's quite original in her talk, too; one of those untaught wits that help to stock a country with proverbs. I told you that capital thing I heard her say about Craig – that he was like a cock who thought the sun had risen to hear him crow. Now that's an Æsop's fable[3] in a sentence.'

'But it will be a bad business if the old gentleman turns them out of the farm next Michaelmas, eh?' said Mrs Irwine.

'Oh, that must not be; and Poyser is such a good tenant, that Donnithorne is likely to think twice, and digest his spleen rather than turn them out. But if he should give them notice at Lady-day, Arthur and I must move heaven and earth to mollify him. Such old parishioners as they are must not go.'

'Ah, there's no knowing what may happen before Lady-day,' said Mrs Irwine. 'It struck me on Arthur's birthday that the old man was a little shaken: he's eighty-three, you know. It's really an unconscionable age. It's only women who have a right to live as long as that.'

'When they've got old-bachelor sons who would be forlorn without them,' said Mr Irwine, laughing, and kissing his mother's hand.

Mrs Poyser, too, met her husband's occasional forebodings of a notice to quit with 'There's no knowing what may happen before Lady-day': – one of those undeniable general propositions which are usually intended to convey a particular meaning very far from undeniable. But it is really too hard upon human nature that it should be held a criminal offence to imagine the death even of the king when he is turned eighty-three. It is not to be believed that any but the dullest Britons can be good subjects under that hard condition.

Apart from this foreboding, things went on much as usual in the Poyser household. Mrs Poyser thought she noticed a surprising improvement in Hetty. To be sure, the girl got 'closer tempered, and sometimes she seemed as if there'd be no drawing a word from her with cart-ropes'; but she thought much less about her dress, and went after the work quite eagerly, without any telling. And it was wonderful how she never wanted to go out now – indeed, could hardly be persuaded to go; and she bore her aunt's putting a stop to her weekly lesson in fine-work at the Chase, without the least grumbling or pouting. It must be, after all, that she had set her heart on Adam at last, and her sudden freak of wanting to be a lady's-maid must have been caused by some little pique or misunderstanding between them, which had passed by. For whenever Adam came to the Hall Farm, Hetty seemed to be in better spirits, and to talk more than at other times, though she was almost sullen when Mr Craig or any other admirer happened to pay a visit there.

Adam himself watched her at first with trembling anxiety, which gave way to surprise and delicious hope. Five days after delivering Arthur's letter, he had ventured to go to the Hall Farm again – not without dread lest the sight of him might be painful to her. She was not in the house-place when he entered, and he sat talking to Mr and Mrs Poyser for a few minutes with a heavy fear on his heart that they might presently tell him Hetty was ill. But by-and-by there came a light step that he knew, and when Mrs Poyser said, 'Come, Hetty, where have you been?' Adam was obliged to turn round, though he was afraid to see the changed look there must be in her face. He almost started when he saw her smiling as if she were pleased to see him – looking the same as ever at a first glance, only that she had her cap on, which he had never seen her in before when he came of an evening. Still, when he looked at her again and again as she moved about or sat at her work, there was a change: the cheeks were as pink as ever, and she smiled as much as she had ever done of late, but there was something different in her eyes, in the expression of her face, in all her movements, Adam thought – something harder, older, less child-like. 'Poor thing!' he said to himself, 'that's allays likely. It's because she's had her first heartache. But she's got a spirit to bear up under it. Thank God for that.'

As the weeks went by, and he saw her always looking pleased to see him – turning up her lovely face towards him as if she meant him to understand that she was glad for him to come – and going about her work in the same equable way, making no sign of sorrow, he began to believe that her feeling towards Arthur must have been much slighter than he had imagined in his first indignation and alarm, and that she had been able to think of her girlish fancy that Arthur was in love with her and would marry her, as a folly of which she was timely cured. And it perhaps was, as he had sometimes in his more cheerful moments hoped it would be – her heart was really turning with all the more warmth towards the man she knew to have a serious love for her.

Possibly you think that Adam was not at all sagacious in his interpretations, and that it was altogether extremely unbecoming in a sensible man to behave as he did – falling in love with a girl who really had nothing more than her beauty to recommend her, attributing imaginary virtues to her, and even condescending to cleave to her after she had fallen in love with another man, waiting for her kind looks as a patient trembling dog waits for his master's eye to be turned upon him. But in so complex a thing as human nature, we must consider, it is hard to find rules without exceptions. Of course, I know that, as a rule, sensible men fall in love with the most sensible women of their acquaintance, see through all the pretty deceits of coquettish beauty, never imagine themselves loved when they are not loved, cease loving on all proper occasions, and marry the woman most fitted for them in every respect – indeed, so as to compel the approbation of all the maiden ladies in their neighbourhood. But even to this rule an exception will occur now and then in the lapse of centuries, and my friend Adam was one. For my own part, however, I respect him none the less; nay, I think the deep love he had for that sweet, rounded, blossom-like, dark-eyed Hetty, of whose inward self he was really very ignorant, came out of the very strength of his nature, and not out of any inconsistent weakness. Is it any weakness,

pray, to be wrought on by exquisite music? – to feel its wondrous harmonies searching the subtlest windings of your soul,
the delicate fibres of life where no memory can penetrate, and
binding together your whole being past and present in one
unspeakable vibration: melting you in one moment with all the
tenderness, all the love that has been scattered through the
toilsome years, concentrating in one emotion of heroic courage
or resignation all the hard-learnt lessons of self-renouncing
sympathy, blending your present joy with past sorrow, and
your present sorrow with all your past joy? If not, then neither
is it a weakness to be so wrought upon by the exquisite curves
of a woman's cheek and neck and arms, by the liquid depths of
her beseeching eyes, or the sweet childish pout of her lips. For
the beauty of a lovely woman is like music: what can one say
more? Beauty has an expression beyond and far above the one
woman's soul that it clothes, as the words of genius have a
wider meaning than the thought that prompted them: it is more
than a woman's love that moves us in a woman's eyes – it seems
to be a far-off mighty love that has come near to us, and made
speech for itself there; the rounded neck, the dimpled arm,
move us by something more than their prettiness – by their
close kinship with all we have known of tenderness and peace.
The noblest nature sees the most of this *impersonal* expression
in beauty (it is needless to say that there are gentlemen with
whiskers dyed and undyed who see none of it whatever), and
for this reason, the noblest nature is often the most blinded to
the character of the one woman's soul that the beauty clothes.
Whence, I fear, the tragedy of human life is likely to continue
for a long time to come, in spite of mental philosophers who
are ready with the best receipts for avoiding all mistakes of
the kind.

Our good Adam had no fine words into which he could put
his feeling for Hetty: he could not disguise mystery in this way
with the appearance of knowledge; he called his love frankly a
mystery, as you have heard him. He only knew that the sight
and memory of her moved him deeply, touching the spring of
all love and tenderness, all faith and courage within him. How
could he imagine narrowness, selfishness, hardness in her? He

created the mind he believed in out of his own, which was large, unselfish, tender.

The hopes he felt about Hetty softened a little his feeling towards Arthur. Surely his attentions to Hetty must have been of a slight kind; they were altogether wrong, and such as no man in Arthur's position ought to have allowed himself, but they must have had an air of playfulness about them, which had probably blinded him to their danger, and had prevented them from laying any strong hold on Hetty's heart. As the new promise of happiness rose for Adam, his indignation and jealousy began to die out: Hetty was not made unhappy; he almost believed that she liked him best; and the thought sometimes crossed his mind that the friendship which had once seemed dead for ever might revive in the days to come, and he would not have to say 'good-bye' to the grand old woods, but would like them better because they were Arthur's. For this new promise of happiness, following so quickly on the shock of pain, had an intoxicating effect on the sober Adam, who had all his life been used to much hardship and moderate hope. Was he really going to have an easy lot after all? It seemed so; for at the beginning of November, Jonathan Burge, finding it impossible to replace Adam, had at last made up his mind to offer him a share in the business, without further condition than that he should continue to give his energies to it, and renounce all thought of having a separate business of his own. Son-in-law or no son-in-law, Adam had made himself too necessary to be parted with, and his headwork was so much more important to Burge than his skill in handicraft, that his having the management of the woods made little difference in the value of his services; and as to the bargains about the Squire's timber, it would be easy to call in a third person. Adam saw here an opening into a broadening path of prosperous work, such as he had thought of with ambitious longing ever since he was a lad: he might come to build a bridge, or a town-hall, or a factory, for he had always said to himself that Jonathan Burge's building business was like an acorn, which might be the mother of a great tree. So he gave his hand to Burge on that bargain, and went home with his mind full of happy visions, in which (my refined reader will perhaps be shocked when I say it) the image of Hetty hovered, and smiled over plans for seasoning timber at a trifling expense, calculations as to the cheapening of bricks per thousand by water-carriage,[4] and a favourite scheme for the strengthening of roofs and walls with a peculiar form of iron girder. What then? Adam's enthusiasm lay in these things; and our love is inwrought in our enthusiasm as electricity is inwrought in the air, exalting its power by a subtle presence.

Adam would be able to take a separate house now, and provide for his mother in the old one; his prospects would justify his marrying very soon, and if Dinah consented to have Seth, their mother would perhaps be more contented to live apart from Adam. But he told himself that he would not be hasty he would not try Hetty's feeling for him until it had had time to grow strong and firm. However, to-morrow, after church, he would go to the Hall Farm, and tell them the news. Mr Poyser, he knew, would like it better than a five-pound note, and he should see if Hetty's eyes brightened at it. The months would be short with all he had to fill his mind, and this foolish eagerness which had come over him of late must not hurry him into any premature words. Yet when he got home and told his mother the good news, and ate his supper, while she sat by almost crying for joy, and wanting him to eat twice as much as usual because of his good luck, he could not help preparing her gently for the coming change, by talking of the old house being too small for them all to go on living in it always.

CHAPTER XXXIV

The Betrothal

It was a dry Sunday, and really a pleasant day for the 2nd of November. There was no sunshine, but the clouds were high, and the wind was so still that the yellow leaves which fluttered down from the hedgerow elms must have fallen from pure decay. Nevertheless, Mrs Poyser did not go to church, for she had taken a cold too serious to be neglected; only two winters ago she had been laid up for weeks with a cold; and since his wife did not go to church, Mr Poyser considered that on the whole it would be as well for him to stay away too and 'keep her company'. He could perhaps have given no precise form to the reasons that determined this conclusion; but it is well known to all experienced minds that our firmest convictions are often dependent on subtle impressions for which words are quite too coarse a medium. However it was, no one from the Poyser family went to church that afternoon except Hetty and the boys; yet Adam was bold enough to join them after church, and say that he would walk home with them, though all the way through the village he appeared to be chiefly occupied with Marty and Tommy, telling them about the squirrels in Binton Coppice, and promising to take them there some day. But when they came to the fields he said to the boys, 'Now, then, which is the stoutest walker? Him as gets to th' home-gate first shall be the first to go with me to Binton Coppice on the donkey. But Tommy must have the start up to the next stile, because he's the smallest.'

Adam had never behaved so much like a determined lover before. As soon as the boys had both set off, he looked down at Hetty, and said, 'Won't you hang on my arm, Hetty?' in a pleading tone, as if he had already asked her and she had refused. Hetty looked up at him smilingly and put her round arm through his in a moment. It was nothing to her – putting her arm through Adam's; but she knew he cared a great deal about having her arm through his, and she wished him to care. Her heart beat no faster, and she looked at the half-bare hedgerows and the ploughed field with the same sense of oppressive dulness as before. But Adam scarcely felt that he was walking; he thought Hetty must know that he was pressing her arm a little – a very little; words rushed to his lips that he dared not utter – that he had made up his mind not to utter yet; and so he was silent for the length of that field. The calm patience with which he had once waited for Hetty's love, content only with her presence and the thought of the future, had forsaken him since that terrible shock nearly three months ago. The agitations of jealousy had given a new restlessness to his passion – had made fear and uncertainty too hard almost to bear. But though he might not speak to Hetty of his love, he would tell her about his new prospects, and see if she would be pleased. So when he was enough master of himself to talk, he said –

'I'm going to tell your uncle some news that'll surprise him, Hetty; and I think he'll be glad to hear it too.'

'What's that?' Hetty said, indifferently.

'Why, Mr Burge has offered me a share in his business, and I'm going to take it.'

There was a change in Hetty's face, certainly not produced by any agreeable impression from this news. In fact she felt a momentary annoyance and alarm; for she had so often heard it hinted by her uncle that Adam might have Mary Burge and a share in the business any day if he liked, that she associated the two objects now, and the thought immediately occurred that perhaps Adam had given her up because of what had happened lately, and had turned towards Mary Burge. With that thought, and before she had time to remember any reasons why it could not be true, came a new sense of forsakenness and disappointment: the one thing – the one person – her mind had rested on in its dull weariness, had slipped away from her, and peevish misery filled her eyes with tears. She was looking on

the ground, but Adam saw her face, saw the tears, and before
he had finished saying, 'Hetty, dear Hetty, what are you crying
for?' his eager rapid thought had flown through all the causes
conceivable to him, and had at last alighted on half the true
one. Hetty thought he was going to marry Mary Burge – she
didn't like him to marry – perhaps she didn't like him to marry
any one but herself? All caution was swept away – all reason
for it was gone, and Adam could feel nothing but trembling
joy. He leaned towards her and took her hand, as he said –

'I could afford to be married now, Hetty – I could make a
wife comfortable; but I shall never want to be married if you
won't have me.'

Hetty looked up at him, and smiled through her tears as she
had done to Arthur that first evening in the wood when she had
thought he was not coming, and yet he came. It was a feebler
relief, a feebler triumph she felt now, but the great dark eyes
and the sweet lips were as beautiful as ever, perhaps more
beautiful, for there was a more luxuriant womanliness about
Hetty of late. Adam could hardly believe in the happiness of
that moment. His right hand held her left, and he pressed her
arm close against his heart as he leaned down towards her.

'Do you really love me, Hetty? Will you be my own wife, to
love and take care of as long as I live?'

Hetty did not speak, but Adam's face was very close to hers,
and she put up her round cheek against his, like a kitten. She
wanted to be caressed – she wanted to feel as if Arthur were
with her again.

Adam cared for no words after that, and they hardly spoke
through the rest of the walk. He only said, 'I may tell your
uncle and aunt, mayn't I, Hetty?' and she said, 'Yes.'

The red fire-light on the hearth at the Hall Farm shone on
joyful faces that evening, when Hetty was gone up-stairs and
Adam took the opportunity of telling Mr and Mrs Poyser and
the grandfather that he saw his way to maintaining a wife now,
and that Hetty had consented to have him.

'I hope you have no objections against me for her husband,'
said Adam; 'I'm a poor man as yet, but she shall want nothing
as I can work for.'

'Objections?' said Mr Poyser, while the grandfather leaned forward and brought out his long 'Nay, nay.' 'What objections can we ha' to you, lad? Never mind your being poorish as yet; there's money in your head-piece as there's money i' the sown field, but it must ha' time. You'n got enough to begin on, and we can do a deal tow'rt the bit o' furniture you'll want. Thee'st got feathers and linen to spare – plenty, eh?'

This question was of course addressed to Mrs Poyser, who was wrapped up in a warm shawl, and was too hoarse to speak with her usual facility. At first she only nodded emphatically, but she was presently unable to resist the temptation to be more explicit.

'It 'ud be a poor tale if I hadna feathers and linen,' she said, hoarsely, 'when I never sell a fowl but what's plucked,[1] and the wheel's a-going every day o' the week.'

'Come, my wench,' said Mr Poyser, when Hetty came down, 'come and kiss us, and let us wish you luck.'

Hetty went very quietly and kissed the big good-natured man.

'There!' he said, patting her on the back, 'go and kiss your aunt and your grandfather. I'm as wishful t' have you settled well as if you was my own daughter; and so's your aunt, I'll be bound, for she's done by you this seven 'ear, Hetty, as if you'd been her own. Come, come, now,' he went on, becoming jocose, as soon as Hetty had kissed her aunt and the old man, 'Adam wants a kiss too, I'll warrant, and he's a right to one now.'

Hetty turned away, smiling, towards her empty chair.

'Come, Adam, then, take one,' persisted Mr Poyser, 'else y' arena half a man.'

Adam got up, blushing like a small maiden – great strong fellow as he was – and, putting his arm round Hetty, stooped down and gently kissed her lips.

It was a pretty scene in the red fire-light: for there were no candles; why should there be, when the fire was so bright, and was reflected from all the pewter and the polished oak? No one wanted to work on a Sunday evening. Even Hetty felt something like contentment in the midst of all this love. Adam's attachment to her, Adam's caress, stirred no passion in her, were no

longer enough to satisfy her vanity; but they were the best her
life offered her now – they promised her some change.

There was a great deal of discussion before Adam went away,
about the possibility of his finding a house that would do for
him to settle in. No house was empty except the one next to
Will Maskery's in the village, and that was too small for Adam
now. Mr Poyser insisted that the best plan would be for Seth
and his mother to move, and leave Adam in the old home,
which might be enlarged after a while, for there was plenty
of space in the woodyard and garden; but Adam objected to
turning his mother out.

'Well, well,' said Mr Poyser at last, 'we needna fix everything
to-night. We must take time to consider. You canna think o'
getting married afore Easter. I'm not for long courtships, but
there must be a bit o' time to make things comfortable.'

'Ay, to be sure,' said Mrs Poyser, in a hoarse whisper;
'Christian folks can't be married like cuckoos,[2] I reckon.'

'I'm a bit daunted, though,' said Mr Poyser, 'when I think as
we may have notice to quit, and belike be forced to take a farm
twenty mile off.'

'Eh,' said the old man, staring at the floor, and lifting his
hands up and down, while his arms rested on the elbows of his
chair, 'it's a poor tale if I mun leave th' ould spot, an' be buried
in a strange parish. An' you'll happen ha' double rates to pay,'
he added, looking up at his son.

'Well, thee mustna fret beforehand, father,' said Martin the
younger. 'Happen the Captain 'ull come home and make our
peace wi' th' old Squire. I build upo' that, for I know the
Captain 'll see folks righted if he can.'

CHAPTER XXXV

The Hidden Dread

It was a busy time for Adam – the time between the beginning of November and the beginning of February, and he could see little of Hetty, except on Sundays. But a happy time, nevertheless; for it was taking him nearer and nearer to March, when they were to be married; and all the little preparations for their new housekeeping marked the progress towards the longed-for day. Two new rooms had been 'run up' to the old house, for his mother and Seth were to live with them after all. Lisbeth had cried so piteously at the thought of leaving Adam, that he had gone to Hetty and asked her if, for the love of him, she would put up with his mother's ways, and consent to live with her. To his great delight, Hetty said, 'Yes; I'd as soon she lived with us as not.' Hetty's mind was oppressed at that moment with a worse difficulty than poor Lisbeth's ways, she could not care about them. So Adam was consoled for the disappointment he had felt when Seth had come back from his visit to Snowfield and said 'it was no use – Dinah's heart wasna turned towards marrying'. For when he told his mother that Hetty was willing they should all live together, and there was no more need of them to think of parting, she said, in a more contented tone than he had heard her speak in since it had been settled that he was to be married, 'Eh, my lad, I'll be as still as th' ould tabby, an' ne'er want to do aught but the offal work,[1] as *she* wonna like t' do. An' then, we needna part the platters an' things, as ha' stood on the shelf together sin' afore thee wast born.'

There was only one cloud that now and then came across Adam's sunshine: Hetty seemed unhappy sometimes. But to all his anxious, tender questions, she replied with an assurance that she was quite contented and wished nothing different; and the next time he saw her she was more lively than usual. It might be that she was a little overdone with work and anxiety now, for soon after Christmas Mrs Poyser had taken another cold, which had brought on inflammation, and this illness had confined her to her room all through January. Hetty had to manage everything down-stairs, and half supply Molly's place too, while that good damsel waited on her mistress; and she seemed to throw herself so entirely into her new functions, working with a grave steadiness which was new in her, that Mr Poyser often told Adam she was wanting to show him what a good housekeeper he would have; but he 'doubted the lass was o'er-doing it – she must have a bit o' rest when her aunt could come down-stairs'.

This desirable event of Mrs Poyser's coming down-stairs happened in the early part of February, when some mild weather thawed the last patch of snow on the Binton Hills. On one of these days, soon after her aunt came down, Hetty went to Treddleston to buy some of the wedding things which were wanting, and which Mrs Poyser had scolded her for neglecting, observing that she supposed 'it was because they were not for th' outside, else she'd ha' bought 'em fast enough'.

It was about ten o'clock when Hetty set off, and the slight hoar-frost that had whitened the hedges in the early morning had disappeared as the sun mounted the cloudless sky. Bright February days have a stronger charm of hope about them than any other days in the year. One likes to pause in the mild rays of the sun, and look over the gates at the patient plough-horses turning at the end of the furrow, and think that the beautiful year is all before one. The birds seem to feel just the same: their notes are as clear as the clear air. There are no leaves on the trees and hedgerows, but how green all the grassy fields are! and the dark purplish brown of the ploughed earth and of the bare branches is beautiful too. What a glad world this looks like, as one drives or rides along the valleys and over the hills! I have often thought so when, in foreign countries, where the fields and woods have looked to me like our English Loamshire – the rich land tilled with just as much care, the woods rolling down the gentle slopes to the green meadows – I have come on something by the roadside which has reminded me that I am not in Loamshire: an image of a great agony – the agony of the Cross.[2] It has stood perhaps by the clustering apple-blossoms, or in the broad sunshine by the cornfield, or at a turning by the wood where a clear brook was gurgling below; and surely, if there came a traveller to this world who knew nothing of the story of man's life upon it, this image of agony would seem to him strangely out of place in the midst of this joyous nature. He would not know that hidden behind the apple-blossoms, or among the golden corn, or under the shrouding boughs of the wood, there might be a human heart beating heavily with anguish; perhaps a young blooming girl, not knowing where to turn for refuge from swift-advancing shame; understanding no more of this life of ours than a foolish lost lamb wandering farther and farther in the nightfall on the lonely heath; yet tasting the bitterest of life's bitterness.

Such things are sometimes hidden among the sunny fields and behind the blossoming orchards; and the sound of the gurgling brook, if you came close to one spot behind a small bush, would be mingled for your ear with a despairing human sob. No wonder man's religion has much sorrow in it: no wonder he needs a suffering God.

Hetty, in her red cloak and warm bonnet, with her basket in her hand, is turning towards a gate by the side of the Treddleston road, but not that she may have a more lingering enjoyment of the sunshine, and think with hope of the long unfolding year. She hardly knows that the sun is shining; and for weeks, now, when she has hoped at all, it has been for something at which she herself trembles and shudders. She only wants to be out of the highroad, that she may walk slowly, and not care how her face looks, as she dwells on wretched thoughts; and through this gate she can get into a field-path behind the wide thick hedgerows. Her great dark eyes wander blankly over the fields like the eyes of one who is desolate, homeless, unloved, not the promised bride of a brave, tender man. But there are no tears in them: her tears were all wept away in the weary night, before she went to sleep. At the next stile the pathway branches off:

there are two roads before her – one along by the hedgerow, which will by-and-by lead her into the road again; the other across the fields, which will take her much farther out of the way into the Scantlands, low shrouded pastures where she will see nobody. She chooses this, and begins to walk a little faster, as if she had suddenly thought of an object towards which it was worth while to hasten. Soon she is in the Scantlands, where the grassy land slopes gradually downwards, and she leaves the level ground to follow the slope. Farther on there is a clump of trees on the low ground, and she is making her way towards it. No, it is not a clump of trees, but a dark shrouded pool, so full with the wintry rains that the under boughs of the elder-bushes lie low beneath the water. She sits down on the grassy bank, against the stooping stem of the great oak that hangs over the dark pool. She has thought of this pool often in the nights[3] of the month that has just gone by, and now at last she is come to see it. She clasps her hands round her knees and leans forward, and looks earnestly at it, as if trying to guess what sort of bed it would make for her young round limbs.

No, she has not courage to jump into that cold watery bed, and if she had, they might find her – they might find out why she had drowned herself. There is but one thing left to her: she must go away, go where they can't find her.

After the first on-coming of her great dread, some weeks after her betrothal to Adam, she had waited and waited, in the blind vague hope that something would happen to set her free from her terror; but she could wait no longer. All the force of her nature had been concentrated on the one effort of concealment, and she had shrunk with irresistible dread from every course that could tend towards a betrayal of her miserable secret. Whenever the thought of writing to Arthur had occurred to her, she had rejected it: he could do nothing for her that would shelter her from discovery and scorn among the relatives and neighbours who once more made all her world, now her airy dream had vanished. Her imagination no longer saw happiness with Arthur, for he could do nothing that would satisfy or soothe her pride. No, something else would happen – something *must* happen – to set her free from this dread. In young, childish, ignorant souls there is constantly this blind trust in some unshapen chance: it is as hard to a boy or girl to believe that a great wretchedness will actually befall them, as to believe that they will die.

But now necessity was pressing hard upon her – now the time of her marriage was close at hand – she could no longer rest in this blind trust. She must run away; she must hide herself where no familiar eyes could detect her; and *then* the terror of wandering out into the world, of which she knew nothing, made the possibility of going to Arthur a thought which brought some comfort with it. She felt so helpless now, so unable to fashion the future for herself, that the prospect of throwing herself on him had a relief in it which was stronger than her pride. As she sat by the pool, and shuddered at the dark cold water, the hope that he would receive her tenderly – that he would care for her and think for her – was like a sense of lulling warmth, that made her for the moment indifferent to everything else; and she began now to think of nothing but the scheme by which she should get away.

She had had a letter from Dinah lately, full of kind words about the coming marriage, which she had heard of from Seth; and when Hetty had read this letter aloud to her uncle, he had said, 'I wish Dinah 'ud come again now, for she'd be a comfort to your aunt when you're gone. What do you think, my wench, o' going to see her as soon as you can be spared, and persuading her to come back wi' you? You might happen persuade her wi' telling her as her aunt wants her, for all she writes o' not being able to come.' Hetty had not liked the thought of going to Snowfield, and felt no longing to see Dinah, so she only said, 'It's so far off, uncle.' But now she thought this proposed visit would serve as a pretext for going away. She would tell her aunt when she got home again, that she should like the change of going to Snowfield for a week or ten days. And then, when she got to Stoniton, where nobody knew her, she would ask for the coach that would take her on the way to Windsor. Arthur was at Windsor, and she would go to him.

As soon as Hetty had determined on this scheme, she rose from the grassy bank of the pool, took up her basket, and went on her way to Treddleston, for she must buy the wedding things she had come out for, though she would never want them. She must be careful not to raise any suspicion that she was going to run away.

Mrs Poyser was quite agreeably surprised that Hetty wished to go and see Dinah, and try to bring her back to stay over the wedding. The sooner she went the better, since the weather was pleasant now; and Adam, when he came in the evening, said, if Hetty could set off to-morrow, he would make time to go with her to Treddleston, and see her safe into the Stoniton coach.

'I wish I could go with you and take care of you, Hetty,' he said, the next morning, leaning in at the coach door; 'but you won't stay much beyond a week – the time 'll seem long.'

He was looking at her fondly, and his strong hand held hers in its grasp. Hetty felt a sense of protection in his presence – she was used to it now: if she could have had the past undone, and known no other love than her quiet liking for Adam! The tears rose as she gave him the last look.

'God bless her for loving me,' said Adam, as he went on his way to work again, with Gyp at his heels.

But Hetty's tears were not for Adam – not for the anguish that would come upon him when he found she was gone from him for ever. They were for the misery of her own lot, which took her away from this brave tender man who offered up his whole life to her, and threw her, a poor helpless suppliant, on the man who would think it a misfortune that she was obliged to cling to him.

At three o'clock that day, when Hetty was on the coach that was to take her, they said, to Leicester – part of the long, long way to Windsor – she felt dimly that she might be travelling all this weary journey towards the beginning of new misery.

Yet Arthur was at Windsor; he would surely not be angry with her. If he did not mind about her as he used to do, he had promised to be good to her.

BOOK FIFTH

CHAPTER XXXVI

The Journey in Hope

A long, lonely journey, with sadness in the heart; away from the familiar to the strange; that is a hard and dreary thing even to the rich, the strong, the instructed: a hard thing, even when we are called by duty, not urged by dread.

What was it then to Hetty? With her poor narrow thoughts, no longer melting into vague hopes, but pressed upon by the chill of definite fear; repeating again and again the same small round of memories – shaping again and again the same childish, doubtful images of what was to come – seeing nothing in this wide world but the little history of her own pleasures and pains; with so little money in her pocket, and the way so long and difficult. Unless she could afford always to go in the coaches – and she felt sure she could not, for the journey to Stoniton was more expensive than she had expected – it was plain that she must trust to carriers' carts or slow waggons;[1] and what a time it would be before she could get to the end of her journey! The burly old coachman from Oakbourne, seeing such a pretty young woman among the outside passengers, had invited her to come and sit beside him; and feeling that it became him as a man and a coachman to open the dialogue with a joke, he applied himself as soon as they were off the stones to the elaboration of one suitable in all respects. After many cuts with his whip and glances at Hetty out of the corner of his eye, he lifted his lips above the edge of his wrapper and said –

'He's pretty nigh six foot, I'll be bound, isna he, now?'

'Who?' said Hetty, rather startled.

'Why, the sweetheart as you've left behind, or else him as you're goin' arter – which is it?'

Hetty felt her face flushing and then turning pale. She thought this coachman must know something about her. He must know Adam, and might tell him where she was gone, for it is difficult to country people to believe that those who make a figure in their own parish are not known everywhere else, and it was equally difficult to Hetty to understand that chance words could happen to apply closely to her circumstances. She was too frightened to speak.

'Hegh, hegh!' said the coachman, seeing that his joke was not so gratifying as he had expected, 'you munna take it too ser'ous; if he's behaved ill, get another. Such a pretty lass as you can get a sweetheart any day.'

Hetty's fear was allayed by-and-by, when she found that the coachman made no further allusion to her personal concerns; but it still had the effect of preventing her from asking him what were the places on the road to Windsor. She told him she was only going a little way out of Stoniton, and when she got down at the inn where the coach stopped, she hastened away with her basket to another part of the town. When she had formed her plan of going to Windsor, she had not foreseen any difficulties except that of getting away; and after she had overcome this by proposing the visit to Dinah, her thoughts flew to the meeting with Arthur, and the question how he would behave to her – not resting on any probable incidents of the journey. She was too entirely ignorant of travelling to imagine any of its details, and with all her store of money – her three guineas – in her pocket, she thought herself amply provided. It was not until she found how much it cost her to get to Stoniton that she began to be alarmed about the journey, and then, for the first time, she felt her ignorance as to the places that must be passed on her way. Oppressed with this new alarm, she walked along the grim Stoniton streets, and at last turned into a shabby little inn, where she hoped to get a cheap lodging for the night. Here she asked the landlord if he could tell her what places she must go to, to get to Windsor.

'Well, I can't rightly say. Windsor must be pretty nigh London, for it's where the king lives,'[2] was the answer. 'Any-how, you'd best go t' Ashby next – that's south'ard. But there's

as many places from here to London as there's houses in
Stoniton, by what I can make out. I've never been no traveller
myself. But how comes a lone young woman like you, to be
thinking o' taking such a journey as that?'

'I'm going to my brother – he's a soldier at Windsor,' said
Hetty, frightened at the landlord's questioning look. 'I can't
afford to go by the coach; do you think there's a cart goes
toward Ashby in the morning?'

'Yes, there may be carts if anybody knowed where they
started from; but you might run over the town before you
found out. You'd best set off and walk, and trust to summat
overtaking you.'

Every word sank like lead on Hetty's spirits; she saw the
journey stretch bit by bit before her now; even to get to Ashby
seemed a hard thing: it might take the day, for what she knew,
and that was nothing to the rest of the journey. But it must be
done – she must get to Arthur: oh, how she yearned to be again
with somebody who would care for her! She who had never
got up in the morning without the certainty of seeing familiar
faces, people on whom she had an acknowledged claim; whose
farthest journey had been to Rosseter on the pillion with her
uncle; whose thoughts had always been taking holiday in
dreams of pleasure, because all the business of her life was
managed for her: – this kitten-like Hetty, who till a few months
ago had never felt any other grief than that of envying Mary
Burge a new ribbon, or being girded at by her aunt for neglecting Totty, must now make her toilsome way in loneliness,
her peaceful home left behind for ever, and nothing but a
tremulous hope of distant refuge before her. Now for the first
time, as she lay down to-night in the strange hard bed, she felt
that her home had been a happy one, that her uncle had been
very good to her, that her quiet lot at Hayslope among the
things and people she knew, with her little pride in her one best
gown and bonnet, and nothing to hide from any one, was what
she would like to wake up to as a reality, and find that all the
feverish life she had known besides was a short nightmare. She
thought of all she had left behind with yearning regret for her
own sake: her own misery filled her heart: there was no room

in it for other people's sorrow. And yet, before the cruel letter, Arthur had been so tender and loving: the memory of that had still a charm for her, though it was no more than a soothing draught that just made pain bearable. For Hetty could conceive no other existence for herself in future than a hidden one, and a hidden life, even with love, would have had no delights for her; still less a life mingled with shame. She knew no romances, and had only a feeble share in the feelings which are the source of romance, so that well-read ladies may find it difficult to understand her state of mind. She was too ignorant of every-thing beyond the simple notions and habits in which she had been brought up, to have any more definite idea of her probable future than that Arthur would take care of her somehow, and shelter her from anger and scorn. He would not marry her and make her a lady; and apart from that she could think of nothing he could give towards which she looked with longing and ambition.

The next morning she rose early, and taking only some milk and bread for her breakfast, set out to walk on the road towards Ashby, under a leaden-coloured sky, with a narrowing streak of yellow, like a departing hope, on the edge of the horizon. Now in her faintness of heart at the length and difficulty of her journey, she was most of all afraid of spending her money, and becoming so destitute that she would have to ask people's charity; for Hetty had the pride not only of a proud nature but of a proud class – the class that pays the most poor-rates,[3] and most shudders at the idea of profiting by a poor-rate. It had not yet occurred to her that she might get money for her locket and earrings which she carried with her, and she applied all her small arithmetic and knowledge of prices to calculating how many meals and how many rides were contained in her two guineas, and the odd shillings, which had a melancholy look, as if they were the pale ashes of the other bright-flaming coin.

For the first few miles out of Stoniton she walked on bravely, always fixing on some tree or gate or projecting bush at the most distant visible point in the road as a goal, and feeling a faint joy when she had reached it. But when she came to the fourth milestone,[4] the first she had happened to notice among the long grass by the roadside, and read that she was still only four miles beyond Stoniton, her courage sank. She had come only this little way, and yet felt tired, and almost hungry again in the keen morning air; for ¹ough Hetty was accustomed to much movement and exertion indoors, she was not used to long walks, which produce quite a different sort of fatigue from that of household activity. As she was looking at the milestone she felt some drops falling on her face – it was beginning to rain. Here was a new trouble which had not entered into her sad thoughts before; and quite weighed down by this sudden addition to her burden, she sat down on the step of a stile and began to sob hysterically. The beginning of hardship is like the first taste of bitter food – it seems for a moment unbearable; yet, if there is nothing else to satisfy our hunger, we take another bite and find it possible to go on. When Hetty recovered from her burst of weeping, she rallied her fainting courage: it was raining, and she must try to get on to a village where she might find rest and shelter. Presently, as she walked on wearily, she heard the rumbling of heavy wheels behind her; a covered waggon was coming, creeping slowly along with a slouching driver cracking his whip beside the horses. She waited for it, thinking that if the waggoner were not a very sour-looking man, she would ask him to take her up. As the waggon approached her, the driver had fallen behind, but there was something in the front of the big vehicle which encouraged her. At any previous moment in her life she would not have noticed it; but now, the new susceptibility that suffering had awakened in her caused this object to impress her strongly. It was only a small white-and-liver coloured spaniel which sat on the front ledge of the waggon, with large timid eyes, and an incessant trembling in the body, such as you may have seen in some of these small creatures. Hetty cared little for animals, as you know, but at this moment she felt as if the helpless timid creature had some fellowship with her, and without being quite aware of the reason, she was less doubtful about speaking to the driver, who now came forward – a large ruddy man, with a sack over his shoulders by way of scarf or mantle.

'Could you take me up in your waggon, if you're going towards Ashby?' said Hetty. 'I'll pay you for it.'

'Aw,' said the big fellow, with that slowly dawning smile which belongs to heavy faces, 'I can take y' up fawst enough wi'out bein' paid for't if you dooant mind lyin' a bit closish a-top o' the wool-packs. Where do you coom from? and what do you want at Ashby?'

'I come from Stoniton. I'm going a long way – to Windsor.'

'What! arter some service, or what?'

'Going to my brother – he's a soldier there.'

'Well, I'm going no furder nor Leicester – and fur enough too – but I'll take you, if you dooant mind being a bit long on the road. Th' hosses wooant feel *your* weight no more nor they feel the little doog there, as I puck up on the road a fortni't agoo. He war lost, I b'lieve, an's been all of a tremble iver sin'. Come, gi' us your basket, an' come behind and let me put y' in.'

To lie on the wool-packs, with a cranny left between the curtains of the awning to let in the air, was luxury to Hetty now, and she half slept away the hours till the driver came to ask her if she wanted to get down and have 'some victual'; he himself was going to eat his dinner at this 'public'. Late at night they reached Leicester, and so this second day of Hetty's journey was past. She had spent no money except what she had paid for her food, but she felt that this slow journeying would be intolerable for her another day, and in the morning she found her way to a coach-office to ask about the road to Windsor, and see if it would cost her too much to go part of the distance by coach again. Yes! the distance was too great – the coaches were too dear – she must give them up; but the elderly clerk at the office, touched by her pretty anxious face, wrote down for her the names of the chief places she must pass through. This was the only comfort she got in Leicester, for the men stared at her as she went along the street, and for the first time in her life Hetty wished no one would look at her. She set out walking again; but this day she was fortunate, for she was soon over-taken by a carrier's cart which carried her to Hinckley, and by the help of a return chaise, with a drunken postilion, – who

frightened her by driving like Jehu the son of Nimshi,[5] and
shouting hilarious remarks at her, twisting himself backwards
on his saddle, – she was before night in the heart of woody
Warwickshire: but still almost a hundred miles from Windsor,
they told her. Oh what a large world it was, and what hard
work for her to find her way in it! She went by mistake to
Stratford-on-Avon, finding Stratford set down in her list of
places, and then she was told she had come a long way out of
the right road. It was not till the fifth day that she got to Stony
Stratford.[6] That seems but a slight journey as you look at the
map, or remember your own pleasant travels to and from the
meadowy banks of the Avon. But how wearily long it was to
Hetty! It seemed to her as if this country of flat fields and
hedgerows, and dotted houses, and villages, and market-towns
– all so much alike to her indifferent eyes – must have no end,
and she must go on wandering among them for ever, waiting
tired at toll-gates[7] for some cart to come, and then finding the
cart went only a little way – a very little way – to the miller's a
mile off perhaps; and she hated going into the public-houses,
where she must go to get food and ask questions, because there
were always men lounging there, who stared at her and joked
her rudely. Her body was very weary too with these days of
new fatigue and anxiety; they had made her look more pale
and worn than all the time of hidden dread she had gone
through at home. When at last she reached Stony Stratford,
her impatience and weariness had become too strong for her
economical caution; she determined to take the coach for the
rest of the way, though it should cost her all her remaining
money. She would need nothing at Windsor but to find Arthur.
When she had paid the fare for the last coach, she had only a
shilling; and as she got down at the sign of the Green Man in
Windsor[8] at twelve o'clock in the middle of the seventh day,
hungry and faint, the coachman came up, and begged her to
'remember him'. She put her hand in her pocket, and took out
the shilling, but the tears came with the sense of exhaustion
and the thought that she was giving away her last means of
getting food, which she really required before she could go in
search of Arthur. As she held out the shilling, she lifted up her

dark tear-filled eyes to the coachman's face and said, 'Can you give me back sixpence?'

'No, no,' he said, gruffly, 'never mind – put the shilling up again.'

The landlord of the Green Man had stood near enough to witness this scene, and he was a man whose abundant feeding served to keep his good-nature, as well as his person, in high condition. And that lovely tearful face of Hetty's would have found out the sensitive fibre in most men.

'Come, young woman, come in,' he said, 'and have a drop o' something; you're pretty well knocked up: I can see that.'

He took her into the bar and said to his wife, 'Here, missis, take this young woman into the parlour; she's a little over-come,' – for Hetty's tears were falling fast. They were merely hysterical tears: she thought she had no reason for weeping now, and was vexed that she was too weak and tired to help it. She was at Windsor at last, not far from Arthur.

She looked with eager, hungry eyes at the bread and meat and beer that the landlady brought her, and for some minutes she forgot everything else in the delicious sensations of satisfying hunger and recovering from exhaustion. The landlady sat oppo-site to her as she ate, and looked at her earnestly. No wonder: Hetty had thrown off her bonnet, and her curls had fallen down: her face was all the more touching in its youth and beauty because of its weary look; and the good woman's eyes presently wandered to her figure, which in her hurried dressing on her journey she had taken no pains to conceal; moreover, the stranger's eye detects what the familiar unsuspecting eye leaves unnoticed.

'Why, you're not very fit for travelling,' she said, glancing while she spoke at Hetty's ringless hand. 'Have you come far?'

'Yes,' said Hetty, roused by this question to exert more self-command, and feeling the better for the food she had taken. 'I've come a good long way, and it's very tiring. But I'm better now. Could you tell me which way to go to his place?' Here Hetty took from her pocket a bit of paper: it was the end of Arthur's letter on which he had written his address.

While she was speaking, the landlord had come in, and had

begun to look at her as earnestly as his wife had done. He took up the piece of paper which Hetty handed across the table, and read the address.

'Why, what do you want at this house?' he said. It is in the nature of innkeepers, and all men who have no pressing business of their own, to ask as many questions as possible before giving any information.

'I want to see a gentleman as is there,' said Hetty.

'But there's no gentleman there,' returned the landlord. 'It's shut up – been shut up this fortnight. What gentleman is it you want? Perhaps I can let you know where to find him.'

'It's Captain Donnithorne,' said Hetty, tremulously, her heart beginning to beat painfully at this disappointment of her hope that she should find Arthur at once.

'Captain Donnithorne? Stop a bit,' said the landlord, slowly. 'Was he in the Loamshire Militia? A tall young officer with a fairish skin and reddish whiskers – and had a servant by the name o' Pym?'

'Oh yes,' said Hetty; 'you know him – where is he?'

'A fine sight o' miles away from here: the Loamshire Militia's gone to Ireland;⁹ it's been gone this fortnight.'

'Look there! she's fainting,' said the landlady, hastening to support Hetty, who had lost her miserable consciousness and looked like a beautiful corpse. They carried her to the sofa and loosened her dress.

'Here's a bad business, I suspect,' said the landlord, as he brought in some water.

'Ah, it's plain enough what sort of business it is,' said the wife. 'She's not a common flaunting dratchell, I can see that. She looks like a respectable country girl, and she comes from a good way off, to judge by her tongue. She talks something like that ostler we had that come from the north: he was as honest a fellow as we ever had about the house – they're all honest folks in the north.'

'I never saw a prettier young woman in my life,' said the husband. 'She's like a pictur in a shop-winder. It goes to one's 'eart to look at her.'

'It 'ud have been a good deal better for her if she'd been

uglier and had more conduct,' said the landlady, who on any charitable construction must have been supposed to have more 'conduct' than beauty. 'But she's coming to again. Fetch a drop more water.'

CHAPTER XXXVII

The Journey in Despair

Hetty was too ill through the rest of that day for any questions to be addressed to her – too ill even to think with any distinctness of the evils that were to come. She only felt that all her hope was crushed, and that instead of having found a refuge she had only reached the borders of a new wilderness where no goal lay before her. The sensations of bodily sickness, in a comfortable bed, and with the tendance of the good-natured landlady, made a sort of respite for her; such a respite as there is in the faint weariness which obliges a man to throw himself on the sand, instead of toiling onward under the scorching sun.

But when sleep and rest had brought back the strength necessary for the keenness of mental suffering, – when she lay the next morning looking at the growing light which was like a cruel taskmaster returning to urge from her a fresh round of hated hopeless labour, – she began to think what course she must take, to remember that all her money was gone, to look at the prospect of further wandering among strangers with the new clearness shed on it by the experience of her journey to Windsor. But which way could she turn? It was impossible for her to enter into any service, even if she could obtain it: there was nothing but immediate beggary before her. She thought of a young woman who had been found against the church wall at Hayslope one Sunday, nearly dead with cold and hunger – a tiny infant in her arms: the woman was rescued and taken to the parish.[1] 'The parish!' You can perhaps hardly understand the effect of that word on a mind like Hetty's, brought up among people who were somewhat hard in their feelings even towards poverty, who lived among the fields, and had little pity

for want and rags as a cruel inevitable fate such as they sometimes seem in cities, but held them a mark of idleness and vice
– and it was idleness and vice that brought burthens on the
parish. To Hetty the 'parish' was next to the prison in obloquy;
and to ask anything of strangers – to beg – lay in the same
far-off hideous region of intolerable shame that Hetty had all
her life thought it impossible she could ever come near. But
now the remembrance of that wretched woman whom she had
seen herself, on her way from church, being carried into Joshua
Rann's, came back upon her with the new terrible sense that
there was very little now to divide *her* from the same lot. And
the dread of bodily hardship mingled with the dread of shame;
for Hetty had the luxurious nature of a round, soft-coated pet
animal.

How she yearned to be back in her safe home again, cherished
and cared for as she had always been! Her aunt's scolding about
trifles would have been music to her ears now: she longed for
it: she used to hear it in a time when she had only trifles to hide.
Could she be the same Hetty that used to make up the butter
in the dairy with the Gueldres roses peeping in at the window
– she, a runaway whom her friends would not open their doors
to again, lying in this strange bed, with the knowledge that she
had no money to pay for what she received, and must offer
those strangers some of the clothes in her basket? It was then
she thought of her locket and earrings, and seeing her pocket[2]
lie near, she reached it and spread the contents on the bed
before her. There were the locket and earrings in the little
velvet-lined boxes, and with them there was a beautiful silver
thimble which Adam had bought her, the words 'Remember
me' making the ornament of the border; a steel purse, with her
one shilling in it, and a small red-leather case, fastening with a
strap. Those beautiful little earrings, with their delicate pearls
and garnet, that she had tried in her ears with such longing in
the bright sunshine on the 30th of July! She had no longing to
put them in her ears now: her head with its dark rings of hair
lay back languidly on the pillow, and the sadness that rested
about her brow and eyes was something too hard for regretful
memory. Yet she put her hands up to her ears: it was because

XXXVII THE JOURNEY IN DESPAIR

there were some thin gold rings in them, which were also worth a little money. Yes, she could surely get some money for her ornaments: those Arthur had given her must have cost a great deal of money. The landlord and landlady had been good to her; perhaps they would help her to get the money for these things.

But this money would not keep her long: what should she do when it was gone? Where should she go? The horrible thought of want and beggary drove her once to think she would go back to her uncle and aunt, and ask them to forgive her and have pity on her. But she shrank from that idea again, as she might have shrunk from scorching metal: she could never endure that shame before her uncle and aunt, before Mary Burge, and the servants at the Chase, and the people at Broxton, and everybody who knew her. They should never know what had happened to her. What *could* she do? She would go away from Windsor – travel again as she had done the last week, and get among the flat green fields with the high hedges round them, where nobody could see her or know her; and there, perhaps, when there was nothing else she could do, she should get courage to drown herself in some pond like that in the Scantlands. Yes, she would get away from Windsor as soon as possible: she didn't like these people at the inn to know about her, to know that she had come to look for Captain Donnithorne: she must think of some reason to tell them why she had asked for him.

With this thought she began to put the things back into her pocket, meaning to get up and dress before the landlady came to her. She had her hand on the red-leather case, when it occurred to her that there might be something in this case which she had forgotten – something worth selling; for without knowing what she should do with her life, she craved the means of living as long as possible; and when we desire eagerly to find something, we are apt to search for it in hopeless places. No, there was nothing but common needles and pins, and dried tulip-petals between the paper leaves where she had written down her little money-accounts. But on one of these leaves there was a name, which, often as she had seen it before, now flashed on Hetty's mind like a newly-discovered message. The name was – *Dinah Morris, Snowfield.* There was a text above it, written, as well as the name, by Dinah's own hand with a little pencil, one evening that they were sitting together and Hetty happened to have the red case lying open before her. Hetty did not read the text now: she was only arrested by the name. Now, for the first time she remembered without indifference the affectionate kindness Dinah had shown her, and those words of Dinah in the bed-chamber – that Hetty must think of her as a friend in trouble. Suppose she were to go to Dinah, and ask her to help her? Dinah did not think about things as other people did: she was a mystery to Hetty, but Hetty knew she was always kind. She couldn't imagine Dinah's face turning away from her in dark reproof or scorn, Dinah's voice willingly speaking ill of her, or rejoicing in her misery, as a punishment. Dinah did not seem to belong to that world of Hetty's, whose glance she dreaded like scorching fire. But even to her Hetty shrank from beseeching and confession: she could not prevail on herself to say, 'I will go to Dinah'; she only thought of that as a possible alternative, if she had not courage for death.

The good landlady was amazed when she saw Hetty come down-stairs soon after herself, neatly dressed, and looking resolutely self-possessed. Hetty told her she was quite well this morning: she had only been very tired and overcome with her journey, for she had come a long way to ask about her brother, who had run away, and they thought he was gone for a soldier, and Captain Donnithorne might know, for he had been very kind to her brother once. It was a lame story, and the landlady looked doubtfully at Hetty as she told it; but there was a resolute air of self-reliance about her this morning, so different from the helpless prostration of yesterday, that the landlady hardly knew how to make a remark that might seem like prying into other people's affairs. She only invited her to sit down to breakfast with them, and in the course of it Hetty brought out her earrings and locket, and asked the landlord if he could help her to get money for them: her journey, she said, had cost her much more than she expected, and now she had no money to get back to her friends, which she wanted to do at once.

It was not the first time the landlady had seen the ornaments, for she had examined the contents of Hetty's pocket yesterday, and she and her husband had discussed the fact of a country girl having these beautiful things, with a stronger conviction than ever that Hetty had been miserably deluded by the fine young officer.

'Well,' said the landlord, when Hetty had spread the precious trifles before him, 'we might take 'em to the jeweller's shop, for there's one not far off; but Lord bless you, they wouldn't give you a quarter o' what the things are worth. And you wouldn't like to part with 'em?' he added, looking at her inquiringly.

'Oh, I don't mind,' said Hetty, hastily, 'so as I can get money to go back.'

'And they might think the things were stolen, as you wanted to sell 'em,' he went on; 'for it isn't usual for a young woman like you to have fine jewellery like that.'

The blood rushed to Hetty's face with anger. 'I belong to respectable folks,' she said; 'I'm not a thief.'

'No, that you aren't, I'll be bound,' said the landlady; 'and you'd no call to say that', looking indignantly at her husband. 'The things were gev to her: that's plain enough to be seen.'

'I didn't mean as I thought so,' said the husband, apologetically, 'but I said it was what the jeweller might think, and so he wouldn't be offering much money for 'em.'

'Well,' said the wife, 'suppose you were to advance some money on the things yourself, and then if she liked to redeem 'em when she got home, she could. But if we heard nothing from her after two months, we might do as we liked with 'em.'

I will not say that in this accommodating proposition the landlady had no regard whatever to the possible reward of her good-nature in the ultimate possession of the locket and earrings: indeed, the effect they would have in that case on the mind of the grocer's wife had presented itself with remarkable vividness to her rapid imagination. The landlord took up the ornaments and pushed out his lips in a meditative manner. He wished Hetty well, doubtless; but pray, how many of your well-wishers would decline to make a little gain out of you? Your landlady is sincerely affected at parting with you, respects you highly, and will really rejoice if any one else is generous to you; but at the same time she hands you a bill by which she gains as high a percentage as possible.

'How much money do you want to get home with, young woman?' said the well-wisher, at length.

'Three guineas,' answered Hetty, fixing on the sum she set out with, for want of any other standard, and afraid of asking too much.

'Well, I've no objections to advance you three guineas,' said the landlord; 'and if you like to send it me back and get the jewellery again, you can, you know: the Green Man isn't going to run away.'

'Oh yes, I'll be very glad if you'll give me that,' said Hetty, relieved at the thought that she would not have to go to the jeweller's, and be stared at and questioned.

'But if you want the things again, you'll write before long,' said the landlady, 'because when two months are up, we shall make up our minds as you don't want 'em.'

'Yes,' said Hetty, indifferently.

The husband and wife were equally content with this arrangement. The husband thought, if the ornaments were not redeemed, he could make a good thing of it by taking them to London and selling them: the wife thought she would coax the good man into letting her keep them. And they were accommodating Hetty, poor thing: – a pretty, respectable-looking young woman, apparently in a sad case. They declined to take anything for her food and bed: she was quite welcome. And at eleven o'clock Hetty said 'Good-bye' to them, with the same quiet, resolute air she had worn all the morning, mounting the coach that was to take her twenty miles back along the way she had come.

There is a strength of self-possession which is the sign that the last hope has departed. Despair no more leans on others than perfect contentment, and in despair pride ceases to be counteracted by the sense of dependence.

Hetty felt that no one could deliver her from the evils that would make life hateful to her; and no one, she said to herself, should ever know her misery and humiliation. No; she would not confess even to Dinah: she would wander out of sight, and drown herself where her body would never be found, and no one should know what had become of her.

When she got off this coach, she began to walk again, and take cheap rides in carts, and get cheap meals, going on and on without distinct purpose, yet strangely, by some fascination, taking the way she had come, though she was determined not to go back to her own country. Perhaps it was because she had fixed her mind on the grassy Warwickshire fields, with the bushy tree-studded hedgerows that made a hiding-place even in this leafless season. She went more slowly than she came, often getting over the stiles, and sitting for hours under the hedgerows, looking before her with blank, beautiful eyes; fancying herself at the edge of a hidden pool, low down, like that in the Scantlands; wondering if it were very painful to be drowned, and if there would be anything worse after death than what she dreaded in life. Religious doctrines had taken no hold on Hetty's mind: she was one of those numerous people who have had godfathers and godmothers, learned their catechism, been confirmed, and gone to church every Sunday,[3] and yet, for any practical result of strength in life, or trust in death, have never appropriated a single Christian idea or Christian feeling. You would misunderstand her thoughts during these wretched days, if you imagined that they were influenced either by religious fears or religious hopes.

She chose to go to Stratford-on-Avon again, where she had gone before by mistake; for she remembered some grassy fields on her former way towards it – fields among which she thought she might find just the sort of pool she had in her mind. Yet she took care of her money still; she carried her basket: death seemed still a long way off, and life was so strong in her! She craved food and rest – she hastened towards them at the very moment she was picturing to herself the bank from which she would leap towards death. It was already five days since she had left Windsor, for she had wandered about, always avoiding speech or questioning looks, and recovering her air of proud self-dependence whenever she was under observation, choosing her decent lodging at night, and dressing herself neatly in the morning, and setting off on her way steadily, or remaining under shelter if it rained, as if she had a happy life to cherish.

And yet, even in her most self-conscious moments, the face was sadly different from that which had smiled at itself in the old specked glass, or smiled at others when they glanced at it admiringly. A hard and even fierce look had come in the eyes, though their lashes were as long as ever, and they had all their dark brightness. And the cheek was never dimpled with smiles now. It was the same rounded, pouting, childish prettiness, but with all love and belief in love departed from it – the sadder for its beauty, like that wondrous Medusa-face,[4] with the passionate, passionless lips.

At last she was among the fields she had been dreaming of, on a long narrow pathway leading towards a wood. If there should be a pool in that wood! It would be better hidden than one in the fields. No, it was not a wood, only a wild brake, where there had once been gravel-pits, leaving mounds and hollows studded with brushwood and small trees. She roamed up and down, thinking there was perhaps a pool in every hollow before she came to it, till her limbs were weary, and she sat down to rest. The afternoon was far advanced, and the leaden sky was darkening, as if the sun were setting behind it. After a little while Hetty started up again, feeling that darkness would soon come on; and she must put off finding the pool till to-morrow, and make her way to some shelter for the night. She had quite lost her way in the fields, and might as well go in one direction as another, for aught she knew. She walked through field after field, and no village, no house was in sight; but *there*, at the corner of this pasture, there was a break in the hedges; the land seemed to dip down a little, and two trees leaned towards each other across the opening. Hetty's heart gave a great beat as she thought there must be a pool there. She walked towards it heavily over the tufted grass, with pale lips and a sense of trembling: it was as if the thing were come in spite of herself, instead of being the object of her search.

There it was, black under the darkening sky: no motion, no sound near. She set down her basket, and then sank down herself on the grass, trembling. The pool had its wintry depth now:[5] by the time it got shallow, as she remembered the pools did at Hayslope, in the summer, no one could find out that it was her body. But then there was her basket – she must hide that too: she must throw it into the water – make it heavy with stones first, and then throw it in. She got up to look about for stones, and soon brought five or six, which she laid down beside her basket, and then sat down again. There was no need to hurry – there was all the night to drown herself in. She sat leaning her elbow on the basket. She was weary, hungry. There were some buns in her basket – three, which she had supplied herself with at the place where she ate her dinner. She took them out now, and ate them eagerly, and then sat still again, looking at the pool. The soothed sensation that came over her from the satisfaction of her hunger, and this fixed dreamy attitude, brought on drowsiness, and presently her head sank down on her knees. She was fast asleep.

When she awoke it was deep night, and she felt chill. She was frightened at this darkness – frightened at the long night before her. If she *could* but throw herself into the water! No, not yet. She began to walk about that she might get warm again, as if she would have more resolution then. Oh how long the time was in that darkness! The bright hearth and the warmth and the voices of home, – the secure uprising and lying down, – the familiar fields, the familiar people, the Sundays and holidays with their simple joys of dress and feasting, – all the sweets of her young life rushed before her now, and she seemed to be stretching her arms towards them across a great gulf. She set her teeth when she thought of Arthur: she cursed him, without knowing what her cursing would do: she wished he too might know desolation, and cold, and a life of shame that he dared not end by death.

The horror of this cold, and darkness, and solitude – out of all human reach – became greater every long minute: it was almost as if she were dead already, and knew that she was dead, and longed to get back to life again. But no: she was alive still; she had not taken the dreadful leap. She felt a strange contradictory wretchedness and exultation: wretchedness, that she did not dare to face death; exultation, that she was still in life – that she might yet know light and warmth again. She walked backwards and forwards to warm herself, beginning to discern something of the objects around her, as her eyes became accustomed to the night: the darker line of the hedge, the rapid motion of some living creature – perhaps a field-mouse – rushing across the grass. She no longer felt as if the darkness hedged her in: she thought she could walk back across the field, and get over the stile; and then, in the very next field, she thought she remembered there was a hovel of furze[6] near a sheepfold. If she could get into that hovel, she would be warmer; she could pass the night there, for that was what Alick did at Hayslope in lambing-time. The thought of this hovel brought the energy of a new hope: she took up her basket and walked across the field, but it was some time before she got in the right direction for the stile. The exercise and the occupation of finding the stile were a stimulus to her, however, and lightened the horror of the darkness and solitude. There were sheep in the next field, and she startled a group as she set down her basket and got over the stile; and the sound of their movement comforted her, for it assured her that her impression was right: this *was* the field where she had seen the hovel, for it was the field where the sheep were. Right on along the path, and she would get to it. She reached the opposite gate, and felt her way along its rails, and the rails of the sheepfold, till her hand encountered the pricking of the gorsy wall. Delicious sensation! She had found the shelter: she groped her way, touching the prickly gorse, to the door, and pushed it open. It was an ill-smelling close place, but warm, and there was straw on the ground: Hetty sank down on the straw with a sense of escape. Tears came – she had never shed tears before since she left Windsor – tears and sobs of hysterical joy that she had still hold of life, that she was still on the familiar earth, with the sheep near her. The very consciousness of her own limbs was a delight to her: she turned up her sleeves, and kissed her arms with the passionate love of life. Soon warmth and weariness lulled her in the midst of her sobs, and she fell continually into dozing, fancying herself at the brink of the pool again – fancying that she had jumped into the water, and then awaking with a start, and wondering where she was. But at last deep dreamless sleep came; her head, guarded by her bonnet, found a pillow against the gorsy wall; and the poor soul, driven to and fro between two equal terrors, found the one relief that was possible to it – the relief of unconsciousness.

Alas! that relief seems to end the moment it has begun. It seemed to Hetty as if those dozing dreams had only passed into another dream – that she was in the hovel, and her aunt was standing over her with a candle in her hand. She trembled under her aunt's glance, and opened her eyes. There was no candle, but there was light in the hovel – the light of early morning through the open door. And there was a face looking down on her; but it was an unknown face, belonging to an elderly man in a smock-frock.

'Why, what do you do here, young woman?' the man said, roughly.

Hetty trembled still worse under this real fear and shame than she had done in her momentary dream under her aunt's glance. She felt that she was like a beggar already – found sleeping in that place. But in spite of her trembling, she was so eager to account to the man for her presence here, that she found words at once.

'I lost my way,' she said. 'I'm travelling – north'ard, and I got away from the road into the fields, and was overtaken by the dark. Will you tell me the way to the nearest village?'

She got up as she was speaking, and put her hands to her bonnet to adjust it, and then laid hold of her basket.

The man looked at her with a slow bovine gaze, without giving her any answer, for some seconds. Then he turned away and walked towards the door of the hovel, but it was not till he got there that he stood still, and, turning his shoulder half round towards her, said –

'Aw, I can show you the way to Norton, if you like. But what do you do gettin' out o' the highroad?' he added, with a tone of gruff reproof. 'Y'ull be gettin' into mischief, if you dooant mind.'

'Yes,' said Hetty, 'I won't do it again. I'll keep in the road, if you'll be so good as show me how to get to it.'

'Why dooant you keep where there's finger-poasses an' folks to ax the way on?' the man said, still more gruffly. 'Anybody 'ud think you was a wild woman, an' look at yer.'

Hetty was frightened at this gruff old man, and still more at this last suggestion that she looked like a wild woman. As she followed him out of the hovel she thought she would give him a sixpence for telling her the way, and then he would not suppose she was wild. As he stopped to point out the road to her, she put her hand in her pocket to get the sixpence ready, and when he was turning away, without saying good-morning, she held it out to him and said, 'Thank you; will you please to take something for your trouble?'

He looked slowly at the sixpence, and then said, 'I want none o' your money. You'd better take care on't, else you'll get it stool from yer, if you go trapesin' about the fields like a mad woman a-that-way.'

The man left her without further speech, and Hetty held on her way. Another day had risen, and she must wander on. It was no use to think of drowning herself – she could not do it, at least while she had money left to buy food, and strength to journey on. But the incident on her waking this morning heightened her dread of that time when her money would be all gone; she would have to sell her basket and clothes then, and she would really look like a beggar or a wild woman, as the man had said. The passionate joy in life she had felt in the night, after escaping from the brink of the black cold death in the pool, was gone now. Life now, by the morning light, with the impression of that man's hard wondering look at her, was as full of dread as death; – it was worse; it was a dread to which she felt chained, from which she shrank and shrank as she did from the black pool, and yet could find no refuge from it.

She took out her money from her purse, and looked at it; she had still two-and-twenty shillings; it would serve her for many days more, or it would help her to get on faster to Stonyshire, within reach of Dinah. The thought of Dinah urged itself more strongly now, since the experience of the night had driven her shuddering imagination away from the pool. If it had been only going to Dinah – if nobody besides Dinah would ever know –

Hetty could have made up her mind to go to her. The soft voice, the pitying eyes, would have drawn her. But afterwards the other people must know, and she could no more rush on that shame than she could rush on death.

She must wander on and on, and wait for a lower depth of despair to give her courage. Perhaps death would come to her, for she was getting less and less able to bear the day's weariness. And yet – such is the strange action of our souls, drawing us by a lurking desire towards the very ends we dread – Hetty, when she set out again from Norton, asked the straightest road northward towards Stonyshire, and kept it all that day.

Poor wandering Hetty, with the rounded childish face, and the hard unloving despairing soul looking out of it – with the narrow heart and narrow thoughts, no room in them for any sorrows but her own, and tasting that sorrow with the more intense bitterness! My heart bleeds for her as I see her toiling along on her weary feet, or seated in a cart, with her eyes fixed vacantly on the road before her, never thinking or caring whither it tends, till hunger comes and makes her desire that a village may be near.

What will be the end? – the end of her objectless wandering, apart from all love, caring for human beings only through her pride, clinging to life only as the hunted wounded brute clings to it?

God preserve you and me from being the beginners of such misery!

CHAPTER XXXVIII

The Quest

The first ten days after Hetty's departure passed as quietly as any other days with the family at the Hall Farm, and with Adam at his daily work. They had expected Hetty to stay away a week or ten days at least, perhaps a little longer if Dinah came back with her, because there might then be something to detain them at Snowfield. But when a fortnight had passed they began to feel a little surprise that Hetty did not return; she must surely have found it pleasanter to be with Dinah than any one could have supposed. Adam, for his part, was getting very impatient to see her, and he resolved that, if she did not appear the next day (Saturday), he would set out on Sunday morning to fetch her. There was no coach on a Sunday; but by setting out before it was light, and perhaps getting a lift in a cart by the way, he would arrive pretty early at Snowfield, and bring back Hetty the next day – Dinah too, if she were coming. It was quite time Hetty came home, and he would afford to lose his Monday for the sake of bringing her.

His project was quite approved at the Farm when he went there on Saturday evening. Mrs Poyser desired him emphatically not to come back without Hetty, for she had been quite too long away, considering the things she had to get ready by the middle of March, and a week was surely enough for any one to go out for their health. As for Dinah, Mrs Poyser had small hope of their bringing her, unless they could make her believe the folks at Hayslope were twice as miserable as the folks at Snowfield. 'Though,' said Mrs Poyser, by way of conclusion, 'you might tell her she's got but one aunt left, and *she's* wasted pretty nigh to a shadder;[1] and we shall p'rhaps all be gone twenty mile further off her next Michaelmas, and shall die o' broken hearts among strange folks, and leave the children fatherless and motherless.'

'Nay, nay,' said Mr Poyser, who certainly had the air of a man perfectly heart-whole, 'it isna so bad as that. Thee't looking rarely now, and getting flesh every day. But I'd be glad for Dinah t' come, for she'd help thee wi' the little uns: they took t' her wonderful.'

So at daybreak, on Sunday, Adam set off. Seth went with him the first mile or two, for the thought of Snowfield, and the possibility that Dinah might come again, made him restless, and the walk with Adam in the cold morning air, both in their best clothes, helped to give him a sense of Sunday calm. It was the last morning in February, with a low grey sky, and a slight hoar-frost on the green border of the road and on the black hedges. They heard the gurgling of the full brooklet hurrying down the hill, and the faint twittering of the early birds. For they walked in silence, though with a pleased sense of companionship.

'Good-bye, lad,' said Adam, laying his hand on Seth's shoulder, and looking at him affectionately as they were about to part, 'I wish thee wast going all the way wi' me, and as happy as I am.'

'I'm content, Addy, I'm content,' said Seth, cheerfully. 'I'll be an old bachelor, belike, and make a fuss wi' thy children.'

They turned away from each other, and Seth walked leisurely homeward, mentally repeating one of his favourite hymns – he was very fond of hymns: –

> 'Dark and cheerless is the morn
>   Unaccompanied by thee:
> Joyless is the day's return
>   Till thy mercy's beams I see:
> Till thou inward light impart,
> Glad my eyes and warm my heart.

Visit, then, this soul of mine,
  Pierce the gloom of sin and grief, –
Fill me, Radiancy Divine,
  Scatter all my unbelief.
More and more thyself display,
Shining to the perfect day.'[2]

   Adam walked much faster, and any one coming along the
Oakbourne road at sunrise that morning must have had a
pleasant sight in this tall broad-chested man, striding along
with a carriage as upright and firm as any soldier's, glancing
with keen glad eyes at the dark-blue hills as they began to show
themselves on his way. Seldom in Adam's life had his face been
so free from any cloud of anxiety as it was this morning; and
this freedom from care, as is usual with constructive practical
minds like his, made him all the more observant of the objects
round him, and all the more ready to gather suggestions from
them towards his own favourite plans and ingenious contrivances. His happy love – the knowledge that his steps were
carrying him nearer and nearer to Hetty, who was so soon to
be his – was to his thoughts what the sweet morning air was to
his sensations: it gave him a consciousness of wellbeing that
made activity delightful. Every now and then there was a rush
of more intense feeling towards her, which chased away other
images than Hetty; and along with that would come a wondering thankfulness that all this happiness was given to him – that
this life of ours had such sweetness in it. For Adam had a devout
mind, though he was perhaps rather impatient of devout words;
and his tenderness lay very close to his reverence, so that the
one could hardly be stirred without the other. But after feeling
had welled up and poured itself out in this way, busy thought
would come back with the greater vigour; and this morning it
was intent on schemes by which the roads might be improved
that were so imperfect all through the country, and on picturing
all the benefits that might come from the exertions of a single
country gentleman, if he would set himself to getting the roads
made good in his own district.[3]
   It seemed a very short walk, the ten miles to Oakbourne, that

pretty town within sight of the blue hills, where he breakfasted. After this, the country grew barer and barer: no more rolling woods, no more wide-branching trees near frequent home-steads, no more bushy hedgerows; but grey stone walls inter-secting the meagre pastures, and dismal wide-scattered grey stone houses on broken lands where mines had been and were no longer. 'A hungry land,' said Adam to himself. 'I'd rather go south'ard, where they say it's as flat as a table, than come to live here; though if Dinah likes to live in a country where she can be the most comfort to folks, she's i' the right to live o' this side; for she must look as if she'd come straight from heaven, like th' angels in the desert, to strengthen them as ha' got nothing t' eat.'[4] And when at last he came in sight of Snowfield, he thought it looked like a town that was 'fellow to the country', though the stream through the valley where the great mill stood gave a pleasant greenness to the lower fields. The town lay, grim, stony, and unsheltered, up the side of a steep hill, and Adam did not go forward to it at present, for Seth had told him where to find Dinah. It was at a thatched cottage outside the town, a little way from the mill – an old cottage, standing sideways towards the road, with a little bit of potato-ground[5] before it. Here Dinah lodged with an elderly couple; and if she and Hetty happened to be out, Adam could learn where they were gone, or when they would be at home again. Dinah might be out on some preaching errand, and perhaps she would have left Hetty at home. Adam could not help hoping this, and as he recognized the cottage by the road-side before him, there shone out in his face that involuntary smile which belongs to the expectation of a near joy.

He hurried his step along the narrow causeway, and rapped at the door. It was opened by a very clean old woman, with a slow palsied shake of the head.[6]

'Is Dinah Morris at home?' said Adam.

'Eh? . . . no,' said the old woman, looking up at this tall stranger with a wonder that made her slower of speech than usual. 'Will you please to come in?' she added, retiring from the door, as if recollecting herself. 'Why, ye're brother to the young man as come afore, arena ye?'

'Yes,' said Adam, entering. 'That was Seth Bede. I'm his brother Adam. He told me to give his respects to you and your good master.'

'Ay, the same t' him: he was a gracious young man. An' ye feature him,[7] on'y ye're darker. Sit ye down i' th' arm-chair. My man isna come home from meeting.'[8]

Adam sat down patiently, not liking to hurry the shaking old woman with questions, but looking eagerly towards the narrow twisting stairs in one corner, for he thought it was possible Hetty might have heard his voice, and would come down them.

'So you're come to see Dinah Morris?' said the old woman, standing opposite to him. 'An' you didna know she was away from home, then?'

'No,' said Adam, 'but I thought it likely she might be away, seeing as it's Sunday. But the other young woman – is she at home, or gone along with Dinah?'

The old woman looked at Adam with a bewildered air.

'Gone along wi' her?' she said. 'Eh, Dinah's gone to Leeds, a big town ye may ha' heard on, where there's a many o' the Lord's people. She's been gone sin' Friday was a fortnight: they sent her the money for her journey. You may see her room here,' she went on, opening a door, and not noticing the effect of her words on Adam. He rose and followed her, and darted an eager glance into the little room, with its narrow bed, the portrait of Wesley on the wall, and the few books lying on the large Bible. He had had an irrational hope that Hetty might be there. He could not speak in the first moment after seeing that the room was empty; an undefined fear had seized him – something had happened to Hetty on the journey. Still the old woman was so slow of speech and apprehension, that Hetty might be at Snowfield after all.

'It's a pity ye didna know,' she said. 'Have ye come from your own country o' purpose to see her?'

'But Hetty – Hetty Sorrel,' said Adam, abruptly; 'where is *she*?'

'I know nobody by that name,' said the old woman, wonderingly. 'Is it anybody ye've heard on at Snowfield?'

'Did there come no young woman here – very young and pretty – Friday was a fortnight, to see Dinah Morris?'

'Nay; I'n seen no young woman.'

'Think; are you quite sure? A girl, eighteen years old, with dark eyes and dark curly hair, and a red cloak on, and a basket on her arm? You couldn't forget her if you saw her.'

'Nay; Friday was a fortnight – it was the day as Dinah went away – there come nobody. There's ne'er been nobody asking for her till you come, for the folks about know as she's gone. Eh dear, eh dear, is there summat the matter?'

The old woman had seen the ghastly look of fear in Adam's face. But he was not stunned or confounded: he was thinking eagerly where he could inquire about Hetty.

'Yes; a young woman started from our country to see Dinah, Friday was a fortnight. I came to fetch her back. I'm afraid something has happened to her. I can't stop. Good-bye.'

He hastened out of the cottage, and the old woman followed him to the gate, watching him sadly with her shaking head, as he almost ran towards the town. He was going to inquire at the place where the Oakbourne coach stopped.

No! no young woman like Hetty had been seen there. Had any accident happened to the coach a fortnight ago? No. And there was no coach to take him back to Oakbourne that day. Well, he would walk: he couldn't stay here, in wretched inaction. But the innkeeper, seeing that Adam was in great anxiety, and entering into this new incident with the eagerness of a man who passes a great deal of time with his hands in his pockets looking into an obstinately monotonous street, offered to take him back to Oakbourne in his own 'taxed cart'[9] this very evening. It was not five o'clock; there was plenty of time for Adam to take a meal, and yet to get to Oakbourne before ten o'clock. The innkeeper declared that he really wanted to go to Oakbourne, and might as well go to-night; he should have all Monday before him then. Adam, after making an ineffectual attempt to eat, put the food in his pocket, and, drinking a draught of ale, declared himself ready to set off. As they approached the cottage, it occurred to him that he would do well to learn from the old woman where Dinah was to be found in Leeds: if there was trouble at the Hall Farm – he only half admitted the foreboding that there would be – the Poysers might

like to send for Dinah. But Dinah had not left any address, and
the old woman, whose memory for names was infirm, could
not recall the name of the 'blessed woman' who was Dinah's
chief friend in the Society[10] at Leeds.

During that long, long journey in the taxed cart, there was
time for all the conjectures of importunate fear and struggling
hope. In the very first shock of discovering that Hetty had not
been to Snowfield, the thought of Arthur had darted through
Adam like a sharp pang: but he tried for some time to ward off
its return by busying himself with modes of accounting for the
alarming fact, quite apart from that intolerable thought. Some
accident had happened. Hetty had, by some strange chance, got
into a wrong vehicle from Oakbourne: she had been taken ill,
and did not want to frighten them by letting them know. But
this frail fence of vague improbabilities was soon hurled down
by a rush of distinct agonizing fears. Hetty had been deceiving
herself in thinking that she could love and marry him: she had
been loving Arthur all the while: and now, in her desperation
at the nearness of their marriage, she had run away. And she
was gone to *him*. The old indignation and jealousy rose again,
and prompted the suspicion that Arthur had been dealing falsely
– had written to Hetty – had tempted her to come to him –
being unwilling, after all, that she should belong to another man
besides himself. Perhaps the whole thing had been contrived by
him, and he had given her directions how to follow him to
Ireland: for Adam knew that Arthur had been gone thither
three weeks ago, having recently learnt it at the Chase. Every
sad look of Hetty's, since she had been engaged to Adam,
returned upon him now with all the exaggeration of painful
retrospect. He had been foolishly sanguine and confident. The
poor thing hadn't perhaps known her own mind for a long
while; had thought that she could forget Arthur; had been
momentarily drawn towards the man who offered her a protecting, faithful love. He couldn't bear to blame her: she never
meant to cause him this dreadful pain. The blame lay with that
man who had selfishly played with her heart – had perhaps
even deliberately lured her away.

At Oakbourne, the ostler at the Royal Oak remembered

such a young woman as Adam described getting out of the Treddleston coach more than a fortnight ago – wasn't likely to forget such a pretty lass as that in a hurry – was sure she had not gone on by the Buxton coach that went through Snowfield, but had lost sight of her while he went away with the horses, and had never set eyes on her again. Adam then went straight to the house from which the Stoniton coach started: Stoniton was the most obvious place for Hetty to go to first, whatever might be her destination, for she would hardly venture on any but the chief coach-roads. She had been noticed here too, and was remembered to have sat on the box by the coachman; but the coachman could not be seen, for another man had been driving on that road in his stead the last three or four days: he could probably be seen at Stoniton, through inquiry at the inn where the coach put up. So the anxious, heart-stricken Adam must of necessity wait and try to rest till morning – nay, till eleven o'clock, when the coach started.

At Stoniton another delay occurred, for the old coachman who had driven Hetty would not be in the town again till night. When he did come he remembered Hetty well, and remembered his own joke addressed to her, quoting it many times to Adam, and observing with equal frequency that he thought there was something more than common, because Hetty had not laughed when he joked her. But he declared, as the people had done at the inn, that he had lost sight of Hetty directly she got down. Part of the next morning was consumed in inquiries at every house in the town from which a coach started – (all in vain; for you know Hetty did not start from Stoniton by coach, but on foot in the grey morning) – and then in walking out to the first toll-gates on the different lines of road, in the forlorn hope of finding some recollection of her there. No, she was not to be traced any farther; and the next hard task for Adam was to go home, and carry the wretched tidings to the Hall Farm. As to what he should do beyond that, he had come to two distinct resolutions amidst the tumult of thought and feeling which was going on within him while he went to and fro. He would not mention what he knew of Arthur Donnithorne's behaviour to Hetty till there was a clear necessity for it: it was still possible

Hetty might come back, and the disclosure might be an injury or an offence to her. And as soon as he had been home, and done what was necessary there to prepare for his further absence, he would start off to Ireland: if he found no trace of Hetty on the road, he would go straight to Arthur Donnithorne, and make himself certain how far he was acquainted with her movements. Several times the thought occurred to him that he would consult Mr Irwine; but that would be useless unless he told him all, and so betrayed the secret about Arthur. It seems strange that Adam, in the incessant occupation of his mind about Hetty, should never have alighted on the probability that she had gone to Windsor, ignorant that Arthur was no longer there. Perhaps the reason was, that he could not conceive Hetty's throwing herself on Arthur uncalled; he imagined no cause that could have driven her to such a step, after that letter written in August. There were but two alternatives in his mind: either Arthur had written to her again and enticed her away, or she had simply fled from her approaching marriage with himself, because she found, after all, she could not love him well enough, and yet was afraid of her friends' anger if she retracted.

With this last determination on his mind, of going straight to Arthur, the thought that he had spent two days in inquiries which had proved to be almost useless, was torturing to Adam; and yet, since he would not tell the Poysers his conviction as to where Hetty was gone, or his intention to follow her thither, he must be able to say to them that he had traced her as far as possible.

It was after twelve o'clock on Tuesday night when Adam reached Treddleston; and, unwilling to disturb his mother and Seth, and also to encounter their questions at that hour, he threw himself without undressing on a bed at the 'Waggon Overthrown', and slept hard from pure weariness. Not more than four hours, however; for before five o'clock he set out on his way home in the faint morning twilight. He always kept a key of the workshop door in his pocket, so that he could let himself in; and he wished to enter without awaking his mother, for he was anxious to avoid telling her the new trouble himself by seeing Seth first, and asking him to tell her when it should be necessary. He walked gently along the yard, and turned the key gently in the door; but, as he expected, Gyp, who lay in the workshop, gave a sharp bark. It subsided when he saw Adam, holding up his finger at him to impose silence; and in his dumb, tailless joy he must content himself with rubbing his body against his master's legs.

Adam was too heart-sick to take notice of Gyp's fondling. He threw himself on the bench, and stared dully at the wood and the signs of work around him, wondering if he should ever come to feel pleasure in them again; while Gyp, dimly aware that there was something wrong with his master, laid his rough grey head on Adam's knee, and wrinkled his brows to look up at him. Hitherto, since Sunday afternoon, Adam had been constantly among strange people and in strange places, having no associations with the details of his daily life; and now that by the light of this new morning he was come back to his home, and surrounded by the familiar objects that seemed for ever robbed of their charm, the reality – the hard, inevitable reality – of his troubles pressed upon him with a new weight. Right before him was an unfinished chest of drawers, which he had been making in spare moments for Hetty's use, when his home should be hers.

Seth had not heard Adam's entrance, but he had been roused by Gyp's bark, and Adam heard him moving about in the room above, dressing himself. Seth's first thoughts were about his brother: he would come home to-day, surely, for the business would be wanting him sadly by to-morrow, but it was pleasant to think he had had a longer holiday than he had expected. And would Dinah come too? Seth felt that that was the greatest happiness he could look forward to for himself, though he had no hope left that she would ever love him well enough to marry him; but he had often said to himself, it was better to be Dinah's friend and brother than any other woman's husband. If he could but be always near her, instead of living so far off!

He came down-stairs and opened the inner door leading from the kitchen into the workshop, intending to let out Gyp; but he stood still in the doorway, smitten with a sudden shock at the sight of Adam seated listlessly on the bench, pale, unwashed, with sunken blank eyes, almost like a drunkard in the morning. But Seth felt in an instant what the marks meant: not drunkenness, but some great calamity. Adam looked up at him without speaking, and Seth moved forward towards the bench, himself trembling so that speech did not come readily.

'God have mercy on us, Addy,' he said, in a low voice, sitting down on the bench beside Adam, 'what is it?'

Adam was unable to speak: the strong man, accustomed to suppress the signs of sorrow, had felt his heart swell like a child's at this first approach of sympathy. He fell on Seth's neck and sobbed.

Seth was prepared for the worst now, for, even in his recollections of their boyhood, Adam had never sobbed before.

'Is it death, Adam? Is she dead?' he asked, in a low tone, when Adam raised his head and was recovering himself.

'No, lad; but she's gone – gone away from us. She's never been to Snowfield. Dinah's been gone to Leeds ever since last Friday was a fortnight, the very day Hetty set out. I can't find out where she went after she got to Stoniton.'

Seth was silent from utter astonishment: he knew nothing that could suggest to him a reason for Hetty's going away.

'Hast any notion what she's done it for?' he said, at last.

'She can't ha' loved me: she didn't like our marriage when it came nigh – that must be it,' said Adam. He had determined to mention no further reason.

'I hear mother stirring,' said Seth. 'Must we tell her?'

'No, not yet,' said Adam, rising from the bench, and pushing the hair from his face, as if he wanted to rouse himself. 'I can't have her told yet; and I must set out on another journey directly, after I've been to the village and th' Hall Farm. I can't tell thee where I'm going, and thee must say to her I'm gone on business as nobody is to know anything about. I'll go and wash myself now.' Adam moved towards the door of the workshop, but after a step or two he turned round, and, meeting Seth's eyes with a calm sad glance, he said, 'I must take all the money out o' the tin box, lad; but if anything happens to me, all the rest'll be thine, to take care o' mother with.'

Seth was pale and trembling: he felt there was some terrible secret under all this. 'Brother,' he said, faintly – he never called Adam 'brother' except in solemn moments – 'I don't believe you'll do anything as you can't ask God's blessing on.'

'Nay, lad,' said Adam, 'don't be afraid. I'm for doing nought but what's a man's duty.'

The thought that if he betrayed his trouble to his mother, she would only distress him by words, half of blundering affection, half of irrepressible triumph that Hetty proved as unfit to be his wife as she had always foreseen, brought back some of his habitual firmness and self-command. He had felt ill on his journey home – he told her when she came down, – had stayed all night at Treddleston for that reason; and a bad headache, that still hung about him this morning, accounted for his pale-ness and heavy eyes.

He determined to go to the village, in the first place; attend to his business for an hour, and give notice to Burge of his being obliged to go on a journey, which he must beg him not to mention to any one; for he wished to avoid going to the Hall Farm near breakfast-time, when the children and servants would be in the house-place, and there must be exclamations in their hearing about his having returned without Hetty. He waited until the clock struck nine before he left the work-yard at the village, and set off, through the fields towards the Farm. It was an immense relief to him, as he came near the Home Close, to see Mr Poyser advancing towards him, for this would spare him the pain of going to the house. Mr Poyser was walking briskly this March morning, with a sense of Spring business on his mind: he was going to cast the master's eye on the shoeing of a new cart-horse, carrying his spud[11] as a useful companion by the way. His surprise was great when he caught sight of Adam, but he was not a man given to presentiments of evil.

'Why, Adam, lad, is't you? Have ye been all this time away, and not brought the lasses back, after all? Where are they?'

'No, I've not brought 'em,' said Adam, turning round, to indicate that he wished to walk back with Mr Poyser.

'Why,' said Martin, looking with sharper attention at Adam, 'ye look bad. Is there anything happened?'

'Yes,' said Adam, heavily. 'A sad thing's happened. I didna find Hetty at Snowfield.'

Mr Poyser's good-natured face showed signs of troubled astonishment. 'Not find her? What's happened to her?' he said, his thoughts flying at once to bodily accident.

'That I can't tell, whether anything's happened to her. She never went to Snowfield – she took the coach to Stoniton, but I can't learn nothing of her after she got down from the Stoniton coach.'

'Why, you donna mean she's run away?' said Martin, standing still, so puzzled and bewildered that the fact did not yet make itself felt as a trouble by him.

'She must ha' done,' said Adam. 'She didn't like our marriage when it came to the point – that must be it. She'd mistook her feelings.'

Martin was silent for a minute or two, looking on the ground, and rooting up the grass with his spud, without knowing what he was doing. His usual slowness was always trebled when the subject of speech was painful. At last he looked up, right in Adam's face, saying –

'Then she didna deserve t' ha' ye, my lad. An' I feel i' fault myself, for she was my niece, and I was allays hot for her marr'ing ye. There's no amends I can make ye, lad – the more's the pity: it's a sad cut-up for ye, I doubt.'

Adam could say nothing; and Mr Poyser, after pursuing his walk for a little while, went on: –

'I'll be bound she's gone after trying to get a lady's-maid's place, for she'd got that in her head half a year ago, and wanted me to gi' my consent. But I'd thought better on her,' he added, shaking his head slowly and sadly – 'I'd thought better on her, nor to look for this, after she'd gi'en y' her word, an' everything been got ready.'

Adam had the strongest motives for encouraging this supposition in Mr Poyser, and he even tried to believe that it might possibly be true. He had no warrant for the *certainty* that she was gone to Arthur.

'It was better it should be so,' he said, as quietly as he could, 'if she felt she couldn't like me for a husband. Better run away before than repent after. I hope you won't look harshly on her if she comes back, as she may do if she finds it hard to get on away from home.'

'I canna look on her as I've done before,' said Martin, decisively. 'She's acted bad by you, and by all of us. But I'll not turn my back on her: she's but a young un, and it's the first harm I've knowed on her. It'll be a hard job for me to tell her aunt. Why didna Dinah come back wi' ye? – she'd ha' helped to pacify her aunt a bit.'

'Dinah wasn't at Snowfield. She's been gone to Leeds this fortnight; and I couldn't learn from th' old woman any direction where she is at Leeds, else I should ha' brought it you.'

'She'd a deal better be staying wi' her own kin,' said Mr Poyser, indignantly, 'than going preaching among strange folks a-that'n.'

'I must leave you now, Mr Poyser,' said Adam, 'for I've a deal to see to.'

'Ay, you'd best be after your business, and I must tell the missis when I go home. It's a hard job.'

'But,' said Adam, 'I beg particular, you'll keep what's happened quiet for a week or two. I've not told my mother yet, and there's no knowing how things may turn out.'

'Ay, ay; least said, soonest mended. We'n no need to say why the match is broke off, an' we may hear of her after a bit. Shake hands wi' me, lad; I wish I could make thee amends.'

There was something in Martin Poyser's throat at that moment which caused him to bring out those scanty words in rather a broken fashion. Yet Adam knew what they meant all the better; and the two honest men grasped each other's hard hands in mutual understanding.

There was nothing now to hinder Adam from setting off. He had told Seth to go to the Chase, and leave a message for the Squire, saying that Adam Bede had been obliged to start off suddenly on a journey, – and to say as much, and no more, to any one else who made inquiries about him. If the Poysers learned that he was gone away again, Adam knew they would infer that he was gone in search of Hetty.

He had intended to go right on his way from the Hall Farm;

but now the impulse which had frequently visited him before – to go to Mr Irwine, and make a confidant of him – recurred with the new force which belongs to a last opportunity. He was about to start on a long journey – a difficult one – by sea – and no soul would know where he was gone. If anything happened to him? or, if he absolutely needed help in any matter concerning Hetty? Mr Irwine was to be trusted; and the feeling which made Adam shrink from telling anything which was *her* secret, must give way before the need there was that she should have some one else besides himself, who would be prepared to defend her in the worst extremity. Towards Arthur, even though he might have incurred no new guilt, Adam felt that he was not bound to keep silence when Hetty's interest called on him to speak.

'I must do it,' said Adam, when these thoughts, which had spread themselves through hours of his sad journeying, now rushed upon him in an instant, like a wave that had been slowly gathering 'it's the right thing. I can't stand alone in this way any longer.'

CHAPTER XXXIX

The Tidings

Adam turned his face towards Broxton and walked with his swiftest stride, looking at his watch with the fear that Mr Irwine might be gone out – hunting, perhaps. The fear and haste together produced a state of strong excitement before he reached the Rectory gate; and outside it he saw the deep marks of a recent hoof on the gravel.

But the hoofs were turned towards the gate, not away from it; and though there was a horse against the stable door, it was not Mr Irwine's: it had evidently had a journey this morning, and must belong to some one who had come on business. Mr Irwine was at home, then; but Adam could hardly find breath and calmness to tell Carroll that he wanted to speak to the Rector. The double suffering of certain and uncertain sorrow had begun to shake the strong man. The butler looked at him wonderingly, as he threw himself on a bench in the passage and stared absently at the clock on the opposite wall: the master had somebody with him, he said, but he heard the study door open – the stranger seemed to be coming out, and as Adam was in a hurry, he would let the master know at once.

Adam sat looking at the clock: the minute-hand was hurrying along the last five minutes to ten, with a loud hard indifferent tick, and Adam watched the movement and listened to the sound as if he had had some reason for doing so. In our times of bitter suffering, there are almost always these pauses, when our consciousness is benumbed to everything but some trivial perception or sensation. It is as if semi-idiocy came to give us rest from the memory and the dread which refuse to leave us in our sleep.

Carroll, coming back, recalled Adam to the sense of his burthen. He was to go into the study immediately. 'I can't think what that strange person's come about,' the butler added, from mere incontinence of remark, as he preceded Adam to the door, 'he's gone i' the dining-room. And master looks unaccountable – as if he was frightened.' Adam took no notice of the words: he could not care about other people's business. But when he entered the study and looked in Mr Irwine's face, he felt in an instant that there was a new expression in it, strangely different from the warm friendliness it had always worn for him before. A letter lay open on the table, and Mr Irwine's hand was on it; but the changed glance he cast on Adam could not be owing entirely to preoccupation with some disagreeable business, for he was looking eagerly towards the door, as if Adam's entrance were a matter of poignant anxiety to him.

'You want to speak to me, Adam,' he said, in that low constrainedly quiet tone which a man uses when he is determined to suppress agitation. 'Sit down here.' He pointed to a chair just opposite to him, at no more than a yard's distance from his own, and Adam sat down with a sense that this cold manner of Mr Irwine's gave an additional unexpected difficulty to his disclosure. But when Adam had made up his mind to a measure, he was not the man to renounce it for any but imperative reasons.

'I come to you, sir,' he said, 'as the gentleman I look up to most of anybody. I've something very painful to tell you – something as it'll pain you to hear, as well as me to tell. But if I speak o' the wrong other people have done, you'll see I didn't speak till I'd good reason.'

Mr Irwine nodded slowly, and Adam went on rather tremulously.

'You was t' ha' married me and Hetty Sorrel, you know, sir, o' the fifteenth o' this month. I thought she loved me, and I was th' happiest man i' the parish. But a dreadful blow's come upon me.'

Mr Irwine started up from his chair, as if involuntarily, but then, determined to control himself, walked to the window and looked out.

'She's gone away, sir, and we don't know where. She said she was going to Snowfield o' Friday was a fortnight, and I went last Sunday to fetch her back; but she'd never been there, and she took the coach to Stoniton, and beyond that I can't trace her. But now I'm going a long journey to look for her, and I can't trust t' anybody but you where I'm going.'

Mr Irwine came back from the window and sat down.

'Have you no idea of the reason why she went away?' he said.

'It's plain enough she didn't want to marry me, sir,' said Adam. 'She didn't like it when it came so near. But that isn't all, I doubt. There's something else I must tell you, sir. There's somebody else concerned besides me.'

A gleam of something – it was almost like relief or joy[1] – came across the eager anxiety of Mr Irwine's face at that moment. Adam was looking on the ground, and paused a little: the next words were hard to speak. But when he went on, he lifted up his head and looked straight at Mr Irwine. He would do the thing he had resolved to do, without flinching.

'You know who's the man I've reckoned my greatest friend,' he said, 'and used to be proud to think as I should pass my life i' working for him, and had felt so ever since we were lads' . . .

Mr Irwine, as if all self-control had forsaken him, grasped Adam's arm, which lay on the table, and, clutching it tightly like a man in pain, said, with pale lips and a low hurried voice –

'No, Adam, no – don't say it, for God's sake!'

Adam, surprised at the violence of Mr Irwine's feeling, repented of the words that had passed his lips, and sat in distressed silence. The grasp on his arm gradually relaxed, and Mr Irwine threw himself back in his chair, saying, 'Go on – I must know it.'

'That man played with Hetty's feelings, and behaved to her as he'd no right to do to a girl in her station o' life – made her presents, and used to go and meet her out a-walking: I found it out only two days before he went away – found him a-kissing her as they were parting in the Grove. There'd been nothing said between me and Hetty then, though I'd loved her for a long while, and she knew it. But I reproached him with his

wrong actions, and words and blows passed between us; and
he said solemnly to me, after that, as it had been all nonsense,
and no more than a bit o' flirting. But I made him write a letter
to tell Hetty he'd meant nothing; for I saw clear enough, sir, by
several things as I hadn't understood at the time, as he'd got
hold of her heart, and I thought she'd belike go on thinking of
him, and never come to love another man as wanted to marry
her. And I gave her the letter, and she seemed to bear it all after
a while better than I'd expected ... and she behaved kinder
and kinder to me ... I daresay she didn't know her own feelings
then, poor thing, and they came back upon her when it was too
late ... I don't want to blame her ... I can't think as she meant
to deceive me. But I was encouraged to think she loved me, and
– you know the rest, sir. But it's on my mind as he's been false
to me, and 'ticed her away, and she's gone to him – and I'm
going now to see; for I can never go to work again till I know
what's become of her.'

During Adam's narrative, Mr Irwine had had time to recover
his self-mastery in spite of the painful thoughts that crowded
upon him. It was a bitter remembrance to him now – that
morning when Arthur breakfasted with him, and seemed as if
he were on the verge of a confession. It was plain enough *now*
what he had wanted to confess. And if their words had taken
another turn ... if he himself had been less fastidious about
intruding on another man's secrets ... it was cruel to think
how thin a film had shut out rescue from all this guilt and
misery. He saw the whole history now by that terrible illumination which the present sheds back upon the past. But every
other feeling as it rushed upon him was thrown into abeyance
by pity, deep respectful pity, for the man who sat before him,
– already so bruised, going forth with sad blind resignedness to
an unreal sorrow, while a real one was close upon him, too far
beyond the range of common trial for him ever to have feared
it. His own agitation was quelled by a certain awe that comes
over us in the presence of a great anguish; for the anguish he
must inflict on Adam was already present to him. Again he put
his hand on the arm that lay on the table, but very gently this
time, as he said solemnly –

'Adam, my dear friend, you have had some hard trials in your life. You can bear sorrow manfully, as well as act manfully: God requires both tasks at our hands. And there is a heavier sorrow coming upon you than any you have yet known. But you are not guilty – you have not the worst of all sorrows. God help him who has!'

The two pale faces looked at each other; in Adam's there was trembling suspense, in Mr Irwine's hesitating, shrinking pity. But he went on.

'I have had news of Hetty this morning. She is not gone to *him*. She is in Stonyshire – at Stoniton.'

Adam started up from his chair, as if he thought he could have leaped to her that moment. But Mr Irwine laid hold of his arm again, and said, persuasively, 'Wait, Adam, wait.' So he sat down.

'She is in a very unhappy position – one which will make it worse for you to find her, my poor friend, than to have lost her for ever.'

Adam's lips moved tremulously, but no sound came. They moved again, and he whispered, 'Tell me.'

'She has been arrested . . . she is in prison.'

It was as if an insulting blow had brought back the spirit of resistance into Adam. The blood rushed to his face, and he said, loudly and sharply –

'For what?'

'For a great crime – the murder of her child.'

'It *can't be!*' Adam almost shouted, starting up from his chair, and making a stride towards the door; but he turned round again, setting his back against the book-case, and looking fiercely at Mr Irwine. 'It isn't possible. She never had a child. She can't be guilty. *Who* says it?'

'God grant she may be innocent, Adam. We can still hope she is.'

'But who says she is guilty?' said Adam, violently. 'Tell me everything.'

'Here is a letter from the magistrate before whom she was taken, and the constable who arrested her is in the dining-room. She will not confess her name or where she comes from; but I

fear, I fear, there can be no doubt it is Hetty. The description
of her person corresponds, only that she is said to look very
pale and ill. She had a small red-leather pocket-book in her
pocket with two names written in it – one at the beginning,
"Hetty Sorrel, Hayslope", and the other near the end, "Dinah
Morris, Snowfield". She will not say which is her own name
– she denies everything, and will answer no questions; and
application has been made to me, as a magistrate, that I may
take measures for identifying her, for it was thought probable
that the name which stands first is her own name.'

'But what proof have they got against her, if it *is* Hetty?' said
Adam, still violently, with an effort that seemed to shake his
whole frame. 'I'll not believe it. It couldn't ha' been, and none
of us know it.'

'Terrible proof that she was under the temptation to commit
the crime; but we have room to hope that she did not really
commit it. Try and read that letter, Adam.'

Adam took the letter between his shaking hands, and tried
to fix his eyes steadily on it. Mr Irwine meanwhile went out to
give some orders. When he came back, Adam's eyes were still
on the first page – he couldn't read – he could not put the words
together, and make out what they meant. He threw it down at
last, and clenched his fist.

'It's *his* doing,' he said; 'if there's been any crime, it's at his
door, not at hers. *He* taught her to deceive – *he* deceived me
first. Let 'em put *him* on his trial – let him stand in court beside
her, and I'll tell 'em how he got hold of her heart, and 'ticed
her t' evil, and then lied to me. Is *he* to go free, while they lay
all the punishment on her . . . so weak and young?'

The image called up by these last words gave a new direction
to poor Adam's maddened feelings. He was silent, looking at
the corner of the room as if he saw something there. Then he
burst out again, in a tone of appealing anguish –

'I *can't* bear it . . . O God, it's too hard to lay upon me – it's
too hard to think she's wicked.'

Mr Irwine had sat down again in silence: he was too wise to
utter soothing words at present, and indeed the sight of Adam
before him, with that look of sudden age which sometimes

comes over a young face in moments of terrible emotion – the hard bloodless look of the skin, the deep lines about the quivering mouth, the furrows in the brow – the sight of this strong firm man shattered by the invisible stroke of sorrow, moved him so deeply that speech was not easy. Adam stood motionless, with his eyes vacantly fixed in this way for a minute or two; in that short space he was living through all his love again.

'She can't ha' done it,' he said, still without moving his eyes, as if he were only talking to himself: 'it was fear made her hide it . . . I forgive her for deceiving me . . . I forgive thee, Hetty . . . thee wast deceived too . . . it's gone hard wi' thee, my poor Hetty . . . but they'll never make me believe it.'

He was silent again for a few moments, and then he said, with fierce abruptness –

'I'll go to him – I'll bring him back – I'll make him go and look at her in her misery – he shall look at her till he can't forget it – it shall follow him night and day – as long as he lives it shall follow him – he shan't escape wi' lies this time – I'll fetch him, I'll drag him myself.'

In the act of going towards the door, Adam paused automatically and looked about for his hat, quite unconscious where he was, or who was present with him. Mr Irwine had followed him, and now took him by the arm, saying, in a quiet but decided tone –

'No, Adam, no; I'm sure you will wish to stay and see what good can be done for *her*, instead of going on a useless errand of vengeance. The punishment will surely fall without your aid. Besides, he is no longer in Ireland: he must be on his way home – or would be, long before you arrived; for his grandfather, I know, wrote for him to come at least ten days ago. I want you now to go with me to Stoniton. I have ordered a horse for you to ride with us, as soon as you can compose yourself.'

While Mr Irwine was speaking, Adam recovered his consciousness of the actual scene: he rubbed his hair off his forehead and listened.

'Remember,' Mr Irwine went on, 'there are others to think of, and act for, besides yourself, Adam: there are Hetty's friends, the good Poysers, on whom this stroke will fall more heavily than I can bear to think. I expect it from your strength of mind, Adam – from your sense of duty to God and man – that you will try to act as long as action can be of any use.'

In reality, Mr Irwine proposed this journey to Stoniton for Adam's own sake. Movement, with some object before him, was the best means of counteracting the violence of suffering in these first hours.

'You *will* go with me to Stoniton, Adam?' he said again, after a moment's pause. 'We have to see if it is really Hetty who is there, you know.'

'Yes, sir,' said Adam, 'I'll do what you think right. But the folks at th' Hall Farm?'

'I wish them not to know till I return to tell them myself. I shall have ascertained things then which I am uncertain about now, and I shall return as soon as possible. Come now, the horses are ready.'

CHAPTER XL

The Bitter Waters[1] Spread

Mr Irwine returned from Stoniton in a post-chaise that night, and the first words Carroll said to him, as he entered the house, were, that Squire Donnithorne was dead – found dead in his bed at ten o'clock that morning – and that Mrs Irwine desired him to say she should be awake when Mr Irwine came home, and she begged him not to go to bed without seeing her.

'Well, Dauphin,' Mrs Irwine said, as her son entered her room, 'you're come at last. So the old gentleman's fidgetiness and low spirits, which made him send for Arthur in that sudden way, really meant something. I suppose Carroll has told you that Donnithorne was found dead in his bed this morning. You will believe my prognostications another time, though I daresay I shan't live to prognosticate anything but my own death.'

'What have they done about Arthur?' said Mr Irwine. 'Sent a messenger to await him at Liverpool?'

'Yes, Ralph was gone before the news was brought to us. Dear Arthur, I shall live now to see him master at the Chase, and making good times on the estate, like a generous-hearted fellow as he is. He'll be as happy as a king now.'

Mr Irwine could not help giving a slight groan: he was worn with anxiety and exertion, and his mother's light words were almost intolerable.

'What are you so dismal about, Dauphin? Is there any bad news? Or are you thinking of the danger for Arthur in crossing that frightful Irish Channel at this time of year?'

'No, mother, I'm not thinking of that; but I'm not prepared to rejoice just now.'

'You've been worried by this law business that you've been

to Stoniton about. What in the world is it, that you can't tell me?'

'You will know by-and-by, mother. It would not be right for me to tell you at present. Good-night: you'll sleep now you have no longer anything to listen for.'

Mr Irwine gave up his intention of sending a letter to meet Arthur, since it would not now hasten his return: the news of his grandfather's death would bring him as soon as he could possibly come. He could go to bed now and get some needful rest, before the time came for the morning's heavy duty of carrying his sickening news to the Hall Farm and to Adam's home.

Adam himself was not come back from Stoniton, for though he shrank from seeing Hetty, he could not bear to go to a distance from her again.

'It's no use, sir,' he said to the Rector – 'it's no use for me to go back. I can't go to work again while she's here; and I couldn't bear the sight o' the things and folks round home. I'll take a bit of a room here, where I can see the prison walls, and perhaps I shall get, in time, to bear seeing *her*.'

Adam had not been shaken in his belief that Hetty was innocent of the crime she was charged with, for Mr Irwine, feeling that the belief in her guilt would be a crushing addition to Adam's load, had kept from him the facts which left no hope in his own mind. There was not any reason for thrusting the whole burthen on Adam at once, and Mr Irwine, at parting, only said, 'If the evidence should tell too strongly against her, Adam, we may still hope for a pardon. Her youth and other circumstances will be a plea for her.'

'Ah, and it's right people should know how she was tempted into the wrong way,' said Adam, with bitter earnestness. 'It's right they should know it was a fine gentleman made love to her, and turned her head wi' notions. You'll remember, sir, you've promised to tell my mother, and Seth, and the people at the Farm, who it was as led her wrong, else they'll think harder of her than she deserves. You'll be doing her a hurt by sparing him, and I hold him the guiltiest before God, let her ha' done what she may. If you spare him, I'll expose him!'

'I think your demand is just, Adam,' said Mr Irwine, 'but when you are calmer, you will judge Arthur more mercifully. I say nothing now, only that his punishment is in other hands than ours.'

Mr Irwine felt it hard upon him that he should have to tell of Arthur's sad part in the story of sin and sorrow – he who cared for Arthur with fatherly affection – who had cared for him with fatherly pride. But he saw clearly that the secret must be known before long, even apart from Adam's determination, since it was scarcely to be supposed that Hetty would persist to the end in her obstinate silence.[2] He made up his mind to withhold nothing from the Poysers, but to tell them the worst at once, for there was no time to rob the tidings of their suddenness. Hetty's trial must come on at the Lent assizes,[3] and they were to be held at Stoniton the next week. It was scarcely to be hoped that Martin Poyser could escape the pain of being called as a witness, and it was better he should know everything as long beforehand as possible.

Before ten o'clock on Thursday morning the home at the Hall Farm was a house of mourning for a misfortune felt to be worse than death. The sense of family dishonour was too keen even in the kind-hearted Martin Poyser the younger, to leave room for any compassion towards Hetty. He and his father were simple-minded farmers, proud of their untarnished character, proud that they came of a family which had held up its head and paid its way as far back as its name was in the parish register; and Hetty had brought disgrace on them all – disgrace that could never be wiped out. That was the all-conquering feeling in the mind both of father and son – the scorching sense of disgrace, which neutralized all other sensibility; and Mr Irwine was struck with surprise to observe that Mrs Poyser was less severe than her husband. We are often startled by the severity of mild people on exceptional occasions; the reason is, that mild people are most liable to be under the yoke of traditional impressions.

'I'm willing to pay any money as is wanted towards trying to bring her off,' said Martin the younger when Mr Irwine was gone, while the old grandfather was crying in the opposite chair, 'but I'll not go nigh her, nor ever see her again, by my own will. She's made our bread bitter to us, for all our lives to come, an' we shall ne'er hold up our heads i' this parish nor i' any other. The parson talks o' folks pitying us; it's poor amends pity 'ull make us.'

'Pity?' said the grandfather, sharply. 'I ne'er wanted folks's pity i' *my* life afore . . . an' I mun begin to be looked down on now, an' me turned seventy-two last St Thomas's,[4] an' all th' under-bearers and pall-bearers as I'n picked for my funeral are i' this parish and the next to't. . . . It's o' no use now . . . I mun be ta'en to the grave by strangers.'

'Don't fret so, father,' said Mrs Poyser, who had spoken very little, being almost overawed by her husband's unusual hardness and decision. 'You'll have your children wi' you; an' there's the lads and the little un 'ull grow up in a new parish as well as i' th' old un.'

'Ah, there's no staying i' this country for us now,' said Mr Poyser, and the hard tears trickled slowly down his round cheeks. 'We thought it 'ud be bad luck if the old Squire gave us notice this Lady Day, but I must gi' notice myself now, an' see if there can anybody be got to come an' take to the crops as I'n put i' the ground; for I wonna stay upo' that man's land a day longer nor I'm forced to't. An' me as thought him such a good upright young man, as I should be glad when he come to be our landlord. I'll ne'er lift my hat to him again, nor sit i' the same church wi' him . . . a man as has brought shame on respectable folks . . . an' pretended to be such a friend t' everybody. . . . Poor Adam there . . . a fine friend he's been t' Adam, making speeches an' talking so fine, an' all the while poisoning the lad's life, as it's much if he can stay i' this country any more nor we can.'

'An' you t' ha' to go into court, and own you're akin t' her,' said the old man. 'Why, they'll cast it up to the little un, as isn't four 'ear old, some day – they'll cast it up t' her as she'd a cousin tried at the 'sizes for murder.'

'It'll be their own wickedness, then,' said Mrs Poyser, with a sob in her voice. 'But there's One above 'ull take care o' the inicent child, else it's but little truth they tell us at church. It'll be harder nor ever to die an' leave the little uns, an' nobody to be a mother to 'em.'

'We'd better ha' sent for Dinah, if we'd known where she is,' said Mr Poyser; 'but Adam said she'd left no direction where she'd be at Leeds.'

'Why, she'd be wi' that woman as was a friend t' her aunt Judith,' said Mrs Poyser, comforted a little by this suggestion of her husband's. 'I've often heard Dinah talk of her, but I can't remember what name she called her by. But there's Seth Bede; he's like enough to know, for she's a preaching woman as the Methodists think a deal on.'

'I'll send to Seth,' said Mr Poyser. 'I'll send Alick to tell him to come, or else to send us word o' the woman's name, an' thee canst write a letter ready to send off to Treddles'on as soon as we can make out a direction.'

'It's poor work writing letters when you want folks to come to you i' trouble,' said Mrs Poyser. 'Happen it'll be ever so long on the road, an' never reach her at last.'

Before Alick arrived with the message, Lisbeth's thoughts too had already flown to Dinah, and she had said to Seth –

'Eh, there's no comfort for us i' this world any more, wi'out thee couldst get Dinah Morris to come to us, as she did when my old man died. I'd like her to come in an' take me by th' hand again, an' talk to me: she'd tell me the rights on't, belike – she'd happen know some good i' all this trouble an' heart-break comin' upo' that poor lad, as ne'er done a bit o' wrong in's life, but war better nor anybody else's son, pick the country round. Eh, my lad . . . Adam, my poor lad!'

'Thee wouldstna like me to leave thee, to go and fetch Dinah?' said Seth, as his mother sobbed, and rocked herself to and fro.

'Fetch her?' said Lisbeth, looking up, and pausing from her grief, like a crying child, who hears some promise of consolation. 'Why, what place is't she's at, do they say?'

'It's a good way off, mother – Leeds, a big town. But I could be back in three days, if thee couldst spare me.'

'Nay, nay, I canna spare thee. Thee must go an' see thy brother, an' bring me word what he's a-doin'. Mester Irwine said he'd come an' tell me, but I canna make out so well what

it means when he tells me. Thee must go thysen, sin' Adam
wonna let me go to him. Write a letter to Dinah, canstna?
Thee't fond enough o' writin' when nobody wants thee.'

'I'm not sure where she'd be i' that big town,' said Seth. 'If
I'd gone myself, I could ha' found out by asking the members o'
the Society. But perhaps, if I put Sarah Williamson, Methodist
preacher, Leeds,[5] o' th' outside, it might get to her; for most
like she'd be wi' Sarah Williamson.'

Alick came now with the message, and Seth, finding that Mrs
Poyser was writing to Dinah, gave up the intention of writing
himself; but he went to the Hall Farm to tell them all he could
suggest about the address of the letter, and warn them that
there might be some delay in the delivery, from his not knowing
an exact direction.

On leaving Lisbeth, Mr Irwine had gone to Jonathan Burge,
who had also a claim to be acquainted with what was likely to
keep Adam away from business for some time; and before six
o'clock that evening there were few people in Broxton and
Hayslope who had not heard the sad news. Mr Irwine had not
mentioned Arthur's name to Burge, and yet the story of his
conduct towards Hetty, with all the dark shadows cast upon it
by its terrible consequences, was presently as well known as
that his grandfather was dead, and that he was come into the
estate. For Martin Poyser felt no motive to keep silence towards
the one or two neighbours who ventured to come and shake
him sorrowfully by the hand on the first day of his trouble; and
Carroll, who kept his ears open to all that passed at the Rectory,
had framed an inferential version of the story, and found early
opportunities of communicating it.

One of those neighbours who came to Martin Poyser and
shook him by the hand without speaking for some minutes,
was Bartle Massey. He had shut up his school, and was on his
way to the Rectory, where he arrived about half-past seven in
the evening, and, sending his duty to Mr Irwine, begged pardon
for troubling him at that hour, but had something particular
on his mind. He was shown into the study, where Mr Irwine
soon joined him.

'Well, Bartle?' said Mr Irwine, putting out his hand. That

was not his usual way of saluting the schoolmaster, but trouble
makes us treat all who feel with us very much alike. 'Sit down.'

'You know what I'm come about as well as I do, sir, I
daresay,' said Bartle.

'You wish to know the truth about the sad news that has
reached you . . . about Hetty Sorrel?'

'Nay, sir, what I wish to know is about Adam Bede. I understand you left him at Stoniton, and I beg the favour of you to
tell me what's the state of the poor lad's mind, and what he
means to do. For as for that bit o' pink-and-white they've taken
the trouble to put in jail, I don't value her a rotten nut – not a
rotten nut – only for the harm or good that may come out of
her to an honest man – a lad I've set such store by – trusted to,
that he'd make my bit o' knowledge go a good way in the
world. . . . Why, sir, he's the only scholar I've had in this stupid
country that ever had the will or the head-piece for mathe-
matics. If he hadn't had so much hard work to do, poor fellow,
he might have gone into the higher branches, and then this
might never have happened – might never have happened.'

Bartle was heated by the exertion of walking fast in an agitated frame of mind, and was not able to check himself on this
first occasion of venting his feelings. But he paused now to rub
his moist forehead, and probably his moist eyes also.

'You'll excuse me, sir,' he said, when this pause had given
him time to reflect, 'for running on in this way about my own
feelings, like that foolish dog of mine, howling in a storm, when
there's nobody wants to listen to me. I came to hear you speak,
not to talk myself; if you'll take the trouble to tell me what the
poor lad's doing.'

'Don't put yourself under any restraint, Bartle,' said Mr
Irwine. 'The fact is, I'm very much in the same condition as you
just now; I've a great deal that's painful on my mind, and I find
it hard work to be quite silent about my own feelings and only
attend to others. I share your concern for Adam, though he is
not the only one whose sufferings I care for in this affair. He
intends to remain at Stoniton till after the trial: it will come on
probably a week to-morrow. He has taken a room there, and I
encouraged him to do so, because I think it better he should be

away from his own home at present; and, poor fellow, he still believes Hetty is innocent – he wants to summon up courage to see her if he can; he is unwilling to leave the spot where she is.'

'Do you think the creatur's guilty, then?' said Bartle. 'Do you think they'll hang her?'

'I'm afraid it will go hard with her: the evidence is very strong. And one bad symptom is that she denies everything – denies that she has had a child, in the face of the most positive evidence. I saw her myself, and she was obstinately silent to me; she shrank up like a frightened animal when she saw me. I was never so shocked in my life as at the change in her. But I trust that, in the worst case, we may obtain a pardon for the sake of the innocent who are involved.'

'Stuff and nonsense!' said Bartle, forgetting in his irritation to whom he was speaking – 'I beg your pardon, sir, I mean it's stuff and nonsense for the innocent to care about her being hanged. For my own part, I think the sooner such women are put out o' the world the better; and the men that help 'em to do mischief had better go along with 'em for that matter. What good will you do by keeping such vermin alive? eating the victual that 'ud feed rational beings. But if Adam's fool enough to care about it, I don't want him to suffer more than's needful. . . . Is he very much cut up, poor fellow?' Bartle added, taking out his spectacles and putting them on, as if they would assist his imagination.

'Yes, I'm afraid the grief cuts very deep,' said Mr Irwine. 'He looks terribly shattered, and a certain violence came over him now and then yesterday, which made me wish I could have remained near him. But I shall go to Stoniton again to-morrow, and I have confidence enough in the strength of Adam's principle to trust that he will be able to endure the worst without being driven to anything rash.'

Mr Irwine, who was involuntarily uttering his own thoughts rather than addressing Bartle Massey in the last sentence, had in his mind the possibility that the spirit of vengeance towards Arthur, which was the form Adam's anguish was continually taking, might make him seek an encounter that was likely to end more fatally than the one in the Grove. This possibility heightened the anxiety with which he looked forward to Arthur's arrival. But Bartle thought Mr Irwine was referring to suicide, and his face wore a new alarm.

'I'll tell you what I have in my head, sir,' he said, 'and I hope you'll approve of it. I'm going to shut up my school: if the scholars come, they must go back again, that's all: and I shall go to Stoniton and look after Adam till this business is over. I'll pretend I'm come to look on at the assizes; he can't object to that. What do you think about it, sir?'

'Well,' said Mr Irwine, rather hesitatingly, 'there would be some real advantages in that . . . and I honour you for your friendship towards him, Bartle. But . . . you must be careful what you say to him, you know. I'm afraid you have too little fellow-feeling in what you consider his weakness about Hetty.'

'Trust to me, sir – trust to me. I know what you mean. I've been a fool myself in my time, but that's between you and me. I shan't thrust myself on him – only keep my eye on him, and see that he gets some good food, and put in a word here and there.'

'Then,' said Mr Irwine, reassured a little as to Bartle's discretion, 'I think you'll be doing a good deed; and it will be well for you to let Adam's mother and brother know that you're going.'

'Yes, sir, yes,' said Bartle, rising, and taking off his spectacles, 'I'll do that, I'll do that; though the mother's a whimpering thing – I don't like to come within earshot of her; however, she's a straight-backed, clean woman, none of your slatterns. I wish you good-bye, sir, and thank you for the time you've spared me. You're everybody's friend in this business – everybody's friend. It's a heavy weight you've got on your shoulders.'

'Good-bye, Bartle, till we meet at Stoniton, as I daresay we shall.'

Bartle hurried away from the Rectory, evading Carroll's conversational advances, and saying in an exasperated tone to Vixen, whose short legs pattered beside him on the gravel –

'Now, I shall be obliged to take you with me, you good-for-nothing woman. You'd go fretting yourself to death if I left you – you know you would, and perhaps get snapped up by some

tramp; and you'll be running into bad company, I expect, putting your nose in every hole and corner where you've no
business! but if you do anything disgraceful, I'll disown you –
mind that, madam, mind that!'

CHAPTER XLI

The Eve of the Trial

An upper room[1] in a dull Stoniton street, with two beds in it – one laid on the floor. It is ten o'clock on Thursday night, and the dark wall opposite the window shuts out the moonlight that might have struggled with the light of the one dip candle by which Bartle Massey is pretending to read, while he is really looking over his spectacles at Adam Bede, seated near the dark window.

You would hardly have known it was Adam without being told. His face has got thinner this last week: he has the sunken eyes, the neglected beard of a man just risen from a sick-bed. His heavy black hair hangs over his forehead, and there is no active impulse in him which inclines him to push it off, that he may be more awake to what is around him. He has one arm over the back of the chair, and he seems to be looking down at his clasped hands. He is roused by a knock at the door.

'There he is,' said Bartle Massey, rising hastily and unfastening the door. It was Mr Irwine.

Adam rose from his chair with instinctive respect, as Mr Irwine approached him and took his hand.

'I'm late, Adam,' he said, sitting down on the chair which Bartle placed for him; 'but I was later in setting off from Broxton than I intended to be, and I have been incessantly occupied since I arrived. I have done everything now, however – everything that can be done to-night, at least. Let us all sit down.'

Adam took his chair again mechanically, and Bartle, for whom there was no chair remaining, sat on the bed in the background.

'Have you seen her, sir?' said Adam, tremulously.

'Yes, Adam; I and the chaplain have both been with her this evening.'

'Did you ask her, sir . . . did you say anything about me?'

'Yes,' said Mr Irwine, with some hesitation, 'I spoke of you. I said you wished to see her before the trial, if she consented.'

As Mr Irwine paused, Adam looked at him with eager, questioning eyes.

'You know she shrinks from seeing any one, Adam. It is not only you – some fatal influence seems to have shut up her heart against her fellow-creatures. She has scarcely said anything more than "No", either to me or the chaplain. Three or four days ago, before you were mentioned to her, when I asked her if there was any one of her family whom she would like to see – to whom she could open her mind, she said, with a violent shudder, "Tell them not to come near me – I won't see any of them."'

Adam's head was hanging down again, and he did not speak. There was silence for a few minutes, and then Mr Irwine said –

'I don't like to advise you against your own feelings, Adam, if they now urge you strongly to go and see her to-morrow morning, even without her consent. It is just possible, notwithstanding appearances to the contrary, that the interview might affect her favourably. But I grieve to say I have scarcely any hope of that. She didn't seem agitated when I mentioned your name; she only said "No", in the same cold, obstinate way as usual. And if the meeting had no good effect on her, it would be pure, useless suffering to you – severe suffering, I fear. She is very much changed' . . .

Adam started up from his chair, and seized his hat which lay on the table. But he stood still then, and looked at Mr Irwine, as if he had a question to ask, which it was yet difficult to utter. Bartle Massey rose quietly, turned the key in the door, and put it in his pocket.

'Is he come back?' said Adam at last.

'No, he is not,' said Mr Irwine, quietly. 'Lay down your hat, Adam, unless you like to walk out with me for a little fresh air. I fear you have not been out again to-day.'

'You needn't deceive me, sir,' said Adam, looking hard at Mr

Irwine, and speaking in a tone of angry suspicion. 'You needn't be afraid of me. I only want justice. I want him to feel what she feels. It's his work . . . she was a child as it 'ud ha' gone t' anybody's heart to look at . . . I don't care what she's done . . . it was him brought her to it. And he shall know it . . . he shall feel it . . . if there's a just God, he shall feel what it is t' ha' brought a child like her to sin and misery.'

'I'm not deceiving you, Adam,' said Mr Irwine. 'Arthur Donnithorne is not come back – was not come back when I left. I have left a letter for him: he will know all as soon as he arrives.'

'But you don't mind about it,' said Adam, indignantly. 'You think it doesn't matter as she lies there in shame and misery, and he knows nothing about it – he suffers nothing.'

'Adam, he *will* know – he *will* suffer, long and bitterly. He has a heart and a conscience: I can't be entirely deceived in his character. I am convinced – I am sure he didn't fall under temptation without a struggle. He may be weak, but he is not callous, not coldly selfish. I am persuaded that this will be a shock of which he will feel the effects all his life. Why do you crave vengeance in this way? No amount of torture that you could inflict on *him* could benefit *her*.'

'No – O God, no,' Adam groaned out, sinking on his chair again; 'but then, that's the deepest curse of all . . . that's what makes the blackness of it . . . *it can never be undone*. My poor Hetty . . . she can never be my sweet Hetty again . . . the prettiest thing God had made – smiling up at me . . . I thought she loved me . . . and was good' . . .

Adam's voice had been gradually sinking into a hoarse under-tone, as if he were only talking to himself; but now he said abruptly, looking at Mr Irwine –

'But she isn't as guilty as they say? You don't think she is, sir? She can't ha' done it.'

'That perhaps can never be known with certainty, Adam,' Mr Irwine answered, gently. 'In these cases we sometimes form our judgement on what seems to us strong evidence, and yet, for want of knowing some small fact, our judgement is wrong. But suppose the worst: you have no right to say that the guilt of her crime lies with him, and that he ought to bear the punishment. It is not for us men to apportion the shares of moral guilt and retribution. We find it impossible to avoid mistakes even in determining who has committed a single criminal act, and the problem how far a man is to be held responsible for the unforeseen consequences of his own deed, is one that might well make us tremble to look into it. The evil consequences that may lie folded in a single act of selfish indulgence, is a thought so awful that it ought surely to awaken some feeling less presumptuous than a rash desire to punish. You have a mind that can understand this fully, Adam, when you are calm. Don't suppose I can't enter into the anguish that drives you into this state of revengeful hatred; but think of this: if you were to obey your passion – for it *is* passion, and you deceive yourself in calling it justice – it might be with you precisely as it has been with Arthur; nay, worse; your passion might lead you yourself into a horrible crime.'

'No, not worse,' said Adam, bitterly; 'I don't believe it's worse – I'd sooner do it – I'd sooner do a wickedness as I could suffer for by myself, than ha' brought *her* to do wickedness and then stand by and see 'em punish her while they let me alone; and all for a bit o' pleasure, as, if he'd had a man's heart in him, he'd ha' cut his hand off sooner than he'd ha' taken it. What if he didn't foresee what's happened? He foresaw enough: he'd no right to expect anything but harm and shame to her. And then he wanted to smooth it off wi' lies. No – there's plenty o' things folks are hanged for, not half so hateful as that: let a man do what he will, if he knows he's to bear the punishment himself, he isn't half so bad as a mean selfish coward as makes things easy t' himself, and knows all the while the punishment 'ull fall on somebody else.'

'There again you partly deceive yourself, Adam. There is no sort of wrong deed of which a man can bear the punishment alone; you can't isolate yourself, and say that the evil which is in you shall not spread. Men's lives are as thoroughly blended² with each other as the air they breathe: evil spreads as necessarily as disease. I know, I feel the terrible extent of suffering this sin of Arthur's has caused to others; but so does every sin cause suffering to others besides those who commit it. An act of vengeance on your part against Arthur would simply be another evil added to those we are suffering under: you could not bear the punishment alone; you would entail the worst sorrows on every one who loves you. You would have committed an act of blind fury, that would leave all the present evils just as they were, and add worse evils to them. You may tell me that you meditate no fatal act of vengeance: but the feeling in your mind is what gives birth to such actions, and as long as you indulge it, as long as you do not see that to fix your mind on Arthur's punishment is revenge, and not justice, you are in danger of being led on to the commission of some great wrong. Remember what you told me about your feelings after you had given that blow to Arthur in the Grove.'

Adam was silent: the last words had called up a vivid image of the past, and Mr Irwine left him to his thoughts, while he spoke to Bartle Massey about old Mr Donnithorne's funeral and other matters of an indifferent kind. But at length Adam turned round and said, in a more subdued tone –

'I've not asked about 'em at th' Hall Farm, sir. Is Mr Poyser coming?'

'He is come; he is in Stoniton to-night. But I could not advise him to see you, Adam. His own mind is in a very perturbed state, and it is best he should not see you till you are calmer.'

'Is Dinah Morris come to 'em, sir? Seth said they'd sent for her.'

'No. Mr Poyser tells me she was not come when he left. They're afraid the letter has not reached her. It seems they had no exact address.'

Adam sat ruminating a little while, and then said –

'I wonder if Dinah 'ud ha' gone to see her. But perhaps the Poysers would ha' been sorely against it, since they won't come nigh her themselves. But I think she would, for the Methodists are great folks for going into the prisons; and Seth said he thought she would. She'd a very tender way with her, Dinah had; I wonder if she could ha' done any good. You never saw her, sir, did you?'

'Yes, I did: I had a conversation with her – she pleased me a good deal. And now you mention it, I wish she would come; for it is possible that a gentle, mild woman like her might move Hetty to open her heart. The jail chaplain is rather harsh in his manner.'

'But it's o' no use if she doesn't come,' said Adam, sadly.

'If I'd thought of it earlier, I would have taken some measures for finding her out,' said Mr Irwine, 'but it's too late now, I fear ... Well, Adam, I must go now. Try to get some rest to-night. God bless you. I'll see you early to-morrow morning.'

CHAPTER XLII

The Morning of the Trial

At one o'clock the next day, Adam was alone in his dull upper room; his watch lay before him on the table, as if he were counting the long minutes. He had no knowledge of what was likely to be said by the witnesses on the trial, for he had shrunk from all the particulars connected with Hetty's arrest and accusation. This brave active man, who would have hastened towards any danger or toil to rescue Hetty from an apprehended wrong or misfortune, felt himself powerless to contemplate irremediable evil and suffering. The susceptibility which would have been an impelling force where there was any possibility of action, became helpless anguish when he was obliged to be passive, or else sought an active outlet in the thought of inflicting justice on Arthur. Energetic natures, strong for all strenuous deeds, will often rush away from a hopeless sufferer, as if they were hard-hearted. It is the over-mastering sense of pain that drives them. They shrink by an ungovernable instinct, as they would shrink from laceration. Adam had brought himself to think of seeing Hetty, if she would consent to see him, because he thought the meeting might possibly be a good to her – might help to melt away this terrible hardness they told him of. If she saw he bore her no ill-will for what she had done to him, she might open her heart to him. But this resolution had been an immense effort; he trembled at the thought of seeing her changed face, as a timid woman trembles at the thought of the surgeon's knife; and he chose now to bear the long hours of suspense, rather than encounter what seemed to him the more intolerable agony of witnessing her trial.

Deep, unspeakable suffering may well be called a baptism, a regeneration, the initiation into a new state. The yearning memories, the bitter regret, the agonized sympathy, the struggling appeals to the Invisible Right – all the intense emotions which had filled the days and nights of the past week, and were compressing themselves again like an eager crowd into the hours of this single morning, made Adam look back on all the previous years as if they had been a dim sleepy existence, and he had only now awaked to full consciousness. It seemed to him as if he had always before thought it a light thing that men should suffer; as if all that he had himself endured and called sorrow before, was only a moment's stroke that had never left a bruise. Doubtless a great anguish may do the work of years, and we may come out from that baptism of fire with a soul full of new awe and new pity.

'O God,' Adam groaned, as he leaned on the table, and looked blankly at the face of the watch, 'and men have suffered like this before . . . and poor helpless young things have suffered like her. . . . Such a little while ago looking so happy and so pretty . . . kissing 'em all, her grandfather and all of 'em, and they wishing her luck. . . . Oh my poor, poor Hetty . . . dost think on it now?'

Adam started and looked round towards the door. Vixen had begun to whimper, and there was a sound of a stick and a lame walk on the stairs. It was Bartle Massey come back. Could it be all over?

Bartle entered quietly, and, going up to Adam, grasped his hand and said, 'I'm just come to look at you, my boy, for the folks are gone out of court for a bit.'

Adam's heart beat so violently, he was unable to speak – he could only return the pressure of his friend's hand; and Bartle, drawing up the other chair, came and sat in front of him, taking off his hat and his spectacles.

'That's a thing never happened to me before,' he observed – 'to go out o' door with my spectacles on. I clean forgot to take 'em off.'

The old man made this trivial remark, thinking it better not to respond at all to Adam's agitation: he would gather, in an indirect way, that there was nothing decisive to communicate at present.

'And now,' he said, rising again, 'I must see to your having a bit of the loaf, and some of that wine Mr Irwine sent this morning. He'll be angry with me if you don't have it. Come, now,' he went on, bringing forward the bottle and the loaf, and pouring some wine into a cup, 'I must have a bit and a sup myself. Drink a drop with me, my lad – drink with me.'

Adam pushed the cup gently away, and said, entreatingly, 'Tell me about it, Mr Massey – tell me all about it. Was she there? Have they begun?'

'Yes, my boy, yes – it's taken all the time since I first went; but they're slow, they're slow; and there's the counsel they've got for her puts a spoke in the wheel whenever he can, and makes a deal to do with cross-examining the witnesses, and quarrelling with the other lawyers. That's all he can do for the money they give him; and it's a big sum – it's a big sum. But he's a 'cute fellow, with an eye that 'ud pick the needles out of the hay in no time. If a man had got no feelings, it 'ud be as good as a demonstration to listen to what goes on in court; but a tender heart makes one stupid. I'd have given up figures for ever only to have had some good news to bring to you, my poor lad.'

'But does it seem to be going against her?' said Adam. 'Tell me what they've said. I must know it now – I must know what they have to bring against her.'

'Why, the chief evidence yet has been the doctors; all but Martin Poyser – poor Martin. Everybody in court felt for him – it it was like one sob, the sound they made when he came down again. The worst was, when they told him to look at the prisoner at the bar. It was hard work, poor fellow – it was hard work. Adam, my boy, the blow falls heavily on him as well as you: you must help poor Martin; you must show courage. Drink some wine now, and show me you mean to bear it like a man.'

Bartle had made the right sort of appeal. Adam, with an air of quiet obedience, took up the cup, and drank a little.

'Tell me how *she* looked,' he said, presently.

'Frightened, very frightened, when they first brought her in; it was the first sight of the crowd and the judge, poor creatur. And there's a lot o' foolish women in fine clothes, with gewgaws all up their arms and feathers on their heads, sitting near the judge: they've dressed themselves out in that way, one 'ud think, to be scarecrows and warnings against any man ever meddling with a woman again; they put up their glasses, and stared and whispered. But after that she stood like a white image, staring down at her hands, and seeming neither to hear nor see anything. And she's as white as a sheet. She didn't speak when they asked her if she'd plead "guilty" or "not guilty", and they pled "not guilty" for her. But when she heard her uncle's name, there seemed to go a shiver right through her; and when they told him to look at her, she hung her head down, and cowered, and hid her face in her hands. He'd much ado to speak, poor man, his voice trembled so. And the counsellors, – who look as hard as nails mostly, – I saw, spared him as much as they could. Mr Irwine put himself near him, and went with him out o' court. Ah, it's a great thing in a man's life to be able to stand by a neighbour, and uphold him in such trouble as that.'

'God bless him, and you too, Mr Massey,' said Adam, in a low voice, laying his hand on Bartle's arm.

'Ay, ay, he's good metal; he gives the right ring when you try him, our parson does. A man o' sense – says no more than's needful. He's not one of those that think they can comfort you with chattering, as if folks who stand by and look on knew a deal better what the trouble was than those who have to bear it. I've had to do with such folks in my time – in the south, when I was in trouble myself. Mr Irwine is to be a witness himself, by-and-by, on her side, you know, to speak to her character and bringing up.'

'But the other evidence . . . does it go hard against her?' said Adam. 'What do you think, Mr Massey? Tell me the truth.'

'Yes, my lad, yes: the truth is the best thing to tell. It must come at last. The doctor's evidence is heavy on her – is heavy. But she's gone on denying she's had a child from first to last: these poor silly women-things – they've not the sense to know it's no use denying what's proved. It'll make against her with the jury, I doubt, her being so obstinate: they may be less for recommending her to mercy, if the verdict's against her. But Mr Irwine 'll leave no stone unturned with the judge – you may rely upon that, Adam.'

'Is there nobody to stand by her, and seem to care for her, in the court?' said Adam.

'There's the chaplain o' the jail sits near her, but he's a sharp ferrety-faced man – another sort o' flesh and blood to Mr Irwine. They say the jail chaplains are mostly the fag-end o' the clergy.'

'There's one man as ought to be there,' said Adam, bitterly. Presently he drew himself up, and looked fixedly out of the window, apparently turning over some new idea in his mind.

'Mr Massey,' he said at last, pushing the hair off his forehead, 'I'll go back with you. I'll go into court. It's cowardly of me to keep away. I'll stand by her – I'll own her – for all she's been deceitful. They oughtn't to cast her off – her own flesh and blood. We hand folks over to God's mercy, and show none ourselves. I used to be hard sometimes: I'll never be hard again. I'll go, Mr Massey – I'll go with you.'

There was a decision in Adam's manner which would have prevented Bartle from opposing him, even if he had wished to do so. He only said –

'Take a bit, then, and another sup, Adam, for the love of me. See, I must stop and eat a morsel. Now, you take some.'

Nerved by an active resolution, Adam took a morsel of bread and drank some wine. He was haggard and unshaven, as he had been yesterday, but he stood upright again, and looked more like the Adam Bede of former days.

CHAPTER XLIII

The Verdict

The place fitted up that day as a court of justice[1] was a grand
old hall, now destroyed by fire. The mid-day light that fell on
the close pavement of human heads, was shed through a line of
high pointed windows, variegated with the mellow tints of old
painted glass. Grim dusty armour hung in high relief in front
of the dark oaken gallery at the farther end; and under the
broad arch of the great mullioned window opposite was spread
a curtain of old tapestry, covered with dim melancholy figures,
like a dozing indistinct dream of the past. It was a place that
through the rest of the year was haunted with the shadowy
memories of old kings and queens, unhappy, discrowned,
imprisoned; but to-day all those shadows had fled, and not a
soul in the vast hall felt the presence of any but a living sorrow,
which was quivering in warm hearts.

But that sorrow seemed to have made itself feebly felt
hitherto, now when Adam Bede's tall figure was suddenly seen,
being ushered to the side of the prisoner's dock. In the broad
sunlight of the great hall, among the sleek shaven faces of other
men, the marks of suffering in his face were startling even to
Mr Irwine, who had last seen him in the dim light of his small
room; and the neighbours from Hayslope who were present,
and who told Hetty Sorrel's story by their fire-sides in their old
age, never forgot to say how it moved them when Adam Bede,
poor fellow, taller by the head than most of the people round
him, came into court, and took his place by her side.

But Hetty did not see him. She was standing in the same
position Bartle Massey had described, her hands crossed over
each other, and her eyes fixed on them. Adam had not dared to

look at her in the first moments, but at last, when the attention of the court was withdrawn by the proceedings, he turned his face towards her with a resolution not to shrink.

Why did they say she was so changed? In the corpse we love, it is the *likeness* we see – it is the likeness, which makes itself felt the more keenly because something else *was* and *is not*. There they were – the sweet face and neck, with the dark tendrils of hair, the long dark lashes, the rounded cheek and the pouting lips: pale and thin – yes – but like Hetty, and only Hetty. Others thought she looked as if some demon had cast a blighting glance upon her, withered up the woman's soul in her, and left only a hard despairing obstinacy. But the mother's yearning, that completest type of the life in another life which is the essence of real human love, feels the presence of the cherished child even in the debased, degraded man; and to Adam, this pale, hard-looking culprit was the Hetty who had smiled at him in the garden under the apple-tree boughs – she was that Hetty's corpse, which he had trembled to look at the first time, and then was unwilling to turn away his eyes from.

But presently he heard something that compelled him to listen, and made the sense of sight less absorbing. A woman was in the witness-box, a middle-aged woman, who spoke in a firm distinct voice. She said –

'My name is Sarah Stone. I am a widow, and keep a small shop licensed to sell tobacco, snuff, and tea, in Church Lane, Stoniton. The prisoner at the bar is the same young woman who came, looking ill and tired, with a basket on her arm, and asked for a lodging at my house on Saturday evening, the 27th of February. She had taken the house for a public, because there was a figure against the door.[2] And when I said I didn't take in lodgers, the prisoner began to cry, and said she was too tired to go anywhere else, and she only wanted a bed for one night. And her prettiness, and her condition, and something respectable about her clothes and looks, and the trouble she seemed to be in, made me as I couldn't find in my heart to send her away at once. I asked her to sit down, and gave her some tea, and asked her where she was going, and where her friends were. She said she was going home to her friends: they were farming

folks a good way off, and she'd had a long journey that had
cost her more money than she expected, so as she'd hardly any
money left in her pocket, and was afraid of going where it
would cost her much. She had been obliged to sell most of the
things out of her basket; but she'd thankfully give a shilling for
a bed. I saw no reason why I shouldn't take the young woman
in for the night. I had only one room, but there were two beds
in it, and I told her she might stay with me. I thought she'd
been led wrong, and got into trouble, but if she was going to
her friends, it would be a good work to keep her out of further
harm.'

The witness then stated that in the night a child was born,
and she identified the baby-clothes then shown to her as those
in which she had herself dressed the child.

'Those are the clothes. I made them myself, and had kept
them by me ever since my last child was born. I took a deal of
trouble both for the child and the mother. I couldn't help taking
to the little thing and being anxious about it. I didn't send for
a doctor, for there seemed no need. I told the mother in the
day-time she must tell me the name of her friends, and where
they lived, and let me write to them. She said, by-and-by she
would write herself, but not to-day. She would have no nay,
but she would get up and be dressed, in spite of everything I
could say. She said she felt quite strong enough; and it was
wonderful what spirit she showed. But I wasn't quite easy what
I should do about her, and towards evening I made up my mind
I'd go, after Meeting was over, and speak to our minister[3] about
it. I left the house about half-past eight o'clock. I didn't go out
at the shop door, but at the back door, which opens into a
narrow alley. I've only got the ground-floor of the house, and
the kitchen and bedroom both look into the alley. I left the
prisoner sitting up by the fire in the kitchen with the baby on
her lap. She hadn't cried or seemed low at all, as she did the
night before. I thought she had a strange look with her eyes,
and she got a bit flushed towards evening. I was afraid of the
fever,[4] and I thought I'd call and ask an acquaintance of mine,
an experienced woman, to come back with me when I went
out. It was a very dark night. I didn't fasten the door behind

me: there was no lock: it was a latch with a bolt inside, and
when there was nobody in the house I always went out at the
shop door. But I thought there was no danger in leaving it
unfastened that little while. I was longer than I meant to be, for
I had to wait for the woman that came back with me. It was an
hour and a half before we got back, and when we went in, the
candle was standing burning just as I left it, but the prisoner
and the baby were both gone. She'd taken her cloak and bonnet,
but she'd left the basket and the things in it. . . . I was dreadful
frightened, and angry with her for going. I didn't go to give
information, because I'd no thought she meant to do any harm,
and I knew she had money in her pocket to buy her food and
lodging. I didn't like to set the constable after her, for she'd a
right to go from me if she liked.'

The effect of this evidence on Adam was electrical; it gave
him new force. Hetty could not be guilty of the crime – her
heart must have clung to her baby – else why should she have
taken it with her? She might have left it behind. The little
creature had died naturally, and then she had hidden it: babies
were so liable to death – and there might be the strongest
suspicions without any proof of guilt. His mind was so occupied
with imaginary arguments against such suspicions, that he
could not listen to the cross-examination by Hetty's counsel,
who tried, without result, to elicit evidence that the prisoner
had shown some movements of maternal affection towards the
child. The whole time this witness was being examined, Hetty
had stood as motionless as before: no word seemed to arrest
her ear. But the sound of the next witness's voice touched a
chord that was still sensitive; she gave a start and a frightened
look towards him, but immediately turned away her head and
looked down at her hands as before. This witness was a man,
a rough peasant. He said –

'My name is John Olding. I am a labourer, and live at Tedd's
Hole, two miles out of Stoniton. A week last Monday, towards
one o'clock in the afternoon, I was going towards Hetton
Coppice, and about a quarter of a mile from the coppice I saw
the prisoner, in a red cloak, sitting under a bit of a haystack
not far off the stile. She got up when she saw me, and seemed

as if she'd be walking on the other way. It was a regular road through the fields, and nothing very uncommon to see a young woman there, but I took notice of her because she looked white and scared. I should have thought she was a beggar-woman, only for her good clothes. I thought she looked a bit crazy, but it was no business of mine. I stood and looked back after her, but she went right on while she was in sight. I had to go to the other side of the coppice to look after some stakes.[5] There's a road right through it, and bits of openings here and there, where the trees have been cut down, and some of 'em not carried away. I didn't go straight along the road, but turned off towards the middle, and took a shorter way towards the spot I wanted to get to. I hadn't got far out of the road into one of the open places, before I heard a strange cry. I thought it didn't come from any animal I knew, but I wasn't for stopping to look about just then. But it went on, and seemed so strange to me in that place, I couldn't help stopping to look. I began to think I might make some money of it, if it was a new thing. But I had hard work to tell which way it came from, and for a good while I kept looking up at the boughs. And then I thought it came from the ground; and there was a lot of timber-choppings lying about, and loose pieces of turf, and a trunk or two. And I looked about among them, but could find nothing; and at last the cry stopped. So I was for giving it up, and I went on about my business. But when I came back the same way pretty nigh an hour after, I couldn't help laying down my stakes to have another look. And just as I was stooping and laying down the stakes, I saw something odd and round and whitish lying on the ground under a nut-bush by the side of me. And I stooped down on hands and knees to pick it up. And I saw it was a little baby's hand.'

At these words a thrill ran through the court. Hetty was visibly trembling: now, for the first time, she seemed to be listening to what a witness said.

'There was a lot of timber-choppings put together just where the ground went hollow, like, under the bush, and the hand came out from among them. But there was a hole left in one place, and I could see down it, and see the child's head; and I made haste and did away the turf and the choppings, and took out the child. It had got comfortable clothes on, but its body was cold, and I thought it must be dead. I made haste back with it out of the wood, and took it home to my wife. She said it was dead, and I'd better take it to the parish and tell the constable. And I said, "I'll lay my life it's that young woman's child as I met going to the coppice." But she seemed to be gone clean out of sight. And I took the child on to Hetton parish and told the constable,[6] and we went on to Justice Hardy. And then we went looking after the young woman till dark at night, and we went and gave information at Stoniton, as they might stop her. And the next morning another constable came to me, to go with him to the spot where I found the child. And when we got there, there was the prisoner a-sitting against the bush where I found the child; and she cried out when she saw us, but she never offered to move. She'd got a big piece of bread on her lap.'

Adam had given a faint groan of despair while this witness was speaking. He had hidden his face on his arm, which rested on the boarding in front of him. It was the supreme moment of his suffering: Hetty was guilty: and he was silently calling to God for help. He heard no more of the evidence, and was unconscious when the case for the prosecution had closed – unconscious that Mr Irwine was in the witness-box, telling of Hetty's unblemished character in her own parish, and of the virtuous habits in which she had been brought up. This testimony could have no influence on the verdict, but it was given as part of that plea for mercy which her own counsel would have made if he had been allowed to speak for her – a favour not granted to criminals in those stern times.[7]

At last Adam lifted up his head, for there was a general movement round him. The judge had addressed the jury, and they were retiring. The decisive moment was not far off. Adam felt a shuddering horror that would not let him look at Hetty, but she had long relapsed into her blank hard indifference. All eyes were strained to look at her, but she stood like a statue of dull despair.

There was a mingled rustling, whispering, and low buzzing

throughout the court during this interval. The desire to listen was suspended, and every one had some feeling or opinion to express in under-tones. Adam sat looking blankly before him, but he did not see the objects that were right in front of his eyes – the counsel and attorneys talking with an air of cool business, and Mr Irwine in low earnest conversation with the judge: did not see Mr Irwine sit down again in agitation, and shake his head mournfully when somebody whispered to him. The inward action was too intense for Adam to take in outward objects until some strong sensation roused him.

It was not very long, hardly more than a quarter of an hour, before the knock which told that the jury had come to their decision, fell as a signal for silence on every ear. It is sublime – that sudden pause of a great multitude, which tells that one soul moves in them all. Deeper and deeper the silence seemed to become, like the deepening night, while the jurymen's names were called over, and the prisoner was made to hold up her hand, and the jury were asked for their verdict.

'Guilty.'

It was the verdict every one expected, but there was a sigh of disappointment from some hearts, that it was followed by no recommendation to mercy. Still the sympathy of the court was not with the prisoner: the unnaturalness of her crime stood out the more harshly by the side of her hard immovability and obstinate silence. Even the verdict, to distant eyes, had not appeared to move her; but those who were near saw her trembling.

The stillness was less intense until the judge put on his black cap, and the chaplain in his canonicals[8] was observed behind him. Then it deepened again, before the crier had had time to command silence. If any sound were heard, it must have been the sound of beating hearts. The judge spoke –

'Hester Sorrel.' . . .

The blood rushed to Hetty's face, and then fled back again, as she looked up at the judge, and kept her wide-open eyes fixed on him, as if fascinated by fear. Adam had not yet turned towards her: there was a deep horror, like a great gulf, between them. But at the words – 'and then to be hanged by the neck till you be dead', a piercing shriek rang through the hall. It was Hetty's shriek. Adam started to his feet and stretched out his arms towards her; but the arms could not reach her: she had fallen down in a fainting-fit, and was carried out of court.

CHAPTER XLIV

Arthur's Return

When Arthur Donnithorne landed at Liverpool, and read the letter from his aunt Lydia, briefly announcing his grandfather's death, his first feeling was, 'Poor grandfather! I wish I could have got to him to be with him when he died. He might have felt or wished something at the last that I shall never know now. It was a lonely death.'

It is impossible to say that his grief was deeper than that. Pity and softened memory took place of the old antagonism, and in his busy thoughts about the future, as the chaise carried him rapidly along towards the home where he was now to be master, there was a continually recurring effort to remember anything by which he could show a regard for his grandfather's wishes, without counteracting his own cherished aims for the good of the tenants and the estate. But it is not in human nature – only in human pretence – for a young man like Arthur, with a fine constitution and fine spirits, thinking well of himself, believing that others think well of him, and having a very ardent intention to give them more and more reason for that good opinion, – it is not possible for such a young man, just coming into a splendid estate through the death of a very old man whom he was not fond of, to feel anything very different from exultant joy. *Now* his real life was beginning; now he would have room and opportunity for action, and he would use them. He would show the Loamshire people what a fine country gentleman was; he would not exchange that career for any other under the sun. He felt himself riding over the hills in the breezy autumn days, looking after favourite plans of drainage and enclosure; then admired on sombre mornings as the best rider on the best

horse in the hunt; spoken well of on market-days as a first-rate
landlord; by-and-by making speeches at election dinners, and
showing a wonderful knowledge of agriculture; the patron of
new ploughs and drills, the severe upbraider of negligent landowners, and withal a jolly fellow that everybody must like, –
happy faces greeting him everywhere on his own estate, and
the neighbouring families on the best terms with him. The
Irwines should dine with him every week, and have their own
carriage to come in, for in some very delicate way that Arthur
would devise, the lay-impropriator of the Hayslope tithes[1]
would insist on paying a couple of hundreds more to the Vicar;
and his aunt should be as comfortable as possible, and go on
living at the Chase, if she liked, in spite of her old-maidish
ways, – at least until he was married; and that event lay in
the indistinct background, for Arthur had not yet seen the
woman who would play the lady-wife to the first-rate country
gentleman.

These were Arthur's chief thoughts, so far as a man's
thoughts through hours of travelling can be compressed into a
few sentences, which are only like the list of names telling you
what are the scenes in a long, long panorama, full of colour, of
detail, and of life. The happy faces Arthur saw greeting him
were not pale abstractions, but real ruddy faces, long familiar
to him: Martin Poyser was there – the whole Poyser family.

What – Hetty?

Yes; for Arthur was at ease about Hetty: not quite at ease
about the past, for a certain burning of the ears would come
whenever he thought of the scenes with Adam last August, –
but at ease about her present lot. Mr Irwine, who had been a
regular correspondent, telling him all the news about the old
places and people, had sent him word nearly three months ago
that Adam Bede was not to marry Mary Burge, as he had
thought, but pretty Hetty Sorrel. Martin Poyser and Adam
himself had both told Mr Irwine all about it; – that Adam had
been deeply in love with Hetty these two years, and that now
it was agreed they were to be married in March. That stalwart
rogue Adam was more susceptible than the Rector had thought;
it was really quite an idyllic love affair; and if it had not been

too long to tell in a letter, he would have liked to describe to
Arthur the blushing looks and the simple strong words with
which the fine honest fellow told his secret. He knew Arthur
would like to hear that Adam had this sort of happiness in
prospect.

Yes, indeed! Arthur felt there was not air enough in the room
to satisfy his renovated life, when he had read that passage in
the letter. He threw up the windows, he rushed out of doors
into the December air, and greeted every one who spoke to him
with an eager gaiety, as if there had been news of a fresh
Nelson victory. For the first time that day since he had come to
Windsor, he was in true boyish spirits: the load that had been
pressing upon him was gone; the haunting fear had vanished.
He thought he could conquer his bitterness towards Adam now
– could offer him his hand, and ask to be his friend again, in
spite of that painful memory which would still make his ears
burn. He had been knocked down, and he had been forced to
tell a lie: such things make a scar, do what we will. But if Adam
were the same again as in the old days, Arthur wished to be the
same too, and to have Adam mixed up with his business and his
future, as he had always desired before that accursed meeting
in August. Nay, he would do a great deal more for Adam than
he should otherwise have done, when he came into the estate;
Hetty's husband had a special claim on him – Hetty herself
should feel that any pain she had suffered through Arthur in
the past, was compensated to her a hundredfold. For really she
could not have felt much, since she had so soon made up her
mind to marry Adam.

You perceive clearly what sort of picture Adam and Hetty
made in the panorama of Arthur's thoughts on his journey
homeward. It was March now; they were soon to be married:
perhaps they were already married. And *now* it was actually in
his power to do a great deal for them. Sweet – sweet little Hetty!
The little puss hadn't cared for him half as much as he cared
for her; for he was a great fool about her still – was almost
afraid of seeing her – indeed, had not cared much to look at
any other woman since he parted from her. That little figure
coming towards him in the Grove, those dark-fringed childish

eyes, the lovely lips put up to kiss him – that picture had got no fainter with the lapse of months. And she would look just the same. It was impossible to think how he could meet her: he should certainly tremble. Strange, how long this sort of influence lasts; for he was certainly not in love with Hetty now: he had been earnestly desiring, for months, that she should marry Adam, and there was nothing that contributed more to his happiness in these moments than the thought of their marriage. It was the exaggerating effect of imagination that made his heart still beat a little more quickly at the thought of her. When he saw the little thing again, as she really was, as Adam's wife, at work quite prosaically in her new home, he should perhaps wonder at the possibility of his past feelings. Thank heaven it had turned out so well! He should have plenty of affairs and interests to fill his life now, and not be in danger of playing the fool again.

Pleasant the crack of the postboy's whip! Pleasant the sense of being hurried along in swift ease through English scenes, so like those round his own home, only not quite so charming. Here was a market-town – very much like Treddleston – where the arms of the neighbouring lord of the manor were borne on the sign of the principal inn: then mere fields and hedges, their vicinity to a market-town carrying an agreeable suggestion of high rent, till the land began to assume a trimmer look, the woods were more frequent, and at length a white or red mansion looked down from a moderate eminence, or allowed him to be aware of its parapet and chimneys among the dense-looking masses of oaks and elms – masses reddened now with early buds. And close at hand came the village: the small church, with its red-tiled roof, looking humble even among the faded half-timbered houses; the old green grave-stones with nettles round them; nothing fresh and bright but the children, opening round eyes at the swift post-chaise; nothing noisy and busy but the gaping curs of mysterious pedigree. What a much prettier village Hayslope was! And it should not be neglected like this place: vigorous repairs should go on everywhere among farm-buildings and cottages, and travellers in post-chaises, coming along the Rosseter road, should do nothing but admire as they

went. And Adam Bede should superintend all the repairs, for
he had a share in Burge's business now, and, if he liked, Arthur
would put some money into the concern, and buy the old man
out in another year or two. That was an ugly fault in Arthur's
life, that affair last summer; but the future should make amends.
Many men would have retained a feeling of vindictiveness
towards Adam; but *he* would not – he would resolutely overcome all littleness of that kind, for he had certainly been very
much in the wrong; and though Adam had been harsh and
violent, and had thrust on him a painful dilemma, the poor
fellow was in love, and had real provocation. No; Arthur had
not an evil feeling in his mind towards any human being: he
was happy, and would make every one else happy that came
within his reach.

And here was dear old Hayslope at last, sleeping on the hill,
like a quiet old place as it was, in the late afternoon sunlight;
and opposite to it the great shoulders of the Binton Hills, below
them the purplish blackness of the hanging woods, and at last
the pale front of the Abbey, looking out from among the oaks
of the Chase, as if anxious for the heir's return. 'Poor grandfather! and he lies dead there. *He* was a young fellow once,
coming into the estate, and making his plans. So the world goes
round! Aunt Lydia must feel very desolate, poor thing; but she
shall be indulged as much as she indulges her fat Fido.'

The wheels of Arthur's chaise had been anxiously listened
for at the Chase, for to-day was Friday, and the funeral had
already been deferred two days. Before it drew up on the gravel
of the courtyard, all the servants in the house were assembled
to receive him with a grave, decent welcome, befitting a house
of death. A month ago, perhaps, it would have been difficult
for them to have maintained a suitable sadness in their faces,
when Mr Arthur was come to take possession; but the hearts
of the head-servants were heavy that day for another cause than
the death of the old Squire, and more than one of them was
longing to be twenty miles away, as Mr Craig was, knowing
what was to become of Hetty Sorrel – pretty Hetty Sorrel –
whom they used to see every week. They had the partisanship
of household servants who like their places, and were not

inclined to go the full length of the severe indignation felt against him by the farming tenants, but rather to make excuses for him; nevertheless, the upper servants, who had been on terms of neighbourly intercourse with the Poysers for many years, could not help feeling that the longed-for event of the young Squire's coming into the estate had been robbed of all its pleasantness.

To Arthur it was nothing surprising that the servants looked grave and sad: he himself was very much touched on seeing them all again, and feeling that he was in a new relation to them. It was that sort of pathetic emotion which has more pleasure than pain in it – which is perhaps one of the most delicious of all states to a good-natured man, conscious of the power to satisfy his good-nature. His heart swelled agreeably as he said –

'Well, Mills, how is my aunt?'

But now Mr Bygate, the lawyer, who had been in the house ever since the death, came forward to give deferential greetings and answer all questions, and Arthur walked with him towards the library, where his aunt Lydia was expecting him. Aunt Lydia was the only person in the house who knew nothing about Hetty: her sorrow as a maiden daughter was unmixed with any other thoughts than those of anxiety about funeral arrangements and her own future lot; and, after the manner of women, she mourned for the father who had made her life important, all the more because she had a secret sense that there was little mourning for him in other hearts.

But Arthur kissed her tearful face more tenderly than he had ever done in his life before.

'Dear aunt,' he said affectionately, as he held her hand, '*your* loss is the greatest of all, but you must tell me how to try and make it up to you all the rest of your life.'

'It was so sudden and so dreadful, Arthur,' poor Miss Lydia began, pouring out her little plaints; and Arthur sat down to listen with impatient patience. When a pause came, he said –

'Now, aunt, I'll leave you for a quarter of an hour just to go to my own room, and then I shall come and give full attention to everything.'

'My room is all ready for me, I suppose, Mills?' he said to the butler, who seemed to be lingering uneasily about the entrance-hall.

'Yes, sir, and there are letters for you; they are all laid on the writing-table in your dressing-room.'

On entering the small anteroom which was called a dressing-room, but which Arthur really used only to lounge and write in, he just cast his eyes on the writing-table, and saw that there were several letters and packets lying there; but he was in the uncomfortable dusty condition of a man who has had a long hurried journey, and he must really refresh himself by attending to his toilette a little, before he read his letters. Pym was there, making everything ready for him; and soon, with a delightful freshness about him, as if he were prepared to begin a new day, he went back into his dressing-room to open his letters. The level rays of the low afternoon sun entered directly at the window, and as Arthur seated himself in his velvet chair with their pleasant warmth upon him, he was conscious of that quiet wellbeing which perhaps you and I have felt on a sunny afternoon, when, in our brightest youth and health, life has opened a new vista for us, and long to-morrows of activity have stretched before us like a lovely plain which there was no need for hurrying to look at, because it was all our own.

The top letter was placed with its address upwards: it was in Mr Irwine's handwriting, Arthur saw at once; and below the address was written, 'To be delivered as soon as he arrives'. Nothing could have been less surprising to him than a letter from Mr Irwine at that moment: of course there was something he wished Arthur to know earlier than it was possible for them to see each other. At such a time as that it was quite natural that Irwine should have something pressing to say. Arthur broke the seal with an agreeable anticipation of soon seeing the writer.

'*I send this letter to meet you on your arrival, Arthur, because I may then be at Stoniton, whither I am called by the most painful duty it has ever been given me to perform; and it is right that you should know what I have to tell you without delay.*

'*I will not attempt to add by one word of reproach to the retribution that is now falling on you: any other words that I could write at this moment must be weak and unmeaning by the side of those in which I must tell you the simple fact.*

'*Hetty Sorrel is in prison, and will be tried on Friday for the crime of child-murder.*' ...

Arthur read no more. He started up from his chair, and stood for a single minute with a sense of violent convulsion in his whole frame, as if the life were going out of him with horrible throbs; but the next minute he had rushed out of the room, still clutching the letter – he was hurrying along the corridor, and down the stairs into the hall. Mills was still there, but Arthur did not see him, as he passed like a hunted man across the hall and out along the gravel. The butler hurried out after him as fast as his elderly limbs could run: he guessed, he knew, where the young Squire was going.

When Mills got to the stables, a horse was being saddled, and Arthur was forcing himself to read the remaining words of the letter. He thrust it into his pocket as the horse was led up to him, and at that moment caught sight of Mills's anxious face in front of him.

'Tell them I'm gone – gone to Stoniton,' he said, in a muffled tone of agitation – sprang into the saddle, and set off at a gallop.

CHAPTER XLV

In the Prison

Near sunset that evening an elderly gentleman was standing with his back against the smaller entrance-door of Stoniton jail, saying a few last words to the departing chaplain. The chaplain walked away, but the elderly gentleman stood still, looking down on the pavement, and stroking his chin with a ruminating air, when he was roused by a sweet clear woman's voice, saying –

'Can I get into the prison, if you please?'

He turned his head, and looked fixedly at the speaker for a few moments without answering.

'I have seen you before,' he said at last. 'Do you remember preaching on the village green at Hayslope in Loamshire?'

'Yes, sir, surely. Are you the gentleman that stayed to listen on horseback?'

'Yes. Why do you want to go into the prison?'

'I want to go to Hetty Sorrel, the young woman who has been condemned to death – and to stay with her, if I may be permitted. Have you power in the prison, sir?'

'Yes; I am a magistrate, and can get admittance for you. But did you know this criminal, Hetty Sorrel?'

'Yes, we are kin: my own aunt married her uncle, Martin Poyser. But I was away at Leeds, and didn't know of this great trouble in time to get here before to-day. I entreat you, sir, for the love of our heavenly Father, to let me go to her and stay with her.'

'How did you know she was condemned to death, if you are only just come from Leeds?'

'I have seen my uncle since the trial, sir. He is gone back to

his home now, and the poor sinner is forsaken of all. I beseech
you to get leave for me to be with her.'

'What! have you courage to stay all night in the prison?
She is very sullen, and will scarcely make answer when she is
spoken to.'

'Oh, sir, it may please God to open her heart still. Don't let
us delay.'

'Come, then,' said the elderly gentleman, ringing and gaining
admission; 'I know you have a key to unlock hearts.'

Dinah mechanically took off her bonnet and shawl as soon
as they were within the prison court, from the habit she had of
throwing them off when she preached or prayed, or visited the
sick; and when they entered the jailer's room, she laid them
down on a chair unthinkingly. There was no agitation visible
in her, but a deep concentrated calmness, as if, even when she
was speaking, her soul was in prayer reposing on an unseen
support.

After speaking to the jailer, the magistrate turned to her and
said, 'The turnkey will take you to the prisoner's cell, and leave
you there for the night, if you desire it; but you can't have a
light during the night – it is contrary to rules. My name is
Colonel Townley: if I can help you in anything, ask the jailer
for my address, and come to me. I take some interest in this
Hetty Sorrel, for the sake of that fine fellow, Adam Bede: I
happened to see him at Hayslope the same evening I heard you
preach, and recognized him in court to-day, ill as he looked.'

'Ah, sir, can you tell me anything about him? Can you tell
me where he lodges? For my poor uncle was too much weighed
down with trouble to remember.'

'Close by here. I inquired all about him of Mr Irwine. He
lodges over a tinman's shop, in the street on the right hand as
you entered the prison. There is an old schoolmaster with him.
Now, good-bye: I wish you success.'

'Farewell, sir. I am grateful to you.'

As Dinah crossed the prison court with the turnkey, the
solemn evening light seemed to make the walls higher than they
were by day, and the sweet pale face in the cap was more than
ever like a white flower on this background of gloom. The

turnkey looked askance at her all the while, but never spoke: he somehow felt that the sound of his own rude voice would be grating just then. He struck a light as they entered the dark corridor leading to the condemned cell,[1] and then said in his most civil tone, 'It'll be pretty nigh dark in the cell a'ready; but I can stop with my light a bit, if you like.'

'Nay, friend, thank you,' said Dinah. 'I wish to go in alone.'

'As you like,' said the jailer, turning the harsh key in the lock, and opening the door wide enough to admit Dinah. A jet of light from his lantern fell on the opposite corner of the cell, where Hetty was sitting on her straw pallet with her face buried in her knees. It seemed as if she were asleep, and yet the grating of the lock would have been likely to waken her.

The door closed again, and the only light in the cell was that of the evening sky, through the small high grating – enough to discern human faces by. Dinah stood still for a minute, hesitating to speak, because Hetty might be asleep; and looking at the motionless heap with a yearning heart. Then she said, softly –

'Hetty!'

There was a slight movement perceptible in Hetty's frame – a start such as might have been produced by a feeble electrical shock; but she did not look up. Dinah spoke again, in a tone made stronger by irrepressible emotion –

'Hetty . . . it's Dinah.'

Again there was a slight, startled movement through Hetty's frame, and without uncovering her face, she raised her head a little, as if listening.

'Hetty . . . Dinah is come to you.'

After a moment's pause, Hetty lifted her head slowly and timidly from her knees, and raised her eyes. The two pale faces were looking at each other: one with a wild hard despair in it, the other full of sad, yearning love. Dinah unconsciously opened her arms and stretched them out.

'Don't you know me, Hetty? Don't you remember Dinah? Did you think I wouldn't come to you in trouble?'

Hetty kept her eyes fixed on Dinah's face, – at first like an animal that gazes, and gazes, and keeps aloof.

'I'm come to be with you, Hetty – not to leave you – to stay with you – to be your sister to the last.'

Slowly, while Dinah was speaking, Hetty rose, took a step forward, and was clasped in Dinah's arms.

They stood so a long while, for neither of them felt the impulse to move apart again. Hetty, without any distinct thought of it, hung on this something that was come to clasp her now, while she was sinking helpless in a dark gulf; and Dinah felt a deep joy in the first sign that her love was welcomed by the wretched lost one. The light got fainter as they stood, and when at last they sat down on the straw pallet together, their faces had become indistinct.

Not a word was spoken. Dinah waited, hoping for a spontaneous word from Hetty; but she sat in the same dull despair, only clutching the hand that held hers, and leaning her cheek against Dinah's. It was the human contact she clung to, but she was not the less sinking into the dark gulf.

Dinah began to doubt whether Hetty was conscious who it was that sat beside her. She thought suffering and fear might have driven the poor sinner out of her mind. But it was borne in upon her, as she afterwards said, that she must not hurry God's work: we are over-hasty to speak – as if God did not manifest himself by our silent feeling, and make his love felt through ours. She did not know how long they sat in that way, but it got darker and darker, till there was only a pale patch of light on the opposite wall: all the rest was darkness. But she felt the Divine presence more and more, – nay, as if she herself were a part of it, and it was the Divine pity that was beating in her heart, and was willing the rescue of this helpless one. At last she was prompted to speak, and find out how far Hetty was conscious of the present.

'Hetty,' she said, gently, 'do you know who it is that sits by your side?'

'Yes,' Hetty answered, slowly, 'it's Dinah.'

'And do you remember the time when we were at the Hall Farm together, and that night when I told you to be sure and think of me as a friend in trouble?'

'Yes,' said Hetty. Then, after a pause, she added, 'But you can do nothing for me. You can't make 'em do anything. They'll hang me o' Monday – it's Friday now.'

As Hetty said the last words, she clung closer to Dinah, shuddering.

'No, Hetty, I can't save you from that death. But isn't the suffering less hard when you have somebody with you, that feels for you – that you can speak to, and say what's in your heart? . . . Yes, Hetty: you lean on me: you are glad to have me with you.'

'You won't leave me, Dinah? You'll keep close to me?'

'No, Hetty, I won't leave you. I'll stay with you to the last. . . . But, Hetty, there is some one else in this cell besides me, some one close to you.'

Hetty said, in a frightened whisper, 'Who?'

'Some one who has been with you through all your hours of sin and trouble – who has known every thought you have had – has seen where you went, where you lay down and rose up again, and all the deeds you have tried to hide in darkness. And on Monday, when I can't follow you, – when my arms can't reach you, – when death has parted us, – He who is with us now, and knows all, will be with you then. It makes no difference – whether we live or die, we are in the presence of God.'

'O Dinah, won't nobody do anything for me? *Will* they hang me for certain? . . . I wouldn't mind if they'd let me live.'

'My poor Hetty, death is very dreadful to you. I know it's dreadful. But if you had a friend to take care of you after death – in that other world – some one whose love is greater than mine – who can do everything? . . . If God our Father was your friend, and was willing to save you from sin and suffering, so as you should neither know wicked feelings nor pain again? If you could believe he loved you and would help you, as you believe I love you and will help you, it wouldn't be so hard to die on Monday, would it?'

'But I can't know anything about it,' Hetty said, with sullen sadness.

'Because, Hetty, you are shutting up your soul against him, by trying to hide the truth. God's love and mercy can overcome

all things – our ignorance, and weakness, and all the burthen
of our past wickedness – all things but our wilful sin; sin that
we cling to, and will not give up. You believe in my love and
pity for you, Hetty; but if you had not let me come near you, if
you wouldn't have looked at me or spoken to me, you'd have
shut me out from helping you: I couldn't have made you feel
my love; I couldn't have told you what I felt for you. Don't
shut God's love out in that way, by clinging to sin. . . . He
can't bless you while you have one falsehood in your soul; his
pardoning mercy can't reach you until you open your heart to
him, and say, "I have done this great wickedness; O God, save
me, make me pure from sin."[2] While you cling to one sin and
will not part with it, it must drag you down to misery after
death, as it has dragged you to misery here in this world, my
poor, poor Hetty. It is sin that brings dread, and darkness, and
despair: there is light and blessedness for us as soon as we cast
it off: God enters our souls then, and teaches us, and brings us
strength and peace. Cast it off now, Hetty – now: confess the
wickedness you have done – the sin you have been guilty of
against your heavenly Father. Let us kneel down together, for
we are in the presence of God.'

Hetty obeyed Dinah's movement, and sank on her knees.
They still held each other's hands, and there was long silence.
Then Dinah said –

'Hetty, we are before God: he is waiting for you to tell the
truth.'

Still there was silence. At last Hetty spoke, in a tone of
beseeching –

'Dinah . . . help me . . . I can't feel anything like you . . . my
heart is hard.'

Dinah held the clinging hand, and all her soul went forth in
her voice:

'Jesus, thou present Saviour! Thou hast known the depths of
all sorrow: thou hast entered that black darkness where God is
not, and hast uttered the cry of the forsaken.[3] Come, Lord, and
gather of the fruits of thy travail and thy pleading: stretch forth
thy hand, thou who art mighty to save to the uttermost, and

rescue this lost one. She is clothed round with thick darkness: the fetters of her sin are upon her, and she cannot stir to come to thee: she can only feel her heart is hard, and she is helpless. She cries to me, thy weak creature. . . . Saviour! it is a blind cry to thee. Hear it! Pierce the darkness! Look upon her with thy face of love and sorrow that thou didst turn on him who denied thee;[4] and melt her hard heart.

'See, Lord, – I bring her, as they of old brought the sick and helpless, and thou didst heal them:[5] I bear her on my arms and carry her before thee. Fear and trembling have taken hold on her; but she trembles only at the pain and death of the body: breathe upon her thy life-giving Spirit, and put a new fear within her – the fear of her sin. Make her dread to keep the accursed thing within her soul: make her feel the presence of the living God, who beholds all the past, to whom the darkness is as noonday;[6] who is wanting now, at the eleventh hour,[7] for her to turn to him, and confess her sin, and cry for mercy – now, before the night of death comes, and the moment of pardon is for ever fled, like yesterday that returneth not.

'Saviour! it is yet time – time to snatch this poor soul from everlasting darkness. I believe – I believe in thy infinite love. What is *my* love or *my* pleading? It is quenched in thine. I can only clasp her in my weak arms, and urge her with my weak pity. Thou – thou wilt breathe on the dead soul, and it shall arise from the unanswering sleep of death.

'Yea, Lord, I see thee, coming through the darkness, coming, like the morning, with healing on thy wings.[8] The marks of thy agony are upon thee – I see, I see thou art able and willing to save – thou wilt not let her perish for ever.

'Come, mighty Saviour! let the dead hear thy voice; let the eyes of the blind be opened:[9] let her see that God encompasses her; let her tremble at nothing but at the sin that cuts her off from him. Melt the hard heart; unseal the closed lips: make her cry with her whole soul, "Father, I have sinned."[10] . . .'

'Dinah,' Hetty sobbed out, throwing her arms round Dinah's neck, 'I will speak . . . I will tell . . . I won't hide it any more.'

But the tears and sobs were too violent. Dinah raised her

gently from her knees, and seated her on the pallet again, sitting down by her side. It was a long time before the convulsed throat was quiet, and even then they sat some time in stillness and darkness, holding each other's hands. At last Hetty whispered –

'I did do it, Dinah . . . I buried it in the wood . . . the little baby . . . and it cried . . . I heard it cry . . . ever such a way off . . . all night . . . and I went back because it cried.'

She paused, and then spoke hurriedly in a louder, pleading tone.

'But I thought perhaps it wouldn't die – there might some-body find it. I didn't kill it – I didn't kill it myself. I put it down there and covered it up, and when I came back it was gone. . . . It was because I was so very miserable, Dinah . . . I didn't know where to go . . . and I tried to kill myself before, and I couldn't. Oh, I tried so to drown myself in the pool, and I couldn't. I went to Windsor – I ran away – did you know? I went to find him, as he might take care of me; and he was gone; and then I didn't know what to do. I daredn't go back home again – I couldn't bear it. I couldn't have bore to look at anybody, for they'd have scorned me. I thought o' you sometimes, and thought I'd come to you, for I didn't think you'd be cross with me, and cry shame on me: I thought I could tell you. But then the other folks 'ud come to know it at last, and I couldn't bear that. It was partly thinking o' you made me come toward Stoniton; and, besides, I was so frightened at going wandering about till I was a beggar-woman, and had nothing; and some-times it seemed as if I must go back to the Farm sooner than that. Oh, it was so dreadful, Dinah . . . I was so miserable . . . I wished I'd never been born into this world. I should never like to go into the green fields again – I hated 'em so in my misery.'

Hetty paused again, as if the sense of the past were too strong upon her for words.

'And then I got to Stoniton, and I began to feel frightened that night, because I was so near home. And then the little baby was born, when I didn't expect it; and the thought came into my mind that I might get rid of it, and go home again. The thought came all of a sudden, as I was lying in the bed, and it

got stronger and stronger . . . I longed so to go back again . . .
I couldn't bear being so lonely, and coming to beg for want.
And it gave me strength and resolution to get up and dress
myself. I felt I must do it . . . I didn't know how . . . I thought
I'd find a pool, if I could, like that other, in the corner of the
field, in the dark. And when the woman went out, I felt as if I
was strong enough to do anything . . . I thought I should get
rid of all my misery, and go back home, and never let 'em know
why I ran away. I put on my bonnet and shawl, and went out
into the dark street, with the baby under my cloak; and I walked
fast till I got into a street a good way off, and there was a
public, and I got some warm stuff to drink and some bread.
And I walked on and on, and I hardly felt the ground I trod on;
and it got lighter, for there came the moon – O Dinah, it
frightened me when it first looked at me out o' the clouds – it
never looked so before; and I turned out of the road into the
fields, for I was afraid o' meeting anybody with the moon
shining on me. And I came to a haystack, where I thought I
could lie down and keep myself warm all night. There was a
place cut into it, where I could make me a bed; and I lay
comfortable, and the baby was warm against me; and I must
have gone to sleep for a good while, for when I woke it was
morning, but not very light, and the baby was crying. And I
saw a wood a little way off . . . I thought there'd perhaps be a
ditch or a pond there . . . and it was so early I thought I could
hide the child there, and get a long way off before folks was up.
And then I thought I'd go home – I'd get rides in carts and go
home, and tell 'em I'd been to try and see for a place, and
couldn't get one. I longed so for it, Dinah, I longed so to be
safe at home. I don't know how I felt about the baby. I seemed
to hate it – it was like a heavy weight hanging round my neck;[11]
and yet its crying went through me, and I daredn't look at its
little hands and face. But I went on to the wood, and I walked
about, but there was no water' . . .

Hetty shuddered. She was silent for some moments, and when
she began again, it was in a whisper.

'I came to a place where there was lots of chips and turf, and
I sat down on the trunk of a tree to think what I should do.

And all of a sudden I saw a hole under the nut-tree, like a little grave. And it darted into me like lightning – I'd lay the baby there, and cover it with the grass and the chips. I couldn't kill it any other way. And I'd done it in a minute; and, oh, it cried so, Dinah – I *couldn't* cover it quite up – I thought perhaps somebody 'ud come and take care of it, and then it wouldn't die. And I made haste out of the wood, but I could hear it crying all the while; and when I got out into the fields, it was as if I was held fast – I couldn't go away, for all I wanted so to go. And I sat against the haystack to watch if anybody 'ud come: I was very hungry, and I'd only a bit of bread left; but I couldn't go away. And after ever such a while – hours and hours – the man came – him in a smock-frock, and he looked at me so, I was frightened, and I made haste and went on. I thought he was going to the wood, and would perhaps find the baby. And I went right on, till I came to a village, a long way off from the wood; and I was very sick, and faint, and hungry. I got something to eat there, and bought a loaf. But I was frightened to stay. I heard the baby crying, and thought the other folks heard it too, – and I went on. But I was so tired, and it was getting towards dark. And at last, by the roadside there was a barn – ever such a way off any house – like the barn in Abbot's Close; and I thought I could go in there and hide myself among the hay and straw, and nobody 'ud be likely to come. I went in, and it was half full o' trusses of straw, and there was some hay, too. And I made myself a bed, ever so far behind, where nobody could find me; and I was so tired and weak, I went to sleep. . . . But oh, the baby's crying kept waking me; and I thought that man as looked at me so was come and laying hold of me. But I must have slept a long while at last, though I didn't know; for when I got up and went out of the barn, I didn't know whether it was night or morning. But it was morning, for it kept getting lighter; and I turned back the way I'd come. I couldn't help it, Dinah; it was the baby's crying made me go: and yet I was frightened to death. I thought that man in the smock-frock 'ud see me, and know I put the baby there. But I went on, for all that: I'd left off thinking about going home – it had gone out o' my mind. I saw nothing but

that place in the wood where I'd buried the baby . . . I see it
now. O Dinah! shall I allays see it?'

Hetty clung round Dinah, and shuddered again. The silence
seemed long before she went on.

'I met nobody, for it was very early, and I got into the
wood. . . . I knew the way to the place . . . the place against the
nut-tree; and I could hear it crying at every stop. . . . I thought
it was alive. . . . I don't know whether I was frightened or glad
. . . I don't know what I felt. I only know I was in the wood,
and heard the cry. I don't know what I felt till I saw the baby
was gone. And when I'd put it there, I thought I should like
somebody to find it, and save it from dying; but when I saw it
was gone, I was struck like a stone, with fear. I never thought
o' stirring, I felt so weak. I knew I couldn't run away, and
everybody as saw me 'ud know about the baby. My heart went
like a stone: I couldn't wish or try for anything; it seemed like
as if I should stay there for ever, and nothing 'ud ever change.
But they came and took me away.'

Hetty was silent, but she shuddered again, as if there were
still something behind; and Dinah waited, for her heart was so
full, that tears must come before words. At last Hetty burst out,
with a sob –

'Dinah, do you think God will take away that crying and the
place in the wood, now I've told everything?'

'Let us pray, poor sinner: let us fall on our knees again, and
pray to the God of all mercy.'

CHAPTER XLVI

The Hours of Suspense

On Sunday morning, when the church bells in Stoniton were ringing for morning service, Bartle Massey re-entered Adam's room, after a short absence, and said –

'Adam, here's a visitor wants to see you.'

Adam was seated with his back towards the door, but he started up and turned round instantly, with a flushed face and an eager look. His face was even thinner and more worn than we have seen it before, but he was washed and shaven this Sunday morning.

'Is it any news?' he said.

'Keep yourself quiet, my lad,' said Bartle; 'keep quiet. It's not what you're thinking of: it's the young Methodist woman come from the prison. She's at the bottom o' the stairs, and wants to know if you think well to see her, for she has something to say to you about that poor castaway; but she wouldn't come in without your leave, she said. She thought you'd perhaps like to go out and speak to her. These preaching women are not so back'ard commonly,' Bartle muttered to himself.

'Ask her to come in,' said Adam.

He was standing with his face towards the door, and as Dinah entered, lifting up her mild grey eyes towards him, she saw at once the great change that had come since the day when she had looked up at the tall man in the cottage. There was a trembling in her clear voice as she put her hand into his, and said –

'Be comforted, Adam Bede: the Lord has not forsaken her.'

'Bless you for coming to her,' Adam said. 'Mr Massey brought me word yesterday as you was come.'

They could neither of them say any more just yet, but stood

before each other in silence; and Bartle Massey, too, who had put on his spectacles, seemed transfixed, examining Dinah's face. But he recovered himself first, and said, 'Sit down, young woman, sit down', placing the chair for her, and retiring to his old seat on the bed.

'Thank you, friend; I won't sit down,' said Dinah, 'for I must hasten back: she entreated me not to stay long away. What I came for, Adam Bede, was to pray you to go and see the poor sinner, and bid her farewell. She desires to ask your forgiveness, and it is meet you should see her to-day, rather than in the early morning, when the time will be short.'

Adam stood trembling, and at last sank down on his chair again.

'It won't be,' he said; 'it'll be put off – there'll perhaps come a pardon. Mr Irwine said there was hope: he said, I needn't quite give it up.'

'That's a blessed thought to me,' said Dinah, her eyes filling with tears. 'It's a fearful thing hurrying her soul away so fast.'

'But let what will be,' she added, presently, 'you will surely come, and let her speak the words that are in her heart. Although her poor soul is very dark, and discerns little beyond the things of the flesh, she is no longer hard: she is contrite – she has confessed all to me. The pride of her heart has given way, and she leans on me for help, and desires to be taught. This fills me with trust; for I cannot but think that the brethren sometimes err in measuring the Divine love by the sinner's knowledge. She is going to write a letter to the friends at the Hall Farm for me to give them when she is gone; and when I told her you were here, she said, "I should like to say good-bye to Adam, and ask him to forgive me." You will come, Adam? – perhaps you will even now come back with me.'

'I can't,' Adam said: 'I can't say good-bye, while there's any hope. I'm listening, and listening – I can't think o' nothing but that. It can't be as she'll die that shameful death – I can't bring my mind to it.'

He got up from his chair again, and looked away out of the window, while Dinah stood with compassionate patience. In a minute or two he turned round and said –

'I *will* come, Dinah . . . to-morrow morning . . . if it must be. I may have more strength to bear it, if I know it *must* be. Tell her, I forgive her; tell her I will come – at the very last.'

'I will not urge you against the voice of your own heart,' said Dinah. 'I must hasten back to her, for it is wonderful how she clings now, and was not willing to let me out of her sight. She used never to make any return to my affection before, but now tribulation has opened her heart. Farewell, Adam: our heavenly Father comfort you, and strengthen you to bear all things.' Dinah put out her hand, and Adam pressed it in silence.

Bartle Massey was getting up to lift the stiff latch of the door for her, but before he could reach it, she had said, gently, 'Farewell, friend', and was gone, with her light step, down the stairs.

'Well,' said Bartle, taking off his spectacles, and putting them into his pocket, 'if there must be women to make trouble in the world, it's but fair there should be women to be comforters under it; and she's one – she's one. It's a pity she's a Methodist; but there's no getting a woman without some foolishness or other.'

Adam never went to bed that night: the excitement of suspense, heightening with every hour that brought him nearer the fatal moment, was too great; and in spite of his entreaties, in spite of his promises that he would be perfectly quiet, the schoolmaster watched too.

'What does it matter to me, lad?' Bartle said: 'a night's sleep more or less? I shall sleep long enough, by-and-by, underground. Let me keep thee company in trouble while I can.'

It was a long and dreary night in that small chamber. Adam would sometimes get up, and tread backwards and forwards along the short space from wall to wall; then he would sit down and hide his face, and no sound would be heard but the ticking of the watch on the table, or the falling of a cinder from the fire which the schoolmaster carefully tended. Sometimes he would burst out into vehement speech –

'If I could ha' done anything to save her – if my bearing anything would ha' done any good . . . but t' have to sit still, and know it, and do nothing . . . it's hard for a man to bear . . .

and to think o' what might ha' been now, if it hadn't been for *him*. . . . O God, it's the very day we should ha' been married.'

'Ay, my lad,' said Bartle, tenderly, 'it's heavy – it's heavy. But you must remember this: when you thought of marrying her, you'd a notion she'd got another sort of a nature inside her. You didn't think she could have got hardened in that little while to do what she's done.'

'I know – I know that,' said Adam. 'I thought she was loving and tender-hearted, and wouldn't tell a lie, or act deceitful. How could I think any other way? And if he'd never come near her, and I'd married her, and been loving to her, and took care of her, she might never ha' done anything bad. What would it ha' signified – my having a bit o' trouble with her? It 'ud ha' been nothing to this.'

'There's no knowing, my lad – there's no knowing what might have come. The smart's bad for you to bear now: you must have time – you must have time. But I've that opinion of you, that you'll rise above it all, and be a man again; and there may good come out of this that we don't see.'

'Good come out of it!' said Adam, passionately. 'That doesn't alter th' evil: *her* ruin can't be undone. I hate that talk o' people, as if there was a way o' making amends for everything. They'd more need be brought to see as the wrong they do can never be altered. When a man's spoiled his fellow-creatur's life, he's no right to comfort himself with thinking good may come out of it: somebody else's good doesn't alter her shame and misery.'

'Well, lad, well,' said Bartle, in a gentle tone, strangely in contrast with his usual peremptoriness and impatience of contradiction, 'it's likely enough I talk foolishness: I'm an old fellow, and it's a good many years since I was in trouble myself. It's easy finding reasons why other folks should be patient.'

'Mr Massey,' said Adam, penitently, 'I'm very hot and hasty. I owe you something different; but you mustn't take it ill of me.'

'Not I, lad – not I.'

So the night wore on in agitation, till the chill dawn and the growing light brought the tremulous quiet that comes on the brink of despair. There would soon be no more suspense.

'Let us go to the prison now, Mr Massey,' said Adam, when he saw the hand of his watch at six. 'If there's any news come, we shall hear about it.'

The people were astir already, moving rapidly, in one direction,[1] through the streets. Adam tried not to think where they were going, as they hurried past him in that short space between his lodging and the prison gates. He was thankful when the gates shut him in from seeing those eager people.

No; there was no news come – no pardon – no reprieve.

Adam lingered in the court half an hour before he could bring himself to send word to Dinah that he was come. But a voice caught his ear: he could not shut out the words.

'The cart is to set off at half-past seven.'

It must be said – the last good-bye: there was no help.

In ten minutes from that time, Adam was at the door of the cell. Dinah had sent him word that she could not come to him, she could not leave Hetty one moment; but Hetty was prepared for the meeting.

He could not see her when he entered, for agitation deadened his senses, and the dim cell was almost dark to him. He stood a moment after the door closed behind him, trembling and stupefied.

But he began to see through the dimness – to see the dark eyes lifted up to him once more, but with no smile in them. O God, how sad they looked! The last time they had met his was when he parted from her with his heart full of joyous, hopeful love, and they looked out with a tearful smile from a pink, dimpled, childish face. The face was marble now; the sweet lips were pallid and half-open, and quivering; the dimples were all gone – all but one, that never went; and the eyes – Oh! the worst of all was the likeness they had to Hetty's. They were Hetty's eyes looking at him with that mournful gaze, as if she had come back to him from the dead to tell him of her misery.

She was clinging close to Dinah; her cheek was against Dinah's. It seemed as if her last faint strength and hope lay in that contact; and the pitying love that shone out from Dinah's face looked like a visible pledge of the Invisible Mercy.

When the sad eyes met – when Hetty and Adam looked at
each other, she felt the change in *him* too, and it seemed to
strike her with fresh fear. It was the first time she had seen any
being whose face seemed to reflect the change in herself: Adam
was a new image of the dreadful past and the dreadful present.
She trembled more as she looked at him.

'Speak to him, Hetty,' Dinah said; 'tell him what is in your
heart.'

Hetty obeyed her, like a little child.

'Adam . . . I'm very sorry . . . I behaved very wrong to you
. . . will you forgive me . . . before I die?'

Adam answered with a half-sob: 'Yes, I forgive thee, Hetty:
I forgave thee long ago.'

It had seemed to Adam as if his brain would burst with the
anguish of meeting Hetty's eyes in the first moments; but the
sound of her voice uttering these penitent words touched a
chord which had been less strained: there was a sense of relief
from what was becoming unbearable, and the rare tears came
– they had never come before, since he had hung on Seth's neck
in the beginning of his sorrow.

Hetty made an involuntary movement towards him; some of
the love that she had once lived in the midst of was come near
her again. She kept hold of Dinah's hand, but she went up to
Adam and said, timidly –

'Will you kiss me again, Adam, for all I've been so wicked?'

Adam took the blanched wasted hand she put out to him,
and they gave each other the solemn unspeakable kiss of a
life-long parting.

'And tell him,' Hetty said, in rather a stronger voice, 'tell him
. . . for there's nobody else to tell him . . . as I went after him
and couldn't find him . . . and I hated him and cursed him once
. . . but Dinah says, I should forgive him . . . and I try . . . for
else God won't forgive me.'

There was a noise at the door of the cell now – the key was
being turned in the lock, and when the door opened, Adam
saw indistinctly that there were several faces there: he was too
agitated to see more – even to see that Mr Irwine's face was
one of them. He felt that the last preparations were beginning,

and he could stay no longer. Room was silently made for him to depart, and he went to his chamber in loneliness, leaving Bartle Massey to watch and see the end.

CHAPTER XLVII

The Last Moment

It was a sight that some people remembered better even than their own sorrows – the sight in that grey clear morning, when the fatal cart with the two young women in it was descried by the waiting watching multitude, cleaving its way towards the hideous symbol of a deliberately-inflicted sudden death.

All Stoniton had heard of Dinah Morris, the young Methodist woman who had brought the obstinate criminal to confess, and there was as much eagerness to see her as to see the wretched Hetty.

But Dinah was hardly conscious of the multitude. When Hetty had caught sight of the vast crowd in the distance, she had clutched Dinah convulsively.

'Close your eyes, Hetty,' Dinah said, 'and let us pray without ceasing to God.'[1]

And in a low voice, as the cart went slowly along through the midst of the gazing crowd, she poured forth her soul with the wrestling intensity of a last pleading, for the trembling creature that clung to her and clutched her as the only visible sign of love and pity.

Dinah did not know that the crowd was silent, gazing at her with a sort of awe – she did not even know how near they were to the fatal spot, when the cart stopped, and she shrank appalled at a loud shout hideous to her ear, like a vast yell of demons. Hetty's shriek mingled with the sound, and they clasped each other in mutual horror.

But it was not a shout of execration – not a yell of exultant cruelty.

It was a shout of sudden excitement at the appearance of a

horseman cleaving the crowd at full gallop. The horse is hot and distressed, but answers to the desperate spurring; the rider looks as if his eyes were glazed by madness, and he saw nothing but what was unseen by others. See, he has something in his hand – he is holding it up as if it were a signal.

The Sheriff[2] knows him: it is Arthur Donnithorne, carrying in his hand a hard-won release from death.

CHAPTER XLVIII

Another Meeting in the Wood

The next day, at evening, two men were walking from opposite points towards the same scene, drawn thither by a common memory. The scene was the Grove by Donnithorne Chase: you know who the men were.

The old Squire's funeral had taken place that morning, the will had been read, and now in the first breathing-space, Arthur Donnithorne had come out for a lonely walk, that he might look fixedly at the new future before him, and confirm himself in a sad resolution. He thought he could do that best in the Grove

Adam, too, had come from Stoniton on Monday evening, and to-day he had not left home, except to go to the family at the Hall Farm, and tell them everything that Mr Irwine had left untold. He had agreed with the Poysers that he would follow them to their new neighbourhood, wherever that might be; for he meant to give up the management of the woods, and, as soon as it was practicable, he would wind up his business with Jonathan Burge, and settle with his mother and Seth in a home within reach of the friends to whom he felt bound by a mutual sorrow.

'Seth and me are sure to find work,' he said. 'A man that's got our trade at his finger ends is at home everywhere; and we must make a new start. My mother won't stand in the way, for she's told me, since I came home, she'd made up her mind to being buried in another parish, if I wished it, and if I'd be more comfortable elsewhere. It's wonderful how quiet she's been ever since I came back. It seems as if the very greatness o' the trouble had quieted and calmed her. We shall all be better in a new country; though there's some I shall be loth to leave behind. But I won't part from you and yours, if I can help it, Mr Poyser, Trouble's made us kin.'

'Ay, lad,' said Martin. 'We'll go out o' hearing o' that man's name. But I doubt we shall ne'er go far enough for folks not to find out as we've got them belonging to us as are transported o'er the seas,[1] and were like to be hanged. We shall have that flyin' up in our faces, and our children's after us.'

That was a long visit to the Hall Farm, and drew too strongly on Adam's energies for him to think of seeing others, or re-entering on his old occupations till the morrow. 'But to-morrow,' he said to himself, 'I'll go to work again. I shall learn to like it again some time, maybe; and it's right, whether I like it or not.'

This evening was the last he would allow to be absorbed by sorrow: suspense was gone now, and he must bear the unalterable. He was resolved not to see Arthur Donnithorne again, if it were possible to avoid him. He had no message to deliver from Hetty now, for Hetty had seen Arthur; and Adam distrusted himself: he had learned to dread the violence of his own feeling. That word of Mr Irwine's – that he must remember what he had felt after giving the last blow to Arthur in the Grove – had remained with him.

These thoughts about Arthur, like all thoughts that are charged with strong feeling, were continually recurring, and they always called up the image of the Grove – of that spot under the overarching boughs where he had caught sight of the two bending figures, and had been possessed by sudden rage.

'I'll go and see it again to-night for the last time,' he said; 'it'll do me good; it'll make me feel over again what I felt when I'd knocked him down. I felt what poor empty work it was, as soon as I'd done it, *before* I began to think he might be dead.'

In this way it happened that Arthur and Adam were walking towards the same spot at the same time.

Adam had on his working-dress again, now, – for he had thrown off the other with a sense of relief as soon as he came home; and if he had had the basket of tools over his shoulder, he might have been taken, with his pale wasted face, for the spectre of the Adam Bede who entered the Grove on that August evening eight months ago. But he had no basket of tools, and he was not walking with the old erectness, looking keenly round him; his hands were thrust in his side pockets, and his eyes rested chiefly on the ground. He had not long entered the Grove, and now he paused before a beech. He knew that tree well; it was the boundary mark of his youth – the sign, to him, of the time when some of his earliest, strongest feelings had left him. He felt sure they would never return. And yet, at this moment, there was a stirring of affection at the remembrance of that Arthur Donnithorne whom he had believed in before he had come up to this beech eight months ago. It was affection for the dead: *that* Arthur existed no longer.

He was disturbed by the sound of approaching footsteps, but the beech stood at a turning in the road, and he could not see who was coming, until the tall slim figure in deep mourning suddenly stood before him at only two yards' distance. They both started, and looked at each other in silence. Often, in the last fortnight, Adam had imagined himself as close to Arthur as this, assailing him with words that should be as harrowing as the voice of remorse, forcing upon him a just share in the misery he had caused; and often, too, he had told himself that such a meeting had better not be. But in imagining the meeting he had always seen Arthur, as he had met him on that evening in the Grove, florid, careless, light of speech; and the figure before him touched him with the signs of suffering. Adam knew what suffering was – he could not lay a cruel finger on a bruised man. He felt no impulse that he needed to resist: silence was more just than reproach. Arthur was the first to speak.

'Adam,' he said, quietly, 'it may be a good thing that we have met here, for I wished to see you. I should have asked to see you to-morrow.'

He paused, but Adam said nothing.

'I know it is painful to you to meet me,' Arthur went on, 'but it is not likely to happen again for years to come.'

'No, sir,' said Adam, coldly, 'that was what I meant to write to you to-morrow, as it would be better all dealings should be at an end between us, and somebody else put in my place.'

Arthur felt the answer keenly, and it was not without an effort that he spoke again.

'It was partly on that subject I wished to speak to you. I don't want to lessen your indignation against me, or ask you to do anything for my sake. I only wish to ask you if you will help me to lessen the evil consequences of the past, which is unchangeable. I don't mean consequences to myself, but to others. It is but little I can do, I know. I know the worst consequences will remain; but something may be done, and you can help me. Will you listen to me patiently?'

'Yes, sir,' said Adam, after some hesitation; 'I'll hear what it is. If I can help to mend anything, I will. Anger 'ull mend nothing, I know. We've had enough o' that.'

'I was going to the Hermitage,' said Arthur. 'Will you go there with me and sit down? We can talk better there.'

The Hermitage had never been entered since they left it together, for Arthur had locked up the key in his desk. And now, when he opened the door, there was the candle burnt out in the socket; there was the chair in the same place where Adam remembered sitting; there was the waste-paper basket full of scraps, and deep down in it, Arthur felt in an instant, there was the little pink silk handkerchief. It would have been painful to enter this place if their previous thoughts had been less painful.

They sat down opposite each other in the old places, and Arthur said, 'I'm going away, Adam; I'm going into the army.'

Poor Arthur felt that Adam ought to be affected by this announcement – ought to have a movement of sympathy towards him. But Adam's lips remained firmly closed, and the expression of his face unchanged.

'What I want to say to you,' Arthur continued, 'is this: one of my reasons for going away is, that no one else may leave Hayslope – may leave their home on my account. I would do anything, there is no sacrifice I would not make, to prevent any further injury to others through my – through what has happened.'

Arthur's words had precisely the opposite effect to that he had anticipated. Adam thought he perceived in them that notion of compensation for irretrievable wrong, that self-soothing attempt to make evil bear the same fruits as good, which most of all roused his indignation. He was as strongly impelled to look painful facts right in the face as Arthur was to turn away his eyes from them. Moreover, he had the wakeful suspicious pride of a poor man in the presence of a rich man. He felt his old severity returning as he said –

'The time's past for that, sir. A man should make sacrifices to keep clear of doing a wrong; sacrifices won't undo it when it's done. When people's feelings have got a deadly wound, they can't be cured with favours.'

'Favours!' said Arthur, passionately; 'no; how can you suppose I meant that? But the Poysers – Mr Irwine tells me the Poysers mean to leave the place where they have lived so many years – for generations. Don't you see, as Mr Irwine does, that if they could be persuaded to overcome the feeling that drives them away, it would be much better for them in the end to remain on the old spot, among the friends and neighbours who know them?'

'That's true,' said Adam, coldly. 'But then, sir, folks's feelings are not so easily overcome. It'll be hard for Martin Poyser to go to a strange place, among strange faces, when he's been bred up on the Hall Farm, and his father before him; but then it 'ud be harder for a man with his feelings to stay. I don't see how the thing's to be made any other than hard. There's a sort o' damage, sir, that can't be made up for.'

Arthur was silent some moments. In spite of other feelings, dominant in him this evening, his pride winced under Adam's mode of treating him. Wasn't he himself suffering? Was not he too obliged to renounce his most cherished hopes? It was now as it had been eight months ago – Adam was forcing Arthur to feel more intensely the irrevocableness of his own wrongdoing: he was presenting the sort of resistance that was the most irritating to Arthur's eager, ardent nature. But his anger was subdued by the same influence that had subdued Adam's when they first confronted each other – by the marks of suffering in a long familiar face. The momentary struggle ended in the feeling that he could bear a great deal from Adam, to whom he had been the occasion of bearing so much; but there was a touch of pleading, boyish vexation in his tone as he said –

'But people may make injuries worse by unreasonable conduct – by giving way to anger and satisfying that for the moment, instead of thinking what will be the effect in the future.

'If I were going to stay here and act as landlord,' he added, presently, with still more eagerness – 'if I were careless about what I've done – what I've been the cause of, you would have some excuse, Adam, for going away and encouraging others to go. You would have some excuse then for trying to make the evil worse. But when I tell you I'm going away for years – when you know what that means for me, how it cuts off every plan of happiness I've ever formed – it is impossible for a sensible man like you to believe that there is any real ground for the Poysers refusing to remain. I know their feeling about disgrace, – Mr Irwine has told me all; but he is of opinion that they might be persuaded out of this idea that they are disgraced in the eyes of their neighbours, and that they can't remain on my estate, if you would join him in his efforts, – if you would stay yourself, and go on managing the old woods.'

Arthur paused a moment, and then added, pleadingly, 'You know that's a good work to do for the sake of other people, besides the owner. And you don't know but that they may have a better owner soon, whom you will like to work for. If I die, my cousin Tradgett will have the estate, and take my name.[2] He is a good fellow.'

Adam could not help being moved: it was impossible for him not to feel that this was the voice of the honest, warm-hearted Arthur whom he had loved and been proud of in old days; but nearer memories would not be thrust away. He was silent; yet Arthur saw an answer in his face that induced him to go on, with growing earnestness.

'And then, if you would talk to the Poysers – if you would talk the matter over with Mr Irwine – he means to see you tomorrow – and then if you would join your arguments to his to prevail on them not to go. . . . I know, of course, that they would not accept any favour from me: I mean nothing of that kind: but I'm sure they would suffer less in the end. Irwine thinks so too; and Mr Irwine is to have the chief authority on the estate – he has consented to undertake that. They will really be under no man but one whom they respect and like. It would be the same with you, Adam; and it could be nothing but a desire to give me worse pain that could incline you to go.'

Arthur was silent again for a little while, and then said, with some agitation in his voice –

'I wouldn't act so towards you, I know. If you were in my place and I in yours, I should try to help you to do the best.'

Adam made a hasty movement on his chair, and looked on the ground. Arthur went on –

'Perhaps you've never done anything you've had bitterly to repent of in your life, Adam; if you had, you would be more generous. You would know then that it's worse for me than for you.'

Arthur rose from his seat with the last words, and went to one of the windows, looking out and turning his back on Adam, as he continued, passionately –

'Haven't *I* loved her too? Didn't I see her yesterday? Shan't I carry the thought of her about with me as much as you will? And don't you think you would suffer more if you'd been in fault?'

There was silence for several minutes, for the struggle in Adam's mind was not easily decided. Facile natures, whose emotions have little permanence, can hardly understand how much inward resistance he overcame before he rose from his seat and turned towards Arthur. Arthur heard the movement, and, turning round, met the sad but softened look with which Adam said –

'It's true what you say, sir: I'm hard – it's in my nature. I was too hard with my father, for doing wrong. I've been a bit hard t' everybody but *her*. I felt as if nobody pitied her enough – her suffering cut into me so; and when I thought the folks at the Farm were too hard with her, I said I'd never be hard to anybody myself again. But feeling overmuch about her has perhaps made me unfair to you. I've known what it is in my life to repent and feel it's too late: I felt I'd been too harsh to my father when he was gone from me – I feel it now, when I think of him. I've no right to be hard towards them as have done wrong and repent.'

Adam spoke these words with the firm distinctness of a man who is resolved to leave nothing unsaid that he is bound to say; but he went on with more hesitation.

'I wouldn't shake hands with you once, sir, when you asked me – but if you're willing to do it now, for all I refused then' . . .

Arthur's white hand was in Adam's large grasp in an instant, and with that action there was a strong rush, on both sides, of the old, boyish affection.

'Adam,' Arthur said, impelled to full confession now, 'it would never have happened if I'd known you loved her. That would have helped to save me from it. And I *did* struggle: I never meant to injure her. I deceived you afterwards – and that led on to worse; but I thought it was forced upon me, I thought it was the best thing I could do. And in that letter I told her to let me know if she were in any trouble: don't think I would not have done everything I could. But I was all wrong from the very first, and horrible wrong has come of it. God knows, I'd give my life if I could undo it.'

They sat down again opposite each other, and Adam said, tremulously –

'How did she seem when you left her, sir?'

'Don't ask me, Adam,' Arthur said; 'I feel sometimes as if I should go mad with thinking of her looks and what she said to me, and then, that I couldn't get a full pardon – that I couldn't save her from that wretched fate of being transported – that I can do nothing for her all those years; and she may die under it, and never know comfort any more.'

'Ah, sir,' said Adam, for the first time feeling his own pain merged in sympathy for Arthur, 'you and me'll often be thinking o' the same thing, when we're a long way off one another. I'll pray God to help you, as I pray him to help me.'

'But there's that sweet woman – that Dinah Morris,' Arthur said, pursuing his own thoughts, and not knowing what had been the sense of Adam's words, 'she says she shall stay with her to the very last moment – till she goes; and the poor thing clings to her as if she found some comfort in her. I could worship that woman; I don't know what I should do if she were not there. Adam, you will see her when she comes back: I could say nothing to her yesterday – nothing of what I felt towards her. Tell her,' Arthur went on hurriedly, as if he wanted to hide the emotion with which he spoke, while he took off his chain and watch – 'tell her I asked you to give her this in remembrance of me – of the man to whom she is the one source of comfort, when he thinks of . . . I know she doesn't care about such things – or anything else I can give her for its own sake. But she will use the watch – I shall like to think of her using it.'

'I'll give it to her, sir,' Adam said, 'and tell her your words. She told me she should come back to the people at the Hall Farm.'

'And you *will* persuade the Poysers to stay, Adam?' said Arthur, reminded of the subject which both of them had forgotten in the first interchange of revived friendship. 'You *will* stay yourself, and help Mr Irwine to carry out the repairs and improvements on the estate?'

'There's one thing, sir, that perhaps you don't take account of,' said Adam, with hesitating gentleness, 'and that was what made me hang back longer. You see, it's the same with both me and the Poysers: if we stay, it's for our own worldly interest, and it looks as if we'd put up with anything for the sake o' that. I know that's what they'll feel, and I can't help feeling a little of it myself. When folks have got an honourable, independent spirit, they don't like to do anything that might make 'em seem base-minded.'

'But no one who knows you will think that, Adam: that is not a reason strong enough against a course that is really more generous, more unselfish than the other. And it will be known – it shall be made known, that both you and the Poysers stayed at my entreaty. Adam, don't try to make things worse for me; I'm punished enough without that.'

'No, sir, no,' Adam said, looking at Arthur with mournful affection. 'God forbid I should make things worse for you. I used to wish I could do it, in my passion; – but that was when I thought you didn't feel enough. I'll stay, sir: I'll do the best I can. It's all I've got to think of now – to do my work well, and make the world a bit better place for them as can enjoy it.'

'Then we'll part now, Adam. You will see Mr Irwine tomorrow, and consult with him about everything.'

'Are you going soon, sir?' said Adam.

'As soon as possible – after I've made the necessary arrangements. Good-bye, Adam. I shall think of you going about the old place.'

'Good-bye, sir. God bless you.'

The hands were clasped once more, and Adam left the Hermitage, feeling that sorrow was more bearable now hatred was gone.

As soon as the door was closed behind him, Arthur went to the waste-paper basket and took out the little pink silk handkerchief.

BOOK SIXTH

CHAPTER XLIX

At the Hall Farm

The first autumnal afternoon sunshine of 1801 – more than eighteen months after that parting of Adam and Arthur in the Hermitage – was on the yard at the Hall Farm, and the bulldog was in one of his most excited moments; for it was that hour of the day when the cows were being driven into the yard for their afternoon milking. No wonder the patient beasts ran confusedly into the wrong places, for the alarming din of the bulldog was mingled with more distant sounds which the timid feminine creatures, with pardonable superstition, imagined also to have some relation to their own movements – with the tremendous crack of the waggoner's whip, the roar of his voice, and the booming thunder of the waggon, as it left the rick-yard empty of its golden load.

The milking of the cows was a sight Mrs Poyser loved, and at this hour on mild days she was usually standing at the house door, with her knitting in her hands, in quiet contemplation, only heightened to a keener interest when the vicious yellow cow, who had once kicked over a pailful of precious milk, was about to undergo the preventive punishment of having her hinder-legs strapped.

To-day, however, Mrs Poyser gave but a divided attention to the arrival of the cows, for she was in eager discussion with Dinah, who was stitching Mr Poyser's shirt-collars, and had borne patiently to have her thread broken three times by Totty pulling at her arm with a sudden insistence that she should look at 'Baby', that is, at a large wooden doll with no legs and a long skirt, whose bald head Totty, seated in her small chair at Dinah's side, was caressing and pressing to her fat cheek with much fervour. Totty is larger by more than two years' growth than when you first saw her, and she has on a black frock under her pinafore: Mrs Poyser too has on a black gown, which seems to heighten the family likeness between her and Dinah. In other respects there is little outward change now discernible in our old friends, or in the pleasant house-place, bright with polished oak and pewter.

'I never saw the like to you, Dinah,' Mrs Poyser was saying, 'when you've once took anything into your head: there's no more moving you than the rooted tree. You may say what you like, but I don't believe *that's* religion; for what's the Sermon on the Mount[1] about, as you're so fond o' reading to the boys, but doing what other folks 'ud have you do? But if it was anything unreasonable they wanted you to do, like taking your cloak off and giving it to 'em, or letting 'em slap you i' the face, I daresay you'd be ready enough: it's only when one 'ud have you do what's plain common-sense and good for yourself, as you're obstinate th' other way.'

'Nay, dear aunt,' said Dinah, smiling slightly as she went on with her work. 'I'm sure your wish 'ud be a reason for me to do anything that I didn't feel it was wrong to do.'

'Wrong! You drive me past bearing. What is there wrong, I should like to know, i' staying along wi' your own friends, as are th' happier for having you with 'em, an' are willing to provide for you, even if your work didn't more nor pay 'em for the bit o' sparrow's victual y' eat, and the bit o' rag you put on? An' who is it, I should like to know, as you're bound t' help and comfort i' the world more nor your own flesh and blood – an' me th' only aunt you've got above-ground, an' am brought to the brink o' the grave welly every winter as comes, an' there's the child as sits beside you 'ull break her little heart when you go, an' the grandfather not been dead a twelvemonth, an' your uncle 'ull miss you so as never was – a-lighting his pipe an' waiting on him, an' now I can trust you wi' the butter, an' have had all the trouble o' teaching you, and there's all the sewing to be done, an' I must have a strange gell out o' Treddles'on to do it – an' all because you must go back to that bare heap o' stones as the very crows fly over an' won't stop at.'

'Dear aunt Rachel,' said Dinah, looking up in Mrs Poyser's face, 'it's your kindness makes you say I'm useful to you. You don't really want me now; for Nancy and Molly are clever at their work, and you're in good health now, by the blessing of God, and my uncle is of a cheerful countenance again, and you have neighbours and friends not a few – some of them come to sit with my uncle almost daily. Indeed, you will not miss me; and at Snowfield there are brethren and sisters in great need, who have none of those comforts you have around you. I feel that I am called back to those amongst whom my lot was first cast: I feel drawn again towards the hills where I used to be blessed in carrying the word of life to the sinful and desolate.'

'You feel! yes,' said Mrs Poyser, returning from a parenthetic glance at the cows. 'That's allays the reason I'm to sit down wi', when you've a mind to do anything contrairy. What do you want to be preaching for more than you're preaching now? Don't you go off, the Lord knows where, every Sunday a-preaching and praying? an' haven't you got Methodists enow at Treddles'on to go and look at, if church folks's faces are too handsome to please you? an' isn't there them i' this parish as you've got under hand, and they're like enough to make friends wi' Old Harry again as soon as your back's turned? There's that Bessy Cranage – she'll be flaunting i' new finery three weeks after you're gone, I'll be bound: she'll no more go on in her new ways without you, than a dog 'ull stand on its hindlegs when there's nobody looking. But I suppose it doesna matter so much about folks's souls i' this country, else you'd be for staying with your own aunt, for she's none so good but what you might help her to be better.'

There was a certain something in Mrs Poyser's voice just then, which she did not wish to be noticed, so she turned round hastily to look at the clock and said: 'See there! It's tea-time; an' if Martin's i' the rick-yard, he'll like a cup. Here, Totty, my chicken, let mother put your bonnet on, and then you go out into the rick-yard, and see if father's there, and tell him he mustn't go away again without coming t' have a cup o' tea; and tell your brothers to come in too.'

Totty trotted off in her flapping bonnet, while Mrs Poyser

set out the bright oak table, and reached down the tea-cups.

'You talk o' them gells Nancy and Molly being clever i' their work,' she began again; – 'it's fine talking. They're all the same, clever or stupid – one can't trust 'em out o' one's sight a minute. They want somebody's eye on 'em constant if they're to be kept to their work. An' suppose I'm ill again this winter, as I was the winter before last, who's to look after 'em then, if you're gone? An' there's that blessed child – something's sure t' happen to her – they'll let her tumble into the fire, or get at the kettle wi' the boiling lard in't, or some mischief as 'ull lame her for life; an' it'll be all your fault, Dinah.'

'Aunt,' said Dinah, 'I promise to come back to you in the winter if you're ill. Don't think I will ever stay away from you if you're in real want of me. But indeed it is needful for my own soul that I should go away from this life of ease and luxury, in which I have all things too richly to enjoy – at least that I should go away for a short space. No one can know but myself what are my inward needs, and the besetments I am most in danger from. Your wish for me to stay is not a call of duty which I refuse to hearken to because it is against my own desires; it is a temptation that I must resist, lest the love of the creature should become like a mist in my soul shutting out the heavenly light.'

'It passes my cunning to know what you mean by ease and luxury,' said Mrs Poyser, as she cut the bread and butter. 'It's true there's good victual enough about you, as nobody shall ever say I don't provide enough and to spare, but if there's ever a bit o' odds and ends as nobody else 'ud eat, you're sure to pick it out . . . but look there! there's Adam Bede a-carrying the little un in. I wonder how it is he's come so early.'

Mrs Poyser hastened to the door for the pleasure of looking at her darling in a new position, with love in her eyes but reproof on her tongue.

'Oh for shame, Totty! Little gells o' five year old should be ashamed to be carried. Why, Adam, she'll break your arm, such a big gell as that; set her down – for shame!'

'Nay, nay,' said Adam, 'I can lift her with my hand, I've no need to take my arm to it.'

Totty, looking as serenely unconscious of remark as a fat white puppy, was set down at the door-place, and the mother enforced her reproof with a shower of kisses.

'You're surprised to see me at this hour o' the day,' said Adam.

'Yes, but come in,' said Mrs Poyser, making way for him; 'there's no bad news, I hope?'

'No, nothing bad,' Adam answered, as he went up to Dinah and put out his hand to her. She had laid down her work and stood up, instinctively, as he approached her. A faint blush died away from her pale cheek as she put her hand in his, and looked up at him timidly.

'It's an errand to you brought me, Dinah,' said Adam, apparently unconscious that he was holding her hand all the while; 'mother's a bit ailing, and she's set her heart on your coming to stay the night with her, if you'll be so kind. I told her I'd call and ask you as I came from the village. She overworks herself, and I can't persuade her to have a little girl t' help her. I don't know what's to be done.'

Adam released Dinah's hand as he ceased speaking, and was expecting an answer; but before she had opened her lips Mrs Poyser said –

'Look there now! I told you there was folks enow t' help i' this parish, wi'out going further off. There's Mrs Bede getting as old and cas'alty² as can be, and she won't let anybody but you go a-nigh her hardly. The folks at Snowfield have learnt by this time to do better wi'out you nor she can,'

'I'll put my bonnet on and set off directly, if you don't want anything done first, aunt,' said Dinah, folding up her work.

'Yes, I do want something done. I want you t' have your tea, child; it's all ready; and you'll have a cup, Adam, if y' arena in too big a hurry.'

'Yes, I'll have a cup, please; and then I'll walk with Dinah. I'm going straight home, for I've got a lot o' timber valuations to write out.'

'Why, Adam lad, are you here?' said Mr Poyser, entering warm and coatless, with the two black-eyed boys behind him, still looking as much like him as two small elephants are like a large one. 'How is it we've got sight o' you so long before foddering-time?'

'I came on an errand for mother,' said Adam. 'She's got a touch of her old complaint, and she wants Dinah to go and stay with her a bit.'

'Well, we'll spare her for your mother a little while,' said Mr Poyser. 'But we wonna spare her for anybody else, on'y her husband.'

'Husband!' said Marty, who was at the most prosaic and literal period of the boyish mind. 'Why, Dinah hasn't got a husband.'

'Spare her?' said Mrs Poyser, placing a seed-cake on the table, and then seating herself to pour out the tea. 'But we must spare her, it seems, and not for a husband neither, but for her own megrims. Tommy, what are you doing to your little sister's doll? making the child naughty, when she'd be good if you'd let her. You shanna have a morsel o' cake if you behave so.'

Tommy, with true brotherly sympathy, was amusing himself by turning Dolly's skirt over her bald head, and exhibiting her truncated body to the general scorn – an indignity which cut Totty to the heart.

'What do you think Dinah's been a-telling me since dinner-time?' Mrs Poyser continued, looking at her husband.

'Eh! I'm a poor un at guessing,' said Mr Poyser.

'Why, she means to go back to Snowfield again, and work i' the mill, and starve herself, as she used to do, like a creatur as has got no friends.'

Mr Poyser did not readily find words to express his unpleasant astonishment; he only looked from his wife to Dinah, who had now seated herself beside Totty, as a bulwark against brotherly playfulness, and was busying herself with the children's tea. If he had been given to making general reflections, it would have occurred to him that there was certainly a change come over Dinah, for she never used to change colour; but, as it was, he merely observed that her face was flushed at that moment. Mr Poyser thought she looked the prettier for it: it was a flush no deeper than the petal of a monthly rose.[3] Perhaps it came because her uncle was looking at her so fixedly; but there is no knowing; for just then Adam was saying, with quiet surprise –

'Why, I hoped Dinah was settled among us for life. I thought she'd given up the notion o' going back to her old country.'

'Thought! yes,' said Mrs Poyser; 'and so would anybody else ha' thought, as had got their right end up'ards. But I suppose you must *be* a Methodist to know what a Methodist 'ull do. It's ill guessing what the bats are flying after.'

'Why, what have we done to you, Dinah, as you must go away from us?' said Mr Poyser, still pausing over his tea-cup. 'It's like breaking your word, welly; for your aunt never had no thought but you'd make this your home.'

'Nay, uncle,' said Dinah, trying to be quite calm. 'When I first came, I said it was only for a time, as long as I could be of any comfort to my aunt.'

'Well, an' who said you'd ever left off being a comfort to me?' said Mrs Poyser. 'If you didna mean to stay wi' me, you'd better never ha' come. Them as ha' never had a cushion don't miss it.'

'Nay, nay,' said Mr Poyser, who objected to exaggerated views. 'Thee mustna say so; we should ha' been ill off wi'out her, Lady Day was a twelvemont': we mun be thankful for that, whether she stays or no. But I canna think what she mun leave a good home for, to go back int' a country where the land, most on't, isna worth ten shillings an acre, rent and profits.'

'Why, that's just the reason she wants to go, as fur as she can give a reason,' said Mrs Poyser. 'She says this country's too comfortable, an' there's too much t' eat, an' folks arena miserable enough. And she's going next week: I canna turn her, say what I will. It's allays the way wi' them meekfaced people; you may's well pelt a bag o' feathers as talk to 'em. But *I* say it isna religion, to be so obstinate – is it now, Adam?'

Adam saw that Dinah was more disturbed than he had ever seen her by any matter relating to herself, and, anxious to relieve her, if possible, he said, looking at her affectionately –

'Nay, I can't find fault with anything Dinah does. I believe her thoughts are better than our guesses, let 'em be what they may. I should ha' been thankful for her to stay among us; but if she thinks well to go, I wouldn't cross her, or make it hard to her by objecting. We owe her something different to that.'

As it often happens, the words intended to relieve her were just too much for Dinah's susceptible feelings at this moment. The tears came into the grey eyes too fast to be hidden; and she got up hurriedly, meaning it to be understood that she was going to put on her bonnet.

'Mother, what's Dinah crying for?' said Totty. 'She isn't a naughty dell.'

'Thee'st gone a bit too fur,' said Mr Poyser. 'We've no right t' interfere with her doing as she likes. An' thee'dst be as angry as could be wi' me, if I said a word against anything she did.'

'Because you'd very like be finding fault wi'out reason,' said Mrs Poyser. 'But there's reason i' what I say, else I shouldna say it. It's easy talking for them as can't love her so well as her own aunt does. An' me got so used to her! I shall feel as uneasy as a new sheared sheep when she's gone from me. An' to think of her leaving a parish where she's so looked on. There's Mr Irwine makes as much of her as if she was a lady, for all her being a Methodist, an' wi' that maggot o' preaching in her head; – God forgi'e me if I'm i' the wrong to call it so.'

'Ay,' said Mr Poyser, looking jocose; 'but thee dostna tell Adam what he said to thee about it one day. The missis was saying, Adam, as the preaching was th' only fault to be found wi' Dinah, and Mr Irwine says, "But you mustn't find fault with her for that, Mrs Poyser; you forget she's got no husband to preach to. I'll answer for it, you give Poyser many a good sermon." The parson had thee there,' Mr Poyser added, laughing unctuously. 'I told Bartle Massey on it, an' he laughed too.'

'Yes, it's a small joke sets men laughing when they sit a-staring at one another with a pipe i' their mouths,' said Mrs Poyser. 'Give Bartle Massey his way, and he'd have all the sharpness to himself. If the chaff-cutter[4] had the making of us, we should all be straw, I reckon. Totty, my chicken, go upstairs to cousin Dinah, and see what she's doing, and give her a pretty kiss.'

This errand was devised for Totty as a means of checking certain threatening symptoms about the corners of the mouth;

for Tommy, no longer expectant of cake, was lifting up his eyelids with his fore-fingers, and turning his eyeballs towards Totty, in a way that she felt to be disagreeably personal.

'You're rare and busy now – eh, Adam?' said Mr Poyser. 'Burge's getting so bad wi' his asthmy,[5] it's well if he'll ever do much riding about again.'

'Yes, we've got a pretty bit o' building on hand now,' said Adam: 'what with the repairs on th' estate, and the new houses at Treddles'on.'

'I'll bet a penny that new house Burge is building on his own bit o' land is for him and Mary to go to,' said Mr Poyser. 'He'll be for laying by business soon, I'll warrant, and be wanting you to take to it all, and pay him so much by th' 'ear. We shall see you living on th' hill before another twelvemont's over.'

'Well,' said Adam, 'I should like t' have the business in my own hands. It isn't as I mind much about getting any more money: we've enough and to spare now, with only our two selves and mother; but I should like t' have my own way about things: I could try plans then, as I can't do now.'

'You get on pretty well wi' the new steward, I reckon?' said Mr Poyser.

'Yes, yes; he's a sensible man enough: understands farming – he's carrying on the draining, and all that, capital. You must go some day towards the Stonyshire side, and see what alterations they're making. But he's got no notion about buildings: you can so seldom get hold of a man as can turn his brains to more nor one thing; it's just as if they wore blinkers like th' horses, and could see nothing o' one side of 'em. Now, there's Mr Irwine has got notions o' building more nor most architects; for as for th' architects, they set up to be fine fellows, but the most of 'em don't know where to set a chimney so as it shan't be quarrelling with a door. My notion is, a practical builder, that's got a bit o' taste, makes the best architect for common things; and I've ten times the pleasure i' seeing after the work when I've made the plan myself.'

Mr Poyser listened with an admiring interest to Adam's discourse on building; but perhaps it suggested to him that the building of his corn-rick had been proceeding a little too long without the control of the master's eye; for when Adam had done speaking, he got up and said –

'Well, lad, I'll bid you good-bye now, for I'm off to the rick-yard again.'

Adam rose too, for he saw Dinah entering, with her bonnet on, and a little basket in her hand, preceded by Totty.

'You're ready, I see, Dinah,' Adam said; 'so we'll set off, for the sooner I'm at home the better.'

'Mother,' said Totty, with her treble pipe, 'Dinah was saying her prayers and crying ever so.'

'Hush, hush,' said the mother: 'little gells mustn't chatter.'

Whereupon the father, shaking with silent laughter, set Totty on the white deal table, and desired her to kiss him. Mr and Mrs Poyser, you perceive, had no correct principles of education.

'Come back to-morrow if Mrs Bede doesn't want you, Dinah,' said Mrs Poyser: 'but you can stay, you know, if she's ill.'

So, when the good-byes had been said, Dinah and Adam left the Hall Farm together.

CHAPTER L

In the Cottage

Adam did not ask Dinah to take his arm when they got out into the lane. He had never yet done so, often as they had walked together; for he had observed that she never walked arm-in-arm with Seth, and he thought, perhaps, that kind of support was not agreeable to her. So they walked apart, though side by side, and the close poke of her little black bonnet[1] hid her face from him.

'You can't be happy, then, to make the Hall Farm your home, Dinah?' Adam said, with the quiet interest of a brother, who has no anxiety for himself in the matter. 'It's a pity, seeing they're so fond of you.'

'You know, Adam, my heart is as their heart, so far as love for them and care for their welfare goes; but they are in no present need, their sorrows are healed, and I feel that I am called back to my old work, in which I found a blessing that I have missed of late in the midst of too abundant worldly good. I know it is a vain thought to flee from the work that God appoints us, for the sake of finding a greater blessing to our own souls, as if we could choose for ourselves where we shall find the fulness of the Divine Presence, instead of seeking it where alone it is to be found, in loving obedience. But now, I believe, I have a clear showing that my work lies elsewhere – at least for a time. In the years to come, if my aunt's health should fail, or she should otherwise need me, I shall return.'

'You know best, Dinah,' said Adam. 'I don't believe you'd go against the wishes of them that love you, and are akin to you, without a good and sufficient reason in your own conscience. I've no right to say anything about my being sorry: you

know well enough what cause I have to put you above every
other friend I've got; and if it had been ordered so that you
could ha' been my sister, and lived with us all our lives, I should
ha' counted it the greatest blessing as could happen to us now;
but Seth tells me there's no hope o' that: your feelings are
different; and perhaps I'm taking too much upon me to speak
about it.'

Dinah made no answer, and they walked on in silence for
some yards, till they came to the stone stile; where, as Adam
had passed through first, and turned round to give her his
hand while she mounted the unusually high step, she could not
prevent him from seeing her face. It struck him with surprise;
for the grey eyes, usually so mild and grave, had the bright
uneasy glance which accompanies suppressed agitation, and the
slight flush in her cheeks, with which she had come down-stairs,
was heightened to a deep rose-colour. She looked as if she
were only sister to Dinah. Adam was silent with surprise and
conjecture for some moments, and then he said –

'I hope I've not hurt or displeased you, by what I've said,
Dinah: perhaps I was making too free. I've no wish different
from what you see to be best; and I'm satisfied for you to live
thirty mile off, if you think it right. I shall think of you just as
much as I do now; for you're bound up with what I can no
more help remembering, than I can help my heart beating.'

Poor Adam! Thus do men blunder. Dinah made no answer,
but she presently said –

'Have you heard any news from that poor young man, since
we last spoke of him?'

Dinah always called Arthur so; she had never lost the image
of him as she had seen him in the prison.

'Yes,' said Adam. 'Mr Irwine read me part of a letter from
him yesterday. It's pretty certain, they say, that there'll be a
peace soon, though nobody believes it'll last long;[2] but he says
he doesn't mean to come home. He's no heart for it yet; and
it's better for others that he should keep away. Mr Irwine thinks
he's in the right not to come: – it's a sorrowful letter. He asks
about you and the Poysers, as he always does. There's one thing
in the letter cut me a good deal: – "You can't think what an

old fellow I feel," he says; "I make no schemes now. I'm the best when I've a good day's march or fighting before me."'

'He's of a rash, warm-hearted nature, like Esau, for whom I have always felt great pity,' said Dinah. 'That meeting between the brothers, where Esau is so loving and generous, and Jacob so timid and distrustful,[3] notwithstanding his sense of the Divine favour, has always touched me greatly. Truly I have been tempted sometimes to say that Jacob was of a mean spirit. But that is our trial: – we must learn to see the good in the midst of much that is unlovely.'

'Ah,' said Adam, 'I like to read about Moses best, in th' Old Testament. He carried a hard business well through, and died when other folks were going to reap the fruits:[4] a man must have courage to look at his life so, and think what'll come of it after he's dead and gone. A good solid bit o' work lasts: if it's only laying a floor down, somebody's the better for it being done well, besides the man as does it.'

They were both glad to talk of subjects that were not personal, and in this way they went on till they passed the bridge across the Willow Brook, when Adam turned round and said –

'Ah, here's Seth. I thought he'd be home soon. Does he know of your going, Dinah?'

'Yes, I told him last Sabbath.'

Adam remembered now that Seth had come home much depressed on Sunday evening, a circumstance which had been very unusual with him of late, for the happiness he had in seeing Dinah every week seemed long to have outweighed the pain of knowing she would never marry him. This evening he had his habitual air of dreamy benignant contentment, until he came quite close to Dinah, and saw the traces of tears on her delicate eyelids and eyelashes. He gave one rapid glance at his brother; but Adam was evidently quite outside the current of emotion that had shaken Dinah: he wore his everyday look of unexpectant calm. Seth tried not to let Dinah see that he had noticed her face, and only said –

'I'm thankful you're come, Dinah, for mother's been hungering after the sight of you all day. She began to talk of you the first thing in the morning.'

When they entered the cottage, Lisbeth was seated in her arm-chair, too tired with setting out the evening meal, a task she always performed a long time beforehand, to go and meet them at the door as usual, when she heard the approaching footsteps.

'Coom, child, thee't coom at last,' she said, when Dinah went towards her. 'What dost mane by lavin' me a week, an' ne'er coomin' a-nigh me?'

'Dear friend,' said Dinah, taking her hand, 'you're not well. If I'd known it sooner, I'd have come.'

'An' how's thee t' know if thee dostna coom? Th' lads on'y know what I tell 'em: as long as ye can stir hand and foot the men think ye're hearty. But I'm none so bad, on'y a bit of a cold sets me achin'. An' th' lads tease me so t' ha' somebody wi' me t' do the work – they make me ache worse wi' talkin'. If thee'dst come and stay wi' me, they'd let me alone. The Poysers canna want thee so bad as I do. But take thy bonnet off, an' let me look at thee.'

Dinah was moving away, but Lisbeth held her fast while she was taking off her bonnet, and looked at her face, as one looks into a newly-gathered snowdrop, to renew the old impressions of purity and gentleness.

'What's the matter wi' thee?' said Lisbeth, in astonishment; 'thee'st been a-cryin'.'

'It's only a grief that'll pass away,' said Dinah, who did not wish just now to call forth Lisbeth's remonstrances by disclosing her intention to leave Hayslope. 'You shall know about it shortly – we'll talk of it to-night. I shall stay with you to-night.'

Lisbeth was pacified by this prospect; and she had the whole evening to talk with Dinah alone; for there was a new room in the cottage, you remember, built nearly two years ago, in the expectation of a new inmate; and here Adam always sat when he had writing to do, or plans to make. Seth sat there too this evening, for he knew his mother would like to have Dinah all to herself.

There were two pretty pictures on the two sides of the wall in the cottage. On one side there was the broad-shouldered, large-featured, hardy old woman, in her blue jacket and buff

kerchief, with her dim-eyed anxious looks turned continually
on the lily face and the slight form in the black dress that were
either moving lightly about in helpful activity, or seated close
by the old woman's arm-chair, holding her withered hand, with
eyes lifted up towards her to speak a language which Lisbeth
understood far better than the Bible or the hymn-book. She
would scarcely listen to reading at all to-night. 'Nay, nay, shut
the book,' she said. 'We mun talk. I want t' know what thee
wast cryin' about. Hast got troubles o' thy own, like other
folks?'

On the other side of the wall there were the two brothers, so
like each other in the midst of their unlikeness: Adam, with
knit brows, shaggy hair, and dark vigorous colour, absorbed
in his 'figuring'; Seth, with large rugged features, the close copy
of his brother's, but with thin wavy brown hair and blue dreamy
eyes, as often as not looking vaguely out of the window instead
of at his book although it was a newly-bought book – Wesley's
abridgment of Madame Guyon's life,[5] which was full of wonder
and interest for him. Seth had said to Adam, 'Can I help thee
with anything in here to-night? I don't want to make a noise in
the shop.'

'No, lad,' Adam answered, 'there's nothing but what I must
do myself. Thee'st got thy new book to read.'

And often, when Seth was quite unconscious, Adam, as he
paused after drawing a line with his ruler, looked at his brother
with a kind smile dawning in his eyes. He knew 'th' lad liked
to sit full o' thoughts he could give no account of; they'd never
come t' anything, but they made him happy'; and in the last
year or so, Adam had been getting more and more indulgent to
Seth. It was part of that growing tenderness which came from
the sorrow at work within him.

For Adam, though you see him quite master of himself,
working hard and delighting in his work after his inborn
inalienable nature, had not outlived his sorrow – had not felt it
slip from him as a temporary burthen, and leave him the same
man again. Do any of us? God forbid. It would be a poor result
of all our anguish and our wrestling, if we won nothing but our
old selves at the end of it – if we could return to the same blind

loves, the same self-confident blame, the same light thoughts of human suffering, the same frivolous gossip over blighted human lives, the same feeble sense of that Unknown towards which we have sent forth irrepressible cries in our loneliness. Let us rather be thankful that our sorrow lives in us as an indestructible force, only changing its form, as forces do, and passing from pain into sympathy – the one poor word which includes all our best insight and our best love. Not that this transformation of pain into sympathy had completely taken place in Adam yet: there was still a great remnant of pain, and this he felt would subsist as long as *her* pain was not a memory, but an existing thing, which he must think of as renewed with the light of every new morning. But we get accustomed to mental as well as bodily pain, without, for all that, losing our sensibility to it: it becomes a habit of our lives, and we cease to imagine a condition of perfect ease as possible for us. Desire is chastened into submission; and we are contented with our day when we have been able to bear our grief in silence, and act as if we were not suffering. For it is at such periods that the sense of our lives having visible and invisible relations beyond any of which either our present or prospective self is the centre, grows like a muscle that we are obliged to lean on and exert.

That was Adam's state of mind in this second autumn of his sorrow. His work, as you know, had always been part of his religion, and from very early days he saw clearly that good carpentry was God's will – was that form of God's will that most immediately concerned him; but now there was no margin of dreams for him beyond this daylight reality, no holiday-time in the working-day world: no moment in the distance when duty would take off her iron glove and breastplate, and clasp him gently into rest. He conceived no picture of the future but one made up of hard-working days such as he lived through, with growing contentment and intensity of interest, every fresh week: love, he thought, could never be anything to him, but a living memory – a limb lopped off, but not gone from consciousness. He did not know that the power of loving was all the while gaining new force within him; that the new sensibilities bought by a deep experience were so many new fibres by which it was possible, nay, necessary to him, that his nature should intertwine with another. Yet he was aware that common affection and friendship were more precious to him than they used to be, – that he clung more to his mother and Seth, and had an unspeakable satisfaction in the sight or imagination of any small addition to their happiness. The Poysers, too – hardly three or four days passed but he felt the need of seeing them, and interchanging words and looks of friendliness with them: he would have felt this, probably, even if Dinah had not been with them; but he had only said the simplest truth in telling Dinah that he put her above all other friends in the world. Could anything be more natural? For in the darkest moments of memory the thought of her always came as the first ray of returning comfort: the early days of gloom at the Hall Farm had been gradually turned into soft moonlight by her presence; and in the cottage, too, – for she had come at every spare moment to soothe and cheer poor Lisbeth, who had been stricken with a fear that subdued even her querulousness, at the sight of her darling Adam's grief-worn face. He had become used to watching her light quiet movements, her pretty loving ways to the children, when he went to the Hall Farm; to listen for her voice as for a recurrent music; to think everything she said and did was just right, and could not have been better. In spite of his wisdom, he could not find fault with her for her over-indulgence of the children, who had managed to convert Dinah the preacher, before whom a circle of rough men had often trembled a little, into a convenient household slave; though Dinah herself was rather ashamed of this weakness, and had some inward conflict as to her departure from the precepts of Solomon.[6] Yes, there was one thing that might have been better; she might have loved Seth, and consented to marry him. He felt a little vexed, for his brother's sake; and he could not help thinking regretfully how Dinah, as Seth's wife, would have made their home as happy as it could be for them all – how she was the one being that would have soothed their mother's last days into peacefulness and rest.

'It's wonderful she doesn't love th' lad,' Adam had said sometimes to himself; 'for anybody 'ud think he was just cut

out for her. But her heart's so taken up with other things. She's
one o' those women that feel no drawing towards having a
husband and children o' their own. She thinks she should be
filled up with her own life then; and she's been used so to living
in other folks's cares, she can't bear the thought of her heart
being shut up from 'em. I see how it is, well enough. She's cut
out o' different stuff from most women: I saw that long ago.
She's never easy but when she's helping somebody, and marriage 'ud interfere with her ways, – that's true. I've no right to
be contriving and thinking it 'ud be better if she'd have Seth, as
if I was wiser than she is; – or than God either, for He made
her what she is, and that's one o' the greatest blessings I've ever
had from His hands, and others besides me.'

This self-reproof had recurred strongly to Adam's mind,
when he gathered from Dinah's face that he had wounded her
by referring to his wish that she had accepted Seth, and so he
had endeavoured to put into the strongest words his confidence
in her decision as right – his resignation even to her going away
from them, and ceasing to make part of their life otherwise
than by living in their thoughts, if that separation were chosen
by herself. He felt sure she knew quite well enough how much
he cared to see her continually – to talk to her with the silent
consciousness of a mutual great remembrance. It was not possible she should hear anything but self-renouncing affection and
respect in his assurance that he was contented for her to go
away; and yet there remained an uneasy feeling in his mind that
he had not said quite the right thing – that, somehow, Dinah
had not understood him.

Dinah must have risen a little before the sun the next morning, for she was down-stairs about five o'clock. So was Seth;
for, through Lisbeth's obstinate refusal to have any woman-
helper in the house, he had learned to make himself, as Adam
said, 'very handy in the housework', that he might save his
mother from too great weariness; on which ground I hope you
will not think him unmanly, any more than you can have
thought the gallant Colonel Bath unmanly when he made the
gruel for his invalid sister.[7] Adam, who had sat up late at his
writing, was still asleep, and was not likely, Seth said, to be

down till breakfast-time. Often as Dinah had visited Lisbeth during the last eighteen months, she had never slept in the cottage since that night after Thias's death, when, you remember, Lisbeth praised her deft movements, and even gave a modified approval to her porridge. But in that long interval Dinah had made great advances in household cleverness: and this morning, since Seth was there to help, she was bent on bringing everything to a pitch of cleanliness and order that would have satisfied her aunt Poyser. The cottage was far from that standard at present, for Lisbeth's rheumatism had forced her to give up her old habits of dilettante scouring and polishing.[8] When the kitchen was to her mind, Dinah went into the new room, where Adam had been writing the night before, to see what sweeping and dusting were needed there. She opened the window and let in the fresh morning air, and the smell of the sweetbrier, and the bright low-slanting rays of the early sun, which made a glory about her pale face and pale auburn hair as she held the long brush, and swept, singing to herself in a very low tone – like a sweet summer murmur that you have to listen for very closely – one of Charles Wesley's hymns:

> 'Eternal Beam of Light Divine,
>   Fountain of unexhausted love,
> In whom the Father's glories shine,
>   Through earth beneath and heaven above;
>
> Jesus! the weary wanderer's rest,
>   Give me thy easy yoke to bear;
> With steadfast patience arm my breast,
>   With spotless love and holy fear.
>
> Speak to my warring passions, "Peace!"
>   Say to my trembling heart, "Be still!"
> Thy power my strength and fortress is,
>   For all things serve thy sovereign will.'

She laid by the brush and took up the duster; and if you had ever lived in Mrs Poyser's household, you would know how

the duster behaved in Dinah's hand – how it went into every
small corner, and on every ledge in and out of sight – how it
went again and again round every bar of the chairs, and every
leg, and under and over everything that lay on the table, till it
came to Adam's papers and rulers, and the open desk near
them. Dinah dusted up to the very edge of these, and then
hesitated, looking at them with a longing but timid eye. It was
painful to see how much dust there was among them. As she
was looking in this way, she heard Seth's step just outside the
open door, towards which her back was turned, and said,
raising her clear treble –

'Seth, is your brother wrathful when his papers are stirred?'

'Yes, very, when they are not put back in the right places,'
said a deep strong voice, not Seth's.

It was as if Dinah had put her hands unawares on a vibrating
chord; she was shaken with an intense thrill, and for the instant
felt nothing else; then she knew her cheeks were glowing, and
dared not look round, but stood still, distressed because she
could not say good-morning in a friendly way. Adam, finding
that she did not look round so as to see the smile on his face,
was afraid she had thought him serious about his wrathfulness,
and went up to her, so that she was obliged to look at him.

'What! you think I'm a cross fellow at home, Dinah?' he said,
smilingly.

'Nay,' said Dinah, looking up with timid eyes, 'not so. But
you might be put about by finding things meddled with; and
even the man Moses, the meekest of men, was wrathful
sometimes.'[9]

'Come, then,' said Adam, looking at her affectionately, 'I'll
help you move the things, and put 'em back again, and then
they can't get wrong. You're getting to be your aunt's own
niece, I see, for particularness.'

They began their little task together, but Dinah had not
recovered herself sufficiently to think of any remark, and Adam
looked at her uneasily. Dinah, he thought, had seemed to dis-
approve him somehow lately; she had not been so kind and
open to him as she used to be. He wanted her to look at him
and be as pleased as he was himself with doing this bit of playful

work. But Dinah did not look at him – it was easy for her to avoid looking at the tall man; and when at last there was no more dusting to be done, and no further excuse for him to linger near her, he could bear it no longer, and said, in rather a pleading tone –

'Dinah, you're not displeased with me for anything, are you? I've not said or done anything to make you think ill of me?'

The question surprised her, and relieved her by giving a new course to her feeling. She looked up at him now, quite earnestly, almost with the tears coming, and said –

'Oh, no, Adam! how could you think so?'

'I couldn't bear you not to feel as much a friend to me as I do to you,' said Adam. 'And you don't know the value I set on the very thought of you, Dinah. That was what I meant yester-day, when I said I'd be content for you to go, if you thought right. I meant, the thought of you was worth so much to me, I should feel I ought to be thankful, and not grumble, if you see right to go away. You know I do mind parting with you, Dinah?'

'Yes, dear friend,' said Dinah, trembling, but trying to speak calmly, 'I know you have a brother's heart towards me, and we shall often be with one another in spirit; but at this season I am in heaviness through manifold temptations; you must not mark me. I feel called to leave my kindred for a while; but it is a trial: the flesh is weak.'[10]

Adam saw that it pained her to be obliged to answer.

'I hurt you by talking about it, Dinah,' he said: 'I'll say no more. Let's see if Seth's ready with breakfast now.'

That is a simple scene, reader. But it is almost certain that you, too, have been in love – perhaps, even, more than once, though you may not choose to say so to all your feminine friends. If so, you will no more think the slight words, the timid looks, the tremulous touches, by which two human souls approach each other gradually, like two little quivering rain-streams, before they mingle into one – you will no more think these things trivial than you will think the first-detected signs of coming spring trivial, though they be but a faint, indescribable something in the air and in the song of the birds, and the tiniest perceptible budding on the hedgerow branches. Those slight words and looks and touches are part of the soul's language; and the finest language, I believe, is chiefly made up of unimposing words, such as 'light', 'sound', 'stars', 'music', – words really not worth looking at, or hearing, in themselves, any more than 'chips' or 'sawdust': it is only that they happen to be the signs of something unspeakably great and beautiful. I am of opinion that love is a great and beautiful thing too; and if you agree with me, the smallest signs of it will not be chips and sawdust to you: they will rather be like those little words, 'light' and 'music', stirring the long-winding fibres of your memory, and enriching your present with your most precious past.

CHAPTER LI

Sunday Morning

Lisbeth's touch of rheumatism could not be made to appear serious enough to detain Dinah another night from the Hall Farm, now she had made up her mind to leave her aunt so soon: and at evening the friends must part. 'For a long while,' Dinah had said; for she had told Lisbeth of her resolve.

'Then it'll be for all my life, an' I shall ne'er see thee again,' said Lisbeth. 'Long while! I'n got no long while t' live. An' I shall be took bad an' die, an' thee canst ne'er come a-nigh me, an' I shall die a-longing for thee.'

That had been the key-note of her wailing talk all day; for Adam was not in the house, and so she put no restraint on her complaining. She had tried poor Dinah by returning again and again to the question, why she must go away; and refusing to accept reasons, which seemed to her nothing but whim and 'contrairiness'; and still more, by regretting that she 'couldna ha' one o' the lads', and be her daughter.

'Thee couldstna put up wi' Seth,' she said; 'he isna cliver enough for thee, happen; but he'd ha' been very good t' thee – he's as handy as can be at doin' things for me when I'm bad; an' he's as fond o' the Bible an' chapellin' as thee art thysen. But happen, thee'dst like a husband better as isna just the cut o' thysen: the runnin' brook isna athirst for th' rain. Adam 'ud ha' done for thee – I know he would; an' he might come t' like thee well enough, if thee'dst stop. But he's as stubborn as th' iron bar – there's no bending him no way but's own. But he'd be a fine husband for anybody, be they who they will, so looked-on an' so cliver as he is. And he'd be rare an' lovin': it does me good on'y a look o' the lad's eye, when he means kind tow'rt me.'

Dinah tried to escape from Lisbeth's closest looks and questions by finding little tasks of housework, that kept her moving about; and as soon as Seth came home in the evening she put on her bonnet to go. It touched Dinah keenly to say the last good-bye, and still more to look round on her way across the fields, and see the old woman still standing at the door, gazing after her till she must have been the faintest speck in the dim aged eyes. 'The God of love and peace be with them,' Dinah prayed, as she looked back from the last stile. 'Make them glad according to the days wherein thou hast afflicted them, and the years wherein they have seen evil. It is thy will that I should part from them; let me have no will but thine.'[1]

Lisbeth turned into the house at last, and sat down in the workshop near Seth, who was busying himself there with fitting some bits of turned wood he had brought from the village, into a small workbox which he meant to give to Dinah before she went away.

'Thee't see her again o' Sunday afore she goes,' were her first words. 'If thee wast good for anything, thee'dst make her come in again o' Sunday night wi' thee, an' see me once more.'

'Nay, mother,' said Seth, 'Dinah 'ud be sure to come again if she saw right to come. I should have no need to persuade her. She only thinks it 'ud be troubling thee for nought, just to come in to say good-bye over again.'

'She'd ne'er go away, I know, if Adam 'ud be fond on her an' marry her; but everything's so contrairy,' said Lisbeth, with a burst of vexation.

Seth paused a moment, and looked up, with a slight blush, at his mother's face. 'What! has she said anything o' that sort to thee, mother?' he said, in a lower tone.

'Said? nay, she'll say nothin'. It's on'y the men as have to wait till folks say things afore they find 'em out.'

'Well, but what makes thee think so, mother? What's put it into thy head?'

'It's no matter what's put it into my head: my head's none so hollow as it must get in, an' nought to put it there. I know she's fond on him, as I know th' wind's comin' in at the door, an' that's anoof. An' he might be willin' to marry her if he know'd she's fond on him, but he'll ne'er think on't if somebody doesna put it into's head.'

His mother's suggestion about Dinah's feeling towards Adam was not quite a new thought to Seth, but her last words alarmed him, lest she should herself undertake to open Adam's eyes. He was not sure about Dinah's feeling, and he thought he *was* sure about Adam's.

'Nay, mother, nay,' he said, earnestly, 'thee mustna think o' speaking o' such things to Adam. Thee'st no right to say what Dinah's feelings are if she hasna told thee; and it 'ud do nothing but mischief to say such things to Adam: he feels very grateful and affectionate toward Dinah, but he's no thoughts towards her that 'ud incline him to make her his wife; and I don't believe Dinah 'ud marry him either. I don't think she'll marry at all.'

'Eh,' said Lisbeth, impatiently. 'Thee think'st so 'cause she wouldna ha' thee. She'll ne'er marry thee; thee mightst as well like her t' ha' thy brother.'

Seth was hurt. 'Mother,' he said, in a remonstrating tone, 'don't think that of me. I should be as thankful t' have her for a sister as thee wouldst t' have her for a daughter. I've no more thoughts about myself in that thing, and I shall take it hard if ever thee say'st it again.'

'Well, well, then thee shouldstna cross me wi' sayin' things arena as I say they are.'

'But, mother,' said Seth, 'thee'dst be doing Dinah a wrong by telling Adam what thee think'st about her. It 'ud do nothing but mischief; for it 'ud make Adam uneasy if he doesna feel the same to her. And I'm pretty sure he feels nothing o' the sort.'

'Eh, donna tell me what thee't sure on; thee know'st nought about it. What's he allays goin' to the Poysers' for, if he didna want t' see her? He goes twice where he used t' go once. Happen he knowsna as he wants t' see her; he knowsna as I put salt in's broth, but he'd miss it pretty quick if it warna there. He'll ne'er think o' marrying if it isna put into's head; an' if thee'dst any love for thy mother, thee'dst put him up to't, an' not let her go away out o' my sight, when I might ha' her to make a bit o' comfort for me afore I go to bed to my old man under the white thorn.'

'Nay, mother,' said Seth, 'thee mustna think me unkind; but I should be going against my conscience if I took upon me to say what Dinah's feelings are. And besides that, I think I should give offence to Adam by speaking to him at all about marrying; and I counsel thee not to do't. Thee may'st be quite deceived about Dinah; nay, I'm pretty sure, by words she said to me last Sabbath, as she's no mind to marry.'

'Eh, thee't as contrairy as the rest on 'em. If it war summat I didna want, it 'ud be done fast enough.

Lisbeth rose from the bench at this, and went out of the workshop, leaving Seth in much anxiety lest she should disturb Adam's mind about Dinah. He consoled himself after a time with reflecting that, since Adam's trouble, Lisbeth had been very timid about speaking to him on matters of feeling, and that she would hardly dare to approach this tenderest of all subjects. Even if she did, he hoped Adam would not take much notice of what she said.

Seth was right in believing that Lisbeth would be held in restraint by timidity; and during the next three days, the intervals in which she had an opportunity of speaking to Adam were too rare and short to cause her any strong temptation. But in her long solitary hours she brooded over her regretful thoughts about Dinah, till they had grown very near that point of unmanageable strength when thoughts are apt to take wing out of their secret nest in a startling manner. And on Sunday morning, when Seth went away to chapel at Treddleston, the dangerous opportunity came.

Sunday morning was the happiest time in all the week to Lisbeth; for as there was no service at Hayslope church till the afternoon, Adam was always at home, doing nothing but reading, an occupation in which she could venture to interrupt him. Moreover, she had always a better dinner than usual to prepare for her sons – very frequently for Adam and herself alone, Seth being often away the entire day; and the smell of the roast-meat before the clear fire in the clean kitchen, the clock ticking in a peaceful Sunday manner, her darling Adam

seated near her in his best clothes, doing nothing very important, so that she could go and stroke her hand across his hair if
she liked, and see him look up at her and smile, while Gyp,
rather jealous, poked his muzzle up between them, – all these
things made poor Lisbeth's earthly paradise.

The book Adam most often read on a Sunday morning was
his large pictured Bible, and this morning it lay open before
him on the round white deal table in the kitchen; for he sat
there in spite of the fire, because he knew his mother liked to
have him with her, and it was the only day in the week when
he could indulge her in that way. You would have liked to see
Adam reading his Bible: he never opened it on a week-day, and
so he came to it as a holiday book, serving him for history,
biography, and poetry. He held one hand thrust between his
waistcoat buttons, and the other ready to turn the pages; and
in the course of the morning you would have seen many changes
in his face. Sometimes his lips moved in semi-articulation – it
was when he came to a speech that he could fancy himself
uttering, such as Samuel's dying speech to the people; then his
eyebrows would be raised, and the corners of his mouth would
quiver a little with sad sympathy – something, perhaps old
Isaac's meeting with his son, touched him closely; at other
times, over the New Testament, a very solemn look would come
upon his face, and he would every now and then shake his
head in serious assent, or just lift up his hand and let it fall
again; and on some mornings, when he read in the Apocrypha,
of which he was very fond, the son of Sirach's keen-edged
words would bring a delighted smile, though he also enjoyed
the freedom of occasionally differing from an Apocryphal
writer. For Adam knew the Articles[2] quite well, as became a
good churchman.

Lisbeth, in the pauses of attending to her dinner, always sat
opposite to him and watched him, till she could rest no longer
without going up to him and giving him a caress, to call his
attention to her. This morning he was reading the Gospel
according to St Matthew, and Lisbeth had been standing close
by him for some minutes, stroking his hair, which was smoother
than usual this morning, and looking down at the large page

with silent wonderment at the mystery of letters. She was encouraged to continue this caress, because when she first went up to him, he had thrown himself back in his chair to look at her affectionately and say, 'Why, mother, thee look'st rare and hearty this morning. Eh, Gyp wants me t' look at him: he can't abide to think I love thee the best.' Lisbeth said nothing, because she wanted to say so many things. And now there was a new leaf to be turned over, and it was a picture – that of the angel seated on the great stone that has been rolled away from the sepulchre. This picture had one strong association in Lisbeth's memory, for she had been reminded of it when she first saw Dinah; and Adam had no sooner turned the page, and lifted the book sideways that they might look at the angel, than she said, 'That's her – that's Dinah.'

Adam smiled, and, looking more intently at the angel's face, said –

'It *is* a bit like her; but Dinah's prettier, I think.'

'Well, then, if thee think'st her so pretty, why arn't fond on her?'

Adam looked up in surprise. 'Why, mother, dost think I don't set store by Dinah?'

'Nay,' said Lisbeth, frightened at her own courage, yet feeling that she had broken the ice, and the waters must flow, whatever mischief they might do. 'What's th' use o' settin' store by things as are thirty mile off? If thee wast fond enough on her thee wouldstna let her go away.'

'But I've no right t' hinder her, if she thinks well,' said Adam, looking at his book as if he wanted to go on reading. He foresaw a series of complaints tending to nothing. Lisbeth sat down again in the chair opposite to him, as she said –

'But she wouldna think well if thee wastna so contrairy.' Lisbeth dared not venture beyond a vague phrase yet.

'Contrairy, mother?' Adam said, looking up again in some anxiety. 'What have I done? What dost mean?'

'Why, thee't never look at nothin', nor think o' nothin', but thy figurin' an' thy work,' said Lisbeth, half crying. 'An' dost think thee canst go on so all thy life, as if thee wast a man cut out o' timber? An' what wut do when thy mother's gone, an' nobody to take care on thee as thee gett'st a bit o' victual comfortable i' the mornin'?'

'What hast got i' thy mind, mother?' said Adam, vexed at this whimpering. 'I canna see what thee't driving at. Is there anything I could do for thee as I don't do?'

'Ay, an' that there is. Thee might'st do as I should ha' somebody wi' me to comfort me a bit, an' wait on me when I'm bad, an' be good to me.'

'Well, mother, whose fault is it there isna some tidy body i' th' house t' help thee? It isna by my wish as thee hast a stroke o' work to do. We can afford it – I've told thee often enough. It 'ud be a deal better for us.'

'Eh, what's the use o' talkin' o' tidy bodies, when thee mean'st one o' th' wenches out o' th' village, or somebody from Treddles'on as I ne'er set eyes on i' my life? I'd sooner make a shift an' get into my own coffin afore I die, nor ha' them folks to put me in.'

Adam was silent, and tried to go on reading. That was the utmost severity he could show towards his mother on a Sunday morning. But Lisbeth had gone too far now to check herself, and after scarcely a minute's quietness she began again.

'Thee mightst know well enough who 'tis I'd like t' ha' wi' me. It isna many folks I send for t' come an' see me, I reckon. An' thee'st had the fetchin' on her times enow.'

'Thee mean'st Dinah, mother, I know,' said Adam. 'But it's no use setting thy mind on what can't be. If Dinah 'ud be willing to stay at Hayslope, it isn't likely she can come away from her aunt's house, where they hold her like a daughter, and where she's more bound than she is to us. If it had been so that she could ha' married Seth, that 'ud ha' been a great blessing to us, but we can't have things just as we like in this life. Thee must try and make up thy mind to do without her.'

'Nay, but I canna ma' up my mind, when she's just cut out for thee; an' nought shall ma' me believe as God didna make her an' send her there o' purpose for thee. What's it sinnify about her being a Methody? It 'ud happen wear out on her wi' marryin'.'

Adam threw himself back in his chair and looked at his

mother. He understood now what she had been aiming at from the beginning of the conversation. It was as unreasonable, impracticable a wish as she had ever urged, but he could not help being moved by so entirely new an idea. The chief point, however, was to chase away the notion from his mother's mind as quickly as possible.

'Mother,' he said, gravely, 'thee't talking wild. Don't let me hear thee say such things again. It's no good talking o' what can never be. Dinah's not for marrying; she's fixed her heart on a different sort o' life.'

'Very like,' said Lisbeth, impatiently, 'very like she's none for marr'ing, when them as she'd be willin' t' marry wonna ax her. I shouldna ha' been for marr'ing thy feyther if he'd ne'er axed me; an' she's as fond o' thee as e'er I war o' Thias, poor fellow.'

The blood rushed to Adam's face, and for a few moments he was not quite conscious where he was: his mother and the kitchen had vanished for him, and he saw nothing but Dinah's face turned up towards his. It seemed as if there were a resurrection of his dead joy. But he woke up very speedily from that dream (the waking was chill and sad); for it would have been very foolish in him to believe his mother's words; she could have no ground for them. He was prompted to express his disbelief very strongly – perhaps that he might call forth the proofs, if there were any to be offered.

'What dost say such things for, mother, when thee'st got no foundation for 'em? Thee know'st nothing as gives thee a right to say that.'

'Then I knowna nought as gi'es me a right to say as the year's turned, for all I feel it fust thing when I get up i' th' mornin'. She isna fond o' Seth, I reckon, is she? She doesna want to marry *him*? But I can see as she doesna behave tow'rt thee as she does tow'rt Seth. She makes no more o' Seth's coming a-nigh her nor if he war Gyp, but she's all of a tremble when thee't a-sittin' down by her at breakfast, an' a-looking at her. Thee think'st thy mother knows nought, but she war alive afore thee wast born.'

'But thee canstna be sure as the trembling means love?' said Adam, anxiously.

'Eh, what else should it mane? It isna hate, I reckon. An' what should she do but love thee? Thee't made to be loved – for where's there a straighter, cliverer man? An' what's it sinnify her bein' a Methody? It's on'y the marigold i' th' parridge.'

Adam had thrust his hands in his pockets, and was looking down at the book on the table, without seeing any of the letters. He was trembling like a gold-seeker, who sees the strong promise of gold, but sees in the same moment a sickening vision of disappointment. He could not trust his mother's insight; she had seen what she wished to see. And yet – and yet, now the suggestion had been made to him, he remembered so many things, very slight things, like the stirring of the water by an imperceptible breeze, which seemed to him some confirmation of his mother's words.

Lisbeth noticed that he was moved. She went on –

'An' thee't find out as thee't poorly aff when she's gone. Thee't fonder on her nor thee know'st. Thy eyes follow her about, welly as Gyp's follow thee.'

Adam could sit still no longer. He rose, took down his hat, and went out into the fields.

The sunshine was on them: that early autumn sunshine which we should know was not summer's, even if there were not the touches of yellow on the lime and chestnut: the Sunday sunshine, too, which has more than autumnal calmness for the working man: the morning sunshine, which still leaves the dew-crystals on the fine gossamer webs in the shadow of the bushy hedgerows.

Adam needed the calm influence; he was amazed at the way in which this new thought of Dinah's love had taken possession of him, with an overmastering power that made all other feelings give way before the impetuous desire to know that the thought was true. Strange, that till that moment the possibility of their ever being lovers had never crossed his mind, and yet now, all his longing suddenly went out towards that possibility; he had no more doubt or hesitation as to his own wishes than the bird that flies towards the opening through which the daylight gleams and the breath of heaven enters.

The autumnal Sunday sunshine soothed him; but not by

preparing him with resignation to the disappointment if his
mother – if he himself, proved to be mistaken about Dinah: it
soothed him by gentle encouragement of his hopes. Her love
was so like that calm sunshine that they seemed to make one
presence to him, and he believed in them both alike. And Dinah
was so bound up with the sad memories of his first passion,
that he was not forsaking them, but rather giving them a new
sacredness by loving her. Nay, his love for her had grown out
of that past: it was the noon of that morning.

But Seth? Would the lad be hurt? Hardly; for he had seemed
quite contented of late, and there was no selfish jealousy in him;
he had never been jealous of his mother's fondness for Adam.
But had *he* seen anything of what their mother talked about?
Adam longed to know this, for he thought he could trust Seth's
observation better than his mother's. He must talk to Seth
before he went to see Dinah; and, with this intention in his
mind, he walked back to the cottage and said to his mother –

'Did Seth say anything to thee about when he was coming
home? Will he be back to dinner?'

'Ay, lad; he'll be back for a wonder. He isna gone to
Treddles'on. He's gone somewhere else a-preachin' and
a-prayin'.'

'Hast any notion which way he's gone?' said Adam.

'Nay, but he aften goes to th' Common. Thee know'st more
o's goings nor I do.'

Adam wanted to go and meet Seth, but he must content
himself with walking about the near fields and getting sight of
him as soon as possible. That would not be for more than an
hour to come, for Seth would scarcely be at home much before
their dinner-time, which was twelve o'clock. But Adam could
not sit down to his reading again, and he sauntered along by
the brook and stood leaning against the stiles, with eager,
intense eyes, which looked as if they saw something very vividly;
but it was not the brook or the willows, not the fields or the
sky. Again and again his vision was interrupted by wonder at
the strength of his own feeling, at the strength and sweetness
of this new love – almost like the wonder a man feels at the
added power he finds in himself for an art which he had laid

aside for a space. How is it that the poets have said so many fine things about our first love, so few about our later love? Are their first poems their best? or are not those the best which come from their fuller thought, their larger experience, their deeper-rooted affections? The boy's flute-like voice has its own spring charm; but the man should yield a richer, deeper music.

At last, there was Seth, visible at the farthest stile, and Adam hastened to meet him. Seth was surprised, and thought something unusual must have happened: but when Adam came up, his face said plainly enough that it was nothing alarming.

'Where hast been?' said Adam, when they were side by side.

'I've been to the Common,' said Seth. 'Dinah's been speaking the Word to a little company of hearers at Brimstone's, as they call him. They're folks as never go to church hardly – them on the Common – but they'll go and hear Dinah a bit. She's been speaking with power this forenoon from the words, "I came not to call the righteous, but sinners to repentance."[3] And there was a little thing happened as was pretty to see. The women mostly bring their children with 'em, but to-day there was one stout curly-headed fellow about three or four year old, that I never saw there before. He was as naughty as could be at the beginning while I was praying, and while we was singing, but when we all sat down and Dinah began to speak, th' young un stood stock-still all at once, and began to look at her with's mouth open, and presently he ran away from's mother and went up to Dinah, and pulled at her, like a little dog, for her to take notice of him. So Dinah lifted him up and held th' lad on her lap, while she went on speaking; and he was as good as could be till he went to sleep – and the mother cried to see him.'

'It's a pity she shouldna be a mother herself,' said Adam, 'so fond as the children are of her. Dost think she's quite fixed against marrying, Seth? Dost think nothing 'ud turn her?'

There was something peculiar in his brother's tone, which made Seth steal a glance at his face before he answered.

'It 'ud be wrong of me to say nothing 'ud turn her,' he answered. 'But if thee mean'st it about myself, I've given up all thoughts as she can ever be *my* wife. She calls me her brother, and that's enough.'

'But dost think she might ever get fond enough of anybody else to be willing to marry 'em?' said Adam, rather shyly.

'Well,' said Seth, after some hesitation, 'it's crossed my mind sometimes o' late as she might; but Dinah 'ud let no fondness for the creature draw her out o' the path as she believed God had marked out for her. If she thought the leading was not from Him, she's not one to be brought under the power of it. And she's allays seemed clear about that – as her work was to minister t' others, and make no home for herself i' this world.'

'But suppose,' said Adam, earnestly, 'suppose there was a man as 'ud let her do just the same and not interfere with her, – she might do a good deal o' what she does now, just as well when she was married as when she was single. Other women of her sort have married – that's to say, not just like her, but women as preached and attended on the sick and needy. There's Mrs Fletcher[4] as she talks of.'

A new light had broken in on Seth. He turned round, and laying his hand on Adam's shoulder, said, 'Why, wouldst like her to marry *thee*, brother?'

Adam looked doubtfully at Seth's inquiring eyes, and said, 'Wouldst be hurt if she was to be fonder o' me than o' thee?'

'Nay,' said Seth, warmly, 'how canst think it? Have I felt thy trouble so little, that I shouldna feel thy joy?'

There was silence a few moments as they walked on, and then Seth said –

'I'd no notion as thee'dst ever think of her for a wife.'

'But is it o' any use to think of her?' said Adam – 'what dost say? Mother's made me as I hardly know where I am, with what she's been saying to me this forenoon. She says she's sure Dinah feels for me more than common, and 'ud be willing t' have me. But I'm afraid she speaks without book.[5] I want to know if thee'st seen anything.'

'It's a nice point to speak about,' said Seth, 'and I'm afraid o' being wrong; besides, we've no right t' intermeddle with people's feelings when they wouldn't tell 'em themselves.'

Seth paused.

'But thee mightst ask her,' he said, presently. 'She took no offence at *me* for asking, and thee'st more right than I had, only thee't not in the Society. But Dinah doesn't hold wi' them as are for keeping the Society so strict to themselves. She doesn't mind about making folks enter the Society, so as they're fit t' enter the kingdom o' God. Some o' the brethren at Treddles'on are displeased with her for that.'

'Where will she be the rest o' the day?' said Adam.

'She said she shouldn't leave the Farm again to-day,' said Seth, 'because it's her last Sabbath there, and she's going t' read out o' the big Bible wi' the children.'

Adam thought – but did not say – 'Then I'll go this afternoon; for if I go to church my thoughts 'ull be with her all the while. They must sing th' anthem without me to-day.'

CHAPTER LII

Adam and Dinah

It was about three o'clock when Adam entered the farmyard and roused Alick and the dogs from their Sunday dozing. Alick said everybody was gone to church 'but th' young missis' – so he called Dinah; but this did not disappoint Adam, although the 'everybody' was so liberal as to include Nancy the dairy-maid, whose works of necessity were not unfrequently incompatible with church-going.

There was perfect stillness about the house: the doors were closed, and the very stones and tubs seemed quieter than usual. Adam heard the water gently dripping from the pump – that was the only sound; and he knocked at the house door rather softly, as was suitable in that stillness.

The door opened, and Dinah stood before him, colouring deeply with the great surprise of seeing Adam at this hour, when she knew it was his regular practice to be at church. Yesterday he would have said to her without any difficulty, 'I came to see you, Dinah: I knew the rest were not at home.' But to-day something prevented him from saying that, and he put out his hand to her in silence. Neither of them spoke, and yet both wished they could speak, as Adam entered, and they sat down. Dinah took the chair she had just left; it was at the corner of the table near the window, and there was a book lying on the table, but it was not open: she had been sitting perfectly still, looking at the small bit of clear fire in the bright grate. Adam sat down opposite her, in Mr Poyser's three-cornered chair.

'Your mother is not ill again, I hope, Adam?' Dinah said, recovering herself. 'Seth said she was well this morning.'

'No, she's very hearty to-day,' said Adam, happy in the signs of Dinah's feeling at the sight of him, but shy.

'There's nobody at home, you see,' Dinah said; 'but you'll wait. You've been hindered from going to church to-day, doubtless.'

'Yes,' Adam said, and then paused, before he added, 'I was thinking about you: that was the reason.'

This confession was very awkward and sudden, Adam felt; for he thought Dinah must understand all he meant. But the frankness of the words caused her immediately to interpret them into a renewal of his brotherly regrets that she was going away, and she answered calmly –

'Do not be careful and troubled for me, Adam. I have all things and abound at Snowfield. And my mind is at rest, for I am not seeking my own will in going.'

'But if things were different, Dinah,' said Adam, hesitatingly – 'if you knew things that perhaps you don't know now.' . . .

Dinah looked at him inquiringly, but instead of going on, he reached a chair and brought it near the corner of the table where she was sitting. She wondered and was afraid – and the next moment her thoughts flew to the past: was it something about those distant unhappy ones that she didn't know?

Adam looked at her: it was so sweet to look at her eyes, which had now a self-forgetful questioning in them, – for a moment he forgot that he wanted to say anything, or that it was necessary to tell her what he meant.

'Dinah,' he said suddenly, taking both her hands between his, 'I love you with my whole heart and soul. I love you next to God who made me.'

Dinah's lips became pale, like her cheeks, and she trembled violently under the shock of painful joy. Her hands were cold as death between Adam's. She could not draw them away, because he held them fast.

'Don't tell me you can't love me, Dinah. Don't tell me we must part, and pass our lives away from one another.'

The tears were trembling in Dinah's eyes, and they fell before she could answer. But she spoke in a quiet low voice.

'Yes, dear Adam, we must submit to another Will. We must part.'

'Not if you love me, Dinah – not if you love me,' Adam said, passionately. 'Tell me – tell me if you can love me better than a brother?'

Dinah was too entirely reliant on the Supreme guidance to attempt to achieve any end by a deceptive concealment. She was recovering now from the first shock of emotion, and she looked at Adam with simple sincere eyes as she said –

'Yes, Adam, my heart is drawn strongly towards you; and of my own will, if I had no clear showing to the contrary, I could find my happiness in being near you, and ministering to you continually. I fear I should forget to rejoice and weep with others; nay, I fear I should forget the Divine presence, and seek no love but yours.'[1]

Adam did not speak immediately. They sat looking at each other in delicious silence, – for the first sense of mutual love excludes other feelings; it will have the soul all to itself.

'Then, Dinah,' Adam said at last, 'how can there be anything contrary to what's right in our belonging to one another, and spending our lives together? Who put this great love into our hearts? Can anything be holier than that? For we can help one another in everything as is good. I'd never think o' putting myself between you and God, and saying you oughtn't to do this, and you oughtn't to do that. You'd follow your conscience as much as you do now.'

'Yes, Adam,' Dinah said, 'I know marriage is a holy state[2] for those who are truly called to it, and have no other drawing; but from my childhood upward I have been led towards another path; all my peace and my joy have come from having no life of my own, no wants, no wishes for myself, and living only in God and those of his creatures whose sorrows and joys he has given me to know. Those have been very blessed years to me, and I feel that if I was to listen to any voice that would draw me aside from that path, I should be turning my back on the light that has shone upon me, and darkness and doubt would take hold of me. We could not bless each other, Adam, if there were doubts in my soul, and if I yearned, when it was too late, after that better part[3] which had once been given me and I had put away from me.'

'But if a new feeling has come into your mind, Dinah, and if you love me so as to be willing to be nearer to me than to other people, isn't that a sign that it's right for you to change your life? Doesn't the love make it right when nothing else would?'

'Adam, my mind is full of questionings about that; for now, since you tell me of your strong love towards me, what was clear to me has become dark again. I felt before that my heart was too strongly drawn towards you, and that your heart was not as mine; and the thought of you had taken hold of me, so that my soul had lost its freedom, and was becoming enslaved to an earthly affection, which made me anxious and careful about what should befall myself. For in all other affection I had been content with any small return, or with none; but my heart was beginning to hunger after an equal love from you. And I had no doubt that I must wrestle against that as a great temptation; and the command was clear that I must go away.'

'But now, dear, dear Dinah, now you know I love you better than you love me . . . it's all different now. You won't think o' going: you'll stay, and be my dear wife, and I shall thank God for giving me my life as I never thanked him before.'

'Adam, it's hard to me to turn a deaf ear . . . you know it's hard; but a great fear is upon me. It seems to me as if you were stretching out your arms to me, and beckoning me to come and take my ease, and live for my own delight, and Jesus, the Man of Sorrows, was standing looking towards me, and pointing to the sinful, and suffering, and afflicted. I have seen that again and again when I have been sitting in stillness and darkness, and a great terror has come upon me lest I should become hard, and a lover of self,[4] and no more bear willingly the Redeemer's cross.'

Dinah had closed her eyes, and a faint shudder went through her. 'Adam,' she went on, 'you wouldn't desire that we should seek a good through any unfaithfulness to the light that is in us; you wouldn't believe that could be a good. We are of one mind in that.'

'Yes, Dinah,' said Adam, sadly, 'I'll never be the man t' urge you against your conscience. But I can't give up the hope that you may come to see different. I don't believe your loving me could shut up your heart; it's only adding to what you've been before, not taking away from it; for it seems to me it's the same with love and happiness as with sorrow – the more we know of it the better we can feel what other people's lives are or might be, and so we shall only be more tender to 'em, and wishful to help 'em. The more knowledge a man has, the better he'll do's work; and feeling's a sort o' knowledge.'

Dinah was silent; her eyes were fixed in contemplation of something visible only to herself. Adam went on presently with his pleading –

'And you can do almost as much as you do now. I won't ask you to go to church with me of a Sunday; you shall go where you like among the people, and teach 'em; for though I like church best, I don't put my soul above yours, as if my words was better for you to follow than your own conscience. And you can help the sick just as much, and you'll have more means o' making 'em a bit comfortable; and you'll be among all your own friends as love you, and can help 'em and be a blessing to 'em till their dying day. Surely, Dinah, you'd be as near to God as if you was living lonely and away from me.'

Dinah made no answer for some time. Adam was still holding her hands, and looking at her with almost trembling anxiety, when she turned her grave loving eyes on his, and said, in rather a sad voice –

'Adam, there is truth in what you say, and there's many of the brethren and sisters who have greater strength than I have, and find their hearts enlarged by the cares of husband and kindred. But I have not faith that it would be so with me, for since my affections have been set above measure on you, I have had less peace and joy in God; I have felt as it were a division in my heart. And think how it is with me, Adam: – that life I have led is like a land I have trodden in blessedness since my childhood; and if I long for a moment to follow the voice which calls me to another land that I know not, I cannot but fear that my soul might hereafter yearn for that early blessedness which I had forsaken;[5] and where doubt enters, there is not perfect love. I must wait for clearer guidance: I must go from you, and we must submit ourselves entirely to the Divine Will. We are sometimes required to lay our natural, lawful affections on the altar.'

Adam dared not plead again, for Dinah's was not the voice of caprice or insincerity. But it was very hard for him; his eyes got dim as he looked at her.

'But you may come to feel satisfied . . . to feel that you may come to me again, and we may never part, Dinah?'

'We must submit ourselves, Adam. With time, our duty will be made clear. It may be, when I have entered on my former life, I shall find all these new thoughts and wishes vanish, and become as things that were not. Then I shall know that my calling is not towards marriage. But we must wait.'

'Dinah,' said Adam, mournfully, 'you can't love me so well as I love you, else you'd have no doubts. But it's natural you shouldn't; for I'm not so good as you. I can't doubt it's right for me to love the best thing God's ever given me to know.'

'Nay, Adam; it seems to me that my love for you is not weak; for my heart waits on your words and looks, almost as a little child waits on the help and tenderness of the strong on whom it depends. If the thought of you took slight hold of me, I should not fear that it would be an idol in the temple. But you will strengthen me – you will not hinder me in seeking to obey to the uttermost.'

'Let us go out into the sunshine, Dinah, and walk together. I'll speak no word to disturb you.'

They went out and walked towards the fields, where they would meet the family coming from church. Adam said, 'Take my arm, Dinah', and she took it. That was the only change in their manner to each other since they were last walking together. But no sadness in the prospect of her going away – in the uncertainty of the issue – could rob the sweetness from Adam's sense that Dinah loved him. He thought he would stay at the Hall Farm all that evening. He would be near her as long as he could.

'Heyday! there's Adam along wi' Dinah,' said Mr Poyser, as he opened the far gate into the Home Close. 'I couldna think how he happened away from church. Why,' added good

Martin, after a moment's pause, 'what dost think has just jumped into my head?'

'Summat as hadna far to jump, for it's just under our nose. You mean as Adam's fond o' Dinah.'

'Ay! hast ever had any notion of it before?'

'To be sure I have,' said Mrs Poyser, who always declined, if possible, to be taken by surprise. 'I'm not one o' those as can see the cat i' the dairy, an' wonder what she's come after.'

'Thee never saidst a word to me about it.'

'Well, I aren't like a bird-clapper, forced to make a rattle when the wind blows on me. I can keep my own counsel when there's no good i' speaking.'

'But Dinah 'ull ha' none o' him; dost think she will?'

'Nay,' said Mrs Poyser, not sufficiently on her guard against a possible surprise; 'she'll never marry anybody, if he isn't a Methodist and a cripple.'

'It 'ud ha' been a pretty thing though for 'em t' marry,' said Martin, turning his head on one side, as if in pleased contemplation of his new idea. 'Thee'dst ha' liked it too, wouldstna?'

'Ah! I should. I should ha' been sure of her then, as she wouldn't go away from me to Snowfield, welly thirty mile off, and me not got a creatur to look to, only neighbours, as are no kin to me, an' most of 'em women as I'd be ashamed to show my face, if *my* dairy things war like their'n. There may well be streaky butter i' the market. An' I should be glad to see the poor thing settled like a Christian woman, with a house of her own over her head; and we'd stock her well wi' linen and feathers; for I love her next to my own children. An' she makes one feel safer when she's i' the house; for she's like the driven snow: anybody might sin for two as had her at their elbow.'

'Dinah,' said Tommy, running forward to meet her, 'mother says you'll never marry anybody but a Methodist cripple. What a silly you must be!' a comment which Tommy followed up by seizing Dinah with both arms, and dancing along by her side with incommodious fondness.

'Why, Adam, we missed you i' the singing to-day,' said Mr Poyser. 'How was it?'

'I wanted to see Dinah: she's going away so soon,' said Adam.

'Ah, lad! can you persuade her to stop somehow? Find her a good husband somewhere i' the parish. If you'll do that, we'll forgive you for missing church. But, anyway, she isna going before the harvest-supper o' Wednesday, and you must come then. There's Bartle Massey comin', an' happen Craig. You'll be sure an' come, now, at seven? The missus wunna have it a bit later.'

'Ay,' said Adam, 'I'll come if I can. But I can't often say what I'll do beforehand, for the work often holds me longer than I expect. You'll stay till the end o' the week, Dinah?'

'Yes, yes!' said Mr Poyser; 'we'll have no nay.'

'She's no call to be in a hurry,' observed Mrs Poyser. 'Scarceness o' victual 'ull keep: there's no need to be hasty wi' the cooking. An' scarceness is what there's the biggest stock of i' that country.'

Dinah smiled, but gave no promise to stay, and they talked of other things through the rest of the walk, lingering in the sunshine to look at the great flock of geese grazing, at the new corn-ricks, and at the surprising abundance of fruit on the old pear-tree; Nancy and Molly having already hastened home, side by side, each holding, carefully wrapped in her pocket-handkerchief, a prayer-book, in which she could read little beyond the large letters and the Amens.

Surely all other leisure is hurry compared with a sunny walk through the fields from 'afternoon church', – as such walks used to be in those old leisurely times, when the boat, gliding sleepily along the canal, was the newest locomotive wonder; when Sunday books had most of them old brown-leather covers, and opened with remarkable precision always in one place. Leisure is gone – gone where the spinning-wheels are gone, and the pack-horses, and the slow waggons, and the pedlars, who brought bargains to the door on sunny afternoons. Ingenious philosophers tell you, perhaps, that the great work of the steam-engine is to create leisure for mankind. Do not believe them: it only creates a vacuum for eager thought to rush in. Even idleness is eager now – eager for amusement: prone to excursion-trains, art-museums, periodical literature, and exciting novels: prone even to scientific theorizing, and cursory peeps through microscopes. Old Leisure was quite a different personage: he only read one newspaper, innocent of leaders, and was free from that periodicity of sensations which we call post-time.[6] He was a contemplative, rather stout gentleman, of excellent digestion, – of quiet perceptions, undiseased by hypothesis: happy in his inability to know the causes of things, preferring the things themselves. He lived chiefly in the country, among pleasant seats and homesteads, and was fond of saunter-ing by the fruit-tree wall, and scenting the apricots when they were warmed by the morning sunshine, or of sheltering himself under the orchard boughs at noon, when the summer pears were falling. He knew nothing of week-day services, and thought none the worse of the Sunday sermon if it allowed him to sleep from the text to the blessing – liking the afternoon service best, because the prayers were the shortest, and not ashamed to say so; for he had an easy, jolly conscience, broad-backed like himself, and able to carry a great deal of beer or port-wine, – not being made squeamish by doubts and qualms and lofty aspirations. Life was not a task to him, but a sinecure: he fingered the guineas in his pocket, and ate his dinners, and slept the sleep of the irresponsible; for had he not kept up his charter by going to church on the Sunday afternoons?

Fine old Leisure! Do not be severe upon him, and judge him by our modern standard: he never went to Exeter Hall, or heard a popular preacher, or read *Tracts for the Times* or *Sartor Resartus*.[7]

CHAPTER LIII

The Harvest Supper

As Adam was going homewards, on Wednesday evening, in the six o'clock sunlight, he saw in the distance the last load of barley winding its way towards the yard-gate of the Hall Farm, and heard the chant of 'Harvest Home!'[1] rising and sinking like a wave. Fainter and fainter, and more musical through the growing distance, the falling dying sound still reached him, as he neared the Willow Brook. The low westering sun shone right on the shoulders of the old Binton Hills, turning the unconscious sheep into bright spots of light; shone on the windows of the cottage too, and made them a-flame with a glory beyond that of amber or amethyst. It was enough to make Adam feel that he was in a great temple, and that the distant chant was a sacred song.

'It's wonderful,' he thought, 'how that sound goes to one's heart almost like a funeral-bell, for all it tells one o' the joy-fullest time o' the year, and the time when men are mostly the thankfullest. I suppose it's a bit hard to us to think anything's over and gone in our lives; and there's a parting at the root of all our joys. It's like what I feel about Dinah: I should never ha' come to know that her love 'ud be the greatest o' blessings to me, if what I counted a blessing hadn't been wrenched and torn away from me, and left me with a greater need, so as I could crave and hunger for a greater and a better comfort.'

He expected to see Dinah again this evening, and get leave to accompany her as far as Oakbourne; and then he would ask her to fix some time when he might go to Snowfield, and learn whether the last best hope that had been born to him must be resigned like the rest. The work he had to do at home, besides putting on his best clothes, made it seven before he was on his way again to the Hall Farm, and it was questionable whether, with his longest and quickest strides, he should be there in time even for the roast-beef, which came after the plum-pudding;² for Mrs Poyser's supper would be punctual.

Great was the clatter of knives and pewter plates and tin cans when Adam entered the house, but there was no hum of voices to this accompaniment: the eating of excellent roast-beef, provided free of expense, was too serious a business to those good farm-labourers to be performed with a divided attention, even if they had had anything to say to each other, – which they had not; and Mr Poyser, at the head of the table, was too busy with his carving to listen to Bartle Massey's or Mr Craig's ready talk.

'Here, Adam,' said Mrs Poyser, who was standing and looking on to see that Molly and Nancy did their duty as waiters, 'here's a place kept for you between Mr Massey and the boys. It's a poor tale you couldn't come to see the pudding when it was whole.'

Adam looked anxiously round for a fourth woman's figure; but Dinah was not there. He was almost afraid of asking about her; besides, his attention was claimed by greetings, and there remained the hope that Dinah was in the house, though perhaps disinclined to festivities on the eve of her departure.

It was a goodly sight – that table with Martin Poyser's round good-humoured face and large person at the head of it, helping his servants to the fragrant roast-beef, and pleased when the empty plates came again. Martin, though usually blest with a good appetite, really forgot to finish his own beef to-night – it was so pleasant to him to look on in the intervals of carving, and see how the others enjoyed their supper; for were they not men who, on all the days of the year except Christmas Day and Sundays, ate their cold dinner, in a make-shift manner, under the hedgerows, and drank their beer out of wooden bottles – with relish certainly, but with their mouths towards the zenith, after a fashion more endurable to ducks than to human bipeds. Martin Poyser had some faint conception of the flavour such men must find in hot roast-beef and fresh-drawn ale. He held his head on one side, and screwed up his mouth, as he nudged Bartle Massey, and watched half-witted Tom Tholer, otherwise known as 'Tom Saft',[3] receiving his second plateful of beef. A grin of delight broke over Tom's face as the plate was set down before him, between his knife and fork, which he held erect, as if they had been sacred tapers; but the delight was too strong to continue smouldering in a grin – it burst out the next instant in a long-drawn 'haw, haw!' followed by a sudden collapse into utter gravity, as the knife and fork darted down on the prey. Martin Poyser's large person shook with his silent unctuous laugh: he turned towards Mrs Poyser to see if she, too, had been observant of Tom, and the eyes of husband and wife met in a glance of good-natured amusement.

'Tom Saft' was a great favourite on the farm, where he played the part of the old jester, and made up for his practical deficiencies by his success in repartee. His hits, I imagine, were those of the flail, which falls quite at random, but nevertheless smashes an insect now and then. They were much quoted at sheep-shearing and haymaking times; but I refrain from recording them here, lest Tom's wit should prove to be like that of many other bygone jesters eminent in their day – rather of a temporary nature, not dealing with the deeper and more lasting relations of things.

Tom excepted, Martin Poyser had some pride in his servants and labourers, thinking with satisfaction that they were the best worth their pay of any set on the estate. There was Kester Bale, for example (Beale, probably, if the truth were known, but he was called Bale, and was not conscious of any claim to a fifth letter), – the old man with the close leather cap, and the network of wrinkles on his sun-browned face. Was there any man in Loamshire who knew better the 'natur' of all farming work? He was one of those invaluable labourers who can not only turn their hand to everything, but excel in everything they turn their hand to. It is true Kester's knees were much bent outward by this time, and he walked with a perpetual curtsy, as if he were among the most reverent of men. And so he was; but I am obliged to admit that the object of his reverence was his own skill, towards which he performed some rather affecting acts of worship. He always thatched the ricks;[4] for if anything were his forte more than another, it was thatching; and when the last touch had been put to the last beehive rick, Kester, whose home lay at some distance from the farm, would take a walk to the rick-yard in his best clothes on a Sunday morning, and stand in the lane, at a due distance, to contemplate his own thatching, – walking about to get each rick from the proper point of view. As he curtsied along, with his eyes upturned to the straw knobs imitative of golden globes at the summits of the beehive ricks, which indeed were gold of the best sort, you might have imagined him to be engaged in some pagan act of adoration. Kester was an old bachelor, and reputed to have stockings full of coin, concerning which his master cracked a joke with him every pay-night: not a new, unseasoned joke, but a good old one, that had been tried many times before, and had worn well. 'Th' young measter's a merry mon,' Kester frequently remarked; for having begun his career by frightening away the crows under the last Martin Poyser but one, he could never cease to account the reigning Martin a young master. I am not ashamed of commemorating old Kester: you and I are indebted to the hard hands of such men – hands that have long ago mingled with the soil they tilled so faithfully, thriftily making the best they could of the earth's fruits, and receiving the smallest share as their own wages.

Then, at the end of the table, opposite his master, there was Alick, the shepherd and head man, with the ruddy face and broad shoulders, not on the best terms with old Kester; indeed, their intercourse was confined to an occasional snarl, for though they probably differed little concerning hedging and ditching and the treatment of ewes, there was a profound difference of opinion between them as to their own respective merits. When Tityrus and Meliboeus[5] happen to be on the same farm, they are not sentimentally polite to each other. Alick, indeed, was not by any means a honeyed man: his speech had usually something of a snarl in it, and his broad-shouldered aspect something of the bull-dog expression – 'Don't you meddle with me, and I won't meddle with you'; but he was honest even to the splitting

of an oat-grain rather than he would take beyond his acknowledged share, and as 'close-fisted' with his master's property as
if it had been his own, – throwing very small handfuls of
damaged barley to the chickens, because a large handful affected his imagination painfully with a sense of profusion. Good-
tempered Tim, the waggoner, who loved his horses, had his
grudge against Alick in the matter of corn: they rarely spoke to
each other, and never looked at each other, even over their dish
of cold potatoes; but then, as this was their usual mode of
behaviour towards all mankind, it would be an unsafe conclusion that they had more than transient fits of unfriendliness.
The bucolic character at Hayslope, you perceive, was not of
that entirely genial, merry, broad-grinning sort, apparently
observed in most districts visited by artists. The mild radiance
of a smile was a rare sight on a field labourer's face, and there
was seldom any gradation between bovine gravity and a laugh.
Nor was every labourer so honest as our friend Alick. At
this very table, among Mr Poyser's men, there is that big Ben
Tholoway, a very powerful thresher, but detected more than
once in carrying away his master's corn in his pockets: an action
which, as Ben was not a philosopher, could hardly be ascribed
to absence of mind. However, his master had forgiven him, and
continued to employ him; for the Tholoways had lived on the
Common, time out of mind, and had always worked for
the Poysers. And on the whole, I daresay, society was not much
the worse because Ben had not six months of it at the treadmill;
for his views of depredation were narrow, and the House of
Correction[6] might have enlarged them. As it was, Ben ate his
roast-beef to-night with a serene sense of having stolen nothing
more than a few peas and beans as seed for his garden, since
the last harvest-supper, and felt warranted in thinking that
Alick's suspicious eye, for ever upon him, was an injury to his
innocence.

But *now* the roast-beef was finished, and the cloth was drawn,
leaving a fair large deal table for the bright drinking-cans, and
the foaming brown jugs, and the bright brass candle-sticks,
pleasant to behold. *Now*, the great ceremony of the evening

was to begin – the harvest-song, in which every man must join:
he might be in tune, if he liked to be singular, but he must not
sit with closed lips. The movement was obliged to be in triple
time; the rest was *ad libitum*.[7]

As to the origin of this song – whether it came in its actual
state from the brain of a single rhapsodist, or was gradually
perfected by a school or succession of rhapsodists, I am ignorant. There is a stamp of unity, of individual genius, upon it,
which inclines me to the former hypothesis, though I am not
blind to the consideration that this unity may rather have arisen
from that consensus of many minds which was a condition of
primitive thought, foreign to our modern consciousness. Some
will perhaps think that they detect in the first quatrain an indication of a lost line, which later rhapsodists, failing in imaginative vigour, have supplied by the feeble device of iteration:
others, however, may rather maintain that this very iteration is
an original felicity, to which none but the most prosaic minds
can be insensible.

The ceremony connected with the song was a drinking ceremony. (That is perhaps a painful fact, but then, you know, we
cannot reform our forefathers.) During the first and second
quatrain, sung decidedly *forte*, no can was filled.

> 'Here's a health unto our master,
>   The founder of the feast;
> Here's a health unto our master
>   And to our mistress!
>
> And may his doings prosper,
>   Whate'er he takes in hand,
> For we are all his servants,
>   And are at his command.'

But now, immediately before the third quatrain or chorus, sung
fortissimo, with emphatic raps of the table, which gave the
effect of cymbals and drum together, Alick's can was filled, and
he was bound to empty it before the chorus ceased.

> 'Thon drink, boys, drink!
> And see ye do not spill,
> For if ye do, ye shall drink two,
> For 'tis our master's will.'[8]

When Alick had gone successfully through this test of steady-handed manliness, it was the turn of old Kester, at his right hand, – and so on, till every man had drunk his initiatory pint under the stimulus of the chorus. Tom Saft – the rogue – took care to spill a little by accident; but Mrs Poyser (too officiously, Tom thought) interfered to prevent the exaction of the penalty.

To any listener outside the door it would have been the reverse of obvious why the 'Drink, boys, drink!' should have such an immediate and often-repeated encore; but once entered, he would have seen that all faces were at present sober, and most of them serious: it was the regular and respectable thing for those excellent farm-labourers to do, as much as for elegant ladies and gentlemen to smirk and bow over their wine-glasses. Bartle Massey, whose ears were rather sensitive, had gone out to see what sort of evening it was, at an early stage in the ceremony; and had not finished his contemplation until a silence of five minutes declared that 'Drink, boys, drink!' was not likely to begin again for the next twelvemonth. Much to the regret of the boys and Totty: on them the stillness fell rather flat, after that glorious thumping of the table, towards which Totty, seated on her father's knee, contributed with her small might and small fist.

When Bartle re-entered, however, there appeared to be a general desire for solo music after the choral. Nancy declared that Tim the waggoner knew a song and was 'allays singing like a lark i' the stable'; whereupon Mr Poyser said encouragingly, 'Come, Tim, lad, let's hear it.' Tim looked sheepish, tucked down his head, and said he couldn't sing; but this encouraging invitation of the master's was echoed all round the table. It was a conversational opportunity: everybody could say 'Come, Tim', – except Alick, who never relaxed into the frivolity of unnecessary speech. At last, Tim's next neighbour, Ben Tholoway, began to give emphasis to his speech by nudges, at which Tim, growing rather savage, said, 'Let me alooan, will ye? else I'll ma' ye sing a toon ye wonna like.' A good-tempered waggoner's patience has limits, and Tim was not to be urged further.

'Well, then, David, ye're the lad to sing,' said Ben, willing to show that he was not discomfited by this check. 'Sing "My loove's a roos wi'out a thorn".'[9]

The amatory David was a young man of an unconscious abstracted expression, which was due probably to a squint of superior intensity rather than to any mental characteristic; for he was not indifferent to Ben's invitation, but blushed and laughed and rubbed his sleeve over his mouth in a way that was regarded as a symptom of yielding. And for some time the company appeared to be much in earnest about the desire to hear David's song. But in vain. The lyrism of the evening was in the cellar at present, and was not to be drawn from that retreat just yet.

Meanwhile the conversation at the head of the table had taken a political turn. Mr Craig was not above talking politics occasionally, though he piqued himself rather on a wise insight than on specific information. He saw so far beyond the mere facts of a case, that really it was superfluous to know them.

'I'm no reader o' the paper myself,' he observed to-night, as he filled his pipe, 'though I might read it fast enough if I liked, for there's Miss Lyddy has 'em, and 's done with 'em i' no time; but there's Mills, now, sits i' the chimney-corner and reads the paper pretty nigh from morning to night, and when he's got to th' end on't he's more addleheaded than he was at the beginning. He's full o' this peace now, as they talk on; he's been reading and reading, and thinks he's got to the bottom on't. "Why, Lor' bless you, Mills," says I, "you see no more into this thing nor you can see into the middle of a potato. I'll tell you what it is: you think it'll be a fine thing for the country; and I'm not again' it – mark my words – I'm not again' it. But it's my opinion as there's them at th' head o' this country as are worse enemies to us nor Bony and all the mounseers he's got at's back; for as for the mounseers, you may skewer half-a-dozen of 'em at once as if they war frogs." '[10]

'Ay, ay,' said Martin Poyser, listening with an air of much

intelligence and edification, 'they ne'er ate a bit o' beef i' their lives. Mostly sallet,[11] I reckon.'

'And says I to Mills,' continued Mr Craig, '"Will *you* try to make me believe as furriners[12] like them can do us half th' harm them ministers do with their bad government? If King George 'ud turn 'em all away and govern by himself, he'd see everything righted. He might take on Billy Pitt[13] again if he liked; but I don't see myself what we want wi' anybody besides King and Parliament. It's that nest o' ministers does the mischief, I tell you."'

'Ah, it's fine talking,' observed Mrs Poyser, who was now seated near her husband, with Totty on her lap – 'it's fine talking. It's hard work to tell which is Old Harry when every-body's got boots on.'[14]

'As for this peace,' said Mr Poyser, turning his head on one side in a dubitative manner, and giving a precautionary puff to his pipe between each sentence, 'I don't know. Th' war's a fine thing for the country, an' how'll you keep up prices wi'out it? An' them French are a wicked sort o' folks, by what I can make out; what can you do better nor fight 'em?'

'Ye're partly right there, Poyser,' said Mr Craig, 'but I'm not again' the peace – to make a holiday for a bit. We can break it when we like, an' *I'm* in no fear o' Bony, for all they talk so much o' his cliverness. That's what I says to Mills this morning. Lor' bless you, he sees no more through Bony! . . . why, I put him up to more in three minutes than he gets from 's paper all the year round. Says I, "Am I a gardener as knows his business, or aren't I, Mills? answer me that." "To be sure y' are, Craig," says he – he's not a bad fellow, Mills isn't, for a butler, but weak i' the head. "Well," says I, "you talk o' Bony's cliverness; would it be any use my being a first-rate gardener if I'd got nought but a quagmire to work on?" "No," says he. "Well," I says, "that's just what it is wi' Bony. I'll not deny but he may be a bit cliver – he's no Frenchman born,[15] as I understand; but what's he got at's back but mounseers?"'

Mr Craig paused a moment with an emphatic stare after this triumphant specimen of Socratic argument, and then added, thumping the table rather fiercely –

'Why, it's a sure thing – and there's them 'ull bear witness to't – as i' one regiment where there was one man a-missing, they put the regimentals on a big monkey, and they fit him as the shell fits the walnut, and you couldn't tell the monkey from the mounseers!'

'Ah! think o' that now!' said Mr Poyser, impressed at once with the political bearings of the fact, and with its striking interest as an anocdote in natural history.

'Come, Craig,' said Adam, 'that's a little too strong. You don't believe that. It's all nonsense about the French being such poor sticks. Mr Irwine's seen 'em in their own country, and he says they've plenty o' fine fellows among 'em. And as for knowledge, and contrivances, and manufactures, there's a many things as we're a fine sight behind 'em in. It's poor foolishness to run down your enemies. Why, Nelson and the rest of 'em 'ud have no merit i' beating 'em, if they were such offal as folks pretend.'

Mr Poyser looked doubtfully at Mr Craig, puzzled by this opposition of authorities. Mr Irwine's testimony was not to be disputed; but, on the other hand, Craig was a knowing fellow, and his view was less startling. Martin had never 'heard tell' of the French being good for much. Mr Craig had found no answer but such as was implied in taking a long draught of ale, and then looking down fixedly at the proportions of his own leg, which he turned a little outward for that purpose, when Bartle Massey returned from the fireplace, where he had been smoking his first pipe in quiet, and broke the silence by saying, as he thrust his forefinger into the canister[16] –

'Why, Adam, how happened you not to be at church on Sunday? answer me that, you rascal. The anthem went limping without you. Are you going to disgrace your schoolmaster in his old age?'

'No, Mr Massey,' said Adam. 'Mr and Mrs Poyser can tell you where I was. I was in no bad company.'

'She's gone, Adam – gone to Snowfield,' said Mr Poyser, reminded of Dinah for the first time this evening. 'I thought you'd ha' persuaded her better. Nought 'ud hold her, but she must go yesterday forenoon. The missis has hardly got over it. I thought she'd ha' no sperrit for the harvest supper.'

Mrs Poyser had thought of Dinah several times since Adam had come in, but she had had 'no heart' to mention the bad news.

'What!' said Bartle, with an air of disgust. 'Was there a woman concerned? Then I give you up, Adam.'

'But it's a woman you'n spoke well on, Bartle,' said Mr Poyser. 'Come, now, you canna draw back; you said once as women wouldna ha' been a bad invention if they'd all been like Dinah.'

'I meant her voice, man – I meant her voice, that was all,' said Bartle. 'I can bear to hear her speak without wanting to put wool in my ears. As for other things, I daresay she's like the rest o' the women – thinks two and two 'ull come to make five, if she cries and bothers enough about it.'

'Ay, ay!' said Mrs Poyser; 'one 'ud think, an' hear some folks talk, as the men war 'cute enough to count the corns in a bag o' wheat wi' only smelling at it. They can see through a barn-door, *they* can. Perhaps that's the reason they can see so little o' this side on't.'

Martin Poyser shook with delighted laughter, and winked at Adam, as much as to say the schoolmaster was in for it now.

'Ah!' said Bartle, sneeringly, 'the women are quick enough – they're quick enough. They know the rights of a story before they hear it, and can tell a man what his thoughts are before he knows 'em himself.'

'Like enough,' said Mrs Poyser; 'for the men are mostly so slow, their thoughts overrun 'em, an' they can only catch 'em by the tail. I can count a stocking-top while a man's getting's tongue ready; an' when he outs wi' his speech at last, there's little broth to be made on't. It's your dead chicks take the longest hatchin'. Howiver, I'm not denyin' the women are foolish: God Almighty made 'em to match the men.'

'Match!' said Bartle; 'ay, as vinegar matches one's teeth. If a man says a word, his wife 'll match it with a contradiction; if he's a mind for hot meat, his wife 'll match it with cold bacon;

if he laughs, she'll match him with whimpering. She's such a match as the horse-fly is to th' horse: she's got the right venom to sting him with – the right venom to sting him with.'

'Yes,' said Mrs Poyser, 'I know what the men like – a poor soft, as 'ud simper at 'em like the pictur o' the sun, whether they did right or wrong, an' say thank you for a kick, an' pretend she didna know which end she stood uppermost, till her husband told her. That's what a man wants in a wife, mostly; he wants to make sure o' one fool as 'ull tell him he's wise. But there's some men can do wi'out that – they think so much o' themselves a'ready; an' that's how it is there's old bachelors.'

'Come, Craig,' said Mr Poyser, jocosely, 'you mun get married pretty quick, else you'll be set down for an old bachelor; an' you see what the women 'ull think on you.'

'Well,' said Mr Craig, willing to conciliate Mrs Poyser, and setting a high value on his own compliments, '*I* like a cleverish woman – a woman o' sperrit – a managing woman.'

'You're out there, Craig,' said Bartle, dryly; 'you're out there. You judge o' your garden-stuff on a better plan than that: you pick the things for what they can excel in – for what they can excel in. You don't value your peas for their roots, or your carrots for their flowers. Now, that's the way you should choose women: their cleverness 'll never come to much – never come to much; but they make excellent simpletons, ripe and strong-flavoured.'

'What dost say to that?' said Mr Poyser, throwing himself back and looking merrily at his wife.

'Say!' answered Mrs Poyser, with dangerous fire kindling in her eye; 'why, I say as some folks' tongues are like the clocks as run on strikin', not to tell you the time o' the day, but because there's summat wrong i' their own inside' . . .

Mrs Poyser would probably have brought her rejoinder to a further climax, if every one's attention had not at this moment been called to the other end of the table, where the lyrism, which had at first only manifested itself by David's *sotto voce* performance of 'My love's a rose without a thorn', had gradually assumed a rather deafening and complex character. Tim,

thinking slightly of David's vocalization, was impelled to super-
sede that feeble buzz by a spirited commencement of 'Three
Merry Mowers';[17] but David was not to be put down so easily,
and showed himself capable of a copious crescendo, which was
rendering it doubtful whether the rose would not predominate
over the mowers, when old Kester, with an entirely unmoved
and immovable aspect, suddenly set up a quavering treble, –
as if he had been an alarum, and the time was come for him to
go off.

The company at Alick's end of the table took this form of
vocal entertainment very much as a matter of course, being free
from musical prejudices; but Bartle Massey laid down his pipe
and put his fingers in his ears; and Adam, who had been longing
to go, ever since he had heard Dinah was not in the house, rose
and said he must bid good-night.

'I'll go with you, lad,' said Bartle; 'I'll go with you before my
ears are split.'

'I'll go round by the Common, and see you home, if you like,
Mr Massey,' said Adam.

'Ay, ay!' said Bartle; 'then we can have a bit o' talk together.
I never get hold of you now.'

'Eh! it's a pity but you'd sit it out,' said Martin Poyser.
'They'll all go soon; for th' missus niver lets 'em stay past ten.'

But Adam was resolute, so the good-nights were said, and
the two friends turned out on their starlight walk together.

'There's that poor fool, Vixen, whimpering for me at home,'
said Bartle. 'I can never bring her here with me for fear she
should be struck with Mrs Poyser's eye, and the poor bitch
might go limping for ever after.'

'I've never any need to drive Gyp back,' said Adam, laughing.
'He always turns back of his own head when he finds out I'm
coming here.'

'Ay, ay,' said Bartle. 'A terrible woman! – made of needles –
made of needles. But I stick to Martin – I shall always stick to
Martin. And he likes the needles, God help him! He's a cushion
made on purpose for 'em.'

'But she's a downright good-natur'd woman, for all that,'
said Adam, 'and as true as the daylight. She's a bit cross wi' the

dogs when they offer to come in th' house, but if they depended on her, she'd take care and have 'em well fed. If her tongue's keen her heart's tender: I've seen that in times o' trouble. She's one o' those women as are better than their word.'

'Well, well,' said Bartle, 'I don't say th' apple isn't sound at the core; but it sets my teeth on edge – it sets my teeth on edge.'

CHAPTER LIV

The Meeting on the Hill

Adam understood Dinah's haste to go away, and drew hope rather than discouragement from it. She was fearful lest the strength of her feeling towards him should hinder her from waiting and listening faithfully for the ultimate guiding voice from within.

'I wish I'd asked her to write to me, though,' he thought. 'And yet even that might disturb her a bit, perhaps. She wants to be quite quiet in her old way for a while. And I've no right to be impatient and interrupting her with my wishes. She's told me what her mind is; and she's not a woman to say one thing and mean another. I'll wait patiently.'

That was Adam's wise resolution, and it throve excellently for the first two or three weeks on the nourishment it got from the remembrance of Dinah's confession that Sunday afternoon. There is a wonderful amount of sustenance in the first few words of love. But towards the middle of October the resolution began to dwindle perceptibly, and showed dangerous symptoms of exhaustion. The weeks were unusually long: Dinah must surely have had more than enough time to make up her mind. Let a woman say what she will after she has once told a man that she loves him, he is a little too flushed and exalted with that first draught she offers him to care much about the taste of the second: he treads the earth with a very elastic step as he walks away from her, and makes light of all difficulties. But that sort of glow dies out: memory gets sadly diluted with time, and is not strong enough to revive us. Adam was no longer so confident as he had been: he began to fear that perhaps Dinah's old life would have too strong a grasp upon her for any new feeling to triumph. If she had not felt this, she would surely have written to him to give him some comfort; but it appeared that she held it right to discourage him. As Adam's confidence waned, his patience waned with it, and he thought he must write himself; he must ask Dinah not to leave him in painful doubt longer than was needful. He sat up late one night to write her a letter, but the next morning he burnt it, afraid of its effect. It would be worse to have a discouraging answer by letter than from her own lips, for her presence reconciled him to her will.

You perceive how it was: Adam was hungering for the sight of Dinah; and when that sort of hunger reaches a certain stage, a lover is likely to still it though he may have to put his future in pawn.

But what harm could he do by going to Snowfield? Dinah could not be displeased with him for it: she had not forbidden him to go: she must surely expect that he would go before long. By the second Sunday in October this view of the case had become so clear to Adam, that he was already on his way to Snowfield; on horseback this time, for his hours were precious now, and he had borrowed Jonathan Burge's good nag for the journey.

What keen memories went along the road with him! He had often been to Oakbourne and back since that first journey to Snowfield, but beyond Oakbourne the grey stone walls, the broken country, the meagre trees, seemed to be telling him afresh the story of that painful past which he knew so well by heart. But no story is the same to us after a lapse of time; or rather, we who read it are no longer the same interpreters: and Adam this morning brought with him new thoughts through that grey country – thoughts which gave an altered significance to its story of the past.

That is a base and selfish, even a blasphemous, spirit, which rejoices and is thankful over the past evil that has blighted or crushed another, because it has been made a source of unforeseen good to ourselves: Adam could never cease to mourn over that mystery of human sorrow which had been brought so close to him: he could never thank God for another's misery. And if

I were capable of that narrow-sighted joy in Adam's behalf, I should still know he was not the man to feel it for himself: he would have shaken his head at such a sentiment, and said, 'Evil's evil, and sorrow's sorrow, and you can't alter its natur by wrapping it up in other words. Other folks were not created for my sake, that I should think all square when things turn out well for me.'

But it is not ignoble to feel that the fuller life which a sad experience has brought us is worth our own personal share of pain: surely it is not possible to feel otherwise, any more than it would be possible for a man with a cataract to regret the painful process by which his dim blurred sight of men as trees walking had been exchanged for clear outline[1] and effulgent day. The growth of higher feeling within us is like the growth of faculty, bringing with it a sense of added strength: we can no more wish to return to a narrower sympathy, than a painter or a musician can wish to return to his cruder manner, or a philosopher to his less complete formula.

Something like this sense of enlarged being was in Adam's mind this Sunday morning as he rode along in vivid recollection of the past. His feeling towards Dinah, the hope of passing his life with her, had been the distant unseen point towards which that hard journey from Snowfield eighteen months ago had been leading him. Tender and deep as his love for Hetty had been – so deep that the roots of it would never be torn away – his love for Dinah was better and more precious to him; for it was the outgrowth of that fuller life which had come to him from his acquaintance with deep sorrow. 'It's like as if it was a new strength to me,' he said to himself, 'to love her, and know as she loves me. I shall look t' her to help me to see things right. For she's better than I am – there's less o' self in her, and pride. And it's a feeling as gives you a sort o' liberty, as if you could walk more fearless, when you've more trust in another than y' have in yourself. I've always been thinking I knew better than them as belonged to me, and that's a poor sort o' life, when you can't look to them nearest to you t' help you with a bit better thought than what you've got inside you a'ready.'

It was more than two o'clock in the afternoon when Adam came in sight of the grey town on the hill-side, and looked searchingly towards the green valley below, for the first glimpse of the old thatched roof near the ugly red mill. The scene looked less harsh in the soft October sunshine than it had done in the eager time of early spring; and the one grand charm it possessed in common with all wide-stretching woodless regions – that it filled you with a new consciousness of the overarching sky – had a milder, more soothing influence than usual, on this almost cloudless day. Adam's doubts and fears melted under this influence as the delicate web-like clouds had gradually melted away into the clear blue above him. He seemed to see Dinah's gentle face assuring him, with its looks alone, of all he longed to know.

He did not expect Dinah to be at home at this hour, but he got down from his horse and tied it at the little gate, that he might ask where she was gone to-day. He had set his mind on following her and bringing her home. She was gone to Sloman's End, a hamlet about three miles off, over the hill, the old woman told him: had set off directly after morning chapel, to preach in a cottage there, as her habit was. Anybody at the town would tell him the way to Sloman's End. So Adam got on his horse again and rode to the town, putting up at the old inn, and taking a hasty dinner there in the company of the too chatty landlord, from whose friendly questions and reminiscences he was glad to escape as soon as possible, and set out towards Sloman's End. With all his haste, it was nearly four o'clock before he could set off, and he thought that as Dinah had gone so early, she would perhaps already be near returning. The little, grey, desolate-looking hamlet, unscreened by sheltering trees, lay in sight long before he reached it; and as he came near he could hear the sound of voices singing a hymn. 'Perhaps that's the last hymn before they come away,' Adam thought: 'I'll walk back a bit, and turn again to meet her, further off the village.' He walked back till he got nearly to the top of the hill again, and seated himself on a loose stone, against the low wall, to watch till he should see the little black figure leaving the hamlet and winding up the hill. He chose this spot, almost at the top of the hill, because it was away from all eyes – no house, no cattle, not even a nibbling sheep near – no presence but the still lights and shadows, and the great embracing sky.

She was much longer coming than he expected: he waited an hour at least watching for her and thinking of her, while the afternoon shadows lengthened, and the light grew softer. At last he saw the little black figure coming from between the grey houses, and gradually approaching the foot of the hill. Slowly, Adam thought; but Dinah was really walking at her usual pace, with a light quiet step. Now she was beginning to wind along the path up the hill, but Adam would not move yet: he would not meet her too soon; he had set his heart on meeting her in this assured loneliness. And now he began to fear lest he should startle her too much; 'Yet,' he thought, 'she's not one to be overstartled; she's always so calm and quiet, as if she was prepared for anything.'

What was she thinking of as she wound up the hill? Perhaps she had found complete repose without him, and had ceased to feel any need of his love. On the verge of a decision we all tremble: hope pauses with fluttering wings.

But now at last she was very near, and Adam rose from the stone wall. It happened that just as he walked forward, Dinah had paused and turned round to look back at the village: who does not pause and look back in mounting a hill? Adam was glad; for, with the fine instinct of a lover, he felt that it would be best for her to hear his voice before she saw him. He came within three paces of her and then said, 'Dinah!' She started without looking round, as if she connected the sound with no place. 'Dinah!' Adam said again. He knew quite well what was in her mind. She was so accustomed to think of impressions as purely spiritual monitions, that she looked for no material visible accompaniment of the voice.

But this second time she looked round. What a look of yearning love it was that the mild grey eyes turned on the strong dark-eyed man! She did not start again at the sight of him; she said nothing, but moved towards him so that his arm could clasp her round.

And they walked on so in silence, while the warm tears fell.

Adam was content, and said nothing. It was Dinah who spoke first.

'Adam,' she said, 'it is the Divine Will. My soul is so knit to yours that it is but a divided life I live without you. And this moment, now you are with me, and I feel that our hearts are filled with the same love, I have a fulness of strength to bear and do our heavenly Father's Will, that I had lost before.'

Adam paused and looked into her sincere eyes.

'Then we'll never part any more, Dinah, till death parts us.'[2]

And they kissed each other with a deep joy.

What greater thing is there for two human souls, than to feel that they are joined for life – to strengthen each other in all labour, to rest on each other in all sorrow, to minister to each other in all pain, to be one with each other in silent unspeakable memories at the moment of the last parting?

CHAPTER LV

Marriage Bells

In little more than a month after that meeting on the hill – on a rimy morning in departing November – Adam and Dinah were married.

It was an event much thought of in the village. All Mr Burge's men had a holiday, and all Mr Poyser's; and most of those who had a holiday appeared in their best clothes at the wedding. I think there was hardly an inhabitant of Hayslope specially mentioned in this history and still resident in the parish on this November morning, who was not either in church to see Adam and Dinah married, or near the church door to greet them as they came forth. Mrs Irwine and her daughters were waiting at the churchyard gates in their carriage (for they had a carriage now) to shake hands with the bride and bridegroom, and wish them well; and in the absence of Miss Lydia Donnithorne at Bath, Mrs Best, Mr Mills, and Mr Craig had felt it incumbent on them to represent 'the family' at the Chase on the occasion. The churchyard walk was quite lined with familiar faces, many of them faces that had first looked at Dinah when she preached on the Green; and no wonder they showed this eager interest on her marriage morning, for nothing like Dinah and the history which had brought her and Adam Bede together had been known at Hayslope within the memory of man.

Bessy Cranage, in her neatest cap and frock, was crying, though she did not exactly know why; for, as her cousin Wiry Ben, who stood near her, judiciously suggested, Dinah was not going away, and if Bessy was in low spirits, the best thing for her to do was to follow Dinah's example, and marry an honest fellow who was ready to have her. Next to Bessy, just within

the church door, there were the Poyser children, peeping round
the corner of the pews to get a sight of the mysterious ceremony;
Totty's face wearing an unusual air of anxiety at the idea of
seeing cousin Dinah come back looking rather old, for in Totty's
experience no married people were young.

I envy them all the sight they had when the marriage was
fairly ended and Adam led Dinah out of church. She was not
in black this morning; for her aunt Poyser would by no means
allow such a risk of incurring bad luck, and had herself made
a present of the wedding dress, made all of grey, though in the
usual Quaker form, for on this point Dinah could not give way.
So the lily face looked out with sweet gravity from under a grey
Quaker bonnet, neither smiling nor blushing, but with lips
trembling a little under the weight of solemn feelings. Adam,
as he pressed her arm to his side, walked with his old erectness
and his head thrown rather backward as if to face all the world
better; but it was not because he was particularly proud this
morning, as is the wont of bridegrooms, for his happiness was
of a kind that had little reference to men's opinion of it. There
was a tinge of sadness in his deep joy; Dinah knew it, and did
not feel aggrieved.

There were three other couples, following the bride and
bridegroom: first, Martin Poyser, looking as cheery as a bright
fire on this rimy morning, led quiet Mary Burge, the bridesmaid;
then came Seth, serenely happy, with Mrs Poyser on his arm;
and last of all Bartle Massey, with Lisbeth – Lisbeth in a new
gown and bonnet, too busy with her pride in her son, and her
delight in possessing the one daughter she had desired, to devise
a single pretext for complaint.

Bartle Massey had consented to attend the wedding at
Adam's earnest request, under protest against marriage in
general, and the marriage of a sensible man in particular. Nevertheless, Mr Poyser had a joke against him after the wedding
dinner, to the effect that in the vestry he had given the bride
one more kiss than was necessary.

Behind this last couple came Mr Irwine, glad at heart over
this good morning's work of joining Adam and Dinah. For he
had seen Adam in the worst moments of his sorrow; and what

better harvest from that painful seed-time could there be than this? The love that had brought hope and comfort in the hour of despair, the love that had found its way to the dark prison cell and to poor Hetty's darker soul – this strong, gentle love was to be Adam's companion and helper till death.

There was much shaking of hands mingled with 'God bless you's', and other good wishes to the four couples, at the church-yard gate, Mr Poyser answering for the rest with unwonted vivacity of tongue, for he had all the appropriate wedding-day jokes at his command. And the women, he observed, could never do anything but put finger in eye at a wedding. Even Mrs Poyser could not trust herself to speak as the neighbours shook hands with her; and Lisbeth began to cry in the face of the very first person who told her she was getting young again.

Mr Joshua Rann, having a slight touch of rheumatism, did not join in the ringing of the bells this morning, and, looking on with some contempt at these informal greetings which required no official co-operation from the clerk, began to hum in his musical bass, 'Oh what a joyful thing it is', by way of preluding a little to the effect he intended to produce in the wedding psalm[1] next Sunday.

'That's a bit of good news to cheer Arthur,' said Mr Irwine to his mother, as they drove off. 'I shall write to him the first thing when we get home.'

EPILOGUE

It is near the end of June, in 1807. The workshops have been shut up half an hour or more in Adam Bede's timber-yard, which used to be Jonathan Burge's, and the mellow evening light is falling on the pleasant house with the buff walls and the soft grey thatch, very much as it did when we saw Adam bringing in the keys on that June evening nine years ago.

There is a figure we know well, just come out of the house, and shading her eyes with her hands as she looks for something in the distance; for the rays that fall on her white borderless cap and her pale auburn hair are very dazzling. But now she turns away from the sunlight and looks towards the door. We can see the sweet pale face quite well now: it is scarcely at all altered – only a little fuller, to correspond to her more matronly figure, which still seems light and active enough in the plain black dress.

'I see him, Seth,' Dinah said, as she looked into the house. 'Let us go and meet him. Come, Lisbeth, come with mother.'

The last call was answered immediately by a small fair creature with pale auburn hair and grey eyes, little more than four years old, who ran out silently and put her hand into her mother's.

'Come, uncle Seth,' said Dinah.

'Ay, ay, we're coming,' Seth answered from within, and presently appeared stooping under the doorway, being taller than usual by the black head of a sturdy two-year-old nephew, who had caused some delay by demanding to be carried on uncle's shoulder.

'Better take him on thy arm, Seth,' said Dinah, looking fondly at the stout black-eyed fellow. 'He's troublesome to thee so.'

'Nay, nay: Addy likes a ride on my shoulder. I can carry him so for a bit.' A kindness which young Addy acknowledged by drumming his heels with promising force against uncle Seth's chest. But to walk by Dinah's side, and be tyrannized over by Dinah's and Adam's children, was uncle Seth's earthly happiness.

'Where didst see him?' asked Seth, as they walked on into the adjoining field. 'I can't catch sight of him anywhere.'

'Between the hedges by the roadside,' said Dinah. 'I saw his hat and his shoulder. There he is again.'

'Trust thee for catching sight of him if he's anywhere to be seen,' said Seth, smiling. 'Thee't like poor mother used to be. She was always on the look-out for Adam, and could see him sooner than other folks, for all her eyes got dim.'

'He's been longer than he expected,' said Dinah, taking Arthur's watch from a small side-pocket and looking at it; 'it's nigh upon seven now.'

'Ay, they'd have a deal to say to one another,' said Seth, 'and the meeting'ud touch 'em both pretty closish. Why, it's getting on towards eight years since they parted.'

'Yes,' said Dinah, 'Adam was greatly moved this morning at the thought of the change he should see in the poor young man, from the sickness he has undergone, as well as the years which have changed us all. And the death of the poor wanderer, when she was coming back to us, has been sorrow upon sorrow.'

'See, Addy,' said Seth, lowering the young one to his arm now, and pointing, 'there's father coming – at the far stile.'

Dinah hastened her steps, and little Lisbeth ran on at her utmost speed till she clasped her father's leg. Adam patted her head and lifted her up to kiss her, but Dinah could see the marks of agitation on his face as she approached him, and he put her arm within his in silence.

'Well, youngster, must I take you?' he said, trying to smile, when Addy stretched out his arms – ready, with the usual baseness of infancy, to give up his uncle Seth at once, now there was some rarer patronage at haud.

'It's cut me a good deal, Dinah,' Adam said at last, when they were walking on.

'Didst find him greatly altered?' said Dinah.

'Why, he's altered and yet not altered. I should ha' known him anywhere. But his colour's changed, and he looks sadly. However, the doctors say he'll soon be set right in his own country air. He's all sound in th' inside; it's only the fever shattered him so. But he speaks just the same, and smiles at me just as he did when he was a lad. It's wonderful how he's always had just the same sort o' look when he smiles.'

'I've never seen him smile, poor young man,' said Dinah.

'But thee *wilt* see him smile, to-morrow,' said Adam. 'He asked after thee the first thing when he began to come round, and we could talk to one another. "I hope she isn't altered," he said, "I remember her face so well." I told him, "no,"' Adam continued, looking fondly at the eyes that were turned up towards his, 'only a bit plumper, as thee'dst a right to be after seven year. "I may come and see her to-morrow, mayn't I?" he said; "I long to tell her how I've thought of her all these years."'

'Didst tell him I'd always used the watch?' said Dinah.

'Ay; and we talked a deal about thee, for he says he never saw a woman a bit like thee. "I shall turn Methodist some day," he said, "when she preaches out of doors, and go to hear her." And I said, "Nay, sir, you can't do that, for Conference has forbid the women preaching,[1] and she's given it up, all but talking to the people a bit in their houses."'

'Ah,' said Seth, who could not repress a comment on this point, 'and a sore pity it was o' Conference; and if Dinah had seen as I did, we'd ha' left the Wesleyans and joined a body that 'ud put no bonds on Christian liberty.'

'Nay, lad, nay,' said Adam, 'she was right and thee wast wrong. There's no rule so wise but what it's a pity for somebody or other. Most o' the women do more harm nor good with their preaching – they've not got Dinah's gift nor her sperrit; and she's seen that, and she thought it right to set th' example o' submitting, for she's not held from other sorts o' teaching. And I agree with her, and approve o' what she did.'

Seth was silent. This was a standing subject of difference rarely alluded to, and Dinah, wishing to quit it at once, said –

'Didst remember, Adam, to speak to Colonel Donnithorne the words my uncle and aunt intrusted to thee?'

'Yes, and he's going to the Hall Farm with Mr Irwine the day after to-morrow. Mr Irwine came in while we were talking about it, and he would have it as the Colonel must see nobody but thee to-morrow: he said – and he's in the right of it – as it'll be bad for him t' have his feelings stirred with seeing many people one after another. "We must get you strong and hearty," he said, "that's the first thing to be done, Arthur, and then you shall have your own way. But I shall keep you under your old tutor's thumb till then." Mr Irwine's fine and joyful at having him home again.'

Adam was silent a little while, and then said –

'It was very cutting when we first saw one another. He'd never heard about poor Hetty till Mr Irwine met him in London, for the letters missed him on his journey. The first thing he said to me, when we'd got hold o' one another's hands, was, "I could never do anything for her, Adam – she lived long enough for all the suffering – and I'd thought so of the time when I might do something for her. But you told me the truth when you said to me once, 'There's a sort of wrong that can never be made up for.'"'

'Why, there's Mr and Mrs Poyser coming in at the yard gate,' said Seth.

'So there is,' said Dinah. 'Run, Lisbeth, run to meet aunt Poyser. Come in, Adam, and rest; it has been a hard day for thee.'

THE END

Appendix I
George Eliot's History of
Adam Bede

George Eliot wrote these notes on 'The History of Adam Bede' in her journal, 30 November 1858. It was printed by J. W. Cross in his *George Eliot's Life* (1885, vol. II, pp. 65–71) and is reprinted here, with the kind permission of Yale University Press, from Gordon S. Haight's *Letters*, II, pp. 502–5.

History of 'Adam Bede'

The germ of 'Adam Bede' was an anecdote told me by my Methodist Aunt Samuel (the wife of my Father's younger brother): an anecdote from her own experience. We were sitting together one afternoon during her visit to me at Griffe, probably in 1839 or 40,[1] when it occurred to her to tell me how she had visited a condemned criminal, a very ignorant girl who had murdered her child and refused to confess – how she had stayed with her praying, through the night and how the poor creature at last broke out into tears, and confessed her crime. My Aunt afterwards went with her in the cart to the place of execution, and she described to me the great respect with which this ministry of hers was regarded by the official people about the gaol. The story, told by my aunt with great feeling, affected me deeply, and I never lost the impression of that afternoon and our talk together; but I believe I never mentioned it, through all the intervening years, till something prompted me to tell it to George in December 1856, when I had begun to write the 'Scenes of Clerical Life.' He remarked that the scene in the prison would make a fine element in a story, and I afterwards began to think of blending this and some other recollections of my aunt in one story with some points in my father's early life and character. The problem of construction that remained was to make the unhappy girl one of the chief *dramatis personae* and connect her

1. It was in 1839.

with the hero. At first I thought of making the story one of the series of 'Scenes,' but afterwards, when several motives had induced me to close these with 'Janet's Repentance,' I determined on making what we always called in our conversations 'My Aunt's Story,' the subject of a long novel: which I accordingly began to write on the 22d October 1857.

The character of Dinah grew out of my recollections of my aunt, but Dinah is not at all like my aunt, who was a very small, black-eyed woman, and (as I was told, for I never heard her preach) very vehement in her style of preaching. She had left off preaching when I knew her, being, probably, sixty years old, and in delicate health; and she had become, as my father told me, much more gentle and subdued than she had been in the days of her active ministry and bodily strength, when she could not rest without exhorting and remonstrating in season and out of season. I was very fond of her, and enjoyed the few weeks of her stay with me greatly. She was loving and kind to me, and I could talk to her about my inward life, which was closely shut up from those usually round me. I saw her only twice again, for much shorter periods: once at her own home at Wirksworth in Derbyshire,[2] and once at my Father's last residence, Foleshill.[3]

The character of Adam, and one or two incidents connected with him were suggested by my Father's early life; but Adam is not my father any more than Dinah is my aunt. Indeed, there is not a single *portrait* in 'Adam Bede'; only the suggestions of experience wrought up into new combinations. When I began to write it, the only elements I had determined on besides the character of Dinah were the character of Adam, his relation to Arthur Donnithorne and their mutual relation to Hetty, i.e. to the girl who commits child-murder: the scene in the prison being of course the climax towards which I worked. Everything else grew out of the characters and their mutual relations. Dinah's ultimate relation to Adam was suggested by George, when I had read to him the first part of the first volume: he was so delighted with the presentation of Dinah and so convinced that the readers' interest would centre in her, that he wanted her to be the principal figure at the last. I accepted the idea at once, and from the end of the third chapter worked with it constantly in view.

The first volume was written at Richmond and given to Blackwood in March. He expressed great admiration of its freshness and vividness,

2. 18 June 1840, when GE and her father spent the night with Samuel Evans at Wirksworth (Robert Evans's Journal).
3. 30 April–4 May 1842 (Robert Evans's Journal).

but seemed to hesitate about putting it in the Magazine, which was the form of publication he, as well as myself, had previously contemplated. He still *wished* to have it for the Mag., but desired to know the course of the story; at *present*, he saw nothing to prevent its reception in Maga, but he would like to see more. I am uncertain whether his doubts rested solely on Hetty's relation to Arthur, or whether they were also directed towards the treatment of Methodism by the Church. I refused to tell my story beforehand, on the ground that I would not have it judged apart from my *treatment*, which alone determines the moral quality of art; and ultimately I proposed that the notion of publication in Maga should be given up, and that the novel should be published in three volumes, at Christmas, if possible. He assented.

I began the second volume in the second week of my stay at Munich, about the middle of April. While we were at Munich, George expressed his fear that Adam's part was too passive throughout the drama, and that it was important for him to be brought into more direct collision with Arthur. This doubt haunted me, and out of it grew the scene in the Wood between Arthur and Adam: the fight came to me as a *necessity* one night at the Munich opera when I was listening to *William Tell*.[4] Work was slow and interrupted at Munich, and when we left I had only written to the beginning of the dance on the Birthday Feast:[5] but at Dresden, I wrote <in quiet> uninterruptedly and with great enjoyment in the long, quiet mornings, and there I nearly finished the second volume – all, I think, but the last chapter, which I wrote here in the old room at Richmond in the first week of September, and then sent the M.S. off to Blackwood. The opening of the third volume – Hetty's journeys[6] – was, I think written more rapidly than the rest of the book, and was left without the slightest alteration of the first draught. Throughout the book, I have altered little, and the only cases, I think, in which George <has> suggested more than a verbal alteration, when I <have> read the M.S. aloud to him, <have been> were the first scene at the Farm and the scene in the Wood between Arthur and Adam,[7] both of which he recommended me to 'space out' a little, which I did.

When, on October 29, I had written to the end of the love scene at the Farm, between Adam and Dinah, I sent the M.S. to Blackwood, since the remainder of the third volume could not affect the judgment

4. 30 May 1858 (GHL's Journal).
5. Ch. XXVI. They left Munich 6 July 1858 (GHL's Journal).
6. Ch. XXXVI.   7. Chs. VI and XXVII.

passed on what had gone before. He wrote back in warm admiration, and offered me, on the part of the firm, £800 for four years' copyright. I accepted the offer. The last words of the third volume were written and dispatched on their way to Edinburgh November the 16th, and now on this last day of the same month I have written this slight history of my book. I love it very much and am deeply thankful to have written it, whatever the public may say to it – a result which is still in darkness, for I have at present had only four sheets of the proof. The book would have been published at Christmas, or rather, early in December, but that Bulwer's 'What will he do with it?' was to be published by Blackwoods at that time, and it was thought that this novel might interfere with mine.

8 Park Shot, Richmond. | November 30. 1858.

Appendix II
Contemporary Broadsheets
on Mary Voce

Reproduced by kind permission of Nottinghamshire County Council, Leisure Services (Nottingham Central Library Local Studies).

AN ACCOUNT OF THE
Experience and Happy Death of
Mary Voce,

Who was EXECUTED on NOTTINGHAM GALLOWS, on TUESDAY, March 16, 1802, for the MURDER OF HER OWN CHILD.

JOHN CLARKE, Miss Richards, and a few other serious friends visited her repeatedly for several weeks before her trial, explaining the plan of salvation, praying with her, and exhorting her to confess her sins and earnestly seek the Lord; but it does not appear that she was deeply awakened to a proper sense of her dangerous and lost situation by nature and practice, till early on Saturday morning last. On Friday after her condemnation, though in the most agonizing distress, she remained as hardened and impenitent as ever, persisting in denying her guilt, (and as she afterwards told us) determined to destroy herself if possible; it is evident that all the anguish she experienced on Friday was merely worldly sorrow, but very early on Saturday morning her conscience was truly awakened, and she declared she was *now* convinced that Hell must be her portion, unless she both confessed her guilt and obtained pardon through Jesus Christ. About two o'clock the same morning she confessed the Murder, but remained still much distressed with a load of guilt on her soul, for she became very sensible that she was under the condemnation of the law of God; all that forenoon she manifested real penitence and earnestly sought the Lord, but in the afternoon, her distress on account of her sins increased very much; she frequently said, she had such a weight of guilt upon her soul, that she thought her heart would certainly break, exclaiming, Oh, my heart will break! my heart will break! The danger of her final condemnation appeared to her so great, that she repeatedly declared, she feared she must after all go to Hell, that she thought the very Devil had the possession of her, for she saw it was quite necessary to give up the man with whom she had been wickedly connected, but felt unable to do it, till a very little time before the Lord graciously set her soul at liberty. About five o'clock her mind was much softened, and she freely and fully confessed with real penitential contrition of soul all the sins she recollected being guilty off, continuing in earnest agonizing prayer to God for mercy. Miss UNWIN and Miss RICHARDS were shortly after engaged in prayer imploring the mercy of God in her behalf, when she suddenly stopped them, by exclaiming in a surprise of gratitude and joy, 'Oh, what has the Lord done for me!' On being asked what he had done for her, she replied, 'He has forgiven me all my sins, I feel it in my heart!' Her load of guilt and misery was instantly gone, peace and resignation flowed into her happy soul! She immediately exclaimed, 'How happy I am, I don't wonder at your taking such pains with me, if you feel as happy as I do, I could not have thought it possible, what happy lives you must live! Shortly after, when JOHN CLARKE, Miss RICHARDS, and ELIZABETH TOMLINSON were at prayer with her, she felt the evidence of her pardon much clearer, her consolation was amazingly increased, she never after felt any doubt, nor the least degree of the fear of death.

After she found peace, her sins appeared in their true light, and she repeatedly declared that hanging was too good for her, she deserved Hell. She felt she not only forgave but loved her enemies, and often assured us that she had *now* rather die than live. She observed that her imprisonment was the best thing that ever happened to her. Before her soul was set at liberty, she was much concerned at the thought of being made such a public spectacle, but ever after, all shame was banished from her mind. She could scarcely take any nourishment after her condemnation, till she experienced the pardoning love of God, but afterwards could take her food, and sleep, as usual. She frequently said that God loved her, and she felt she loved him. The prison was indeed a Bethel to all who had the privilege of visiting her. The few hours we were with her, were some of the happiest of our lives, she was *so* triumphant, so delivered from every degree of fear, so lost in wonder, love and praise, was such a proof that perfect love casteth out all fear that hath torment, that our grateful souls felt an increasing love to God for his goodness to her, and at the same time the most perfect union of spirit, and the most ardent christian affection with her's. Mr Bonington very humanely requested JOHN CLARKE to prepare her mind for the entrance of the Sheriff, and his Officers, she immediately said, 'They might come forward, for she had no fear of death;' She met the Executioner with a smile, and gave him her hand, saying, when he asked her to forgive him, 'Bless you, I have nothing against you, somebody must do it,' and assisted him in placing the ropes. – She told them, that God had helped her to confess her sins, and that she was happy, that she knew the Lord had pardoned her, and that she was going to Heaven. Some of the gentlemen who had seen her on the Friday after her condemnation, remarked that they could not have conceived such a change could possibly have been effected: She took the most affectionate leave of Mr Bonington's servant-maid and the female prisoners, embracing them all, and assuring them (although they all wept very much at parting with her) that she was so happy she could not weep, for she had rather die than live. On the road to the gallows she frequently said to Miss RICHARDS, ELIZ. TOMLINSON, and JOHN CLARKE, who at her request attended her in the cart to the place of execution, 'This is the best day I ever saw, I am quite happy, I had rather die than live,' and frequently uttered short ejaculatory sentences chiefly of praise to God; it seemed indeed that her prayer was almost all turned into praise. – On the road she observed, 'I am so happy, I cannot cry, I cannot shed one tear;' when the cart arrived at the fatal tree, Miss RICHARDS said to her, We are got there, Mary; 'Well,' she said, 'Bless the Lord,' with a triumphant and heavenly smile on her countenance.

After her condemnation our friends who visited her never left her, there were always at least two of the young women with her, which was certainly made an infinite blessing, and for which privilege, she very sensibly felt her obligation to the Sheriffs and Mr Bonington, often expressing her thankfulness on that account to those of us who were with her.

She desired the people at the gallows to take warning by her, and assured them that she was happy, and that she was confident she should be in Glory directly, observing, that indeed Glory had already begun in her happy soul.

After the cap was drawn over her face, while the Executioner was fastening the rope, she repeated her former exclamations of 'Glory! Glory to Jesus!' adding, 'I shall soon be in Glory, – Glory is indeed already begun in my soul, and the angels of God are about me!' which were her last words.

In the evening Mr KANE preached a sermon on the occasion, to a very crouded audience, in the Methodist Chapel, *Halifax Lane*, from these words, '*Is not this a Brand plucked from the fire?*'

HENRY TAFT.

Some things through haste were omitted in a few of the first
copies which are here inserted.

Printed and Sold by C. SUTTON, Bridlesmith gate.

The Life, Character, Behaviour at the Place of Execution and
Dying Speech of

MARY VOCE,

Who was Executed on Nottingham Gallows, on Tuesday the
16th of March, 1802,

For the Wilful Murder of Elizabeth Voce, her own Child.

AT the Lent Assizes for the Town of Nottingham, held on THURSDAY,
March 11, 1802, before the Hon. Sir Robert Graham, Knt. one of the
Barons of his Majesty's Court of Exchequer, MARY VOCE, aged
24, wife of ———— Voce, bricklayer, was indicted for the wilful
murder of her daughter, Elizabeth Voce, an infant, in the parish of
St Mary, in the town of Nottingham, by administering a certain
poisonous substance, called arsenic, mixed in water in a tea-cup, to
the said Elizabeth Voce, of which she languished a few hours in
extreme agony, and then expired.

This horrid act was perpetrated in November last, and the alledged
causes came out in evidence at the trial, and more particularly in the
under-mentioned voluntary Confession, which she desired might be
published to the world, for the sake of deterring those unhappy married females from forming polluted connexions with other men, whose
ways are ways of wickedness, and whose paths are paths of wretchedness. – Her Trial came on on Friday noon, March 12, which lasted
nearly four hours; and it appeared that this unhappy creature had
made several attempts to purchase the fatal drug before she could
finally obtain it. The witnesses were clear and circumstantial in their
evidence, as to the day and hour on which she purchased it, and the
Judge, whose humanity on all occasions is so conspicuous, seeing no
hope whereby he could put in a plea for her, asked if she had any
thing to say in her defence? Upon this she produced a written paper,
which being immediately handed to his Lordship, contained a refu-
tation of the direct charge on which she stood indicted, saying that
the poison was given by some of her neighbours' children to the child,
through mistake, whilst she was absent in the yard a few minutes; that

the child being thirsty, they had hastily taken the tea-cup from the hob, and given it to her, and that she had just swallowed the contents at the moment she (Mary Voce) returned into the house; that moreover, she did not deny buying the arsenic, but declared it was her solemn intention to destroy herself by taking it, in consequence of the long repeated ill usage she had sustained from her husband. This was the only circumstance which could be construed any ways favourable for her, and on which the Judge dwelt for the space of half an hour; but then she had no evidence to corroborate her declaration.

The Judge here recapitulated the evidence, coupled with the Prisoner's defence, and left it with the Jury to decide on the whole fact; observing, however, that possibly it might be true that she had bore with ill treatment from her husband, and that her life might be rendered burthensome to her; but the motive and the cause for such treatment, was, alas! too apparent; she had embraced the allurements of infidelity, and unable to withstand the resentment of an injured husband, she says she had recourse to the dreadful expedient aforesaid; – 'it may be so,' said his Lordship, but there is no one who appears to substantiate this written document. She may have been constrained to destroy this child in revenge for the bad usage; and it is necessary to state, that her husband having left her, she had herself and infant to maintain by the labor of her own hands.

The Jury retired out of Court, and after a consultation of ten minutes, pronounced the Prisoner 'GUILTY of Wilful Murder.' The Judge immediately passed the awful Sentence of the Law, 'That she be hanged by the neck 'til she was dead, and that afterwards her body be given to the Surgeons to be dissected and anatomised;' which dreadful judgment the Prisoner heard with a tolerable degree of fortitude, if we except her eyes being suffused with tears. His Lordship and the whole Court were deeply affected, on beholding a woman, in the prime of life and comeliness of person, stand before God and her country, a guilty creature unworthy to live any longer in this world, and not sufficiently prepared to enter that of another, 'where the worm dyeth not.'

THE following account of her Birth and Parentage was received verbally from her own mouth, on the morning of her execution, and committed to writing by a friend:

'I MARY VOCE, was born at Snenton, near Nottingham, in the year 1778; my father and mother are both dead, and fortunate it is they are no more. My maiden name was Hallam; I wish it had been so still. I met with the man who took me for his wife, at ————; there we were united by the spiritual law, but at Nottingham – O how

I tremble while I speak it – at this place the dominion of Lust seized my soul, I quitted the protecting partner of my virgin heart, and rambling after new delights, became intoxicated with a succession of carnal pleasures; nor did I awake from my reverie, till my husband became so exasperated by my conduct, that he left me a prey to remorse. I had one child* by him, but I believe he suspected it was not his own, which gave rise to the most violent recriminations before he left me. Having torn himself from me, I thought of subsisting my child by batting cotton, and by other methods which it is too painful to relate.

'I came to dwell in Fishergate, and had work for some time; but that at length failing, I was at a loss how to act; to beg I was ashamed, to steal I did not like, though I could kill my child; – my husband sent me no money, in a fit of revenge I sought the deadly poison; with a view, at first, to destroy myself, but Satan, always watchful for our destruction, dictated to me the infernal spirit of murdering that sweet innocent, and prompted me to continue onwards in the wages of prostitution. I obeyed his mandates, and was undone. It was in vain I pleaded the excuse of Self-murder before the Judge and Jury, their penetrating minds knew better.

'One Wm. Jackson went with me to purchase the arsenic in Warsergate; I wish he had persuaded me to the contrary, it might have been better for his conscience.

'I hope God will accept this my sincere repentance, and thro' the merits of Christ's blood, if my sins be as scarlet, yet they shall be as wool. This is a town full of vice and misery, many there be that sit in darkness and in the valley of death; yet the Gospel is preached unto them, and they awake not; may my fate, however, awake them.

'Lastly, I forgive those who have reflected on me. – I hope they will reflect on me no more after my decease. I have an affectionate sister who will weep at my sad exit; this is all I have to say.

                                                        'MARY VOCE.'

'Condemned Cell, Town-gaol, Nottingham, Monday night, March 15, 1802.'

The resident Clergymen have alternately visited her, both before and since condemnation, and have found her very desirous of prayer, and anxious to express her contrition. On Sunday night she felt quite comfortable and resigned, and asked the Ministers many questions

---

* She had besides a little boy in breeches, and it is surprising she has not mentioned him in her declaration; possibly she had some reason for it.

relative to a future state, who assured her that Jesus will wait 'til the
last hour to save to the uttermost all those who seek him by faith and
repentance; at which she seemed greatly submissive and thankful.

The morning at length arrived when she was to bid adieu to the
transactions of this world; at ten o'clock, the Undersheriff, with his
posse of constables, arrived at the gaol to demand her body, and being
seated backwards in the cart, was drawn to the place of execution
amidst a crowd of spectators, where after being some time engaged
in devotion, she was launched into that gulph 'whence no traveller
returns.'

Her remains, after dissection, were publicly exposed.

Beware of buying those printed the day before her Execution.

Burbage and Stretton, Printers.

A full and particular Account of the Life, Trial, and Behaviour of

MARY VOCE,

Who was EXECUTED on NOTTINGHAM GALLOWS,
on TUESDAY March 16, 1802, for

Poisoning her own CHILD.

HOW frequently are we called upon to lament the untimely Death of
our fellow-creatures, who are cut off by the stroke of Justice, for the
perpetration of crimes which make humanity shudder! – Of all the
atrocious acts which are committed by Mortals, that of Murder is of
the greatest magnitude: 'Tis a Sin of the deepest dye: and calls loudly
to Heaven for immediate Vengeance. If the guilty wretch escape the
sword of Justice, yet sooner or later we generally find that necessary
observation verified, 'Be sure your Sin will find you out.' We cannot
but be deeply affected at the depravity of human nature, when we find
it arrive to that degree of barbarity as to destroy, 'The noblest work
of God.' The Creator enquires, 'Can a woman forget her sucking child,
that she should not have compassion on the fruit of her womb?' Which
question implies the almost impossibility of such a depraved conduct,
and were it not that we have seen and heard of such things, we should
be ready to say, 'It is impossible.' But matters of fact compel us to say
such inhuman wretches are found among the sons of men, as the
following account will fully prove.

MARY VOCE, the unfortunate subject of our narrative, was on

Friday, the 12th of March, arraigned at the Bar, before the Hon. Sir Richard Graham, Knight, and stood charged with having poisoned her Child, an Infant about six weeks old.

It appears from the evidence given on Trial, that she had applied at a respectable Druggist's shop to purchase arsenick, but not having any person with her, they refused selling her any; she then applied at another shop, and for the same reason as before she was refused. She then applied at another shop, and was also refused till she brought another person with her, whom they properly interrogated respecting the purpose for which she wanted the poison; He answered, he knew she wanted it to poison rats with. Here she succeeded in her purpose. During the course of the Trial she presented a Letter to his Lordship, the substance of which is as follows, That her Husband having left her she was apprehensive of coming to poverty and distress, and during the anxiety of her mind, she resolved upon the desperate plan of terminating her own existence: That she mixed the fatal draught in a cup, but before she had time to put her horrid resolution in effect, a neighbour called upon her and invited her out to breakfast, which invitation she accepted of, and that during her absence, some Children or person unknown to her, must have given the poison to the Child. A Witness was then called upon, who declared that the Prisoner had been out to breakfast that morning as stated in the Letter.

After two hours or more had been employed in the examination of Witnesses, during which the Judge displayed great candour towards the unfortunate Prisoner; He then proceeded to sum up the evidence, taking particular notice of every circumstance which had appeared in her favour, more especially he called the attention of the Jury to the apparent state of her mind during the illness of her Infant; That she was found *wringing her hands and weeping bitterly*, this, he said, was worthy their attention; for the Evidence deposed, that she saw the Tears, &c. all of which were signs of real Grief.

After having summed up the evidence, the Jury withdrew, and in about ten minutes returned a Verdict GUILTY.

The Judge then proceeded to pronounce Sentence of Death, and gave her a very impressive exhortation to improve the few hours she had to live, in imploring Pardon for her Sins, and in particular for the very horrid and unnatural Crime, the Murder of her own Infant. During the whole time the Prisoner seemed much affected, and when the awful sentence was pronounced, she was unable to stand under it.

For a few hours after her condemnation she was almost frantic, and afterward acknowledged that had she had an opportunity, she would have put an end to her existence; but one person or other being

APPENDIX II 603

constantly with her, who were solicitous for her eternal Welfare, she became more calm and thoughtful, hearkened to their seasonable admonitions, and manifested signs of genuine Repentance. She fully confessed her crime and acknowledged she had been guilty of administering the poison to the Child, and earnestly implored Heaven to have mercy on her Soul. – Which Mercy we hope she has found.

This poor unfortunate woman whose untimely death we are now deploring, was born at Snenton, near Nottingham, and was a natural Child of the late Paul Simpson of Bobbers Mill. Her mother's name was Hallam, and she resided at Snenton about three years, when she left, and went to live near Newark, and was married to a Boatman, but we understand she is since dead. She left her Child in the care of a distant relation at Snenton, where she was brought up, and where she continued to reside till the time of her marriage to her surviving husband Thomas Voce. She has had four children, one of which only is living, a Boy about five years of age; Her husband is a Pensioner, and is obliged to go to Chatham once in three years on account of his Pension; during the time he was absent on one of these Journies, which was sometime in March, 1801, she had entertained another Man in her house, and cohabited with him, refusing to admit her legal husband. They lived separate till the latter end of September, when her husband was informed she was in the greatest distress, having been brought to bed, and the person she had been familiar with had forsaken her. In this situation he visited her, and she manifested tokens of sorrow for her misconduct, acknowledged how ill she had used him, and that if he would forgive the past, she would treat him with greater kindness in future; he hearkened to her invitations, and was prevailed upon to receive her into his favour, but alas! their reunion was but of short duration, she fell into the same crime again, on account of which together with some difference which arose on another occasion, a separation took place again, which happened on Friday, the 7th of Nov. and on the Monday following she perpetrated the horrid crime for which she has forfeited her Life.

Her general Character has been very indifferent, she acknowledged to having lived a very dissolute Life, and has been guilty of several petty crimes. During the short interval between her Condemnation, and her Execution, she sent a message to her husband, hoping he would forgive her, but did not wish to see him, as it would only have a tendency to disturb her mind, and augment her grief. She saw her Son, and took a most affectionate and parting Farewel, committing him to the care of Providence.

May every such awful occurrence as we have now been recording, operate as a powerful warning to all those Persons who find themselves tempted to evil, that they may not be drawn away by their own lust and enticed. How needful that divine caution, 'Watch and Pray that ye enter not into Temptation.' May we be found frequently invoking Heaven to keep us back from presumptuous sins, that they may not have dominion over us, that we may be innocent, and free from the great Transgression. *(Sutton, Printer.)*

Notes

New readers should be aware that these annotations discuss details of the plot.

Biblical quotations refer to the Authorized Version, and Eliot's minor misquotations are not corrected.

The following abbreviations are used:

GEJ   *The Journals of George Eliot*, ed. Margaret Harris and Judith Johnston (Cambridge: Cambridge University Press, 1999).

Letters   *The George Eliot Letters*, ed. Gordon S. Haight, 9 vols. (New Haven and London: Yale University Press, 1954–78).

Wiesenfarth   Joseph Wiesenfarth, 'George Eliot's Notes for *Adam Bede*', *Nineteenth-Century Fiction*, 32:2 (September 1977), pp. 127–65. Eliot's notebook is in the Beinecke Rare Books and Manuscript Library, Yale University.

[EPIGRAPH]

1.   '*So that . . .*' WORDSWORTH: From William Wordsworth's long philosophical poem *The Excursion* (1814), Book VI, lines 651–8, in a section where a pastor tells the stories of his dead parishioners, including Ellen, a young mother buried with her dead baby – 'a virtuous woman, in pure youth . . . delivered to distress and shame' when she becomes pregnant and her lover abandons her. George Eliot read all of Wordsworth's poems at an early age, and bought herself a six-volume set of his works when she was twenty-one. She especially admired *The Excursion* which she read with George Henry Lewes in February 1858: it 'repaid us for going to the end by an occasional fine passage even

to the last' (2–3 February 1858, *GEJ*, p. 73). Eliot's epigraphs
for her novels and chapter headings are always highly significant,
and Wordsworth figures more frequently than any other author
except Shakespeare. On her attitude to Wordsworth's poetry, see
Stephen Gill, *Wordsworth and the Victorians* (Oxford: Clarendon Press, 1998), pp. 145–67.

BOOK FIRST

CHAPTER I

The Workshop

1. *With a single drop of ink . . . visions of the past*: A tiny pool of
   ink poured into the palm of any person, but especially a child's,
   was said to allow gifted individuals the means of 'scrying' past
   and future. See Introduction, pp. 1–2. See also Wiesenfarth,
   p. 128, and Letters III, 301.
2. *the eighteenth of June, in the year of our Lord 1799*: Napoleon
   Bonaparte's Egyptian campaign (Chapter XXXIII) was one of
   his most successful. He left Egypt in August 1799 and slipped
   through the British blockade. On his return to France in November he overthrew the ruling Directorate in France in the *coup
   d'état* of the 18th Brumaire and made himself First Consul. In
   the meantime, French troops were campaigning in Italy against
   the combined forces of Austria, Russia and Britain. On 15 August
   1799 the French general Barthélemy-Catherine Joubert was killed
   at the battle of Novi Ligure where the French were defeated.
   When back in France, Napoleon turned his attention to annexing
   Italy and was eventually to succeed in taking Venice and penetrating as far as Rome. These events were to have serious consequences in England, which had been at war with Revolutionary
   France since 1793, in that they led to the Napoleonic wars which
   dominated public life until his defeat at Waterloo in 1815.

   In the Epilogue the narrator tells us that the date is 1807 and
   that the events of the novel began 'nine years' ago, but this
   mistake does not affect the essence of the story.
3. *wainscoting*: Wooden panelling for interior use tacked on over
   plaster, providing both warmth and decoration.
4. *'Awake my soul . . . noonday clear'*: From the first and third
   stanzas of a hymn by Bishop Thomas Ken (1637–1711), also
   quoted at the end of the chapter. It is the third morning hymn

in the hymnal published with the Anglican Book of Common Prayer.

5. *Adam Bede was a Saxon, and justified his name*: From the Old English 'bede', to bid, command or pray; connected to the German 'gebiet'. His biblical first name is that of the first man and the father of the human race; the second suggests his ancient lineage and authority. His occupation as a carpenter indicates his relation to Christ.

6. *Seth's*: Seth was the third son – after Cain and Abel (see also Chapter VIII, note 6) – of Adam and Eve. Seth's hair and eye colour changes in Chapter L.

7. *the exact contour of a coronal arch*: The coronal or frontal bone shapes the forehead and the crown. In the study of phrenology, developed by Franz Joseph Gall (1757–1828) and Johann Gaspar Spurzheim (1776–1832) personality and temperament are said to be revealed by the contours and proportions of the skull, and the frontal bone governs the learning, and observing faculties. Eliot's friend Charles Bray was converted to the pseudo-science of phrenology by the writings of George Combe. In August 1851 Combe observed Eliot's own head and pronounced that her Destructiveness was prominent and her Amativeness undeveloped. She was rather proud that her own 'organ of affectiveness' was considered 'highly developed' (Gordon Haight, *George Eliot: A Biography* (Oxford: Clarendon Press, 1968), pp. 100–101).

8. *thee'st*: 'Thee' is an intimate form of address, often used by Quakers and other dissenting groups in the eighteenth and nineteenth centuries.

9. *Methody*: A slang term for Methodist, the followers of John and Charles Wesley (1703–91 and 1707–88) who founded a religious society at Oxford University in 1729, and were so called because they favoured a simple and methodical approach to faith. Along with their friend George Whitefield, they initiated a campaign for reform in the established Church of England, but this was not well received, and they gradually broke away to become best known for their efforts to extend the teaching of the Gospel to working people and had a greater success rate in the new industrial towns among factory workers, miners and mill-workers than in rural areas (see Chapter II). John Wesley himself was reluctant to make this break and remained a priest in Anglican orders all his life. To begin with, the Methodists preached in the open air in public places, but later the movement built simple

chapels. By the end of the eighteenth century Methodism had splintered into many separate factions, e.g. Eliot's aunt Elizabeth Evans (whom she called 'Aunt Samuel'), and on whom the character of Dinah is partly based, was a Wesleyan, then a Primitive Methodist and was later associated with the Arminian Methodists of Derby, called the Derby Faith Folk (see also Chapter VIII, note 3). For an account of the rise of Methodism, see *A History of the Methodist Church in Great Britain*, ed. R. Davies, R. George and G. Rupp, 4 vols. (London: Epworth Press, 1965–88). For the story of the literary influence of the movement, see Valentine Cunningham's *Everywhere Spoken Against: Dissent in the Victorian Novel* (Oxford: Clarendon Press, 1975). Eliot made extensive notes on material drawn from Robert Southey's *The Life of Wesley, and Rise and Progress of Methodism*, ed. Charles Cuthbert Southey, 3rd edn (1846), see Wiesenfarth, pp. 131–7, 151–3.

10. *th' red-pot*: A marking dye used by carpenters for setting out patterns and specifications on pieces of wood.

11. *sarmunt*: Sermon.

12. *'What come ye out for to see . . . a prophetess'*: A reference to Christ's words about John the Baptist: 'But what went ye out for to see? A prophet? Yea, I say unto you, and more than a prophet' (Matthew 11:9).

13. *women preachin'*: Women, as well as men, preached in the informal early days of Methodism, but many within the movement felt that the display was inappropriate and immodest. See Mary Anne Schofield, '"Women's Speaking Justified": The Feminine Quaker Voice, 1662–1797', *Tulsa Studies in Women's Literature*, 6:1 (Spring 1987), pp. 61–77. See also Epilogue, note 1.

14. *jest-book*: A book of jokes or amusing stories cheaply produced for the lower end of the market.

15. *dissenters*: Those members of Protestant religious groups who disagreed with some or all of the established doctrines and practices of the Church of England, e.g. Methodist, Baptist, Nonconformists, Presbyterians, Congregationalists and Quakers.

16. *canals . . . Cromford*: During the eighteenth century Britain was at the centre of the great developments of the Industrial Revolution. As a practical working man Adam takes an interest in all the new inventions and engineering enterprises, including the canal system, unfolding all across England (see Chapter XXXIII, note 4); the aqueducts that brought water supplies to the major cities; the coal-pit engines which harnessed power for digging

and lifting – operations previously carried out by hand or by man or horse power; and the new machines invented for spinning yarn developed by Richard Arkwright (1732–92) in his cloth factories at Cromford.

17. *the tabernacle*: In Exodus 25–7 the Lord instructed Moses and the children of Israel as to how they should build an ark and the trappings of the tabernacle, or sacred place, that would hold it.

18. *the bakehouse*: Many working people did not have an oven in their own house even well into the nineteenth century. Each village or town district would have a local bakehouse, and the housewife took her loaves of bread or meat to be baked there for a small fee.

19. *a-praying and a-groaning*: A great deal of histrionic display was characteristic of some aspects of dissenting religions.

20. *a wool-gathering chap*: A colloquial expression for a daydreamer.

21. *Mum Taft . . . true to his name, had kept silence*: To 'keep mum' is a slang term for to 'keep silent'.

22. *grindstone*: A heavy rotating stone driven by hand or power and used to file knives to a fine point or to grind wheat ears into flour.

23. *the door-stone*: The threshold stone.

24. *portmanteau*: From French: literally for 'carrying cloaks', a suitcase.

CHAPTER II
The Preaching

1. *a pretty take of land*: The Donnithorne Arms would have been part of the Donnithorne estate, let to Casson, the former butler, along with a substantial piece of land.

2. *a piece of unenclosed ground*: Up until the eighteenth century most land in England was not enclosed, that is fenced in, and much of it was 'common land', available for use to all local inhabitants for grazing and firewood. With the agricultural and industrial revolutions, large landowners started to fence off such land for more efficient management, but this became a serious cause for discontent in rural areas.

3. *a 'spotty globe', as Milton*: John Milton, *Paradise Lost* (1667), Book I, line 291.

4. *ostler . . . smock-frock*: An ostler is one who looks after the riding and carriage horses so essential for transport up until the middle

of the nineteenth century. A smock-frock was a long shirt commonly worn by country workers, where threads are sewn criss-
cross, pulling the fabric tight, across the top, so that it gave a
snug fit to the breast while allowing unrestricted movement for
the limbs.

5. *Parson Irwine ... doesn't live here*: It was common for vicars to
hold the livings for two or more parishes (see Chapter V, note
2), so they could choose in which they lived depending on the
state of the accommodation.

6. *a grey cob*: An English or Irish breed, generally defined as a
horse of any colour of between 14.2 to 15.1 hands and of good
workmanlike appearance. (A hand is approximately 4 inches or
10 cm.)

7. *umbels*: Cup-shaped flowers, from the Latin, *umbella* or shade.

8. *Sehon ... endureth for ever*: Psalm 136:19–20. Joshua Rann is
the parish clerk and therefore responsible for reading the psalms
during the Anglican service (and uses the Book of Common
Prayer's version of names for the Authorized Version's 'Sihon'
and 'Bashan').

9. *Quaker-like costume*: 'Quakers' is a nickname for the seven-
teenth-century Society of Friends founded by George Fox. It
comes from the notion that they 'quaked' with emotion at their
religious meetings. They were distinguished by the adoption of a
severe form of dress, usually grey or black with a plain white
collar and no ornament.

10. *olive-branch*: The biblical allusion (e.g. Psalm 128:3) extends the
notion of the family 'tree', rather than a peace symbol.

11. *Ye gallows young dog*: A reproof uttered as an endearment. The
child is naughty; see Chapter VI, note 11.

12. *groon*: Groan.

13. *Dinah*: According to the biblical story, Dinah was the only
daughter of Jacob and Leah (she is raped and her brothers take
a terrible revenge – Genesis 34).

14. *works at a mill*: The new cloth mills in the industrial North
employed a great many people, including women and children.
Through the nineteenth century commercial competition meant
that conditions for the workforce deteriorated rapidly. By the
mid nineteenth century legislation was passed to restrict working
hours and conditions for women and for children.

15. *when a poor woman, laden with sins ... she found Thee sitting
at the well*: See John 4:4–30. Dinah's text for her sermon is Luke

4:18, but she also draws on Psalms 63:6, 119:148; Luke 24:32; Psalm 119:151; Acts 26:18; Matthew 11:28; John 10:10; Luke 23:34; Matthew 24:30; and 2 Timothy 4:1. Luke 4:18 was John Wesley's text when he preached his first sermon in the open air to the miners of Kingswood in Bristol, and Dinah's rhetorical technique is adapted from his.

16. *oat-cake*: As opposed to bread which, being made from wheat flour, was more expensive.

17. *the Ranter*: Originally the name for a mid-seventeenth-century sect, the Antinomians, which stressed the individual's direct communication with God (see Chapter V, note 31), but subsequently a common term for dissenters of all kinds, who were popularly distinguished by their inclination to 'rant' enthusiastically.

18. *'curcheyed'*: Curtsied. A respectful form of greeting conventionally offered by their inferiors to all the gentry.

19. *'an egg, an apple, or a nut'*: An old English proverb: 'An apple, an egg and a nut, you may eat though dressed by a slut.'

20. *visible manifestations of Jesus*: Visions or emanations that testified to the actual presence of Christ in the world.

21. *Its streams the whole creation reach ... Enough for evermore*: The fourth stanza of Hymn 241 ('Thy ceaseless, unexhausted love'), by Charles Wesley, in *A Collection of Hymns, For the Use of the People Called Methodists* (1780). Unlike the Quakers (for instance), Methodism endorsed the use of hymn-singing in the act of worship.

CHAPTER III

After the Preaching

1. *It was borne in upon my mind*: An expression used by dissenters to describe their experience of God's will communicated directly to their understanding.

2. *"And after we had seen the vision ... go into Macedonia"*: As Eliot explains later in this chapter, opening the Bible at random in search of spiritual and practical guidance was common practice among the early Methodists. Here it is Acts 16:10 where the Apostle Paul, travelling with Silas, has a vision of a 'man of Macedonia' asking them to 'Come over ... and help us' (verse 9).

3. *Hetty Sorrel*: It seems highly likely that Eliot was influenced in her choice of first name by Nathaniel Hawthorne's novel *The*

NOTES

Scarlet Letter (1850), where Hester Prynne was seduced by Arthur Dimmesdale. Hetty's proper name is only used once (Chapter LXXIII). Sorrel is a plant with bitter leaves used in salad.

4. *"And Jacob served seven years for Rachel . . . for the love he had to her"*: Genesis 29:20. Rachel was the daughter of Laban who promised her to Jacob in return for seven years' labour. At the expiry Laban deceived Jacob by marrying him to his elder daughter Leah. Jacob then had to undertake another seven years of service in order to marry Rachel. On Jacob, see also note 11, Chapter VIII, note 2 and Chapter L, note 3.

5. *"She that's married . . . how she may please her husband"*: 1 Corinthians 7:34. Seth's second, positive, quotation about marriage (1 Timothy 5:14) is Paul writing specifically about young widows and how to govern their behaviour. Unless it is Eliot who has misremembered (which I doubt) I think we may assume that Dinah would have known that Seth is interpreting Scripture. For 'two are better than one' he is again reapplying Ephesians 5:31: 'For this cause shall a man leave his father and mother, and shall be joined unto his wife, and they two shall be one flesh', and conflating it with Ecclesiastes 4:9: 'Two are better than one, because they have a good reward for their labour', and with Acts 4:32: 'the multitude of them that believed were of one heart and of one soul'.

6. *two tall stones, which performed the office of a stile*: The point of these two tall stones is that a person can manoeuvre their way from field to field, but the livestock cannot.

7. *"as God has distributed to every man . . . so let him walk"*: 1 Corinthians 7:17.

8. *a leading of Providence*: Dinah construes her understanding of God's wishes as 'provided' by Him.

9. *passing the love of women*: From the story of David and Jonathan in 2 Samuel 1:26.

10. *"In darkest shades . . . she my rising sun"*: 'My God, the spring of all my joys', by Isaac Watts, which was included in the revised collection of Methodist hymns in 1797. Seth adapts, as the pronouns should be masculine, for the hymn is in praise of God.

11. *this land of Goshen*: Joseph, second youngest son of Jacob by his favourite wife Rachel (see note 4), was sold into slavery by his jealous brothers. But in Egypt he found favour with the Pharaoh and rose to an eminent position. When his brothers

came to him seeking food, he arranged that they should be shamed into acknowledging their crime. He was subsequently reconciled with them and reunited with his father and his younger brother Benjamin in the 'land of Goshen' where there was plenty (Genesis 45:10). See also Chapter VIII, note 12.

12. *the three concords*: The grammatical principle of formal agreement between words as parts of speech which requires, for instance, that the verb should match the subject in terms of case, number, gender and person. In Samuel Johnson's *Dictionary of the English Language* (1755) under the heading 'Concordance' 3: 'A concord in grammar; one of the three chief relations in speech. It is not now in use in this sense. "After the three *concordances* learned, let the master read unto him the epistles of Cicero." Ascham' (9th edition, London, 1806).

To make sense of the reference, the reader needs to look back a few lines to Eliot's remarks on the old-fashioned Methodists' belief in a 'literal way of interpreting the Scriptures' and to her humorous apology for her own inability to 'represent their diction as correct, or their instruction as liberal'. Her argument is that one can never expect complete consistency – or agreement, or concord – between people's feelings, actions and principles.

13. *loftier sorrows ... fiery passions*: The fashion for 'silver-fork' novels published in the mid nineteenth century was one that Eliot roundly condemned in 'Silly Novels by Lady Novelists', *Westminster Review*, 66 (October 1856), pp. 442–61. This essay followed on from one in which she had set out her own theories for an Ideal modern fiction in 'The Natural History of German Life', *Westminster Review*, 66 (July 1856), pp. 51–79 (see Introduction, p. xxxi). Both are reprinted in George Eliot's *Selected Essays, Poems and Other Writings*, ed. A. S. Byatt and Nicholas Warren (Harmondsworth: Penguin, 1990).

CHAPTER IV

Home and its Sorrows

1. *short bed-gown ... a considerable length of linsey-wolsey*: An undergarment worn either or both in bed and underneath one's outer clothes. Linsey-wolsey is a coarse cloth made of flax or cotton and wool.

2. *till the last child's born*: A colloquial saying, i.e. Adam will always finish every piece of work undertaken.

3. *chapellin'*: Going to chapel, or to the preaching or dissenting worship of whatever kind.

4. *workhus*: The workhouse. Poor people who could not support themselves had to throw themselves upon 'the Parish', which established workhouses to provide a roof, clothing, food and minimal care, under the Poor Law acts of 1601. Obviously these were not lavish, and gradually there came to grow up not only a fear of conditions in the workhouse, but of the social stigma attached to the public acknowledgement of destitution.

5. *the house-place*: The main living-room which would have included the kitchen.

6. *if Solomon was as wise . . . rainy day*: Proverbs 27: 15: 'A continual dropping in a very rainy day and a contentious woman are alike.'

7. *day-clock*: A clock with a relatively simple mechanism which needs winding up every day. Below, 'in advance of the day' means the clock runs fast.

8. *the school*: Evening classes for working men run by the schoolmaster.

9. *paying his savings . . . from going for a soldier*: During the Revolutionary and Napoleonic wars, a shortage of manpower meant that men were conscripted into the army or press-ganged into the navy. Only by paying for a substitute could a young and healthy man be excused his turn. See J. R. Western, *The English Militia in the Eighteenth Century: The Story of a Political Issue 1660–1802* (London: Routledge & Kegan Paul, 1965), pp. 205–71.

10. *Take no thought for the morrow*: Matthew 6:34, which continues 'for the morrow shall take thought for the things of itself. Sufficient unto the day is the evil thereof.' See also Chapter XXX.

11. *a peck o' thy own words out o' a pint o' the Bible's*: A peck is a measure of dry goods, equivalent to one quarter of a bushel, or two gallons. A pint is a considerably smaller liquid measure, equivalent to one-eighth of a gallon (in metric to about half a litre).

12. *"God helps them as helps theirsens"*: A proverb which was collected in Benjamin Franklin's *Poor Richard's Almanac* for June 1736. This is one of the books that Adam has read (see Chapter XIX and note 3).

13. *a flick*: A flitch, or leg joint.

14. *to set up his tent in a far country . . . all the days of her pilgrimage*: A mix of biblical allusions, to Genesis 47:9, Hebrews 11:13, etc.,

as well as a thematic reference to the Christian life as a pilgrimage. The image also suggests the biblical fathers living in tents and continually moving on, as Abraham does in Genesis 13:18, and refers also to the story of the Prodigal Son who becomes a wanderer in a 'far country' in Luke 15:11–32 (see also Chapter XLV, note 6).

15. *dear times*: The cost of living went up considerably during times of war and shortages.

16. *a diorama*: A series of painted canvases set up along a tunnel that you look down which would be selectively illuminated so that it appeared to be a succession of moving pictures, invented by Daguerre and Bouton and first exhibited in London in a specially built theatre in Regent's Park in 1823.

17. *the wonderful pigeon-house at Broxton parsonage*: From the Middle Ages on the gentry kept pigeons to provide them with fresh meat.

18. *his 'mensuration book'*: A quick guide to calculations and measuring figures.

19. *"They that are strong . . . please themselves"*: Adam seems to have adapted this proverb from Romans 15:1: 'We then that are strong ought to bear the infirmities of the weak, and not to please ourselves.'

20. *prognostics . . . willow wand*: After the publication of the first edition, Eliot felt that she had not sufficiently explained the nature of Adam's reliance on superstition. John Chapman had specifically mentioned the introduction of superstition as a 'disfigurement' in a realist novel in his review of *Adam Bede* in the *Westminster* Review NS 15 (April 1859), p. 510. She wrote to her publisher John Blackwood on 29 April 1859 that she wanted to expand this explanation: 'Some readers seem not to have understood what I meant, namely – that it was in Adam's peasant blood and nurture to believe in this, and that he narrated it with awed belief to his dying day. That is not a fancy of my own brain, but a matter of observation, and is in my mind an important feature in Adam's character' (*Letters*, III, 60). Accordingly Eliot prepared an additional passage which appeared in the fourth edition in 1859: 'prognostics, and to his dying day . . . the sympathy that comprehends them'. The first edition had read 'prognostics, and you see he shuddered at the idea of the stroke with the willow wand'.

Various superstitions accrue around willow: in some parts of England it was considered unlucky to burn willow, to bring the

catkins of pussy willow into the house, and a child or an animal
struck with a willow rod was believed likely to sicken or die.

CHAPTER V

The Rector

1. *Provence roses*: Large blowsy roses originating from the south
    of France.
2. *a pluralist at whom the severest Church-reformer*: A pluralist
    was a vicar who held more than one living in order to keep up
    his income. Church reformers objected to such abuses because
    this often meant that he would neglect some congregations. Eliot
    made notes on the practice in the late eighteenth and early nine-
    teenth centuries, see Wiesenfarth, pp. 143–4, 160–61.
3. *president*: Anyone who presides over a scene or a meeting.
4. *mullioned oriel window . . . the walls . . . not yet painted*: This
    room has been built recently, and its plastered walls are not yet
    dry enough to be painted. A mullion is the window upright,
    in stone or wood. An oriel window projects from the wall, is
    supported by brackets and does not extend to the ground.
5. *a massive silver waiter*: A large platter used like a tray.
6. *a coat of arms conspicuous*: Parson Irwine's old silver is engraved
    with a heraldic device, once the exclusive right of the aristocracy.
    The implication is that he comes from a family that was once
    both wealthy and noble.
7. *powdered hair*: For most of the eighteenth century the upper
    classes wore either wigs or powdered their own hair with a
    variety of concoctions made from flour or rice. By 1799 this style
    was quite old-fashioned. Eliot made notes on eighteenth-century
    costume and even made little drawings of fashionable hats for the
    period in her notebook, see Wiesenfarth, pp. 137–8, 154–5.
8. *Ceres*: The Greek goddess of the harvest.
9. *right divine*: Eliot plays here on the idea of Mrs Irwine's aristo-
    cratic credentials, and the divine right of kings.
10. *Dauphin*: The title for the heir presumptive to the French throne.
    In 1799 the French royal family had but recently been deposed,
    and the King, Queen and young Dauphin executed. The pet name
    suggests the reactionary character of Mrs Irwine's politics and
    attitudes, as well as her royalist leanings.
11. *witch-mother, you sorceress*: The pagan references in this pass-
    age, along with the close connection to a Catholic royal family,

indicates that Eliot knows that Irwine – classically educated as he would have been – does not take his religious duties altogether seriously.

12. *Juno*: Juno or Hera was the Queen of the Greek and Roman gods, patron of marriage and childbirth.

13. *St Thomas . . . th' Easter dues*: St Thomas's falls on 3 July. Each person qualified by property in any parish was expected to give a tithe (dues) to the Church which would provide an income for the vicar.

14. *the quire . . . counter-singin'*: The choir; singing in counterpoint, with different parts of the choir taking different tunes.

15. *church lead*: The drains, parapets and windows of churches were often dressed in lead as a long-lasting material, but it was also useful and valuable – and an easy target for thieves and unscrupulous workmen.

16. *if his comb isn't cut a bit*: If he is not curbed. The analogy is with a boisterous cockerel's flamboyant comb.

17. *a blind Pharisee*: In the Gospels the Pharisees, a privileged religious sect, figure as the worst kind of arrogant and hypocritical teachers. In Matthew 15:12–14 they appear as the 'blind leaders of the blind'; see also Matthew 23:16.

18. *"dumb dog" . . . "idle shepherd"*: Isaiah 56:10: 'His watchmen are . . . all ignorant, they are all dumb dogs'; Zechariah 11:17: 'Woe to the idle shepherd that leaveth the flock!'

19. *coxy*: Cocky; that is, bumptious and arrogant; behaving like a coxcomb. See also Chapter XVI.

20. *cracklin' o' thorns under a pot*: Ecclesiastes 7:6: 'For as the crackling of thorns under a pot, so is the laughter of the fool.'

21. *the Sacriment-cup*: The precious cup used in the Communion service to hold the wine which transubstantiates into the blood of Christ.

22. *only a captain in the Loamshire Militia . . . His Majesty's regulars*: The Loamshire Militia would have been volunteers recruited locally in the time of national emergency, while the King's regular troops were professional soldiers.

23. *crowner*: The coroner, who is called in to investigate suspicious deaths of any kind.

24. *grand-vizier*: Chief minister. The Grand Vizier was the officer who assisted Muslim rulers, especially the Sultan of Turkey. In England the term is best known through Oriental tales.

25. *St Catherine*: The most famous of the many saints with this name is Catherine of Alexandria (d. *c.* 310) who was martyred on

a wheel. Arthur's familiarity with her appearance is probably indicative of his having seen a number of pictures in churches that he might have visited in Catholic countries abroad.

26. *a story of hatred and persecution . . . their magazine*: The *Arminian Magazine*, published 1778–97, became the *Methodist Magazine*, 1798–1821, and then the *Wesleyan Methodist Magazine*. It included stories of Methodist heroism in the face of persecution.

27. *poor lean cobblers*: Shoemakers were popularly supposed to be notorious radicals.

28. *my majority*: Arthur's coming of age when he turns twenty-one in July.

29. *an Olympian goddess*: Mount Olympus was the home of the gods and goddesses of ancient Greece.

30. *"Lyrical Ballads" . . . "The Ancient Mariner"*: Wordsworth and Samuel Taylor Coleridge's first volume of poems was published anonymously in 1798. Coleridge wrote 'The Ancient Mariner' (see Chapter XLV and note 7).

31. *Antinomianism and Evangelicalism*: Eliot is generalizing about the state of religious and social ferment that characterized the late eighteenth century. Antinomianism or 'lawlessness' is the idea that members of a particular religious dispensation are not obliged to adhere to moral or ethical law (see also Chapter II, note 17). Evangelicalism centres on the idea that belief comes through personal experience of conversion, a concept fundamental to the practice of Methodism.

32. *the King's health . . . Lord Dacey's lawsuit*: King George III suffered periodic bouts of 'madness' from 1760 to 1820, probably due to a metabolism problem. Eventually he was declared unfit to rule and his son acted as Prince Regent. In August 1799 Napoleon Bonaparte returned to France from his continuing campaign in Egypt. Lord Dacey is a fictional local aristocrat.

33. *epicurean*: The Greek philosopher Epicurus (341–270 BC) is often mistakenly attributed with a creed of pleasure for its own sake. In fact, his theories advocate freedom from pain as the greatest good.

34. *the 'travelling preacher'*: The Wesley brothers travelled across the country to preach the Word of God, and insisted their preachers, whether professional or lay, did the same.

35. *lusts of the flesh . . . receiving money*: See 1 John 2:16, 1 Kings 7:1, Matthew 6:31, John 10:12, John 6:48 and Matthew 21:12 (like the moneychangers in the Temple).

36. *honourable members*: Members of Parliament.

37. *Sophocles or Theocritus*: Greek tragedian (496–406 BC); Greek lyric poet (*fl. c.* 270 BC), author of the pastoral *Idylls*. (Isaiah and Amos are books in the Old Testament.)

38. *body to be burned . . . charity*: 1 Corinthians 13:3: 'And though I bestow all my goods to feed the poor, and though I give my body to be burned, and have not charity, it profiteth me nothing.'

39. *panegyric*: A rhetorical term for a complimentary speech.

CHAPTER VI

The Hall Farm

1. *a chancery suit*: The Court of Chancery dealt with disputes over property and wills but it was notoriously slow in its deliberations, and was most famously attacked in Charles Dickens's *Bleak House* (1851–2).

2. *dogs*: A metal frame for supporting large logs in a fireplace.

3. *a pillion*: A light saddle for a woman, or else a secondary saddle designed for the person who rides behind the horseman.

4. *the finest Greek sculpture*: The marble sculptures of antiquity were much admired in the eighteenth and nineteenth centuries. One major collection was in the sculpture galleries of the Vatican museum, described by Eliot in *Middlemarch* (1871–2). Such surviving statues had often lost their protruding parts simply because they were vulnerable to accident. See Francis Haskell and Nicholas Penny, *Taste and the Antique: The Lure of Classical Sculpture 1500–1900* (New Haven and London: Yale University Press, 1981).

5. *a watering-place*: During the eighteenth century a new fashion grew up for sea bathing and fresh air which led to many English coastal towns such as Brighton and Hastings becoming the haunt of the rich and famous. Their decline marked their adoption as holiday locations by a different class.

6. *eight-day clock*: An elaborate piece of machinery designed to require winding only once a week.

7. *the 'whittaw'*: A dialect version of 'whittawer', the saddler and harness maker.

8. *shone like jasper*: The walls of the new Jerusalem are built of semi-precious stone, see Revelation 21:11.

9. *Martha and Mary*: See Luke 10:38–42. Friends of Jesus, two sisters: Martha is the bustling practical housewife, Mary the contemplative, listening to him.

10. *churning-day*: The day when the collected milk was churned into butter.

11. *gallowsness*: A common threat addressed to the young, the idle and the mischievous – that they will end their lives with being hanged on the gallows.

12. *since last Michaelmas, and I hired you ... without a bit o' character*: The contracted time of servants' hire was measured out with set dates in the calendar. Michaelmas (29 September) and Lady Day (25 March), quarter-days, were the prime dates for hiring. Molly came to Mrs Poyser with no 'character', that is, no references from her previous employers. 'Treddles'on stattits' is a fair held on a regular basis by official statute.

13. *mawkin*: The scarecrow, which mopes, or 'mawks' because it does nothing, but, as a noun, originally a kitchenmaid (or a slattern) by association with the mop cloths used by the kitchen servant.

14. *the flax you've spoiled learning to spin*: Molly has been learning how to spin bundles of vegetable flax into long strands of linen thread for weaving.

15. *Comb the wool for the whittaws*: The wool is for stuffing the new-made saddle.

16. *Dantean picture*: That is, of the refined circles of particular hells devised for each specific crime, as portrayed in Dante's *Inferno*, the first section of his long poem *The Divine Comedy* (1300– 1318).

17. *the dairy thralls*: The stands in the dairy set out for the milk churns.

18. *like a jack as is run down, istead o' getting your wheel out*: A jack, or clockwork machine, was suspended before the fire to turn the meat for roasting. 'Wheel' is a spinning wheel.

19. *bring up with a spoon*: As opposed to breast feeding.

20. *cunning*: Clever.

21. *i' the Catechism and the Prayer-book ... in the Bible*: Mrs Poyser resorts to the authority of the Catechism, the formulaic expression of the tenets of faith in the Church of England learned by rote by every child before confirmation, and the Book of Common Prayer, the official guide to services in the Church of England, whereas Dinah uses only the Bible.

22. *without direction*: That is, without what Dinah felt to be God's direction and authority. 'Assurance', used just above, is another Evangelical word for confidence in a decision that comes directly from God. Both were received by signs or inner certainty.

23. *statty*: Statue.

24. *the factor*: An agent, who buys and sells on behalf of others.

CHAPTER VII
The Dairy

1. *calenture*: A tropical fever which afflicted sailors so that they believed the sea to be green fields and wanted to jump overboard.
2. *pattens*: High wooden shoes designed to go over the wearer's more closely fitting shoes to raise the feet out of the mud.
3. *a millennial abundance*: A fantasized time of plenty which comes only once in a thousand years.
4. *blue-bag*: The blue powder used as a whitening agent to bleach clothes.

CHAPTER VIII
A Vocation

1. *the good seed might fall on that soil*: Dinah is thinking of Jesus's parable of the Sower in Matthew 13:3–23.
2. *a good land . . . scarceness*: Deuteronomy 8:7, 9.
3. *a Wesleyan*: Reference to the first split in Methodism, between the Wesley brothers and Whitefield (see also Chapter I, note 9 and Chapter XVII, note 8).
4. *Miss Bosanquet*: Mary Bosanquet (1739–1815) married John Fletcher, Vicar of Madeley in Shropshire, in 1781; she had worked in London and Manchester. Eliot borrowed Henry Moore's *Life of Mrs Mary Fletcher, Consort and Relict of the Rev. John Fletcher . . . Compiled from her Journal* (Birmingham, 1817) from her aunt Elizabeth Evans in March 1839 (*Letters*, I, 18). See also Chapter I, note 9. The first woman whose ministry was endorsed by John Wesley was Sarah Crosby (see Chapter XL, note 5), a friend of the Mrs Robinson of Derby who encouraged Elizabeth Evans to become a Methodist class-leader.
5. *deceive the brethren . . . his own way*: see Matthew 24:24; James 1:22; Hebrews 13:17; Isaiah 53:6.
6. *'Am I my brother's keeper'*: Genesis 4:9: Cain's famous response when questioned by God as to the whereabouts of his brother Abel.
7. *my besetment*: My problem, my besetting sin or difficulty.
8. *heavens stretched out . . . given to me abundantly*: See Isaiah 40:22; Deuteronomy 33:27; Matthew 26:41 (see also Chapter L, note 11); 1 John 1:1; Ephesians 3:20.

9. *a lovely young woman on whom men's eyes are fixed*: The preacher Mrs Fletcher had worried about the possibility of her being perceived 'as a bad woman, or as a stage player' (*Life of Mrs Mary Fletcher*, ed. Moore, p. 89). Actresses in the late eighteenth and early nineteenth centuries had a popular reputation as loose women.

10. *Moses . . . saw the brightness of the Lord*: See Exodus 3:2: God spoke to Moses from the bushing bush, so the analogy is that it does not matter who speaks – whether man or woman – as long as they speak the Word of the Lord. On Moses, see also Chapter XII, note 1 and Chapter L, notes 4 and 10.

11. *lead a quiet life among the green pastures and the still waters*: Psalm 23:2.

12. *the patriarch Joseph*: As the father of one of the twelve tribes of Israel, descended from the twelve sons of Jacob, Joseph is a patriarch, forefather. He was expert in the skills of divination and prophecy. For his treatment of his father and brothers, see Chapter III, note 11.

13. *a Pyrrhic dance*: A dance devised by the ancient Greeks of Sparta in which the warlike motions of the battlefield were mimicked in a performance set to music.

14. *a worldly Sadducee*: The Sadducees were an aristocratic Jewish religious sect who supported the interests of rank and the rich. Along with the Pharisees, Jesus saw them as opposed to true godliness: see, e.g., Matthew 16:12.

15. *bare-ribbed runts on a common*: Thin, malnourished livestock, usually the weakest and last born, which graze the thin grass of common land.

16. *bacon-sword and sour-cake*: Bacon rind, and cheap filling biscuits made from oats and fermented dough.

17. *the key of B with five sharps to the frank and genial C*: The key of B major has five sharps, the key of C major has none. Music in C major has a broad warm tone. Eliot was a keen lover of music, and many of her works include portraits of singers and performers, including Mirah in *Scenes of Clerical Life* (1858); Rosamund in *Middlemarch*; Gwendolen, the Princess Alcharisi, and the composer Klesmer in *Daniel Deronda* (1876).

18. *a bunch of dock-leaves*: The leaves of the common dock weed were used to pack up butter because they allowed moisture to penetrate to the butter and to keep it fresh.

CHAPTER IX

Hetty's World

1. *occasional regimentals*: The uniform of the local militia.
2. *Memnon's statue*: A huge black 'singing' statue at Thebes, said to be of Memnon, an Ethiopian prince killed in the Trojan war (but more likely of King Amenophis of the eighteenth Egyptian dynasty). The statue was supposed to give out a musical strain when touched by the rays of the rising sun and superstition explained this as Amenophis' greeting to his mother, the goddess of Dawn. In fact the statue was hollow, and the sun caused the warm air inside to be expelled through the throat.
3. *a master-man*: A master craftsman, so a man who works for himself, as opposed to a journeyman who is employed by another.
4. *Lady-day*: See Chapter VI, note 12.
5. *geck*: A fool, a simpleton.
6. *Nottingham lace*: At the end of the eighteenth century the town of Nottingham became famous for its lace, as the industry exploited the new inventions of the spinning-jenny by James Hargreaves and the spinning frame by Richard Arkwright.
7. *an amateur of damp quarries and skimming-dishes*: Quarries, floor tiles, which would be cool and damp in order to maintain a low temperature in the dairy. Skimming-dishes have a low spout, so that when the fresh milk is left to stand the cream rises to the top and allows the skimmed milk to be poured away from underneath.
8. *Hebe*: The goddess of youth and spring who waited on the ancient Greek gods and served their food and drink.
9. *phiz*: Short for 'physiognomy', that is, appearance, the arrangement of facial features.
10. *one might have escaped from Socrates himself*: Socrates (469–399 BC), an irascible and argumentative ancient Greek philosopher likely to engage opponents in debate in public places.

CHAPTER X

Dinah Visits Lisbeth

1. *ceiled houses*: Houses with plaster ceilings as opposed to bare rafters.

2. *churched*: A service of thanksgiving and cleansing offered when the woman went to church after the birth of a child.

3. *when I war ill an' cumbered wi' th' babby, an' made me the posset*: 'To be ill' was a euphemism for being either pregnant or in labour. 'Cumbered' is to be hampered. A 'posset' is a sweet drink made of milk flavoured with spices and wine taken as a remedy.

4. *cumber*: Burdensome rubbish.

5. *haft*: The handle of a knife or other cutting tool.

6. *a journeyman tramp*: A working farmhand who tramps from place to place offering his services for hire.

7. *queechy*: Feeble.

8. *a cade lamb . . . franzy*: A lamb abandoned by its mother which has to be fed by bottle and which may be undernourished as a result. 'Franzy' is difficult or irritable.

9. *the thack*: The thatched roof.

10. *what David did, when God took away his child from him*: See 2 Samuel 12: 15–23. When his son from his adultery with Bathsheba died, David accepted God's will.

CHAPTER XI
In the Cottage

1. *the burthen and heat of the day*: Matthew 20:12, from Christ's parable of the vineyard (verses 1–16).

2. *carrier*: The cart would pass through the locality on a regular basis carrying goods and people.

CHAPTER XII
In the Wood

1. *Pharaoh's daughter . . . minding the infant Moses*: As the Israelites became a powerful presence in the land of Egypt (see Chapter III, note 11), Pharaoh – who had been warned that a boy child would be his downfall – declared that they should be culled. Miriam persuaded her mother to allow her baby brother Moses to be placed in a cradle and floated in the water where Pharaoh's daughter bathed. Just according to plan, she was attracted to the baby and brought him up as her own. See Exodus 2:1–10.

2.   *his favourite song . . . 'When the heart . . . with care'*: John Gay's
      The Beggar's Opera (1728) includes 'When the heart of a man',
      composed by Thomas d'Urfey. In the play (II.iii, Air 21) it is sung
      by the villain and seducer of women, MacHeath:

> If the heart of a Man is deprest with Cares,
> The Mist is dispell'd when a Woman appears;
> Like the Notes of a Fiddle, she sweetly, sweetly
> Raises the Spirits, and charms our Ears.
> > Roses and Lillies her Cheeks disclose.
> > But her ripe lips are more sweet than those.
> > Press her,
> > Caress her,
> > With Blisses,
> > Her Kisses
> > Dissolve us in Pleasure, and Soft Repose.

3.   *a hobble*: An awkward situation. Derived from an agricultural
      term where a horse or other animal is closely tethered.
4.   *to increase Irwine's income for the vicarage of Hayslope*: The
      'living' for each individual vicar was raised by the squire from
      his tithes drawn on the local tenantry.
5.   *the age of frocks and trousers*: That is, when he was a child. Both
      girls and boys wore dresses in infancy.
6.   *college*: Oxford or Cambridge.
7.   *the whole sex*: 'The sex' was a common slang term for women
      in the eighteenth century.
8.   *the Centaurs*: Mythical creatures, half man and half horse, who
      lived wild lives and had a lusty disposition.
9.   *haimabler*: More amiable.
10.   *Dr Moore's Zeluco*: In the novel (1786) by Dr John Moore,
      Zeluco is a noble Sicilian who begins his career by strangling a
      canary and graduates to the seduction and abandonment of a
      young girl. He was an influence on Byron's *Don Juan* (1819–
      24). Zeluco ends badly.
11.   *the ottoman*: A stuffed, cushioned seat (from Arabic). Like the
      Persian word 'sofa', these luxurious pieces of furniture were
      associated with a decadent East, appearing in depictions of har-
      ems and other places of indulgence in the Western imagination.

CHAPTER XIII

Evening in the Wood

1. *If a chest . . . from some unknown source*: An allusion to Goethe's
    Faust (Part I, 1808), where Gretchen finds a chest of jewels
    outside her door. It is a gift conjured by Mephistopheles who
    has promised to win her for the rejuvenated Faust, and the
    seduction duly takes place. Gretchen bears a child, is repudiated
    by her brother and dies insane, while Faust is filled with remorse
    and dissatisfaction.
       Lewes carried out much of the research for his *Life of Goethe*
    (1855) during his and Eliot's first trip to Germany. In 1863
    Charles Gounod's opera *Faust* (1859), which is based on
    Goethe's story, was performed at Covent Garden. Eliot went to
    see it three times (29 July 1863, *GEJ*, p. 118). The opera includes
    the famous 'jewel song'.
2. *leveret*: A young hare.
3. *a shepherd in Arcadia . . . lips of Psyche*: Arcadia is the ancient
    name for a mountainous region in Greece, but in legend an ideal
    world of idyllic pastoral happiness. Eros, the Greek god of love,
    fell in love with Psyche, but Aphrodite forbade her son to see
    Psyche so he visited her only at night. When she took a candle
    to steal a look at him, he abandoned her.

CHAPTER XIV

The Return Home

1. *No more nor the cake 'ull come wi'out the leaven*: Breads or
    cakes will only rise with the inclusion of some raising agent,
    generally yeast or eggs or bicarbonate of soda.
2. *'Pilgrim's Progress'*: *The Pilgrim's Progress, From This World
    To That Which Is To Come* (1678, 1684), an allegory of religious
    endeavour by John Bunyan (1628–88). Many editions, a number
    of them illustrated, were published.
3. *wisdom and knowledge*: According to Isaiah 11:2, these are two
    of the attributes of the Messianic descendant of Jesse in a passage
    which is interpreted in Christian tradition as referring to the
    coming of Christ.
4. *the momentous subject of the Hebrew points*: Written Hebrew
    originally had no vowels, and small marks indicated where they

should go. It is an arcane study, but in the nineteenth century – especially among women who aspired to an intellectual education – to know Hebrew was regarded as the apogee of attainment. Eliot learned Hebrew for her biblical research and for her 1846 translation of D. F. Strauss's *Life of Jesus*. Cf. *Middlemarch*, Chapter 7, where Dorothea aspires to learn Hebrew.

5. *cowcumber*: Cucumber.
6. *dilling*: Darling.
7. *a kettle-cake*: A homemade bread cooked in a kettle, that is, a pot.
8. *the safe*: A ventilated cupboard or box designed to keep food cool and safe from flies.
9. *a crab*: A crab apple, growing wild, is sour to the taste.
10. *the rushlight*: A cheap form of illumination made by dipping a rush in tallow or wax.

CHAPTER XV
The Two Bed-Chambers

1. *hyacinthine*: That is, like hyacinths, but a standard poetical trope for describing hair, derived from Homer's *Odyssey*, Book VI, 231. In the English poets – and the epithet is used by Milton and Pope – the assumption is that they are describing dark blue-black hair like Hetty's. Hyacinthus was a beautiful boy beloved of Apollo who died when struck accidentally during a game of quoits, and the flower was said to have sprung up from the ground where he lay.
2. *white stockings, perhaps with silk clocks*: A fashion where the stocking is made of cotton ornamented with silk clocks woven down the sides.
3. *peculation*: Embezzlement of money or property.
4. *a fishy eye*: An eye with a vacant expression.
5. *the Jacob's Ladder*: A tall blue spiked flower that flowers in June, seeds itself and grows rampant. That Hetty does 'not like' this flower may suggest her lack of aspirational spiritual values: see the story of Jacob's dream in Genesis 28:10–22.
6. *the milch cows*: The dairy cows in milk.
7. *And they all wept ... exhortation and warning*: Acts 20:37: when Paul is about to depart from Ephesus, he calls together all the leaders of his newly established Church to warn them to

beware of the wolves that will come among the flock after his departure (verses 17–36).

8.   *trouble is appointed for us all here below*: See Job 5:7 and 14:1.

9.   *the things of this life*: See 1 Corinthians 6:3.

10. *we set our hearts on things . . . for us to have*: See Colossians 3:2; see also Chapter XLI.

11. *the evil day*: See Ephesians 6:13.

CHAPTER XVI
Links

1.   *when you have put your mouth . . . expectant ear at the other end*: Allusion to the practice of the Catholic confessional which promises anonymity.

2.   *a proletaire with democratic ideas*: A proletarian or person of the lowest class. An allusion, given the French spelling, to the hopes and aims of the French Revolution, with its influence continuing well into the nineteenth century.

3.   *fairings*: Gifts or treats purchased at local fairs.

4.   *scagliola pillar*: A plaster imitation of a stone or marble pillar.

5.   *the Foulis Æschylus*: Robert Foulis (1707–76) was a printer based in Glasgow who produced many classics. His two-volume Greek–Latin edition (1746) of the tragedies of the playwright Aeschylus (525–456 BC) included the trilogy of the *Oresteia*, which Eliot was reading while she was working on *Adam Bede* (see Chapter XXII, note 10). Eliot also read Aeschylus' *Prometheus Bound* during this period (10 February 1858, *GEJ*, p. 73).

6.   *the glebe*: The parish.

7.   *"Cras ingens iterabimus aequor"*: Horace, *Odes*, I.vii.32: 'Tomorrow we will set forth again on the vast sea.'

8.   *Arthur Young's* books: Arthur Young (1741–1820) was secretary of the Board of Agriculture from 1793 and a prominent theorist on farming methods. He edited the *Annals of Agriculture* (1784–1809).

9.   *tithe*: One-tenth. From the Middles Ages, church activities were supported by the 'tithe' exacted from the populace of one-tenth of their produce.

10. *the chorus in the Prometheus*: A reference to Aeschylus' *Prometheus Bound*, II, 887–93, where there is a warning against marrying out of one's class:

Chorus

Ah, sage, sage in sooth, was he who first pondered
this truth in his mind and with his tongue gave
it utterance – that to marry in one's own degree is far
the best, and that neither among them that are puffed
up by riches nor among them that are mighty in pride
of birth should marriage be desired by him who toileth
with his hands.

(Loeb edn., trans. Herbert Weir Smyth (Cambridge Mass.:
Harvard University Press, 1922), I, p. 295).

11. *Nemesis*: Most exactly, just punishment for wrong-doing, but
more generally, fate or destiny. In Greek legend Nemesis was the
name of the goddess of retributive justice. Stephen Gill argues
that Eliot drew on her own reading of Greek drama for her
definitions of tragedy and discussed these issues in increasingly
complex ways in her novels *Felix Holt* (1866) and *Middlemarch*
(1871–2). See her 'Notes on the Spanish Gypsy', which includes
an analysis of the purpose and effects of tragedy, published by
John Walter Cross in *George Eliot's Life as Related in Her
Letters and Journals* (Edinburgh and London, 1885), vol. 3,
pp. 48–51, and see also Darrel Mansell Jr., 'George Eliot's Conception of Tragedy', *Nineteenth-Century Fiction*, 22 (1967),
pp. 155–71, and Robert E. Norton, 'The Aesthetic Education
of Humanity: George Eliot's *Romola* and Schiller's Theory of
Tragedy', *Journal of Aesthetic Education*, 25:4 (Winter 1991),
pp. 3–20. See also Deborah Guth, *George Eliot and Schiller:
Intertextuality and Cross-Cultural Discourse* (London: Ashgate,
2003).

12. *transparencies that made a great effect ... 'generous youth'*:
During the late eighteenth and early nineteenth centuries there
was a great vogue for spectaculars. A transparency was a thin
gauze used as a canvas upon which the picture was painted and
then illuminated by candles. The movement of the cloth, and the
judicious placement of the candles, led to the sense that the
picture was alive.

In writing *Adam Bede* Eliot made copious notes to perfect her
period detail. In the *Gentleman's Magazine* 69:1 (January 1799),
pp. 73–5, there was a report on the celebrations at Belvoir Castle
to mark the coming of age of John Henry, fifth Duke of Rutland:
'On this day, every magnificence which could fill the polished
mind was exhibited at the Castle, and every joy which mirth and

entertainment could give the rustic was found in its walls.' Inside the castle, 'fronting the grand staircase were two transparencies . . . One, Britannia trampling upon Faction, and with her spear piercing the monster through his head . . . On the other, a medallion of the Duke of Rutland. Motto: "Hail generous Youth" . . . At the celebrations the Duke appeared in the regimental dress of the Leicestershire militia.' Eliot jotted down details in her notebook, see Wiesenfarth, pp. 139, 155–6.

BOOK SECOND

CHAPTER XVII

In Which the Story Pauses a Little

1. *In Which the Story Pauses a Little*: Philosophical asides of this kind are typical of Eliot's method, but nowhere else does she set out her literary manifesto on the novelist's duty to be faithful to 'life' quite so clearly.

    Eliot made substantial revisions to the opening passages of this chapter when she compiled the corrections published in the one-volume 'Tenth Edition' of 1862. In the revised version she drops the pretence of addressing a 'lady reader' and tones down the sarcasm. In the first edition of 1859 the second paragraph reads:

    > Certainly I could, my fair critic, if I were a clever novelist, not obliged to creep servilely after nature and fact, but able to represent things as they never have been and never will be. Then, of course, my characters would be entirely of my own choosing, and I could select the most unexceptionable type of clergyman, and put my own admirable opinions into his mouth on all occasions. But you must have perceived long ago that I have no such lofty vocation, and that I aspire to give no more than a faithful account of men and things as they have mirrored themselves in my mind. The mirror is doubtless defective; the outlines will sometimes be disturbed; the reflection faint or confused; but I feel as much bound to tell you, as precisely as I can, what that reflection is, as if I were in the witness-box narrating my experience on oath.

    Doreen Roberts speculates that Eliot's outburst was initially prompted by her response to John Blackwood's letters written in March and April of 1858 where, among other things, he remarked that 'the passage page 53 about the identity of Love, religious feeling, and Love of Art would be better modified a little' (*Letters*, II, 444–6).

2. *many Dutch paintings*: During April 1858, while she was working on *Adam Bede*, Eliot and Lewes lived in Munich where they visited the art galleries, particularly the Glyptothek (*Letters*, II, 451, 454–5). She especially appreciated the paintings of the Dutch and Flemish schools, and the details of an 'old woman' she describes here have been linked to Gerard Dou's *Betende Spinnerin* which is at Munich.

3. *Apollo . . . Diana*: In Greek legend, Phoebus Apollo is the sun god, famous for his beauty. Eliot may have been thinking particularly of the ancient Greek statue called the Apollo Belvedere housed in the Vatican museum, but another candidate is the Apollo Barberini in the Glyptothek in Munich. Diana is the Greek (as Artemis) and Roman goddess of the moon. She was the twin sister of Apollo, famed for her skill in hunting, and considered the perfection of female beauty, although perpetually virgin.

4. *pot-house*: A public house, an ale house.

5. *lazzaroni*: Neapolitan beggars, thieves and street dwellers.

6. *an Oberlin or a Tillotson*: Jean Oberlin (1740–1826), clergyman from Alsace, who was famous for his efforts to improve the roads, schools and agricultural methods in his district. John Tillotson (1630–94), Archbishop of Canterbury, composed many famous sermons notable for their tone of tolerance and understanding.

7. *the doctrines of the Reformation*: When the Church of England was established in the fifteenth century, part of the break with the Catholic Church of Rome was attributable to the philosophies of a number of religious theorists across Europe who saw a need for 'Reform', especially in matters to do with patronage and ceremony.

8. *Arminians and the Calvinists*: The Dutch Protestant Jacobus Arminius (1560–1609) argued that any person might save their soul by good works and therefore was responsible for their own salvation. The followers of the French theologian John Calvin (1509–64), by contrast, believed that the salvation or damnation of each human soul is preordained by God. This radical split in Evangelical teachings was one of the reasons for dissension among the Methodists: the Wesleys followed the Arminian line, George Whitefield and other Evangelical Anglicans espoused the Calvinist view.

9. *an epigram . . . French literature*: Eliot is being ironic, but it may

be that she refers to the famous *bon mot* of Madame Cornuel, society hostess and letter writer: 'Il n'y a point de heros pour son valet de chambre' ('No man is a hero to his valet'), in *Lettres de Mlle Aisse a Madame Cornuel* (1787), Letter 13, 'De Paris, 1728'.

CHAPTER XVIII

Church

1. *'dizening*: Bedizening, or adorning.
2. *drab*: A woollen cloth, lightish-brown to olive in colour and which gives its name to that shade.
3. *a large cornelian seal*: A personalized seal cut into the red gem-stone cornelian, which is a variety of chalcedony, used for sealing the wax on letters.
4. *tippet*: A kind of scarf, small cape or neckerchief.
5. *Christmas Day, Easter Sunday, and 'Whissuntide'*: The chief Christian festivals which were also used to mark out the accounting and farming year – the last is properly Whitsuntide, which falls on the seventh day after Easter and marks the events of Pentecost (Acts 2), when the followers of Jesus spoke 'in tongues' inspired by the Holy Spirit.
6. *to turn the milk an' save the rennet*: Rennet, a digestive juice obtained from the stomach of a cow, is used to curdle milk to make junkets and other set milk dishes.
7. *"Love your neighbour as yourself"*: See Matthew 22:39 and Mark 12:31.
8. *megrims*: Originally, fancies, wild notions. Later, headache, or bad temper (related to 'migraine').
9. *sweltered*: Overcome by heat exhaustion.
10. *key-bugles*: A relatively sophisticated trumpet instrument because the introduction of keys allowed for the more precise pitching of notes.
11. *Bishop Ken's evening hymn*: Beginning 'Glory to Thee, my God, this night'.
12. *Melodies die out, like the pipe of Pan*: Pan, the Greek god of flocks and shepherds, played a musical pipe of seven reeds. The legend is that with the coming of Christianity, Pan died and so his songs faded in memory.
13. *the General Confession*: In this recitation, which begins the Anglican service morning and evening, the whole congregation makes

a confession of sin and pleads for forgiveness: 'We have erred, and strayed from thy ways like lost sheep.'

14. *smelling-bottle*: Smelling salts, a strong concoction, usually including carbonate of ammonia, were a universal lady's remedy through the eighteenth and nineteenth centuries. Of course they should smell powerfully.

15. *those early Christians . . . in catacombs*: In the early years of the establishment of the Christian faith, believers were persecuted. In Rome especially, many took to the warren of catacombs, burial places below ground, outside the city walls where they built secret churches.

16. *a large occiput, and a prominent crown*: The back and the top of the human skull. Eliot is referring again to the study of phrenology.

17. *Thou sweep'st us . . . like dreams*: From Psalm 90:5, one of the funeral psalms. This is the revised wording of the 'New Version' of the Psalms by Nahum Tate and Nicholas Brady (1696), generally printed in the Book of Common Prayer.

18. *'In the midst of life we are in death'*: From the Burial Service in the Book of Common Prayer.

19. *a Scotch name, she supposed*: It is actually more likely to be a Latin name, but Eliot is playing up the fact of Hetty's ignorance.

20. *th' anchor's Nelson*: Horatio Nelson was the Admiral in Chief of the British navy, and would go on to defeat the French at the Battle of Trafalgar in 1805.

21. *spoon-meat*: Food for invalids, chopped up small and eaten with a spoon.

CHAPTER XIX

Adam on a Working Day

1. *Hetty, like a bright-cheeked apple hanging over the orchard wall . . . everybody must long for her*: A generalized metaphor, associated with young and desirable girls. See, for example, the ancient Greek legend of the Hesperides, who guarded the tree which grew golden apples. Otherwise, it may refer to the Greek lyric poet Sappho (late seventh to early sixth century BC), whose Fragment 105a was well known in the nineteenth century:

'Like the sweet apple which reddens upon the topmost bough,
A-top on the top-most twig, – which the pluckers forgot, somehow, –
Forgot it not, nay, but got it not, for none could get it till now.
(Fragment 105a: Translation by Dante Gabriel Rossetti, *Poems* (1870))

2. *the Old and New Version*: Of the metrical Psalms. The Old
   Version was mainly by Thomas Sternhold and John Hopkins and
   was added to the Prayer Book in 1562. On the New Version, see
   Chapter XVIII, note 17.

3. *the apocryphal books . . . a 'History of Babylon'*: Adam's reading
   includes the 'apocryphal books' of the Old Testament, not generally accepted now in the Protestant churches; *Poor Richard's
   Almanac*, a series of books of information, mottoes and sayings
   by Benjamin Franklin, published between 1732 and 1757; Jeremy
   Taylor's *Holy Living* (1650) and *Holy Dying* (1651), Anglican
   religious guide books that Eliot admired when she was young;
   on John Bunyan's *Pilgrim's Progress*, see Chapter XIV, note 2,
   and his *The Holy War* (1682) is another religious allegory;
   Nathan (or Nathaniel) Bailey's *Universal Etymological English
   Dictionary* (1721), the first dictionary to attempt a list of all the
   words in the English language; *Valentine and Orson*, an early
   French romance about two brothers, one brought up as a gentleman, while the other was carried away by a bear and grew up as
   a wild man, was first translated into English in around 1550
   by Henry Watson as the *History of two Valyannte Brethren,
   Valentyne and Orson*, and remained a hugely popular tale; it is
   not obvious which history of Babylon Adam might have read.

4. *Where shall I find their like*: Possibly a reminiscence of William
   Shakespeare's *Hamlet* (1601), I.ii.187–8: 'He was a man, take
   him all in all, / I shall not look upon his like again.'

CHAPTER XX

Adam Visits the Hall Farm

1. *dratchell*: Slut, or 'loose' woman.
2. *Gueldres roses*: An old-fashioned name for *viburnum opulus*
   which flowers in the spring and early summer.
3. *The very rose-trees . . . the union of the houses of York and
   Lancaster*: A longstanding feud between two branches of the
   English royal family led to the Wars of the Roses, so called
   because the emblem of the House of Lancaster was a white rose

and of the House of York a red one. The conflict came to an end
in 1485 with the death of Richard III. His successor Henry Tudor,
later Henry VII, a Lancastrian, married Elizabeth of York.

4.   *wort*: The boiling infusion of malt or other grain which after
     fermentation becomes beer.

5.   *St Vitus's Dance*: Chorea; a disorder of the face and the limbs
     where the afflicted person is subject to convulsive and uncontrol-
     lable fits. The disease is popularly named after St Vitus to whom
     a sufferer prayed for a cure.

6.   *hollodays*: Holidays.

                            CHAPTER XXI

                The Night-School and the Schoolmaster

1.   *thin dips*: Cheap candles made by 'dipping' the wick into tallow.

2.   *a well-seasoned meerschaum*: Strictly a Meerschaum-pipe, where
     the bowl is made of meerschaum, or sepiolite, a hydrous silicate
     of magnesium which has an appearance like a white clay. The
     pipe is well-seasoned because it has been used often.

3.   *his old soubriquet of 'Brimstone'*: His old nickname of Brim-
     stone, a chemical also called saltpetre, which is highly inflam-
     mable and associated with the devil.

4.   *the old carved oaken press ... at a high price in aristocratic
     houses*: A press is a substantial piece of furniture with a cupboard
     above and drawers below. Bartle Massey's furniture presumably
     dates from the seventeenth or early eighteenth century. Eliot
     makes the point that a heavier style of furniture was popular
     again by the mid nineteenth century.

5.   *friggling*: Fussy, fiddly.

6.   *Jacob and Rachel a-kissing one another among the sheep*: See
     Genesis 29: 10–11 and Chapter III, note 4.

7.   *a guinea*: A golden guinea was worth twenty-one silver shillings
     (one more than an ordinary pound).

8.   *'cute*: Acute, discerning.

BOOK THIRD

CHAPTER XXII

Going to the Birthday Feast

1. *the psychology of a canary bird*: One of Eliot's favourite terms of criticism for an empty-headed woman. Cf. *Middlemarch*, Chapter 20, where the narrator considers Mr Casaubon's unexpressed wish that Dorothea might observe 'his abundant pen scratches and amplitude of paper with the uncritical awe of an elegant-minded canary-bird'.

2. *water-nixies, and such lovely things without souls*: Water elves. Another one of Eliot's favoured terms of condemnation for the flighty woman: Rosamund in *Middlemarch* is described as a 'water nixie'.

3. *a rancorous poisoned garment*: When her husband Jason repudiated her in favour of a younger bride, Medea pretended to be reconciled to his plans and sent Creusa a wedding gift of a beautiful garment, but it was poisoned and when Creusa put it on the virulent fabric ate into her flesh. (Medea also killed her sons by Jason.) Another legend tells how Deianeira gave her husband Hercules a garment that she believed was treated with a love potion in the hope of restoring his love for her. It turned out to be poison, and he died.

4. *collogue*: Connive.

5. *Old Harry*: The devil.

6. *in honour of 'th' heir'*: Such large celebrations where all the tenants and local farmers were included in the festivities were commonplace in the eighteenth and nineteenth centuries. On the coming of age of the fifth Duke of Rutland, see Chapter XVI, note 12.

7. *the Benefit Club*: An organization of the local community in order to help each other in sickness or old age. Everyone paid in a regular small subscription and an individual in need could draw on the collective resource.

8. *the Scotch raybels*: In 1745 the Scottish Jacobite army was led by Charles Edward, the Young Pretender or 'Bonnie Prince Charlie'.

9. *portraits of Queen Elizabeth ... his Commentaries in his hand*: Historical portraits of Elizabeth I (1533–1603) and General Monk (1608–70), who led Parliamentary troops during the Civil War, but later went over to the Royalist side; a picture of a

biblical scene – Darius, King of Babylon, threw Daniel into a lion's den to test his faith (see Daniel 6:16–24); Julius Caesar (*c.* 102–44 BC) was Consul of Rome and the author of the *Commentarii*, an account of the conquest of Gaul and the Civil War.

10. *it is not only woman's love that is ἀπέρωτος ἔρως, as old Æschylus calls it*: A reference to the 'unloving love', that is, a destructive or obsessive love, described in Aeschylus' *Choephorae* (Libation bearers), I, 576, the second part of the *oresteia* trilogy. Eliot's copy of *Des Aeschylos Oresteia, Griechisch und Deutsch*, ed. Johannes Franz (Leipzig, 1846) is now in Dr Williams's Library, 14 Gordon Square, London, and this line is marked. See also Wiesenfarth, pp. 149–50.

11. *the old Fogy*: From the adjective 'foggy', fat, bloated or covered with moss. A 'fogy' was an invalid soldier, or one who spent all his time in the garrison. 'Old Fogy' came to be a disrespectful term for anyone holding old-fashioned ideas.

CHAPTER XXIII
Dinner-Time

1. *"Over the hills and far away"*: A popular tune dating from the seventeenth century which also appeared, in a re-worked version, as Air XVI in Gay's *Beggar's Opera*: see Chapter XII, note 2.

2. *Give the lads a bagpipes instead of a rattle, and I'll answer for it the corn' ll be safe*: A rattle was commonly used to scare off birds eating the seed corn in the fields, and Bartle Massey's argument is that the bagpipes are as tuneless as such a rattle. He does not approve of the Scottish. This is partly to do with what Bartle Massey considers as the barbarism of Scotland, and partly with a denigration left over from the Jacobite rebellions of the early eighteenth century in 1715 and 1745.

CHAPTER XXIV
The Health-Drinking

1. *da capo*: From the head, or from the beginning (Italian). A musical term for repetition.

2. *a bailiff ... a steward*: A bailiff is someone to look after the farm, but an employee, rather than a tenant who would have

leased the farm and thus brought in an income for the squire as
he proposed in Chapter XXXII. A steward is the professional
manager appointed to look after an estate, its lands and tenancies.

CHAPTER XXV

The Games

1. *the band of the Benefit Club ... hornpipes*: The band of local
    musicians play country dances and sailors' hornpipes.
2. *the grand socialistic idea*: The term 'socialism', advocating the
    equality of all men, did not become common currency until the
    earlier part of the nineteenth century when it referred particularly
    to the theories of writers such as Charles François-Marie Fourier
    (1772–1837), who published his ideas for social reform in
    Théorie des Quatre Mouvements et des Destinées Générales
    (1808) and *Le Nouveau Monde Industriel* (1829–30).
3. *'airs from heaven'*: Shakespeare, *Hamlet*, I. iv. 41.
4. *an excellent grogram gown and a piece of flannel*: Grogram is a
    strong coarse cloth made of a mixture of silk, mohair and wool
    stiffened with gum. Flannel is a thick serviceable material made
    of wool.
5. *the yearly Wake*: A local annual festival, usually held on the
    saint's day associated with the parish church.
6. *the 'White Cockade'*: A popular Jacobite song. In Robert Burns's
    version (there are several others), the first verse runs: 'My love
    was born in Aberdeen, / The bonniest lad that e'vr was seen, /
    But now he makes our hearts fr' sad, / He takes the Field wi' his
    white cockade.' The Jacobite soldiers had no formal uniform but
    wore a white cockade (a knot of ribbons) on a blue bonnet.
7. *the 'Bird Waltz'*: There were many tunes of this name in the
    nineteenth century. The most popular was that by Francis
    Panormo (1765–1844) which by the 1850s had been through
    more than forty print issues. This might be seen as one of the
    anachronisms remarked upon by Eliot's contemporary reviewers,
    as the waltz did not become a widely popular dance until the
    1840s. However, Carol A. Martin points out that here Eliot is
    directly addressing her readers in the 'realist' mode, treating them
    as her own 1859 contemporaries (George Eliot, *Adam Bede*, ed.
    Carol A. Martin (Oxford: Clarendon Press, 2001), p. 519).

CHAPTER XXVI

The Dance

1.   *Christmas boxes*: Tips and presents of money given at Christmas.

BOOK FOURTH

CHAPTER XXIX

The Next Morning

1.   *Our deeds determine us, as much as we determine our deeds*: A
typical moral stand taken by Eliot's narrative persona. Cf., the
epigraph to Chapter 4 of *Middlemarch* by Eliot herself:

> *1st gent*   Our deeds are fetters that we forge ourselves.
> *2nd gent*   Ay, truly: but I think it is the world
>   That brings the iron.

2.   *Europe adjusts itself to a fait accompli*: Possibly a reference to
Louis Napoleon's *coup d'état* in December 1852 which made
him Emperor of France. It was later confirmed by a plebiscite,
but many felt that his retrospective attention to the wishes of the
people was something of a sham. If Eliot is alluding to this event,
it figures as one of the anachronisms in the novel.

3.   *he war let blood*: Letting blood either through cuts or the use of
leeches was a common treatment for ills of all kinds in the
eighteenth and nineteenth centuries.

CHAPTER XXX

The Delivery of the Letter

1.   *'cob-nut'*: A game resembling 'conkers' where the filbert nuts
(one or more) are threaded on a string and hit against another
until one splits. Otherwise the nuts might be piled and shied at
from a distance.

2.   *Ganymede*: Beautiful young shepherd boy who was carried off
by Jupiter (or the Greek Zeus) in the form of an eagle to become
cup-bearer to the Gods, serving the nectar which made them
immortal. Given that this comparison is rather inappropriate in

relation to Adam and Totty, Martin suggests that Eliot may have had a particular image in mind and proposes the statue after Leochares in the Vatican Museum or a half-size polychrome terracotta of Jupiter and Ganymede in the museum at Olympia (Eliot, *Adam Bede*, ed. Martin, p. 520).

3. *Aristides the Just*: Athenian general and statesman (530?–468? BC), who assessed fairly contributions by states to the Delian league.

4. *vally*: Value.

5. *a state of perfection*: An old Christian idea that John Wesley adapted for Methodism in his book *A Plain Account of Christian Perfection as Believed and Taught by the Rev. Mr John Wesley from the Year 1725 to 1765* (1767). The knowledge of 'perfection' may come to the individual some time after conversion, but before death. At this point followers reach a state of grace where they are purified from the stain of original sin.

6. *clemmed*: Starved.

7. *to pay the carriage*: Before the introduction of the uniform Penny Post (see Chapter LII, note 6), postage costs were paid by the recipient, not the sender. The rates of such charges depended on the weight of the letter. By the 1830s the cost of receiving a letter sent from Edinburgh to London could be as much as a labourer's day's wages.

8. *the laying up of the manna*: See Exodus 16:14–21. When the Lord sent manna to the people of Israel who were starving in the wilderness, Moses instructed them that they were to eat it that day. However, some disobeyed, and tried to store it, but it went rotten and 'bred worms, and stank' (verse 20).

9. *wherewith the whole creation . . . the Man of Sorrows*: Romans 8:22. The 'Man of Sorrows' is Christ, whose coming was predicted in Isaiah 53:3: 'He is despised and rejected of men; a man of sorrows, and acquainted with grief.'

10. *'If any man . . . sufficient for the day*: See, for example, Matthew 10:37–8, and 16:24; Matthew 20:22–3; Philippians 4:18 (also Chapter LII); 1 Kings 18:17–40; see Chapter IV, note 10.

11. *There may be some leading here*: Another one of Dinah's ways of accounting for what she sees as the inspiration of God's will or Providence.

CHAPTER XXXI

In Hetty's Bed-Chamber

1. *a gentleman's handwriting*: Hetty might find this hard to read because it would be florid and ornamented, as opposed to the plain copperplate style taught to workmen.
2. *'Let that man . . . its moorings'*: If this is a quotation, it is unidentified.

CHAPTER XXXII

Mrs Poyser 'Has Her Say Out'

1. *misbehave towards her betters, and fly in the face of the cat-echism*: Part of the response to the Bishop's question 'What is thy duty towards thy Neighbour?' is: 'To order myself lowly and reverently to all my betters.'
2. *'pitching'*: Throwing up sheaves of hay with a pitchfork as they are being collected for storage.
3. *a withered crab*: That is, an old crab apple.
4. *palaver*: Persuasiveness, ability to wheedle, cajole or flatter; probably from the Spanish *palavra* for word, speech or talk.
5. *board wage*: A common arrangement in great houses which usually retained a large retinue of staff. When the family were away from home, the servants would have no work to do, and so their wages would be reduced to enough to buy food only. Mrs Poyser is worried that without the squire actually in residence, very little would be required in the way of dairy products for his table.
6. *the plagues o' Egypt*: When Pharaoh refused to allow the enslaved Israelites to leave Egypt, God sent a series of plagues to the land, including one of frogs. See Exodus 8–12.
7. *got the lash i' their hands, for want o' knowing how t' undo the tackle*: The 'lash' is a whip, and the 'tackle' is the bridle and reins that harness the horse or oxen. Mrs Poyser may be alluding to the institution of slavery which was a hotly contested topic in the 1790s.
8. *two-three old folks as you think o' saving your soul by giving 'em a bit o' flannel and a drop o' porridge*: The squire has perhaps built some almshouses or gives charity to some of the elderly poor in the parish. Mrs Poyser is thinking of the ancient practice which gave its name to the 'almshouse' where the gentry would

provide for impoverished persons in return for prayers offered up for the donor's welfare.

CHAPTER XXXIII

More Links

1. *the harvest suppers*: To celebrate and give thanks for the safe bringing in of the harvest. Traditionally a country custom where all the labourers were treated to a feast. See Chapter LIII.
2. *'Bony' was come back from Egypt . . . French in Italy*: Bonaparte (see Chapter I, note 2).
3. *an Æsop's fable*: Aesop (about the middle of the sixth century BC) was said to be the inventor of a series of fables which pointed morals for human life, including such famous stories as 'The Tortoise and the Hare', 'The Fox and the Grapes' and 'The Man and the Lion'.
4. *the cheapening of bricks per thousand by water-carriage*: Bricks were expensive to make because of their firing ovens, and, because they were so heavy to carry, their cost went up even further when transport was added, but the new network of canals carrying industrial goods by water meant that many items were reduced in price (see Chapter I, note 16).

CHAPTER XXXIV

The Betrothal

1. *I never sell a fowl but what's plucked*: Mrs Poyser collects feathers from her chickens to provide the stuffing for quilts for the winter.
2. *Christian folks can't be married like cuckoos*: Cuckoos are the most obvious in their distinctive mating calls, which sound is popularly taken as signalling the arrival of spring. Folk traditions ascribe lascivious and promiscuous habits to the bird, in part associated with its well-known appropriation of other birds' nests for laying its eggs.

CHAPTER XXXV

The Hidden Dread

1. *I'll be as still as th' ould tabby, . . . do aught but the offal work*: Lisbeth promises to placate Hetty by keeping quiet like an old tabby cat and only doing the harder jobs.

2. *something by the roadside . . . the agony of the Cross*: Crucifix statues are frequently found at crossroads in France, Germany and Italy.

3. *She has thought of this pool often in the nights*: In the mid nineteenth century it was very common for women to commit suicide by drowning. All too frequently the reason for their despair was the fact that they were pregnant with an illegitimate child. So familiar was this circumstance that the words 'Found Drowned' often posted on police notices were enough for a contemporary audience in the 1850s to be able to surmise the situation. See Lynda Nead, *Myths of Sexuality: Representations of Women in Victorian Britain* (Oxford: Basil Blackwell, 1988).

BOOK FIFTH

CHAPTER XXXVI

The Journey in Hope

1. *she must trust to carriers' carts or slow waggons*: The regular coach routes were prohibitively dear. So Hetty has to hitch lifts with carriers (see Chapter XI, note 2) or hope that a farm wagon might pick her up.

2. *Windsor . . . it's where the king lives*: At Windsor Castle, one of the main royal residences. This may indicate a slight anachronism. It was not until after 1804 that George III made the castle an important residence for his family of thirteen children. From 1811 he was confined to his apartments there as his deranged state worsened.

3. *poor-rates*: A local tax levied by the parish to pay for the running of the workhouse.

4. *milestone*: Marked the distances between major towns and were an important feature of the English countryside.

5. *a drunken postilion, – who frightened her by driving like Jehu the son of Nimshi*: Jehu drove 'furiously' (2 Kings 9:20). This

journey would have been cheaper because the chaise had made the timetabled journey to its destination with paying passengers, and was now returning to base. This also explains why the postilion, who rode one of the horses but also was the sole driver, was in this unfit state, as he had clearly been relaxing after his official journey.

6. *Stratford-on-Avon ... Stony Stratford*: In Warwickshire and Buckinghamshire, respectively. Stony Stratford is an ancient coaching town on the Roman road called Watling Street, near Milton Keynes now. Hetty has gone fifty to sixty miles out of her way.

7. *toll-gates*: Each stretch of road was owned privately, and a toll was levied at points to pay for the upkeep. (Bridges were similarly owned and subject to such tolls.)

8. *the Green Man in Windsor*: A coaching inn, and a popular name for public houses set in wooded districts.

9. *the Loamshire Militia's gone to Ireland*: During the French Revolutionary and Napoleonic Wars, nationalist dissidents in Ireland sometimes threw in their lot with the French. Arthur's volunteer regiment would have been sent to Ireland to suppress threats of rebellion.

CHAPTER XXXVII

The Journey in Despair

1. *taken to the parish*: That is, taken to the workhouse in her own parish.

2. *her pocket*: Hetty would have had a detachable pocket for her valuables, which could be tied or buttoned into her dress or petticoats.

3. *have had godfathers ... to church every Sunday*: Eliot marks out the rituals of a life in the Anglican church. At the time of Christening chosen friends would stand as godparents for the child, charged with being responsible for their Christian upbringing. During her childhood she would have learnt the catechism, and the tenets of the Anglican faith set out in the Book of Common Prayer. In youth she would have been confirmed in the faith.

4. *that wondrous Medusa-face*: In Greek legend Medusa, one of the three Gorgons, had her hair turned into snakes as punishment for defiling the temple of Athene, and her terrifying gaze turned

men to stone. She was slain by Perseus, who set her head into his shield. Later artistic representations of Medusa tended to portray her face as a death-mask. Eliot may have had in mind here the sculpture known as the Rondanini Medusa which she saw at the Munich Glyptothek Museum (*Letters*, II, 451 and 460). In her notebook Eliot copied out a passage about Medusa from Adolf Stahn's *Torso. Kunst, Künstler und Kunst werk den Alten*, 2 vols. (Brunswick, 1854), vol. 1, pp. 314–15. She reviewed *Torso* three times, and in 'The Art of the Ancients', *Leader*, 6 (1855), pp. 257–8, she referred to 'the terrible beauty of the Medusa Rondanini'. See Wiesenfarth, pp. 130, 148–9.

5. *The pool had its wintry depth now*: The winter rains had filled up the pool which would be shallower in the drought of summer.
6. *a hovel of furze*: A makeshift hut of woody brush and undergrowth designed to provide a shelter for animals.

CHAPTER XXXVIII
The Quest

1. *a shadder*: A shadow.
2. *Dark and cheerless . . . the perfect day*: Hymn by Charles Wesley, which begins 'Christ, whose glory fills the skies.'
3. *getting the roads made good in his own district*: Since roads belonged to individuals or companies (see Chapter XXXVI, note 7), Adam hopes to persuade Arthur to invest in improving the local roads.
4. *like th' angels in the desert, to strengthen them as ha' got nothing t' eat*: Possibly a reference to the manna delivered to the children of Israel (see Chapter XXX, note 8), or an allusion to Christ's temptation during forty days and nights in the wilderness when angels came to strengthen him against the temptations of the devil (Matthew 4:11).
5. *potato-ground*: A plot for growing vegetables.
6. *a slow palsied shake of the head*: An involuntary twitch associated with palsy or a stroke.
7. *feature him*: Look like him.
8. *meeting*: The Methodist service. A common term for any gathering of Nonconformists for the purpose of worship.
9. *'taxed cart'*: During the wars at the end of the eighteenth century the Prime Minister William Pitt was forced to be inventive in ways of raising money to pay for them. In 1794 he introduced a

tax on carriage horses and in 1795 one on open carts drawn by one horse. Each cart bore the sign 'A taxed Cart' and the owner's name and address.

10. *the Society*: A name for the Methodist group.

11. *his spud*: A sharp narrow spade.

CHAPTER XXXIX
The Tidings

1. *it was almost like relief or joy*: Irwine has feared that Adam was responsible for Hetty's pregnancy.

CHAPTER XL
The Bitter Waters Spread

1. *Bitter Waters*: A reference to the bitter waters of Marah encountered by the children of Israel during their exile in the wilderness (Exodus 15:23).

2. *Hetty would persist to the end in her obstinate silence*: Much effort would have been put into persuading an unmarried mother to confess the name of the father of her child.

3. *the Lent assizes*: In country areas temporary courts were set up three times a year and travelling judges would hear all the cases of the most serious crimes that had accrued in the interval.

4. *St Thomas's*: Most likely the Feast of St Thomas the Apostle (3 July).

5. *Sarah Williamson, Methodist preacher, Leeds*: Presumably the unnamed 'holy woman who preaches' at Leeds (p. 101). She may have been based on the Methodist preacher Sarah Crosby (see Chapter VIII, note 4).

CHAPTER XLI
The Eve of the Trial

1. *An upper room*: This scene is designed to echo the events of the Last Supper, when Christ met his disciples in an 'upper room' (Mark 14:15, Luke 22:12), had bread and wine, and acknowledged the imminence of Judas's betrayal.

2. *Men's lives are as thoroughly blended*: With Adam, Irwine takes

up the responsible moral role that he had abjured in not tackling
Arthur about his anxieties in Chapter XVI. This thesis on the
connectedness of social life was taken up again in *Middlemarch*.

CHAPTER XLIII

The Verdict

1. *The place fitted up that day as a court of justice*: The temporary
   courtroom chosen for the hearing of the Lent assizes.
2. *for a public, because there was a figure against the door*: It was
   customary well into the nineteenth century for public houses,
   inns and shops to advertise with a statuette or sign of some kind:
   tobacconists displayed a red Indian, marine stores a black doll,
   and public houses might have a man drinking or the figure of a
   black boy acting as a hitching post for the horses of the customers.
3. *after Meeting was over, and speak to our minister*: Hetty seems
   to have been looked after by a dissenter, not a member of the
   Church of England.
4. *the fever*: Puerperal fever, a form of blood poisoning, common
   in newly delivered mothers, and often fatal in the eighteenth and
   nineteenth centuries.
5. *the coppice to look after some stakes*: Coppicing was a common
   practice when wood was an important source of fuel, where
   young trees were pruned regularly to encourage new growth.
6. *the constable*: The overseer of the parish (not a police constable).
7. *her own counsel ... a favour not granted to criminals in those
   stern times*: In the eighteenth century accused felons were not
   permitted representation by 'counsel'. They were allowed to seek
   advice on points of law, but if they wished to question the
   evidence or put forward a defence they had to do that themselves.
   See J. M. Beattie, 'Scales of Justice: Defense Counsel and the
   English Criminal Trial in the Eighteenth and Nineteenth Centuries', *Law and History Review*, 9:2 (Autumn 1991), pp. 221–
   67. (The jury would of course all have been men.)
8. *the judge put on his black cap, and the chaplain in his canonicals*:
   Thus the courtroom knows the sentence before it is pronounced.
   The judge covers his wig with a black cap and the chaplain wears
   his full robes of canonical office.

CHAPTER XLIV

Arthur's Return

1. *the lay-impropriator of the Hayslope tithes*: A secular official whose job it was to collect tithes and then to calculate payment to the clergy.

CHAPTER XLV

In the Prison

1. *the condemned cell*: Prisoners condemned to die were confined alone.
2. *his pardoning mercy can't reach you . . . from sin*: The idea that God's forgiveness relies upon the repentance of the sinner.
3. *the cry of the forsaken*: 'My God, my God, why hast thou forsaken me?' were the words of Jesus spoken in Hebrew on the cross (Matthew 27:46 and Mark 15:34).
4. *him who denied thee*: Christ prophesied that Peter, his chief disciple, would deny him three times before dawn. So he did, but Christ forgave him (see Luke 22:61).
5. *as they of old brought the sick . . . thou didst heal them*: See Matthew 4:24.
6. *God . . . to whom the darkness is as noonday*: See Isaiah 58:10.
7. *the eleventh hour: See Matthew 20:6 and 9.*
8. *I see thee . . . with healing on thy wings*: See Malachi 4:2.
9. *let the eyes of the blind be opened*: See Isaiah 35:5.
10. *'Father, I have sinned'*: The formula for the beginning of confession, as well the words of the returning Prodigal Son according to Christ's parable (Luke 15:18).
11. *like a heavy weight hanging round my neck*: Specifically a reference to Christ's words on children, 'But whoso shall offend one of these little ones which believe in me, it were better for him that a millstone were hanged about his neck, and that he drowned in the depth of the sea' (Matthew 18:6; Mark 9:42; Luke 17:2). But also like the albatross to the mariner in Coleridge's 'The Ancient Mariner': see Chapter V, note 30.

CHAPTER XLVI
The Hours of Suspense

1. *The people were . . . moving rapidly, in one direction*: Executions were held in public up until the first half of the nineteenth century, and were a popular draw for the crowd, especially when the victim was young and pretty.

CHAPTER XLVII
The Last Moment

1. *let us pray without ceasing to God*: See 1 Thessalonians 5:17.
2. *The Sheriff*: The Sheriff of the County, a legal officer, who would be responsible for seeing that executions were carried out according to the jurisdiction of the law.

CHAPTER XLVIII
Another Meeting in the Wood

1. *transported o'er the seas*: From the early eighteenth century it was the practice of several European countries to transport criminals to their colonies to serve their sentence. People went from England to America, and from 1787 to Australia. Conditions on board the transport ships were degrading and unsanitary, and many convicts died on the journey, while many more died before the completion of their sentence. Women especially suffered as they were at the mercy of both their gaolers and their fellow prisoners. Even if they were assigned to domestic or farm work on arrival in the colony they were likely to suffer harsh treatment and abuse. (Transportation was abolished in 1868.) See Robert Hughes, *The Fatal Shore: A History of the Transportation of Convicts to Australia, 1787–1868* (1986; London: Harvill Panther, 1996).
2. *If I die, my cousin Tradgett will have the estate, and take my name*: As he is unmarried and an only child, Arthur has no heirs, and his death will mean that his family line would die out. His cousin (on the female side) would take on the family name.

BOOK SIXTH

CHAPTER XLIX

At the Hall Farm

1. *the Sermon on the Mount*: Matthew 5–7, includes the passage beginning, 'Blessed are the poor in spirit, for theirs is the Kingdom of Heaven.' Later on, Christ's advice also includes examples of the practice of humility: 'whosoever shall smite thee on thy right cheek, turn to him the other also. And if any man will sue thee at law, and take away thy coat, let him have thy cloke also' (Matthew 5:39–40).

2. *cas'alty*: Casualty, that is, infirm, shaky, liable to accident.

3. *a monthly rose*: Possibly a name for the briar or wild rose which is a very pale pink and which only blooms for about a month in the summer.

4. *the chaff-cutter*: The man who chops up the stalks, or chaff, left after the harvesting of the ears of wheat or corn, in order to make straw.

5. *asthmy*: Asthma.

CHAPTER L

In the Cottage

1. *the close poke of her little black bonnet*: The poke is the brim of Dinah's round bonnet. The poke-bonnet style was associated with the dress adopted by Quakers and Methodists.

2. *peace soon, though nobody believes it'll last long*: Britain and France made peace under the Treaty of Amiens in March 1802, but hostilities resumed in May 1803.

3. *That meeting between the brothers . . . timid and distrustful*: In Genesis 32–3 Jacob tricked his elder brother Esau out of his inheritance by impersonating him, and when the two brothers were to meet again twenty years later, Jacob feared that his reception would not be warm but Esau 'ran to meet him, and embraced him' (33:4).

4. *Moses . . . died when other folks were going to reap the fruits*: Moses successfully led the children of Israel through the wilderness and to the sanctuary of the Promised Land, but dies in sight of it (Deuteronomy 34: 1–5).

5. *Wesley's abridgment of Madame Guyon's life*: Madame Jeanne Marie Bouvier de la Motte Guyon (1648–1717), French Roman Catholic mystic. John Wesley published *An Extract of the Life of Madame Guion* (1776), which is referred to in Moore's *Life of Mrs Mary Fletcher* (see Chapter VIII, note 4).
6. *the precepts of Solomon*: On the training of children, see Proverbs 13:24 and 22:6. The book is traditionally supposed to have been written by Solomon.
7. *the gallant Colonel Bath unmanly when he made the gruel for his invalid sister*: In Henry Fielding's *Amelia* (1751), Book III, Chapter VIII, the not-very-attractive character of Colonel Bath – famous for his sharp tongue – is embarrassed to be found in the act of preparing a posset for his sister.
8. *dilettante scouring and polishing*: The strict meaning of *dilettante* is to be passionately devoted to something. So here, to cleaning.
9. *Moses, the meekest of men, was wrathful sometimes*: Numbers 12:3: 'very meek, above all the men which were upon the face of the earth'. Nonetheless Moses did lose his temper with the Israelites' lack of faith – especially when he found them worshipping the golden calf.
10. *be with one another in spirit ... the flesh is weak*: See 1 Corinthians 5:3; 1 Peter 1:6; John 7:33; Ezekiel 21:13; Matthew 26:41 ('the spirit indeed is willing, but the flesh is weak' – words from the prayer Jesus uttered in the Garden of Gethsemane just before his arrest).

CHAPTER LI

Sunday Morning

1. *have no will but thine*: Cf. Luke 22:42: 'not my will, but thine, be done'.
2. *Samuel's dying speech ... Adam knew the Articles*: See 1 Samuel 12; Genesis 27:1–40; Apochryphal Ecclesiasticus (Sirach). The Thirty-Nine Articles of Faith are included in the Book of Common Prayer. Adam disagrees with Article 6, as it states that while the Church sanctions the reading of the Apochryphal books 'for example of life and instruction in manners', it does not regard them as canonical and 'doth not apply them to establish any doctrine'.
3. *'I came not ... to repentance'*: Mark 2:17 and Luke 5:32.
4. *Mrs Fletcher*: See Chapter VIII, note 4.

5. *without book*: Without knowledge or authority, originally scriptural authority, but here generally.

CHAPTER LII
Adam and Dinah

1. *I fear I should forget the Divine presence, and seek no love but yours*: An interesting echo of Charlotte Brontë's *Jane Eyre* (1847), Chapter 24: 'My future husband was becoming to me my whole world; and more than the world: almost my hope of heaven. He stood between me and every thought of religion, as an eclipse intervenes between man and the broad sun. I could not, in those days, see God for his creature of whom I had made an idol.'

2. *marriage is a holy state*: From the introductory words of the marriage service in the Book of Common Prayer ('Dearly beloved, we are gathered together in the sight of God, and in the face of the congregation to join together this Man and this Woman in holy Matrimony; which is an honourable estate . . .').

3. *that better part*: As in the story of Martha and Mary (Chapter VI, note 9), 'Mary hath chosen that good part', Luke 10:42.

4. *an earthly affection . . . a lover of self*: See Colossians 3:2; 2 Timothy 3:1–2.

5. *that early blessedness which I had forsaken:* Cf. William Cowper's poem 'Walking with God (Genesis, v. 24)', often sung as a hymn, 'O! for a closer walk with God'. The second verse begins 'Where is the blessedness I knew/When first I saw the Lord?' It was first published in *Olney Hymns* by John Newton and William Cowper (1779).

6. *the boat, gliding sleepily along the canal . . . post-time*: The narrator contrasts the ways of the late eighteenth and early nineteenth centuries with the innovations of the 1850s. A complicated network of canals was built (see Chapter I, note 16) and products were transported in this economic way, as opposed to pack-horses, and door-to-door pedlars. The invention of the steam engine meant that mechanized manufacturing supplanted the spinning wheel, and eventually gave rise to the development of the railway network which, in its turn, made the canals obsolete. By the 1850s there was great interest in education and many museums had been founded and periodicals established to pro-

vide for the interests of the growing middle classes. In the eighteenth century a tax on paper meant that there were fewer newspapers from which to choose, but by the 1850s there were several prominent newspapers competing for readers with opinionated 'leaders' on the political questions of the day. And finally, in the 1840s the Uniform Penny Post had been introduced, making the sending of letters not only cheaper (see Chapter XXX, note 7) but more regular, with city dwellers having two, if not three, postal deliveries a day.

7.   *Exeter Hall ... Sartor Resartus*: Exeter Hall in London was identified with Evangelist philosophies and was often the venue chosen by radical religious thinkers in the nineteenth century including such men as Edward Irving (1792–1834), who established the dissenting Holy Catholic Apostolic Church in 1832, and the preacher Charles Haddon Spurgeon (1834–92), who filled it to capacity when he preached there in 1854. Eliot read his sermons in September 1858 (*Letters*, II, 478) and eventually heard him speak in 1870 when she described his tone as the 'most superficial, Grocer's-back-parlour view of Calvinistic Christianity' (*Letters*, V, 121–2.).

     Tracts for the Times was a series of ninety influential pamphlets (1833–41) written by a group of Oxford High Church men led by John Henry Newman, called the 'Oxford Movement'. Their endeavours were part of an effort to challenge the secularization of the Anglican Church. As a young woman Eliot borrowed some copies from the local squire in Warwickshire (Haight, *George Eliot*, p. 24).

     Sartor Resartus (The Tailor Refashioned) (1833–4) by Thomas Carlyle (1795–1881), part autobiography, part social criticism condemning the materialism of the age. Eliot admired his writings and sent her first two books to his wife Jane Carlyle in the hopes that her husband would read them.

CHAPTER LIII

The Harvest Supper

1.   *Harvest Home*: See Chapter XXXIII, note 1.
2.   *the plum-pudding*: Here a savoury dish, served before the meat. The equivalent today is the practice of serving Yorkshire pudding and gravy before the beef.
3.   *'Tom Saft'*: Or 'Soft', as in 'soft in the head'.

4. *thatched the ricks*: The newly harvested crops would be stored in ricks and then thatched over in order to keep the rain off.

5. *Tityrus and Melibœus*: Two shepherds introduced in Virgil's (70–19 BC) first *Eclogue*. Tityrus is a generalized name for a shepherd and he also appears in Theocritus (see Chapter V, note 37).

6. *the treadmill . . . the House of Correction*: Persons convicted of minor crimes would be sentenced to a spell in the House of Correction and condemned to hard labour; picking oakum, that is tar, off ropes; breaking stones; or walking on the treadmill grinding corn.

7. *ad libitum*: A musical term; the performer is at liberty to sing the passage freely as regards rhythm or tempo.

8. *Here's a health . . . our master's will*: A drinking song which would be repeated for several verses as each person is named and their health drunk by the assembled company.

9. *"M loove's a roos wi'out a thorn"*: 'The Lass of Richmond Hill' (*c.* 1790) by James Hook (1746–1827): 'On Richmond Hill there lives a Lass, / More bright than May-day morn, / Whose charms all other maids surpass, / A rose without a thorn'. Perhaps a glancing reference to the plot here. Some sources suggest the song was about the longstanding, cross-class relationship between the Prince of Wales and Mrs Fitzherbert.

10. *the mounseers . . . as if they war frogs*: The French ('monsieurs'), whom English prejudice derogates as French 'frogs'.

11. *ne'er ate a bit o' beef i' their lives. Mostly sallet*: The eating of beef is proof of manly British virtue as opposed to an effeminate French preference for salad.

12. *furriners*: Foreigners.

13. *If King George 'ud turn 'em all away . . . He might take on Billy Pitt*: As a constitutional monarch, King George III was obliged to defer to the wishes of Parliament, but his insanity (see Chapter V, note 32) meant that he relied on ministers appointed by the Crown to make political decisions. William Pitt the Younger (1759–1806) was Prime Minister for seventeen years up until March 1801 when he fell from power. (He did return again as Prime Minister in May 1804.)

14. *which is Old Harry when everybody's got boots on*: The Devil traditionally has cloven hoofs.

15. *he's no Frenchman born*: Napoleon was born in Ajaccio on the island of Corsica, off the coast of Italy.

16. *thrust his forefinger into the canister*: Of tobacco.

17. *'Three Merry Mowers'*: Another popular song.

CHAPTER LIV
The Meeting on the Hill

1. *a man with a cataract to regret the painful process . . . exchanged for clear outline*: A reference to the blind man's description of his partly restored sight when Jesus laid hands on him: see Mark 8:24. Cataracts could be removed by surgery in the nineteenth century, but it was performed without anaesthetic.

2. *till death parts us*: A reference to the words of the marriage service as included in the Book of Common Prayer: 'till death do us part'.

CHAPTER LV
Marriage Bells

1. *'Oh what a joyful thing it is' . . . the wedding psalm*: Either Psalm 128 in the Bible or 67 in the Book of Common Prayer.

EPILOGUE

1. *Conference has forbid the women preaching*: In July 1803 the annual Conference and legislative meeting of the Methodist clergy and lay-preachers considered the matter of women preaching. The decision was that women 'in general' should not preach, 'But if any woman among us think she has an extraordinary call from God to speak in public . . . we are of the opinion she should, in general, address *her own sex*, and *those only*.' See *Minutes of the Methodist Conferences from the first, held in London, by the late Rev. John Wesley, A. M. in the year* 1774 (1813), vol. II, p. 188. In the early nineteenth century there was a general reactionary movement throughout Europe with regard to women's rights. Some Methodists, such as the Primitive Methodists, still endorsed women preachers and Eliot's Aunt Elizabeth Evans joined them.

THE STORY OF PENGUIN CLASSICS

Before 1946 ... 'Classics' are mainly the domain of academics and students; readable editions for everyone else are almost unheard of. This all changes when a little-known classicist, E. V. Rieu, presents Penguin founder Allen Lane with the translation of Homer's *Odyssey* that he has been working on in his spare time.

1946 Penguin Classics debuts with *The Odyssey*, which promptly sells three million copies. Suddenly, classics are no longer for the privileged few.

1950s Rieu, now series editor, turns to professional writers for the best modern, readable translations, including Dorothy L. Sayers's *Inferno* and Robert Graves's unexpurgated *Twelve Caesars*.

1960s The Classics are given the distinctive black covers that have remained a constant throughout the life of the series. Rieu retires in 1964, hailing the Penguin Classics list as 'the greatest educative force of the twentieth century.'

1970s A new generation of translators swells the Penguin Classics ranks, introducing readers of English to classics of world literature from more than twenty languages. The list grows to encompass more history, philosophy, science, religion and politics.

1980s The Penguin American Library launches with titles such as *Uncle Tom's Cabin*, and joins forces with Penguin Classics to provide the most comprehensive library of world literature available from any paperback publisher.

1990s The launch of Penguin Audiobooks brings the classics to a listening audience for the first time, and in 1999 the worldwide launch of the Penguin Classics website extends their reach to the global online community.

The 21st Century Penguin Classics are completely redesigned for the first time in nearly twenty years. This world-famous series now consists of more than 1300 titles, making the widest range of the best books ever written available to millions – and constantly redefining what makes a 'classic'.

The Odyssey continues ...

The best books ever written

PENGUIN ( ) CLASSICS

SINCE 1946

Find out more at www.penguinclassics.com